select
editions

Reader's
Digest

Reader's Digest

The names, characters and incidents portrayed in the novels in this volume are the work of the authors' imaginations. Any resemblance to actual persons, living or dead, events or localities is entirely coincidental.

www.readersdigest.co.uk

Published in the United Kingdom by Vivat Direct Limited (t/a Reader's Digest), 157 Edgware Road, London W2 2HR

For information as to ownership of copyright in the material of this book, and acknowledgments, see last page.

Printed in Germany
ISBN 978 0 276 44669 6

THE READER'S DIGEST ASSOCIATION, INC.

contents

author in focus

In 1981, Linwood Barclay joined the *Toronto Star* as a reporter and held a variety of posts there until 2008, when he left to become a full-time novelist. Barclay says that he loves newspapers and, in *Never Look Away,* he puts forward some of his concerns for their future. 'The examples I invent in my novel are the kind of mistakes that could be made,' he explains. 'Recently I read about a paper in Pasadena that was getting people in India to watch council meetings on the Internet and write about them. To cover local news events from the other side of the world—that appalls me.'

in the spotlight

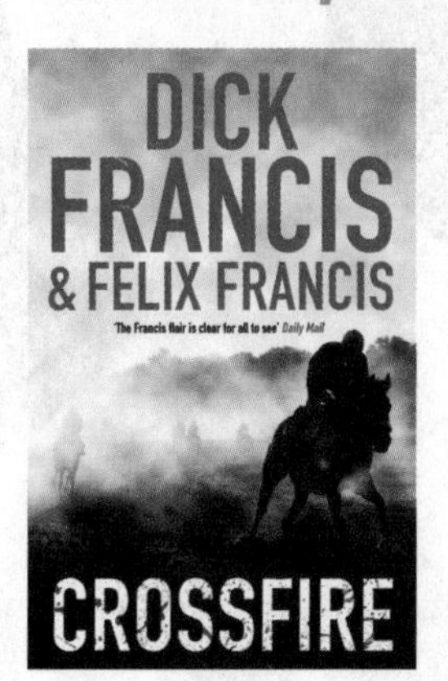

In the racing world, Dick Francis, who died in 2010, will be remembered as one of the most successful National Hunt jockeys of his era—and as the jockey who failed to win the 1956 Grand National on Devon Loch, the Queen Mother's horse, when it collapsed near the finishing line. Dick Francis will also be remembered as a best-selling author, aided by his wife Mary and his younger son, Felix, who was co-writer on the last four novels. 'His legacy will live on beyond him with the publication of *Crossfire*, the book we were working on before his death last February,' Felix says. 'I do miss him so much, but I rejoice in having been the son of such an extraordinary man, and I share in the joy that he brought to so many over such a long life.'

Cross-fire

Dick Francis

and Felix Francis

Captain Tom Forsyth is blown up
in a bomb attack in Afghanistan.
Invalided home to Berkshire, he discovers
that his mother is being blackmailed,
forced to make her beloved horses lose
at the racecourse. When he decides
to investigate, Tom faces a new
battleground . . . one that proves just as
life-threatening as war.

Prologue

Helmand Province, Afghanistan, October 2009

'Medic! Medic!'

I could see that my company sergeant major was shouting, but strangely, the sound of his voice seemed muffled, as if I were in a neighbouring room rather than out in the open.

I was lying on the dusty ground with my back up against a low bank so that I was actually half sitting. Sergeant O'Leary was kneeling beside me.

'Medic!' he shouted again urgently over his shoulder. He turned his head and looked me in the eyes. 'Are you all right, sir?' he asked.

'What happened?' I said, my voice sounding loud in my head.

'A bloody IED,' he said. He turned away, looked behind him, and shouted again. 'Where's that bloody medic?'

An IED. I knew that I should have known what IED meant, but my brain seemed to be working in slow motion. I finally remembered. IED—improvised explosive device—a roadside bomb.

The sergeant was talking loudly into his personal radio.

'Alpha four,' he said in a rush. 'This is Charlie six three. IED, IED. One CAT A, several CAT C. Request IRT immediate back-up and medevac. Over.'

I couldn't hear any response, if there was one. I seemed to have lost my radio headset, along with my helmet.

CAT A, he'd said. CAT A was army-speak for a seriously injured soldier requiring immediate medical help to prevent loss of life. CAT Cs were walking wounded. The sergeant turned back to me.

'You still all right, sir?' he asked, the stress apparent on his face.

'Yes,' I said, but in truth I didn't really feel that great. I was cold yet sweaty. 'How are the men?' I asked him.

'Don't worry about the men, sir. I'll look after the men.'

'How many are injured?' I asked.

'A few. Minor, mostly,' he said. He turned away and shouted at the desert-camouflaged figure nearest to him. 'Johnson, go and fetch the medic kit from Cummings. Little rat's too scared to move.'

He turned back to me once more.

'You said on the radio there's a CAT A. Who is it?'

'The CAT A is you, sir,' he said. 'Your foot's been blown off.'

1

Four months later

I realised as soon as I walked out of the hospital that I had nowhere to go. I stood holding my bag at the side of the road, watching a line of passengers board a red London bus.

Simply being discharged from National Health Service care had been my overriding aim for weeks, without any thought to what was to come next.

Progress had been painfully slow, with painful being the appropriate word. However, I was now able to walk reasonably well on an artificial foot. I might even have been able to run a few strides to catch that bus, if only I'd wanted to go wherever it was bound.

I looked around me. No one had turned up to collect me, nor had I expected them to. None of my family actually knew that 25198241 Captain Thomas Vincent Forsyth was being discharged on that particular Saturday morning, and quite likely, they would not have turned up even if they had. I had always preferred to do things for myself, and they knew it.

The army had been my life since the night I left home after another unpleasant argument with my stepfather. I had slept on the steps of the army recruiting office in Oxford, and when the office opened at nine the following morning, I had signed on for Queen and Country as a private soldier in the Grenadier Guards.

Guardsman Forsyth had taken to service life like the proverbial duck to water and had risen through the ranks to officer cadet at the Royal Military Academy in Sandhurst, followed by a commission back in my old regiment.

The army had been much more to me than just a job. It had been my wife, my friend and my family; it had been all I had known for fifteen years, and I loved it. But now it appeared that my army career might be over, blown apart for ever by an Afghan IED.

Consequently, I had not been a happy bunny during the previous four months, and it showed. In fact, I was an angry young man.

I TURNED LEFT out of the hospital gates and began walking. Perhaps, I thought, I would see where I had got to by the time I became too tired to continue.

'Tom,' shouted a female voice. 'Tom!'

I stopped and turned around. Vicki, one of the physiotherapists from the rehabilitation centre, was in her car, turning out of the hospital parking lot. She had the passenger window down.

'Do you need a lift?' she asked. 'I was going to Hammersmith, but I can take you somewhere else if you like.'

'Hammersmith would be fine.'

I threw my bag onto the back seat and climbed in beside her.

'So they've let you out, then?' she said.

'Glad to see the back of me, I expect,' I said.

Vicki tactfully didn't say anything. So it was true.

'It's been a very difficult time for you,' she said eventually. 'It can't have been easy.'

I sat in silence. Of course it hadn't been easy.

Losing my foot had, in retrospect, been the most straightforward part. The doctors had managed to save the rest of my right leg so that it now finished some seven inches below my knee.

My stump had healed well, and I had quickly become proficient at putting on and taking off my new prosthetic leg: a wonder of steel, leather and plastic that had turned me from a cripple into a normal-looking human being; at least on the outside.

But there had been other physical injuries, too. The bomb had driven Afghan desert dust deep into my torn lungs, to say nothing of the blast damage and lacerations to the rest of my body. Pneumonia had almost finished off what the explosion had failed to do.

'Where do you live?' Vicki asked, bringing me back to reality.

That was a good question. I supposed I was technically homeless.

For the past fifteen years, I had lived in army accommodation of one form or another: barracks, officers' messes, tents. More often than I cared to remember, I had slept where I sat or lay on the ground, half an ear open for the sound of an approaching enemy.

However, the army had now sent me 'home' for six months.

The major from the Ministry of Defence, the Wounded Personnel liaison officer, had been fair but firm during his recent visit. 'Six months leave on full pay,' he'd said. 'To recover. Then we'll see.'

'I don't need six months,' I'd insisted. 'I'll be ready to go back to my regiment in half that time.'

'We'll see,' he'd repeated. 'I'm not sure that going back to your regiment will be possible. You might be more suited for a civilian job. You wouldn't be passed fit for combat. Not without a foot.'

We'll see, indeed. I'd show them.

'Will the tube station do?' Vicki said.

'Sorry?' I said.

'The tube station,' she repeated. 'Is that OK?'

'Fine,' I said. 'Anywhere.'

'Where are you going?' she asked.

'My mother lives in Lambourn,' I said. 'Near Newbury.'

'Is that where you're going now?'

Was it? I didn't particularly want to. But where else? I could hardly sleep on the streets.

'Probably,' I said. 'I'll get the train.'

I STOOD AT THE bottom of the steep driveway to my mother's home and experienced the same reluctance to go up that I had so often felt in the past.

I had taken a taxi from Newbury station to Lambourn, asking the driver to drop me some way along the road from my mother's gate so that I could walk the last hundred yards. It was force of habit: I felt happier approaching anywhere on foot. It must have to do with being in the infantry. On foot I could hear the sounds that vehicle engines would drown out. And I could get a proper feel of the lie of the land, essential to anticipate an ambush.

I shook my head and smiled at my folly. There was unlikely to be a Taliban ambush in a Berkshire village, but I could recall the words of my colour sergeant at Sandhurst. 'You can never be too careful,' he would say. 'Never assume anything; always check.'

No IEDs went bang as I safely negotiated the climb up from the road to the house, a redbrick affair built between the world wars.

As usual in the middle of the day, all was quiet as I wandered around the side of the house towards the back door. A few equine residents put their heads out of their stalls in the nearest stable yard as I crunched across the gravel, inquisitive to see a new arrival.

My mother was out. I knew she would be. Perhaps that was why I hadn't phoned ahead to say I was coming. Perhaps I needed to be here alone first, to get used to the idea of being back.

My mother was a racehorse trainer. But she was much more than that. She was a phenomenon. In a sport where there were plenty of big egos, my mother had the biggest ego of them all. She did, however, have some justification. In only her fifth year in the sport, she had been the first lady to be crowned Jump Racing Champion Trainer, a feat she had repeated for each of the next six seasons. Her horses had won three Cheltenham Gold Cups and two Grand Nationals, and she was recognised as the First Lady of British Racing.

She was also a highly opinionated workaholic and no sufferer of fools. Her politics made Genghis Khan seem like an indecisive liberal, but everybody loved her, nonetheless. She was a 'character'.

Everyone, that is, except her ex-husbands and her children.

For about the twentieth time, I asked myself why I had come here. There had to be somewhere else I could go. But there wasn't.

I struggled to get down low enough with my artificial leg to find the key that my mother habitually left under a stone in the flowerbed, but I couldn't find it. I sat down on the doorstep and leaned against the locked door.

I knew where she was. She was at Cheltenham races. I had looked up the runners in the morning paper, as I always did. She had four horses declared, including the favourite in the big race, and my mother would never miss a day at her beloved Cheltenham. I could visualise her holding court in the parade ring before the races and welcoming the winner back after them. I had seen it so often. It had been my childhood.

It was now beginning to get cold. I put my head back against the wood and rested my eyelids.

'Can I help you?' said a voice.

I reopened my eyes. A short man in his mid-thirties wearing faded jeans and a puffy anorak stood on the gravel in front of me. I must have briefly drifted off to sleep.

'I'm waiting for Mrs Kauri,' I said.

Mrs Kauri was my mother, Mrs Josephine Kauri, although Josephine had not been the name with which she had been christened. It was her name of choice. Long before I was born, she had decided that Jane, her real name, was not classy enough. Kauri had been the surname of her first husband; she was now on her third.

'Mrs Kauri is at the races,' replied the man.

'I know,' I said. 'I'll just wait for her here. I'm her son.'

'The soldier?' he asked.

'Yes,' I said, somewhat surprised that he would know.

But he did know. It was only fleeting, but I didn't miss his glance down at my right foot. He knew only too well.

'I'm Mrs Kauri's head lad,' he said. 'Ian Norland.'

He held out a hand, and I used it to help me up.

'Tom,' I said. 'Tom Forsyth. What happened to old Basil?'

'He retired. I've been here three years now.'

'It's been a while longer than that since I've been here,' I said.

Ian nodded. 'I saw you from the window of my flat,' he said, pointing to a row of windows above the stables. 'Would you like to come in and watch the racing on the telly? It's cold out here.'

'I'd love to.'

We climbed the stairs to what I remembered had once been a storage loft over the stables.

'The horses provide great central heating,' Ian said as he led the way. 'I never have to turn the boiler on until it freezes outside.'

The narrow stairway opened out into a long, open-plan living area with a kitchen at the near end and doors at the far end that presumably led to a bedroom and bathroom. There was no sign of any Mrs Norland, and the place had a 'man look' about it, with stacked-up dishes in the sink and newspapers spread over much of the floor.

'Take a pew,' Ian said, waving at a brown corduroy-covered sofa placed in front of a huge plasma television. 'Fancy a beer?'

'Sure,' I said. I'd not had a beer in more than five months.

Ian went to the fridge, which appeared to contain nothing but beers. He tossed me a can.

We sat in easy companionship watching the racing from Cheltenham. My mother's horse won the second race, and Ian punched the air in delight.

'Good young novice, that,' he said. 'He'll make a good chaser in time.'

He took pleasure in the success of his charges, as I had done in the progress of a guardsman from raw recruit into battle-hardened warrior, a man who could then be trusted with one's life.

'Now for the big one,' Ian said. 'Pharmacist should win. He's frightened off most of the opposition.'

'Pharmacist?' I asked.

'Our Gold Cup hope,' he said. 'This is his last warm-up for the Festival. He loves Cheltenham.' He was referring to the Cheltenham Gold Cup at the Steeple Chase Festival in March, the pinnacle of British jump racing.

'What do you mean, he's frightened off the opposition?' I asked.

'Mrs Kauri's been saying all along that old Pharm will run in this race and so the other Gold Cup big guns have gone elsewhere. Not good for them to be beaten today with only a few weeks left to the Festival.'

Ian became more and more nervous, continually getting up and walking around the room.

'God, I hope he wins,' he said, sitting down.

'I thought you said he would,' I said.

'He should do, he's streaks better than the rest, but . . .'

'But what?' I asked.

'Nothing.' He paused. 'I just hope nothing strange happens, that's all.'

'Do you think something strange might happen?'

'Maybe,' he said. 'Something bloody strange has been happening to our horses recently.'

'What sort of things?'

'Bloody strange things,' he repeated. 'Like not winning when they should,' he said. 'Especially in the big races. Then they come home unwell. You can see it in their eyes. Some have even had diarrhoea, and I've never seen racehorses with that before.'

We watched as my mother was shown on the screen tossing the jockey up onto Pharmacist's back, the black-and-white-check silks appearing bright against the dull green of the February grass. My stepfather stood nearby, observing events as he always did.

Ian became more and more nervous as the race time approached.

We watched as the horses walked around in circles at the start. Then the starter called them into line and they were off.

Pharmacist appeared to be galloping along with relative ease in about third place of the eight runners as they passed the grandstand on the first circuit. But only when they started down the hill towards the finishing straight for the last time did the pace pick up.

Pharmacist seemed to be going well and even jumped to the front. But then the horse appeared to fade rapidly, jumping the final fence and almost coming to a halt on landing. He was easily passed by the others and crossed the finish line in last place, almost walking.

I didn't know what to say. Pharmacist certainly did not look like a horse that could win a Gold Cup in six weeks' time.

Ian sat rigidly on the sofa. 'Bastards,' he spat. 'I'll kill the bastards who did this.'

I was not the only angry young man in Lambourn.

TO SAY MY HOMECOMING was not a happy event would not be an exaggeration. No, 'Hello, darling,' no kiss on the cheek, no fatted calf, nothing. But no surprise, either.

My mother walked past me as if I were invisible, her face taut. I knew that look. She was about to cry but would not do so in public.

'Oh, hello,' my stepfather, said by way of greeting.

Lovely to see you, too, I thought, but decided not to say so.

My stepfather and I had never really got on. In the mixed-up mind of an unhappy child, I had tried to make my mother feel guilty for driving away my father and had ended up alienating not only her but everyone else.

My father had packed his bags and left when I was just eight, finally fed up with being well behind the horses in my mother's affection. Her horses had always come first, then her dogs, then her stable staff, and finally, if there was time, her family.

How my mother had ever had the time to have three children had always been a mystery to me. Both my siblings were older than I and had been fathered by my mother's first husband, whom she had married when she was seventeen. Richard Kauri had been a rich New Zealand playboy who toyed at being a racehorse trainer. My mother had used his money to further her own ambition in racing, taking over the house and stables as part of their divorce settlement after ten years of turbulent marriage. Their young son and daughter had both sided with their father, a situation I now believed my mother had encouraged, as it gave her more chance of acquiring the training business if her ex-husband had the children.

Almost immediately, she had married again, to my father, a local seed merchant, and had produced me like a present on her twenty-ninth birthday. But I had never been a much-loved child. I think my mother looked upon me as just another of her charges to be fed and watered twice a day, mucked out and exercised as required, and expected to stay quietly in my stable for the rest of the time.

I suppose it had been a lonely childhood, but I'd been happy enough. What I missed in human contact I made up for with dogs and horses. They were my friends.

When my parents divorced, there had been a protracted argument over custody of me. Years later, I realised that they had argued because neither of them had wanted the responsibility of bringing up an eight-year-old misfit. My mother had lost the argument, so I lived with her, and my father had disappeared from my life for good. I hadn't thought it a great loss at the time, and I still didn't.

'SO, DARLING, how was Afghanistan? You know, before you were injured?' my mother asked rather tactlessly. 'Were you able to enjoy yourself at all?'

My mother had always managed to call me 'darling' without any of the emotion the word was designed to convey.

'I wasn't sent there to enjoy myself,' I said, slightly irritated. 'I was there to fight the Taliban.'

'I know that,' she said. 'But did you have any good times?'

We were sitting around the kitchen table having dinner, and my mother and stepfather both looked at me expectantly.

What should I say? In truth, I had enjoyed myself immensely before I was blown up, but I wondered if I should say so. Recording my first confirmed kill of a Taliban had been exhilarating; it had sent my adrenaline levels to maximum. One wasn't meant to enjoy killing other human beings, but I had.

'I suppose it was OK,' I said. 'Lots of sitting round doing nothing, really. That, and playing cards.'

'Did you see anything of the Taliban?' my stepfather asked.

'A little,' I said matter-of-factly. 'But mostly at a distance.'

A distance of about two feet, impaled on my bayonet.

'You're not very talkative,' my mother said. 'I thought that soldiers liked nothing better than to recount stories of past battles.'

'There's not much to tell you, really,' I said.

Not much to tell, I thought, that wouldn't put her off her dinner.

'I saw you on the television today,' I said, changing the subject, 'at Cheltenham. Good win in the novice chase. Shame about Pharmacist. At one point, I thought he was going to win as well.'

My mother kept her eyes down as she pushed a potato around on her plate.

'Your mother doesn't want to talk about it,' my stepfather said.

'Your head lad seems to think the horse was nobbled,' I said.

My mother's head came up quickly. 'Ian doesn't know what he's talking about,' she said angrily. 'And he shouldn't have been talking to *you*.'

I hoped that I hadn't dropped Ian into too much hot water. But I wasn't finished yet.

'Shouldn't have been talking to me about what?' I asked.

No reply.

'So are the horses being nobbled?' I asked into the silence.

'No, of course not,' my mother said. 'Pharmacist simply had a bad day. He'll be fine next time out.'

I stoked the fire a little more. 'Ian Norland said it wasn't the first time that your horses haven't run as well as expected.'

'Ian knows nothing!' She was almost shouting. 'We've just had some bad luck of late. It'll pass.'

'And Mrs Kauri doesn't need you spreading any rumours,' my stepfather interjected, somewhat clumsily.

I looked at my stepfather, and I wondered what he really thought of his wife still using the name of another man.

Only when the other children at my primary school had asked me why I was Thomas Forsyth and not Thomas Kauri had I ever questioned the matter. 'My father is Mr Forsyth,' I'd told them. 'Then why isn't your mother Mrs Forsyth?' It had been a good question, and one I hadn't been able to answer.

Mrs Josephine Kauri had been born Miss Jane Brown and was now, by rights, Mrs Derek Philips, although woe betide anyone who called her that in her hearing. Since first becoming a bride at seventeen, Josephine Kauri had worn the trousers in each of her three marriages, and it was no coincidence that she had retained the marital home in each of her divorces. From the look she had just delivered across the kitchen table, I thought Mr Derek Philips might soon be outstaying his welcome at Kauri House Stables.

We ate in silence for a while, finishing off the chicken casserole that my mother's cleaner-cum-housekeeper had prepared.

But I couldn't resist having one more go.

'So will Pharmacist still run in the Gold Cup?'

I thought my stepfather might kick me under the table, such was the fury in his eyes. My mother, however, was more controlled.

'We'll see,' she said. 'It depends on how he is in the morning.'

'Is he not back here yet, then?' I asked.

'Yes,' she said, without further explanation.

'And have you been out to see him?' I persisted.

'In the morning,' my mother replied brusquely. 'I said I'd see how he was in the morning. Now, can we drop the subject?'

Even I didn't have the heart to go on. There were limits to the pleasure one could obtain from other people's distress, and distressed she clearly was.

But as Ian Norland had said, something very strange was going on.

I WENT FOR a walk outside before going to bed. I wandered around the garden and along the concrete path to the stables. Not much had changed since I had run away all those years before.

A light went on in the first-floor room above my head.

'Why the hell does he have to turn up? That's all we need at the moment.' I could clearly hear my mother.

'Keep your voice down. He'll hear you.'

That was my stepfather.

'No, he won't,' she said at full volume. 'He's gone outside.'

'Josephine,' my stepfather said angrily, 'half the bloody village will hear you if you're not careful.'

I was quite surprised that he would talk to her like that. Perhaps there was more to him than I thought. My mother even took notice, and they continued their conversation more quietly. I couldn't hear anything other than a faint murmur. Presently the lights went out.

I lifted the leather flap that covered the face of my watch. The luminous hands showed me it was only ten thirty. Clearly, racehorse trainers went to bed as early as hospital patients, even on Saturday nights. I was neither, and I enjoyed being outside in the dark.

I had always been completely at home in darkness. I supposed it was one thing I should thank my mother for. When I was a child, she had always insisted I sleep with my bedroom lights off and my door firmly closed. Since then, the dark had always been my friend.

Eventually the cold drove me inside. I went quietly through the house so as not to disturb those sleeping. Good as it was, my new right leg made an annoying metallic clinking noise every time I put it down. An enemy sentry would have heard me coming from a mile away. I would have to do something about that.

I went up the stairs to my old bedroom. My childhood things had long gone. However, the bed looked the same.

This wasn't the first night I had been back in this bed. There had been other occasional visits, all started with good intentions but invariably ending in argument. To be fair, I was as much, if not more, to blame than my mother and stepfather. There was just something about the three of us together that caused the ire in us to rise.

Maybe I shouldn't have come, but somehow I had needed to. This place was where I grew up, and in some odd way, it still represented safety and security. And it was the only home I'd ever had.

I sat down on the edge of the bed and removed my prosthesis, rolling down the flesh-coloured rubber sleeve that gripped over my real knee, keeping the false lower leg and foot from falling off. I slowly eased my stump out of the tight-fitting cup. It was all very clever. Moulded to fit me exactly by the boys at Dorset Orthopaedic, they had constructed a limb that I could walk on all day without causing so much as a pressure sore, let alone a blister.

But it still wasn't *me*. I shook my head. Feeling sorry for myself wasn't going to help me get back to combat-ready fitness.

2

'HAS JOSEPHINE LOST HER MAGIC?'

The headline of Sunday's *Racing Post* couldn't have been more blunt. The paper lay on the kitchen table when I went downstairs at eight o'clock to make myself some coffee after a disturbed night.

I wondered if my mother or stepfather had seen the headline yet. I heard my mother coming down the stairs.

'That bastard Rambler,' she was shouting. 'He knows sod all.'

She swept into the kitchen in a light blue quilted dressing gown and white slippers, snatched up the newspaper from the table, and studied the front-page article intently.

'It says here that Pharmacist was distressed after the race.' My mother was shouting over her shoulder, obviously for the benefit of my stepfather, who had sensibly stayed upstairs. 'That's not true. How would Rambler know, anyway?'

I shifted on my feet, my false leg making its familiar clink.

'Oh, hello,' said my mother, apparently seeing me for the first time. 'Have you read this rubbish?' she demanded.

'No,' I said.

'Well, don't,' she said, throwing the paper back down on the table. 'It's a load of crap.' She turned on her heel and disappeared back upstairs as quickly as she had arrived, shouting obscenities.

I leaned down and turned the paper round so I could read it.

'FROM OUR SENIOR CORRESPONDENT GORDON RAMBLER AT CHELTENHAM' was printed under the headline. I read on:

> Josephine Kauri was at a loss for words after her eight-year-old Gold Cup prospect, Pharmacist, finished last in the Janes Bank Trophy yesterday at Cheltenham. The horse finished at a walk and in some distress. The Cheltenham steward ordered that the horse be drugs tested.
>
> This is not the first time in recent weeks that Kauri's horses have seemingly run out of puff in big races. Her promising novice chaser, Scientific, suffered the same fate at Kempton in December, and questions were asked about another Kauri horse, Oregon, at Newbury last week, when it failed to finish in the first half dozen when a heavily backed favourite.
>
> With the Cheltenham Festival now only five weeks away, can we expect a repeat of last year's fantastic feats, or have the Kauri horses simply flattered to deceive?

Rambler had pulled no punches. He went on to speculate that Mrs Kauri might be over-training the horses, such that they had passed their peak by the time they reached the racetrack. I would be surprised if my mother had, not after so many years of experience. Not unless, as the paper said, she had lost her magic touch.

She hadn't lost her touch for shouting. I could hear her upstairs in full flow, although I couldn't quite make out the words. No doubt my stepfather was suffering the wrath of her tongue. I almost felt sorry for him. But only almost.

I decided it might be prudent for me to get out of the house for a while, so I went for a wander around the stables. The block nearest the house, the one over which Ian Norland lived, was one side of three quadrangles of stables, each containing twenty-four stalls, which stretched away from the house. Even on a Sunday morning the stables were a hive of activity.

'Good morning,' Ian Norland called to me as he came out of one of the stalls. 'Still here, then?'

'Yes,' I said. 'Why wouldn't I still be here?'

'No reason,' he said, smiling. 'Just that Mrs Kauri doesn't seem to like guests staying overnight. Most go home after dinner.'

'This is my home,' I said.

'Oh,' he said, slightly flustered. 'I suppose it is.'

'And how is Pharmacist this morning?' I asked, half hoping for some more indiscretion.

'Fine,' he said. 'He's a bit tired after yesterday, but he's OK.'

'No diarrhoea?' I asked.

He gave me a look that I took to imply he wished he hadn't mentioned anything about diarrhoea to me yesterday.

'No,' he said. 'Like I said, he's just tired.' He picked up a bucket and began to fill it under a tap. 'Sorry, I have to get on.' It was my cue that the conversation was over.

'Yes, of course,' I said. I started to walk on, but I stopped and turned around. 'Which stall is Pharmacist in?'

'Mrs Kauri wouldn't want anyone seeing him now,' Ian said.

'Why on earth not?' I said, aggrieved.

'Mrs Kauri doesn't like anyone snooping round the yard.'

'Nonsense,' I said. 'I'm not just anyone. I'm her son.'

He wavered, and I thought he was about to tell me, when he was saved by the arrival of his employer.

'Morning, Ian,' my mother called, striding towards us.

'Morning, ma'am,' Ian replied. 'I was just talking to your son.'

'So I see,' she said, in a disapproving tone. 'Well, don't. You've talked to him too much already.'

Ian blushed, and he stole a glance of displeasure at me.

'Sorry, ma'am,' he said.

She nodded firmly at him as if to close the matter and turned her attention to me.

'What are you doing out here, exactly?' she asked.

'I was just having a look round,' I said as innocently as I could.

'Well, don't,' she said.

'Why not?' I said. 'Have you something to hide?'

Ian almost choked. I could see the irritation level rise in my mother's eyes. However, she managed to remain in control.

'Of course not,' she said, with a forced smile. 'I just don't want anyone upsetting the horses.'

I couldn't actually see how wandering around the stable blocks would upset the horses, but I decided not to say so.

'And how is Pharmacist this morning?' I asked again.

'I was on my way to see him right now,' my mother replied. 'Come on, Ian,' she said, and set off briskly with Ian in tow.

'Good,' I said, walking behind them. 'I'll come with you.'

My mother said nothing but simply increased her pace, with Ian almost running behind her to keep up. Perhaps she thought that with my false foot, I wouldn't be able to. Maybe she was right.

I followed as quickly as I could into the next stable rectangle. If my mother thought she could go fast enough so that I wouldn't see where she had gone, she was mistaken. I watched as she slid the bolts and went into a stall on the far side, almost pushing Ian through the gap and pulling the door shut behind them. As if that would make them unreachable. Even I knew that stable doors are bolted only from the outside. Perhaps I should lock them in and wait. Now, that would be fun.

Instead, I opened the top half of the door, leaned on the lower portion, and looked in.

My mother was bent over, running her hands down the backs of Pharmacist's legs, feeling for heat that would imply a soreness of the tendon. 'Nothing,' she said, standing up. 'Not even a twinge.'

'That must be good,' I said.

'How would you know?' my mother said caustically.

'Surely it's good if there's no heat in his tendons,' I said.

'Not really,' she replied. 'It means there must be another reason for him finishing so badly yesterday.'

That's true, I thought. 'Does he look all right?' I asked.

'No. He's got two heads.' My mother's attempts at humour rarely came off. 'Of course he looks all right.'

'Has he got diarrhoea?' I asked.

Ian gave me a pained look.

'And why would he have diarrhoea?' my mother asked haughtily.

'I just wondered,' I said. 'I know horses can't vomit, so I wondered if he had a stomach upset that might show as diarrhoea.'

'Nonsense,' my mother said. 'Horses only get diarrhoea with dirty or mouldy feed, and we are very careful to keep our feed clean.'

The inspection of Pharmacist was over, and my mother came out through the door, followed by Ian, who slid home the door bolts.

If it had been my best horse that had inexplicably run so badly, I would have had a vet out here last night giving him the full once-over. Strangely, my mother seemed satisfied with just a quick look.

'How long before the dope-test results are out?' I said.

'How do you know they ordered a dope test?' she demanded.

'It says so in today's *Racing Post*.'

'I told you not to read that paper,' she said crossly.

'I don't always do what I'm told,' I said.

'No,' my mother said, 'that's the problem. You never did.'

She turned and strode away, leaving Ian and me standing alone.

'So what do *you* think?' I asked him.

'Don't involve me,' he said. 'I need this job.'

'You do realise there won't be a job if someone has been nobbling the horses? The yard will be closed down.'

'Don't you think I know that?' he said, through clenched teeth. 'Something strange is going on. That's all I know. Now let me get on with my job while I still have it.'

He strode away, leaving me alone outside Pharmacist's stall.

THE ATMOSPHERE back in the house was frosty, to put it mildly, and it had nothing to do with Pharmacist. It had to do with money.

'Josephine, we simply can't afford it.'

I could hear my stepfather almost shouting. He and my mother were in the office off the hallway. I was in the kitchen, eavesdropping. They must not have heard me come in from the yard.

'We must be able to afford it,' wailed my mother. 'I've had the best year ever with the horses.'

'Yes, you have, but we've also had other things to contend with, not least the ongoing fallout from your disastrous little scheme.' My stepfather's voice was full of incrimination and displeasure.

'Please don't start all that again.' Her tone was suddenly more conciliatory and apologetic.

'But it's true,' my stepfather went on mercilessly. 'Without that, we would've easily been able to buy you a new BMW. As it is, let's just hope our old Ford doesn't need too much work done.'

I wondered what disastrous little scheme could have resulted in things being so tight financially that one of the top trainers in the country was unable to upgrade her old Ford to a new BMW.

I would have loved to listen to them longer. However, I didn't want to get caught snooping, so I silently swivelled back and forth on my good foot from the kitchen table to the back door. It was a technique I had developed to get around my hospital bed at night once I had removed my prosthesis. I was getting quite good at heel-and-toeing, as the physiotherapists had called it.

I could still hear my mother at high volume. 'For God's sake, Derek, there must be something we can do.'

'What do you suggest?' Derek shouted back at her. 'We don't even know who it is.'

I opened the back door a few inches, then closed it with a bang. Their conversation stopped. I walked to the hall, my right foot making its familiar clink. My mother came out of the open office door.

'Hello,' I said, as genially as I could.

'Hello, darling,' she replied. She took a step towards me. 'Tell me,' she said, 'how much longer are you planning to stay?'

'I've only just arrived,' I said. 'I hadn't thought about leaving just yet. I haven't really worked out where I would go.'

'But you would go back to the army.'

'It's not that simple. They're not sure they want me any more.'

'What?' She sounded genuinely shocked. 'Surely they must have an obligation to go on employing you.'

'Mum, it's not like any other job,' I said. 'I would have to be fit and able to fight. That's what soldiers do.'

'But there must be something else you could do,' she argued. 'They must need people to organise things, to do the paperwork.'

My stepfather came to the office door and leaned on the frame.

'Josephine, my dear. I don't think Tom would be prepared to be in the army simply to push paper around a desk.' He looked me in the eye, and for the first time in twenty-four years, I thought there might be some flicker of understanding between us.

'Derek is right,' I said.

'For how long has the army sent you home?' my mother asked.

'Six months.'

'Six months! But you can't possibly stay here six months.'

That was true. I had already been there too long for her liking.

'I'll look for somewhere else to go this week,' I said.

'Oh, darling, it's not that I want to throw you out, you understand,' she said, 'but I think it might be for the best.'

Best for her, I thought. But perhaps it would be the best for us all. A full-scale shouting match couldn't be very far away.

'I could pay you rent,' I said, purposely fishing for a reaction.

'Don't be silly,' my mother said. 'This is your home.'

'A contribution towards your food might be welcome,' my stepfather interjected.

Things must have been tight. Very tight indeed.

THE REMAINDER of Sunday proved to be quiet at Kauri House.

In the afternoon, I ventured out into Lambourn, deciding to go for a walk, mostly to get out of the house but also because I was curious about how much the place had changed over fifteen years.

There were a few more houses than I remembered, but overall the village was as familiar as it had been when I'd delivered the morning papers as a teenager. I went into the general store to buy a sandwich for lunch and waited for my turn at the checkout.

'Oh, hello,' said the woman behind the till, looking at me intently. 'It's Tom, isn't it? Tom Kauri?'

I looked at her. She was about my age, with long, fair hair tied back in a ponytail. She wore a loose-fitting dark grey sweatshirt that camouflaged the fairly substantial body beneath.

'Tom Forsyth,' I said, correcting her.

'Oh, yes,' she said. 'That's right. But your mum is Mrs Kauri, isn't she?'

I nodded, and she smiled. I handed her my sandwich.

'You don't remember me, do you?' she said.

I looked at her more closely. 'Sorry,' I said. 'No.'

'I'm Virginia Bayley,' she said expectantly. 'Ginny.' She paused. 'From primary school. I was Ginny Worthington then.' She laughed nervously. 'Dyed my hair since then. And put on a few pounds, you know, due to having had the kids.'

Virginia Bayley, plump and blonde, née Ginny Worthington, skinny and brunette. One and the same person.

'How nice to see you again,' I said, not really meaning it.

'Staying with your mother, are you?' she asked.

'Yes,' I said.

She handed me my sandwich in a plastic bag. 'Lovely to see you.'

'Thanks,' I said, taking the bag. 'You, too.' I started to turn away from her.

'You can come and buy me a drink later if you like. My old man has arranged a bit of a get-together at seven o'clock at the Wheelwright Arms for my birthday. There'll be others there, too. Some from school. You're welcome to come.'

'Thank you,' I said. 'So is it your birthday today?'

'Yeah,' she said, grinning.

'Then, happy birthday, Ginny,' I said with a flourish.

'Ta,' she said, smiling broadly. 'Come tonight if you can. It'll be fun.'

I couldn't think of a less fun-filled evening than going to the pub-birthday party of someone I couldn't really remember, where there would be other people I also wouldn't be able to remember. But I supposed anything might be preferable to sitting through another excruciating dinner with my mother and stepfather.

'OK,' I said. 'I will.'

THE EVENING PROVED to be better than I had expected, and I very nearly hadn't gone.

By seven o'clock, rain had been falling vertically out of the dark sky with huge droplets splashing back from the flooded area between the house and the stables. I looked at my black leather shoes, my only shoes, and wondered if staying at home in front of the television might be wiser.

I decided instead to find out if it would be possible to pull a Wellington over my false leg. I borrowed the largest pair of wellies I could find in the boot room and had surprisingly little difficulty in getting them on. I also borrowed my mother's long Barbour coat and my stepfather's cap.

I set off for the Wheelwright relatively well protected but still with the rain running down my neck.

'I thought you wouldn't come,' said Ginny as I stood in the bar, removing my mother's coat. 'Not with the weather this bad.'

'Crazy,' I agreed.

'You or me?' she said.

'Both.'

She laughed. Ginny was trying very hard to make me feel welcome. Too hard, in fact. Her husband didn't like it, which I took to be a good sign for their marriage. But he had no worries with me. Ginny was nice enough but not my sort.

What *was* my sort? I wondered.

I'd slept with plenty of girls, but they had all been casual affairs. I was, in truth, married to the military.

There were seven of us standing in a circle near the bar. As well as Ginny and her husband, there were two other couples. I didn't recognise any of them and none of the four looked old enough to have been at school with me.

One of the men stepped forward to buy a round at the bar.

'Should I know any of these?' I said quietly to Ginny, waving a hand at the others.

'No, not these,' she said. 'I think the weather has put some people off.'

I was beginning to wish it had put me off as well, when the door of the pub opened and another couple came in.

At least, I thought they were a couple, until they removed their coats. Both of them were young women, and one of them I knew the instant she removed her hat and shook out her long, blonde hair.

'Hello, Isabella,' I said.

'My God,' she replied. 'No one's called me Isabella for years.' She looked closely at my face. 'Bloody hell. It's Tom Kauri.'

'Tom Forsyth,' I corrected.

'I know, I know,' she said, laughing. 'I was just winding you up. As usual.'

It was true. She had teased me mercilessly, ever since I had told her, about age ten, that I was deeply in love with her, and I had asked her to marry me.

She had clearly filled out a bit since then, and in all the right places.

'So what do people call you now?' I asked.

'Bella,' she said. 'Or Issy. Only my mother calls me Isabella, and then only when I've displeased her.'

'And do you displease her often?' I asked flippantly.

She looked me in the eyes and smiled. 'As often as possible.'

Wow, I thought.

BOTH ISABELLA AND I ignored Ginny's birthday celebration as we renewed our friendship and, in my case, my feelings of longing.

'Are you married?' I asked her almost immediately.

'Why do you want to know?' she replied.

'To know where I stand,' I said, somewhat clumsily.

'And where exactly do you think you stand?' she said.

I stand on only one leg. Now what would she say to that?

'You tell me,' I said.

She never did answer my question. I took her silence on the matter to be answer enough, and I wondered who was the lucky man.

At ten o'clock, as people were beginning to drift away, I asked her if I could walk her home.

She smiled. 'OK. But just a walk home. No bonus.'

'I've never heard it called a bonus before.' I laughed.

She also laughed, and we left in congenial companionship.

I positively ached to have a 'bonus' with Isabella. But there was little likelihood of that, and my chances weren't helped when she suddenly stopped.

'What's that noise?' she asked.

'What noise?' I said, stopping next to her.

'That clicking noise.' She listened. 'That's funny. It's stopped.'

She walked on, and I followed.

'There it is,' she said triumphantly. 'It's you, when you walk.'

'It's nothing,' I said quietly. 'Just the boots.'

I could see she was confused. I was wearing rubber boots.

'No, come on,' she said. 'That's definitely a sharp metal sound, and you've got wellies on. So what is it?'

'Leave it,' I said sharply, embarrassed and angry. In truth, more angry with myself for not saying than with her for asking.

'Come on,' she said again, laughing. 'What have you got down there?' She looked for the source of the noise.

I had no choice. 'I've got a false leg,' I said quietly.

'What?' She stood still, looking at me. 'Oh, Tom, I'm so sorry.'

'It's all right,' I said. But it wasn't.

Isabella stood in the street, getting wetter, while I told her everything. She listened—first with horror and then with concern. She tried to comfort me, and I despised it. I didn't want her pity.

Suddenly I knew why I had come back to Lambourn, to my 'home'. I must have subconsciously understood that my mother would not have tried to be reassuring and sympathetic. I preferred the Kauri 'Get on with your own life and let me get on with mine' attitude. Grief was easier to cope with alone.

'Please don't patronise me,' I said.

Isabella stopped talking in mid sentence. 'I wasn't,' she said. 'I was only trying to help.'

'Well, don't,' I said, rather cruelly. 'I'm fine without it.'

'OK,' she said, obviously hurt. 'If that's the way you feel, then I'll bid you good night.'

She turned abruptly and walked away, leaving me standing alone in the rain, confused and bewildered. I felt like I wanted to run away, but I couldn't, not without a cacophony of metallic clinking.

ON MONDAY MORNING, I went to Aldershot to try to collect my car and my other belongings out of storage. Isabella came with me.

In fact, to be totally accurate, I went with her. She drove her VW Golf in a manner akin to a world-championship rally driver.

'Do you always drive like this?' I asked as we almost collided with an oncoming truck during a dodgy overtaking manoeuvre.

'Only when I'm not being patronising,' she said.

She had phoned the house early. Too early. I'd still been in bed.

'That Warren woman called for you,' my mother had said with distaste when I went down to breakfast.

'Warren woman?'

'Married to Jackson Warren.'

'Who's Jackson Warren?'

'You must know,' my mother had said. 'Lives in the Hall. Family made pots of money in the colonies. Married that young girl when his wife died. She must be thirty years younger than him. That's who called. Brazen hussy.' The last two words had been spoken under her breath but had been clearly audible nonetheless.

'Is her name Isabella?' I'd asked.

'That's the one.'

So she was married.

'What did she want?' I'd asked.

'She wanted to speak to you; that's all I know.'

I'd gone into the office to return the call to Isabella.

'I'm so sorry about last night,' she'd said. 'Can we meet again today so that I can apologise in person?'

'I can't,' I'd said. 'I'm going to Aldershot.'

'Can't I take you?' she had replied, rather too eagerly. 'It's the least I can do after being so crass last night.'

So here we were, dodging trucks on the Bracknell bypass.

Everything I owned, other than my kit for war, had been locked away in a metal cage at an army barracks in Aldershot prior to the regiment's move to Afghanistan. Everything, that is, except my car, which I hoped was still sitting at one end of the huge parking lot set aside for that purpose within the military camp down the road from Aldershot, at Pirbright.

'Let's get my car first,' I said. 'Then I can load it with my stuff.'

'OK,' she said. She drove in silence for a while.

'Why didn't you just tell me you were married?' I asked.

'Does it matter?' she replied.

'It might.'

'I'm actually amazed you didn't know already. Quite the scandal, it was, when Jackson and I got married.'

'How long ago?' I asked.

'Seven years now,' she said. 'And before you ask, no, it wasn't for his money. I love the old bugger.'

'But the money helped?' I said with some irony.

'Why does everyone assume that it's all about his money? It's not. In fact, I won't get anything when he dies. I said I didn't want it. It all goes to his children.'

'Are any of them your children, too?' I asked.

'No.' I could detect disappointment in her voice. 'Sadly not.'

'You tried?' I asked.

'At the beginning, but not now. It's too late.'

'But you're still young enough.'

'I'm all right. It's Jackson that's the problem. Prostate cancer. The doctors say they've caught it early and it's completely controllable with drugs. But there are some unfortunate side effects.'

'Has he tried Viagra?' I asked.

'Tried it?' She laughed. 'He's swallowed them like M&Ms, but still not a flicker. It's the fault of the Zoladex—that's one of the drugs. It seems to switch off his sex drive completely.'

'I can see that would be a tad frustrating,' I said.

'A tad? I'll tell you it's extremely frustrating. And for both of us.' She looked at me in embarrassment. 'Sorry, I shouldn't have said anything. Far too much information.'

'It's fine,' I said.

Annoyingly, at this point we arrived at Pirbright Camp, so I heard no more juicy revelations.

I FOUND IT was surprisingly easy to drive with a false foot. A few practice circuits of the car park and I was ready for the public highway.

Isabella insisted on following me the nine miles from Pirbright to Aldershot. 'You might need help carrying your things,' she had said. 'And you won't get much of it into that.'

True, my XK Jaguar coupé was pretty small, but Isabella obviously had no idea how little I had acquired in the way of 'stuff' during fifteen years in the army. I could probably have fitted it into my car twice over.

'Is that all?' she was amazed. 'I'd take more than that on a dirty weekend.'

I was standing next to two navy-blue holdalls and a four-foot by four-inch black, heavy-duty cardboard tube. Between them they contained all my meagre worldly possessions.

'I've moved a lot,' I said.

'What's in the tube?'

'My sword. Every officer has a sword, but it's only for ceremonial use these days.'

'But don't you have any furniture?'

'No. I've lived in army barracks all my adult life. I've never known the luxury of an en suite bathroom, except on holiday.'

'You men,' Isabella said. 'Girls wouldn't put up with it.'

'The girls don't fight,' I said. 'At least, not yet.'

'Will you mind when it happens?' she asked.

'No, as long as they fight as well as the men. But they will have to be strong to carry all their kit. The Israeli army scrapped their mixed infantry battalions when they suspected the men were carrying the girls' kits in return for sex.'

'Human nature is human nature,' Isabella said.

'Certainly is,' I replied. 'Any chance of a bonus?'

3

Back at Kauri House Stables, there was still tension in the air between my mother and her husband. I suspected that I'd interrupted an argument as I went into the kitchen with my bags.

'Where has all that stuff come from?' my mother asked.

'It's just my things that were in storage,' I said.

'Well, I don't know why you've brought it all here,' she said.

'Where else would I take it?'

'Oh, I don't know,' she said, almost with a sob. 'I don't know bloody anything.' She stormed out. I thought she was crying.

'What's all that about?' I asked my stepfather.

'Nothing for you to worry about,' he said.

'Let me be the judge of that. It's to do with money, isn't it? Why can't you afford to buy her a new car?'

He was angry. 'Who told you that?' he almost shouted.

'I overheard you talking to my mother.'

'How dare you listen to a private conversation?'

I thought of saying that I couldn't have helped it, so loud had been their voices, but that wasn't completely accurate. I could have chosen not to stay in the kitchen listening.

'So why can't you afford a new car?' I asked him bluntly.

'That's none of your business,' he replied sharply.

'Anything to do with my mother is my business.'

'No, it isn't.' He stormed out of the kitchen.

And I thought I was meant to be the angry one.

I COULD HEAR my mother and stepfather arguing upstairs, so I casually walked into their office off the hall.

My stepfather had said that they would have been able to afford a new car if it hadn't been for the 'ongoing fallout' from my mother's 'disastrous little scheme'. What sort of scheme?

I looked down at the desk. There were two stacks of papers on each side of the standard keyboard and computer monitor.

The one on the far left contained bills and receipts to do with the house: electricity, council tax, etc. All paid by bank direct debit. I scanned through them, but there was nothing out of the ordinary.

The next stack was bills and receipts for the stables: power, heat, feed, together with the salary and tax papers for the staff. Nothing indicated the existence of any 'scheme'.

The third pile was simply magazines and other publications, including the blue-printed booklets of the racing calendar. Nothing unusual there.

But it was in the fourth pile that I found the smoking gun. In fact, there were two smoking guns that together gave the story.

The first was in a pile of bank statements. Clearly, my mother had two separate accounts—one for her training business and one for private use. The statements showed that my mother was withdrawing £2,000 in cash every week from her private account. This in itself would not have been suspicious; many people in racing dealt in cash. But it was a second piece of paper that completed the story. It was a handwritten note in capital letters. I found it inside an envelope addressed to my mother. The message on it was to the point:

THE PAYMENT WAS LATE. IF IT IS LATE ONE MORE TIME, IT WILL INCREASE TO THREE THOUSAND. IF YOU FAIL TO PAY, A CERTAIN PACKAGE WILL BE DELIVERED TO THE AUTHORITIES.

Plain and simple, it was a blackmail note.

The 'ongoing fallout' my stepfather had spoken about was having to pay two thousand pounds a week to a blackmailer. No wonder they couldn't afford a new BMW.

'What the bloody hell do you think you're doing?'

I jumped. My mother was standing in the office doorway. There was no way to hide the fact that I was holding the blackmail note.

I looked at her. She looked at my hand and the paper it held.

'Oh, my God.' Her voice was little more than a whisper, and her legs began to buckle.

I stepped quickly towards her, but she went down fast. Fortunately, she went down vertically, her head making a relatively soft landing on the carpeted floor. But she was out cold in a dead faint.

I decided to leave her where she had fallen. I had to struggle to get down to my knees to place a pillow under her head. She started to come round, opening her eyes with a confused expression.

Then she remembered.

'It's all right,' I said, trying to give her some comfort.

For the first time that I could remember, my mother looked frightened. In fact, she looked scared out of her wits.

'Stay there,' I said to her. 'I'll get you something to drink.'

I went out to the kitchen to fetch a glass of water. When I went back, I found my stepfather kneeling beside his wife, cradling her head. 'What did you do to her?' he shouted at me, in accusation.

'Nothing,' I said calmly. 'She just fainted.'

'Why?' he asked, concerned.

'Derek, he knows everything,' my mother said.

'Knows what?' he demanded, sounding alarmed.

'Everything,' she said.

'He can't!'

'I don't know everything,' I said to him. 'But I do know you're being blackmailed.'

IT WAS BRANDY, not water, that was needed to revive them both. We were sitting in the drawing room in chintz-covered armchairs. My mother's face was pale, and her hands shook. Derek sat tight-lipped on the edge of his chair, knocking back Rémy Martin VSOP.

'So tell me,' I said for the umpteenth time.

Again there was no reply from either of them.

'If you won't tell me,' I said, 'then I will have no choice but to report a case of blackmail to the police.'

I thought for a moment that my mother was going to faint again.

'No.' She did little more than mouth the word. 'Please, no.'

'Then tell me why not,' I said. My voice seemed loud and strong compared to my mother's. I remembered what my colour sergeant said at Sandhurst: 'Command needs to be expressed in the correct tone. Half the struggle is won if your men believe you know what you're doing even if you don't, and a strong, decisive tone will give them that belief.'

I was now 'in command' of the present situation, whether my mother or stepfather believed it or not.

'Because your mother would go to prison,' Derek said slowly. 'And me, too, probably, as an accessory.'

'An accessory to what?' I said. 'Have you murdered someone?'

'No.' He almost smiled. 'Not quite that bad. Evading tax.'

I looked at my mother. She was crying openly, as I had never seen her. She suddenly looked much older than her sixty-one years.

'So what are we going to do about it?' I said in my voice-of-command. 'You can't go on paying two thousand pounds a week.'

Derek sighed. 'It's not just the money.'

'What else?' I asked him.

His shoulders slumped. 'The horses.'

'What about the horses?'

'No,' my mother said, but it was barely a whisper.

'Have the horses had to lose to order?' I asked into the silence. 'Is that what happened to Pharmacist?'

Derek nodded. My mother now had her eyes firmly closed. The crying had abated, but she rocked back and forth in the chair.

'How do you get the orders?' I asked Derek.

'On the telephone,' he said.

There were so many questions: what, when, and, in particular, who? I refilled their brandy glasses and started the inquisition.

'How did you get into this mess?' I asked.

Neither of them said anything.

'Look,' I said. 'If you want me to help you, then you will have to tell me what's been going on.'

'I don't want your help,' my mother said quietly.

'But I'm sure we can sort out the problem,' I said. 'The solution is to find out who is doing this and stop them. And for that I need you to answer my questions.'

'No police,' my mother said.

I paused. 'But we might need the police to find the blackmailer.'

'No!' she almost shouted. 'No police.'

'So tell me about this tax business,' I said.

'No,' she said again. 'No one must know.' She was desperate.

'Josephine, dear,' Derek said. 'We need help from someone.'

'I don't want to go to prison.' She was crying again.

I suddenly felt sorry for her. It wasn't an emotion with which I was very familiar. I had, in fact, spent most of my life wanting to get even with her. I went over to her chair and stroked her shoulder.

'Mum,' I said kindly. 'They won't send you to prison.'

'Yes, they will,' she said. 'He says so.'

'The blackmailer?'

'Yes.'

'Well, I wouldn't take his word for it,' I said. 'Why don't you allow me to give you a second opinion?' I said.

'Because you'll tell the police.'

'No, I won't,' I said. 'I promise.'

I hoped so much that it was a promise I would be able to keep.

GRADUALLY, WITH PLENTY of cajoling and the rest of the bottle of Rémy Martin, I managed to piece together most of the sorry story. And it wasn't good. My mother might indeed go to prison if the police found out. She would almost certainly be convicted of tax evasion. And she would undoubtedly lose her reputation, her home and her business, even if she did manage to retain her liberty.

My mother's 'disastrous little scheme' had been the brainchild of a dodgy young accountant she had met at a party about five years previously. He had convinced her that she should register her training business offshore, in Gibraltar. Then she would enjoy the tax-free status that such a registration would bring. And somehow he had managed to assure her that even though she could go on adding the value added tax to the owners' accounts, she was no longer under any obligation to pay the money to the tax man.

Racehorse training fees are not cheap, and my mother had seventy-two stalls that were always filled. She was in demand and could charge premium prices. The VAT, whether fifteen or seventeen and a half per cent of the fees, must have run into several hundred thousand pounds a year.

'But didn't you think it was suspicious?' I asked her in disbelief.

'Of course not,' she said. 'Roderick told me it was all legal. He even showed me documents that proved it was all right.'

Roderick, it transpired, had been the young accountant.

'Do you still have these documents?'

'No. Roderick kept them.'

I bet he did.

'Roderick said the owners wouldn't be out of pocket, because all racehorse owners can claim back the VAT from the government.'

So it was the government that she was stealing from. She wasn't paying the tax as she should, yet at the same time, the owners were claiming it back. What a mess.

'Which firm does Roderick work for?' I asked.

'He was self-employed,' my mother said. 'He'd only recently qualified at university. We were lucky to find someone so cheap.'

I could hardly believe my ears.

'And what is Roderick's surname?'

'His name was Ward,' she said.

'Was?'

'He's dead. He was in a car accident about six months ago.'

'Are you sure that he's dead and hasn't just run away?' I said. 'Are you certain he's not the blackmailer?'

'Thomas,' she said, 'don't be ridiculous. The car crash was reported in the local paper. Of course I'm sure he's dead.'

I felt like asking her if she had actually seen Roderick Ward's lifeless body. In Afghanistan there were no confirmed Taliban 'kills' without the corpse to prove it.

'So how long did the little scheme of yours run? When did you stop paying the tax man?'

'Nearly four years ago,' my mother said in a whimper.

Four years of non-payment of VAT must add up to nearly a million pounds.

'Who is doing your accounts now?' I asked.

'No one,' she said. 'I was frightened of getting anyone.'

With good reason, I thought.

'Can't you pay the tax now?' I said. 'If you pay everything you owe and explain that you were misled by your accountant, I'm sure that it would prevent you from being sent to prison.'

My mother began to cry again.

'We haven't got the money to pay the tax man,' Derek said.

'But what happened to all of the extra you collected?' I asked.

'It's all gone,' he said. 'We spent a lot of it. In the beginning, mostly on holidays. And Roderick had some of it, of course. Some has gone to the blackmailer.' He sounded resigned. 'I don't honestly know where it went. We've only got fifty thousand left.'

That was a start.

'So how much are the house and stables worth?' I asked.

My mother looked horrified.

'Mother dear,' I said. 'If I'm going to keep you out of prison, then we have to find a way to pay the tax.'

'But you promised me you wouldn't tell the police,' she whined.

'I won't,' I replied. 'But if you really think the tax man won't find out eventually, then you're wrong. It will be much better for you if we go and tell them before they uncover it for themselves.'

'Oh God.'

I said nothing, allowing the awful truth to sink in. It was quite a mess, and I couldn't readily see a way out of it.

MY MOTHER AND STEPFATHER went off to bed at nine o'clock, emotional and tired from the realisation that their secret was out.

I, too, went up to my bedroom, but I didn't go to sleep.

I carefully eased my stump out of the prosthetic leg. I had been over-doing the walking, and my leg was sore and swollen. I raised the stump by placing it on a pillow, and then I lay back to think.

There was little doubt that my mother and stepfather were in real trouble. The solution for them was simple, at least in theory: raise the money, pay it to the tax man, submit a retrospective tax return, report the blackmail to the police, and then pray for forgiveness.

So the first thing to be done was to raise more than a million pounds to hand over to the Revenue. It was easier said than done.

Reluctantly, my mother and stepfather had agreed that the house and stables could fetch about £2,500,000. But the house was heavily mortgaged, and the stables had been used as collateral for a bank loan to the training business.

I thought back to the brief conversation I'd had with my stepfather after my mother had gone upstairs.

'So how much free capital is there altogether?' I'd asked him.

'About five hundred thousand.'

I was surprised that it was so little. 'But surely the training business has been earning good money for years?'

'It's not as lucrative as you might think, and your mother has always used any profits to build more stables.'

'So why is there so little free-capital value in the property?'

'Roderick advised us to increase our borrowing,' he'd said. 'He believed that capital tied up in property wasn't doing anything useful. He told us that our capital wasn't working properly for us.'

'So what did Roderick want you to do with it instead?'

'Buy into an investment fund he was very keen on. We took out another mortgage and invested it in the fund.'

'So that money is still safe?' I had asked, with renewed hope.

'Unfortunately, the fund went into bankruptcy last year.'

Why was I not surprised? 'But surely you were covered by some kind of government bailout protection insurance?'

'Sadly not,' he'd said. 'It was some sort of off-shore fund.'

'A hedge fund?'

'Yes, that's it. I knew it sounded like something to do with gardens.'

I was stunned by his naïveté. 'But didn't you take any advice? From an independent financial adviser or something?'

'Roderick said it wasn't necessary.'

'Didn't you ever think that Roderick might have been wrong?'

'No,' he'd said. 'Roderick showed us a brochure about how well the fund had done. It was all very exciting.'

'And is there any money left?'

'I had a letter that said they were trying to recover some of the funds and they would let investors know if they succeeded.'

I took that to mean no, there was nothing left.

'How much did you invest in this hedge fund?' I'd asked.

'A million US dollars.'

More than £600,000 at the prevailing rate. I supposed it could have been worse, but not much. At least there was some capital left in the real estate, although not enough.

'What about other investments?'

'I've got a few ISAs,' he'd said.

Ironically, an ISA, an individual savings account, was designed for tax-free saving, but there was a limit on investment, and each ISA could amount to only a few thousand pounds per year. They would help, but alone they were not the solution.

I wondered if the training business itself had any value. It would have if my mother was still the trainer, but I doubted that anyone buying the stables would pay much for the business. I had to assume that the business had no intrinsic value other than the real estate in which it operated, plus a bit extra for the tack and the rest of the stable kit.

I lay on my bed and did some mental adding up: the house and stables might raise half a million; the business might fetch fifty thousand, and there was fifty thousand in the bank. Add the ISAs and a few pieces of antique furniture, and we were probably still short by more than four hundred thousand. And my mother and Derek had to live somewhere. Where would they go and what could they earn if Kauri House Stables was sold?

Over the years, I had saved from my army pay and had accumulated a reasonable nest egg. I'd invested it in a more secure manner than my parent, so I had about £60,000 to my name.

I wondered if the Revenue would take instalments.

IN THE MORNING, I set to the task at hand: identifying the blackmailer, recovering the papers and my mother's money, and making things good with the tax man. It sounded deceptively simple. But where would I start?

With Roderick Ward, the con-man accountant. He had been the architect of this misery, so discovering his whereabouts, alive or dead, must be the first goal.

I called Isabella Warren from the phone in the drawing room.

'Oh, hello,' she said.

'What are you up to today?' I asked her.

'Nothing,' she said, 'as usual.'

'Can you pick me up at ten?' I asked.

'I thought you said you'd never let me drive you again.' She was laughing.

'I'll chance it,' I said. 'I need to go into Newbury, and the parking is dreadful. Are you on?'

'Definitely,' she said. 'I'll be there at ten.'

I went into the kitchen to find my mother coming in from the stables.

'Good morning,' I said.

'What's good about it?' she said.

'We're both alive,' I said.

She gave me a look that made me wonder if she had thought about not being alive this morning.

'We will sort out this problem,' I said in reassurance.

Her shoulders drooped, and she slumped onto a chair. 'I'm tired,' she said. 'I don't feel I can carry on. I've spent most of the night thinking about it. If I died, it would solve all the problems.'

'That's crazy,' I said. 'What would Derek do, for a start?'

'It would clear all the problems for him.'

'No, it wouldn't. The training business would still have to pay the tax it owes. The house and stables would be sold. You dying would leave Derek homeless and alone. Is that what you want?'

She looked up at me. 'I don't know what I want.'

'Assuming the tax problems were solved and the blackmailer was stopped, would you want to go on training?'

'I suppose so,' she said. 'It's all I know.'

'And you are so good at it,' I said, trying to raise her spirits. 'But tell me, how did you stop Pharmacist winning on Saturday?'

She almost smiled. 'I gave him a tummy ache. I fed him some rotten food. Green sprouting potatoes.'

'Green potatoes! How on earth did you think of green potatoes?'

'It had worked before,' she said. 'When *he* called the first time and said that Scientific had to lose, I was at my wits' end. If I over-galloped him, everyone in the stable would know.' She gulped. 'I was desperate. But what could I give him? I had some potatoes that had gone green. I remembered one of my dogs being ill after eating a green-skinned potato, so I peeled them and liquidised the peel. I poured it down Scientific's throat and hoped it would make him ill.'

'And it worked?' I asked.

'Seemed to, although the poor old boy was really very ill afterwards. As horses can't vomit, the stuff had to go right through him. I was scared that he'd die. So I reduced the amount the next time.'

'And it still worked?'

'Yes. But I was so frightened about Pharmacist that I used more again that time. I was worried the potatoes weren't green and rotten enough.'

'How many times have you done this?' I asked her.

'Only six,' she said. 'But Perfidio won even though I'd given him the potato peel. It didn't seem to affect him one bit.'

Would the British Horseracing Authority ever have thought of dope testing for liquidised rotten potato peel? I doubted it.

ISABELLA TOOK ME first to the Newbury Public Library. I wanted to look at past editions of the local newspapers to see what they had to say about the supposed death of one Roderick Ward.

The story of his car crash had been prominently covered on page 3 of the *Newbury Weekly News* for Thursday, July 16:

> **Another Fatal Accident at Local Black Spot**
>
> Police are investigating yet another death at one of the most dangerous spots on Oxfordshire's roads. Roderick Ward, 33, was discovered dead in his car at 8 a.m. on Monday. Police assume that Mr Ward's dark blue Renault Megane failed to negotiate the S-bends on the A415 near Standlake and collided with a bridge wall before toppling into the River Windrush. Mr Ward's car was found immersed in water, and he is thought to have died of drowning. An inquest was opened and adjourned on Tuesday at Oxford Coroner's Court.

I used the library's computerised index to check for any other references to Roderick Ward in the *Newbury Weekly News*. There was nothing else about his death, but there was a brief mention from three months before it. The paper reported that a Mr Roderick Ward of Oxford had pleaded guilty in Newbury Magistrates' Court to causing criminal damage to a private home in Hungerford. He had been observed by a police officer throwing a brick through a window of a house in Willow Close. He was ordered to pay £250 to the homeowner in compensation for the broken glass and for the distress caused. Unfortunately, the report gave no further details, for example, the name of the house owner or the identity of the policeman who witnessed the event.

I searched through the index again, but there was no report of any inquest into Roderick Ward's death. For that, I suspected I would have to go to the archive of the *Oxford Mail* or the *Oxford Times*.

'Where to now?' Isabella said as I climbed back into her Golf.

'Hungerford. Willow Close.'

'Where's that?'

'I've no idea,' I said. 'But it's in Hungerford somewhere.'

Isabella looked at me quizzically but resisted the temptation to actually ask why I wanted to go to Willow Close in Hungerford. Instead, she started the car and turned out of the library car park.

WILLOW CLOSE was in a housing estate in the southwestern corner of the town. There were twenty or so houses in the close.

'Which number?' Isabella said.

'I've no idea,' I said again. 'Someone threw a brick through the window of one of these houses, and I'd like to talk to the person whose window was smashed.'

'Why?' she asked. 'What is this all about?'

It was a good question. I didn't particularly want to tell Isabella about Roderick Ward, mostly because I had no intention of explaining anything to her about my mother's tax situation.

'The young man who's been accused of throwing the brick is a soldier in my company,' I lied. 'It's an officer's job to look after his troops, and I promised him I would investigate. That's all.'

She seemed satisfied. 'And do you have a name for the person whose window was broken?'

'No.'

'And no address,' she said.

'No,' I agreed, 'but it was reported in the local newspaper as having happened in Willow Close, Hungerford.'

'Right then,' she said decisively. 'Let's go and ask someone.'

We climbed out of the car. 'Let's start at number sixteen,' I said, pointing to one of the houses. 'I saw the curtains twitch when we arrived. Perhaps they keep an eye on everything that goes on here.'

'I'M NOT BUYING,' an elderly woman shouted through the door of number 16. 'I never buy from door-to-door salesmen.'

'We're not selling,' I shouted back through the wood. 'We'd just like to ask you some questions.'

'I don't want any religion, either,' the woman shouted again.

'Do you remember someone throwing a brick through one of your neighbour's windows?' I asked her.

'That was down the end of the close.'

'Which house?' I asked her, still through the closed door.

'George Sutton's house. I don't know numbers. Now go away.'

'Thank you,' I called through the door. 'Have a nice day.'

We went back to the car and drove towards the end of the close.

'Which house do you fancy?' I asked as we stopped at the end.

'Let's try the one with the car in the drive,' Isabella said.

We walked up the driveway past a Honda Jazz and rang the doorbell. A young woman answered, carrying a baby on her hip.

'Yes?' she said. 'Can I help you?'

'Hello,' said Isabella, jumping in and taking the lead. 'We're trying to find Mr Sutton.'

'Old Man Sutton or his son?' the young woman asked helpfully.

'Either,' Isabella said.

'Old Man Sutton has gone into a old-people's home,' the woman said. 'His son comes round sometimes to collect his mail.'

'How long has Mr Sutton been in a nursing home?' I asked.

'Since just before Christmas.'

'Do you know which home he's in?' I asked her.

'Sorry,' she said, shaking her head.

'Do you remember an incident when someone threw a brick through his window?' I asked.

'I heard about it, but it happened before we moved in,' she said. 'We've only been here eight months or so.'

'Do you know how I can contact Mr Sutton's son?' I asked her.

'Hold on. I've got his telephone number somewhere.' She disappeared into the house but was soon back with a business card.

'Here it is. Fred Sutton.' She read out his number, and Isabella wrote it down.

'Thank you,' I said. 'I'll give him a call.'

'He might be at work,' the woman said. 'He works shifts.'

'I'll try him anyway,' I said. 'What does he do?'

'He's a policeman,' she said. 'A detective sergeant.'

'So why all of a sudden don't you want to call this Fred Sutton?' Isabella demanded. We were again sitting in her car, having driven out of Willow Close and into the centre of Hungerford.

I was beginning to be sorry that I had asked Isabella to drive me. How could I explain to her that I didn't want to discuss anything to do with Willow Close with any member of the police, let alone a detective sergeant, especially if, as I suspected, DS Fred Sutton had been the policeman who had witnessed young Mr Ward throwing the brick through his father's window?

'I can't,' I said. 'I can't involve the police.'

'Why on earth not?' she asked, rather self-righteously.

'I just can't,' I said. 'I promised my young soldier I wouldn't.'

'But why not?' she asked again, imploring me to answer.

I looked at her. 'I'm really sorry,' I said. 'But I can't tell you why.' Even to my ears, I sounded melodramatic.

'Don't be ridiculous.' She was clearly annoyed. 'I think I'd better take you home now.'

'Maybe that would be best,' I said.

My chances of any bonuses had obviously diminished.

I PASSED THE AFTERNOON using my mother's computer to look up reports of inquests using the online service of the *Oxford Mail*. There were thousands.

I searched for an inquest with the name Roderick Ward, and there it was, reported briefly by the paper on Wednesday, July 15. But it had only been the opening and adjournment of the inquest immediately after the accident.

It would appear that the full inquest was yet to be heard. However, the report did contain one interesting piece of information. According to the *Oxford Mail*, Roderick Ward's body had been identified by his sister, a Mrs Stella Beecher, also from Oxford.

Perhaps Mr Roderick Ward really was dead, after all.

4

At nine o'clock sharp on Tuesday evening, my mother received another demand from the blackmailer.

The three residents of Kauri House were suffering through another unhappy dinner around the kitchen table when the telephone rang. Both my mother and stepfather jumped.

'Nine o'clock,' my stepfather said. '*He* always calls at nine.'

I stood up and started to move towards the phone.

'No,' my mother screamed, leaping to her feet. 'I'll get it.'

She pushed past me and grabbed the receiver.

'Hello,' she said. 'Yes, this is Mrs Kauri.' She listened for less than a minute. 'Yes, I understand,' she said, and placed the phone back in its cradle. 'Scientific at Newbury on Saturday.'

'To lose?' I asked.

She nodded. 'In the Game Spirit Steeple Chase.' She walked like a zombie back to her chair and sat down heavily.

'What chance would you expect Scientific to have?' I asked.

'Fairly good. He's only a novice, but I think he's ready for it.' Her shoulders slumped. 'It's not fair on the horse. If I make him ill again, it may ruin him. He'll associate racing with being ill.'

'Would he really remember?' I asked.

'Oh, yes,' she said. 'Lots of my good chasers over the years have been hopeless at home, only to run like the wind on a racetrack because they liked it there. One I had years ago, a chestnut called Butterfield; he only ran well at Sandown.' She smiled, remembering. 'Old boy loved Sandown. He definitely remembered.'

I could see a glimpse of why my mother was such a good trainer. She adored her horses and spoke of Butterfield with real affection.

'But Scientific is not the odds-on sure thing that Pharmacist was meant to be at Cheltenham last week?'

'No,' she said. 'There's another very good chaser in the race, Sovereign Owner, although I think we could beat him. Newark Hall may run as well. He's one of Ewen's and has a reasonable chance.'

'Ewen?' I asked.

'Ewen Yorke,' she said. 'Trains in the village. Has some really good horses this year. The up-and-coming young opposition.'

'So Scientific is far from a dead cert?' I said.

'He should win,' she stressed again. 'Unless he crossfires.'

'Crossfires?' I asked. 'What's that?'

'When a horse leads with a different leg in front than he does at the rear,' she explained.

'OK,' I said slowly, none the wiser. 'Does Scientific do that?'

'Sometimes,' she said. 'But he hasn't done it recently.'

'OK,' I said again. 'So even supposing that Scientific doesn't crossfire, no one would be vastly surprised if he didn't win.'

'No,' she agreed. 'It would be disappointing, but no surprise.'

'So all we have to do is ensure he doesn't win on Saturday without making him so ill he gives up on racing altogether. How about a bit of over-training on Friday so he's worn out on Saturday?'

'But everyone would know,' she said. 'There are always people watching the horses work. Some are from the media, but most are spotters for the bookmaking firms. They would easily see if I gave Scientific anything more than a gentle pipe opener on Friday.'

'Can't you make his saddle slip or something?' I asked.

'But the jockey would fall off,' she said. 'I can't do that.'

'How about if you cut through the reins just enough so that they break during the race? If the jockey can't steer, then he can't win.'

'But I'd be a laughing stock,' she said miserably. 'Horses from Kauri House Stables don't race with substandard tack.'

'Would you rather be laughed at or arrested for tax evasion?'

'Thomas is right, dear,' my stepfather said.

'So it's agreed, then,' I said. 'We will try and arrange for Scientific's reins to break during the race.'

'I suppose so,' my mother said reluctantly.

'Right,' I said positively. 'That's the first decision made.'

'What other decisions do you have in mind?'

'Nothing specific as yet,' I said. 'But I do have some questions. First, when is your next value-added tax return due?'

'I told you, I don't pay the VAT,' my mother said.

'But the stables must have a VAT registration for the other bills, like the horses' feed, the purchase of tack, and all sorts of other stuff. Don't the race entries attract VAT?'

'Roderick cancelled our registration,' she said.

If Roderick hadn't already been dead, I'd have wrung his bloody neck.

'How about the other tax returns?' I said. 'Your personal one and the training business return. When are they due?'

'Roderick dealt with all that.'

'But who has been doing it since Roderick died?' I asked in desperation.

'No one,' she said.

'Where do you keep your tax papers?' I asked.

'Roderick had them.'

'But you must have copies of your tax returns,' I implored.

'They might be in one of the filing cabinets in the office.'

I was amazed that anyone who was so brilliant at the organisation and training of seventy-two racehorses, with all the decisions and red tape that must be involved to satisfy the rules of racing, could be so hopeless when it came to anything financial.

I WAS PRETTY certain that my mother's individual self-assessment tax return, as for every other self-employed person in the United Kingdom, should have been filed with the tax office by midnight on January 31 at the latest, along with the payment of any tax due.

I looked up at the calendar on the wall above her desk. It was already February 9. There were no exceptions to the deadline, so she would have already incurred a penalty for late filing, to say nothing of the interest for late payment.

I'd checked the tax office website on the internet. It confirmed an automatic £100 late-filing penalty plus interest on the overdue tax. It also said that she had until the end of February before a five per cent surcharge of the tax due was added on top of the interest.

Very soon now the Revenue was probably going to start asking difficult questions about my mother's accounts. The time left to sort out the mess was unknown, but it had to be short.

I wondered about my own tax affairs. Sometime soon I would be receiving a tax-free lump sum of nearly £100,000 from the Armed Forces Compensation Scheme. It might keep the tax man's handcuffs from my mother's wrists. But would it be enough? And would it arrive in time?

I searched through my mother's filing cabinets and eventually found her previous year's tax return filed under R, for Roderick. Where else?

The tax return was a piece of art. It clearly showed that my mother had only minimal personal income, well below that which would have incurred any tax to be paid. It stated that her monthly income was just £200 from her business.

Possibly designed to confuse the Revenue, the return was not in the name of Mrs Josephine Kauri, and her address was not recorded as Kauri House Stables. It wasn't even in Lambourn, but at 26 Banbury Drive, Oxford. However, I did recognise the signature as being that of my mother, in her familiar curly handwriting. She had signed the form Jane Philips, her real, legal, married name.

In the same filing cabinet, I also found a Kauri House Stables Ltd corporate tax return for the previous year. It was dated May, so at least we had some breathing space before the next one was due.

I looked through it. Roderick had worked his magic here as well.

How, I wondered, did my mother afford to pay £2,000 a week in blackmail demands if, as according to the tax returns, her personal income was less than two and a half thousand a year and her business made such a small profit that it paid tax only in three figures, in spite of all the extras paid by the horse owners in non-existent VAT?

But, of course, I could find no records of the profits made by the company called Kauri House Stables (Gibraltar) Ltd. In fact, there was no reference to any such entity anywhere in the R for Roderick drawer of the filing cabinet. However, I did find one interesting sheet of paper nestling among the tax returns.

It was a letter from an investment fund manager welcoming my mother and stepfather into the select group of individuals invited to invest in his fund. The letter was dated three years previously and had been signed by a Mr Anthony Cigar of Rock Bank (Gibraltar) Ltd.

Mr Cigar hadn't actually used the term 'hedge fund', but it was quite clear from his letter, and from the attached fee schedule, that a hedge fund was what he'd managed.

I sat at my mother's desk and looked up Rock Bank (Gibraltar) Ltd on the internet. The bank's website was under construction and was unavailable to be displayed.

I went back to the Google page and clicked on the site for the *Gibraltar Chronicle*, one of the search results that had mentioned the Rock Bank. It reported that back in September, Parkin & Cleeve Ltd, a UK-based firm of liquidators, had unsuccessfully filed a suit against the individual directors of Rock Bank (Gibraltar) Ltd in an attempt to recover money on behalf of several of their clients. The directors were not named by the report, and the *Chronicle* had been unable to obtain a response from any representative of the bank. It didn't bode well for the recovery of my mother's million dollars.

I yawned and looked at my watch. It was ten to midnight, and my mother and Derek had long before gone up to bed.

I flicked off the light in the office and went upstairs. My first day as sleuth-in-residence at Kauri House Stables hadn't gone my way. I hoped for better results in the morning.

After breakfast the next morning, I went out to the stable yard in search of Ian Norland.

'You're still here, then?' he said as I found him in the feed store.

'Seems so,' I said.

I watched him measure out oats into metal bowls.

'I'm not talking to you,' he said. 'It nearly cost me my job last time.'

'We've moved on. My mother and I are now on the same side.'

'I'll wait for her to tell me that, if you don't mind.'

'She's in the kitchen right now,' I said. 'Please go and ask her. I need to talk to you.'

He went off reluctantly in the direction of the house. I hoped my mother wouldn't actually bite his head off.

In his absence, I went from the feed store into the tack room next door. It was all very neat and smelled of leather. On the left-hand wall, there were about twenty metal saddle racks, half of which were occupied by saddles. On the opposite wall, there were rows of coat hooks holding bridles. It was the bridles I was interested in.

As I looked at them, one of the stable staff came in and collected a saddle from one of the racks and a bridle from a hook.

'Are these bridles specific to each horse?' I asked him.

'Not usually. The lads have one each, and there are a few spare.'

'Are these saddles also used in the races?'

'Naah,' he said. 'The jocks have their own saddles.'

'And their own bridles?'

'Naah,' he said again. 'But we 'ave special racing ones of those. Jack keeps them in the racing tack room.'

'Who's Jack?' I said.

'Travelling 'ead lad.' He paused. 'Who are you, anyway?'

'I'm Mrs Kauri's son,' I said.

'Oh, yeah,' he said, glancing at my leg. ''Eard you were 'ere.'

'Where is the racing tack room?' I asked him.

'Round the other side,' he said, pointing through the far wall.

'Thank you, Declan,' my mother said domineeringly, coming into the tack room. 'Now get on.'

Declan went pink and scurried away with his saddle and bridle.

'I'll thank you not to interrogate my staff,' she said.

I walked round her and pulled the tack-room door shut.

'Mother,' I said formally, 'if you want me to go now, I will. Or you can let me help you and I might just keep you out of jail.'

She stood tight-lipped in front of me. At that moment, Ian Norland opened the tack-room door behind her and joined us.

'Ian,' my mother said. 'You may say what you like to my son. Please answer any questions and give him whatever help he needs.'

With that, she turned abruptly and marched out.

'I told you something strange was going on,' Ian said. 'I'll answer your questions, but don't ask me to help you if it's illegal.'

'I won't,' I said. 'I promise.'

I hoped it was another promise I'd be able to keep.

WE WERE IN the racing tack room. To my eye, the racing bridles looked identical to those in the general tack room. However, Ian assured me they were newer and of better quality. Both the bridles and the reins were predominantly made of leather, although there was a fair amount of metal and rubber as well.

'Does each horse have its own bridle?' I asked.

'They do on any given race day,' Ian said. 'But we have fifteen racing bridles in here, and they do for all our runners.'

'So say on Saturday, when Scientific runs at Newbury,' I said. 'Can you tell which bridle he'll use?'

Ian looked at me strangely. 'No. Jack will take any one of these.' He waved a hand at the fifteen bridles on their hooks.

I could see that making Scientific's bridle or reins break on Saturday was not going to be as easy as I had imagined.

'How about special nosebands?' I asked. 'Why, for example, do some horses run in sheepskin nosebands?'

'It helps the trainers see which horse is theirs,' Ian said. 'The colours aren't very easy to see when the horses are coming straight at you, especially if it's muddy.'

'Do my mother's horses all wear them?'

'No,' he said. 'Not as a general rule. But we do use them occasionally if a horse tends to run with his head held up.'

'Why's that?'

'If a horse runs with his head too high, he isn't looking at the bottom of the fences, and also, when the jockey pulls the reins, the horse will lift it higher, not put it down like he should. So we put a nice thick sheepskin on him and he has to lower his head a little to see where he's going.'

'Amazing,' I said. 'Does it really work?'

'We wouldn't do it if it didn't work,' Ian replied. 'We also sometimes put an Australian noseband on, which lifts the bit higher in the mouth to stop a horse from putting his tongue over it.'

'Is that important?' I asked.

'It can be,' Ian said. 'If a horse puts his tongue over the bit, it can push on the back of the mouth and put pressure on the airway so the horse can't breathe properly.'

There was clearly much I didn't know about racehorse training.

'I THINK YOU might have to revert to the liquidised green potato peel,' I said to my mother when I went back into the kitchen.

'Why?' she said.

'Because I can't see how we are going to arrange for Scientific's reins to break if we can't be sure which bridle he'll be wearing.'

'I'll ask Jack,' she said.

'That might be suspicious. Can't you run him in a sheepskin noseband?'

'That won't help,' she said. 'We simply fit the sheepskin to a regular bridle using Velcro.'

'How about an Australian noseband?'

'He could run in an Australian, I suppose. That would mean he would have to have the one bridle we have fitted with it.'

'Good,' I said. 'You'll have to show me later, when Ian and Jack have gone. Make sure Scientific is the only horse this week that runs in it.'

The phone rang. I picked it up. 'Hello,' I said.

'Hi, Tom. Would you like to come to supper tomorrow night?' It was Isabella. 'Seven thirty or thereabouts, at the Hall. Very casual. I'll be in jeans. It's just a kitchen supper with friends.'

'OK, thanks. I'll bring a bottle.'

'That would be great,' she said. 'See you tomorrow.'

She disconnected, and I put the phone back.

'Are you going to the races today?' I asked my mother.

'No,' she replied. 'I've no runners today.'

'So you can show me which bridle Scientific will use after lunch when the stable staff are off.'

'Do you really think you can make the reins break during the race?' she asked.

'I think it might be possible. The reins are made of leather, but they have that non-slip rubber covering sewn round them. The rubber is thin and not very strong. If I was able to break the leather inside the rubber, then it wouldn't be visible and the reins would part during the race.'

'It seems very risky,' she said.

'Would you rather use your green-potato-peel soup?' I asked.

'No,' she said adamantly. 'That could ruin the horse for ever.'

'OK,' I said. 'You show me which bridle Scientific will wear and I'll do the rest.'

Was I getting myself in too deep here? Was I about to become an accessory to a fraud on the betting public as well as to tax evasion? Yes. Guilty on both counts.

I SPENT MUCH of Thursday morning on a journey to Oxford.

Banbury Drive was in Summertown, a northern suburb of the city, and number 26 was one of a row of 1950s-built, semi-detached houses. Number 26 was the supposed address of Mrs Jane Philips, my mother, which Roderick Ward had included on her tax return.

I parked my Jaguar down the road so it wouldn't be so visible and walked to the front door of number 26. I rang the bell.

I didn't really know what to expect, but I was a little surprised when the door was opened a fraction by an elderly gentleman.

'What do you want?' he snapped through the narrow gap.

'Does someone called Mr Roderick Ward live here?' I asked.

'Never heard of him,' said the man. 'Now go away.'

The door began to close.

'He was killed in a car crash last July,' I said quickly. 'He had a sister called Stella, Stella Beecher.'

The door stopped and reopened just a fraction.

'Do you know Stella?' I asked him.

'Someone called Stella brings my Meals on Wheels,' he said.

'What time?' I asked. It was already nearly twelve o'clock.

'Around one,' he said.

'Thank you, sir,' I said. 'And what is your name, please?'

'Are you from the council?' he asked.

'Of course,' I said.

'Then you should know my bloody name,' he said, and slammed the door shut.

Damn it, I thought. *That was stupid.*

I stood on the pavement for a while, but it was cold. I took shelter in my car. I started the engine and switched on the heater.

Consequently, I almost missed the arrival of the old man's meal.

A blue Nissan pulled up in front of the house, and a woman leapt out and ran to the old man's door carrying a foil-covered tray. She had a key and let herself in. A few seconds later she emerged and was back in her car almost before I had a chance to get out of mine.

I walked in the road so she couldn't leave without running me over. I put up a hand in a police-style stop signal.

'I'm in a hurry,' she shouted.

'I just need to ask you a question,' I shouted back.

The driver's window slid down a few inches.

'Are you Stella Beecher?' I asked, coming alongside the car.

'No,' she said.

'The old man said Stella delivered his meals.'

She smiled. 'He calls all of us Stella,' she said. 'Someone called Stella used to do it for him, but she hasn't been here for months.' The woman looked at her watch. 'Sorry, I've got to go. The old people don't like me being late with their food.'

'What's his name?' I asked, nodding at the house.

'Mr Horner,' she said. 'He's a cantankerous git. Must dash.'

She revved the engine and was gone.

I walked back up the driveway of number 26 and rang the bell. There was no reply. I leaned down and called through the letterbox, 'Mr Horner, I need to ask you some questions.'

'Go away.' I could hear him in the distance. 'I'm having my lunch.'

'I only want a minute,' I shouted, again through the letterbox. 'I need to ask you about your post.'

'What about my post?' he said, from much closer.

'Do letters arrive for other people with your address on them?'

He opened the door a crack. 'Sometimes,' he said. 'Stella takes them.'

'And did Stella take them today?' I asked, knowing that the lady he called Stella hadn't taken anything away.

'No,' he said.

'Have you got any post for other people at the moment?' I asked.

'Lots of it,' he said.

'Shall I take it away for you?' I asked him.

The door opened wide. 'It's in there,' he said, pointing at a box next to his feet.

I looked down. There must have been at least thirty items of various shapes and sizes lying in a heap in the box.

'I've been wondering about it,' he said. 'Most of it's been there for months. Stella doesn't seem to take it any more.'

I reached down and picked up the contents of the box. 'Don't forget your lunch,' I said, turning towards my car.

He closed the door, and I was back in my car and speeding off before he had time to rethink the last few minutes.

I SPENT THE AFTERNOON in my bedroom impersonating a government official and then knowingly opening other people's mail—I was pretty sure that both actions were dishonest.

First I started calling nursing homes claiming to be an official from the Pensions Office enquiring after the well-being of a Mr George Sutton. I told them that I was checking that Mr Sutton was still alive and entitled to his state pension.

After about fifty fruitless calls, I was at the point of giving up when someone at the Silver Pines Nursing Home on Newbury Road, Andover, informed me that Mr George Sutton was indeed very much alive and kicking and that his pension was an essential part of the payment for his care and I'd better leave it alone or else.

Next I turned to the mail sent to 26 Banbury Drive, Oxford.

In all, there had been forty-two items, but most were junk circulars. Six, however, were of particular interest to me. Three were addressed to Mr R. Ward; a fourth to Mrs Jane Philips, my mother; and the two others to a Mrs Stella Beecher, all three persons supposedly residents of 26 Banbury Drive.

Two of the letters to Roderick Ward were simply tax circulars giving general notes of new tax bands. The third, however, was from Mr Anthony Cigar of Rock Bank (Gibraltar) Ltd formally confirming the closure of the bank's investment fund and the imminent proceedings in the Gibraltar bankruptcy court. It was dated July 7, 2009 and almost certainly did not arrive at Banbury Drive until after Roderick's fatal car accident on July 12.

The letter to Mrs Jane Philips, my mother, was more recent. It was a computer-generated notice of a penalty of £100 for the late filing of her tax return, which had been due just ten days ago.

But the two letters to Mrs Stella Beecher were the real find.

One was from the Oxford coroner's office informing her that the adjourned inquest into the death of her brother, Roderick Ward, was due to be reconvened on February 15—next Monday.

And the other was a handwritten note on lined paper that simply read in capital letters:

I DON'T KNOW WHETHER THIS WILL GET THERE IN TIME, BUT TELL HIM I HAVE THE STUFF HE WANTS.

I picked up the envelope in which it had arrived. It was a standard white envelope. The address had been handwritten in the same manner as the note. The postmark was blurred, and it was difficult to tell where it had been posted. However, the date was clear. The letter had been mailed on July 13, the day after Roderick Ward supposedly died, the very day his body had been discovered.

I sat on my bed for quite a while looking at the note and wondering if 'in time' meant before the 'accident' occurred and if 'the stuff' had anything to do with my mother's tax papers.

I was no handwriting expert, but this message to Stella Beecher looked, to my eyes, to have been written in the same style as the blackmail note that I had found on my mother's desk.

ON THURSDAY EVENING, I carried a bottle of red wine to the Hall in Lambourn for a kitchen supper with Isabella and her guests. I was looking forward to a change in both venue and company.

'Tom,' she squealed, opening the front door wide and taking my offered bottle. 'How lovely. Come and meet the others.'

I followed her towards the kitchen and the noise. The room was already full of guests. Isabella grabbed my arm and pulled me into the throng, where everyone seemed to be talking at once.

'Ewen,' she shouted to a fair-haired man about forty years old. 'Ewen, I want you to meet Tom. Tom, this is Ewen Yorke.'

We shook hands. 'Tom Forsyth,' I said.

'Ah,' he said in a dramatic manner, throwing an arm wide. 'Jackson, we have a spy in our midst.'

'A spy?' Isabella said.

'Yes,' Ewen said. 'A damn spy from Kauri Stables. Come to steal our secrets about Saturday.'

'Ah,' I said. 'You must mean about Newark Hall in the Game Spirit. You've got no chance with Scientific running.'

'There you are,' he boomed. 'What did I tell you? He's a bloody spy. Fetch the firing squad.' He laughed heartily at his own joke, and we all joined in. Little did he know.

'Where is this spy?' said a tall man pushing his way towards me.

'Tom,' said Isabella, 'this is my husband, Jackson Warren.'

'Good to meet you,' I said, shaking his proffered hand and hoping he couldn't see the envy in my eyes—envy that he had managed to snare my beautiful Isabella.

Jackson Warren certainly didn't give the impression of someone suffering from prostate cancer. I knew that he was sixty-one years old because I'd looked him up on the internet, but his lack of any grey hair seemed to belie the fact. Rather unkindly, I wondered if he dyed it, or perhaps just being married to a much younger woman had helped keep him youthful.

'So are you spying on us or on Ewen?' he asked jovially.

'Both,' I said jokily, but I had partially misjudged the moment.

'Not for the Sunday papers, I hope,' he said, changing his mood instantly from amusement to disdain. 'Though I suppose one more bastard won't make any difference.' He laughed once more, but this time the amusement didn't reach his eyes.

'Come on, darling,' said Isabella, sensing his unease. 'Relax. Tom's not a spy. In fact, he's a hero.'

I gave her a stern look, but the message didn't get through.

'A hero?' said Ewen.

Isabella was about to reply, when I cut her off sharply.

'Isabella exaggerates,' I said quickly. 'I'm in the army, that's all. And I've been in Afghanistan.'

'Really,' said an attractive woman in a low-cut dress who was standing next to Ewen. 'Was it very hot?'

'No, not really,' I said. 'It's very hot in the summer, but it's cold in the winter.' *Trust a Brit*, I thought, *to talk about the weather.*

'Did you see any action?' Ewen asked.

'A bit. But I was only there for a couple of months this last time.' Time, I thought, to change the subject. 'So, Ewen,' I said. 'How many horses do you train?'

'There you are,' he said expansively. 'I told you he was a spy.'

We all laughed.

The attractive woman next to Ewen turned out to be his wife, Julie, and I found myself sitting next to her at supper at one of two large round tables set up in the extensive Lambourn Hall kitchen.

On the other side, on my left, was a Mrs Toleron, a rather dull, grey-haired woman who didn't stop telling me about how successful her husband had been in business. She had introduced herself as Mrs Martin Toleron, as if I would recognise her spouse's name.

'You must have heard of him!' she exclaimed, amazed that I hadn't. 'He was head of Toleron Plastics until we sold out a few months ago. It was all in the papers at the time.'

I didn't tell her that a few months ago I had been fighting for my life in a Birmingham hospital.

'We were the biggest plastic drainpipe manufacturer in Europe.'

'Really? Thank goodness for rain.' She didn't get the joke.

As soon as I was able, I managed to stem the tide of plastic drainpipe talk, turning more eagerly to Julie, on my right.

'So how many horses does Ewen train?' I asked as we tucked in to lasagna and garlic bread. 'He never did tell me.'

'About sixty,' she said. 'But it's getting more all the time, so we are looking to buy the Webster place.'

'Webster place?' I asked.

'You must know, on the hill off the Wantage Road. It's been on the market for months. Price is too high, I reckon, and it needs a lot done to it.' She smiled wearily.

'He's lucky in this economic climate to have the option,' I said.

'I know,' she agreed. 'Lots of trainers are having troubles. I hear it all the time from their wives at the races.'

'Do you go racing a lot?' I asked.

'Not as much as I once did,' she said. 'Ewen is always so busy these days that I never see him—either at the races or at home.'

She sighed. Clearly, success had not brought her happiness.

'But enough about me. Tell me about you.' She turned in her chair to give me her full attention and a much better view of her ample cleavage. Ewen should spend more time with her, I thought, both at home and at the races, or he might soon find her straying.

'Not much to tell,' I said.

'Now, come on. You must have lots of stories,' she said, putting her hand on my arm. She fluttered her eyelashes at me. It made me think that it was probably already too late for Ewen—far too late.

ISABELLA INSISTED that everyone move round after the lasagna, and so, in spite of Julie Yorke's best efforts, I escaped her advances before they became too obvious, but not before she'd had the shock of her life trying to play footsie under the table with my prosthesis.

'My God! What's that?' she had exclaimed under her breath.

So I'd been forced to explain about the IED. Far from turning her off, the idea of a man with only one leg excited her further. She had become more determined to invade my privacy with questions.

As soon as Isabella suggested it, I was quick to move seats, opting to sit between Jackson Warren and another man at the second table. I'd had my fill of the female of the species for one night.

'So how long have you been back from Afghanistan?' Jackson asked me as I sat down.

'Four months,' I said.

'In hospital?' he asked.

I nodded. Isabella must have told him.

'In hospital?' the man on my other side asked.

'Yes,' I said. 'I was wounded.'

He looked at me, clearly waiting for me to expand on my answer.

'Tom lost a foot,' Jackson said, filling the silence.

'Really,' said the man with astonishment. 'Which one?'

'Does it matter?' I asked with obvious displeasure.

'Er . . .' He was suddenly uncomfortable. 'No, I suppose not. I'm sorry,' he said, looking down and intently studying his dessert plate.

'Thank you,' I said. I paused. 'It was my right foot.'

'I watched you walk over here just now, and I had no idea.'

'Prosthetic limbs have come a long way.'

'Amazing,' he said.

'I'm Tom Forsyth,' I said.

'Oh, I'm sorry,' he replied. 'Alex Reece. Good to meet you.'

We shook hands. He was a small man in his thirties, with thinning ginger hair and horn-rimmed spectacles. He was wearing a navy cardigan over a white shirt and brown flannel trousers.

'Are you a trainer, too?' I asked.

'Oh, no,' he said with a nervous laugh. 'I'm an accountant.'

'Alex here,' Jackson interjected, 'keeps my hard-earned income out of the grasping hands of the tax man.'

'I try,' Alex said with a smile.

'Legally?' I asked, smiling.

'Of course legally,' said Jackson, feigning annoyance.

'The line between avoidance, which is legal, and evasion, which isn't, can sometimes be somewhat blurred,' Alex said.

'And what exactly is that meant to mean?' demanded Jackson, the simulated irritation having been replaced by the real thing.

'Nothing,' Alex said, back-pedalling furiously and again embarrassed. 'Just that sometimes what we believe is avoidance may be seen as evasion by the Revenue.'

'And who is right?' I asked.

'We are,' Jackson stated firmly. 'Aren't we, Alex?'

'It is the courts who ultimately decide who's right,' Alex said.

'In what way?' I asked.

'We put in a return based on our understanding of the tax law,' he said, seemingly unaware of Jackson's staring eyes to my left. 'If the Revenue challenges that understanding, they might demand that we pay more tax. If we refuse to pay, they take us to court, and a jury will decide whose interpretation of the law is correct. If you lose in court, you end up paying far more than the tax you should have paid in the first place, because they will fine you on top. And the court can also send you to prison if they think you were trying to evade paying tax on purpose. It's a risk we shouldn't take.'

'Are you trying to tell me something, Alex?' Jackson asked angrily. 'Because I'm warning you, if I end up in court, I will tell them it was all my accountant's idea.'

'What was his idea?' I asked tactlessly.

'Nothing,' said Jackson, suddenly realising he'd said too much.

There was an uncomfortable few moments of silence. The others at the table, who had been listening to the exchange, suddenly decided it was best to start talking amongst themselves, and turned away.

Jackson stood up, scraping his chair on the stone floor, and stomped out of the room.

'So how long have you been Jackson's accountant?' I asked Alex.

He didn't answer but simply watched the door through which Jackson had disappeared.

'Sorry. What did you say?' he said eventually.

'I asked you how long you'd been Jackson's accountant.'

He stared at me. 'Too long,' he said.

THE KITCHEN SUPPER soon broke up, and most of the guests departed, Alex Reece being the first out of the door, almost at a run. Eventually there was only a handful remaining. I had tried, politely, to depart, but Isabella had insisted on my staying for a nightcap, and I had been easily persuaded.

Five of us, including a couple I had only seen at a distance across the room earlier, moved into the drawing room. The man was wearing a dark suit and blue tie, while the woman was in a long, charcoal-coloured jersey over a brown skirt. I placed them both in their early sixties.

'Hello,' I said to them. 'I'm Tom Forsyth.' I held out my hand.

'Yes,' said the man rather sneeringly, not shaking it. 'We know. Bella spoke of little else over dinner.'

'Really?' I said with a laugh. 'All good, I hope. And you are?'

The man said nothing.

'Peter and Rebecca Garraway,' the woman said softly. 'Please excuse my husband. He's just jealous because Bella doesn't speak about him all the time.'

I wasn't sure if she was joking or not. Peter Garraway certainly wasn't laughing. Instead, he turned away and sat down on a sofa. His wife obediently joined him. What a bundle of fun, I thought.

Isabella handed around drinks, while her husband remained conspicuous by his continued absence. But no one mentioned it.

'I thought you trainers went to bed early,' I said to Ewen Yorke as he sat next to me and buried his nose into a brandy snifter.

'You must be joking,' he said. 'And turn down our Bella's best VSOP? Not likely.' He poured the golden liquid down his throat.

Ewen's wife, Julie, had departed with the other guests, saying she was tired and was going home to bed. Her husband seemed to be in no hurry to join her.

'So, Tom,' he said, 'where does the army send you next? Back to Afghanistan? Back to the fight?'

'I think my fighting days are over.'

'So what will you do instead?' Ewen asked.

'I'm not sure,' I said. 'Perhaps I'll take up racehorse training.'

'It's not always as exciting as it appears,' he said. 'Particularly not at seven thirty on cold, wet winter mornings.'

'Especially after a late night out,' said Isabella with a laugh.

'Oh, God,' said Ewen, looking at his watch. 'Quick. Give me another slosh of brandy.'

Isabella and I laughed. Peter Garraway sat stony-faced on the sofa.

'I think it's time I was off,' I said, standing up. 'Isabella, thank you for a lovely evening. Good night, all.'

'Good night,' Ewen and Rebecca called back as Isabella showed me out into the hallway. Peter Garraway said nothing.

'Thank you for tonight,' I said as Isabella opened the front door. 'It's been great fun.'

'I'm sorry about the Garraways,' she whispered. 'They can be strange, especially him. I think he fancies me, but I think he's creepy.'

'And rather rude,' I whispered back. 'Who are they?'

'Old friends of Jackson's.' She rolled her eyes. 'Unfortunately, they're our house guests. The Garraways always come for the end of the pheasant shooting season—Peter is a great shot—and they're staying on for the races at Newbury on Saturday. Are you going?'

'Probably,' I said.

'Great. Maybe I'll see you there.'

'What exactly does Peter Garraway do?' I asked.

'He makes pots of money,' she said. 'And he owns racehorses. Ewen trains some of them.'

I thought that explained a lot.

'I don't think Mr Garraway is impressed by his trainer drinking your brandy until all hours of the night.'

'Oh, that's not the problem,' she said. 'Peter and Jackson had a row earlier. Over some business project they're working on.'

'What sort of business?' I asked.

'Financial services or something,' she said. 'I don't really know.

Business is not my thing.' She laughed. 'But Peter must do very well. We go and stay with them occasionally, and their house makes this place look like a weekend cottage. It's absolutely huge.'

'Where is it?' I asked.

'In Gibraltar.'

5

The Silver Pines Nursing Home was a modern redbrick monstrosity built onto the side of what had once been an attractive Victorian residence on the edge of the town of Andover, in Hampshire.

'Certainly, sir,' said one of the pink-uniformed carers when I asked if I might visit Mr Sutton. 'I think he's in the day room.'

I followed her along the corridor into the day room. There were about fifteen armchairs arranged around the walls. About half of the chairs were occupied, and most of the occupants were asleep.

'Mr Sutton,' called the pink lady, walking towards one elderly gentleman. 'Wake up. You've got a visitor.'

He slowly raised his head and opened his eyes.

'Hello, Mr Sutton.' I spoke in the same loud manner the woman had used. 'Do you remember me? It's John, from Willow Close.' Unsurprisingly, he stared at me without recognition. 'Jimbo and his mum send their love. Has your son, Fred, been in yet today?'

The pink lady seemed satisfied. 'Can I leave you two together, then?' she asked. 'The tea trolley will be here soon.'

'Thank you,' I said.

She walked away, and I sat down on an empty chair next to Old Man Sutton. All the while, he went on staring at me.

'I don't know you,' he said.

I looked around me. There were six other residents in the room, and all had now drifted off to sleep.

'Mr Sutton,' I said straight to his face, 'I want to ask you about a man called Roderick Ward.'

I hadn't been sure what reaction to expect. I'd thought that maybe Old

Man Sutton wouldn't be able to remember what had happened nearly a year previously. I was wrong.

'Roderick Ward is a thieving little bastard,' he said clearly.

'Roderick Ward is dead. He died in a car accident.'

'That was too good for him,' the old man said with venom.

I was slightly taken aback. 'What did he do to you?' I asked. It had to be more than throwing a brick through his window.

'He stole my life savings,' he said.

'How?' I asked.

'Some harebrained scheme of his that went bust,' he said. He shook his head. 'I should never have listened to him.'

'So he didn't exactly steal your savings?'

'As good as,' Mr Sutton replied. 'My son was furious with me. Kept saying I'd gambled away his inheritance.'

I didn't think it had been the most tactful of comments.

'And what exactly was Ward's harebrained scheme?' I asked.

'I borrowed some money against my house to invest in some fancy investment fund that Ward guaranteed would make me rich.' He sighed. 'All that happened was the fund went bust and I now have a bloody great mortgage, and I can't afford the interest.'

'How come Ward threw a brick through your window?'

He smiled. 'I poured tea in his lap. He came to tell me that I'd lost all my money. He told me I should have realised that investments could go down as well as up.' He smiled again. 'So I poured the hot tea from the teapot I was holding straight into his lap.'

'So he went out and threw the brick through your window?'

'Yeah, as he was leaving, but my son saw him do it and arrested him.' He stopped smiling. 'But then I had to tell Fred the whole story about losing the money.'

So he had lost his money about a year ago. Before the same fate had befallen my mother.

'Mr Sutton,' I said. 'Can you remember anything about the investment fund that went bust? Was it an off-shore fund?' I asked.

He looked quizzically at me. 'I don't think so.' He shook his head. 'I can't remember.' He had begun to dribble from the corner of his mouth, and there were tears in his eyes.

It was time for me to go.

SATURDAY MORNING dawned crisp and bright, with the winter sun doing its best to thaw the frosty ground.

I had spent an hour in the racing tack room on Friday doing my best to ensure that Scientific's reins would part during his race. My mother had shown me the bridle that had the Australian noseband, and I had been dismayed to see its pristine condition.

I'd looked at where the reins were attached to the metal rings on either side of the bit. The leather was sewn back on itself with multiple stitches of strong thread. I had tested it with all my strength without even an iota of separation. How about if I cut through most of the stitches? But with what? And wouldn't it show?

There were four green first-aid boxes stacked on a shelf in the racing tack room, and I'd opened one looking for a pair of scissors. I'd found something better: a surgical scalpel.

With great care, I cut through the stitches on the right side of the bridle. I'd been careful to cut only the stitches in the middle, leaving both ends intact so the sabotage was less obvious. I had no idea if it was enough, but it would have to do.

MY MOTHER drove us to Newbury in her old Ford, my stepfather sitting next to her in the front while I was in the back behind her, as I had been so often before, on the way to and from the races.

By the time she pulled into the trainers' car park, it was nearly full.

'Hello, Josephine,' called a voice as we stepped out of the car. Ewen Yorke was standing just in front of us.

'Oh, hello, Ewen,' replied my mother without warmth.

'Hiya, Tom,' Julie Yorke called as she climbed out of their brand-new white BMW, a fact not lost on my mother.

Julie was dressed in a thin, figure-hugging silk dress with a matching but equally thin print-patterned topcoat. Rather inappropriate, I thought, for a cold February afternoon, but it clearly warmed the hearts of several male admirers who walked by.

'Hi, Julie,' I replied with a small wave.

My mother looked at me disapprovingly. I was sure that she would be desperate to discover how I knew them. I'd not mentioned to her where I had gone to dinner on Thursday night. I had let her assume that I had gone down to one of the village pubs.

We hung back, putting on our own coats and hats, as the Yorkes made their way to the entrance. We watched them go.

'If Scientific is not able to win today,' my mother said icily, 'I just hope it's not bloody Newark Hall. I can't stand that man.'

I looked around quickly to see if anyone had heard her comment. 'If I were you,' I said forcefully but quietly, 'I'd keep my voice down. This parking lot is also used by the stewards.'

THE GAME SPIRIT Steeple Chase was the second race on the card. I stood nervously at the entrance to the pre-parade ring waiting for the horses to be led in by the stable lads.

To say that I was relieved when Scientific came into the ring was an understatement. I looked closely at his bridle. It appeared to be the same one that I had tampered with. So far, so good.

I wandered over to the saddling stalls and waited for Scientific to be brought over by Declan, the stable lad. Presently my mother and stepfather arrived; then the travelling head lad, Jack, appeared, trotting into the saddling stall with the jockey's minuscule saddle under his arm.

My mother and Jack busied themselves, one on each side of the animal, applying under-saddle pad, weight cloth, number cloth, and then the saddle. With a slap on his neck from Jack, Scientific was sent to the parade ring for inspection by the betting public.

A racetrack official rang a handbell, and I watched as Declan turned Scientific inwards, waiting for my mother and stepfather to walk over with the horse's owner and jockey. Declan stood impassively as my mother tossed the lightweight rider up onto his equally slight saddle. The jockey placed his feet in the stirrup irons and gathered the reins. The horses moved down the horse walk towards the racetrack, and the crowd moved towards the grandstand.

'Hello, Tom,' said a voice from behind me.

I turned around. 'Oh, hello.' I kissed Isabella on the cheek. Jackson was with her, and they had the Garraways in tow.

'Fancy a drink?' Jackson said, clapping me on the shoulder.

'Later,' I said. 'I want to watch this race.'

'Come on up to our box, and we can do both.'

I had been trying to spot my mother in the throng of people so I could watch the race with her, but I couldn't see her. It was probably just as well.

Together we would be a pair of nervous wrecks.

'Thank you. I'd love to,' I said to Jackson, smiling at Isabella.

'Good,' she said, smiling back.

'And thank you both for a lovely evening on Thursday,' I said.

'It was a pleasure to have you,' said Jackson. 'We all really enjoyed it.' Unsurprisingly, he made no mention of his early departure from supper or his untimely row with Alex Reece.

'How's Alex?' I asked, perhaps unwisely.

'Alex?' he said, looking at me.

'Alex Reece,' I said. 'Your accountant.'

'Oh, him,' Jackson said with a forced smile. 'Bloody little weasel needs a good kick up the arse.' He guffawed loudly.

'Really?' I said. 'I'll be needing an accountant soon myself. I thought I might go and see him. Are you saying I shouldn't?'

I was playing with him, and he suddenly didn't like it.

'Ask whoever you bloody like,' he said dismissively.

As we climbed the few steps to the entrance of the Berkshire Stand, we were joined by the Yorkes.

'Ah, the spy again,' said Ewen, smiling.

I smiled back. I found myself crammed into the lift with my back against the wall and with Julie Yorke standing close in front. We arrived at the fourth floor, and stepped out of the lift. Julie smiled as I held the door of the box open for her, a seductive, inviting smile.

'Come and see me some time,' she whispered as she went past.

Jackson offered me a glass of champagne, and I took it onto the balcony to watch the horses and escape from Julie.

'Do you think he'll win?' It was a moment before I realised that Rebecca Garraway was talking to me.

'Who?' I asked.

'Newark Hall, of course,' she said. 'Our horse.'

I hadn't realised that the Garraways were Newark Hall's owners.

'He has a good chance,' I said back to her.

In truth, he had a better chance than she appreciated.

Ewen Yorke was standing to my left, looking through his binoculars. 'Seems we have a problem,' he said, still looking. 'It's Scientific. Seems his reins have snapped. He's running away.'

I looked down the course in horror, but without the benefit of Ewen's multi-magnification, I was unable to see exactly what was going on.

'Good. They've caught him,' Ewen said. 'No real harm done.'

'So what will happen?' I asked. 'Will Scientific be withdrawn?'

'Oh, no. They'll just fit a new bridle on him down at the start. The starter always has a spare, just in case something breaks. Most unlike your mother to have a tack malfunction.' He almost laughed.

I felt sick. What would the blackmailer do if Scientific won?

'They're off!' announced the public-address system, and all twelve runners moved away slowly, not one of the jockeys eager to set the early pace. They jumped the first fence without breaking into a gallop, and then the horses gathered pace.

Even though I wanted to, I couldn't take my eyes off Scientific.

I suppose I was hoping he might have crossfired and cut into himself, but the horse appeared to gallop along easily, without any problems.

My mother had said that Scientific was a good novice but that the Game Spirit Steeple Chase was a considerable step up in class. It didn't show. The horse jumped all the way round without putting a hoof wrong and he was well placed in the leading trio as they turned into the finishing straight for the second and final time. The other two contenders were Newark Hall and Sovereign Owner.

The three horses jumped the last fence abreast and battled together all the way to the finish line with the crowd cheering.

'Photograph!' announced the judge as the horses flashed past the winning post. No one was sure which of the three had won.

Ewen Yorke and the Garraways rushed out to get to the winner's enclosure, confident that their horse had done enough, and Jackson went with them, leaving me in the box with Isabella and Julie.

The public-address system announced: 'Here is the result of the photograph. First number ten, second number six, third number eleven.'

Number ten, the winner, was Scientific. He'd won by a short head from Newark Hall. Sovereign Owner had been third.

Oh, hell, I thought.

'Oh, well,' said Julie, shrugging her shoulders. 'There's always next time. But Ewen will be like a caged tiger tonight. He hates so much to lose.' She smiled at me again in a seductive manner.

It wasn't Ewen, I thought, who was the caged tiger; it was his wife. And I had no desire to release her.

I watched on the television in the corner of the box as my mother greeted her winner, a genuine smile of triumph on her face. In the euphoria of victory, she had clearly forgotten that she had disobeyed the instructions of the man who might hold the keys to her prison cell.

She might as well enjoy it while she could.

'WHAT THE BLOODY hell is going on?' Ian Norland stood in the middle of the Kauri House kitchen shouting at my mother and me. He had thrown the bridle with the broken reins onto the table.

'Ian, please don't shout at me,' my mother said. 'And what's the problem, anyway? Scientific won, didn't he?'

'More by luck than judgment,' Ian almost shouted at her. 'Why did you make the reins break?'

'Are you accusing us of deliberately sabotaging the reins?' my mother asked in her most pompous manner.

'Yes, I am. This bridle was brand new. If I don't get some answers, I'm leaving here tonight for good and I will take this to the racing authorities on Monday morning.' He picked up the bridle.

'What on earth makes you think we had anything to do with the reins breaking?' I asked him innocently.

Ian gave me a contemptuous look. 'Because you've been so bloody interested in the racing tack all week, asking questions and all. What else am I going to think?'

'Don't be ridiculous,' said my mother.

'And how about the others?' he said. 'Pharmacist last week and Oregon the week before. Did you stop them from winning, too?'

'No, of course not.' My mother sounded affronted.

'Why should I believe you?' Ian said.

'Because, Ian,' I said in my best voice of command, 'you must. If you choose to leave here, I will have to insist that you do not take any of my mother's property with you. That includes that bridle.'

I held out my hand. Reluctantly, he passed the bridle over to me.

'Good,' I said. 'Now, my mother's stable is committed to winning. My mother will not tolerate any of her employees who might suggest otherwise. Do I make myself clear?'

He looked at me in mild surprise. 'I suppose so,' he said. 'But you have to promise me that there will be no more of this.' He pointed at the bridle.

'I do promise,' I said. There was no way I would be trying this cutting-the-reins malarkey again. 'Does that mean you're staying?'

'Maybe,' he said slowly. 'I'll decide in the morning.'

'OK,' I said. 'We'll see you in the morning, then.' I said it by way of dismissal, and he reluctantly turned away.

DINNER ON SATURDAY night was a grim affair. As before, the three of us sat at the kitchen table, eating a casserole that had been slow-cooking while we had been at the races.

'So what do we do now?' I asked into the silence. 'Do we just sit and wait for the blackmailer to come a-calling?'

'What else do you suggest?' my mother asked.

'Oh, I don't know,' I said in frustration. 'I just feel it's time for us to start controlling him, not the other way round.'

We sat there in silence for a while.

'When you paid him this week, how did you pay?' I asked.

'In cash,' Derek said. 'By post to somewhere in Newbury.'

'And how did you get the address in the first place?'

'It was included with the first blackmail note.'

'And when did that arrive?'

'In July last year.'

When Roderick Ward had his accident. 'And the address has been the same since the beginning?' I asked him.

'Yes,' he said. 'I have to place two thousand pounds in fifty-pound notes in a padded envelope and post it each Thursday.'

'Can you get me the address?' I asked.

As he stood up to fetch it, the telephone rang. As one, we all looked at the kitchen clock. It was exactly nine o'clock.

'Let me answer it,' I said, striding across the kitchen.

'No,' my mother shouted, jumping up. But I ignored her.

'Hello,' I said into the phone.

There was a click on the line. The person had hung up.

I replaced the receiver back on its cradle.

'Talkative, isn't he?' I said, smiling at my mother.

She was cross. 'Why did you do that?' she demanded.

'Because he has to learn that we aren't going to just roll over and do everything he says.'

The phone rang again.

'Hello,' I said. 'Kauri House Stables.'

'Mrs Kauri, please,' said a whispered voice.

'She can't speak just now,' I said. 'Can I give her a message?'

'Give me Mrs Kauri,' the person whispered again.

'No,' I said. 'You will have to talk to me.'

The line went click again as he hung up.

My mother was crosser than ever. 'Thomas,' she said, 'please do not do that again.' She was almost crying. 'We must do as he says. He'll send the stuff to the tax man if we don't.'

'No, he won't,' I said. 'What has he to gain? In fact, he has everything to lose. You are paying him two thousand a week, and he won't get that if he tips off the tax man.'

'But why are you antagonising him?' my stepfather said.

'Because I need to see who it is,' I said. 'If I knew the identity of the enemy, I could then start to fight him.'

'I don't want you to fight him,' my mother said forlornly.

'Well, we have to do something.'

The phone rang again. I picked it up.

'Kauri House Stables,' I said.

Silence.

'Now listen here, you little creep. You can't speak to Mrs Kauri. You'll have to speak to me. I'm her son, Thomas Forsyth.'

More silence.

'And another thing,' I said. 'All the horses from these stables will, in the future, be trying their best to win. Do you understand?'

There was a click as he disconnected.

I had just committed a tactical gamble. I had exposed myself to the enemy.

SUNDAY HAD BEEN an uneventful day with no further telephone calls from the blackmailer.

My mother had responded to my initiative of Saturday evening by withdrawing into her shell and not appearing at all from her bedroom.

Ian Norland had not made another appearance in the house on Sunday morning, and I had watched through the kitchen window as he had directed the stable staff in the feeding and watering of the horses. I had taken it to mean that he had decided to stay.

At noon on Sunday, I had driven into Newbury, using the Jaguar's satellite navigation to find the address that Derek had finally given me, the address where he sent the weekly cash payments.

'But it's so close,' I'd said to my stepfather. 'Surely you've been to see where it is you send all this money.'

'He said not to,' he'd replied.

'And you obeyed him?' I'd asked incredulously. 'Didn't you just drive past to see? Even in the middle of the night?'

'We mustn't. We have to do exactly what he says.' He had been close to tears. 'We're so frightened.'

I could see. 'So when did the telephone calls start?'

'Just before Christmas.' Two months ago.

I hadn't really expected the address to provide any great revelation into the identity of the blackmailer, and I'd been right.

Number 46 Cheap Street, Newbury, turned out to be a shop with rentable mailboxes, and suite 116 was a single six-by-four-inch grey mailbox at shoulder level. The shop was closed on Sundays.

I had returned to Kauri House from Newbury via the Wheelwright Arms for a lunch of roast beef with all the trimmings.

EARLY THE NEXT morning, I drove to Oxford and parked near the Westgate shopping centre. The city centre was quiet.

Oxford Coroner's Court was housed next to the Oxfordshire County Council building in New Road, near the old prison. According to the court proceedings notice, the case of Roderick Ward, deceased, was the first on the coroner's list for the day.

I went inside and sat in the public gallery. Into the courtroom came men in suits, plus one in a sweater and jeans who joined me in the public gallery. He looked familiar, but I didn't know him.

There was no young woman in the court who might have been Stella Beecher. But then, she had never received the letter sent to her at 26 Banbury Drive by the coroner's office to inform her that the inquest was going to reconvene today. I was sure of that, because the letter was currently in my pocket.

The inquest began with the coroner giving the details of the deceased, Mr Roderick Ward. His address was given as 26 Banbury Drive, Oxford, but I knew that was false. The coroner went on to say that the body of the deceased had been identified by his sister, Mrs Stella Beecher, of the same address. Another lie.

The first witness was a policeman from the Thames Valley Police road traffic accident investigation team, who described the circumstances surrounding the death of Roderick Ward on July 12.

'Mr Ward had been proceeding along the A415 in a southerly direction. He veered over to the wrong side of the road and struck the concrete parapet of the bridge over the River Windrush. The vehicle then went into the river, where it was found by a fisherman the morning of July thirteen. The deceased's body was discovered inside the vehicle when it was lifted. The vehicle had been slightly damaged but was found to be in full working order. It appeared that this collision was unlikely to have been of sufficient force to prove fatal. From the position and directions of the marks on the grass, I conclude that the driver might have fallen asleep at the wheel.'

The policeman stopped and waited while the coroner made notes.

'Has anyone any questions for this officer?' said the coroner, raising his head from his notebook.

'Yes, sir,' said a tall gentleman in a pin-striped suit, standing up.

The coroner nodded at him, clearly in recognition.

'Officer,' the tall man said, 'in your opinion, would this life have been saved if a crash barrier had been fitted at the point where the car went off the road into the water?'

'Most probably, yes,' said the policeman.

'And would you agree,' the pin-striped suit went on, 'that the failure of the Oxfordshire County Council to erect a crash barrier at that known accident black spot was tantamount to negligence on their behalf, negligence that resulted in the death of Roderick Ward?'

'Objection,' said another suit. 'Counsel is leading the witness.'

'Thank you, Mr Sims,' said the coroner. 'I know the procedures of this court.' He turned towards the first suit.'Now, Mr Hoogland, I agreed that you could ask questions of the witnesses, but this question is not answerable by this court, and would be better asked in any civil case that may be brought in a county court,' said the coroner. 'I uphold the objection. Are there any further questions of this witness?'

There was no fresh movement from Mr Hoogland other than to sit down. He had made his point.

I wanted to stand up and ask the officer if the circumstances of this death could have been staged such that it only appeared that the deceased had fallen asleep, hit the bridge, and ended up in the river when, in fact, he had been murdered? But, of course, I didn't.

'Thank you, Officer,' said the coroner. 'You may step down.'

The policeman left the witness box and was replaced by a balding man wearing a tweed suit. He stated his name as Dr Geoffrey Vegas, pathologist at the John Radcliffe Hospital in Oxford.

'Now, Dr Vegas,' said the coroner, 'can you please tell the court what knowledge you have concerning Mr Roderick Ward?'

'Certainly,' replied the doctor. 'On the morning of July thirteenth, I examined the body in situ and gave instructions that the body be removed to my laboratory at the John Radcliffe.'

'Did you perform a post-mortem examination at the hospital?'

'Yes,' replied Dr Vegas. 'I concluded that death was due to asphyxia, resulting in cardiac arrest. The asphyxia appeared to be due to prolonged immersion in water. Put simply, he drowned. There was water in the lungs and in the stomach, both of which indicate that the deceased was alive when he entered the water.'

'Are there any other findings that you would like to bring to the court's attention?' asked the coroner.

'A blood test indicated that the deceased had been more than three times over the legal alcohol limit for driving a vehicle.'

'Thank you, Doctor,' said the coroner. 'Does anyone else have any questions for this witness?'

I wanted to ask if he had done a test to confirm that the water in the lungs had come from the river. Could the man not have been forced to drink heavily, then been drowned elsewhere and tipped into the river when he was already dead? But, of course, again I didn't.

The coroner, using his notes, summed up the evidence and then recorded a verdict of accidental death with Mr Ward's excessive alcohol consumption as a contributory factor.

No one objected; no one cried foul; no one believed that a whitewash had occurred. No one other than me, that is.

I stood and followed the man in the sweater out of the courtroom.

'Are you family?' I asked his back.

He turned towards me, and I thought again that I recognised him.

'No,' he said. 'Are you?'

'No,' I said.

He smiled and turned away. In profile, I suddenly realised who he must be. I'd spoken to his father the previous Friday. They had the same shape of head. The man was Fred Sutton, the son of Old Man Sutton, he of the broken window.

I HUNG BACK as Fred Sutton made his way out of the building. I didn't want to talk to him, but I did want to speak to Mr Hoogland.

I caught up with him in the lobby.

'Excuse me, Mr Hoogland,' I said. 'I was in the court just now, and I wondered who you were acting for.'

He turned and looked at me. 'And who are you?' he demanded.

'Just a friend of Roderick Ward's,' I said.

'I am acting for a life insurance company,' he said.

'Really,' I said. 'So was Roderick's life insured?'

'I couldn't say,' he said, but it was obvious it had been; otherwise, why was he asking questions and trying to imply negligence by the county council?

'So were you satisfied with the verdict?' I asked.

'It's what we expected,' Mr Hoogland said dismissively.

'Are you sure that the dead man in the car was Roderick Ward?'

'What?' he said, suddenly giving me his full attention. 'Yes, of course. The body was identified by his sister.'

'Yes, but where is the sister today?' I said. 'And is she the beneficiary of your client's insurance policy?'

He stared at me. 'What are you implying?'

'Nothing,' I lied. 'I'm just curious. If my brother had died, I'd be at the inquest.' Mr Hoogland wasn't to know that the coroner's letter to Stella Beecher was in my pocket. 'Anyway, I don't have access to the pathologist's report. For all I know, he might have already done a DNA test and checked it against the DNA database.'

'Why would Ward's DNA be in the database?' he asked.

'Because he was arrested for breaking windows,' I replied. 'It should be there.'

Mr Hoogland opened a notebook and made some notes.

'And what is your name?' he asked.

'Is that important?' I said.

'You can't go round making accusations anonymously.'

'I'm not accusing anyone,' I said. 'I just asked you if you were sure it was Roderick Ward in that car.'

'That in itself is an accusation of fraud.'

'Or murder,' I said.

He stared at me again. 'Are you serious?'

'Very,' I said. 'It just seems too easy. Late at night on a road with no traffic, low-speed collision, alcohol, car tips into deep river, no attempt to get out of the car, life insurance. Need I go on?'

'So what are you going to do about your theory?'

'Nothing,' I said. 'It's not me that has the client who's about to pay out a large sum in life insurance.'

I could see in his face that he was having doubts.

'At least find out for sure if the deceased really was Roderick Ward by getting a DNA test done. And ask the pathologist if he determined if the water in the lungs actually came from the river.'

'You have a suspicious mind,' he said.

'Exactly,' I said. 'Do you have a card?'

He fished one out of his jacket pocket and gave it to me.

'I'll call you,' I said, turning away.

'Right,' he shouted to my departing back. 'You do that.'

6

I woke in agony. And in the pitch-black. Where was I?

My arms hurt badly, my head was spinning, and there was some sort of cloth on my face—rough cloth, like a sack.

It felt as if I was hanging by my arms. My back ached, and my head pounded. I felt sick, and I could smell the rancid odour of vomit on the cloth over my face. How did I get here? I tried to remember, but the pain in my arms clouded every thought. My upper body screamed in agony, and I could hear myself screaming with it.

Apart from the ongoing fire in my back and arms, my left leg also hurt. 'Concentrate,' I shouted out loud at myself. Why does my heel hurt? Because it's pressing on the floor. I realised that I wasn't hanging straight down. My left foot was stretched out in front of me. I bent my knee, pulled my foot back, and stood up. The searing agony in my shoulders instantly abated.

Where was I? What had happened? And how had I got here?

I felt dizzy. Why couldn't I stand up properly?

Then I remembered that, too.

I reached down to the floor with my right leg. Nothing. My prosthesis was missing. I could feel the empty right trouser leg flapping against my left calf as I moved my leg back and forth.

Standing up, even on one leg, had vastly improved the pain in my back and shoulders, and feeling was beginning to return to my hands with the onset of horrendous pins and needles. But that was a pain I could bear.

I turned my head from side to side. Not a chink of light was visible through the hood. I listened but could hear nothing. I smelled the air. The stench of vomit clouded everything, but there was a faint sweet smell alongside it, something like an alcoholic solvent.

With my fingers, I searched around the space above my head. My wrists were tightly bound by some sort of thin plastic, which was attached to a chain. I followed the chain along its short length until I came to a ring fixed into the wall. The ring was set just over my head height, six-foot-six or so from the floor, and was about two inches across. The chain was secured to it with a padlock.

I leaned forward against the wall. There was something running horizontally that was sticking into my elbows. I couldn't quite get my hands low enough to feel it, so I used my face through the cloth. The horizontal bar ran in both directions as far as I could feel, with a small ledge above it. Suddenly I knew where I was.

I was in a stable. The horizontal bar and ledge was the top of the wooden boarding that runs around a stall to protect a horse from kicking out at the unforgiving brick or stone. And the ring in the wall was there to tie up the horse or to hang a hay net.

But which stable was I in?

I shouted. 'Can anyone hear me? Help! Help!'

I went on shouting for ages but no one came running. I don't think the hood helped. My voice sounded very loud to me inside it but I wondered if the noise had even penetrated beyond the stable.

I was pretty sure I wasn't at Kauri House Stables. It was too quiet. Even if there had been an empty stall in my mother's yard, there would be horses nearby, and horses make noises, even at night, and especially if someone is shouting their head off next door.

I was beginning to be particularly irritated by the hood, not least by having to breathe vomit fumes, even if it was my own vomit. I tried to hold the material and pull it off but it was tied too tightly round my neck and I couldn't reach down with my hands far enough to untie it. I would just have to stand the irritation. It was nothing compared to the previous pain in my shoulders.

I stood on my one leg for a long time. Occasionally I would lean back against the wall, but mostly I just stood.

Night turned into day. I found that I could tell because a very small amount of light did penetrate the hood, and if I turned my head, I could just tell that there was a window to my left.

The day brought nothing new. I went on standing for hours.

I was hungry and thirsty, and my leg began to ache. And to make matters worse, I desperately needed to pee.

I tried to remember how I had come to be here. I could recall the inquest and speaking to Mr Hoogland. What happened after that?

I had walked back to my car in the multi-storey car park. I could remember being annoyed. The car park was almost empty, but someone had parked within a foot of my car. I remembered wondering how I was going to open the driver's door wide enough to get in. But I had never reached the door to try.

Something had knocked me down, and I remembered feeling a towel on my face. The towel had been soaked in ether. I had known immediately what it was. And the next thing I knew was waking up in this predicament.

Who could have done such a thing?

As time passed, I became hungrier, and the pain in my bladder grew to the extent that, in the end, I had to let go, the urine briefly warming my leg as it ran down to the floor.

But it was the thirst and the fatigue that were becoming my greatest problems. I spent some more time shouting, but no one came and it just made me even thirstier.

What did the people who did this want from me? I would gladly give them everything I owned just to sit down with a glass of water.

Surely someone would come soon?

But they didn't and, as the light from the window went away as day turned into my second night in the stable, eventually it dawned on me that my kidnapper wasn't going to arrive with food and water.

I faced the shocking reality that I wasn't here to be ransomed; I was here to die.

IN SPITE of the pain in my leg, I went to sleep standing up.

I only realised when I lost my balance and was woken by the jerk of the chain attached to my wrists. I twisted and stood up again. I was cold. I'd been wearing an overcoat when I walked back to the car from the coroner's court, but it had been removed.

I shivered, but the cold was the least of my worries.

I was desperately thirsty, and I knew that my body must be getting dehydrated. I knew from my training that human beings could live only a matter of a few days without water.

It was time to save myself. First things first. I had to get myself disconnected from the ring in the wall. It sounded deceptively easy.

I reached up to where the chain was attached by the padlock. The ring stuck straight out from the wall. I grabbed it with my right hand and tried to twist it. It didn't budge. I jerked it with the chain. But still the ring didn't shift. If I couldn't detach myself from the ring, then I would hang here until I died of dehydration.

I rested my head in frustration on the ledge at the top of the wooden panelling. So fed up was I that I bit through the cloth of the hood into the wood. It moved.

I thought I must be imagining it, so I bit the wood again. It definitely moved.

I felt around with my face. The ledge on the top of the panelling was about an inch and a half wide, with its front edge curved, and it was the curved edge that had moved. It was obviously a facing strip that had been glued or nailed to the front of the ledge.

I bit into the wood again. I found I could get my front teeth behind the curved beading. I bit hard and pulled backwards, using my arms to press on the wall. The curved beading strip came away from the ledge far enough for me to get my mouth around it properly. I pulled back again, and it came away some more.

I was pulling so hard with my mouth that, when one end of the strip came completely free, I again lost my balance and ended up hanging from the chain. But I didn't care. I pulled my knee back under me and stood up. The beading was flapping, with one end free and the other not. There had obviously been a join in the wood just a little way to my left.

I held the wood in my mouth and twisted my neck to the right, making the free end bend upwards. I could feel the free end on my arms, and finally I was able to grasp the strip in my hands.

I now bent myself to the right, folding the strip back on itself.

It snapped with a splintering crack, leaving me holding a free length of the beading, which I put through the ring and used like a handle. I leaned on it with as much weight as I dared.

The ring moved. I felt it. I leaned again. It moved some more.

I was so excited that I was laughing.

The ring had moved half a revolution. I reached up and tried to turn it with my fingers. It was stiff, but it turned—slowly at first, then over and over until I could feel it part company with the wall.

I could lower my arms. I was free of my shackle. What bliss!

With difficulty, I sat down on the floor. I still had my wrists tied, but the joy of not having to stand up any longer was immense.

Stage one was complete. Now I had to remove the hood and free my wrists. I lifted my hands to my neck and found the drawstring of the hood. I managed to untie the knot, and I gratefully pulled the fetid cloth from over my head. I breathed deeply.

Stage two complete. Now for my hands.

It was too dark to see how they were tied, but by feeling with my tongue, I worked out that my kidnapper had used the sort of ties that gardeners use to secure saplings to poles. The loose end went through a collar on the other end and was then pulled tight. One tie on each wrist intertwined both with each other and with the chain.

I tried biting my way through the plastic, but it was too tough. I looked around. There was just enough light for me to see the position of the window. I thought that if I could get outside, I might be able to find something to cut the plastic.

How about the glass in the window? Could I use that to cut the plastic? I hopped along the wall to the window.

It wasn't glass; it was Plexiglas. It would be. I suppose the horses would break glass. The window was actually made of two panes of Plexiglas in wooden frames, one above the other, like a sash window. I slid the bottom pane up. The fresh air tasted so sweet.

But now I discovered there was another problem. The window was covered on the outside by metal bars set about four inches apart. I could feel the panic beginning to rise in me. I was so thirsty, and I could hear rain. I held my arms out through the window as far as they would go but they didn't reach the falling water. There was just enough light for me to see that the roof had an overhang. I would have needed arms six feet long to reach the rain. And, to add insult to injury, it began to fall more heavily, beating like a drum against the stable roof.

More in hope than expectation, I hopped further along the wall to the stall doors. As expected, they were bolted. I pushed at them, but unsurprisingly they didn't shift.

I slithered down in the corner by the door until I was again sitting on the floor. I gave up and went to sleep.

IT WAS LIGHT when I woke, and I could see my prison cell properly for the first time. It was a regular stable stall with wooden boarding around the walls and timber roof beams visible above.

I worked myself back into the corner by the door and sat up, leaning against the wall, to inspect the bindings on my wrists.

The black plastic ties looked thin and flimsy, but try as I might, I couldn't break them. The length of chain was still attached to the ties. It was grey and looked like galvanised steel, with a shiny brass padlock still attaching the end link to the now-unscrewed ring.

I looked around the stall for something sharp. Up on the wall opposite the window was a salt-lick housing, a metal slot about four inches wide, seven high, and one inch deep, into which a block of salt or minerals could be dropped so that, as the name suggested, the horse could lick it. The housing was empty, old and rusting.

I struggled up from the floor and hopped over to it. As I'd hoped, the top of the metal slot had been roughened by rust. I hooked the plastic ties over one of the edges, with a wrist on either side, and sawed back and forth. The plastic on my left wrist parted easily.

I massaged the flesh, then set about ridding myself of the remaining tie around my right wrist and the chain that still hung from it. After a few minutes, I was finally free of the damn things.

Stage three was complete. Now to get out of this stable.

Stable doors are always locked from the outside, and this one was no exception. I could just see the locks from the window. By turning sideways I could use my left eye to see the bolts: top and bottom in the lower door and a single bolt in the upper.

The only way out was up.

I could see from the window that the stall where I was imprisoned was just one in a whole line of them that stretched in both directions. The walls between the individual stalls did not go all the way to the pitched roof; they were the same height as the walls at the front and rear of the building, about nine feet high. So there was a triangular space between the top of the wall and the roof. There was plenty of room for someone to get through the gap from one stall to the next. All I had to do was climb the wall.

Easy, I thought. There had been walls much higher than this on the assault course at Sandhurst, walls I had been forced to cross time and time again. However, I'd had two feet to work with then.

I looked at either side of the stall. Which way should I go?

In the end, the decision was simple. In the corner opposite the door was a metal manger set across the angle. It was about four feet from the floor.

I may have had only one foot, but I had two knees, and I was soon using them to kneel on the edge of the manger while reaching up with my fingers for the top of the wall. Fuelled by a massive determination to free myself, I pulled myself up onto the top of the wall and swung my legs into the next stall.

Dropping down was less easy, and I ended up sprawled on my back. But I didn't care; I was laughing again. I turned over and crawled on my hands and knees to the door.

It was locked. My cries of joy turned to tears of frustration.

OK, I thought, *how about the window?*

More bars. Squeezing myself up against them, I could see that there were bars on all the stall windows. I just had to keep going. One of the stalls would have a door that was open.

Having done it once, it was easier the second time. I even managed not to end up horizontal on the floor. But the next door was also locked. What if they were all locked?

Willpower alone pulled me up over the next wall. But I found I wasn't in another stall but in an empty tack room.

The tack-room door was locked. It would be. But suddenly I realised there were no bars on the window. And the pane was glass, not plastic. I sat on one of the saddle racks and removed my shoe. The glass was no match for a thirsty man in a frenzy. I used the shoe to carefully knock all the glass from the frame. The window was small, but it was big enough. I clambered through headfirst.

What a magnificent feeling. Stage four was complete.

I hopped out from under the overhanging roof to stand in the rain with my head held back and my mouth wide open.

Never had anything tasted so sweet.

ESCAPING FROM the stable building, however, was only the first hurdle.

I didn't know where I was, and I could hardly hop very far. The rain did not give me nearly enough water to quench my roaring thirst. I lay down on the concrete and lapped water from a puddle like a dog. Hunger and mobility were now my highest priorities.

What I needed was a crutch, something like a broom, to put under my arm. I crawled on hands and knees back along the line of stalls until I came to the one I had been held in. There was no broom, I knew, but I had decided to take the ring, the chain, and the padlock with me as evidence.

I opened the next stall looking for a broom, but I discovered something a whole lot better. Lying on the floor was my artificial leg, together with my overcoat. I leaned against the doorframe and put the leg on. The joy of walking again on two legs was immense. I picked up my coat and put it on against the cold. I put my hands in the pockets and found, to my surprise, my mobile phone, my wallet, my car keys and the business card from Mr Hoogland.

The phone was off. I turned it on, and the familiar screen appeared. I wondered who I should call. Who did I trust?

I EXPLORED THE stable block to try to find out where I was. I probably could have used my mobile phone to call the police, and they would have been able to trace where the signal came from, but I really wanted to find out for myself.

There were no horses in any of the stalls. And there were no people in the big house alongside them. All the doors were locked. So I walked across the gravel turning area, past the house, and down the driveway. There was just enough brightness for me to see where I was going, but full darkness would not be far away.

The driveway was long but downhill. At the end, there were seven-foot wrought-iron gates between impressive stone pillars. The gates were locked by a length of chain and a padlock.

I looked up at the top of the gates. Did I really have to start climbing again?

No, I didn't. A quick excursion ten yards to the left allowed me to step through a post-and-rail fence. The imposing gates were more for show than for security. There was a plastic sign attached to the outside of one of the gateposts: FOR SALE, it said, then gave the telephone number of an estate agent. I pulled the sign away to reveal a notice beneath: GREYSTONE STABLES, it read. LARRY WEBSTER RACEHORSE TRAINER.

I could remember someone had told me about this place. 'The Webster place,' they'd said. 'On the hill off the Wantage Road.' So I was back in Lambourn, or just outside. And I could see the village lights about half a mile or so away, down the road.

Did I phone my mother and ask her to collect me, or did I call the police and report a kidnapping and attempted murder? It was the right and the sensible thing to do. And then my mother would simply have to take her chances with the tax man.

Something was stopping me from calling the police, and it wasn't only the belief that my mother would then end up losing everything. Maybe it was the need to fight my own battles, to prove to myself that I still could. But, above all, I think it was the desire to inflict personal revenge on the person who had done this to me.

Perhaps it was some sort of madness, but I called no one. I simply started walking towards the lights and home.

I WAS ALIVE and free, and for as long as someone believed that I was tied up and dead, I had the element of surprise on my side. In strategic terms, surprise was everything.

I walked through the village, keeping to the shadows. Only the clink-clink of my right leg could have given me away. I resolved to find, finally, a way to make my walking silent once more.

When I arrived at the driveway of Kauri House, I paused.

Did I really want my mother and stepfather to know what had happened to me? And could I then trust them not to pass on the knowledge to others, even accidentally? Absolute secrecy might be vital. But I urgently needed to drink and eat, and I also wanted to wash and put on some clean clothes.

As I approached, I could see that the lights were on in the stables and the staff were busily mucking out and feeding their charges.

I skirted round the house and went up the stairs and let myself into Ian Norland's flat above the stables. I'd taken a chance that he would not have locked the door while he was downstairs with the horses, and I'd been right.

While I waited for him to finish with the horses, I raided his refrigerator. There were precious few food items, so I helped myself to a bottle of milk. I'd completely finished it by the time I heard him climbing the stairs. I stood tight behind the door as he came in, but he saw me as soon as he closed it.

'What the hell are you doing here?' he demanded.

'Ian, I need your help,' I said quickly.

He looked at me closely. 'Why are you in such a mess?' he asked accusingly. 'What have you been up to?'

'Nothing,' I said. 'I'm just a bit dirty and hungry. I'll explain everything. But I need your help, and I don't want my mother to know I'm here. We had an argument.'

'What over?' he said.

'Over the running of the horses,' I said.

Now he was interested. 'Tell me.'

'Can I use your bathroom first?' I asked. 'I'm desperate for a shower. I don't suppose you have any spare clothes my size?'

'Do you want me to fetch yours?' he asked. 'Your mother and Mr Philips have gone to some big event in London. Saw them go myself round five o'clock. All dressed up to the nines, they were.'

So I could have probably gone into the house all along.

'But my mother's car is in the driveway,' I said.

'They were collected by a big flashy car with a driver,' he said. 'Seems like Mrs Kauri was the guest of honour or something.'

'Will they be back tonight?'

'I don't know,' he said. 'All she said was she'd see me at seven thirty in the morning.'

'Right, then,' I said. 'I'll go over to the house to shower and change while you go to the Chinese takeaway and get us dinner. I'll have beef in black bean sauce.' I held out some money from my wallet. 'And buy some milk as well. I'm afraid I've drunk yours.'

He stood silently looking at me, but he took the money.

I glanced at the clock on his wall. 'I'll be back here in forty-five minutes to eat and talk.'

IT WAS NEARER to fifty minutes by the time I climbed back up the stairs to Ian's flat, having enjoyed a long soak in a hot bath to ease my aching shoulders. And I'd brought some of my stuff with me.

'What's in the tube?' Ian asked.

'My sword,' I said. 'I thought it might be useful.'

'For what?' he said in alarm. 'I'm not doing anything illegal.'

'It's OK,' I said. 'I won't ask you to do anything illegal.'

He relaxed somewhat.

'So can I stay here?' I asked, placing my bag on the floor.

'But I've only got the one bed.'

'That's OK,' I said. 'I only want the floor.'

'You can have the sofa.'

'Even better,' I said. 'Now how about that food? I'm starving.'

He served it out onto two plates on his kitchen table, and I tucked into mine with gusto. Finally, I sat back with a sigh. I was full.

'Blimey,' said Ian, who had only just started his sweet-and-sour pork. 'Anyone would think you hadn't eaten for a week.'

'What day is it?' I asked.

He looked at me strangely. 'Wednesday.'

Had it really only been on Monday that I'd gone to Oxford for the inquest? Just two and a half days ago? It felt like half a lifetime. Did I want to tell Ian why I was so hungry? Perhaps not.

'Not many restaurants about when you're living rough,' I said. 'I've been on the Downs for a couple of nights in a shelter I made.'

'But it's so cold, and it's done nothing but rain all week!'

'Don't I know it. I couldn't light my fire,' I said. 'But it's all good training. Nothing like a bit of discomfort to harden you up.'

'You army blokes are barmy,' Ian said, before continuing: 'So what was it about the running of the horses that you argued with your mother about?'

'Oh, nothing really,' I said, back-pedalling madly. 'And I am sure she wouldn't want me talking to you about it.'

'You might be right there,' he said. 'But tell me anyway.'

'I just told her that in my opinion, and based on his last run at Cheltenham, Pharmacist wasn't ready for the Gold Cup. She told me to stick my opinion up my you-know-where.'

He laughed. 'Did she throw you out just for saying that?'

'Well, there were a few other things,' I said. 'Family things.'

He nodded knowingly. 'So do you still want to stay here?'

'Absolutely,' I said. 'I'm not going home to my mother with my tail between my legs, I can tell you. I'd never hear the end of it.'

He laughed again. 'Fine by me, but I warn you, I get up early.'

'I'll be well gone by six,' I said.

'To avoid your mother?'

'Perhaps,' I said. 'But you can ask her where she thinks I am. I'd love to know what she says, but don't tell her I've been here.'

'OK, I'll ask her. But where are you going?'

'Back to where I've been for these past few days,' I said. 'I've some unfinished business there.'

I TOOK MY SWORD, still safely stowed in its tube, when I slipped out of Ian's flat at five thirty on Thursday morning. I also took the remains of the Chinese takeaway and half the milk Ian had bought.

In addition, I took my freshly charged mobile phone and the card from Mr Hoogland. I might need something to pass the time.

I retraced my path through the still sleeping village and down the Wantage Road to Greystone Stables. I had managed to stop my leg from clinking. The problem, I discovered, had been where the leg post met the ankle. The clink was made by two metal parts coming together when I put my weight on it. I'd eventually silenced it using an adjustable wrench and a square of rubber that Ian had cut from an old Wellington boot. I relished being able to move silently once more.

The gates at the bottom of the driveway were still locked. I stepped back through the post-and-rail fence and climbed the hill, watching for anything unusual. Halfway up, I checked the spot where, the previous evening, I had placed a stick leaning on a small stone. A car's tyre would have had to disturb it to pass by, but the stick was still in place. No one had driven up this hill overnight.

Even so, I was watchful as I approached the house. The sky was lightening in the east with a lovely display of blues, purples and reds. I silently tried the doors of the house. They were still locked.

I went round the house and into the familiar stable yard. I went down to the far end of the left-hand stable block and carefully picked up all the shards of glass that lay below the window I'd broken. I placed them all back through the window and out of sight.

Now all I needed was a place to hide and wait.

Across the concrete stable yard, opposite the block of boxes in which I'd been imprisoned, there was a second row of stables facing them. In the middle of the row, there was a passageway that ran right through the building from front to rear. The passage had a door, but the latch was a simple lever, not a bolt. The door was made from slats of wood screwed to a simple frame with inch-wide gaps between the slats to allow the wind to blow through.

I lifted the latch, pulled open the door, and went through the passageway. Behind the stables was a muck heap that hadn't been cleared for a long while; there were clumps of grass growing through the straw on its surface. The passageway had been placed there to provide access to the muck heap from the stable yard. And it made an ideal hiding place.

Out the back, I found an empty blue plastic drum that would do well as a seat, and I was soon sitting behind the door in the passageway, watching and waiting for my enemy to arrive. I longed to have my trusty SA80 assault rifle beside me, with fixed bayonet. Instead, all I had was my sword, but it was drawn from its scabbard and ready for action.

7

I waited a long time.

Every so often I would stand and walk back and forth a few times along the passageway to get the blood moving in my legs.

At three in the afternoon, while still maintaining a close watch of the stable yard, I called Mr Hoogland.

'Ah, hello,' he said. 'I've got some answers to your questions.'

'And?' I prompted.

'The deceased definitely was Roderick Ward,' he said.

'Oh.'

'You sound disappointed.'

'No, not really,' I said. 'Just a bit surprised. You're sure?'

'I asked the pathologist. He had done a DNA test. There's no doubt that the body in the river was who we thought it was.'

Well, at least that ruled out Roderick as the blackmailer.

'Did the pathologist confirm if the water in Ward's lungs matched that from the river?'

'Oh, sorry. I forgot to ask him.'

'Did you find out anything about Ward's sister?' I asked.

'Yes. It seems her car broke down on the morning of the inquest and she couldn't get to the court in time. The coroner's office told her they would have to proceed without her, and she agreed.'

'But she only lives in Oxford,' I said. 'Couldn't she have got a bus?'

'Apparently, she's moved,' he said. 'They did give me her address. I can't remember it exactly, but it was in Andover.'

'Well, thanks. Seems I may have been barking up the wrong tree.'

'Yeah,' he said. 'Shame. It would have made for a good story. Who are you, anyway? A journalist?'

'I'm just a born sceptic,' I said with a laugh. 'Bye now.'

I hung up, smiling, and turned off my phone.

Still no one came.

I ATE THE COLD REMAINS of the previous evening's Chinese food and drank some of the milk.

Why would anyone want me dead? There was now no doubt that my death was what they had intended. So would they, in fact, bother to come back and check on their handiwork? Wouldn't they just assume that I was dead?

But didn't they want to know? Never assume anything; always check.

The sun went down soon after five o'clock, and the temperature went down with it. Still I waited, and still no one came.

When my telephone told me it was nine o'clock in the evening, I decided that enough was enough and it was time to go back to Ian's flat. I put my sword back in its scabbard, and then I put that back in the cardboard tube, which I swung over my shoulder.

Halfway down the driveway, I checked that the stick was still resting on the stone. It was.

I was climbing through the post-and-rail fence when I saw a car coming from the direction of Lambourn village. I thought nothing of it. I decided, however, that it would not be such a clever idea to be spotted actually climbing through the fence, so I lay down in the long grass and waited for the car to pass by. But it didn't pass by. It pulled off the road and stopped close to the gates. The headlights went out, and I heard, rather than saw, the driver get out of the car and close the door.

I lay silently face-down in the grass about ten yards away.

I could hear the chain jingling as it was pulled through the metal posts of the gates. Whoever had just arrived in the car had brought with them the key to the padlock. This was indeed my enemy.

I heard the gates squeak a little as they were opened wide. I stole a look as the driver returned to the car, but my view was obstructed by the open car door. It had been impossible to see who it was.

I heard the engine start, and the headlights came back on. The car then reversed out onto the road and drove back towards the village. I rose quickly to my knees. I hadn't identified my enemy, but I thought I'd recognised the make of the car, even if I couldn't see the colour.

'SO WHAT DID my mother say?' I asked Ian when I returned to his flat.

'About what?' he said.

'About where I was.'

'Oh, that. She said that you had unexpectedly been called to London by the army and she didn't know when you would be back. Your note hadn't said that.'

'My note?' I said in surprise.

'Yeah. Mrs Kauri said you sent her a note.'

'From London?' I asked.

'She didn't say,' Ian said, 'but there was no note, right?'

'No,' I said truthfully. 'I definitely didn't send her a note.'

But someone else may have.

I WOKE AT FIVE after a restless night on Ian's couch. My mind was too full of questions to relax, and I lay awake, thinking.

Why had my enemy not gone up to the stables to make sure I was dead? Maybe they didn't want to have to see the gruesome results of their handiwork. I didn't blame them on that count. Human bodies—dead ones, that is—are mostly the stuff of nightmares.

If my enemy hadn't bothered to go up the hill the previous evening after unlocking the gates, I didn't expect him ever to go back there again. So I decided not to spend any more of my time waiting for them. Anyway, I had different plans for today: Andover, the lawyer Hoogland had said.

Now, why did that ring a bell?

Old Man Sutton, I thought. He now lived in a nursing home in Andover. And Old Man Sutton's son, Detective Sergeant Fred, had been at Roderick Ward's inquest. And Roderick Ward's sister had moved to Andover. Was that just a coincidence?

I heard Ian get up at six. I sat on the sofa and attached my leg.

'Can I borrow your car?' I asked him over breakfast.

'How long for?' he said.

'I don't know,' I said. 'I've got to go to an ATM to get some money, for a start. And I might be out all morning or even all day.'

'I need to go to the supermarket,' he said. 'I've run out of food.'

'I'll buy you some,' I said.

'All right, then,' he said, smiling. 'I'd much rather stay here and watch the racing from Sandown on the telly.'

'So can I borrow your car?'

'Where's yours?'

'In Oxford,' I said truthfully. 'The head gasket has blown,' I lied. 'It's in a garage.'

I thought that my Jaguar was probably still in the multi-storey in Oxford city centre, and I had decided to leave it there. To move it would be to advertise that I wasn't dead in a deserted stable.

'OK, you can borrow it,' he said, 'provided you're insured.'

'I am,' I said confidently. 'And I'll fill it with fuel for you.'

'That would be great,' Ian said. He tossed me the keys.

I caught them. 'Thanks.'

'Will you be back here tonight?' he asked.

'If you'll have me,' I said. 'Do you fancy Indian?'

'Yeah,' he said. 'Good idea. Get me a chicken balti and some naan.'

'OK,' I said. 'See you later.'

I slipped out of Ian's flat while it was still dark. I drove his wreck of a Vauxhall Corsa down the drive and out into the village.

NEWBURY WAS QUIET at seven o'clock on a Friday morning, although Sainsbury's car park was already bustling with early-morning shoppers eager to beat the weekend rush for groceries.

I parked in a free space, but I didn't go into the supermarket. Instead, I walked out of the car park and into the town centre.

Number 46 Cheap Street was just one among the long rows of shops that lined both sides of the road, most of them with flats or offices above. The mailbox shop that occupied the address opened at eight thirty and closed at six, Monday to Friday.

If, as usual, my stepfather had mailed the weekly package to the blackmailer—the one containing £2,000—on Thursday afternoon, then the package should arrive at 46 Cheap Street some time today and be placed in mailbox 116, ready for collection.

Mailbox 116 was visible through the front window of the shop, and I intended to watch it all day to see if anyone arrived to make a collection. However, I could hardly stand outside scrutinising every customer who came along. That was why I had come to Newbury so early, so that I could make a full reconnaissance of the area.

At first glance, there seemed to be two promising locations from which to observe 46 Cheap Street. The first was an American-style coffee shop about thirty yards away, and the second was the Taj Mahal Indian restaurant, which was directly opposite.

I decided that the restaurant was the better of the two, not only because it was in such a good position but because there was a curtain hanging from a brass bar halfway down the window, behind which I could easily hide. All I needed was to secure the correct table. A notice hanging on the restaurant door told me that it opened for lunch at noon. Until then, I would have to make do with the coffee shop, which began serving at eight o'clock.

I went round the corner and found a bank with an ATM. I drew out £200 and used some of it to buy a newspaper at a newsagents. It wasn't that I needed something to read, but I did need something to hide behind.

AT EIGHT THIRTY SHARP, I watched from behind my newspaper as a man and a woman unlocked the door of the mailbox shop and went in. From my vantage point, I could just see box number 116.

I drank cups of coffee and glasses of orange juice and hoped that I looked like a man idling away the morning reading his newspaper. The street had become gradually busier as the morning wore on, but so far I'd not recognised anyone.

At ten to eleven, I spotted the postman coming down the street. He was pushing a small, four-wheeled, bright red trolley, and he went into the mailbox shop with a huge armful of mail.

I had half an hour to go before the Taj Mahal opened, but I reckoned I couldn't stay in the coffee shop much longer. I stood up, collected my unread newspaper, and walked out. I couldn't just hang around outside, so I went into the shop right next door to the Indian restaurant. It sold computers and all things electronic.

'Can I help you, sir?' asked a young man approaching me.

'No, thanks,' I said. 'I'm just looking.'

Looking through the window.

'Just call if you want anything,' he said.

'I will,' I assured him. I stood by a display case at the window and went on watching the shop across the road. I glanced at the display case. It was full of cameras.

'I'd like to buy a camera,' I said without turning around.

'Certainly, sir,' said the young man. 'Any particular one?'

'I want one I can use straightaway and with a good zoom.'

'How about the new Panasonic?' he said. 'That has an eighteen-times optical zoom and a Leica lens.'

'OK. I'll have one,' I said. 'But will it work straightaway?'

'It should do,' he said. 'You'll have to charge the battery pretty soon, but they usually come with a little bit of charge in them.'

'Can you set it up so it's ready to shoot immediately?'

'Certainly, sir,' said the young man. 'This one records direct to a memory card. Would you like me to include one?'

'Yes, please,' I said. I went on watching the street as the young man checked the battery and installed the memory card.

'Shall I put it back in the box?' he asked.

'No,' I said. 'Leave it out.'

I handed him my credit card and looked down briefly to enter my PIN, and also to check that I wasn't spending a fortune.

'And please leave the camera switched on.'

'The battery won't last if I do that,' he said. 'But it's easy to turn on when you need it. You just push this here.' He pointed. 'Then you just aim and shoot with this.' He pointed to another button.

'Great, thanks,' I said, taking the bag he held out.

I went swiftly out of the camera shop and into the adjacent Taj Mahal Indian restaurant, just as a waiter turned the CLOSED sign on the door to OPEN.

'I'd like that table there, please,' I said, pointing.

'But, sir,' said the waiter, 'that is for four people.'

'I'm expecting three others,' I said, moving over to the table and sitting down before he had a chance to stop me.

I ordered a sparkling mineral water, and when the waiter departed to fetch it, I opened the curtains in the window a few inches so I could clearly see mailbox 116.

THE PACKAGE WAS collected at twenty past one, by which time the Indian waiter no longer really believed that another three people were coming to join me for lunch.

I had almost eaten the restaurant out of poppadoms and mango chutney when I suddenly recognised a face across the road. It took only a few seconds for the collector to open box 116 with a key, remove the contents, close the box again, and leave.

But not before I had snapped away with my new purchase.

I sat at the table and looked through the photos I'd taken.

Quite a few were of the back of the person's head, but there were three perfect shots, in full-zoom close-up. Two of them showed the collector in profile as the package was being removed from the box, and one was full-face as the person left through the shop door.

I hadn't really known who to expect, but the person who looked out at me from the camera screen hadn't even been on my list of possible candidates.

The face in the photograph, the face of my mother's blackmailer, was that of Julie Yorke.

ON SATURDAY MORNING at nine o'clock, I was sitting in Ian's car parked in a gateway halfway up the Baydon Road. I had chosen the position so I could see the traffic that came up the hill towards me out of Lambourn village. I was waiting for one particular vehicle.

I had woken early again after another troubled night's sleep.

The same questions had been revolving round and around in my head since the early hours. How could Julie Yorke be the blackmailer? And who was she working with?

There had to be someone else involved. My mother had always referred to the blackmailer as 'him', and I had heard the whisperer myself on the telephone and was pretty certain it had been a man.

I yawned. I was tired due to lack of sleep, but I knew that I could exist indefinitely on just a few hours a night. Sometimes I'd survived for weeks on far less than that.

I had again left Kauri House in Ian's car. I'd driven into Wantage and parked in the market square under the imposing statue of King Alfred the Great. I'd bought the *Racing Post* from a newsagent in the town. According to the paper, Ewen Yorke had seven horses running that afternoon—three at Haydock Park and four at Ascot, in the afternoon.

Haydock was midway between Manchester and Liverpool and a three-hour drive away. Ascot, meanwhile, was much closer, just a fifty-minute trip down the M4 motorway.

Ewen had a runner in the first race at both courses, and if he was going to be at Haydock Park in time for the first, he would be expected to drive his distinctive white BMW up Baydon Road sometime around ten o'clock, by ten thirty at the very latest.

So I sat and waited.

At nine forty-five, I recognised a car coming towards me. It wasn't a white BMW but an ageing, battered blue Ford—my mother's car.

I sank down in the seat, hoping that she wouldn't recognise the vehicle of her head lad. I gratefully watched as her car disappeared round the corner. As I had expected, my mother was off to the Haydock Park races, where she had Oregon running, his last outing before the Triumph Hurdle at the Cheltenham Festival.

I went back to waiting, but there was no sign of a white BMW.

At ten to eleven, I decided it was time to move. I hadn't seen Ewen's car go past, but that didn't mean he hadn't gone to Haydock; it just meant he hadn't gone there via the Baydon Road.

I moved Ian's car from Baydon Road to Hungerford Hill, another road out of Lambourn. If Ewen Yorke was going to Ascot this afternoon, he would almost certainly pass this way, and would do so by twelve thirty if he was going to saddle his runner in the first race.

The distinctive white, top-of-the-range BMW swept up the hill at five minutes to twelve, and I pulled out behind it.

I had planned to follow him at a safe distance to avoid detection and to make sure he actually did drive towards Ascot. As it was, I had no need to worry about keeping far enough back. Ian Norland's little Corsa struggled up Hungerford Hill, but Ewen Yorke's powerful BMW was already long gone and well out of sight by the time I reached the top of the hill.

I'd have to assume that he had, in fact, gone to Ascot and that he wouldn't be back in Lambourn for at least the next five hours. I drove the Corsa down the hill to Lambourn village and pulled up on the gravel driveway next to the Yorkes' front door.

JULIE SEEMED SURPRISED to see me, but maybe not so surprised as if she had believed me dead.

'What are you doing here?' she asked.

'You said to come and see you sometime,' I said. 'Here I am.'

She blushed slightly across her neck. 'What's in the bag?' she asked, looking at the plastic bag I was holding.

'Champagne,' I said.

She blushed again, and this time it reached her cheeks.

'You had better come in, then,' she said, opening the door wide.

'How lovely,' I said, admiring the white curved staircase in the hallway. 'Which way's the bedroom?'

'My,' she said with a giggle, 'you are an eager boy.'

'No time like the present,' I said. 'Is your husband in?'

'No,' she said, giggling again. 'He's gone to the races.' She breathed deeply, her breasts rising and falling under her sweater.

'Get some glasses,' I said, starting to climb the stairs.

She skipped away while I continued up.

'In the guest room,' she shouted. 'On the left.'

I went into the guest room on the left and pulled back the duvet on the king-size bed.

Was I really going to have sex with this woman? Did I want to? And did I leave my leg on or take it off?

On this occasion, I decided that leaving it on was definitely better, especially as a quick getaway would be a likely necessity.

I went into the en suite bathroom. I stripped, left my clothes on the floor, and climbed into the bed, pulling the duvet to my waist.

Julie appeared in the doorway carrying two champagne flutes in her left hand and wearing a flimsy housecoat that she allowed to fall open, revealing her nakedness beneath.

'Now, just how naughty have you been?' she asked.

'Very,' I said, opening the champagne with a loud pop.

'Oh, goodie,' she replied.

It wasn't quite what I had in mind, but I went along with her little game for a while as she became more and more excited.

'Just a minute,' I said, getting off the bed.

'What?' she gasped. 'Get back here now!'

'Just a minute,' I repeated. 'I need the bathroom.'

She was resting on her elbows, her knees drawn up and her legs spread wide apart. 'Get back here right now,' she cried.

I ignored her, went into the bathroom, and put on my boxer shorts. I then took my new camera from the cupboard under the sink where I had placed it when I arrived. The champagne hadn't been the only thing in the plastic bag.

'Hurry up, you naughty boy,' she shouted.

'Coming,' I shouted back.

I came out of the bathroom taking shot after shot of her naked body as she lay on the bed, still in the same compromising position. She'd had her eyes closed, and it was a few seconds before she realised what I was doing.

'What's going on?' she screamed, grabbing the duvet to cover herself.

'Just taking some photos,' I said calmly.

'What for?' she shouted angrily.

'Blackmail,' I replied. 'Do you want to see?'

I held the camera towards her so she could see the screen. But the photograph I showed her wasn't one of those I'd just taken; it was the one of her reaching into mailbox 116 to collect the money.

SHE CRIED A LOT. We were still in her guest bedroom. I had thrown her the housecoat when I'd gone into the bathroom to put on my shirt and trousers, and when I'd re-emerged, she had been wearing it. She didn't look like someone up to her neck in a criminal conspiracy.

'It was only a game,' she said.

'Murder is never a game,' I said, standing at the end of the bed.

'Murder?' She went very pale. 'Who was murdered?'

'Someone called Roderick Ward,' I said, even though I had no evidence that it was true.

'No,' she wailed. 'Roderick died in a car crash.'

So she knew of Roderick Ward.

'That's what it was meant to look like. Who killed him?'

'I didn't kill anybody,' she shouted.

'Someone did,' I said. 'Was it Ewen?'

'Ewen?' She almost laughed. 'The only thing Ewen is interested in is horses. That and whisky. Horses all day and whisky all night.'

Perhaps that explained her flirtatious nature—she couldn't get any satisfaction in the marital bed, so she had looked elsewhere.

'So who killed Roderick Ward?' I asked her again.

'No one,' she said. 'I told you. He died in a car crash.'

'Who says so?' I asked.

She didn't respond.

I looked down at her. 'Do you know what the sentence is for being an accessory to murder? Life in prison,' I said.

'I told you, I didn't murder anyone.' She was now crying again.

'But do you think a jury will believe you once they've convicted you for blackmail? Are you aware that the maximum sentence for blackmail is fourteen years?'

That brought her head back up. 'No.' It was almost a plea.

'Oh, yes,' I said. I knew. I'd looked it up on the internet.

'Where's the money you collected yesterday?' I asked.

'In my handbag,' she whimpered.

'And how about the rest of it?'

'The rest?' she said.

'Yes. All the packages you've been collecting each week for the past seven months. Where's all that money?'

'I don't have it,' she said.

'So who has?'

She still didn't want to tell me.

'Julie,' I said. 'You are leaving me no alternative but to give the picture of you in Newbury to the police. I can only help you if you will help me. Otherwise, I will also have to send the other photos to Ewen.' Both of us knew what the other photos showed.

'No, please.' She was begging. 'I can't tell you.'

'What are you frightened of?' I asked.

'I don't want to go to prison,' she sobbed, echoing my mother.

'If you tell me who you give the money to, I am sure the courts won't send you to prison.' Not for long, anyway, I thought.

I could see that she still didn't want to say. Was it fear, I wondered, or some misguided sense of loyalty? 'Do you love him?' I asked her.

She looked up at me, still sobbing. But she nodded.

'Then why are you doing *this*?' I waved my arm at her, at the bed. She had hardly acted as if she was in love with someone.

'Habit, I suppose,' she said quietly.

Some habit, I thought. 'Does he love you?' I asked.

'He says so,' she said, but I detected hesitancy in her voice.

'You're not so sure?' I asked. 'Then what on earth are you doing, protecting him?'

She gave me no answer.

'OK,' I said at length. 'Don't say that I haven't warned you.' I took my mobile phone from my pocket. I pushed the nine key three times—the emergency number. I then held the phone to my ear. She wasn't to know that I hadn't also pressed the connect button.

'Hello,' I said into the dead phone. 'Police, please.'

'All right,' she shouted. 'All right, I'll tell you.'

'Sorry,' I said again into the dead phone, 'there's been a mistake. All is well now. Thank you.' I folded my phone together.

'So who is it?' I asked.

'Alex Reece,' she said slowly.

'What?' I said, astounded. 'The weasel accountant?'

'Alex is not a weasel,' she said defensively. 'He's lovely.'

I thought back to the hours I had spent chained to a wall, and I couldn't agree with her. 'So was it you and Alex Reece who chained me to a wall to die?' I was suddenly very angry.

She was shocked. 'I have no idea what you're talking about.'

'But you did help him to kidnap me?' I shouted at her.

'Tom, stop it,' she pleaded. 'I really don't know what you are talking about. I have never kidnapped anyone in my life.'

'Why should I believe you?' I asked. But I had seen the fear in her eyes, and I did believe her. But if she hadn't helped kidnap and chain me to a wall, who had?

Or could Alex Reece, my mother's blackmailer, really not be the same person as my would-be murderer?

There was very little else that Julie had to tell me. She collected the package from the mailbox shop in Newbury only when Alex Reece was unable to do so, and she didn't even know how much money was in it. When we finally went downstairs to her kitchen and she took the package from her handbag, she could hardly believe her eyes when I removed £2,000.

'Two thousand every week is no game,' I told her.

'Alex says it's just redistributing the wealth.'

'Alex is a thief, and the sooner you realise it, the better it will be for you. Or else you'll be in prison with him.'

It was time for me to meet again with Mr Alex Reece, and I had no intention of letting him see me coming.

'When are you meant to give this package to Reece?' I asked.

'He gets back tomorrow.'

'From where?' I asked.

'Gibraltar. He went there with the Garraways on Tuesday.'

So it couldn't have been him who unlocked the gates of Greystone Stables on Thursday evening.

'So when are you meant to give him the package?' I demanded.

'He said to bring it to Newbury on Monday,' she said. 'There's a coffee shop in Cheap Street where we always meet.'

It was far too public a place for what I wanted to do to him.

'Where else do you two get together?' I asked.

'At his place,' she said, blushing slightly. 'In Greenham.'

Greenham was a village that had almost been consumed by the ever-expanding sprawl of Newbury town.

'Where in Greenham?' I demanded.

'What are you going to do to him?'

'Nothing,' I said. 'As long as he cooperates. If he gives me my mother's money back, I'll let him go.' I'd also take back her tax papers.

'And if he doesn't?' she asked.

'Then I'll persuade him.'

8

Bush Close in Greenham was full of modern little box houses. Number 16, Alex Reece's home, was at the end of the cul-de-sac.

It was late Saturday afternoon, and I had just left Julie Yorke in a state of near collapse. I had merely suggested to her that to have any contact whatever with Alex Reece in the next thirty-six hours would be reason enough for me to send the explicit photographs to her husband.

I had parked Ian Norland's car out on Water Lane in Greenham and had walked round the corner into Bush Close.

'What time does Alex get back?' I had asked Julie.

'His plane lands at Heathrow at six twenty tomorrow evening.'

I lingered for a moment outside the front door of number 16. I glanced around looking for suitable hiding places, but the short driveway was bordered by nothing but grass. I walked back towards Ian's car. However, instead of driving away, I walked through a gateway into the adjacent field. Alex Reece's house backed onto farmland, and I spent some time reconnoitring the whole area.

I looked at my watch. It was just after five thirty, and the light was beginning to fade rapidly. Alex Reece couldn't possibly be back here the following evening until eight o'clock at the earliest. By then it would have been dark for hours.

Keeping in the shadows of some trees, I skirted round the backs of the gardens in Bush Close until I arrived at number 16. I quickly rolled my body over the low back fence and into Alex Reece's garden. It was mostly grass, with no flower beds to worry about.

I moved silently to the back of the garage and looked in. I could see the shape of a car in there. So Mr Reece would probably arrive home by taxi. And I'd be waiting for him.

I SPENT SUNDAY morning making my plans and sorting my kit. I had been back into Kauri House on Saturday afternoon after leaving Julie Yorke and before my excursion to Greenham. The house had been empty. My mother and stepfather had been safely away at Haydock races. I had had a quick shower and collected a few things from my room.

Ian left for a Sunday lunch trip with his folks at eleven, telling me that he would be back at five. After he had gone, I sorted the equipment I would need for my mission. Bits of it I had owned previously, but some things I'd bought in Newbury specifically.

I laid out my black pullover, dark jeans, and a black knit ski hat and some matching gloves that I'd bought from the sports shop in Market Street, where I'd also obtained a pair of black trainers.

Next to the clothes, I placed the rest of my kit: a small, dark blue rucksack; some heavy-duty garden ties similar to those that had been used to bind my wrists in the stables; a small, red first-aid kit; three six-by-four-inch prints of the mailbox-shop photos; a certain metal ring with a piece of galvanised steel chain attached to it; my camera; and finally, a roll of grey duct tape. I had decided against taking my sword. It was not as if I intended to kill anyone. Not yet, anyway.

AT TEN MINUTES TO EIGHT, I was in position alongside Alex Reece's house, on the dark side, away from the glow from the solitary streetlamp. Eight o'clock came and went. A fine drizzle began to fall. My dark clothes would blend into the blackness of the background; only my face might be visible, and that was streaked with home-made, mud-based camouflage cream to break up the familiar shape.

Alex Reece arrived home just before nine, but he didn't come by taxi. Isabella's dark blue Volkswagen Golf pulled into the driveway at high speed and stopped abruptly with a slight squeal of its brakes. I pressed myself close to the wall and peeked around the corner so I could see. I couldn't see who was at the wheel, but from past experience of her driving, I was pretty sure it was Isabella herself.

Reece opened the rear door and stood next to the car with a flight bag in his hand. 'Thanks for the lift,' he called before closing the door and removing a small suitcase from the boot. The Golf backed out and drove away again at high speed. The fact that Alex had been sitting in the back seat implied that there was at least one other person in there in addition to Isabella. Maybe it was Jackson.

I watched as Alex fumbled for the key to his front door. I also scanned the road. No one was about. It was time for action.

In the instant after he opened the front door and before he had time to reach down for his suitcase, I struck him hard between his shoulder blades, forcing him through the open doorway and onto the floor in the dark hallway. I crashed down on top of him.

'Shout and I'll kill you,' I said loudly into his ear.

I pulled both his arms around to the small of his back and used the garden ties from my pocket to secure his wrists. Next I used another pair of the ties to bind his ankles together.

I went outside and picked up Alex's suitcase from the step, then stepped back inside again, closing the front door.

Alex was trussed up like a chicken ready for a spot of roasting.

'I HAVE NO IDEA what you're talking about.' It was only to be expected that he would deny any knowledge of blackmail.

He was still lying on the hall floor, but I had rolled him over onto his back so he could see me. I'd patted down his pockets, removed his mobile phone, and turned it off. He had known immediately who I was in spite of my dark clothes, hat and mud-streaked face.

'You deny that you've been blackmailing my mother?' I asked.

'I do,' he said emphatically. 'I've never heard such nonsense.'

I had told Ian that I would be out all night, so I was in no hurry. I left Reece lying on the hall floor and went into the kitchen to find myself a drink. Waiting all that time had made me thirsty.

'Let me go,' he shouted from the hallway.

'No,' I shouted back, putting his phone down on the worktop.

I fetched a can of Heineken from his fridge and returned to the hall. I took a drink, allowing a little of the beer to pour out of the corner of my mouth and drip onto the floor near his legs.

'Do you have any idea how long a human being can live without taking in any fluid?' He went on staring at me. 'How long it would be before dehydration causes kidney failure and death?'

He obviously didn't like the question, but he still wasn't worried.

I dug around in my rucksack for the piece of chain attached to the ring by the padlock. I held it up for him to see, but it was clear that he didn't know where it had come from, or its significance.

He probably wasn't aware that his lack of reaction may have saved his life. Maybe I didn't now want to kill the little weasel, but that didn't mean I didn't want to use him.

'Are you a diabetic?' I asked.

'No,' he said.

'Lucky you.'

I removed the red-coloured first-aid kit from my rucksack. It was what was known in the expedition business as an anti-AIDS kit. It was a small zipped-up pouch containing two each of sterile syringes, hypodermic needles, intravenous drip cannulas, ready-threaded suture needles and scalpels, plus three small, sterile pouches of saline solution for emergency rehydration. I had bought it some years earlier to take on a trip to climb Mount Kilimanjaro.

I removed one of the syringes and attached it to one of the hypodermic needles. Alex watched me.

'What are you doing?' He sounded worried for the first time.

'Time for my insulin,' I said.

Alex watched as I unpacked a pouch of saline solution and hung it on the stair banister. I drew a little of the clear liquid into the syringe, pulled up the front of my sweater, pinched the flesh of my abdomen, inserted the needle, and injected the fluid under my skin. I smiled down at Alex.

'How often do you have to do that?' he asked.

'Two or three times a day,' I said.

'And what exactly is insulin?'

'It's a hormone,' I said, 'that allows the muscles to use the energy from glucose carried in the blood.'

'So what happens if you don't take it?'

'The glucose level in my blood would get so high that my organs would stop working, and I'd eventually go into a coma and die.' I smiled down at him. 'We wouldn't want that now, would we?'

Perhaps me in a coma or dead was exactly what he wanted. But it wasn't going to happen. I wasn't really diabetic, but my best friend at school had been, and I'd watched him inject himself with insulin hundreds of times. Injecting small amounts of sterile saline solution under my skin was harmless.

I went back into the kitchen and picked up his flight bag. Inside, among other things, was a laptop. I removed the computer and turned it on. While it booted up, I took a chair into the hallway and sat down near Alex's feet.

'Now,' I said, 'I have some questions I need you to answer.'

'I'm not answering anything unless you let me go.'

'Oh, I think you will,' I said. 'It's a long night.'

I stood up and went back into the kitchen. I pulled down the blind over the window, turned on a television set, and sat down at the kitchen table with Alex's computer.

'Hey,' he called. 'Are you just going to leave me here?'

'Yes,' I said, turning up the volume on the television.

'How long for?' he shouted louder.

'How long do you need before you will answer my questions?'

'What questions?'

I went back into the hall and sat down again on the chair by his feet.

'How long have you been having an affair with Julie Yorke?'

It wasn't a question he had been expecting, but he recovered.

'I've no idea what you're talking about.'

'Please yourself,' I said, walking back to the kitchen table.

There was a soccer highlights programme on the television, and I turned the volume up even higher so that Alex wouldn't hear me tapping away on his laptop keyboard.

The computer automatically connected to his wireless internet router, so I clicked on his email and opened the inbox. Careless of him, I thought, not to have it password-protected. I highlighted all his messages received during the past two weeks and forwarded them to my own email account. Next I did the same to his sent items folder. One never knew how useful the information might be.

I opened a computer folder called Rock Accounts. There were twenty or so files in the folder, and I highlighted them all, attached them to an email, and again sent them to my computer.

I clicked on the search button on the computer Start menu and asked it to search itself for the terms 'password' or 'username'. Obligingly, it came up with eight references, so I attached those files to another email, and off they went as well.

'OK, OK,' Alex shouted finally. 'I'll answer your question.'

The messages from one more email folder, one simply named Gibraltar, were also dispatched through cyberspace. I then erased the sent records for my forwarded files so Alex would have no knowledge that I had copied them. I closed the lid of the laptop and returned it to the flight bag. I then went out into the hall and sat down once again on the chair.

But I didn't ask him the same question as before. I asked him something completely different.

'Why did you murder Roderick Ward?'

He was shocked. 'I—I didn't,' he stammered.

'So who did?' I asked.

'I don't know.'

'So he *was* murdered?' I said.

'No,' he whined. 'It was an accident.'

'That car crash was too contrived. It had to be a set-up.'

'The car crash wasn't the accident,' he said. 'The fact that he died was the accident. I tried to warn them, but I was too late.'

'Them?' I asked, intrigued.

He clammed up. I removed a piece of paper from my pocket and held it out. He looked at it in disbelief.

I knew the words written there by heart. It was the handwritten note that had been addressed to Stella Beecher at 26 Banbury Drive in Oxford, the note I had found in the pile of mail I had taken from the box that Meals-on-Wheels Mr Horner kept by his front door:

I DON'T KNOW WHETHER THIS WILL GET THERE IN TIME, BUT TELL HIM I HAVE THE STUFF HE WANTS.

'What stuff?' I demanded. 'Tell who? And in time for what?'

He just stared at me.

'You will have to answer my questions, or you will leave me with no alternative but . . .' I trailed off.

'No alternative but what?' he asked in a panic.

'To kill you,' I said calmly.

I quickly grabbed his manacled feet and removed his left shoe and sock. I used the duct tape to bind his foot upright against one of the spindles on the stairway so that it was completely immobile.

'What are you doing?' he screamed.

'Preparations,' I said. 'I always have to make the right preparations before I kill someone.'

'Help,' he yelled.

I took a piece of the duct tape and fixed it firmly over his mouth to stop him from yelling again.

'Now, Alex,' I said. 'You seem not to fully appreciate your predicament. So let me explain it. You have been blackmailing my mother to the tune of two thousand pounds per week for the past seven months, to say nothing about the demands on her to fix races. Some weeks you collect the money from the mailbox in Cheap Street, and sometimes you get Julie Yorke to collect it.'

I removed the three prints of the photos I had taken of Julie through the window of the Taj Mahal restaurant and held them up to him. With the tape on his mouth, it was difficult to fully gauge his reaction, but he went pale.

'And,' I went on, 'you are blackmailing my mother over the knowledge you have that she has not been paying the tax that she should have been. Which means you either have her tax papers in your possession or have had access to them.'

I reached down into my rucksack and again brought out the red anti-AIDS kit. If anything, Alex went paler.

'Now my problem is this,' I said. 'If I let you go, you will still have my mother's tax papers. And even if you gave me back the papers, you would still have the knowledge.'

I took the large syringe out of the kit, attached a new needle, and then drew up a large quantity of the saline solution from the bag that was still hanging on the stair banister.

'So you see,' I said, 'if you won't help me, then I will have no alternative but to prevent you from speaking to the tax authorities.'

I held the syringe up and squirted a little of the fluid out.

'Did you know that insulin is essential for proper body functions?' I asked. 'But that too much of it causes the glucose level in the blood to drop far too low, which in turn triggers a condition called hypoglycaemia? That usually results in a seizure, followed by coma and death.' I touched his foot. 'And do you know that if you inject between someone's toes, it is very difficult, if not impossible, to find the puncture mark on the skin? And that the insulin would be undetectable, because you create it naturally in your body? It would appear that you had died of a seizure followed by a heart attack.'

The statement wasn't entirely accurate. But Alex didn't know that.

'Now then,' I said. 'Between which two toes would you like it?'

I WAS WORRIED that he was going to pass out. His eyes started to roll back in their sockets, and his breathing suddenly became shallower.

'Alex,' I shouted at him. 'You can prevent this. All you have to do is cooperate and answer all my questions. Do you understand?'

He nodded eagerly.

I stepped forwards and tore off the tape from his mouth, then untaped his foot from the spindle and pulled him across the floor so he was sitting up with his back against the wall by the kitchen door.

'Now,' I said. 'Who killed Roderick Ward?'

'His sister,' Alex said.

I looked at him. 'Stella Beecher?'

He seemed surprised I knew her name. He nodded.

'Why would she kill her own brother?'

'She didn't mean to,' he said. 'It was an accident.'

'You mean, the car crash?'

'No,' he said. 'He was already dead when he went into the river. He drowned in the bath.'

'What on earth was Stella Beecher doing giving him a bath?'

'She wasn't exactly giving him a bath. They were trying to get him to tell them where the money had gone.'

'What money?' I asked.

'Fred's father's money.'

Fred Sutton, Old Man Sutton's son. The man I had seen in the public gallery at Roderick Ward's inquest.

'So Fred Sutton and Stella Beecher know each other?' I asked.

'Know each other!' He laughed. 'They live together.'

In Andover, I thought, close to Old Man Sutton's nursing home. So it had been no coincidence that Stella had moved to Andover.

IT TOOK MORE than an hour, but in the end, Alex told me how, and why, Roderick Ward was found dead in his car in the river.

Ward had been introduced to Old Man Sutton by Stella Beecher, who had been in a relationship with Detective Sergeant Fred for some time. Unbeknownst to either Fred or Stella, Roderick had conned the old man into borrowing against his house and investing the cash in a non-existent hedge fund in Gibraltar. Fred found out about it only after he'd seen the brick being thrown through his father's window. It was like a soap opera.

'How do you know this?' I asked. 'What's your connection?'

'I worked with Roderick Ward.'

'So you are implicated in this sham hedge-fund business?'

He didn't want to admit it. He must have known that my mother had been conned in the same way. He looked away, but he nodded.

'So who's the brains behind it?' I asked.

He turned his eyes back to mine. 'Do you think I'm stupid, or something?' he said. 'If I told you who it was then you wouldn't need to kill me because they'd do it for you.'

Actually, I did think him stupid. But not as stupid as Roderick Ward—stealing from the father of his sister's boyfriend, when the boyfriend just happened to be a police detective.

'Let's go back to Roderick Ward,' I said. 'Why did you send a note to Stella Beecher saying you had the stuff? What stuff? And how did you know Stella, anyway?'

'I didn't,' he said. 'But I knew her address because Roderick had said it was the same address he used, the one in Oxford.'

'So what was this about having the stuff, hoping it was in time?'

'Fred Sutton had been harassing Roderick and me at an office we'd rented in Wantage, threatening us. He told me that he'd get a warrant for my arrest. He said I'd get ten years unless I gave him some papers he wanted about where his dad's money had gone.'

'So why the note?' I asked.

'I made the copies of the papers, but he didn't come to collect them on the Monday morning as he'd said he would. He told me he'd be at the office by eight. But he didn't come all day, and Roderick didn't show up either. I thought they must have done a deal and I would end up carrying the can. I was scared, I can tell you. I had no other way of contacting him, so I sent the note.'

So I had been wrong about 'the stuff' being something to do with my mother's tax papers, and also that 'in time' had not been about before Roderick Ward's 'accident', but about before getting an arrest warrant issued. *Never assume anything*, I reminded myself.

'So how do you know that Fred Sutton and Stella killed Roderick Ward?' I asked Reece.

'Fred pitches up first thing the next day and demands the papers, but I told him to get stuffed. If he thought I was going to take the blame for what Roderick had been doing, he had another think coming. But he says Roderick's dead and I'll go the same way if I don't give him the papers.' He paused only to draw breath. 'So I said I didn't believe that Roderick was dead. I told him he was only saying it to frighten me. He tells me that I should be frightened because they murdered him in the bath, but then he thinks better of it and claims it was an accident, that they'd only meant to scare him into telling them where the money had gone. But Fred says that Stella pulled his feet, and his head went under, and he just . . . died. Killed her own brother, just like that.'

'So did you give Fred the papers he wanted?' I asked.

'Yeah,' he said. 'But they wouldn't have done him much good. It's been ages since his money went, and they change the numbers and stuff all the time.'

'"They"?' I asked.

He clammed up, pursing his lips and shaking his head at me.

But I'd been doing a lot of thinking while I'd sat waiting in Greystone Stables and in the Newbury coffee shop, and the more I had thought about it, the more convinced I had become.

'You mean Jackson Warren and Peter Garraway,' I said.

He stared at me with his mouth hanging open. So I was right.

'And who is Mr Cigar?' I asked him.

He laughed. 'No one,' he said. 'That was Roderick's idea. They all thought it a great joke as they puffed on their Havanas.'

'And Rock Bank Ltd,' I said. 'Is that a myth, too?'

'Oh, no, that exists all right,' he said. 'But it's not really a bank. It's just a Gibraltar holding company. When money comes in, it sits there for a while and then leaves again.'

'And where does it go when it leaves Rock Bank?'

'I arrange a transfer into another Gibraltar account, but it doesn't stay long there, either,' he said. 'I don't know where it goes then. I'm pretty sure it ends up in a secret numbered Swiss account.'

'How long does it stay in Rock Bank?'

'About a week,' he said. 'Just long enough to allow for clearance of the transfer and for any problems to get sorted.'

So Rock 'Bank' Ltd had no assets of its own. No wonder the London-based liquidation firm was attempting to pursue the individual directors.

'And where does it come from?' I asked him.

'The mugs,' he said with a laugh.

'You're the mug,' I said. 'You don't look quite so clever at the moment. And I bet you don't get to keep much of the money.'

'I get my cut,' he boasted. 'They need me. I'm the accountant. They need me to square the audit.'

'How do Warren and Garraway know each other?'

'I don't know,' he said. 'But they've done so for years.'

'And how long have you known them?' I asked.

'About four years.'

'Was that when the fake hedge-fund scheme started?'

'Yeah, about then.'

'Is that what you were referring to when you had that little spat with Jackson Warren—you know, that night when I first met you?'

'No,' he said. 'That was over his and Peter's other little fiddle.'

'And what's that?' I asked.

'No way,' he said. 'I've already said too much as it is.'

'You think the Revenue will investigate their other little fiddle?' I asked him, thinking back to the supper exchange between him and Jackson. 'And you're worried about that investigation finding out about everything else?'

It was a guess, but not a bad one.

'Bloody stupid, if you ask me,' he said.

'Why take the risk?' I said.

'Exactly.'

'So their other little fiddle is about tax?'

'Look,' he said, changing the subject, 'I need to take a piss.'

Reluctantly, I took a pair of scissors from my rucksack, leaned down and cut the ties holding Alex's hands behind his back.

'I might run away,' he said, sitting up and rubbing his wrists.

'Not like that you won't.' I pointed at the plastic ties that still bound his ankles together.

He pulled himself up and hopped into the bathroom beneath the stairs. I thought it unlikely that there would be a phone in the bathroom, but nevertheless, I removed the telephone from its cradle in the kitchen. His mobile phone was still lying on the kitchen counter where I'd left it.

Alex was taking his time, and I was beginning to think he might be trying to escape out of the bathroom window, when I heard the flush. Presently he reappeared, hobbling out into the hall.

'Cut these things off,' he demanded. He had obviously been using the time to try to break the plastic ties around his ankles.

'No,' I said.

'What the bloody hell more do you want?' he asked angrily.

'I need some hard evidence,' I said. 'Evidence of conspiracy to defraud my mother of one million US dollars.'

'Dream on,' he said, smiling.

'Maybe I should ring Jackson Warren and ask him about my mother's money, telling him it was you who suggested I do so.'

'He'd bloody kill me just for talking to you.'

Good, I thought. It was much to my advantage that Alex remained more frightened of Jackson Warren than he was of me.

I walked into the kitchen, and he hobbled in behind me.

'Sit down,' I said sharply, pointing to one of the kitchen chairs.

He wavered, but after a few seconds, he pulled the chair out from under the table and sat down while I sat on the chair opposite him.

'Whose idea was it to get my mother's horses to lose?' I asked.

'Julie's,' he said.

'So she could bet against them on the internet?'

'No, nothing like that,' he said. 'She just wanted to give her old man's horses a better chance of winning. He gives her a hard time when they lose.'

Amateurs, I thought. *These people are amateurs*.

The doorbell rang, making us jump. It was followed by a knocking at the door. I glanced at my watch. It was one in the morning.

'Stay there,' I ordered. 'And keep quiet.'

I walked through into the dark front room and looked through the window. Julie Yorke was standing outside the door. I opened it.

'What have you done to him?' Julie asked in a breathless voice.

'Nothing,' I said.

'Where is he, then?' she demanded.

'In the kitchen,' I said, standing aside to let her pass.

When I went back into the kitchen, Julie was stroking Alex's hair. She was wearing a nightdress under her raincoat.

'Couldn't sleep?' I asked sarcastically.

'I had to wait for my bloody husband to drop off,' she said. 'I've taken a big chance coming here. I tried to call, but it was permanently engaged, and Alex's mobile phone went straight to voice mail.'

I looked across the kitchen at the house phone still lying off the hook on the countertop and at the switched-off mobile alongside it.

'I thought I told you not to contact Alex,' I said sharply.

'You said not in the next thirty-six hours,' she replied in a pained tone. 'That ran out at ten forty-five this evening.'

I hadn't been counting, but she obviously had.

'So what happens now?' Alex asked into the silence.

'Well,' I said, 'for a start, you return all the blackmail money to my mother. I reckon that's about sixty thousand pounds.'

'Dream on,' he said. 'We've spent it.'

'OK,' I said. 'If that's your attitude, I will have to go to Jackson Warren and Peter Garraway and ask them for it.'

'You'll be lucky,' he said, laughing. 'They're tight-fisted bastards.'

'I'll tell them you said that.'

The laughter died in his throat.

'What about my pictures?' Julie demanded.

'They prove nothing,' Alex said. 'All they show is you in the mailbox shop. That doesn't mean you were blackmailing anyone.'

'Not those,' Julie said. 'The other pictures he took of me.'

'What other pictures?' Alex demanded, turning to me.

Oh, dear, I thought. *This could get nasty.*

'Er,' she said, backtracking fast. 'They're not that important.'

'But pictures of what?' Alex persisted, still looking at me.

Should I tell him? Should I show him just the sort of girl she was? Or could they still be useful to me as a lever to apply to Julie?

'Just some photos I took outside the Yorkes' house yesterday to record her reaction when I showed her the prints of her in the mailbox shop. That's when I told her not to contact you for thirty-six hours.'

Julie seemed relieved, and Alex appeared satisfied by the answer.

'So what happens now?' he asked again.

It was a good question. I thought about asking Julie if she knew anything of Warren and Garraway's other little fiddle, the tax one, but I decided I might get more from her without Alex being there.

'Well, I don't know about you two,' I said, standing up, 'but I'm going home to bed.' And, I thought, to read Alex's emails.

I collected my 'insulin' bag from the stairs, slung my rucksack onto my back, and left the two lovebirds in the kitchen as I left the house by the front door. But I didn't walk off down the road. I removed the camera from my rucksack and went quickly down the side of the house to the rear garden and the kitchen window.

I had purposely left a space at the bottom when I'd closed the blind, and I looked in. Alex and Julie weren't very discreet. I took twenty or more photos through the window of them kissing and him sliding his hands inside her coat. My lens captured everything.

Presently Julie cut the plastic ties around Alex's ankles, and they went out of the kitchen and, I presumed, up the stairs to bed.

Even then I didn't go home. Instead, I went to where Julie had parked the white BMW. I tried the doors, but she had locked them, so I sat down on the pavement, leaned up against the passenger door, and waited.

I was getting quite used to waiting and thinking.

I WAS JUST beginning to think that Julie was staying for the whole night when, about an hour after I left, I saw her coming towards me.

I pulled myself to my feet but remained crouched so Julie couldn't see me. When she was ten yards away, she pushed the remote UNLOCK button on her key, and the indicator lights flashed in response. As she opened the driver's door, I opened the passenger one, and we ended up sitting down side by side.

Startled, she immediately tried to open the door again, but I grabbed her arm on the steering wheel.

'Don't,' I said. 'Just drive.'

'Where to?' she said.

'Anywhere,' I said with authority. 'Now. Drive out of this road.'

Julie started the car, pulled out into Water Lane, and turned right towards Newbury, towards home. We went a few hundred yards.

'OK,' I said. 'Pull over here.'

She stopped the car at the side of the road.

'Can't you just leave us alone?'

'But why should I?' I exclaimed. 'My mother has paid you more than sixty thousand pounds over the past seven months, and I think that entitles me to demand something from you.'

'But Alex told you,' she said. 'We've spent it.'

'On what?' I asked.

She laughed. 'Coke, of course. Lots of coke. And bottles of bubbly. Only the best. Cases and cases of lovely Dom.'

I realised that she must have been sampling one or the other during the past hour with Alex. 'Does Ewen know you take cocaine?' I asked.

'Don't be stupid. Ewen wouldn't know a line of coke if it ran up his nose. If it hasn't got four legs and a mane, Ewen couldn't care less. I think he'd much rather screw the horses than me.'

'So what is Jackson Warren and Peter Garraway's tax fiddle?'

'You mean their VAT fiddle?' she asked.

'Yes,' I said. I waited in silence.

She paused for a bit, but eventually she started. 'Did you know that race-horse owners can recover the VAT on training fees?'

'My mother said something about it,' I said.

'And on their other costs as well, those they attribute to their racing business, like transport and telephone charges and vet's fees. They can even recover the VAT they have to pay when they buy the horses in the first place.'

Whether VAT was fifteen or seventeen and a half per cent, that was a lot of tax to recover on expensive horseflesh.

'So what's the fiddle?' I asked.

'What makes you think I'd ever tell you?' she said.

'I'll delete the pictures if you tell me.'

Even in her state, she knew that the pictures were the key.

'Do you promise?' she said.

'I promise,' I said formally, holding up my right hand.

'Garraway lives in Gibraltar, and he's not registered for VAT in the UK. He actually could be, but he's obsessive about having anything to do with the tax people here because he's a tax exile. He only lives in Gibraltar to avoid paying tax.' She paused.

'So?' I said, prompting her to continue.

'So all Peter Garraway's horses are officially owned by Jackson Warren. Jackson pays the training fees and all the other bills, and then he claims back the VAT. He even buys the horses for Garraway in the first place and gets the VAT back on that, too. He uses a company called Budsam Ltd.'

'So why is that a fiddle?' I asked. 'If Jackson buys them and pays the fees, then *he* is the owner, not Garraway.'

'Yes, but Garraway pays Jackson back for all the costs.'

'Doesn't that show up in Jackson's accounts?'

'No.' She smiled. 'That's the clever bit. Peter pays Jackson into an off-shore account in Gibraltar that Jackson doesn't declare to the Revenue. Alex says it's very clever because Jackson gets his money off-shore without ever having to transfer anything from a UK bank, which would be required by law to tell the tax people about it.'

'How many horses does Garraway own in this way?' I asked.

'Masses. He has twelve with us and more with other trainers.'

'But don't they pay for themselves with the prize money?'

'No,' she said. 'Most horses don't make in prize money anything like what they cost to keep, especially not jumpers.'

'So why doesn't Peter Garraway register himself as an owner in the UK for the VAT scheme?'

'I told you,' she said. 'He's paranoid about the tax people. They've been trying forever to get him for tax evasion. He's obsessive about the number of days he stays here, and he and his wife travel on separate planes so they won't both be killed in a crash and his family get done here for inheritance tax. There's no way he'll register. Alex thinks it's stupid. He told them it would solve the problem of the VAT without any risk, but Garraway won't listen.'

I listened, all right. Perhaps now I had a lever long enough to pry my mother's money back from under the Rock of Gibraltar.

All I had to do was work out on whom to apply it, and when.

9

I spent much of the night downloading Alex's files and emails onto my laptop using the internet connection in my mother's office.

I had let myself into the kitchen silently using Ian's key. I worked solely by the light of the computer screen and left everything exactly as I'd found it. I didn't know why I still thought it was necessary for my presence to be a secret from my mother, but I wasn't yet ready to try to explain to her what had been going on. It might also have been safer for me if she didn't know where I was.

After I had left Julie to drive herself home in the white BMW, I'd taken Ian's car up the driveway of Greystone Stables. My telltale stick was broken. Someone had been up to the stable; someone who would now know I wasn't dead; someone who might try to kill me again. But they would have to find me first.

I SLEPT FITFULLY on Ian's sofa, and he left me there snoozing when he went out to morning stables at half past six on Monday morning.

By the time he returned around noon, I had read through all of Alex's downloaded information on my laptop. Most of it was boring, but amongst the dross, there were some real gems and three stand-out diamonds.

One of the diamonds was that Alex was not only the accountant for Rock Bank (Gibraltar) Ltd, but also one of the signatories of the company's bank account, and best of all, I had downloaded all the passwords and user names needed to access the account online.

The other diamonds were the emails sent by Jackson Warren to Alex Reece concerning me: the first a message sent on the night of Isabella's kitchen supper, in a fit of anger, soon after storming out of the supper:

> What the hell do you think you were doing talking so openly in front of Thomas Forsyth? His mother was one of those who invested heavily in the scheme. KEEP YOUR LIPS SEALED, YOU HEAR?

The second email was calmer but no less direct and had been sent by Jackson at five o'clock on the day of the Newbury races:

> Thomas Forsyth told me this afternoon that he wants to contact you. I am making arrangements to ensure that he cannot. If he manages to contact you, you are NOT to speak with him. This is important, in light of the company business this coming week.

I knew only too well what arrangements Jackson had taken to stop me from speaking to Alex—my shoulders still ached from them. But what, I wondered, had been the company business?

'SO HOW ARE the horses?' I asked Ian as he slumped down onto the brown sofa and switched on the television.

'They're all right,' he said with a mighty sigh.

'What's wrong, then?' I asked. 'Bad day at the office?'

'Yeah,' he said, 'you could say that.'

I said nothing. He'd tell me if he wanted to.

He did.

'When I took this job, I thought it would be more as an assistant trainer rather than just as head lad. That's what Mrs Kauri implied.'

'And?' I prompted.

'And nothing,' he said. 'I was wrong. She can't delegate anything to anybody. She treats me the same as one of the young boys straight out of school. She tells the staff to do things that I should be telling them to do, and often it is directly opposite to what I've already said. I feel worthless and undermined.'

Story of my life, I thought.

At least, it had been the story of my life until I'd left home to join the army. It seemed that Ian was already on the road to somewhere else. It was a shame. I'd seen him working with the horses, and even I could see that he was good. Losing Ian would be a sad day for Kauri House Stables.

'Have you been looking?' I asked.

'There's a possibility of a new stable opening that's quite exciting,' he said. 'It's some way off yet, but I'm going to keep my options open. But don't go telling your mother. She'd be furious.'

He was right; she would be furious. She demanded loyalty from everyone around her, but sadly, she repaid it in short measure, and she wasn't about to change now.

'Which stables?' I asked.

'Rumour has it that one of the trainers in the village is going to open up a second yard and he'll need a new assistant to run it. I thought I might apply.'

'Which trainer?' I asked.

'Ewen Yorke. Apparently, he's buying Greystone Stables.'

He'd have to fix the broken pane in the tack-room window.

THE STATEMENTS of the bank account of Rock Bank (Gibraltar) Ltd were most revealing.

I had spent the afternoon rereading all the emails that I had downloaded from Alex Reece's computer, as well as the Gibraltar folder. Quite a few of them were communications back and forth with someone named Sigurd Bellido, the senior cashier at the real Gibraltar bank that held the Rock Bank Ltd account, discussing the transfer of funds in and out. Strangely, they all discussed the health of Mr Bellido's mother-in-law.

At two in the morning, I logged on to the online banking system from my mother's office. I could see the transfers discussed with Mr Bellido were reflected in various changes to the account balance.

As Alex had said, money periodically came into the account, presumably from the 'investors' in the UK, and then left again about a week later. If Alex was right, it disappeared eventually into some secret Swiss account belonging to Garraway or Warren.

I looked particularly at the transactions for the past week to see if they showed any evidence of the 'company business' that Jackson had referred to in his email. There had been two large deposits. Both were in American dollars, one for one million and the other for two million. The two million dollars had a name attached to it—Toleron. I knew I'd heard that name before, but I couldn't place where, so I typed 'Toleron' into Google.

'Toleron Plastics' appeared across my screen in large red letters, with 'The largest drainpipe manufacturer in Europe' running underneath. Mrs Martin Toleron had been the rather boring lady I'd sat next to at Isabella's kitchen supper, and who, it appeared, would soon be finding out that her 'wonderful' husband wasn't quite as good at business as she had claimed. I almost felt sorry for her.

I searched further for Martin Toleron. Nearly every reference was connected with the sale of his company the previous November to a Russian conglomerate, reputedly adding more than a hundred million dollars to his personal fortune. Suddenly, I didn't feel quite so sorry for his wife over the loss of a mere two million.

As Alex would have said, they could afford it.

EARLY ON TUESDAY morning, while my mother was away on the gallops watching her horses exercise, I borrowed Ian Norland's car once more and went to see Mr Martin Toleron.

According to the internet, he lived in the village of Hermitage, a few miles to the north of Newbury, and I found the exact address easily enough by asking directions in a village shop.

Martin Toleron's house was a grand affair, in keeping with his 'captain of industry' billing. I pulled up in front of the six-foot-high iron gates and pushed the button on the intercom box.

'Hello,' said a man's voice through the box.

'Mr Toleron?' I asked.

'Yes,' the man said.

'My name is Thomas Forsyth,' I said. 'I'd like to—'

'Look, I'm sorry,' he replied, cutting me off. 'I don't take cold calls at my gate. Goodbye.' The box went dead.

I pushed the button again. No reply. I pushed once more.

Eventually he came back on the line. 'What do you want?'

'Does Rock Bank of Gibraltar mean anything to you?' I asked.

There was a pause before he replied. 'Who did you say you are?'

'Open the gates and you'll find out,' I said.

'Stay there,' he said. 'I'm coming out.'

I waited, and soon a small, portly man emerged, walking down the driveway. I vaguely remembered him from Isabella's supper.

Martin Toleron stopped some ten feet from the gates. 'What do you want?' he demanded. 'Are you from the tax authorities?'

I thought it a strange question. 'No,' I said. 'I was at the same dinner party as you, at Jackson and Isabella Warren's place last week. I want to talk to you about Rock Bank and the investment you have just made with them in Gibraltar.'

'And how do you know about it?' he asked.

'I think it might be better for us to go inside to discuss this.'

He obviously agreed, because he removed a small black box from his pocket and pushed a button. The gates swung open as I returned to Ian's car.

I parked on the gravel drive in front of the mansion.

'Come into my office,' Martin Toleron said, leading the way into a large oak-panelled room with a matching oak desk and bookcases.

'Sit down,' he said decisively, pointing to one of two armchairs, and

I glimpsed the confidence and resolution that would have served him well in his business. I resolved to ensure that Martin Toleron became a valuable friend rather than a challenging enemy.

'What is this about?' he said, sitting in the other chair.

'I believe that you have recently sent a large sum of money to Rock Bank of Gibraltar as an investment in a hedge fund.'

I paused, but he didn't respond.

'I have reason to believe,' I went on, 'that the investment fund does not actually exist and that you're being defrauded.'

'Why are you telling me this?' he demanded.

'I thought you'd like to know so that you didn't send any more. I'm the son of another victim. I hoped that you might have some information that would be helpful in trying to recover her money.'

'What sort of information?' he asked.

'Well, my mother is no financial wizard, and I can see how she was duped, but you . . .' I left the implication hanging in the air.

He stood up and went to the desk. He picked up a large white envelope and tossed it into my lap. It contained the glossy offering document for what it called the 'opportunity-of-a-lifetime investment'. I skimmed through the brochure. It was convincing and gave the impression of being from a legitimate organisation.

'Why do you think it a fraud?' he asked.

'I know of two cases when people, after investing through Rock Bank, have lost all their money. They were told that the hedge fund had gone bankrupt. I have reason to believe that the funds never existed in the first place and the money was simply stolen.'

I flicked through the glossy brochure once more.

'It's a very professional job,' he said. 'It gives all the right information and assurances.'

'But did you check up on any of it?' I asked.

He didn't answer, but I could tell from his face that he hadn't.

'Why didn't your mother complain to the police?' he said. 'Then there might have been a warning issued.'

'She couldn't,' I said, without further clarification.

I thought back to his strange question at the gate about me being from the tax authorities. 'Mr Toleron,' I said. 'Excuse my asking, but are you being blackmailed?'

As in my mother's case, it wasn't the loss of money that worried Martin Toleron the most; for him, it was the potential loss of face because he'd been conned. And if I thought he would thank me for pointing out that his investment was a fake, I was mistaken. Indirectly, he even offered to pay me not to make that knowledge public.

'Of course I won't make it public,' I said.

'Everyone else I know would have,' he said with a sigh. 'They would gleefully sell it to the gutter press.' Toleron may have been a successful businessman, and he had made pots of money, but he'd obviously been accompanied by few real friends on the journey.

He was not being blackmailed, but someone had recently tried to extort money from him, accusing him of falsifying a tax return that stated he was not a tax resident in the UK when, in fact, he was.

'I told him to bugger off,' he said. 'But it took time and money to get things straightened out. The last thing I want is an audit.'

'So you are fiddling something, then?' I asked.

'No. I'm just sailing close to the wind, trying a few things.'

'VAT?' I asked.

'As a matter of fact, yes,' he said. 'Is that why your mother didn't go to the authorities? She was being blackmailed?'

I simply nodded, echoing my mother's belief that in not saying anything out loud, it somehow diminished the admission.

'Did you know someone called Roderick Ward?' I asked.

'Don't you mention that name here,' he said explosively. 'It was thanks to him that I nearly copped it with the Revenue.'

I wondered how on earth a captain of industry had become tangled up with such a dodgy accountant.

'How did you come to know him?' I asked.

'He was my elder daughter's boyfriend for a while. Kept coming round here and telling me how I could save more tax. I should never have listened to him.'

'Do you know what happened to him?' I asked.

'I heard somewhere that he died in a car crash.'

'Actually, he was murdered,' I said.

He was surprised but not shocked. 'Good riddance, I say!' He smiled for the first time since I'd been there. But then the smile vanished. 'Hold on,' he said. 'Didn't Ward die last summer?'

'Yes,' I said. 'In July.'

'So who is robbing me now?'

'Who was it who recommended the investment to you?'

'How do you know someone did?' he asked.

'No one invests in something from a brochure that just drops through their letter box. Certainly not to the tune of two million dollars. You had to have been told about it by someone.'

He seemed surprised I knew the exact size of his investment.

'Did Jackson tell you the amount?' he asked.

'So it was Jackson Warren who recommended it,' I said. 'You asked me who was robbing you, and that's your answer—Jackson Warren, together with Peter Garraway.'

He didn't believe it. I could read the doubt in his face.

'Why would he? Jackson's got lots of money of his own.'

'Maybe that's because he steals it from other people.'

'Don't be ridiculous,' he said.

'I'm not. I'll show you. Do you have an internet connection?'

'BUT HOW DID YOU get access?' Martin Toleron was astounded as I brought up the recent transactions of Rock Bank (Gibraltar) Ltd on my laptop computer screen.

'Don't ask,' I said. 'You don't want to know.'

'Whose is the other investment?' he asked.

'I was hoping you could tell me,' I said.

'I've no idea. I've only spoken about the fund with Jackson. He told me he had made his investment in the past and claimed that it had performed very well. I believed him, and to be fair, you haven't shown me anything substantive to contradict that belief.'

I opened an email from Alex Reece's inbox from the previous week:

> Alex. We should expect a two-unit sum into the account this coming week from our drainpipe friend. Please ensure it takes the usual route and issue the usual note of acceptance. Your commission will be transferred in due course. JW

'That doesn't prove it's a fraud,' Toleron said.

'Not directly,' I said. 'But did Jackson Warren tell you that he was actually running the fund that he was so keen to promote?'

'No, he did not.'

'But he clearly must be running it if he's ordering the issuing of acceptance notes to investors.' I paused to allow that to sink in. 'Is that enough proof for you? If not, there's plenty more.'

'Show me,' Toleron said.

I pulled up another of Alex Reece's emails, this time one he had sent to Sigurd Bellido, the chief cashier in Gibraltar:

> Sigurd. Please transfer the million dollars, received into the Rock Bank Ltd account last week from the UK, into the usual other account at your bank. I trust your mother-in-law's health problems are improving. AR.

Martin Toleron said, 'That doesn't prove anything.'

'No,' I said. 'But read this.'

I pulled up another email from Alex's Gibraltar folder, this one to Jackson Warren, sent on the same day as the previous one:

> Jackson. I have issued the instruction to SB, and the funds should be available in your account later today for further transfer. AR.

'What's all that mother-in-law business about?' he asked.

'I don't know,' I said. 'But it appears in all the emails sent to SB—that's Sigurd Bellido, who makes the transfers in Gibraltar. Thing is, he doesn't ever mention her in his replies.'

Toleron thought for a moment. 'Perhaps it's a code to prove that the transfer request really is from this AR person.'

'Alex Reece,' I said.

'Didn't I meet him at that dinner party? Ginger-haired fellow?'

'That's him,' I said. 'Slightly odd sort of person. He's Jackson Warren's accountant, but he's up to his neck in the fraud.'

'But Warren must surely know that I would suspect him if the fund went bust and I lost all my money.'

'He would simply apologise for the bad investment advice and say that he'd also lost a packet, and if the newspaper reports of your company sale are to be believed, you would have been able to afford the loss more than he would.'

'Don't believe what you read in the papers,' Toleron said. 'But I get your point. The fact that it was a relatively small investment is why I did it in the first place. I can afford to lose it. Not that I want to.'

How lovely it must be for him, I thought, *to be so rich that two million dollars was a relatively small investment.*

'So all we need to do now is to get this Alex Reece chappy to email SB in Gibraltar and get him to return the money from whence it came.' Martin Toleron smiled at me. 'Then I'll have my money back. Shouldn't be too difficult to arrange, surely.'

He certainly made it sound easy, but I was not sure that Alex Reece would play ball.

'I have a better idea,' I said. 'We could send an email to SB pretending to be Alex Reece.'

'But that's not easy without his email account password.'

It was my turn to smile. 'What makes you think I don't have it?'

10

The email to Sigurd Bellido was ready to go by half past eleven: Sigurd. There has been a mix-up at our end, and I need to transfer back to the UK the last two payments that were made into the Rock Bank Ltd account on Thursday and Friday of last week. Please transfer, as soon as possible, from the Rock Bank Ltd account (number 01201030866) at your bank:

(1) US$2,000,000 (two million US dollars) to Barclays Bank plc, SWIFT code BARCGB2LBGA, Belgravia branch, for further credit to Mr Martin Toleron, account number 81634587.

(2) US$1,000,000 (one million US dollars) to HSBC Bank plc, SWIFT code HSBCGB6174A, Hungerford Branch, for further credit to Mrs Josephine Kauri, account number 15638409.

Please carry out these transfers immediately. I trust your mother-in-law continues to recover. Many thanks. AR.

Martin Toleron and I had looked through all the transfer requests in Alex Reece's Gibraltar folder, and we had studied closely the language and layout he had used in the past.

'Do you think it will work?' Martin asked.

'Maybe,' I said. 'But we have nothing to lose by trying.'

'I have,' he said. 'I stand to lose two million dollars.'

'You've already lost it, but this might just get it back. But it's a lot of money for a bank to transfer without making other checks.'

'They'll email him back, though,' Martin said.

'Oh, for sure.'

By looking at all the emails to and from SB and AR, we had discovered a pattern. Alex would email the request around midday UK time. Sigurd would then email straight back, acknowledging receipt and requesting confirmation. Alex would then instantly respond to that with a note that contained some comment, not now about Sigurd's mother-in-law, but about the weather in the UK.

'Are you ready to intercept SB's reply?' Martin asked.

'As ready as I can be,' I said. 'I'm logged on to Alex Reece's email account.'

'Do you have the reply ready?' He was hopping from foot to foot with his nervousness as he stood behind me at his desk.

'Calm down, Martin.' I pushed the send button, and the message disappeared from the screen. It was on its way.

We both waited in silence as I continually refreshed the webmail page. The clock on the computer moved to 12:01. I refreshed the page once more. Nothing. I forced myself to wait for a count of ten before I clicked on the REFRESH button again. Still nothing. I counted again slowly, this time to fifteen, but still nothing came.

The reply arrived at nine minutes past twelve, by which time I had all but given up hope:

> Alex. I acknowledge receipt of your instructions. To which party do I charge the transfer costs? SB.

I had the reply ready to send, but I quickly pulled it up to make the changes. I typed in the new information:

> Sigurd, I confirm receipt of your acknowledgment and I endorse the instructions. Please charge the transfer costs to the recipients. Thank goodness spring is nearly here in the UK and the temperature has begun to rise. AR.

I pushed the SEND button, and again the message disappeared from the screen. Next I deleted SB's reply from the server so it wouldn't appear on Alex's computer when he downloaded his mail.

I went on monitoring the webmail page for another forty minutes before I was happy that SB wasn't going to ask another question.

'Do you think it will work?' Martin said.

'Do you?' I asked in reply.

'Not really,' he said. 'It was much too easy.'

'Yes,' I said. 'Almost as easy as getting you to part with the two million dollars in the first place.'

MARTIN CALLED HIS BANK and asked them to inform him immediately if a large deposit arrived. My mother, meanwhile, might simply have to wait to see if it appeared on her bank statement.

'Call me if you hear anything,' I said, shaking his hand in the driveway.

'Don't worry, I will,' he said with a smile. 'Quite an entertaining morning, I must say. Much more exciting than the boring existence I have now found for myself.'

'You miss running your company, then?' I asked.

'Miss it!' he said. 'I grieve for my loss.'

'But you have all that money.'

'Yes,' he said forlornly. 'But what can I do every day; count it?'

'Why did you sell the company?'

'I'm sixty-eight, and neither of my children is interested in running a drainpipe business. Far too boring for them. But I loved it. I used to get to the factory in Swindon at seven in the morning, and often I'd not leave before ten at night. It was such fun.'

'Didn't your wife object?' I asked.

'I expect so,' he said. 'But she so enjoys shopping in Harrods.'

'What will you do in the future? Will you start something else?'

'No,' he said with a sigh. 'I don't think so. I suppose I'll have to go to Harrods more often with my wife.' The prospect of more shopping with his wife clearly didn't make him happy.

'Shop for some racehorses,' I said. 'I hear that's a great way to spend loads of money, and it can be lots of fun, too.'

'What a great idea,' he said. 'I'll do just that.'

'And,' I said, 'I know a way to save you all the VAT.'

We both laughed. As I had hoped, Martin Toleron and I parted as friends.

MARTIN CALLED MY mobile phone at a quarter past three as I was dozing on Ian's sofa, half watching racing on the television.

'Have you heard from the bank?' I asked, instantly wide awake.

'No,' he said. 'But I've just had a call from Jackson Warren.'

'Wow,' I said. 'And what did he say?'

'He tried to tell me that the bank in Gibraltar had made an error and had returned my two million dollars to my account. He asked if I would mind instructing my bank to send it again.'

'And what did you say?' I asked.

'I expressed surprise that Jackson was calling me, as I had no idea that he was involved with the organisation of the fund. I told him that I thought he was just another satisfied investor.'

'And what did he say then?'

'He tried to tell me that he had been called by the fund manager because he, the manager, knew that Jackson was a friend of mine. I lost my rag a bit. I said that I would not be investing in anything to do with him, as he had purposely misled me. I also told him I'd be reporting the incident to the Financial Services Authority.'

'I bet he didn't take kindly to that.'

'No, he didn't,' Martin said. 'In fact, he threatened me. He told me straight out that if I went to the FSA, I'd regret it. I asked him what exactly he meant by that, but all he said was "Work it out." And, he doesn't seem to be too pleased with you, either. He accused me of conspiring with you to defraud him. I told him that was rich, coming from him.'

'Did he ask if you knew where I was?' I asked.

'Ask me?' He laughed. 'He demanded that I tell him. I simply said that I had no idea where you were.'

'How secure are your gates?' I asked.

'Why?' He sounded slightly worried for the first time.

'I think that Jackson Warren is a very dangerous man,' I said seriously. 'Martin, this is not a game. He already tried to kill me once, and he would do it again without hesitation. Keep your gates locked and watch your back.'

'I will,' he said, and hung up.

Was it now time, I wondered, to involve the police and be damned about the tax consequences? But what could I say to them? 'Well, Officer, Mr Jackson Warren tried to kill me by hanging me up to starve to death in a disused stable, but I escaped and I've only now decided to tell you about it, a week later, after I've been sneaking around Berkshire attacking and torturing one of Mr Warren's associates using fake insulin and a hypodermic needle, and using the information I illegally obtained from him to transfer one million American dollars from Mr Warren's company in Gibraltar into my mother's personal bank account in Hungerford.'

Somehow I didn't think it would bring the Thames Valley Constabulary rushing to Jackson's front door to make an immediate arrest. They would be far more likely to send me to a psychiatrist, and then Jackson would know exactly where I was.

It would be much safer, I thought, *to lie low for a while*.

How mistaken could I be? The answer was badly.

THE FIRST SIGN that things had gone dangerously wrong was a hammering on the door of Ian's flat that woke me from a deep sleep. I turned on the light and looked at the clock. It was one thirty in the morning.

I grabbed my shirt and went over to the door.

'Who is it?' I shouted.

'Derek Philips,' came the reply. My stepfather.

Ian appeared from his bedroom, bleary-eyed.

'What the hell's going on?' he said, squinting.

'It's my stepfather,' I said to him.

'Well, open the door.' He pushed past and unlocked it himself.

Derek almost fell into the room as the door opened. 'Thank God,' he said. Then he saw me. 'What the hell are you doing here?'

I ignored his question. 'Derek, what's wrong?' I asked.

'It's your mother,' he said, clearly distressed. 'She's been kidnapped. By two men. They came looking for you.'

Derek and Ian both looked at me accusingly.

'Who were they?' Ian asked him.

'I don't know,' Derek said. 'They were wearing ski masks, like balaclavas, but I don't think either of them was very young.'

'Why not?'

'Something about the way they moved,' Derek said.

I believed I knew exactly who they were. Two desperate men in their sixties trying to recover the money they had stolen but which I had then stolen back. But where was Alex Reece?

'Are you sure there were just two of them?' I asked.

'I only saw two,' Derek said.

'What exactly did they say?' I asked.

'They had somehow got into our bedroom. One of them poked me with the barrels of a shotgun to wake me up.' He was almost in tears. 'They said they wanted you, but we told them we didn't know where you were.'

So not telling my mother where I was had saved me a visit from the ski-masked duo. But at what cost to her?

'But why did they take her with them?' I asked, but I already knew the answer. They knew that I'd come to them if they had my mother. 'Did they tell you where they were taking her?'

'No. But they did tell me that you'd know where she would be.'

'Have you called the police?' Ian asked.

'No police,' Derek said. 'Call the police and Josephine dies, they said. They told me to call you.' He nodded at me. 'But I didn't know where you were. All I could think of was asking Ian.'

I would know where she would be. That's what the kidnappers had told Derek. And I did.

I APPROACHED Greystone Stables, not from the driveway but from the opposite direction, through the wood on the hill.

I stopped a few feet short of the limit of the trees and knelt down on my left knee. I looked at my watch. It was now 3.42 a.m. The windless night was clear. The moon was sinking rapidly. In forty minutes or so, it would be down completely, and the blackness of the night would deepen. I liked the darkness. It was my friend.

In the last of the moonlight, I studied the layout of the deserted house and stables spread out below me. I could see no lights and no movement, but I was sure this was where my mother would be.

I had left Derek and Ian in the latter's flat, Derek cuddling a bottle of brandy, and Ian with a list of instructions, including one to telephone the police if he hadn't heard from me by 6.30 a.m.

They had both watched with astonishment as I had made my mission preparations. First I'd changed into my dark clothes. Next I had gathered the equipment into my rucksack: garden ties, scissors, duct tape, the red-coloured first-aid kit, the length of chain with the padlock still attached, a torch, and a box of matches. I borrowed one of Ian's kitchen knives, and I'd placed it on top of everything else in the rucksack for easy access. I had then borrowed a pair of racing binoculars from my mother's office, and finally I'd removed my sword from its protective cardboard tube and scabbard.

I scanned the buildings below me once more, using my mother's binoculars, searching for light or movement. There was nothing.

The moonlight was disappearing fast. I took one last look through the binoculars, and there it was, a movement, maybe only a stretching of a cramped leg, but a telltale movement nevertheless. Someone was waiting for me in the line of trees just to the right of the house. From that position, he would have commanded a fine view of the driveway and the road below.

But where was his accomplice?

I stood up and started forward across the grass. I approached the stables in such a way as to take me past the muck heap near the back end of the passageway in which I had hidden the previous week. I eased myself silently through the fence that separated the stable buildings from the paddock behind.

I stood against the stable wall at the back of the passageway, closed my eyes, and listened. Nothing. Confident that there was no one hiding in the passageway, I moved forward slowly, feeling ahead into the darkness with my hands and my real foot. At the door, I looked through the gaps between the wooden slats.

Compared to the total blackness of the passageway, the stable yard beyond seemed bright. I eased open the slatted door from the passageway and stepped out into the yard. I stood very still, listening again for anyone's breathing, but there was no sound. I looked at my watch. It was four forty-seven.

In eighteen minutes, at five minutes past five, a car would drive through the gates at the bottom of the Greystone Stables driveway and stop. The driver would sound the car horn once, and the car would remain there with the engine running for exactly five minutes. Then it would reverse out and drive away. At least, it would do all of those things if Ian obeyed the instructions I had left him.

He hadn't been very keen on the plan, but I'd promised him that he was in no danger provided he kept the car doors locked. It was a dodgy promise.

I moved silently to my right around the quadrangle of stables, keeping in the darkest corners. Where would my mother be? I felt all the bolts on the stable doors. They were all closed. I decided not to try to open any, as it would surely make some noise.

Unsurprisingly, no one had mended the pane of glass in the tack-room window that I'd broken to get out. I leaned right in through the opening, closed my eyes tight, and listened.

I could hear someone whimpering. My mother was indeed here. The sound came from my left. She was in one of the stalls on the same side of the stables as I had been. Maybe she was in the same stall in which I had been imprisoned.

I looked again at my watch: four fifty-nine.

I withdrew my head and shoulders from the broken window and moved very slowly along the line of stalls. I counted four doors; then I stopped. The stall I had been in was the next one.

I stood very still and waited, listening and counting the seconds. I began to doubt that Ian was coming. I was well into the third minute when I heard the car horn, a long two-second blast. Good boy.

There was immediate movement from the end of the row of stalls not twenty yards from where I was standing. Someone had been sitting there in silence, but now I clearly heard the person walk towards the house, crunching across the gravel turning area. I heard him call out to someone else, asking what the noise was, and there was a murmured reply from further away that I couldn't catch.

I went swiftly to the door of the stall and eased back the bolts. The door swung open. 'Mum,' I whispered into the darkness.

I heard her whimper, but it came from some way to my left. She wasn't in this stall, but in one a bit further along.

I moved as quickly as I dared along the row of stalls, carefully sliding back the bolt on the upper half of each door and calling into the space with a whisper. She was in the second stall from the end, close to where the man had been sitting on guard.

When I opened the door and whispered, my mother was unable to answer me properly, but she managed to murmur loudly.

'Shhh,' I said, going towards the sound. It was absolutely pitch-black in the stable. I removed one of my black woollen gloves and 'saw' by feel, moving my left hand around until I found her.

She had tape stuck over her mouth and had been bound hand and foot with the same plastic garden ties as had been used to secure me. She was sitting on the hard floor close to the door.

I laid my sword down carefully, then swung the rucksack off my back and opened the flap. Ian's knife sliced easily through the plastic ties holding my mother's ankles and wrists together.

'Be very, very quiet,' I whispered in her ear, leaning down. 'Leave the tape on your mouth. Come on, let's go.'

I helped her up and was about to bend down for the rucksack and the sword when she turned and hugged me. She held me so tightly that I could hardly breathe. And she was crying. I couldn't tell if it was from pain, from fear, or in joy, but I could feel her tears on my face.

'Mum, let me go,' I whispered. 'We have to get out of here.'

She eased the pressure but didn't let go completely, hanging on to my left arm. I prised her away from me and swung the rucksack over my right shoulder. As I reached down again for my sword, I stumbled slightly, kicking the sword with my unfeeling right foot. It scraped across the floor with a metallic rattle that sounded dreadfully loud in the confines of the stall but probably wouldn't have been audible at more than ten paces outside.

But had there been anyone outside within ten paces to hear it?

I grabbed the sword and led my mother to the door.

Ian must have completed his five-minute linger by now, and I hoped he had safely departed, back to his flat, to sit by the telephone waiting for my call, ready to summon the cavalry if things went wrong. But where, I wondered, were my enemies?

My mother and I stepped through the stable door, out into the yard, with her hanging on to my arm as though she would never let go. There were no shouts of discovery, no running feet. But my enemies were out there, watching and waiting. It was time to leave.

My mother and I were halfway across the stable yard, taking the shortest route to the muck-heap passageway, when the headlights of a car parked close to the house suddenly came on, catching us in their beams. Whoever was in the car couldn't help but see us.

'Run,' I shouted in my mother's ear, but running wasn't really in her exercise repertoire, even when in mortal danger. It was only ten yards or so to the passageway door, but I wasn't sure we would make it. I dragged her along as all hell broke loose behind us.

There were shouts and footsteps on the gravel near the house.

Then there was a shot, and another.

Shotgun pellets peppered my back, stinging my neck and shoulders, but the rucksack took most of them. The shooter was too far away for the shot to inflict much damage, but he would get closer.

We reached the passageway door, and I swung it open, pushing my mother through it ahead of me. 'Mum, please,' I said. 'Go through the passage and out the back. Then hide.'

But she wouldn't let go of my arm. She was too frightened to move.

Another shot rang out, and some of the wood of the door splintered behind us. That was far too close, I thought. The shooter had now closed to within killing range.

'Come on,' I said to my mother. 'Let's get out of here.'

I firmly removed her hand from my arm and then held it in mine as I dragged her down the passageway and out into the space behind. I pulled her behind the muck heap to a tall narrow space between the rear retaining wall of the heap and a hay barn beyond.

'Get in there,' I said quietly. 'And lie face-down.'

She didn't like it, I could tell, but she couldn't protest, as the tape was still over her mouth. She hesitated.

'Mum,' I said. 'Please. Otherwise, we will die.'

There was just enough light for me to see the fear in her eyes. I eased up the corner of the tape over her mouth and peeled it away.

'Mum,' I said. 'Please, do it now.' I kissed her on the forehead.

'Oh, God,' she whispered in despair. 'Help me.'

'It's all right,' I said, trying to reassure her. 'Just lie down here.'

She lay flat on her tummy, as I'd asked. I pulled some of the old straw down off the muck heap and covered her as best I could.

I left her there and went back to the passageway. Whoever had been shooting had not come through, but the car was being driven round so that its lights were about to shine straight towards where I was standing. I stepped again into the passageway.

The car's headlights were both a help and a hindrance. They helped in showing me the position of at least one of my enemies, but at the same time, their brightness destroyed my night vision.

Consequently, the passageway appeared darker than ever, but from my previous visits, I could visualise the location of every obstruction on the floor, and I easily stepped silently round them. I pressed my eyes up against the gaps between the door slats and looked out once more into the stable yard beyond.

Jackson Warren was standing in the centre of the yard talking to Peter Garraway. They were holding shotguns in a manner that suggested that they knew how to use them. And as I could see Warren and Garraway, it must be Alex Reece who was driving the car.

'You go round the back,' Jackson was saying to Garraway. 'Flush him out. I'll stay here in case he comes through.'

I could tell that Peter Garraway didn't like taking orders. 'Why don't I wait here and you go round the back?' he replied.

'Oh, for God's sake,' said Jackson, annoyed. 'All right. But keep your eyes fixed on that door, and if he appears, shoot him.'

Jackson Warren walked off towards the car, leaving a nervous-looking Peter Garraway standing alone in the stable yard.

Reece had finally managed to get the car behind the stables, and I could see the glow of its lights at the back end of the passageway. That was not good. I would soon find myself liable to attack from opposite directions.

I took another quick glimpse through the slats at Peter Garraway in the stable yard. He was resting his double-barrelled shotgun in the crook of his right arm. It was not the way a soldier would hold a weapon—and it was not ready for immediate action.

I threw open the passageway door and ran right at him with my sword held straight out in front of me, the point aimed at his face.

He was quick in raising his gun, but not quick enough. As he swung the barrels up, I struck his right arm, the point of my sword tearing through both his coat and the flesh beneath. In the same motion, I hit him on the nose with the sword's nickel-plated hand guard. He went sprawling onto the concrete floor, dropping the gun.

I stood over him with my sword raised high, like a matador about to deliver the *coup de grâce*. Garraway, meanwhile, curled himself into a ball, whimpering and shaking like a scolded puppy.

I leaned down, picked up his shotgun, and left him where he was, quivering like jelly. I went quickly across the yard and out towards the house with the gun in one hand and my sword in the other. But the sword had outlived its usefulness. I tossed it into the shadows and put both my hands on the gun—that was better.

I had no real plan in mind, but I knew that somehow I had to draw Jackson Warren towards me and away from my mother.

I broke open the shotgun. There was a live cartridge in each of the two chambers, so I had only two shots. I would need to make both of them count. I closed the gun once more.

If I wanted to draw Jackson and Alex away from my mother, I would have to reveal my position. The headlights were still shining down the back of the stables towards the muck heap, but I wasn't there any more. I was about forty yards away, where the driveway met the turning circle near the house. I could see the car clearly from where I stood. How could I attract attention to myself?

I lifted the shotgun and fired one of my precious cartridges at the car. At this range, the shot wouldn't penetrate the vehicle's skin, although it might just break a window. However, one thing was for sure: Alex Reece, in the car, would certainly know all about it.

I could hear Jackson shouting. Now they would know exactly where I was, and the car was already turning my way.

I lingered just long enough for the headlight beams to fall on my departing back. I dived once more into the darkness down the side of the house. A shot rang out, but I was already round the corner.

I moved swiftly, grateful that I had done a reconnaissance here the previous Thursday. I knew that the concrete path alongside the exterior walls ran completely round the rectangular building, the only obstacle being a small gate at one of the back corners.

In no time, I had completed the circuit and approached the front of the house again, but now I was behind the car, its headlights still blazing towards where I had been just seconds before. In the glow, I could see Jackson creeping forwards towards the corner, his gun raised to his shoulder, ready to fire.

The driver's door of the car suddenly opened, and Alex stood up next to the vehicle, facing away from me, watching Jackson intently.

I moved forwards slowly. Alex would have certainly heard me if the engine of the car hadn't been left running. As it was, I was able to approach him completely undetected.

He was wearing a baggy sweatshirt and a large woollen cap.

I lifted the shotgun and placed the ends of the barrels firmly onto the bare skin visible just beneath his left ear.

'Move and you will die,' I said. He disobeyed and turned around. But when I saw his face, I realised it wasn't Alex Reece.

'Hello, Tom,' said Isabella.

I was stunned. I lowered the barrels. 'But why?' I asked.

'I'm so sorry,' she said in answer.

'Was it you who unlocked the gates?' I asked her.

She seemed surprised that I knew, but she nodded. 'Jackson was in Gibraltar.'

It had been a VW Golf that I had seen that night. Perhaps I had been subconsciously convincing myself ever since that it hadn't been Isabella's car, but it had. 'Why didn't you come and help me?'

The misery of those two days in the stable floated into my mind.

She looked down at her feet. 'I didn't know that you were there. I only found out tonight when I heard Peter talking about how he couldn't believe you'd managed to escape.' She gulped. 'Jackson just phoned home on Thursday and asked me to unlock the gates.'

I wanted to believe her, but then why was she driving the car tonight? She couldn't claim that she didn't know what was going on.

'Why are you here?' I asked. 'Why are you doing this?'

She looked towards Jackson. 'Because I love him,' she said.

I, too, looked at Jackson, who was still inching carefully away from me towards the corner of the house, oblivious to the fact that I was standing behind him next to the car. I suddenly wanted nothing more than to shoot him, to kill him in revenge for what his greed had done to us all. I lifted the gun and aimed.

'No,' Isabella screamed, grabbing the barrels.

Jackson turned towards the noise, but he would have been unable to see anything, as he would be looking straight into the headlights. He started to move back towards the car.

I threw Isabella to the ground and raised the shotgun towards Jackson, but I hadn't bargained on Isabella's panic-driven determination. She grabbed my knees and pushed me down onto the ground.

One of the huge disadvantages of having an artificial leg is that it hampers recovery from a horizontal position. I rolled over to be face-down and drew my good leg under me, but Isabella was quicker. She was on her feet and wrenched the shotgun from my hand.

But she didn't turn the gun on me. She simply ran away with it while I struggled to my feet, using the car door to pull myself up.

A shot rang out—very close—followed by a cry of despair.

I turned quickly to see Jackson running towards a figure lying very still on the ground, a figure whose hat had come off, revealing long blonde hair, hair that was already soaking up blood.

Jackson had killed Isabella.

He sank to his knees beside her, dropping his gun alongside the one that Isabella had been carrying. I walked the few yards from the car and picked up both weapons, unloading their second barrels and placing the unfired cartridges in my pocket. There had been enough shooting for one night. In fact, there had been far too much.

Jackson turned his head slightly to see me. 'I thought it was you,' he said. He made it sound like an excuse, as if shooting me would have been acceptable. He turned back and cradled his wife's lifeless head on his lap. 'I told her to stay in the car. I saw someone running with a gun.' He looked up at me again, now with tears in his eyes. 'I just assumed it was you.'

Epilogue

Three weeks later, Pharmacist, this time with no green potato-peel-induced tummy ache, romped up the finishing hill to win the Cheltenham Gold Cup by a neck. It was the second Kauri House Stables success of the afternoon, after Oregon had won the Triumph Hurdle. My mother positively glowed.

In the post-Gold Cup press conference, she stunned the reporters by announcing her retirement from the sport with immediate effect.

'I'm going out on a huge high,' she told them, beaming from ear to ear. 'I'm handing over the reins to the next generation.'

I stood at the back of the room watching her answer all the journalists' questions with ease. Here was the Josephine Kauri that everyone knew: confident and in control.

I believed that she was as happy that day as I had ever seen her. It had been a somewhat different matter when I had returned to her hiding place that night at Greystone Stables to find her frightened, exhausted, bedraggled and on the point of complete mental and physical collapse.

But much had changed since that dreadful night, not least the removal of the imminent threat of public disgrace and the prospect of being arrested for tax evasion. Not that the senior inspector from Her Majesty's Revenue and Customs hadn't been pretty cross. He had. But nowhere near as cross as he would surely have been if we hadn't arrived to see him with a cheque for all the back taxes.

Martin Toleron had worked some magic, producing a team of accountants to sift through the shambles and to bring some order to my mother's business accounts. It had been quite an undertaking.

'It's the least I can do,' Martin had said, happily agreeing also to pay the accountant's bill.

So the previous Monday my mother, Derek, and I had arrived at the tax office in Newbury, not only with a cheque made out for well over a million pounds of back taxes, but with a set of up-to-date business accounts and a series of signed and sworn affidavits as to how and why the tax had not been paid at the correct time.

We had sat in the senior inspector's office as he silently scrutinised our documents, never once putting down the cheque, which he held between the index finger and thumb of his left hand.

'Most unusual,' he'd said. 'Most unusual, indeed.'

The amount on the cheque had taken all of the million dollars that had been returned from Gibraltar, together with every penny that the three of us had been able to muster, including Derek's ISAs and the proceeds from some sales of my mother's antique furniture, as well as all my savings, including the injury-compensation payout that had arrived from the Ministry of Defence.

'Are you sure that's wise?' Martin had asked me, when I'd offered it.

'No,' I had said. 'In fact, I'm damned sure that it's not wise. But what else can I do?'

'You can come and help buy me some racehorses,' he'd replied.

'Now are you sure that's wise?'

We had laughed, but he'd been serious, and he had already engaged a bloodstock agent to find him a top young steeplechaser.

'I have to spend the money on something,' Martin had said. 'I might as well enjoy spending it, and trips to the races will sure as hell beat going to Harrods every week.'

My mother, Derek, and I had sat in the tax inspector's office for nearly three hours in total while he had read through everything.

'Now I have to tell you, Mrs Kauri,' he'd said to my mother. 'We at the Revenue take a very dim view of people who don't pay their taxes on time. However, in the light of these affidavits and the payment of the back tax due, we have decided to take no action against you. And finally, it is an honour to meet you. I'm a great admirer, and over the years, I've backed lots of your winners.'

So it was official: some tax men could be human after all.

THE POST-RACE press conference was still in full swing, and my mother appeared to be absolutely loving it.

'No, of course I'm not ill,' she said, putting Gordon Rambler from the *Racing Post* in his place with a stare. 'I'm retiring, not dying.' She laughed, and the throng laughed with her.

No, I thought. My mother wasn't dying, but Isabella had. The paramedics had tried to revive her, but she had lost too much blood. Strangely, in spite of everything, I grieved for Isabella. I hadn't been wrong when I'd told her at age ten that I loved her. I still did.

Needless to say, the Thames Valley Constabulary had not been greatly impressed by all the nocturnal activity that had been going on at Greystone Stables. I had called them using my mobile phone as soon as Isabella had been hit. They had subsequently arrived in convoy with an ambulance and had promptly arrested everyone.

'You should have called us immediately if someone had been kidnapped,' they said later at Newbury police station, their anger clearly directed at me for having taken things into my own hands.

Alex Reece had apparently wanted nothing to do with Warren and Garraway's plan to recover the money and had decided that flight would be a much better policy. He had consequently boarded a British Airways jumbo from Heathrow to New York just a few hours before the shootout at the Greystone Stables corral began.

However, he had failed to clean out his suitcase properly and had been apprehended by a sniffer dog from the US customs on his arrival at Kennedy Airport. He had been charged with importing cocaine into the United States and was presently languishing in jail on Rikers Island in New York, waiting to be served with extradition papers by the government of Gibraltar on fraud charges.

Garraway, meanwhile, had been singing like a canary and blaming everything on Jackson Warren, so much so that his lawyers had successfully persuaded a judge to grant him bail on the kidnapping charges. However, the judge had ordered that Garraway's passport be confiscated, and as I heard unofficially from the tax inspector, the Revenue were looking forward to the day, very soon, when Peter Garraway's enforced extended stay in the UK would automatically make him resident here for tax purposes. The inspector had smiled broadly. 'We've been trying to get him for years,' he'd said. 'And now we will.'

'SO WHO IS taking over the training licence?' It was Gordon Rambler who asked my mother the inevitable question at the Cheltenham press conference. 'And what will happen to the horses?'

'The horses will all be staying at Kauri House Stables,' she said. 'I spoke to all my owners yesterday and they are all supportive.'

That wasn't entirely true. Some of her owners had been decidedly unsupportive, but they had all been convinced, out of loyalty to her, to stay on board, at least for the immediate future. Martin Toleron had helped there, too, vocally pledging his support, and his future horses, to the new training regime.

'So who is it?' Rambler was becoming impatient. 'Who's taking over?'

They were all expecting one of the sport's up-and-coming young trainers to be moving into the big league.

'My son,' my mother said with a flourish. 'My son, Thomas Forsyth, will henceforth be training the horses at Kauri Stables.'

I think it would be fair to say that there was a slight intake of breath, even amongst the most hardened of the racing journalists.

'And,' she went on, into the silence, 'he will be assisted by Ian Norland, my previous head lad who has been promoted to assistant trainer.'

'Can we all assume,' Gordon Rambler said, recovering his composure, 'that you will still be around to guide and advise them when necessary?'

'Of course,' she said, smiling broadly.

But one should never assume anything.

dick **francis**

Dick Francis is a familiar and beloved name here at Select Editions, and our readers have loved his books over the years. Sadly, Dick Francis passed away at the age of eighty-nine on February 14, 2010. We pay tribute here to a celebrated jockey and internationally acclaimed author.

Richard Stanley Francis was born on October 31, 1920, in Lawrenny, South Wales. As the son of a professional steeplechase rider, Dick Francis was introduced early to horse racing and followed his father into the profession, winning his first race at the age of eight. He went on to become a champion jockey, winning more than 350 races, and was jockey to Queen Elizabeth the Queen Mother for four seasons. However, in the 1956 Grand National, Francis was moments from winning when his horse, Devon Loch, fell flat on its belly with its four legs splayed—and then mysteriously stood up, apparently uninjured—costing him the trophy. This episode was followed soon afterwards by a serious fall, which forced Francis into an early retirement from racing at the age of thirty-seven.

As his second career, Francis started to write for the sports pages of newspapers and became the racing correspondent for the *Sunday Express* for sixteen years. But his real writing career began with the publication of his autobiography, *The Sport of Queens*, in 1957. Inspired by its success, and further spurred by the thought of earning more than a journalist's wages, he began writing his first novel. In *Dead Cert* (1962), his insider knowledge brought the world of racing alive for readers. From that time, he wrote nearly a book a year, setting most of his stories in the world of horse racing.

Francis famously did not revise or rewrite his manuscripts. Instead he laboured over each sentence (writing in pencil in exercise books) until it was as good as he could make it, and then moved on to the next. He used to say, 'My "first draft" is IT.'

From the early days, the writing of Francis's books was a family affair. His wife, Mary, was a close collaborator who did most of the research for his stories. Her thorough approach consisted of doing such things as taking flying lessons, to ensure that he got the details right in *Flying Finish* (1966) and *Rat Race* (1970), two novels that mixed piloting with Francis's standard horse-racing milieu. After her death in

2000, Francis said that he could not imagine writing again, and it was six years before his next book was published.

In all, Francis wrote forty-five books, with sales of more than sixty million. Among his fans was the Queen Mother, to whom he sent an advance copy of every book. She would respond with a handwritten note giving her views on his work.

Dick Francis received many awards, among them the prestigious Crime Writers' Association's Cartier Diamond Dagger in 1989, for his outstanding contribution to the genre. The Mystery Writers of America awarded him its Edgar Award three times—for *Forfeit* in 1970, *Whip Hand* in 1981 and *Come to Grief* in 1996. In 1996 the MWA also gave Francis the Grand Master Award for lifetime achievement.

Dick Francis is survived by his two sons, Merrick and Felix. Merrick followed his father into horse racing, first as a trainer and then as a racehorse transporter. While Felix initially went his own way and became a physics teacher, he also assisted his father with research and became his father's manager. After his mother's death, Felix took on a larger role and co-authored several books. *Crossfire* is the final collaboration between father and son. Dick Francis will be greatly missed. Nonetheless, readers can rejoice in the news that Felix is planning to continue his father's writing legacy.

felix francis

Felix Francis was born in 1953, the younger of Dick Francis's two sons. He studied physics and electronics at London University, and taught physics for seventeen years before taking on the role of managing his father's affairs in 1991.

Felix assisted his father by conducting research for the novels, most notably for *Twice Shy* (1981), in which the hero is a physics teacher. He also contributed to *Shattered* (2000) and *Under Orders* (2006). Both of these books feature expert marksmen, and the detail was much enhanced by Felix's experience as an international marksman in his youth.

Felix then began to assume a greater role in the writing process. The first collaboration produced *Dead Heat* in 2007. *Silks* followed in 2008 and *Even Money* in 2010.

LAUNDRETTE
MINI MARKET

Minding Frankie

Maeve Binchy

Stella Dixon is running out of time and desperately needs to find someone to care for her baby daughter, Frankie. Noel Lynch might not be the most promising of fathers but, with the help of his family and friends, could he make a go of it? Everyone thinks so, except Moira Tierney, Frankie's social worker, who, for some reason, seems determined to make trouble.

Chapter One

Katie Finglas was coming to the end of a tiring day in the salon. She looked at the man standing opposite her, a big priest with sandy hair mixed with grey.

'You're Katie Finglas and I gather you run this establishment,' the priest said, looking around the salon nervously as if it were a high-class brothel.

'That's right, Father,' Katie said.

'It's just that I was talking to some of the girls who work here, down at the centre on the quays, you know, and they were telling me . . .'

Katie employed a couple of school leavers; she paid them properly, trained them. *What* could they have been complaining about to a priest?

'Yes, Father, what exactly is the problem?' she asked.

'Well, it's this woman, Stella Dixon. She's in hospital you see . . .' He seemed a little awkward. 'And she wants a hairdo. I'm Brian Flynn and I am acting chaplain at St Brigid's Hospital at the moment while the real chaplain is in Rome on a pilgrimage.'

'You want me to go and do someone's hair in hospital?'

'She's dying. And she's pregnant. I thought she needed a senior person to talk to. Not, of course, that you look very senior. You're only a girl yourself,' the priest said.

'God, weren't you a sad loss to the women of Ireland when you went for the priesthood,' Katie said. 'Give me her details and I'll go in to see her.'

'Thank you so much, Ms Finglas. I have it all written out here.'

Father Flynn handed her a note.

A middle-aged woman approached the desk. 'I gather you teach people the tricks of hairdressing,' she said.

'Yes, or more the *art* of hairdressing, as we like to call it,' Katie said.

'I have a cousin coming home from America for a few weeks. She did mention that in America there are places where you could get your hair done for near to nothing if you were letting people practise on you.'

'Well, we do have a students' night on Tuesdays; people bring in their own towels and we give them a style. They contribute five euros to a charity.'

'Tonight is Tuesday!' the woman cried triumphantly.

'So it is,' Katie said through gritted teeth.

'So, could I book myself in? I'm Josie Lynch.'

'Great, Mrs Lynch, see you after seven o'clock,' Katie said.

Her eyes met the priest's. There was sympathy and understanding there. It wasn't all champagne and glitter running your own hairdressing salon.

JOSIE AND CHARLES LYNCH had lived in 23 St Jarlath's Crescent since they were married thirty-two years ago. They had seen many changes in the area. The corner shop had become a mini-supermarket; the old laundry, where sheets had been ironed and folded, was now a launderette. There was also a proper medical practice with four doctors, where once there had been just old Dr Gillespie.

During the height of the economic boom, houses in St Jarlath's Crescent had been changing hands for amazing sums of money. Not any longer, but it was still a much more substantial area than it had been three decades ago. After all, just look at Molly and Paddy Carroll with their son Declan—a doctor—a real, qualified doctor! And look at Muttie and Lizzie Scarlet's daughter Cathy. She ran a catering company that was hired for top events.

But a lot of things had changed for the worse. There was no community spirit any more. No church processions went up and down the Crescent as they used to. Josie and Charles Lynch felt that they were alone in St Jarlath's Crescent, in that they knelt down at night and said the Rosary.

When they married, they planned a life based on the maxim that the family that prays together stays together. They had assumed they would have eight or nine children. But this wasn't to happen. After Noel, Josie had been told there would be no more children. It was hard to accept. But then, perhaps, it was all meant to be this way.

They had always hoped Noel would be a priest. The fund to educate him for the priesthood was started before he was three. Money was put aside from Josie's wages at the biscuit factory. And every week a little more was added to the Post Office savings account when Charles got his envelope on a Friday from the hotel where he was a porter.

So it was with disappointment that Josie and Charles learned that their quiet son had no interest in a religious life. The Brothers at his school said that he showed no sign of a vocation. Noel was vague about what he actually *would* like to do, except to say he might like to run an office. However, he showed no interest in studying office management or bookkeeping or accounting. He liked art, he was good at drawing, but he didn't want to paint.

When Noel was sixteen he told his parents that there was no point in his staying on at school. They were hiring office staff up at Hall's, the builders' merchants, and they would train him in office routine. He might as well go to work straight away rather than hang about getting qualifications.

Noel got his place in Hall's. He met his work colleagues but without any great enthusiasm. They would not be his friends and companions. He didn't *want* to be alone all the time but it was often easier.

He arranged with his mother that he would not join them at meals. He would make a snack for himself in the evening. This way he missed the Rosary and the interrogation about what he had done with his day.

He took to coming home later and later. He also took to visiting Casey's pub on the journey home—a big barn of a place—both comforting and anonymous at the same time. It wasn't a trendy pub with fancy prices. People left him alone here. That was worth a lot.

WHEN HE GOT HOME, Noel noticed that his mother looked different. He couldn't work out why. Eventually he realised that it was her hair.

'You got a new hairdo, Mam!' he said.

Josie Lynch patted her head, pleased. 'They did a good job, didn't they?'

'Very nice, Mam,' he said.

'I'll be putting a kettle on if you'd like a cup of tea,' she offered.

'No, Mam, you're all right.'

He was anxious to be out of there, safe in his room. And then Noel remembered that his cousin Emily was coming from America the next day. His mother must be getting ready for her arrival. This Emily was going to stay for a few weeks apparently.

Noel didn't know much about her; she was an older person, in her fifties maybe, the only daughter of his father's eldest brother Martin. She had been an art teacher but her job had ended unexpectedly and she was using her savings to see the world. She would start with a visit to Dublin from where her father had left many years ago to seek his fortune in America.

It had not been a great fortune, Charles reported. The eldest brother of the family had worked in a bar where he was his own best customer. He had never stayed in touch. Any Christmas cards had been sent by this Emily, who had also written to tell first of her father's death and then her mother's. She sounded remarkably businesslike, and said that when she arrived in Dublin she would expect to pay a contribution to the family expenses.

Noel sighed. He hoped that this woman would not disrupt their ways. But mainly he gave the matter very little thought. Noel got along by not thinking too deeply on anything: not about his dead-end job in Hall's; not about the hours and money he spent in Old Man Casey's pub; not about the religious mania of his parents. Noel would not think about the lack of a steady girlfriend in his life. Nor did he worry about the lack of any kind of mates. Noel had decided that the very best way to cope with things not being so great was not to think about them at all. It had worked well so far.

CHARLES LYNCH was being very silent. He had been told that morning that his services as hotel porter would no longer be needed. He and another 'older' porter would go at the end of the month. Charles had been trying to find the words to tell Josie since he got home, but the words weren't there.

He could repeat what the young man in the suit had said to him earlier in the day, about it being no reflection on Charles. He had been there, man and boy, resplendent in his uniform and very much part of the old image. But that's exactly what it was—an old image. The new owners were insisting on a new image and who could stand in the way of the march of progress?

'I WONDER, should we have gone out to the airport to meet her?' Josie Lynch said for the fifth time the next morning.

'She said she would prefer to make her own way here,' Charles said, as he had said on the previous four occasions.

Noel just drank his mug of tea and said nothing.

'She wrote and said the plane could be in early if they got a good wind behind them.' Josie spoke as if she were a frequent flier herself.

There was a ring at the doorbell. Josie's face was all alarm. Patting her new hairdo, she spoke in a high, false voice.

'Answer the door, please, Noel, and welcome your cousin Emily in.'

Noel opened the door to a small woman, forty-something, with frizzy hair and a cream-coloured raincoat. She had two neat, red suitcases on wheels. She looked entirely in charge of the situation. Her first time in the country and she had found St Jarlath's Crescent with no difficulty.

'You must be Noel. I hope I'm not too early for the household.'

'No, we were all up. We're about to go to work, you see, and you are very welcome, by the way.'

'Thank you. Well, shall I come in and say hello and goodbye to them?'

Noel was only half awake. It took him until about eleven, when he had his first vodka and Coke, to be fully in control of the day.

He brought the small American woman into the kitchen, where his mother and father kissed her on the cheek and said this was a great day that Martin Lynch's daughter had come back to the land of her ancestors.

Noel left them to it.

AT THE BISCUIT FACTORY Josie told them all about the arrival of Emily, who had found her own way to St Jarlath's Crescent as if she had been born and reared there. Josie said she was an extremely nice person who had offered to make the supper for everyone that night. She didn't need to go to bed and rest, apparently, because she had slept overnight on the plane coming over.

The other women said that Josie should consider herself very lucky. This American could have easily turned out to be very difficult indeed.

At the hotel, Charles was his normal, pleasant self to everyone he met. He carried suitcases in from taxis, he directed tourists out towards the sights of Dublin, he looked up the times of theatre performances, he looked down at the sad face of a little fat King Charles spaniel that had been tied to the hotel railing. Charles knew this little dog: Caesar. It was often attached to Mrs Monty—an eccentric old lady who wore a huge hat and three strands of pearls, a fur coat and nothing else. If anyone angered her, she opened her coat, rendering them speechless.

The fact she had left the dog there meant that she must have been taken into the psychiatric hospital. If the past was anything to go by, she would discharge herself and come to collect Caesar and take him back to his unpredictable life with her.

Charles sighed. Last time, he had been able to conceal the dog in the hotel until Mrs Monty came back to get him, but things were different now. He would take the dog home at lunchtime.

EMILY HAD SPENT a busy morning shopping. She was surrounded by food when Charles came in. Immediately, she made him a mug of tea and a cheese sandwich.

Charles introduced Emily to Caesar and told her some of the story behind his arrival in St Jarlath's Crescent.

Emily Lynch seemed to think it was the most natural thing in the world.

'I wish I had known he was coming. I could have got him a bone,' she said. 'Still, I met that nice Mr Carroll, the butcher. He might get me one.'

She hadn't been here five minutes and she had got to know the neighbours! Charles looked at her with admiration.

'Well, aren't you a real bundle of energy,' he said. 'You certainly took your retirement very early for someone as fit as you are.'

'Oh no, I didn't choose retirement,' Emily said, as she trimmed the pastry crust round a pie. 'No, indeed, I loved my job. They let me go. Well, they said I *must* go, actually.'

'Why? Why did they do that?' Charles was shocked.

'It was a question of my being the old style, old guard. I would take children to visit galleries and exhibits. They would have a sheet of paper with twenty questions on it and they would spend a morning there trying to find answers. It would give them a great grounding in how to look at a picture or a sculpture. Well, I thought so anyway. Then came this new principal with the notion that teaching art was all about free expression. He really wanted recent graduates who knew how to do all this. I didn't, so I had to go.'

'They can't sack you for being mature, surely?'

'No, they didn't actually say I was dismissed. They just kept me in the background doing filing, away from the children, out of the art studio. It was unbearable, so I left. But they had forced me to go.'

'Were you upset?' Charles was very sympathetic.

'Oh yes, at the start. I was very upset indeed. It kind of made nothing of all the work I had done for years. I had got accustomed to meeting people at art galleries who often said, "Miss Lynch, you started off my whole interest in art," and so I thought it was all written off when they let me go.'

Charles felt tears in his eyes. She was describing exactly his own years as porter in the hotel. Written off. That's what he felt.

'But my friend Betsy told me that I was mad to sit sulking in my corner. I should resign at once and set about doing what I had really wanted to. Begin the rest of my life, she called it.'

'And did you?' Charles asked.

'Yes, I did. I sat down and made a list of what I wanted to do. I had a small savings account so I could afford to be without paid work for a while. Trouble was, I didn't know what I wanted to do, so I did several things.

'First I did a cookery course. Tra-la-la. That's why I can make a chicken pie so quickly. And then I went on an intensive course and learned to use computers and the Internet properly so I could get a job in any office if I wanted to. Then I went to this garden centre where they had window-box and planter classes. So now that I am full of skills, I decided to go and see the world.'

'I see,' Charles nodded. He seemed about to say something else but stopped himself. He fussed about, getting more milk for the tea.

Emily knew he wanted to say something; she knew how to listen. He would say it eventually.

'The thing is,' he said slowly and with great pain, 'the real thing is that these new brooms that are meant to be sweeping clean, they sweep away a lot of what was valuable as well as sweeping out cobwebs or whatever . . .'

Emily saw it then. She looked at him sympathetically.

'Have another mug of tea, Uncle Charles.'

'No, I have to get back,' he said.

'Do you? I mean, think about it for a moment. Do you have to? What more can they do to you? I mean, that they haven't done already . . .'

He gave her a long, level look.

She understood. This woman he had never met until this morning realised, without having to be told, exactly what had happened to Charles Lynch. Something that his own wife and son hadn't seen at all.

THE CHICKEN PIE that evening was a great success. Emily had made a salad as well. They talked easily, all three of them, and Emily introduced the subject of her own retirement.

'It's just amazing, the very thing you most dread can turn out to be a huge blessing in disguise!'

Charles watched in admiration. She was making his path very smooth. He would tell Josie tomorrow . . . or maybe he might tell her now, this minute.

He explained that he had been thinking for a long time about leaving the hotel. The matter had come up recently in conversation and, amazingly, it turned out that it would suit the hotel too and so the departure would be by mutual agreement. All he had to do now was make sure that he was going to get some kind of reasonable compensation. He said that for the whole afternoon his head had been bursting with ideas for what he would like to do.

Josie was taken aback. She looked at Charles anxiously in case this was just a front. But he seemed to be speaking from the heart.

'I suppose it's what Our Lord wants for you,' she said piously.

'Yes, and I'm grabbing it with both hands.'

Charles Lynch was indeed telling the truth. He had not felt so liberated for a long time. Since talking to Emily today at lunchtime, he had begun to feel that there was a whole world out there.

Emily moved in and out clearing dishes, bringing in some dessert, and from time to time she entered the conversation easily. When her uncle said he had to walk Mrs Monty's dog until she was released from wherever she was, Emily suggested that Charles could mind other people's dogs as well.

'That nice man, Paddy Carroll, the butcher, has a dog called Dimples that needs to lose at least ten pounds' weight,' she said enthusiastically.

'I couldn't ask Paddy for money,' Charles protested.

Josie agreed with him. 'You see, Emily, Paddy and Molly Carroll are neighbours. It would be odd to ask them to pay.'

'I see that, of course, but then again he might see a way to giving you some lamb chops or best ground beef from time to time.'

Emily was a great believer in barter and Charles seemed to think that this was completely possible.

'But would there be a real job, Emily, you know, a *profession*, a life like Charles had in the hotel?' Josie asked.

'I wouldn't survive just with dog walking alone, but maybe I could get a job in a kennels. I'd really love that,' Charles said.

'And if there was anything else that you had both *really* wanted to do?'

'Well, do you know what we always wanted to do . . .?' Josie began.

'No. What was that?' Emily was gentle.

Josie continued, 'We always thought that it was a pity that St Jarlath was never properly celebrated in this neighbourhood. I mean, our street is called after him, but nobody you'd meet knows a thing about him. Charles and I were thinking we might raise money to erect a statue to his memory.'

Emily was surprised. Perhaps she had been wrong to have encouraged them to be free thinkers. 'Wasn't he rather a long time ago?'

Josie waved this objection away. 'Oh, that's no problem. If he's a saint does it matter if he died only a few years back or in the sixth century?'

'The *sixth* century?' This was even worse than Emily had feared.

'Yes, he died around AD 520 and his Feast Day is the 6th of June.'

'And was he from around these parts?' Emily asked.

Apparently not. Jarlath was from the other side of the country, the Atlantic coast. He had set up the first Archdiocese of Tuam.

'Of course, the problem would be raising the money for this campaign about the statue *and* actually earning a living at the same time,' Emily said.

That was apparently no problem at all. They had saved money for years, hoping to put it towards the education of Noel as a priest. To give a son to God. But it hadn't taken. They always intended that those savings be given to God in some way, and now this was the perfect opportunity.

Emily Lynch told herself that she must not try to change the world. She would have preferred to see the money going to look after Josie and Charles, and give them a little comfort after a life of working long, hard hours for little reward. But there were some irresistible forces that could never be fought with logic and practicality. Emily knew this for certain.

NOEL HAD BEEN through a long, bad day. Mr Hall had asked him twice if he was all right. There was something menacing behind the question. When he asked for the third time, Noel enquired politely why he was asking.

'There was an empty bottle, which appears to have contained gin before it was empty,' Mr Hall had said.

'And what has that to do with me and whether I'm all right or not?' Noel had asked. He was confident now, emboldened even.

Mr Hall had looked at him long and sternly under his bushy eyebrows.

'That's as may be, Noel. There's many a fellow taking the plane to some faraway part of the world who would be happy to do your job.'

He had moved on and Noel had seen other workers look away.

Noel had never known Mr Hall like this. Usually there was a kindly remark, some kind of encouragement. Mr Hall seemed to think that Noel could do better and had made many positive suggestions in earlier days. But not now. This was more than a reprimand, it was a warning. It had shaken him and on the way home he found his feet taking him into Casey's. He vaguely recalled having had one too many the last time he'd been there but he hesitated only for a moment before going in.

Mossy, Old Man Casey's son, looked nervous. 'Ah, Noel, it's yourself.'

'Could I have a pint, please, Mossy?'

'Ah now, that's not such a good idea, Noel. You know you're barred. My father told me. I'm sorry, but there it is.'

'Well, that's his decision and yours. As it happens, I have given up drink and what I was actually asking for was a pint of lemonade.'

Mossy looked at him open-mouthed. Noel Lynch off the liquor?

'But if I'm not welcome in Casey's, then I'll have to take my custom elsewhere. Give my best to your father.' Noel made as if to leave.

'When did you give up the gargle?' Mossy asked.

'Oh, Mossy, that's not any of your concern.' And Noel walked, head high, out of the place where he had spent so much of his leisure time.

There was a cold wind blowing down the street as Noel leaned against the wall. He had only spoken in order to annoy Mossy. Now he had to live with his words. He could never drink in Casey's again.

He would have to go to that place where Paddy Carroll and Muttie Scarlet went with their dogs, Dimples and Hooves. The place where nobody had 'friends' or 'mates' or 'people' they met there. They called them 'Associates'. Muttie was always conferring with his Associates over the likely outcome of a race or a soccer match. It was not a place that Noel had enjoyed up to now.

Wouldn't it be much easier if he really *had* given up drink? Then he would have all the time in the world to go back to doing the things he really wanted. He might go back and get a business certificate so as to qualify for a promotion. Maybe even move out of St Jarlath's Crescent.

Noel went for a long, thoughtful walk around Dublin, up the canal, down through the Georgian squares. He was going to give himself the twin gifts of sobriety and time: much more time. He checked his watch before letting himself into number 23. They would all be safely in bed by now.

He was wrong. They were all up, awake and alert at the kitchen table. Apparently his father was going to leave the hotel where he had worked all his life. They appeared to have adopted a tiny King Charles spaniel called Caesar. His mother was planning to work fewer hours at the biscuit factory. And, most alarming of all, they were about to start a campaign to build a statue to some saint. They had all been normal when he left the house this morning. What could have happened?

He wasn't able to manage his usual manoeuvre of sliding into his room and retrieving a bottle from the box labelled 'Art Supplies', which contained mainly unused paintbrushes and unopened bottles of gin or wine.

Not, of course, that he was ever going to drink again. He had forgotten this. A sudden heavy gloom settled over him as he sat there, trying to comprehend the bizarre changes that were about to take place in his home.

Noel shifted in his seat slightly and tried to catch the glance of his cousin Emily. She must be responsible for all this sudden change of heart: the idea that today was the first day of everybody's life. Mad, dangerous stuff in a household that had known no change for decades.

In the middle of the night Noel woke up and decided that giving up drink was something that should not be taken lightly or casually. He would do it next week when the world had settled down. But when he reached for the bottle in the box he felt, with a clarity that he had not often known, that somehow next week would never come. So he poured the contents of two bottles of gin down his basin, followed by two bottles of red wine.

Chapter Two

A message came to the hotel from the psychiatric hospital, saying that Caesar's mother, a titled, if eccentric, lady, was unavoidably detained there and that she hoped Caesar was being adequately looked after. The hotel manager, bewildered by this, was relieved to know that the matter was all in hand and somewhat embarrassed to learn that the rescuer had been that old porter he had just made redundant. Charles Lynch seemed to bear him no ill will but let slip the fact that he was looking forward to some kind of retirement ceremony. The manager made a note to remind himself or someone else to organise something for the fellow.

NOEL LYNCH found the days endless in Hall's builders' merchants. The mornings were hard to endure without a strong shot of alcohol that he would swallow in the men's room. The nice fuzzy afternoons were gone and replaced now by hours of mind-numbing checking of delivery dockets against sales slips. His only pleasure was leaving a glass of mineral water on his desk and watching from a distance as Mr Hall either smelled it or tasted it. But in spite of everything he stuck to it and before too long he was able to chalk up a full week without alcohol.

Matters were much helped by Emily's presence at number 23. Every evening there was a well-cooked meal served at seven o'clock and, with no long evenings to spend in Casey's pub, Noel found himself sitting at the kitchen table eating with his parents and cousin.

Emily had even managed to put off the Rosary on the grounds that they all needed this joint time to plan their various crusades, such as what strategy they should use to get the fundraising started for St Jarlath's statue, and how Emily could go out and earn a living for herself, and where they would find dogs for Charles to walk, and if Noel should do night classes in business or accountancy in order to advance himself at Hall's.

Emily had, in one week, managed to get more information out of Noel about the nature of his work than his parents had learned in years. Little by little, she had learned of the mundane, clerical-officer-type work Noel did all day. She discovered that there were young fellows in the company who had 'qualifications', who had a degree or a diploma, and they climbed up what passed for a corporate ladder in Hall's builders' merchants.

When they were alone, Emily said to him that the business of beating a dependency on alcohol was often a question of having adequate support.

'Did I tell you that I was battling against alcohol?' Noel asked her once.

'You don't need to, Noel. I'm the daughter of an alcoholic. I know the territory. Your uncle Martin thought he could do it on his own. He wasn't nearly as good a man as you are. He had a very closed mind.'

'Oh, I think I have a closed mind too.'

'No, you don't. You'll get help if you need it. I know you will.'

'It's just I don't go along with this thing "I'm Noel. I'm an alcoholic" and then they all say, "Ho, Noel" and I'm meant to feel better.'

Emily shrugged. 'Right, so, they don't do it for you. Fine. One day you might need them. The AA will still be there, that's for sure. Now let's have a look at these courses. I know what CPA means, but what are ACA and ACCA? Tell me the difference between them and what they mean.'

And Noel would feel his shoulders relaxing. She wasn't going to nag him. That was the main thing.

KATIE FINGLAS went to the hospital to see Stella Dixon.

'This has got to be a really good hairdo,' Stella said.

'Have you your eye set on someone?' Katie asked.

She wished that she could take a group of her more difficult clients into this ward so they could see the skin-and-bone woman who knew that she would die shortly when they did the Caesarean section to remove her baby. It made their problems so trivial in comparison.

Stella considered the question.

'It's a bit late for me to have my eye on anyone at this stage,' she said. 'But I *am* asking someone to do me a favour, so I have to look normal. That's why I thought a more settled type of hairstyle would be good.'

'Right, we'll make you look settled,' Katie said, taking out the plastic tray that she would put over the handbasin to wash Stella's thin, frail-looking head with its Pre-Raphaelite mass of red, curly hair.

'What kind of a favour is it?' she asked.

'It's the biggest thing you could ever ask anyone to do,' Stella said.

'CALL FOR YOU, NOEL,' Mr Hall said. Nobody ever telephoned Noel at work. He went to Mr Hall's office nervously.

'Noel? Do you remember me, Stella Dixon? We met at the line-dancing night last year.'

'I do, indeed,' he said, pleased.

A lively redhead who matched him drink for drink. She had been good fun.

'We sort of drifted away from each other back then,' she said.

It had been a while ago. 'That's right,' Noel said evasively.

'I need to see you, Noel,' she said.

'I'm afraid I don't go out too much these days, Stella,' he began.

'Me neither. I'm in the oncology ward of St Brigid's.'

He focused on trying to remember her: feisty, jokey, always playing it for a laugh. This was shocking news indeed.

'So would you like me to come and see you sometime? Is that it?'

'Please, Noel, today. At seven.'

'Today . . .?'

'I wouldn't ask unless it was important.'

He saw Mr Hall hovering. He must not be seen to dither.

'See you then, Stella,' he said and wondered what on earth she wanted to see him about.

THE CORRIDORS OF ST BRIGID'S were crowded with visitors at seven o'clock. Noel threaded his way among them. He saw Declan Carroll, who lived along the road from Noel, walking ahead of him, and ran to catch him up.

'Do you know where the female oncology ward is, Declan?'

'This lift over here will take you to the wing. Second floor.'

Declan didn't ask who Noel was visiting and why. He thought Noel seemed a bit down, but then he was never a barrel of laughs.

Declan had a lot on his mind. Their first baby was due in the next few weeks, and his wife Fiona was up to high doh over everything, and his mother had knitted enough tiny garments for a multiple birth even though they knew they were going to have only one baby.

THERE WERE six women in the ward. None of them had red, curly hair.

One very thin woman in the corner bed was waving at him.

'Noel, Noel, it's Stella! Don't tell me I've changed *that* much!'

He was dismayed. She was skin and bone. She had clearly made a huge effort: her hair was freshly washed and blow-dried and she had a trace of lipstick. He remembered her smile, but that was all.

'Stella. Good to see you,' he mumbled. 'How have you been?' he asked, then instantly wished he hadn't. 'I mean, how are things?' he said.

'Things have been better, Noel, to be honest.' She gestured for him to pull the curtains round the bed.

When he had finished, he sat down beside her and tried to imagine what Emily might have said in the circumstances. She had a habit of asking questions that required you to think.

'What's the very worst thing about it all, Stella?'

She paused to think, as he had known she would.

'I think the very worst thing is that you won't believe me,' she said.

'Try me,' he said.

She stood up and paced the tiny cubicle. It was then he realised that she was pregnant. Very pregnant. And at exactly that moment she spoke to him.

'I was hoping not to have to bother you about this, Noel, but you're the father. This is your baby.'

'Ah no, Stella, this is a mistake. This didn't happen.'

'I know I'm not *very* memorable, but you must remember that weekend.'

'We were wasted that weekend, both of us.'

'Not too drunk to create a new life, apparently.'

'I swear it can't be me. Honestly, Stella, if it were, I would accept . . . I wouldn't run away or anything . . . but . . . but . . .'

'But what, exactly?'

'There must have been lots of other people.'

'Thanks a lot for that, Noel.'

'You know what I mean. An attractive woman like you must have had lots of partners.'

'I'm the one who knows. Do you honestly think I would pick *you* out of a list of candidates? That I'd phone you, a drunk in that mausoleum where you work, in some useless job? You live with your parents, for God's sake! Why would I ask *you*, of all people, to be the father of my child if it wasn't true?'

'Well, as you said yourself, thanks a lot for that.' He looked hurt.

'So you asked me what would be the worst thing. I told you and now the worst *has* happened. You don't believe me.' She had a defeated look.

'It's a fantasy. It didn't happen. I'd remember. I haven't slept with that many women in my life, and what good would I be to you anyway? I'd be no support to you. You'll be able to bring this child up fine, give him some guts, fight his battles for him, more than I would ever do. Do it yourself, Stella, and if you think I should make some contribution, I could give you something—not admitting anything—just to help you out.'

Her eyes blazed at him.

'You are such a fool, Noel Lynch. Such a stupid fool. I won't bloody well be here to bring her up. I'm going to die in three or four weeks' time. I mean, if you smoke four packs a day, you get cancer of the lung. If you drink as much as I did, then you get cirrhosis of the liver. I won't survive the Caesarean.' Her eyes were very bright. 'And the baby is a girl, by the way. Her name is Frankie. That's what she's going to be called: Frances Stella.'

'This is only a fantasy, Stella. This illness has made you very unhinged.'

'Ask any of them in the ward. Ask any of the nurses. Wake up to the real world, Noel. This is happening. We have to do something about it.'

'I can't raise a child, Stella.'

'You're going to *have* to,' Stella said. 'Otherwise she'll have to go into care. And I'm not having that.'

'But that would be the very best for her. There are families out there who are dying to have children of their own . . .' he began, blustering slightly.

'Yes, and some other families, like the ones I met when I was in care, where the fathers and the uncles love to have a little plaything in the house. I've been through it all and Frankie's not going to have to cope with it just because she will have no mother.'

'What are you asking me to do?'

'To mind your daughter, to give her a home and a secure childhood, to tell her that her mother wasn't all that bad. The usual things.'

'I can't do it.' He stood up from his chair. 'I'm so sorry. And I'm really sorry to know how bad your illness is, but I think you're painting too black a picture. Cancer can be cured these days. Truly it can, Stella.'

'Goodbye, Noel,' she said.

He walked to the door and looked back once more. She seemed to have shrivelled even further. She looked tiny as she sat there on her bed.

ON THE BUS HOME Noel realised that there was no way he could force himself to sit at the kitchen table eating supper. He headed for the pub where Paddy Carroll, Declan's father, took his huge labrador dog every night.

The beer felt terrific. Like an old friend. He had lowered four pints before he realised it. Noel had hoped that he might have lost the taste for it, but that hadn't happened. Already he was feeling better.

He *must* stay clear and focused. He would have to go back to St Jarlath's Crescent and take up some semblance of ordinary life. Emily would, of course, see through him at once, but he could tell her later. Much later. No need to announce everything to everyone all at once. Or maybe no need to announce anything at all. It was, after all, some terrible mistake. Noel would *know* if he had fathered a child with that girl.

It was ludicrous. It could not be his child.

NOEL HAD ONLY opened the door when Emily looked up at him sharply. It was as if she had called the meeting to order.

'We're all tired now, it's late. Not a good time to discuss the running of a thrift shop.'

'A what?' Noel shook his head. His parents looked disappointed. They were being carried along by the enthusiasm of Emily's planning and they were sorry to see it being cut short.

But Emily was adamant. She had the household ready for bed in no time.

'Noel, I kept you some Italian meatballs.'

'I don't think I really want anything. I stopped on the way home, you see . . .' Noel began.

'I did see,' Emily said, 'but these are good for you, Noel. Go on into your room and I'll bring a tray in to you in five minutes.'

There was no escape. He sat there waiting for her and the storm that would follow. Oddly, there was no storm. She never mentioned the fact that he had taken up drinking again. She was clearing up and about to go when she asked sympathetically if it had been a bad day.

'The worst ever,' he said. 'Something mad and really upsetting happened. That's why I went back to the pints.'

'And did you sort out the upset?'

She looked at him, inviting him to share whatever it was.

'Please sit down, Emily,' Noel begged, and he told her the whole story.

She was very still as she sat and listened to him. It was only when Noel came to the part where he had walked away from Stella that she spoke.

'Why did you do that?' she asked.

'Well, what else could I do?' Noel was surprised. 'It has nothing to do with *me*. There's no point in my being there. The girl's head is unhinged.'

'You walked out and left her there?'

'I *had* to, Emily. You know what a tightrope I'm walking. Things are quite bad enough already without inviting the Lord knows what kind of fantasies in on top of me.'

'You say that things are bad enough with you, Noel? Right?'

'Well, they *are* bad.' He sounded defensive.

'Like you have terminal cancer?' she asked him. 'Like you are going to be dead a month from now before you see the only child you will ever have? No, indeed, Noel, none of these things have happened to you, yet you just said things are very bad for *you*.'

He was stricken.

'That's all you think. You think how things are for *you*, Noel. Shame on you,' she said, her face full of scorn. She was almost at the door. 'Good night. I'm sorry, but that is all I feel capable of saying.'

And she was gone.

NOEL TRIED TO STAY off drink when he was at work, but the sharp pain of Stella's situation and Emily's shocked revulsion kept coming back to him as the day crawled along. When it came to midafternoon he could bear it no longer and made an excuse to go out and get some more stationery supplies. He bought a half-bottle of vodka and decanted it into a bottle that already had a fizzy orange drink in it. As he drank mug after mug, he felt the pain receding. The familiar blur came down like a comforting shawl.

Noel now felt able to face the afternoon again; but what didn't go away was the feeling that he was a loser who had let down three people: the dying Stella, his strong cousin Emily and an unborn child called Frankie, who could not possibly be his daughter.

EMILY WAS IN the launderette with Molly Carroll. She was there on a mission. On a previous visit she had noticed two outhouses that were not in use. They might form the basis of the new thrift shop that would help raise money for the statue of St Jarlath.

Molly and Paddy Carroll had bought the premises some years back. They had never needed the unused part of the premises but had been loath to sell it in case someone built a noisy takeaway food outlet.

Molly thought that a thrift shop would be perfect. She and Emily toured the place and decided to put shelves here and clothes rails there. They would have a secondhand-book section and Emily said she could grow a few plants from seed and sell them too.

They decided to call the place St Jarlath's Thrift Shop. Together they made a list of people to approach, those who might give a few hours every week to working in the charity shop. Molly knew a man who had the unlikely name of Dingo. He would help them with his van, collecting things.

THAT NIGHT IN ST JARLATH'S Crescent Emily was busy explaining her day's negotiations with Molly. Charles and Josie were drinking in every word.

Charles had news too. There would be a goodbye celebration for him in a couple of weeks' time at the hotel—and a presentation. And would you believe who wanted to come to it, but Mrs Monty—who was really Lady Something. The hotel manager was very nervous about letting her in.

Mrs Monty was now going into a residential home where sadly Caesar would not be welcome; and since Charles had agreed to take him, she wanted to thank the kind employee who had given the little spaniel such a good home. She was also going to make a donation to a charity of his choice. It would be a wonderful start to the fundraising.

Charles was being allowed to bring a small number of family and friends. As well as Josie, Emily and Noel, he thought he would invite Paddy and Molly Carroll and the Scarlets, Muttie and Lizzie.

'Will Noel come, do you think?' Emily's voice was slightly tart.

'Well, here he comes now—we can ask him!' Josie cried out happily.

Noel listened carefully, arranging his face in a variety of receptive expressions as the excitement of the goodbye celebrations was revealed.

Emily knew the technique: she recognised it from her father. It was a matter of saying as little as possible and therefore cutting down on the possibility of being discovered to be drunk.

Eventually he had to speak. Slowly and carefully he said that he would be privileged to be part of the ceremony.

'There's some lamb stew left, Noel. I'll heat it and bring it up to you,' she said, giving him permission to leave before his mask of sobriety collapsed.

'Thank you, Emily, I'd love that,' he said, and fled to his room.

When she went in with the tray, he was sitting in his chair with tears streaming down his face.

'Oh Lord, Noel, what is it?' she asked, alarmed.

'I'm *useless*, Emily. I've let everyone down. I have no one to turn to . . .'

'Eat your supper, Noel. I'll be here,' she said.

And she was there while he told her how despairing he was and what a hopeless father he would be to any child.

She listened and then said simply, 'I hear all that and you may well be right. But then again it might be the making of you, *and* Frankie. She might make you into the kind of person you want to be.'

'They'd never let me keep her . . . the Social Welfare people . . .'

'You'll need to show them what you're made of.'

'I couldn't bring the child here,' Noel said.

'It was time for you to move on anyway.'

Emily was as calm as if they were discussing what to have for lunch tomorrow, rather than Noel's future.

NEXT MORNING, Stella looked up from the magazine she was reading as a shadow fell on her bed. It was Noel carrying a small bunch of flowers.

'Am I interrupting you?' he asked.

'Yes, I'm reading about how to put more zing back in my marriage, as if I knew what either zing or marriage were!'

'I came here to ask you to marry me,' he said.

'Oh Christ, Noel, don't be such an eejit. I'll be dead in a few weeks' time! Marriage was never part of it.' Stella was at a complete loss.

'I thought that's what you wanted!' He was perplexed now.

'No. I wanted you to look after her, to be a dad for her, to keep her out of the lottery of the care system.'

'So will we get married then?'

'No, Noel, of course we won't, but if you *do* want to talk about looking after her, tell me why and how.'

'I'm going to change, Stella. I was up all night planning it. I'm going to go to AA today, admit I have a drink problem, and then I'm going to enrol on an evening business course at a college, and then I'm going to find a flat where I can bring up the baby.'

'This is all so sudden. Why aren't you at work today anyway?'

'My cousin Emily has gone to Hall's to say I have a personal crisis today and that I will make up the time next week.'

'Does Emily know about all this?'

'Yes. I had to tell someone. She was very cross with me for walking out on you.'

'You didn't walk, Noel. You ran.'

'I am so sorry. Believe me. I *am* sorry.'

'So what has changed?' She wasn't hostile, just interested.

'I want to amount to something. I'll be thirty soon. I've done nothing except dream and wish and drink. I want to change that.'

She listened in silence.

'So tell me what you'd like if you don't want us to get married?'

'I don't know, Noel. I'd like things to have been different.'

'So do most people walking around,' he said sadly.

'Then I'd like you to meet Moira Tierney, my social worker, tomorrow evening. She's coming in to discuss what she calls "the future" with me.'

'Could I bring Emily in? She said she'd like to come and talk to you.'

'Bring her in then,' Stella said, 'and she's going to have to talk well to deal with Moira.'

He leaned over and put the flowers in a glass.

'Noel?'

'Yes?'

'Thanks, anyway, about the marriage proposal and all. It wasn't what I had in mind but it was decent of you.'

IT WAS HARD to go into the building where the lunchtime AA meeting was taking place. Noel stood for ten minutes in the corridor, watching men and women of every type walking down to the door at the end.

Eventually he could put it off no longer and followed them in. There were about thirty people in the room. A man sat at a desk near the door. He had a tired, lined face and sandy hair.

'I would actually like to join,' Noel said to him.

'And your name?' the man asked.

'Noel Lynch.'

'Right, Noel. Who referred you here?'

'I'm sorry? Referred?'

'I mean, are you coming here because of a treatment centre?'

'Oh heavens, no. I haven't been having any treatment or anything. I just drink too much and I want to cut it down.'

'We encourage each other to cut it out completely. Are you aware of that?'

'Yes, if that were possible, I would be happy to try.'

'My name is Malachy. Come on in,' the man said. 'We're about to begin.'

THAT EVENING AT SUPPER Josie was eager to discuss the thrift shop and its possible date of opening. She was excited. Charles was in good form too. He had more plans for dog walking, and he had been to a local kennels.

But before the conversation could go down either route—thrift shop or dog walking—Emily spoke firmly.

'Noel has something important to talk to us about.'

Noel looked around him, trapped. He had known that this was coming. It was not news he was going to find easy to break. But when he began his tale, sparing nothing but telling it all as it had unfolded, he felt it was easier and fairer to tell them everything. He went through it as if he were talking about someone else and he never once caught their eye as the story went on. He finished by saying that he had tried to give up drinking on his own and had not succeeded, that he now had a sponsor in AA called Malachy, and would attend a meeting every day.

At this point he realised his parents had been very silent, so he raised his eyes to look at them.

Their faces were frozen with horror at the story he was telling. Everything they had feared might happen in a godless world *had* happened. Their son had enjoyed sex outside marriage and a child had resulted, and he was admitting a dependency on alcohol.

But he would not be put off. He struggled on with the explanations and his plans to get out of the situations he had brought on himself. He accepted that it was all his own fault. He blamed no outside circumstances.

'I feel ashamed telling you all this, Mam and Da. You have lived such good lives. You wouldn't even begin to understand, but I got myself into this and I'm going to get myself out of it.'

They were still silent so he dared to look at them again.

To his amazement they both had some sympathy in their faces.

His mother's eyes were full of tears, but there were no recriminations.

'And you had no idea this Stella was expecting your child?' Josie asked.

'None in the wide world, Mam,' Noel said. And there was something so bleak and honest in his tone that everyone believed him.

Emily spoke for the first time. 'So, we are up to speed on Noel's plans now. It's going to be up to us to give him all the support we can.'

'You *knew* all this?' Josie Lynch was shocked and not best pleased.

'I only knew because I could recognise a drunk at fifty feet. I've had a lifetime of knowing when people are drunk. My father was one very unhappy man and he was miles from home with no one to help him or advise him when he had made one wrong decision that wrecked his life.'

'What decision was that?' Charles asked. This evening was full of shocks.

'The decision to leave Ireland. He regretted it every day of his life.'

'But that can't be right. He lost total interest in us. He never came home.' Charles was astonished.

'He never came home, that's true, but he never lost interest. Talking about all he *could* have done if only he had stayed here. All of it fantasy, of course, but still, if he'd had someone to talk to . . .' Her voice trailed away.

'Could you not talk to him?' Charles asked.

'No, I couldn't. You see, my father didn't have the basic decency that Noel here has. He wasn't half the man Noel is.'

Josie, who had in the last half-hour been facing the whole range of disgrace, mortal sin and shame, found some small comfort in this praise.

'You think that Noel will be able to do all this?' she asked Emily pitifully.

'It's up to us to help him, Josie,' Emily said calmly.

And even to Noel it didn't seem quite as impossible as it had at first.

'STELLA, HELLO, I'M EMILY, Noel's cousin. I came a little early in case there's anything I should know before the social worker comes.'

Stella looked at the businesslike woman with the frizzy hair.

'I'm pleased to meet you, Emily. You're very good to take all this on.' Stella looked down somewhat ruefully at her stomach.

'You have enough problems to think about,' Emily said, her voice warm.

'Well, this social worker is a bit of a madam. You know, interested in everything, believing nothing, always trying to trip you up.'

'I suppose they have to be like that on behalf of the child,' Emily said.

'Yes, but not like the secret police. You see, I sort of implied that Noel and I were more of an item than we are.'

'Sure.' Emily nodded approvingly. It made sense.

At that moment Noel came in, closely followed by Moira Tierney.

She was in her early thirties with dark hair swept back with a red ribbon. If it had not been for the frown of concentration, she would have been considered attractive. But Moira was too busy to consider looking attractive.

'You are Noel Lynch?' she said briskly and without much enthusiasm.

He began to shuffle and appear defensive.

Emily moved in quickly. 'Give me your parcels, Noel. I know you want to say hello to Stella properly,' and she nudged him towards the bed.

Stella held up her thin arms to give him an awkward peck on the cheek.

Moira watched suspiciously.

'You and Stella don't share a home, Mr Lynch?' Moira said.

'No, not at the moment,' he agreed, apologetically.

'But there are active plans going ahead so that Noel can get a place of his own to raise Frankie,' Emily said.

'And you are . . .?' Moira looked at Emily enquiringly.

'Emily Lynch. Noel's cousin.'

'Are you the only family he has?' Moira checked her notes.

'Lord, no! He has a mother and father, Josie and Charles . . .' Emily began. 'They'll be in tomorrow to see Stella.'

'They will?' Stella was startled.

'Of course they will.' Emily sounded more confident than she felt.

Moira absorbed it all as she was meant to.

'And where do you intend to live, Mr Lynch, if you *are* given custody?'

'Well, of course he will have custody of the child,' Stella snapped, 'he's the child's father. We are all agreed on that!'

'There may be circumstances that might challenge this.' Moira was prim. 'Such as a background of alcohol abuse.'

'Not from me, Noel,' Stella said apologetically.

'Naturally, we make enquiries,' Moira said.

'But that is all under control now,' Emily said.

'Well, that will be looked into,' Moira said in a clipped voice. 'What kind of accommodation were you thinking of, Mr Lynch?'

Emily spoke again. 'Noel's family have been discussing nothing else but accommodation. We are looking at this apartment in Chestnut Court. It's a small block of flats not far away from where he lives. The one we are all interested in is on the ground floor. Would you like to see a picture of it?'

Moira was looking at Noel and seemed to spot the surprise on his face.

'What do *you* think of this as a place to move to?' she asked him directly.

Stella and Emily waited anxiously.

'As Emily said, this flat seems to be the most suitable so far.'

If Moira heard the breath of relief from the two women, she gave no sign.

'There are some formalities to go through,' she said. 'I will have to talk about it with my team and then the last word will be with the supervisor.'

'But the most influential word will be from *you*, Moira,' Emily said.

Moira gave a brisk little nod and was gone.

JOSIE AND CHARLES were introduced to Stella and, after some awkward shuffling at the start, they found an astonishing amount of common ground. Both Noel's parents and Stella herself seemed entirely convinced that shortly Stella would be going to a better place. There was no pretence that perhaps she might recover.

They had helped Noel by paying a deposit on the flat in Chestnut Court. It was only a seven-minute walk from St Jarlath's Crescent. St Jarlath's image might have to wait a little, but it would happen.

Noel had little time alone with Stella. There were so many practicalities to be sorted out. Did Stella want the child to be brought up as a Catholic?

Stella shrugged. Possibly to please Josie and Charles, there should be a baptism and First Holy Communion and all, but nothing too 'Holy Joe'.

Were there *any* relations on Stella's side that she might want to involve?

'None whatsoever.' She was clipped and firm.

Or anyone at all from the various foster homes from the past?

'No, Noel, don't go there!'

'Right. It's just that when you're gone, I'll have no one to ask.'

Her face softened. 'I know. Sorry for snapping. I'll write her a letter, telling her a bit about myself, and about you and how good you've been.'

'I wish you weren't going to leave,' he said, covering her hand with his.

'Thanks, Noel. I don't want to go either,' she said.

Chapter Three

Lisa Kelly had been very bright at school; she had been good at everything. Her English teacher encouraged her to do a degree in English Literature and aim for a post in the university. Her sports teacher said that with her height—by the age of fourteen she was already nearly six feet tall—she was a natural and could play tennis or hockey, or both, for Ireland. But Lisa decided to go for art. Specifically for graphic art.

She graduated from that, first in her year, and was instantly offered a position in one of the big design firms in Dublin. It was at that point that she should have left the family home.

Her younger sister Katie had gone three years previously, but Katie was very different. No child genius, only barely able to keep up with the class, Katie had taken a holiday job in a hairdresser's and found her life's calling. She had married Garry Finglas and together they set up a salon, which had gone from strength to strength.

Katie had begged Lisa to leave home.

'It's not like that out in the real world, not awful silences like Mum and Dad have. Other people don't shrug at each other the way *they* do, they *talk*.'

But Lisa had waved this away. Katie had always been over-sensitive about the atmosphere at home. If Mum was distant, then *let* her be distant. If Dad was secretive, then what of it? It was just his way.

Dad worked in a bank where, apparently, he had been passed over for promotion. No wonder he was withdrawn and didn't want to make idle chit-chat. Her mother was discontented but she had reason to be. She worked in a very upmarket boutique, where rich, middle-aged women went to buy outfits. Her mother could never have afforded them. When she had married Dad at the age of eighteen he had looked like a man who was going somewhere. Now he went nowhere except to work every morning.

Lisa went to her office and worked hard all day. It was at a lunch for a client that she met Anton Moran. She saw this man crossing the room, pausing at each table and talking with everyone. He was slight and wore his hair quite long. He looked confident and pleasant without being arrogant.

'Who's *he*?' she gasped to Miranda who knew everyone.

'Oh, that's Anton Moran. He's the chef. He's been here for a year, but he's leaving soon. Going to open his own place, apparently. He'll do well.'

'He's gorgeous,' Lisa said.

'Get to the end of the line!' Miranda laughed. 'There's a list as long as my arm waiting for Anton.'

Lisa could see why. Soon he was at their table.

'The lovely Miranda!' he exclaimed.

'The even lovelier Anton!' Miranda said. 'This is my friend Lisa Kelly.'

'Well, hello, Lisa,' he said, as if he had been waiting all his life to meet her.

'How do you do?' Lisa said and felt awkward.

'I'll be opening my own place shortly,' Anton said. 'Tonight is my last night here. I'm going round giving my cellphone number to everyone and I'll expect you all to be there. No excuses now.'

He handed a card to Miranda and then gave one to Lisa.

'Give me a couple of weeks and I'll give you the details. They'll all know I must be doing *something* right if you two gorgeous girls turn up there,' he said, looking from one to the other. It was an easy patter. But Lisa knew that he had meant it. He wanted to see her again.

'I work in a graphic design studio,' she said suddenly, 'in case you ever need a logo or any designs.'

'I'm sure I will,' Anton said. And then he was gone.

Lisa thought about him way into the night. He wasn't conventionally handsome but he had a face that you wouldn't forget. Intense, dark eyes and a marvellous smile. He had a grace you'd expect in an athlete or a dancer.

She was taken aback when he telephoned her the next day.

'Good. I found you,' he said, sounding pleased to hear her voice. 'This is the third place I've tried. Will you have lunch with me?'

'Today?'

'Well, yes, if you're free . . .' And he named Quentins, one of the most highly regarded restaurants in Dublin.

Lisa went to her boss, Kevin. 'I'm going to have lunch with a good contact. A chef who is about to open his own business and I was wondering—'

'—if you can take him to an expensive restaurant, is that it?' Kevin had seen it all, heard it all.

'No. Certainly not. *He's* paying. But I was wondering if I might buy him a glass of champagne?'

'All right,' Kevin said.

'YOU LOOK VERY ELEGANT,' Anton said as he stood up to greet Lisa.

'Thank you. You don't look as if you made too late a night of it yourself.'

'No, indeed. I just gave my phone number to everyone in the restaurant and then went home to my cup of cocoa and my narrow little bed.'

He smiled his infectious smile. Lisa didn't know what she was smiling at—cocoa, the narrow little bed, or an early night . . . But it must mean that he was giving her signals that he was available.

Should she send back a similar signal or was it too early? Lisa had had many boyfriends, and some of them had been lovers. She had never felt a really strong attraction to any of these men. But Anton was different.

His hair looked soft and silky and she longed to reach across the table and run her hands through it. She must shake herself out of this pretty sharpish and get back to the business of designing a look and styling a logo for his new company.

'What will you call the new place?' she asked.

'Well, I know it's a bit of an ego trip, but I was thinking of calling it Anton's,' he said. 'But let's order first. They have a very good cheese soufflé here. I should know, I've made enough of them in my time!'

'That would be perfect,' Lisa said.

BACK AT THE OFFICE, Kevin asked her, 'Any luck with Golden Boy?'

'He's very personable, certainly.'

'Did you give him an outline and our rates?'

'No—that will come later.'

Lisa was almost dreamy as she thought of Anton and how he had kissed her cheek when they parted.

'Yeah, well, as long as he understands it doesn't come free because he's a pretty boy,' Kevin said. He was anxious there would be no grey areas.

'How do you know that he's a pretty boy?' Lisa asked.

'You just said that he was personable and I think he was the guy that my niece had a nervous breakdown over.'

'Your niece?'

'Yes. My brother's daughter. She went out with a chef called Anton Moran once. Nothing but tears and tantrums, then she drops out of college, and he's gone off cooking on a cruise ship.'

Lisa's heart felt like lead. Anton had told her of his wonderful year on board a luxury liner.

'I don't think it could have been the same person.' Lisa's tone was cold.

'No, maybe not . . .' Kevin was anxious for the least trouble possible. 'Just as long as he knows he's getting nothing on tick from us.'

THE SITE FOR THE RESTAURANT was perfect: it was in a small lane just a few yards off a main road, near to the railway station, a tram route and a taxi rank. Anton had suggested a picnic. Lisa brought cheese and grapes, he a bottle of wine. They sat on packing cases and he described his great plans. His sense of excitement was entirely infectious.

By the time they had finished the cheese and grapes, she knew that she would leave Kevin and set up on her own. Perhaps she could move in with Anton; work with him—they could build the place together, but she must not rush her fences. However hard it was, she mustn't look over-eager.

She knew that he was totally right—this place was going to be a huge success and she wanted to be part of it and in at the very start. She gave a sigh of pure pleasure at the thought of a future with him.

IT WOULD BE LOVELY to have someone to tell but Lisa had few close friends. She couldn't tell anyone at work, that was for sure. When she left Kevin's studio she wanted no one to suspect why. Kevin might become difficult and say she had met Anton on *his* time.

Kevin would have been astonished had he known just how long Lisa spent with Anton and how many drawings she had shown him to establish a logo for his new venture. At that moment she had concentrated on the colours of the French flag, and the A of Anton was a big, curly, showy letter. It could not be mistaken for anything else. She had done drawings and projections, shown him how this image would appear on a restaurant sign, on business cards, menus, table napkins and even china.

For the last eighteen days she had spent every evening with Anton—sometimes sitting on the packing cases, sometimes in small restaurants around Dublin, where he was busy seeing what worked and what didn't. Three weeks ago she had never met this man and now he was quite simply the centre of her whole life. She had definitely decided to leave Kevin's office and set up business on her own.

She would shortly leave the cold, friendless home where she lived now, but would wait until Anton suggested that she move in with him. The whole business had been brought up for discussion as early as their fifth date.

'It's a pity to go back alone to my narrow bed . . .' he had said, his voice full of meaning as he ran his hands through her long, honey-coloured hair.

'I know, but what are the alternatives?' Lisa had asked playfully.

'I suppose you could invite me home to *your* narrow bed?' he said.

'Ah, but I live with my parents, you see. That kind of thing couldn't happen,' she said.

'Unless you were to get your own place, of course,' he grumbled.

'Or we were to explore *your* place?' Lisa said.

But he didn't go down that road. Yet.

When he brought the matter up again it was in connection with a hotel. A place thirty miles from Dublin where they might have dinner, steal some ideas for the new restaurant and stay the night.

Lisa saw nothing wrong with this plan and it all worked out perfectly. As she lay in Anton's arms she knew she was the luckiest girl in the whole world. Soon she was going to be living with and working with the man she loved. Wasn't this what every woman in the world wanted?

And it was going to happen to her, Lisa Kelly.

'I ALWAYS KNEW you would fly the coop one day,' Kevin said. 'Have you decided where to go yet?'

'On my own,' Lisa said simply.

'Not a good idea in this economic climate, Lisa,' Kevin advised her.

'*You* took the risk, Kevin, and look how it paid off for you . . .'

'It was different. I had a rich father and a load of contacts.'

'I'll make the contacts,' Lisa said.

'You will in time. Have you an office?'

'I'll start from home.'

'The very best of luck to you, Lisa,' he said, and she managed to get out before he asked her was there any news of Anton.

Kevin, however, knew all about the place Anton had in Lisa's life and the reason for her move. He thought of his niece, who was still in fragile health, and he shivered a little for what might lie ahead for Lisa Kelly, one of the brightest designers he had ever come across.

EVERY FRIDAY, Lisa left her rent on the kitchen dresser. This entitled her to her room and to help herself to tea and coffee. No meals were served to her unless she were to buy them herself.

Lisa wasn't looking forward to telling her parents that shortly there would be no salary coming in, therefore the rent would be hard to pay. She was even less enthusiastic about telling them that she would be using her bedroom as an office.

She wished that Anton was less adamant about their living arrangements. He said that she was lovely, the loveliest thing that had ever happened to him. If this was so, why would he not let her come and live with him?

He had endless excuses: it was a lads' place—he just had a room there, he didn't pay for it, instead he cooked for the lads once a week and that was his rent, he couldn't abuse their hospitality by bringing in someone else.

He had sounded a little impatient. Lisa didn't mention it again. There was no way she could afford a place to live. There were new clothes, picnic meals and the two occasions she pretended to have got hotel vouchers in order to spirit him off for a night of luxury. All this cost money.

Once or twice she wondered whether Anton might possibly be mean? A bit *careful* with money, anyway? But no, he was endearingly honest.

'Lisa, my love, I'm a total parasite at the moment. Every euro I earn doing shifts I have to put away towards the cost of setting the place up. I'll make it up to you. When you and I are sitting in the restaurant toasting our first Michelin star, *then* you'll think it was all worth while.'

They sat together in the new kitchen, which was coming to life under their eyes. Ovens, refrigerators and hot plates were springing up around them. Soon the work would begin on the dining room. They had agreed the logo and it was being worked into the rugs that would be scattered around the wooden floors. The place was going to be a dream and Lisa was part of it.

The reception to her new plans at home was glacial.

'Lisa, you are twenty-five years of age. You have been well educated—expensively educated. Why can't you find a place to live and work like other girls do? Girls with none of your advantages and privileges . . .'

Her father spoke to her as if she were a vagrant who had come into his bank and asked to sleep behind the counter.

'Even poor Katie, and Lord knows she never achieved much, is able to look after herself.' Lisa's mother spoke witheringly of her other daughter.

'I thought you'd be pleased that I was going out on my own,' Lisa said. 'I'm showing initiative.'

'Mad is more like it. These days anyone who has a job holds on to it instead of throwing it up on a whim,' her father said.

'And no rent for the foreseeable future,' her mother sighed.

'Why don't you forget the whole idea and stay where you are, in the agency,' her father suggested. 'Do that, like a good girl, and we'll say no more about any of this.'

Lisa didn't trust herself to speak any more. She walked quickly to the front door and left the house.

She didn't *care* about money. She didn't *mind* working hard and even though she hated self-pity she did begin to feel that the world was conspiring against her. Her own family were so unsupportive and her boyfriend impervious to any signals and hints. He *was* her boyfriend, wasn't he? They had been together every evening.

Lisa caught sight of herself in a shop window: she looked hunched and defeated. This would never do. She brushed her hair, put on more make-up, then held her shoulders back and strode confidently along to Anton's.

Later, she would think about where to live and where to work. Tonight she would just drop into the gourmet shop and buy some smoked salmon and cream cheese. She wouldn't weary him with her problems.

To her great annoyance there were eight people there already, including her friend Miranda. They were sitting around eating pizza.

'Lisa!' Anton managed to sound delighted, welcoming and surprised at the same time, as if Lisa didn't come there every evening.

'Come on in, Lisa, and have some pizza.'

Miranda, who looked as slim as a greyhound but who ate like a hungry horse, was sitting on the ground in her skinny jeans, wolfing down pizza as if she had known no other food. Some of the men were people who shared Anton's flat. The other girls were glamorous and suntanned.

Lisa slipped the smoked salmon and cream cheese into one of the fridges and came to join them.

'Anton has been singing your praises,' Miranda said.

'I was telling them all about your ideas,' Anton said. 'They said I was very lucky to get you.'

These were the words she had wanted to hear for so long. Why did it not seem as wonderful as she had hoped?

Then he said, 'Everyone is here to give some ideas about marketing, so let's start straight away. Lisa, you first . . .'

Lisa didn't want to share her ideas with this cast. 'I'm last in—let's hear what everyone else has to say.' She smiled.

Anton didn't seem disturbed. 'Right, April, what do you think?'

April said that Anton could hold wine appreciation classes there, followed by a dinner serving the most popular choices of the evening.

'Where's the profit?' Lisa asked icily.

'Well, the wine manufacturers would sponsor it,' April said, annoyed.

'Not until the place is up and running, they won't,' Lisa said.

'What do *you* think, Lisa?' April asked. 'Do you have a background in marketing and business as well as graphic art?'

'No, I don't, April. In fact, I've just decided to do an evening course in management and marketing. The term starts next week, so at the moment all I have is my instinct.'

'Which says . . .?' April was obviously keen.

'Just as Anton says, that the food is going to be extraordinary and everything else is second to that.'

Lisa even managed a wide smile. She had surprised herself with her announcement. She'd had the vague notion that such a course would be a good idea, especially now that she was going freelance, but being challenged by April had made her mind up. She was going to do it. She'd show them.

'You didn't tell me you were going back to college,' Anton said when the others had all left.

It had been touch and go as to whether April would *ever* leave, but somehow she realised that Lisa would outstay her and she did go grudgingly.

'Ah, there's lots of things I don't tell you, Anton,' she said.

'Not too many, I hope,' he said.

'No, not *too* many,' Lisa agreed.

This was the way it had to be played. She knew that now.

SHE SIGNED ON for the business diploma the next day. They were very helpful in the college and she gave them a cheque from the last of her savings.

At her first lecture she sat beside a quiet man called Noel Lynch.

'Do you think it will help us, all this?' he asked her.

'I don't know,' Lisa said. 'You hear successful people saying that qualifications don't matter, but I think they do because they give you confidence.'

'Yes. I know. That's why I'm doing it too. But my cousin is paying my fees and I wouldn't want her to think it was a waste . . .'

He was a gentle sort of fellow. Not smart and lively and vibrant like Anton's friends, but restful.

'Will we go and have a drink afterwards?' she asked him.

'No, if you don't mind. I'm actually a recovering alcoholic and I don't find myself at ease in a pub,' he said.

'Well, coffee then?' Lisa said.

'I'd like that,' Noel said with a smile.

LISA WENT BACK to the bleak terraced house that she had called home for so long. Mother was out somewhere and Father was watching television. He barely looked up as she came in.

Lisa felt very, very lonely. Everyone in that lecture hall tonight had someone to talk to about it. Everyone except her.

Anton was out tonight. He and his flatmates were going to some reception, not that he would have been *very* interested in what she had to say, but he would have listened for a little bit anyway.

What the hell? She would call Anton. Nothing heavy, nothing clinging, just to make contact. He answered immediately.

There was a lot of noise in the background and he had to shout.

'*Lisa*, great. Where are you?'

'I'm at home.'

'Oh, I thought you'd be here,' he said and actually sounded disappointed.

Lisa brightened a little. 'No, no, I was at my first lecture tonight.'

'Oh, that's right. Well, why don't you come along now?'

'What is it exactly?'

'No idea, Lisa. I don't know who's running it, some magazine company, I think. April invited us. She's part of the PR for it all. She said there was unlimited champagne and unlimited chances to meet people and she was right. I was expecting you to be here too . . .'

'No, honestly, I have to dash,' she said and just got off the phone before she began to weep as if she was never going to stop crying ever again.

NEXT MORNING, she got a text from Anton: Where <u>are</u> you? I am lost without you to advise me and set me on target again. I'm like a jellyfish with no backbone. Where did you go, lovely Lisa? A totally abandoned Anton.

She forced herself to wait two hours before replying, then she wrote: I went nowhere. I am always here. Love Lisa.

Then he wrote: Dinner here? 8 p.m.? Do say yes.

She forced herself not to reply at once. It was so silly, all this game playing, yet it appeared to work. Eventually she texted: Dinner at 8 sounds lovely.

She made no offer to bring cheese or salmon or artichoke hearts. She couldn't afford them for one thing and for another he was inviting *her*, she must remember that.

HE HAD, OF COURSE, expected she would bring something to eat. She realised that when he went to the freezer to thaw out some frozen Mexican dishes, but she sat and sipped her wine, smiling, and asked him all about the business. She didn't mention the reception that April had invited him to.

He seemed slightly abstracted as he prepared the meal. He was his usual efficient self, expertly slicing avocado, deseeding chillies and squeezing limes over prawns as a starter, but his mind was obviously somewhere else. Eventually he got round to what he wanted to say.

'Have I annoyed you, Lisa?' he asked.

'No, of course not. Why did you think you had?'

'I don't know. You're different. You don't call me. You didn't bring anything for dinner. I didn't know if you were trying to say something to me . . .'

'Like what?' She looked at him expectantly, not helping him out.

'I suppose I was afraid that there had been a misunderstanding between us, you know.'

'No, I don't know. What kind of a misunderstanding?'

'Well, that you might be reading more into our relationship than there is.'

She felt the ground slip away from her.

'It's fine, isn't it?' she said, hearing her own voice as if from very far away.

'Sure. It's just me being silly. I mean, it's not a commitment or anything . . . exclusive like that.'

'We sleep together,' Lisa said bluntly.

'Yes, we have, of course, and will again, but I don't ask you about who you meet after lectures or anything at your college. And you don't ask me about where I go and who I meet . . .'

'Not if you don't want me to.'

'Oh, Lisa, don't take an attitude.' He was frowning now.

The food tasted like lumps of cardboard. Lisa could barely swallow it.

'Will I make you a margarita? You're only nibbling at your food.' Anton feigned concern.

Lisa shook her head. 'Does this relationship mean anything to you?'

'Of course it does. It's just that I've taken a huge risk, I'm scared that I'm going to fall on my face in this new venture, juggling a dozen balls in the air, just ahead of the posse in terms of debt, and I haven't the *time* to think of anything seriously yet like . . . you know . . . permanent things.'

He looked lost and confused.

She hesitated. 'You're right. I'm just tired and intense because I'm doing too much. I think I *would* like a margarita.'

LISA NEVER CALLED round to Anton without letting him know she was on her way. She took an interest in all he was doing and made no more remarks about April's involvement in anything. Instead, she concentrated on making the cleverest and most eye-catching invitations to the pre-launch party.

There was no question of her getting anything new to wear. There wasn't any money to pay for an outfit. She confided this to Noel.

'Does it matter all that much?' he asked.

'It does a bit because, and I know this sounds silly, a lot of the people who will be there sort of judge you by what you wear.'

'They must be mad,' Noel said. 'How could they not take notice of you? You look amazing, with your height and your looks—that hair . . .'

Lisa looked at him sharply, but he was clearly speaking sincerely, not just trying to flatter her.

'Some of them are mad, I'm sure, but I'm being very honest with you. It's a real pain that I can't get anything new.'

'I don't like to suggest this but what about a thrift shop? My cousin sometimes works in one. She says she often gets designer clothes in there.'

'Lead me to it,' Lisa said with a faint feeling of hope.

Molly Carroll had the perfect dress for her. It was scarlet with a blue ribbon threaded round the hem. The colours of Anton's restaurant and the logo she had designed.

Katie treated her to a wash and blow-dry and she set out for the party in high spirits. April was there in a very official capacity welcoming people in.

'Great dress,' April said to Lisa.

'Thanks,' Lisa said, 'it's vintage.' And went to find Anton.

'You look absolutely beautiful,' he said when he caught sight of her.

Just then a photographer approached them.

'And who's this?' he asked, nodding at Lisa.

'My brilliant designer and stylist, Lisa Kelly,' responded Anton instantly.

The photographer wrote her name down and out of the corner of her eye Lisa could see April's disapproval. She smiled all the more broadly.

'You're really gorgeous, you know.' Anton was admiring Lisa openly.

'There's a great crowd here,' Lisa said. 'Did all the people you wanted turn up?' Across the room she saw that April had a face like a sour lemon. 'But I mustn't monopolise you,' she added as she slipped away and knew that his eyes were on her as she went to mingle with the other guests.

What should she do now? Try to outstay April or leave early? Hard though it was to do, she decided to leave early.

Anton's disappointment was honey to her soul.

'You're never going? I thought you were going to sit down with me afterwards and have a real post-mortem.'

'Nonsense! You'll have lots of people. April, for example.'

'Oh God, no. Lisa, rescue me. She'll be talking of column inches of coverage and her biological clock.'

Lisa laughed aloud. 'No, Anton, of course she won't. See you soon. Call me and tell me how it all went.' And she was gone.

Chapter Four

For Noel there weren't enough hours in the day. He had AA meetings every day, since the thought that most things could be sorted out by several pints and three whiskeys was always with him. Any time that he was not slaving in Hall's, going to Twelve Step meetings or catching up on his studies, he spent surfing the Internet for advice on how to cope with a new baby. He had moved into his new place in Chestnut Court and was busy making preparations for the arrival of a newborn. He began to wonder how he had ever found time to drink.

FOR LISA KELLY the time crawled by. She was finding it difficult to get decisions made about her designs for Anton's restaurant, as a decision meant money being spent. Although the restaurant was open and full to bursting every night, there was still no verdict on whether to use her new logos and style on the tableware.

Weeks had gone by and Lisa had never seen Anton alone. The pictures of her and Anton together at the launch had given way to shots of him with any number of beautiful girls, though she would have heard if he had any new real girlfriend. It would have been in the papers. That's the way Anton attracted publicity—he gave free drinks to columnists and photographers, and they always snapped him with several beautiful women, giving the impression that he was busy making up his mind between them all.

And it wasn't as if he had abandoned her or was ignoring her, Lisa reminded herself. A day didn't pass without a text message from Anton. Life was so busy, he would text. They had a rock band in last night, they were going to do a society wedding, a charity auction, a new tasting menu. Nowhere any mention of Lisa or her designs and plans.

It was an unsettling life, to say the least.

DECLAN CARROLL was in the delivery room, holding Fiona's hand as she groaned and whimpered.

'Great, girl. Just three more . . . Just three . . .'

'How do you know it's only three?' gasped Fiona, red-faced, her hair damp and stuck to her forehead.

'Trust me, I'm a doctor,' Declan said.

'You're not a woman, though,' Fiona said, teeth gritted.

But he had been right—there were only three more. Then the head of his son appeared and he began to cry with relief and happiness.

'He's here,' he said, placing the baby in her arms. He took a photograph of them both and a nurse took a picture of all three of them.

'He'll hate this when he grows up,' Fiona said.

The baby, John Patrick Carroll, let out a wail in agreement.

'Only for a while and then he'll love it,' said Declan, who had his fair share of a mother who showed pictures of him to total strangers at the launderette where she worked.

DECLAN LEFT the delivery ward of St Brigid's and headed for oncology. He knew what time Stella Dixon was going down for surgery and he wanted to be there as moral support for Stella and Noel.

They were just putting her on the trolley.

'Declan!' she said, pleased.

'Had to come and wish you well,' he said.

'You know Noel. And this is his cousin Emily.'

Stella was totally at ease, as if she were at a party instead of about to make the last journey of her life.

Declan knew Emily already as she came regularly to the group practice where he worked. She filled in at the desk as a receptionist or made the coffee or cleaned the place. It was never defined exactly what she did except that everyone knew the place would close down without her.

Then Stella was wheeled out of the ward, leaving Noel, Emily and Declan behind.

FRANCES STELLA DIXON LYNCH was delivered by Caesarean section on October 9 at 7 p.m. She was tiny, but perfect. Ten tiny, perfect fingers, ten tiny, perfect toes and a shock of hair on her tiny, perfect head. She frowned at the world around her and wrinkled her tiny nose before opening her mouth and wailing as if it was already all too much.

Her mother died twenty minutes later.

The first person Noel telephoned was Malachy, his sponsor in AA.

'I can't live through this night without a drink,' he told him.

Malachy said he would come straight to the hospital. Noel was not to move until he arrived.

There was a small bundle of papers in an elastic band on Stella's locker. The word 'Noel' was on the outside.

He read them through with blurred eyes. One was an envelope with 'Frankie' written on it. The others were factual: her instructions about the funeral; her wishes that Frankie be raised in the Roman Catholic faith for as long as it seemed sensible to her. And a note dated last night:

Noel, tell Frankie that I wasn't all bad and that once I knew she was on the way I did the very best for her. Tell her that I had courage at the end. And tell her that if things had been different you and I would both have been there to look after her. Oh—and that I'll be looking out for her from up there. Who knows? Maybe I will.

Thanks again, Stella

Noel looked down at the tiny baby with tears in his eyes.

'Your mam didn't want to leave you, little pet,' he whispered. 'She wanted to stay with you, but she had to go away. It's just you and me now. I don't know how we're going to do it, but we'll manage. We've got to look after each other.'

BABY FRANCES was pronounced healthy. A collection of people came to visit her as she lay there in her little cot: Noel came every day; Moira Tierney, the social worker; Father Brian Flynn; Emily, who brought Charles and Josie Lynch to see their grandchild—and who visibly melted at the sight of the baby.

Eventually Noel was told that he could take his baby daughter home to his new apartment. It was a terrifying moment. Frankie, wrapped in a big pink shawl and held tightly in his arms, looked up at him trustingly. And suddenly, from nowhere, Noel felt a wave of protectiveness almost overwhelm him. This poor, helpless baby had no one else in the world. Stella had trusted him with the most precious thing she ever had, the child she knew she wouldn't live to see.

'Little Frankie,' he said. 'Let's go home.'

EMILY HAD SAID she would come and stay with him for a while to tide him over the most frightening bits. There were three bedrooms in the apartment, two reasonably sized and one small one, which would eventually be Frankie's, so she would be perfectly comfortable. The health visitor came every couple of days but even so, there were so many questions.

How could anyone so very small need to be changed ten times a day? Was that breathing normal? Did he dare go to sleep in case she stopped?

How did anyone learn to identify what kind of crying meant hunger, pain or discomfort? To Noel all crying sounded the same: piercing, jagged, shrill, drilling through the deepest, most exhausted sleep. No one ever told you how tiring it was to be up three, four times every night, night after night. After three days he was near to weeping with fatigue; as he walked up and down with his daughter, trying to wind her after her third feed of the night, he found himself stumbling against furniture, almost incapable of remaining upright.

FATHER FLYNN FOUND a gospel choir, who sang at the funeral Mass down at his church at the welcome centre for immigrants. Muttie Scarlet's foster children, twins called Maud and Simon, who did catering, prepared a light lunch in the hall next door. There were no eulogies or speeches. Declan and Fiona sat next to Charles and Josie; Emily had the bag of baby essentials, while Noel held Frankie wrapped in a warm blanket.

Father Flynn spoke simply and movingly about Stella's troubled and all too short life. She had died, he said, leaving behind a very precious legacy. Everyone who had come to know and care for Stella would support Noel as he provided a home for their little daughter . . .

Katie was there with her husband Garry and her sister Lisa. She noticed that Lisa, for once, was not being distant and withdrawn as she so often was. Instead she was being helpful, offering to pass plates of food or pour coffee. She was talking to Noel in terms of practicalities.

'I'll help you whenever I can. If you have to miss any lectures I'll give you the notes,' she offered.

'People are being very kind,' Noel said. 'Kinder than I ever expected.'

'There's something about a baby,' Lisa said.

'There is indeed. She's so very small. I don't know if I'll be able . . . I mean, I'm pretty clumsy.'

'All new parents are clumsy,' Lisa reassured him.

'That's the social worker over there. Moira,' he indicated.

'She's got a very uptight little face,' Lisa said.

'It's a very uptight job. She's always coming across losers like me.'

'I don't think you're a loser, I think you're bloody heroic,' Lisa said.

LISA HAD DONE a job for a garden centre but her heart wasn't in it. All the time that she toyed with images of floral baskets, watering cans and sunflowers in full bloom, she thought of Anton's restaurant. She found herself drawing a bride throwing a bouquet—and then the thought came to her.

Anton could specialise in weddings. Real society weddings. People would have to fight to get a date there. They had an underused courtyard where people often escaped for a furtive cigarette. It could be transformed into a permanent, mirror-lined marquee for weddings.

It was too good an idea to keep to herself.

Anton had sounded fretful in his recent texts. Business was up and down. So Lisa knew that he would love this idea. She would go to his restaurant tonight, straight after her lectures. She would go home and change into a dress first. She wanted to look her very best when she told him about this news, which would turn his fortunes around and change their lives.

TEDDY, THE MAÎTRE D', was surprised to see her at the restaurant.

'You're a stranger round here, Lisa,' he said with his professional smile.

'Too busy thinking up marvellous ideas for this place, that's why.'

She laughed. In her own ears her laughter sounded brittle and false; she didn't much care for Teddy.

'And are you dining here, Lisa?' Teddy was unfailingly polite.

'Yes. I hoped you could squeeze me in. I need to talk to Anton.'

'Alas, full tonight.' Teddy smiled regretfully. 'Not a table left in the place.'

They were having a special event, he said, a four-for-the-price-of-two night in order to get the word out about Anton's. It had been April's idea.

'But I really need to talk to him,' Lisa insisted. 'I've got a great idea for bringing in new business. Look, Teddy,' she continued, becoming aware of the shrillness in her voice. 'He's really going to want to hear my ideas, he's going to be very angry if you don't let me see him.'

'I'm sorry, Lisa,' he said. 'That's just not going to be possible. You see how busy we are.'

'I'll just go into the kitchen and see what Anton has to say about that . . .'

'I think not,' said Teddy, stepping smoothly to one side and gripping her elbow. 'Why don't you telephone tomorrow and make an appointment? Or better still, make a reservation. I will tell Anton you called in.'

As he spoke, he was guiding her firmly towards the door.

Before she knew what had happened, Lisa found herself outside on the street, looking back at the diners who were staring at her as if hypnotised.

She needed to get away quickly; turning on her heels, she fled as quickly as her too-tight dress would allow her.

When she was able to draw breath, she pulled out her cellphone to call a taxi and found, to her annoyance, that she had let the battery run down. The night was going from bad to worse.

THE HOUSE WAS QUIET when she let herself in. Lisa hoped that no one was going to be there tonight. She was in luck. As she reached the bottom of the stairs, there was just silence about the place, as if it were holding its breath.

And that's when it happened. Lisa saw what the newspapers would have called 'a partially clothed woman' come out of the bathroom at the top of the stairs, holding a mobile phone to her ear. She had long, damp hair and was wearing a green satin slip and nothing much else by the look of her.

'Who are *you*?' Lisa asked in shock.

'I might ask you the same,' the woman said. She didn't seem annoyed, put out or even embarrassed. 'Are you here for him? I'm just ringing for a taxi.'

Who could she be? Then she heard her father's voice.

'What is it, Bella? Who are you talking to?' And her father appeared at his bedroom door in a dressing gown. He looked shocked to see Lisa. 'I didn't know *you* were at home,' he said, nonplussed.

'Obviously,' Lisa said, her hand shaking as she reached for the front door.

'Who *is* she?' the girl in the green satin slip asked.

'It doesn't matter,' her father said.

And Lisa realised that it didn't. It had never mattered to him who she was, or Katie either.

The woman called Bella shrugged and went back into the bedroom as, unsteadily, Lisa left the house.

NOEL ALLOWED HIMSELF to think that Stella would have been pleased with how he was coping with their daughter. He had been without an alcoholic drink for nearly two months. He attended an AA meeting at least five times a week and telephoned his friend Malachy on the days he couldn't make it.

He had brought Frankie back to Chestnut Court and was making a home for her. True, he was walking round like a zombie from tiredness, but he had kept her alive, and, what's more, the community nurse seemed to think she was doing well. She slept in a small cot beside him and when she cried he woke and picked her up, then walked round the room with her.

He sang songs to her as he paced up and down. 'Sitting on the Dock of the Bay' . . . 'Let Me Entertain You' . . . Any snippet of any song he could remember. One night he found himself singing the words to 'Frankie and Johnny'. The lyrics made him hesitate, but as soon as he stopped, she started crying again. Why didn't he know the words to proper lullabies?

He had conducted three satisfactory meetings with Moira Tierney, the social worker, and five with Imelda, the community nurse.

His leave was over and he was about to go back to work at Hall's; he wasn't looking forward to it, but babies were expensive and he really needed the money. He was catching up with his lectures from the college—Lisa had been as good as her word—and was back on track again there.

He put his books away in the silent apartment. His cousin Emily was asleep in her room, little Frankie was sleeping in the cot beside his own bed. He looked out of his window in Chestnut Court. It was late, drizzly, dark, and very quiet.

He saw a taxi draw up and a young woman get out. Then, two seconds later, he heard his doorbell ring. Whoever it was, was coming to see him!

'LISA?' NOEL WAS PUZZLED to see her on the entryphone screen at this hour.

'Can I come in for a moment, Noel? I want to ask you something.'

'Yes . . . well . . . I mean . . . the baby's asleep . . . but, sure, come in.'

He pressed the buzzer to release the door.

She looked very woebegone.

'I can't go home, Noel. Can I sleep on your sofa here, please? Just for tonight. Tomorrow I'll sort something out.'

'Did you have a row at home?'

'No.'

'And what about your friend Anton that you talk so much about?'

'I've been there. He doesn't want to see me.'

'And I'm your last hope, is that it?'

'That's it,' she said bleakly.

'All right,' he said. 'You can stay. I can't give you my bed, Frankie's cot is in there and she's due a feed in a couple of hours. We'll all be up pretty early in the morning. It's no picnic being here.'

'I'd be very grateful, Noel.'

'Sure, then have some tea and go to bed. There's a folded rug over there and use one of the cushions as a pillow. Oh, and if you're up before I am, Emily, that's my cousin, will be getting Frankie ready to take her to the health clinic.'

Lisa didn't think she would sleep at all, but she did, stirring slightly a couple of times when she thought she heard a baby crying. She didn't wake again until she heard someone leave a mug of tea beside her.

Cousin Emily, of course. She in turn didn't seem remotely surprised to see a woman waking up on the sofa in a party dress.

'Do you have to be anywhere for work or anything?' the woman asked.

'No. No, I don't. I'll just wait until my parents have left home, then I'll go back and pick up my things and . . . find myself somewhere else to stay. I'm Lisa, by the way.'

Emily looked at her. 'I know, and I'm Emily. We met at Stella's funeral. What time will your parents be gone?' she asked.

'By nine—on a normal morning, anyway.'

'But this might not be a normal morning?' Emily guessed.

'No, it might not. You see—'

'Noel left half an hour ago. It's eight o'clock now. I'm going to open up the thrift shop, when I've given Frankie her bottle; I'll have some fruit and cereal there. I thought you might like to come with me. Would that suit?'

'That would be great, Emily. I'll just go and give myself a quick wash.'

Lisa hopped up and ran to the bathroom. She looked quite terrible. Her make-up was smeared across her face, like a tart down on her luck. She cleaned her face and gave herself a splash wash, then put on over her dress a sweater Emily had given her.

Emily was ready to leave: she was dressed in a fitted green wool dress and she carried a huge tote bag. The baby in the pram was tiny—less than a month old—looking up trustfully at the two women.

It was the most unreal day Lisa had ever lived through. Emily Lynch asked nothing of Lisa's circumstances. Instead she talked admiringly of Noel and the great efforts he was making on every front.

Emily found a dark brown trouser-suit in the thrift shop and asked Lisa to try it on. It fitted her well enough.

'I only have forty euros to see me through today,' Lisa said apologetically, 'and I may need a taxi to take my things out of my parents' home.'

'That's all right. You can pay for it by working, can't you?' Emily said.

'Working?' Lisa asked, bemused.

'Well, you could help in the shop until I take Frankie to the health clinic. After that you could come with me to the medical centre, and then we could walk down St Jarlath's Crescent, where I look after the gardens, and you could push the pram around if Baby Frankie gets bored. That would be a good day's work and would well cover the cost of that trouser-suit.'

'But I have to collect my things and find somewhere to live!'

'We have all day to think about that,' Emily said calmly.

They left the shop and moved to the clinic, where Frankie was weighed and pronounced very satisfactory. Then it was up to the health centre where Emily collected a sheaf of papers and left a parcel for Dr Hat who was expected in shortly. He'd recently retired from full-time practice, but still did a day's locum work at the surgery each week. Emily had discovered that Dr Hat couldn't cook and didn't seem anxious to learn, so she always left a portion of whatever she and Noel had cooked the night before. Today it was a smoked cod, egg and spinach pie, plus instructions on how to reheat it.

'It's the only meal that Hat eats in the week, apparently,' Emily said.

'What's Hat short for?' Lisa was curious.

'Never asked. I think it's because he seems to wear a hat day and night,' Emily said.

'Night?' Lisa asked, with a sort of a laugh.

'Well, I have no way of knowing that.'

Emily looked at her with interest and Lisa realised that this was the first time today she had allowed herself to relax enough to smile, let alone laugh.

'Right. Where to now?' Lisa was determined to keep cheerful.

'We could stop for lunch, give Frankie to her grandmother for a couple of hours, then I can make a start on this paperwork. I'll ask Dingo Duggan to drive you up to collect your things.'

'Hey, wait a minute, Emily, not so fast. I haven't found anywhere to go yet.'

'Oh, you'll find somewhere.' Emily was very confident of this.

'But you don't know how bad things are,' Lisa said.

'I do,' Emily said.

'How do you know? I didn't even tell Noel.'

'It must have been something very bad for you to come to Chestnut Court in the middle of the night,' Emily said.

IT DIDN'T TAKE Dingo long to pack his van. He already had a dress rail installed in it, so he just hung up Lisa's clothes on that. He had cardboard boxes where he packed her computer and files, and more boxes for her personal possessions. It wasn't much to show after a lifetime, Lisa thought.

The house was quiet, but she knew her father was at home. She had seen the curtains of his room move slightly. He made no move to come out and stop her or to explain what she had seen last night. In a way she was relieved, yet it showed how little he cared about whether she stayed or left.

As she and Dingo finished packing the van, she saw the curtains move again. However much of a failure her own life had been, it was nothing compared to his and her mother's.

She wrote a note and left it on the hall table.

I am leaving the house key. You will realise now that I have left permanently. I wish you both well and certainly I wish you more happiness than you have now. I will wait until I am settled, then I will let you have a forwarding address.

Lisa

BACK AT THE LYNCHES' HOUSE, Emily wanted to know how it had all gone. She was relieved that there had been no confrontation.

'I've telephoned Noel,' she said, 'and he'll be here around five. I'll take

Frankie back to Chestnut Court and Dingo can spring into action then.'

Lisa looked at her blankly.

'What action exactly, Emily? I'm a bit confused here. All my things are outside in Dingo's van. Where am I going to live?'

'I thought you could go to live with Noel in Chestnut Court,' Emily said. 'It would sort out everything . . .'

Chapter Five

Moira Tierney had always wanted to be a social worker. When she was very young she had thought she might be a nun, but somehow that idea had changed over the years. Well, nuns had changed for one thing. They didn't live in big quiet convents chanting hymns at dawn and dusk any more. Nuns, more or less, were social workers these days without any of the lovely ritual and ceremony.

Social work was never going to be nine to five; Moira expected to be called by problem families after working hours. In fact, this was often when she was most needed. She lived alone in a small apartment and spent days and nights picking up the pieces for people where love had gone wrong: where marriages had broken down, where children were abandoned, where domestic violence was too regular.

Moira believed that you often had a nose for a situation that wasn't right. After all, it was what those years of training and further years on the job taught you: to recognise when something was wrong. And Moira was worried about Frankie Lynch. It seemed entirely wrong that Noel Lynch should be given custody of the child. Moira had read the file. He hadn't even lived with Stella, the baby's mother. It was only when she was approaching her death and the baby's birth that she had got in touch with Noel.

It was all highly unsatisfactory.

Admittedly, Noel had managed to build up a support system that looked good on paper. The place was clean and warm and adequately stocked with what was necessary for the baby. His cousin, a middle-aged, settled person called Emily, had stayed with him for a time, and she still took the baby out. Sometimes the baby stayed with former nurse, Fiona Carroll, who had a new baby of her own and was married to a doctor. A very safe environment. And there was an older couple called Signora and Aidan who already looked after their own grandchild.

There were other people too. Noel's parents, who were religious maniacs; then there was a couple called Scarlet: Muttie and Lizzie, and their twin foster children, they were part of the team. And there was a retired doctor who seemed to be called Dr Hat. All reliable people, but still . . .

It was all too bitty, Moira thought: a flimsy, daisy chain of people, like the cast of a musical. If one link blew away, everything could crash to the ground. But could she get anyone to support her instinct? Nobody at all. Her immediate superior, who was team leader, said that she was fussing about nothing—everything seemed to be in place.

Moira had to hold back. But she was watching with very sharp eyes for anything to go out of step. And now it had. Noel had brought a woman to live in the flat. He had done up the spare room for her to sleep in.

'I'm not here permanently,' she had said over and over. 'I'm in a relationship elsewhere. With Anton Moran. The chef. Noel is just kindly giving me somewhere to stay and in return I'm helping him with Frankie.'

Moira didn't like her at all. There were too many of these bimbos around the place, leggy, airheaded young women with nothing in their minds except clothes. Whatever doubts Moira had about Noel's judgment, they were increased a hundredfold by the arrival of Lisa Kelly on the scene.

FRANKIE LYNCH and Johnny Carroll, born the same day, minded by all the same people, were to be baptised together.

Moira had been surprised to be invited to the christening. There was a much larger congregation than she had expected at Father Flynn's church. Most of them must be friends of Dr Carroll and his wife. Surely Noel Lynch wouldn't know half the church?

The two godmothers were there, Emily holding Frankie, and Fiona's friend Barbara, who was a nurse in the heart clinic where Fiona worked, carrying Johnny. The babies were beautifully behaved and for the most part slept through the ceremony. Father Flynn kept it brief and to the point, then everyone moved to the hall next door, where there was a buffet and a cake with the names Frankie and Johnny iced on it. Maud and Simon Mitchell were in charge of the catering: Moira remembered the names being listed among Noel's baby sitters for Frankie.

She stood on the outside, watching the people mingle and talk and come up to gurgle at the babies. Noel moved around easily, drinking orange juice and talking to everyone. Moira also noticed Lisa, who was looking very glamorous, her honey-coloured hair coiled up under a little red hat.

Maud saw Moira standing alone and came over to her, offering her serving tray. 'Can I get you another piece of cake?'

'No, thank you. I'm Moira, Frankie's social worker,' she said.

'Yes, I know you are, I'm Maud Mitchell, one of Frankie's baby sitters. She's doing very well, isn't she?'

Moira leaped on this. 'Didn't you expect her to do well?' she asked.

'Oh no, the reverse, Noel's doing a really great job.'

More solidarity in the community, Moira thought. She could still see in her mind the newspaper headlines: SOCIAL SERVICES TO BLAME. THERE WERE MANY WARNINGS. EVERYTHING WAS IGNORED!

THE NEXT MORNING, Moira decided to go and examine this St Jarlath's Thrift Shop where the baby spent a couple of hours a day. The place was clean and well ventilated. No complaints there.

Emily and a neighbour, Molly Carroll, were busy hanging up clothes that had just come in.

'Ah, Moira,' Emily welcomed her. 'Do you want a nice knitted suit? It would look very well on you. It's a lovely heather colour.'

It was a nice suit and ordinarily Moira might have been interested. But this was a work visit, not a social shopping outing.

'I really called to know whether you are satisfied with the situation with the new tenant in Chestnut Court, Ms Lynch.'

'Oh, Lisa! Yes, isn't it great? Noel would be quite lonely there on his own at night and now they go over their college notes together and she wheels Frankie down here in the mornings. It's a huge help.'

Moira was not convinced. 'But her own relationship. She says she's involved with someone else?'

'Oh yes, she's very keen on this young man who runs a restaurant.'

'And where is this "relationship" going?'

'Do you know, Moira, the French—who are very wise about love, cynical but wise—say, "There is always one who kisses and one who turns the cheek to be kissed." I think that's what we have here: Lisa kissing and Anton offering his cheek to be kissed.'

It silenced Moira completely. How had this middle-aged American woman understood everything so quickly and so well?

Moira wondered would she buy the heather knitted suit. But she didn't want them to think that somehow she was in their debt. She might ask someone to go in and buy it later.

THERE WAS A NOTICE on the corridor wall just outside Moira's office. The heart failure clinic in St Brigid's wanted the services of a social worker for a couple of weeks. Dr Clara Casey said they needed a report done, which she could show to the hospital management to prove that the help of a social worker might contribute to the well-being of the patients.

Moira looked at it vaguely. It wasn't of any interest to her. She was surprised and annoyed, therefore, when the team leader dropped in to see her.

'That job in St Brigid's, it's only for two weeks. I'd like you to do it, Moira.'

'It's not my kind of thing,' Moira began.

'Oh, but it is! No one would do it better or more thoroughly. Clara Casey will be delighted with you.'

'And my own case load?'

'Will be divided between us all while you are away.'

Moira didn't have to ask, was it an order. She knew it was.

MOIRA HAD SENT her colleague Dolores in to buy the knitted suit. Dolores was a foot shorter than Moira and two feet wider. Emily knew exactly what had happened.

'Wear it in happiness,' she said to Dolores.

'Oh . . . um . . . thank you,' said Dolores, who would never have got a job in the Secret Service.

Moira wore the heather-coloured suit for her first day at the heart failure clinic. Clara Casey admired it at once.

'I love nice clothes. They are my little weakness. That's a great outfit.'

'I'm not very interested in clothes myself,' Moira said. 'I've seen too many people get distracted by them over the years.'

'Quite.' Clara was crisp in response and Moira felt that she had somehow let herself down. That she had turned away the warmth of this heart specialist by a glib remark. Was it too late to rescue things?

'Dr Casey, I am anxious to do a good job here. Can you outline to me what you hope I will report to you?'

'Well, I am sure that you won't hand my own words back to me, Ms Tierney. You don't seem that sort of person.'

'Please call me Moira.'

'Later, maybe. At the moment Ms Tierney is fine. I have listed the areas where you can investigate. I do urge, however, some sensitivity when talking to both staff and patients. People are often tense when they present with heart failure. We emphasise the positive here.'

Not since she was a student had Moira received such an obvious ticking off. She would love to be able to rewind the day to the point when Clara had admired her outfit. She would thank her enthusiastically—even show her the satin lining. Some day she would learn, but would it be too late?

NEXT DAY, Moira began to understand the nature of her job. She was helped in this by Hilary, the office manager, and a Polish girl, Ania, who seemed devoted to the place and totally loyal to Clara Casey.

There was, apparently, a bad man called Frank Ennis on the hospital board who tried to resist spending one cent on the heart clinic. He said there was absolutely no need for any social services whatsoever in the clinic.

'Why can't Clara Casey speak to him herself?' Moira asked.

'She can and does, but he's a very determined man.'

'Suppose she just took him out to lunch one day?'

'Oh, she does much more than that,' Ania explained. 'She sleeps with him, but it's no use, he keeps his life in different compartments.'

Hilary tried to gloss over what had been said. 'Ania is just giving you the background,' she said hastily to Moira.

'I'm sorry. I thought she was on our side.' Ania was repentant.

'And I am, indeed,' Moira said.

'Oh, that's all right then.' Ania was happy.

MOIRA QUICKLY SAW that there was a case for having a social worker attend the clinic one day a week. It was time to approach the great Frank Ennis.

She made an appointment to see him on her last day in the clinic. He was courteous and gracious—not at all the monster she had been told about.

'You really do need someone part-time, you know,' Moira said. 'Then St Brigid's can really be said to be looking after patients' welfare.'

'All the social workers and people in pastoral care are run off their feet in the hospital already. They don't want to be sent over to the clinic.'

'Get someone new in for two or three days a week.' Moira was firm.

'One day a week.'

'One and a half,' she bargained.

'Clara is right, Ms Tierney, you have all the skills of a negotiator. A day and a half a week and not a minute more.'

'I feel sure that will be fine, Mr Ennis.'

'And will you do it yourself, Ms Tierney?'

Moira was horrified. 'Oh no! No way, Mr Ennis, I am a senior social worker. I have a serious case load. I couldn't make the time.'

'That's a pity. I thought you could be my friend: my eyes and ears, curb them from playing fast and loose with expenses and taxis.'

He seemed genuinely disappointed not to have her around the place, which was rare these days. But of course it was totally impossible. She could barely keep up with her own work, let alone take on something new. And yet she would be sorry to leave the heart clinic.

ANIA HAD BROUGHT in some shortbread for their afternoon tea to mark the fact that Moira was leaving. Clara joined them and made a little speech.

'We were lucky that they sent us Moira Tierney. She has done a superb report and has even braved the lion's den itself. Frank Ennis has just telephoned to say that the Board have agreed to us having the services of a social worker for one and a half days a week.'

'So you'll be coming back!' Ania seemed pleased.

'No, Ms Tierney made it clear that she has much more important work to do elsewhere. We are very grateful to her for putting it on hold for the two weeks that she was here,' Clara said.

Hilary was always practical. 'Maybe Ms Tierney knows someone who might be suitable?' she said.

As if from miles away Moira heard her own voice saying, 'I can easily reorganise my schedule and if you all thought I would be all right, then I would be honoured to come here.'

They all looked at Clara, who was silent for a moment. Then she said, 'I feel that we would all love Moira to join us, but she will have to sign in under the Official Secrets Act. Frank will expect her to be his eyes and ears, but Moira will know that this can never happen.'

Moira smiled. 'I get the message, Clara,' she said.

And to her great surprise she got a round of applause.

IN CHESTNUT COURT, Frankie was crying again. Noel was beginning to think that he would never know what the crying meant. Some nights she didn't sleep for more than ten minutes at a time. There was one level for food, but she'd just been fed and burped. He sat down and laid her chest across his arm while he rubbed her little back to soothe her.

'Frankie, Frankie, please don't cry, little pet, hush now, hush now . . .'

Nothing. Frankie cried on piteously. Perhaps for a nappy that needed changing? Could it be a changing job?

He was right. The nappy was indeed damp. Carefully he placed the baby on a towel spread over the table where they changed her. As soon as he removed her wet nappy, the crying stopped and he was rewarded with a sunny smile and a coo. As Noel stretched out his hand to reach for the cleaning wipes, to his horror she twisted away from him and began to slip off the table. Quick as he was, he was not in time.

It felt as though everything happened in slow motion as the baby began to fall from the table. As Noel froze in horror, she hit the chair beside it, then fell to the floor. There was blood around her head as she started to scream.

'Frankie, *please, Frankie*.'

He wept inconsolably as he picked her up and clutched her to him. He couldn't tell where she was hurt or how badly. Panic overwhelmed him.

'No, please, *dear God, no*, don't take her away from me, make her be all right. Frankie, little Frankie, please, please . . .'

It was a few moments before he pulled himself together and telephoned for an ambulance.

MOIRA GOT A TEXT message on her cellphone. There had been an accident. Frankie had cut her head. Noel had taken her to the A & E of St Brigid's Hospital, and he thought he should let Moira know.

She took the bus straight to St Brigid's. She had *known* that this would happen, but she felt no satisfaction at being proved right. Just anger, a great anger that everyone else's bleeding-heart philosophy said that a drunk and a flighty young girl could be made responsible for raising a child.

It had been an accident waiting to happen.

She found a white-faced Noel at the hospital.

'They say it's just a deep graze and she'll have a bruise. Thank God! There was so much blood, I couldn't imagine what it was.'

'How did it happen?' Moira's voice was like a knife.

'She rolled over when I was changing her and fell off the table,' he said.

'You let her fall from the table?'

'I didn't *let* her fall. She twisted away from me . . .'

Noel looked frightened and almost faint from the stress of it all.

'So, what caused you to let her fall? That's what it was—*you* let her fall. Was your mind distracted?'

'No, no, it wasn't.'

'Did you have a little drink maybe?'

'*No*, I did *not* have a little drink or a big drink, though by God I could do with one now. It put the heart across me and of course I feel guilty but now I have you yapping at me as if I threw the child on the floor.'

'I'm *not* suggesting that. I realise that it was an accident. I am just trying to work out how it happened.'

'It won't happen again,' Noel said.

'How do we know this?'

'We know because we are going to move the table up against the wall.'

'And where was your partner while all this was going on?'

'Partner?'

'Lisa Kelly.'

'Oh, she wasn't there. She's gone away with Anton to some celebrity chef thing in London for a few days.'

'Is Anton happy about his girlfriend living with you, do you think, Noel?'

'I never thought about it one way or the other. It suits her. He knows we aren't a couple in *that* sense. Why do you ask?'

'It's my business to make sure Frankie grows up in a stable household,' Moira said righteously.

ANTON'S RESTAURANT was advertising Saturday lunches. Moira decided to invite Dr Casey.

'There's no need, Moira,' Clara had said.

'No, of course not, but I'd enjoy it. Please say yes.'

It didn't suit Clara at all. Normally she had a relaxed lunch with Frank Ennis on a Saturday and then they went to the cinema or the theatre. It had become an easy and undemanding routine. But she could meet him later.

'That would be delightful, Moira,' she said.

When Moira went to make the table reservation she was greeted by Anton himself. He was indeed very charming. He pointed around the room.

'Where would you like to sit, Ms Tierney? I'd love to give you the nicest table in the room,' he said.

She picked out a table.

'Excellent choice. Are you inviting a friend?'

'Well, my boss actually. She's a doctor in a heart clinic.'

'We'll make sure you both have a good time,' he said.

Moira left feeling ten years younger and much more attractive. No wonder Lisa was so besotted with the boy. He was truly something special.

AND HE HAD not forgotten that they were to be well looked after. As soon as she entered the restaurant, the maître d' greeted her as though she were a regular and valued customer.

'Ah, Ms Tierney!' Teddy said, as she gave her name. 'Anton said to look out for you and to offer you and your guest a house cocktail.'

'Lord, I don't think so,' Clara said.

'Why not? It's free.' Moira giggled.

And they sipped a coloured glass of something that had fresh mint and ice and soda, some exotic liqueur and probably a triple serving of vodka.

'Thank God it's Saturday,' Clara said. 'Nobody could have gone back to work after one of these house cocktails.'

It was a very pleasant lunch. Clara talked about her daughter Linda who was very anxious to have a child and had been having fertility treatment for eighteen months without success.

'Any babies coming up for adoption in your line of business?' Clara asked.

'There might be,' Moira said, 'a little girl, a few months old now.'

'Well, is she available for adoption?' Clara was a cut-and-dried person.

'Not at the moment, but somehow I don't think she is going to last long in the present set-up,' Moira explained.

'Why? Are they cruel to her?'

'No, not at all. They are just not able to manage properly.'

'But do they love her? I mean, they'll never give her up if they are mad about her.'

'They might have no choice in it,' Moira said.

'I won't tell Linda anything about it in case. No point in raising her hopes,' Clara said.

'No. If and when it does come up, I'll let you know immediately.'

Then they chatted about the various patients who came to the heart clinic.

Moira asked about Clara's friend Frank Ennis and learned that he was a very decent man, but had a blind spot about saving St Brigid's money.

Just as Moira was paying the bill, Anton arrived, accompanied by a very pretty girl who looked about twenty. He came over to their table.

'Ms Tierney, I hope everything was all right for you?' he said.

'Lovely,' Moira said. 'This is Dr Casey . . . Clara, this is Anton Moran.'

'It was all delicious,' Clara said. 'I will certainly tell people about it.'

'That's what we need.' Anton had an easy charm. He introduced the young woman. 'This is April Monaghan,' he said.

'Oh, I read about you in the papers. You were in London recently,' Moira said, gushing slightly.

'That's right,' April agreed.

'It's just that I know a friend of yours. A *great* friend, Lisa Kelly, and she was there too at the same time.'

'Yeah, she was,' April agreed.

Anton's smile didn't falter. 'How exactly do you know Lisa, Ms Tierney?'

'Through work. I'm a social worker,' Moira said.

'I thought social workers didn't discuss their cases in public.' His smile was still there, but not in his eyes.

'No, no, Lisa isn't a client. I know her sort of through something else . . .'

Moira was flustered now. She could sense Clara's disapproval. Why had she brought up this matter anyway? It was in order to fill in the missing parts of the jigsaw in Chestnut Court. The unaccustomed house cocktail and the bottle of wine had loosened her tongue. Now she had somehow managed to spoil the whole day.

'I HEAR YOUR AUNT is going back to America for a bit,' Moira said to Noel.

'She's actually my cousin, but you're right, she is going to New York for a wedding. How did you know?' Noel asked, surprised.

'Someone mentioned it.' Moira, who made it her business to know everything, was vague.

'Yes, she's going to her friend Betsy's wedding,' Noel said. 'She's going to be her maid of honour. But then she's coming back again. My parents are very relieved, I tell you. They'd be lost without Emily.'

'And you would too, Noel, wouldn't you?' Moira said.

'Well, I would miss her certainly, but as far as my mother is concerned the thrift shop would close down without Emily.'

'But surely you are the one she has helped most, Noel?' Moira said.

'How do you mean?'

'Well, didn't she pay your tuition fees at the college? Get you this apartment, arrange a baby-sitting roster for you and probably a lot more . . .?'

There was a dull red flush on Noel's face and neck. Had Emily blabbed to this awful woman? *Nobody* was ever going to know about the fees—that was their secret. He felt betrayed, as he had never felt before. There was no way he could know that Moira was only guessing.

She was waiting for a reply but he didn't trust himself to speak.

'You must have thought about who would take over her duties?'

'I thought maybe Dingo might help out,' Noel said in a strangled voice.

'Dingo?' Moira said the name with distaste.

'You know, he does some deliveries to the thrift shop. Dingo Duggan.'

'I don't know him, no.'

'He only helps out the odd time when no one else is available.'

'And you never thought to tell me about him?' Moira asked, horrified.

'Listen to me, Moira, you give me a pain right in the arse,' Noel said.

'I beg your pardon?' She looked at him in disbelief.

'You heard me. I'm breaking my back to do this right. I'm nearly dead on my feet sometimes, but do you ever see any of this? Oh, no, it's constantly moving the goalposts and complaining and behaving like the secret police.'

'Really, Noel. Control yourself.'

'No, I will *not* control myself. You come here investigating me as if I were some sort of criminal. Repeating poor Dingo's name as if he was a mass murderer instead of a decent poor eejit, which is what he is.'

'*A decent poor eejit.* I see.'

She started to write something down, but Noel pushed her clipboard away and it fell to the ground.

'And then you go and pry and question people. And try to get them to say bad things about me, pretending to look out for Frankie's good.'

Moira remained very still during this outburst. Eventually she said, 'I'll leave now, Noel, and come back tomorrow. You will hopefully have calmed down by then.' And she turned and left the apartment.

NOEL SAT AND STARED ahead of him. That woman was bound to bring in some reinforcements and get Frankie taken away from him. His eyes filled with tears. He picked up his phone and called Dingo.

'Mate, can you come and hold the fort for a couple of hours?'

'Sure, Noel. Can I bring a DVD or is the child asleep?'

'She'll sleep through it if it's not too loud.'

Noel waited until Dingo was installed.

'I'm off now,' he said briefly.

Dingo looked at him. 'Are you OK, Noel? You look a bit funny.'

'I'm fine,' Noel said.

'And will you have your phone on?'

'Maybe not, Dingo, but the emergency numbers are all in the kitchen on the wall, you know: Lisa, my parents, Emily, the hospital or anything.'

And then he was gone. He took a bus to the other side of Dublin and in the anonymity of a cavernous bar Noel Lynch drank pints for the first time in months.

They felt great . . . bloody great . . .

Chapter Six

It was Declan who had to pick up the pieces. Dingo phoned him a half an hour after midnight, sounding very upset. 'I'm sorry for waking you, Declan, but I didn't know what to do—she's roaring like a bull.'

'Who is roaring like a bull?' Declan was struggling to wake up.

'Frankie. Can't you hear her?'

'Is she all right? Does she need changing?' Declan suggested.

'I don't do that. I was just holding the fort. That's what he asked me to do.'

'And where is he? Where's Noel?'

'Well, I don't know, do I? I've been here six hours now!'

'His phone?'

'Turned off. God, Declan, what am I to do? She's bright red in the face.'

'I'll be there in ten minutes,' Declan said, getting out of bed.

'Declan, you don't have to go out. You're not on call!' Fiona protested.

'Noel's gone off somewhere,' Declan told her. 'He left the baby with Dingo. I have to go over there. Go back to sleep, Fiona.'

He was dressed and out of the house in minutes. He was worried about Noel Lynch—very worried indeed.

'GOD BLESS YOU,' Dingo said with huge relief when Declan arrived.

He watched, mystified, as Declan expertly changed a nappy, made up the formula and heated the milk, all in seamless movements.

Frankie was peaceful. All they had to do now was to find her father.

'He didn't say where he was going, but I sort of thought it was for an hour or two. I thought he was going home to his parents for something.'

'Was he upset about anything before he went out?'

'God, I don't know, Declan. Maybe the poor lad was hit by a bus and we're all misjudging him. He could be in an A & E with his phone broken.'

'He could.'

Declan didn't know why he felt so certain that Noel had gone back on the drink. The man had been heroic for months. *What* could have changed him?

'Go home, Dingo,' Declan said. 'You've held the fort for long enough. I'll do it now until Noel gets back. I'll call you when he's found.'

NOEL WAS ASLEEP in a shed on the other side of Dublin.

He had no idea how he had got there. The last thing he could remember was some kind of argument in a bar and people refusing him further drink. He had walked for what seemed a very long time and then it got cold, so he decided to have a rest before he went home.

Home? His heart gave a sudden jump. What about the baby?

He remembered Dingo. Noel looked at his watch. That was hours ago. *Hours*. Was Dingo still there? He wouldn't have contacted Moira, would he? Oh please, God, please, let Dingo not have rung Moira.

He felt physically ill at the thought and realised that he was indeed going to be sick. As a courtesy to whoever owned this garden shed, Noel went out to the road. Then his legs felt weak and wouldn't support him. He went back into the shed and passed out.

DECLAN SLEPT for several hours in the chair. When daybreak came he realised that Noel hadn't come home. He went to make himself a cup of tea and decide what to do. He rang Fiona.

'Is today one of Moira's days up in your clinic?'

'Yes, she'll be there for the morning. Are you coming home?'

'Not immediately. Don't say a word to her about any of this. We'll try to cover for him, but she can't know. Not until we've found him.'

'Listen, Signora and Aidan will be here soon. They're collecting Johnny and will pick up Frankie and then take them to their daughter's place . . .'

'I'll wait until they're here. I'll have her ready for them.'

'You really are a saint, Declan,' Fiona said.

'What else can we do? And remember, Moira knows nothing.'

THE CLINIC WAS in a state of fuss because Frank Ennis was paying one of his unexpected visits.

'You were out with him last night—did he not give you *any* idea he was coming in today?' Hilary asked Clara Casey.

'*Me?*' asked Clara in disbelief. 'I'm the very last person on earth that he'd tell. He's always hoping to catch me out in something.'

'Look, he's talking to Moira very intently about something,' she whispered. 'I'll get nearer and see what they're talking about,' Hilary offered.

'Really, Hilary, I *am* surprised at you,' Clara said in mock horror.

'You go away and I'll hover,' said Hilary. 'I'm a great hoverer. That's why I know so much.'

As Clara made for her desk, the phone rang. It was Declan.

'Don't say my name,' he said immediately.

'Sure, right. What can I do for you?'

'Is Moira near you?'

'Quite, yes.'

'Could you find out what she's doing after she leaves you today? I'll make myself clear. We share baby-minding arrangements with a friend and his baby. It's just that they're clients of Moira's and she's been a bit tough on him. He's gone off on a batter. I have to drag him back here and sort things out. We want to keep Moira out of the place until tomorrow, at any rate. If she discovers the set-up, then things will really hit the fan.'

'I see . . .'

'So, if there was any other direction you could head her towards . . .?'

'Leave it with me,' Clara said, 'and cheer up—maybe your worst scenario won't turn out to be right.'

'No, I'm afraid it's only too right. His AA buddy has just called in. He's getting him back here in about half an hour.'

Hilary came over to Clara with a report.

'He's pumping her for information. Like "Does she see any areas of conspicuous waste?" You know, the usual kind of thing he goes on about. If he got her on her own, Lord knows what he'd get out of her.'

'Be more confident, Hilary. We're not doing anything wrong here. But you've given me an idea.'

Clara approached Frank Ennis and Moira.

'Seeing you two together reminded me that Moira hasn't seen the social work set-up in the main hospital. Frank, maybe you could introduce her to some of the team over there—today possibly?'

'Oh, I have a lot of calls to make on my case load.'

Clara gave a tinkling laugh. 'Oh really, Moira, you're so much on top of everything, I imagine your case load is run like clockwork.'

Moira seemed pleased with the praise.

'I *was* hoping, Moira, that you could link up with the whole system, but of course if you feel it's too much for you, then . . .'

Clara had judged it exactly right.

Moira made an arrangement to meet Frank at lunchtime. Clara had managed to give Noel, Declan and the man from AA a bit of a head start.

AIDAN AND SIGNORA DUNNE had arrived with little Johnny Carroll and taken Frankie with them. They would wheel the two baby buggies along the canal to their daughter's house. There Signora would look after all three children—their grandson Joseph Edward along with Frankie and Johnny—while Aidan gave Latin lessons to students who hoped to go to university.

It was a peaceful and undemanding morning. If they had wondered what Dr Carroll was doing in Noel Lynch's place, and why there was no sign of a normally devoted father, they had said nothing.

Malachy arrived, more or less supporting Noel in the doorway. Noel's clothes were filthy and stained and he seemed totally disorientated.

'Is he still drunk?' Declan asked Malachy.

'Hard to say. Possibly.' Malachy was a man of few words.

'I'll turn on the shower. Can you get him into it?'

'Sure.'

Malachy was as good as his word. He propelled Noel into the water, letting it get cooler all the time until it was almost cold. Meanwhile Declan picked up all the dirty clothes and put them into the washing machine. He laid out clean clothes from Noel's room and made them all a pot of tea.

Noel's eyes were more focused now, but still he said nothing.

Declan poured another mug of tea and allowed the silence to become uncomfortable. He would *not* make things easy for Noel.

Eventually Noel asked, 'Where's Frankie?'

'With Aidan and Signora.'

'And where's Dingo?'

'Gone to work,' Declan said tersely.

'And did he phone *you*?' Noel nodded towards Declan.

'Yes, that's why I'm here,' Declan said.

'And are you the only one he phoned?' Noel's voice was a whisper.

Declan shrugged. 'I've no idea,' he said. Let Noel sweat a bit. Let him think that Moira was on the case.

'Oh my God . . .' Noel said. His face had almost dissolved in grief.

'Well, no one else turned up, so I suppose I was the only one,' Declan said.

'I'm so sorry,' Noel began.

'Why?' Declan cut across him.

'I can't remember. I really can't. I felt a bit uptight and I thought one or two drinks might help. I didn't know it was going to turn out like this,' Noel said piteously.

Malachy was silent.

Declan suddenly felt very tired. 'Where do we go from here?' he asked.

'It's up to Noel,' Malachy said. 'If you want to try to kick it again, I'll help you. But it's going to be hell.'

'Of course I want to,' Noel said.

'It's no use if you are just waiting for me to get out of your hair so that you can sneak off and stick your face into it again,' Malachy told him.

'I won't do that,' Noel wailed. 'From tomorrow on it will be back just the same as it was up to now.'

'What do you mean *tomorrow*? What's wrong with *today*?' Malachy asked.

'Well, tomorrow, fresh start and everything.'

'Grow up, Noel,' Malachy said. '*Today*, fresh start and everything.'

'But just a couple of vodkas to straighten me up and then we can start with a clean slate?' Noel was almost begging now.

Declan spoke. 'I can't let you look after our son any more, Noel. Johnny won't come here again unless we know you're off the sauce.'

'Ah, Declan, I wouldn't hurt a hair of that child's head,' Noel said.

'You left your own daughter with Dingo Duggan for hour after hour. No, Noel, I wouldn't risk it. And even if I did, Fiona wouldn't.'

Declan hated doing it, but it was the truth. They couldn't trust Noel any more. And if *he* felt like that, what would Moira feel?

DECLAN CARROLL took his morning surgery. He had been two hours late, so Dr Hat had been called in to help.

'Muttie Scarlet rang. He said you'd have some results for him today.'

'And I do,' Declan said glumly. 'Isn't it a shit life, Hat?'

'It is indeed, but I'm usually the one who says that and you always say it's not so bad.'

'I'm not saying that today. I'm off out to Muttie's house. Can you stay?'

'I'll stay as long as you like. They don't want me, though, they'll ask when the *real* doctor will be back,' Dr Hat said.

MUTTIE ANSWERED the door.

'Ah, Declan, any news yet?' He spoke in a low voice. He didn't want his wife Lizzie to hear the conversation.

'You know how they are,' Declan said. 'They're so laid-back up there in the hospital they give a new urgency to the word *mañana* . . .'

'So?' Muttie asked.

'So I was wondering, would we go and have a pint?' Declan said.

'I'll go and get Hooves,' Muttie suggested.

'No, let's go to Casey's instead of Dad's and your pub—too many of your Associates there . . . we'd get nothing said.'

Declan saw from Muttie's face that he realised that the news wasn't good.

OLD MAN CASEY served them and, since there was no response to his conversation about the weather or the recession, he left them alone.

'Give it to me straight, Declan,' Muttie said.

'They saw a shadow on the X-ray; the scan showed a . . . a small tumour.'

'Tumour?'

'You know . . . a lump. I've made an appointment for you with a specialist next month.'

'Next *month*?'

'The sooner we deal with it, the better, Muttie.'

'But how in the name of God did you get an appointment so soon?'

'I went private,' Declan said.

'I'm a working man, Declan, I can't afford these fancy fees . . .'

'You won a fortune a few years back on some horse. You've got money in the bank—you *told* me.'

'But that's for emergencies and rainy days . . .'

'This is a rainy day, Muttie.'

Declan blew his nose very loudly. This was more than he could bear at the moment.

'You never asked me about the whole business,' Declan said. 'I mean, there are a lot of options: chemotherapy, radiotherapy, surgery . . .'

'Won't I hear all about it next month from the fellow whose Rolls-Royce I'm paying for? No point in thinking about it until I have to. OK?'

'OK,' agreed Declan, who wondered would this day ever end.

BY THE TIME that Moira called at Chestnut Court, things had settled down a lot. Malachy had taken Noel to an AA meeting where nobody had blamed him but everyone had congratulated him on turning up.

Moira viewed Malachy's presence in the house with no great pleasure. 'Are you a baby sitter?' she asked.

'No, I am from Alcoholics Anonymous. That's how I know Noel.'

'Oh really . . .' Her eyes narrowed slightly. 'Any reason for the visit?'

'We were at a meeting together up the road and I came back for some tea with Noel. That's permitted, isn't it?'

'Of course—you mustn't make me into some kind of a monster. I'm merely here for Frankie's sake. It's just that we had a full and frank exchange of views yesterday and I suppose, when I saw you here, I thought that you might . . . that Noel could possibly . . . that all was not well.'

'And so now you are reassured?' Malachy asked silkily.

'Frankie will be coming back shortly. We want to get things ready for her . . . unless there's anything else?' Noel spoke politely.

Moira left.

MR HARRIS, THE CONSULTANT, was a kindly man. He was more than pleased to have Declan along with Muttie for the consultation.

'If I start talking medical jargon, Dr Carroll can turn it into ordinary English,' he said with a smile.

'Declan is the first person who grew up on our street who became a professional man,' Muttie said proudly.

'That so? I was the first in my family to get a degree, too. I bet they have a great graduation picture of you at home.' He seemed genuinely interested.

'It replaces the Sacred Heart lamp.' Declan grinned.

'Right, Mr Scarlet, let's not waste your time here while we go down

Memory Lane.' Mr Harris came back to the main point. 'You've been to St Brigid's and they've given me a very clear picture of your lungs. There are no grey areas, it's black and white. You have a large and growing tumour in your left lung and secondary tumours in your liver.'

Declan noted that there was a carafe of water on the desk and a glass. Mr Harris poured one for Muttie, who was uncharacteristically silent.

'So, now, Mr Scarlet, we have to see how best to manage this.'

Muttie was still wordless.

'Will an operation be an option?' Declan asked.

'No, not at this stage. It's a choice between radiotherapy and chemotherapy at the moment, and arranging palliative care at home or in a hospice.'

'What's palliative care?' Muttie spoke for the first time.

'It's nurses who are trained to deal with diseases like yours. They are marvellous, very understanding people who know all about it—what patients want and how to give you the best quality of life.'

Muttie thought about this for a moment.

'The quality of life I want is to live for a long, *long* time with Lizzie, to see all my children again, to see the twins well settled in a business and to watch my grandson, Thomas Muttance Feather, grow up into a fine young man. I'd like to walk my dog Hooves for years to the pub where I meet my Associates and go to the races three times a year. That would be a great quality of life.'

Declan saw Mr Harris remove his glasses and concentrate on cleaning them. When he trusted himself to speak again he said, 'And you *will* be able to do a good deal of that for a time. So let's look forward to that.'

'Not live for a long, long time, though?'

'Not for a long, long time, Mr Scarlet, no. So the important thing is how we use what time is left.'

'How long?'

'It's difficult to say exactly . . .'

'*How long?*'

'Months. Six months? Maybe longer, if we're lucky . . .'

'Well, thank you, Mr Harris. I must say you've been very clear. Not worth hundreds of euros, but you were straight and you were kind as well. How much exactly do I owe you?'

Muttie took his wallet from his pocket and laid it on the desk.

'No, Mr Scarlet, you were brought here by Dr Carroll, a fellow doctor.

There's a tradition that we never charge fellow doctors for a consultation.'

'But there's nothing wrong with Declan,' Muttie said, confused.

'You're his friend. He brought you here. Please accept this for what it is, normal procedure, and put that away. I will write my report and recommendations to Dr Carroll who will look after you very well.'

FIONA KNEW there was something wrong the moment he came in the door.

'Declan, you're white as a sheet! What happened? Was it Noel?'

'It's Muttie,' he said, head in his hands. 'He has just a few months.'

'Never!' She was so shocked she had to sit down.

'Yes. I was at the specialist this morning with him.'

'He'll have to tell Lizzie,' Fiona said.

'It's done. I was there.' Declan looked stricken.

'And?'

'It was as bad as you'd think. Worse. Lizzie said she still had so many things to do with Muttie. She had been planning to take him to the Grand National in Liverpool. You know, Fiona, Muttie is never going to make it over to Aintree.'

And then he sobbed like a child.

MAUD AND SIMON, who had grown up with Muttie and Lizzie and hardly remembered any former life, were heartbroken.

'It's not as if he was really old,' Maud said.

'Sixty is meant to be only middle-aged nowadays,' Simon agreed.

'We'll have to put off going to America,' Maud said.

'We can't do that. They won't keep the job for us.' Simon was anxious.

'There will be other jobs. Later, you know, afterwards. We can try to get shifts in good Dublin restaurants.'

'They'd never take us on. We don't have enough experience.'

'Oh, come on, Simon, don't be such a defeatist. We have terrific references from all the people we did catering for. I bet they'll take us on.'

'Where will we start?'

'I think we should invest a little money first, have dinner in somewhere like Quentins or Anton's. You know, top places. And we'd regard it as research, keep our eyes open and *then* go back and ask for a job.'

'It seems a heartless thing to be doing when Muttie is in such bad shape.'

'It's better than going to the other side of the earth,' Maud said.

THEY DECIDED ON chemotherapy for Muttie and by this stage everyone in St Jarlath's Crescent knew about him and had offered a variety of cures. Josie and Charles Lynch said that in recognition for Muttie's interest in the campaign for his statue, St Jarlath would put in a word for him. Dr Hat said that he would be happy to drive Muttie to the pub any evening he wanted to go.

Declan's parents saw that there was half a leg of lamb left over at the end of the day or four fillet steaks. Muttie and Lizzie's daughter Cathy called every day, usually with something to eat. Often she brought her son Thomas with her. He was a lively lad and kept Muttie well entertained.

In fact, it was all going better than Declan could have hoped. He had thought that the normally cheerful Muttie would have fallen into a serious depression. But it was far from being the case. Declan's father said that Muttie was still the life and soul with his Associates up at the pub and he had the same number of pints as ever on the grounds that there wasn't much damage they could do to him now.

DECLAN'S SURGERY BEGAN at 10 a.m. so he would have time to call in to see Muttie and discuss the palliative care nurse who was arriving for the first time today. Declan knew the nurse. She was an experienced, gentle woman called Jessica, trained in making the abnormal seem reasonable and quick to anticipate anything that might be needed.

Moira was bustling down St Jarlath's Crescent when Declan went out. She seemed surgically attached to her clipboard of notes. Declan had never seen her without them. He waved and kept walking, but she stopped him.

'Where are you heading?' he asked easily.

'I heard there was a house for sale in this street,' Moira said. 'I've always wanted a little garden. Do you know anything about it? It's number 22.'

Declan thought quickly; it belonged to an old lady who was going into an old people's home, but it was exactly next door to Noel's parents. Noel would not welcome that.

'Might be in poor condition,' Declan said. 'She was a bit of a recluse.'

'Well, that might make it cheaper,' Moira said cheerfully.

She looked nice when she smiled.

'Noel still OK?' she asked.

'You actually see him more than I do, Moira,' Declan said.

'Yes, well, it's my job. But he can be touchy at times, don't you find?'

'Touchy? No, I never found that.'

'Just one day there recently, he pushed my notes out of my hands and shouted at me.'

'What was all that about?'

'About someone called Dingo Duggan who had been appointed as an extra baby sitter. I asked about him and Noel shouted at me that he was a *decent poor eejit* and used most abusive language. It was quite intolerable.'

Declan looked at her steadily. So *that* was what had tilted Noel that night. He hardly trusted himself to speak.

'Is anything wrong, Declan?' Moira asked. 'I get the feeling that something is being kept from me.'

'Well, when you discover what it is, you'll let me know, won't you?'

Declan managed to fix a smile on his face and moved on.

DECLAN HAD BOOKED a table at Anton's restaurant for dinner. He wanted to talk to Fiona in good surroundings, not in the house they shared with his parents where everything could be heard in some degree anyway.

Fiona was in great form. She said she had starved herself at lunchtime. She was all dressed up in a new outfit: a pink dress with a black jacket. Declan looked at her proudly as they were settled in at the restaurant. She looked so beautiful. She had a style equal to any of the other guests. He took her face in his hands and kissed her for a long time.

'Declan, really! What will people think?' she asked.

'They'll think we are alive and that we are happy,' he said simply. Then added, 'I was thinking . . . I was wondering, should we buy number 22 in the Crescent? It would be a home of our own.'

Chapter Seven

'I have a bit of a problem,' Frank Ennis said to Clara Casey as he picked her up at the heart clinic.

'Let me guess,' she said, laughing. 'We used one can of air freshener too many in the cloakroom last month?'

'No, nothing like that,' he said impatiently, as he negotiated the traffic. 'Clara, are you wedded to this concert tonight?'

'Is anything wrong?' She looked at him sharply. Frank never cancelled arrangements.

'No, nothing is *wrong* exactly, but I do need to talk to you,' he said.

'All right then. Sure we'll cancel the concert. Will we go out to a meal somewhere?'

'Come home with me. I asked a caterer to leave in a dinner for us,' he said, embarrassed.

'Caterers. I see . . .'

'Well, they're quite young. Semi-professional, I'd say. Haven't learned to charge fancy prices yet.'

'Slave labour? Ripe for exploitation, yes?' Clara wondered.

'Oh, Clara, will you give over just for one night?' Frank Ennis begged.

MAUD AND SIMON were in Frank's apartment. They had set the table and brought their own paper napkins and a rose.

'Is that over the top?' Simon was worried.

'No, he's going to propose to her. I know he is,' Maud said. 'Why else is he making a meal for a woman in his flat?' To Maud it was obvious.

They had laid out the smoked salmon with the avocado mousse and a little rosette carved from a Sicilian lemon. The chicken and mustard dish was in the oven. An apple tart and cream were on the sideboard.

'Well, I hope she says yes,' Simon said. 'It's a heavy outlay for that man, all this food and the cost of our catering and everything.'

They let themselves out and posted the keys through the front door.

CLARA HAD ALWAYS thought Frank's apartment rather bleak and soulless. Tonight, though, it looked different. There was subdued lighting and a lovely dinner table prepared.

And she noticed the red rose. This wasn't Frank's speed. Suddenly she felt a great thud-like shock. He couldn't possibly be about to propose to her. Could he? Surely not. Frank and she had been very clear about where they were going, which was a commitment-free relationship. Surely Frank could not have got his wires so hopelessly crossed? Definitely not!

He went into his study and came out with a sheaf of papers.

'This all looks very nice.' Clara admired the place.

'Well, good. And thank you for agreeing to change your plans so readily.'

'Not at all. It must be important . . .'

Frank poured her a glass of wine and then passed the papers over to her. 'This is my problem, Clara. I've had a letter from a boy in Australia. He says he's my son.'

Clara looked at the letter that Frank had handed to her. 'Are you sure you want me to read it?' she asked. 'He didn't write to me . . .'

'Read it, Clara.'

So she began to read a letter from a young man:

You will be surprised to hear from me. My name is Des Raven and I believe that I am your son. This will probably strike terror into your heart and you will expect someone searching for a fortune turning up on your doorstep. Let me say at once that this is not at all the case.

I live very happily here in New South Wales where I'm a teacher and—just to reassure you—where I will go on living!

If my presence in Dublin will cause embarrassment to you and your family, I will quite understand. I just hope it might be possible for us to meet at least once when I am in Ireland. My mother, Rita Raven, died last year.

Funny thing, I never asked her any questions about where I came from and what kind of a guy my father was. I didn't ask because she didn't seem very easy about the whole thing. She would say she had been very young and very foolish at the time and hadn't it all worked out so well? She said she never regretted one day of having me.

She kept in touch with her married sister who lives in England. She was forty-two when she died, although she claimed to be thirty-nine, and I'd say, all in all, she had a good and happy life.

Of you, Frank Ennis, I know nothing except your name on my birth certificate. I found you on the Internet and called the hospital from here and asked were you still working there and they said yes.

You have only my assurance that I will not make trouble for you and your present wife and family.

I truly hope that we will meet. Until then . . .

Des Raven

Clara put the letter down and looked at Frank. His eyes were too bright and there was a tear on his face. She went across to him with her arms out.

'Isn't this *wonderful*, Frank!' she cried. 'You've got a son! Isn't that the best news in the world?'

'Well, yes, but we've got to be cautious,' Frank began.

'What do we have to be cautious about? There was a woman called Rita Raven, wasn't there?'

'Yes, but—'

'And she disappeared off the scene?'

'She went to some cousins in the USA,' he said.

'Or to some non-cousins in Australia . . .' Clara corrected him.

'But it will all have to be checked out . . .' he began to bluster.

She deliberately mistook his meaning. 'Of course the airlines and everything, but let him do that, Frank. The main thing is, what time is it in Australia? You can ring him straight away.'

He didn't move. He couldn't bring himself to tell her he had had the letter for two weeks and hadn't been able to decide what to do.

'Come on, Frank, it's surely morning there and if you leave it any longer he'll have gone out to school. Call him now, will you?'

'HOW WAS FRANK last night?' Hilary asked Clara the next day at the clinic.

'Amazing,' Clara said and left it there.

'And did you enjoy the concert?' Hilary persisted.

'We didn't go. He arranged a catered meal in his apartment.'

'My God, this sounds serious!' Hilary was delighted.

'Frank is as he always was and always will be: cautious and watchful, never spontaneous. Stop trying to matchmake, will you, Hilary?'

Frank had dithered so long last night that the telephone had rung unanswered in Des Raven's home on the other side of the world. He had missed talking to the son he hadn't known he had, just because he was anxious to talk it over and check it out. But Clara told none of this to Hilary.

'Linda rang you earlier,' Hilary said. 'You were busy so I took the call.'

Hilary's son, Nick, was married to Clara's daughter, Linda. The two women had schemed to introduce their children to each other and it had worked spectacularly well. Apart from producing a grandchild. Despite intervention, there'd been no success, and Nick and Linda were despondent.

YET AGAIN THE CALL went to voicemail. Frank was unreasonably annoyed. Did this guy spend *any* time at home? It must be about six thirty in the morning. Where *was* he?

Absently, during the evening he dialled again and to his surprise the phone was answered by a girl with what seemed a very strong Australian accent. Frank realised that Des Raven probably spoke like that too.

'I was looking for Des Raven . . .' he began.

'You missed him, mate,' she said cheerfully.

'And who am I talking to?' Frank asked.

'I'm Eva. I'm house-sitting.'

'And when will he be back?'

'Three months. I'm walking his dog and looking after his garden.'

'Oh, and are you his girlfriend?'

'Who are *you*?' she asked with spirit.

'Sorry, I'm just a . . . friend . . . from Ireland.'

'Well, he's on his way to you, then.' Eva was pleased to have it all settled so easily. 'Probably there now. He knows where to find you.'

'He does?'

'Well, he left here with a briefcase full of papers and notes and letters. I think they were all from people he had written to who had written back.'

'Yes, yes, indeed . . .' Frank was miserable. The boy would have to get in touch through the hospital. He didn't know Frank's home address. He wished Des had sent a picture of himself, then he realised that Des didn't know what his father looked like either. What would Des Raven think of the father he had waited so long to meet?

WHEN IT HAPPENED it was curiously flat.

Miss Gorman, who had been hired by Frank ten years previously because she was not flighty, came in to see him. A man with an Australian accent was on the phone, wishing to talk to Mr Ennis on a personal matter.

He waited until she was off the line, then he asked, 'Des? Is that you?'

'So you *did* get my letter?' Very Australian but not very warm.

'Yes, I tried to call you but first it was the answering machine and then it was Eva. She told me that you had set out. I've been waiting for your call.'

'I nearly didn't ring . . .'

'Why was that? Was it nerves?' Frank asked.

'No, I thought, why bother? You don't want to be involved with me. You've made that clear.'

'That's *so* wrong,' Frank cried out, stung by the unfairness of this. 'I do indeed want to be involved with you. Why else would I have called you in Australia and talked to Eva? Why would I do that?'

Frank felt hollow. Somehow Clara had been right. He had paused when he should have gone enthusiastically forward. But that wasn't his nature.

'You probably thought I was coming to claim my inheritance,' Des said.

'It never crossed my mind. You said you wanted to get in touch. That's what I thought it was. I was as astonished as you. You know, I only just heard of your existence and now I'm delighted!'

'Delighted?' Des sounded unconvinced.

'Yes, sure, I was delighted.' Frank was stammering now. 'Des, will you come and have lunch with me today?'

'Where do you suggest?' Des asked.

Frank breathed out in relief. 'Depends what you'd like . . . this new place, Anton's, is talked about a lot. Will we say one o'clock?'

'Why *don't* we say one o'clock?' Des sounded faintly mocking.

'I'll tell you how to get there—' Frank began.

'I'll find it,' Des said and hung up.

Frank buzzed through to Miss Gorman. Could she kindly find him the number for Anton's restaurant? No, he would make the reservation himself. Perhaps she would cancel all appointments for the afternoon.

She called back with the number and Frank rang the restaurant.

'Can I speak to Anton Moran, please? . . . Mr Moran? Today I arranged to meet for the first time a son I never knew I had and I picked your restaurant. I am hoping you will be able to find me a table. I don't know where to contact my son . . . It will be such a messy start to our relationship if, when we meet, I have to tell him we couldn't get a booking.'

The man at the other end was courteous.

'This is far too important a matter to mess up,' he said gracefully. 'Of course you can have a table. Service today isn't full,' he added, 'but your story sounds so dramatic, and so obviously true, that I would have found a table for you even if I had to kneel down on all fours and pretend to be one.'

Frank smiled and suddenly he remembered Clara saying that he should be more immediate, more up front with people.

He was in the restaurant early. He watched the door and every time some man came in, who might be about twenty-five, his heart gave a lurch.

Then he saw him. He was so like Rita Raven that it almost hurt. Same little freckles on the nose, same thick fair hair and the same huge dark eyes.

Frank swallowed. The boy was talking to Teddy, the maître d', at the door. Then Teddy was leading him over to the table.

'Your guest, Mr Ennis,' he said and slipped away.

'Des!' he said and held out his hand.

The boy looked at him appraisingly. 'Well, well, well . . .' he said. He had ignored the hand that had been offered to him.

'You found the place,' Frank said foolishly. This was going to be much harder than he had thought.

NEAR THE KITCHEN DOOR Teddy spoke to Anton.

'I've had Lisa on the phone.'

'Not again.' Anton sighed.

'She wants to come in for a meal sometime when we are not too busy.'

'Try and head her off, will you, Teddy?' Anton said.

'Not easy . . .' Teddy said.

'Just buy me a week then. Tell her Wednesday of next week.'

'She does work her butt off for this place. I don't think we ever pay her anything.'

'Nobody asked her to slave.'

'WHAT'S WRONG, DES? What has changed? In your letter you were eager to meet . . . Why are you so different?'

'I didn't know the whole story. I didn't know what your family did.'

'What did they do?' Frank cried.

'As if you didn't know.'

'I don't know,' Frank protested.

'You don't fool me. I've got documents, receipts, signed forms—I know the whole story now.'

'You know more than I do,' Frank said. 'Who was writing these documents and filling in these forms?'

'My mother was a frightened girl of seventeen. Your father gave her a choice. She could leave Ireland for ever and she would get a thousand pounds. That's how much my life was worth. A miserable grand. And for this she was to sign an undertaking that she would never approach the Ennis family, claiming any responsibility for her pregnancy.'

'This can't be true!' Frank's voice was weak with shock.

'Why did you think she had gone away?'

'Her mother told me she had gone to America to stay with cousins.'

'Yes, that's the story they all put out.'

'But why shouldn't I believe them?'

'Because you weren't a fool. If you played according to their rules you were in a win-win situation. Troublesome girl, irritatingly pregnant, out of your hair, out of the country. Everything sorted. You leapt at the chance.'

'No, I didn't. I didn't know there was anything *to* sort out. I never knew until I got your letter that I had a child.'

'Pull the other one, Frank.'

'Where did you hear about my parents asking Rita to sign documents?'

'From Nora. Her sister. My aunt Nora. I went to see her in London and she told me everything.'

'She told you wrong, Des. Nothing like that ever happened.'

'You're not going to admit it now if you didn't then.'

'There was nothing to admit.'

'You never got in touch with her. You never wrote to her once.'

'I wrote to her in America every day for three months, but got no reply.'

'Didn't that ring any alarm bells?'

'No, it didn't. I asked her mother if she was forwarding the letters and she said she was.'

'And eventually you gave up?'

'Well, I was getting no response. And her mother said . . .' He stopped as if remembering something.

'Yes?'

'She said I should leave Rita alone. That she had moved on in life. She said the Ravens had done everything according to the letter of the law.'

'And you didn't know what she meant?' Des was not convinced.

'I hadn't an idea what she meant, but now I see . . . No, it couldn't be . . .'

'What couldn't be?'

'My parents—if you had known them, Des. Sex was never mentioned in our house. They would be incapable of any discussion about paying Rita off.'

'Did they like her?'

'Not particularly. They didn't like anyone who was distracting me from my studies and exams.'

'And her folks, did they like you?'

'No, same sort of reasons. Rita was skipping classes to be with me.'

'They thought you were a pig,' Des said.

'Surely not!' Frank was surprised at his calmness in the face of insult.

'That's what Nora says. She says you ruined everyone's life. You and your so-grand family. You broke them all up. Rita never came back from Australia because she had to swear not to. A perfectly decent family, minding its own business, ruined because of you and your snobbish family.'

Des looked very upset and very angry.

Frank knew he had to walk carefully. This boy had been so excited and enthusiastic about meeting him, now he was hostile and barely able to sit at the same table as the father he had crossed the world to meet.

'I *am* sorry. I didn't know *any* of it, Des. Not until I heard from you.'

'Do you believe me?'

'I believe that's what Nora said to you, certainly.'

'So you think *she* was lying?'

'No, I think she believes what she was told. My parents are dead now. Your mother is dead. We have no one to ask.'

He knew that he sounded weak and defeated.

But oddly Des Raven seemed to recognise the honesty in his tone. 'You're right,' he said, almost grudgingly. 'It's up to us now.'

Frank Ennis had seen the waiter hover near them and leave several times.

'Would you like something to eat, Des?'

'I'm sorry, I like to know who I am eating and drinking with.'

'Well, I don't know how well you'll get to know me . . . They say that I'm difficult and that I make a mess of things,' Frank said. 'That's what I'm told.'

'Who tells you that? Your wife?'

'No. I never married.'

Des was surprised. 'So no children then?'

'Apart from you, no.'

'I must have been a shock.'

Frank paused. He must not say the wrong thing here.

'It may sound odd and cold to you, Des, but my first reaction *was* shock. I couldn't believe that I had a child who had lived for a quarter of a century without my having an idea about it. I am a tidy, meticulous sort of person. This was like having my whole world turned upside-down. I had to think about it. That's what I do, Des, I think about things slowly and carefully.'

'Really?' Des sounded slightly scornful.

'Yes, really. I had to get my head round the fact that I had fathered a son. It takes someone like me a bit of time to get used to a new concept and as soon as I did I called you and you had already gone.'

'You must have been afraid what people would say when they found out?'

'No, I wasn't afraid of that. Not at all. I was proud to have a son. I would want people to know.'

'I don't think so . . . Big Catholic hospital manager having an illegitimate child. No, I can't see you wanting people to know. I bet you haven't told anyone about me yet.'

'You are *so* wrong, Des, I have indeed talked about you and said how excited I was to be going to meet you . . .'

At that moment Anton Moran appeared at their side.

'Mr Ennis,' he said, as if Frank was a regular customer. 'I was wondering, would you and your son like to try our lobster? It is this morning's catch, done very simply, with butter and a couple of sauces on the side.'

Anton looked from one to the other. A sudden silence had fallen between the two men. They were looking at each other dumbfounded.

'I'm sorry,' the younger man said.

'No, I'm sorry, Des,' said Frank. 'I'm sorry for all those years . . .'

Anton murmured that he would come back in a few moments. He would never know what was going on there, but they seemed to have turned a corner. At least they were talking and soon they were ordering food.

He looked over again and they were raising a glass of Hunter Valley Chardonnay to each other. That was a relief. As soon as he had mentioned the boy being the man's son, Anton had felt a twinge of anxiety.

Possibly he had been indiscreet? But no, it seemed to be working fine.

IT WAS THE LONG WEEKEND and everyone was going somewhere. The Lynches were taking Baby Frankie to the country for two nights. They had booked a bed-and-breakfast place outside Rossmore. There was a statue of St Anne and a holy well there; Josie and Charles were very interested in it.

Lisa Kelly was going to London. Anton was going to look at restaurants there and she was going to take notes. It would be wonderful. Frank Ennis said that he was going to take a bus tour. It would take in some of Ireland's greatest tourist attractions. He had someone he wanted to show Ireland to and this seemed to be the best way. It was certainly going to be interesting, he told Moira.

Emily said that she was going to see the West of Ireland for the first time. Dingo Duggan was going to drive the van, taking Emily and Declan's parents, Molly and Paddy Carroll, too. They would have a great time.

Dr Declan Carroll and his wife Fiona were taking Johnny to a seaside hotel. Fiona said that she was going to sleep until lunchtime both days. They had baby minders there to look after young children. It would be magical.

Most of Moira's colleagues were going away or else they were having parties or doing their gardens. Moira suddenly felt very much out of it as if she were on the side of things looking on. Why wasn't she going somewhere? The answer was only too clear. She had no friends.

She had never needed them in life—the job was too absorbing, and to do it right you needed to be on duty all hours of the day. But it was lonely and restless to see everyone else with plans for the weekend.

Moira announced that she was going to spend some of the long weekend by the sea. That's what she would do. She would sit beside the sea, go for a paddle maybe. It would calm her, soothe her.

OF COURSE IT DIDN'T really work. Moira did not become calm and mellow. The sun shone on her arms and shoulders but there was a breeze coming in from the sea at the same time and it felt too chilly. There were too many people who had decided their families must go to the seaside.

Moira studied them as she sat silently amid all the families who were calling out to each other on the beach.

To her surprise, a big man with a red face and an open-necked red shirt stopped beside her.

'Moira Tierney as I live and breathe!'

She hadn't an idea who he was. 'Um, hello,' she said cautiously.

He sat down beside her.

'God, isn't this beautiful to be out in the open air? We're blessed to live in a capital city that's so near the sea,' he said.

She still looked at him confused.

'I'm Brian Flynn. We met when Stella was in hospital and then again at the funeral and the christening.'

'Oh, *Father* Flynn. Yes, of course I remember. I just didn't recognise you in the . . . I mean without the . . .'

'A Roman collar wouldn't be very suitable for this weather.'

Brian Flynn was cheerful and dismissive. He was a man who rarely wore clerical garb at all, except when officiating at a ceremony.

'Do you ever feel that your work is hopeless, Father?' Moira asked him unexpectedly.

'No, I don't feel it's hopeless. I think we get things wrong from time to time. I mean, the Church does. It doesn't adapt properly. And I get things wrong myself, quite apart from the Church. But, to answer your question, no, I don't think it's all hopeless. I think we do *something* to help and I certainly see a lot that inspires me. I expect you do too?'

'I don't think I do, Father Flynn, truly I don't. I have a case load of unhappy people, most of them blaming their unhappiness on me.'

'I'm sure that's not true.'

'It *is* true, Father. And I know how there's an army of people lined up against me over that child who is being raised by an alcoholic . . .'

Brian Flynn's voice was a lot more steely now. 'Noel adds up to much more than being just an alcoholic, Moira. He has turned his life around to make a home for that child.'

'And that child will thank us all later for leaving her with a drunken, resentful father?'

'He loves his daughter very much. He's *not* a drunk. He's given it up.'

'Are you telling me, hand on heart, that Noel never strayed, never went back on the drink since he got Frankie?'

Brian Flynn couldn't lie. 'It was only once and it didn't last long,' he said.

Immediately he realised that Moira hadn't known.

'I hope you don't think I'm rude, Moira, but I have to . . . um . . . meet someone . . . um . . . further along here . . .'

'No, of course.'

Moira realised that there was less warmth in his face now. But then that was often the case in her conversations.

Father Flynn moved on. Moira gathered her things together and headed towards the station where a train would take her back into the city. She had been duped. They had even told that priest, who had nothing to do with the set-up. But they hadn't seen fit to tell the social worker assigned to the case.

LISA WAS BACK in Dublin. There had been some crossed wires in London. Lisa had thought that it was a matter of visiting restaurants and talking to various patrons. April had thought it was a PR exercise and had arranged several interviews for Anton on the Monday.

'They don't have a bank holiday in England this weekend, so it will be work as usual,' April had chirruped to them. 'Monday is an ordinary day in London and we can rehearse on Sunday.'

April's face was glowing with achievement and success. It would have been churlish and petty for Lisa not to enthuse. So she had appeared delighted with it all; she decided to get out with her pride intact.

She had loads to see to back in Dublin, she said casually, and saw, to her pleasure, that Anton seemed genuinely sorry to see her go. And now she was back in Dublin with nothing to do and nobody to meet.

As she let herself into Chestnut Court, she saw Moira in the courtyard talking to some of the neighbours. She was here to spy.

Lisa went out again and crossed the courtyard.

'Well, *hello*, Moira,' she said, showing great surprise.

The two middle-aged women that Moira had been interrogating shuffled with embarrassment. Lisa knew them both by sight. She nodded at them.

'Oh, Lisa . . . I thought you were away?'

'Well, yes, I was,' Lisa agreed, 'but I came back. And you? You were going away too?'

'I came back too,' Moira said. 'And are Noel and Frankie back as well?'

'I don't think so. I haven't been into the apartment yet.'

The women neighbours were busy making their excuses.

'Moira is our social worker,' Lisa explained to the fast-retreating neighbours. 'She's great. She drops in at the least expected times in case Noel and I are battering Frankie to death or starving her in a cage or something. So far she hasn't caught us out in anything, but of course time will tell.'

'You completely misunderstand my role, Lisa. I am there for Frankie.'

'We're all bloody there for Frankie,' Lisa said, 'which is something you'd realise if you saw us walking her up and down at night when she can't sleep.'

'Exactly,' Moira cried. 'It's too hard for you both. It's my role to see whether she would be better placed with a more conventional family.'

'But she's Noel's daughter!' Lisa said. 'I thought you people were all meant to be keeping the family together and that sort of thing.'

'Yes, but you are not family, Lisa. You're just a room-mate and Noel, as a father, is unreliable. We have to admit that.'

'I do *not* have to admit that!'

Lisa knew she looked like a fishwife with her hands on her hips, but this was too much. She began to list all that Noel had done and was doing.

Moira cut across her like a knife. 'In all this hymn of praise about Noel,' she said, 'you managed to forget that he went off the rails and was back on the drink. That was a situation where the baby was at risk and not one of you alerted me.'

'It was over before it began,' Lisa said. 'No point in alerting you and starting World War Three!'

Moira looked at her steadily for a moment. 'We are all on the same side,' she said eventually.

'No, we're not,' Lisa said. 'You want to take Frankie away. We want to keep her. How's that the same side?'

'We all want what is *best* for her.' Moira spoke as if to a slow learner.

'It's best for all of us if she stays with Noel, Moira.' Lisa sounded weary suddenly. 'She keeps him off the drink and keeps his head down at his studies so that he'll be a good, educated father for her when the time comes for her to know such things. And she keeps me sane too. I have a lot of worries and considerations in my life, but minding Frankie sort of grounds me. It gives it all some purpose, if you know what I mean.'

Moira sighed. 'I *do* know what you mean. You see, in a way, she does exactly the same for me. Minding Frankie is important to *me* too. I never had a chance as a child. I want her to have a start of some kind, not to get bogged down by a confused childhood like I did.'

Lisa was stunned. Moira had never admitted anything personal before.

'Don't talk to me about childhood! I bet mine could leave yours in the ha'penny place!' Lisa said in a chirpy voice.

'You don't feel like having supper tonight, do you?' Moira said. 'It's just that I'm a bit beaten and there seems to be nobody in town . . .'

Lisa ignored the gracelessness of the invitation. She didn't want to go back to the flat alone.

'Will we agree that Frankie is not on the agenda?' Lisa asked.

'Frankie who?' Moira said, with a strange lopsided look on her face.

Lisa realised that it was meant to be a smile.

THEY CHOSE TO GO to Ennio's trattoria. It was a family restaurant: Ennio cooked and greeted; his son Marco waited tables. Ennio had lived in Dublin for rather more than twenty years and was married to an Irish woman; he knew that to have an Italian accent added to the atmosphere.

Ennio welcomed Lisa and Moira with delight. He gave them huge red and white napkins, a drink on the house and the news that the cannelloni was like the food of angels. Moira started to unwind for the first time for a long time and raised her glass.

'Here's to us. We may have had a bad start but, boy, we're survivors!'

'Here's to surviving,' Lisa said.

Moira was a good listener. Lisa had to hand her that. She was sympathetic when she needed to be, shocked at the right times, curious about why Lisa's mother stayed in such a loveless home. She asked about Lisa's friends and seemed to understand exactly why she never had any. How could anyone bring a friend home to a house like that?

'Now you,' she said to Moira. 'Tell me what was so terrible.'

So Moira began. Every detail from the early days when she came home from school and there was nothing to eat, to her tired father coming in later and finding only a few potatoes peeled. She told it all without self-pity or complaint. Moira, who had kept her private life so very private, was able to speak to this girl because Lisa was even more damaged than she was.

Lisa listened and wished that someone—anyone—had ever said to Moira that there was a way of dealing with all this, that she should be glad for other people instead of appearing to triumph over their downfall. She might have to pretend at first, but soon it would become natural . . .

Chapter Eight

Emily had a wonderful weekend in the West with Paddy and Molly Carroll. Dingo Duggan had been an enthusiastic, if somewhat adventurous, driver. He seemed unable and unwilling to read a map and waved away Emily's attempts to find roads with numbers on them.

'Nobody could understand those numbers, Emily,' he had said. 'They'd do your head in. The main thing is to point west and head for the ocean.'

And they did indeed see beautiful places, such as the Sky Road, and they drove through hills where big mountain goats came down and looked hopefully at the car and its occupants as if they were new playmates come to entertain them. They spent evenings in pubs singing songs and they all said it had been one of the best outings they had ever taken.

Emily had told them about her plans to go to America for Betsy's wedding. The Carrolls were ecstatic; a late marriage, a chance for Emily to dress up and be part of the ceremony, two kindred souls finding each other.

Betsy, however, was having pre-wedding nerves. She'd met and hadn't liked her fiancé Eric's mother, she was disappointed with the grey silk outfit she had bought and her shoes were too tight. Could Emily please come a few days earlier or there might well be no wedding for her to attend?

Emily soothed her by email, but also examined the possibility of getting an earlier flight. Noel helped her sort through the claims and offers of airlines and they found one.

Emily emailed the good news to her friend Betsy; she would be there in three days' time. All would be well.

'I hope you won't want to move on again from here,' Noel said, when it was time to say goodbye.

'I'll wait until Frankie's raised and you've found yourself a nice wife.'

'I'll hold you to that,' Noel said.

He was very pleased. Emily didn't make promises lightly, but if she had to wait for him to find a nice wife . . . Emily might well be here for ever if she were waiting for that!

EVENTUALLY EMILY GOT AWAY. As the plane neared New York, she became excited at all that lay ahead. She tried to force the Irish cast of characters away from the main stage of her mind. She had to focus on Eric's mother and Betsy's dress, but images of the people of St Jarlath's Crescent kept coming back to her and she dropped off to sleep thinking about them all.

Then there she was in JFK. After collecting her luggage and clearing customs, Emily could see Eric and Betsy jumping up and down with excitement. They even had a banner. In uneven writing it said: *Welcome Home, Emily!*

How very odd that it didn't seem like home any more.

But home or not, it was wonderful.

EMILY TALKED to Eric's mother in a woman-of-the-world manner. She managed to convey the impression that Eric was very near his sell-by date and that he was very, *very* lucky that Betsy had been persuaded to consider him.

She sorted the shoes by insisting Betsy bought a pair in the correct size; she sorted the dull dress problem by taking the very plain grey dress to an accessories store and asking everyone's advice. Together, they chose a rose-pink and cream-coloured stole, which transformed it.

The wedding was splendid. Betsy's mother-in-law was charm personified. Betsy cried with happiness; Eric cried and said that this was the best day of his whole life; and Emily cried because it was all so marvellous.

When all the relations had gone home, the bride and groom set off with the maid of honour for Chinatown and had a feast. There would be no honeymoon yet, but a holiday in Ireland would certainly be on the cards before the end of the year.

Emily told them about some of the people they would meet. Eric and Betsy said they could hardly wait. It all sounded so intriguing. They wanted to go right out to Kennedy Airport and fly to Ireland at once.

ERIC AND BETSY, by now an established married couple, saw Emily off at the airport. They waved long after she had disappeared in the crush of people heading into Terminal 4. They would miss her, but they knew that soon she would be sitting on that Aer Lingus flight, resetting her mind and orientating herself towards Dublin again.

It sounded an insane place and it had certainly changed Emily. Normally so reserved and quiet, she seemed to have been seduced by a cast of characters who sounded as if they should be on an off-Broadway variety show . . .

IT WAS EARLY MORNING in Dublin when the transatlantic flight came in. As the crowd from the plane moved out through customs, Emily thought it would be nice if someone had come to meet her, but then who would have been able to?

Just as she came out into the open air, she saw a familiar figure; Dr Hat was standing there waving at her.

'I thought I'd come to meet you,' he said, taking one of her cases.

Emily was thrilled to see him.

'I'm in the short-stay car park,' he said, and led the way.

'It's so good to see you, Hat,' she told him as she settled into his car.

'I brought you a flask of coffee and an egg sandwich. Is that as good as America?' he asked.

'Oh, Hat, how wonderful to be home!' Emily said.

'We were afraid that you would stay out there and get married yourself.' Hat seemed very relieved this was not the case.

'I wouldn't do that,' Emily said, flattered that they had wanted her back. 'Now you can tell me all the news before I get back to St Jarlath's Crescent.'

'There's a lot of news,' Hat said.

'We've a lot of time.'

Emily settled back happily to listen.

It was mixed news.

The bad news was that Muttie had got a great deal worse. His prognosis, though not discussed in public, was no more than a couple of months. Lizzie seemed to find it difficult to take on board and was busy planning a trip to the sunshine. She was even urging the twins to speed up their plans to go to New Jersey—so that she and Muttie could come and visit—but Simon and Maud had started waiting tables at Ennio's . . . and Ennio's son Marco had been seen at the cinema with Maud.

Hat's other good news was that Baby Frankie was going from strength to strength. Emily didn't dare to ask, but Hat knew what she wanted to know.

'And Noel has been a brick. Lisa has been away, but he manages fine.'

'Which means that you help him too.' Emily looked at him gratefully.

'I love the child. She's no trouble.'

'Any more news?' Emily enquired.

'Well, you know the old lady who gave Charles the dog?'

'Mrs Monty, yes? Don't tell me she took Caesar away . . .'

'No. The poor lady died—rest in peace—but didn't she leave all her money to Charles!'

'Isn't that wonderful!' Emily cried.

'It is until you think how it's going to be spent . . .' Dr Hat said, drawing a halo round his head with his finger.

Charles and Josie were waiting for her at number 23; they were fussing over Frankie, who had a bit of a cold and was very fretful, not her usual sunny self. Emily was delighted to see her and lifted her up to examine her. Immediately, the child stopped grizzling.

'She's definitely grown so much in three weeks. Isn't she wonderful?'

She gave the baby a hug and was rewarded with a very chatty babble. Emily realised how much she had missed her. This was the child none of them had expected or, to be honest, really wanted at the start—and look at her now! She was the centre of their world.

Noel rang from work to make sure she really *had* returned and hadn't decided to relocate to New York.

Frankie was fine, he said. The nurse had said she was thriving. Lisa was away again. Oh yes, he had plenty of help. There was this woman called Faith at his lectures who had five younger brothers at home and had no time to study, so she had come to help Noel three evenings a week.

The evenings had slipped into an easy routine: bathtime, bottle, Frankie off to sleep, then revision papers and Internet notes to help them study. Faith sympathised deeply with Noel having to work in a place like Hall's: she was in a fairly dead-end office job but had great hopes that the diploma they were working for would make a difference.

She was a cheerful and optimistic woman of twenty-nine; she had dark curly hair, green eyes, a mobile face and a wide smile, and she loved walking. She showed Noel a great many places he had never known in his own city. She said she needed to walk a lot because it concentrated her mind. She had suffered a great blow: six years ago, her fiancé had been killed in a car accident just weeks before the wedding day. She had coped by walking alone and being very quiet, but recently she had felt the need to get involved with the world about her. That was one of the reasons she had joined the course at the college; and it was one of the reasons she had adapted so easily to Noel's demanding life.

LISA AND ANTON were at a Celtic food celebration in Scotland. They were looking into the possibility of twinning with some similar-type Scottish restaurant where they could do a deal whereby anyone who spent over a certain sum in Anton's could get a voucher for half this amount in the Scottish restaurant and vice versa. It would work because it was tapping into an entirely new market, mainly American.

It was Lisa's idea. She had special cards printed to show how it would work. The Scottish restaurant's name was a blank until the deal was done.

Several times Lisa felt rather than saw Anton's glance of approval, but she knew better now than to look at him for praise. Instead, she concentrated entirely on getting the work done. There would be time later over meals together. It was so cheering to be here with him and to know that April was miles away, not posturing and putting her small bottom in her skintight jeans on Anton's desk or the arm of his chair.

But then the trip was over and it was back to reality. Back to lectures in the college three nights a week, back to Frankie waking up all hours of the night, back to April, who was inching her way again into Anton's life.

MUTTIE LOOKED much more frail even after three weeks. His colour was poor and his face seemed to have hollows in it; his clothes hung off him. His good humour was clearly not affected though.

'Well . . . show us pictures of how the Americans do a wedding,' he said, putting on his spectacles.

'It's not very typical,' Emily explained. 'Fairly mature bride and maid of honour, for one thing.'

'The groom is no spring chicken either,' Muttie agreed.

'Look at the lovely clothes!' Lizzie was delighted with it all. 'And what are all these Chinese signs?'

'Oh, we went to Chinatown for dinner,' Emily said. 'Dozens and dozens of Chinese restaurants, Chinese shops and little pagodas and decorations everywhere.'

'That's where we'll go when we go to New York later on in the year. Emily will mark our card.'

'That's if I can ever get myself on the plane.' Muttie shook his head. 'I seem to have run out of puff, Emily. Hooves here wants me to take him up to have a drink with my Associates, but I find the walk exhausts me.'

'Do you get to see them at all?'

Emily knew how much Muttie loved talking horses to the men in the bar while Hooves sat with his head on Muttie's knee.

'Oh, Dr Hat is very good. And sometimes young Declan Carroll gets a fierce thirst on him and he drives me up there for a few pints.'

Emily knew very well that Declan Carroll would often pretend 'a fierce thirst' and get himself a pint or two of lemonade shandy when he drove his elderly neighbour up to the pub.

'And how are all the family?' Emily enquired.

As she had expected, they all seemed to be planning sudden visits to Ireland from Chicago, or from Sydney, Australia. Muttie was shaking his head at the coincidence of it all.

'I don't know where they get the money, Emily, I really don't. I mean, there's a recession out in those places as well as here.'

'And the twins? Busy as ever?'

'Oh, Maud and Simon are wonderful. There's less chat about their going to New Jersey, but then again Maud has an Italian boyfriend—a really polite, respectful, young man called Marco. They're all setting up this phone for us where you can see the person at the other end. This weekend we'll be calling my daughter Marian in Chicago and we'll see her and all her family. I don't understand it at all.'

'Amazing thing, technology,' Emily agreed.

EMILY WENT to the thrift shop and found Lisa in a corner sighing over her notes. There were no customers.

'Go back to Chestnut Court and study properly, Lisa,' Emily said, taking off her coat. 'I'll do the pricing on the new clothes that have come in. Otherwise you and I will waste the morning and not a penny will be raised for St Jarlath.'

'Thanks, Emily. You're amazing. If I'd come back from America, I'd be on all fours rather than going straight in to work. I'm nearly a basket case and I was only in Scotland!'

'Ah well, you were probably much more active on your holiday than I was on mine,' Emily said.

Rather than work out what Emily might have in mind, Lisa left. As she walked up the road towards her bus-stop she thought about Scotland. They had stayed in five different hotels and in every one of them Anton and she had made love. Twice in the place where they had the honeymoon suite. Why did Anton not miss this and want her to stay with him every night? He had kissed her goodbye when they got to Dublin Airport and said it had been great. Why did he use the past tense? It could all have continued when they were back home. It was meant to continue.

He had said he loved her—four times—two of them were sort of jokey when she had got things right about various hotels and restaurants, but twice when they were making love. And so he must have meant it, because who would say something like that at such an intense time and not mean it?

AT NUMBER 23 St Jarlath's Crescent, Josie and Charles Lynch sat in stunned silence. They had just closed the door behind a very serious lawyer in a pin-stripe suit. He had come to tell them exactly how much they had inherited from the late Meriel Monty. When all the assets were liquidated, the estate would come, the lawyer said very slowly, to a total of approximately 289,000 euros.

EMILY LYNCH WAS shopping for vegetables in the market; she had promised Dr Hat she would teach him how to make a vegetarian curry for his friend Michael who was coming to visit.

'Could you not just . . . er . . . make it for me?' Dr Hat begged.

'No way! I want you to be able to tell Michael how you made it.' She was very firm.

'Emily, *please*. Cooking is women's business.'

'Then why are the great chefs mainly male?' she asked mildly.

'Show-offs,' said Dr Hat mutinously. 'It won't work. I'll burn everything.'

'Don't be ridiculous—we'll have a great time chopping things up—you'll be making this recipe every week.'

'I doubt it,' said Dr Hat. 'I seriously doubt it.'

IT WAS MOIRA'S BIRTHDAY on Friday. It was a sad person who had nobody to celebrate with. Nobody at all. Yet again her thoughts went back to that pleasant evening at Ennio's restaurant. She had felt normal for once.

What would Lisa say if Moira asked her to have a meal with her—except that she wasn't free? Nothing would be lost. She would go round to Chestnut Court now.

'God Almighty, it's Moira *again*!' Lisa said when she had put down the entryphone and buzzed her in. 'What can she want now?'

Noel looked around the flat nervously in case there was something that could be discovered, something that would be a black mark against them.

He continued spooning the purée into Frankie, who enjoyed it mainly as a face-painting activity and something to rub into her hair.

Moira arrived in a grey trouser-suit and sensible shoes. She looked businesslike, but then she was always businesslike.

'Will you have a cup of tea?' Noel asked her.

Moira had taken in the domestic scene at a glance: the child was being well cared for. Anyone could see that. She saw the books and note files out for their studies. These were her so-called hopeless clients; a family at risk, not fit to be minding Frankie, and yet they seemed to have got their act together much better than Moira had.

'I had a tiring day today,' she said unexpectedly.

If the roof had blown off the apartment block, Noel and Lisa could not have been more surprised. Even Frankie looked up startled.

Moira never complained about her workload. She was tireless in her efforts to impose some kind of order on a mad world. This was the very first time she had even given them a hint that she might be human.

'What kind of things were most tiring?' Lisa asked politely.

'Frustration mainly. I know this couple who are desperate for a baby. They would provide a great home, but can they get one? Oh no, they can't. People can ignore babies, harm them, take drugs all around them and that's perfectly fine as long as they are kept with the natural parent. We are meant to be proud of this because we have kept the family unit intact . . .'

Noel found himself involuntarily holding Frankie closer to him.

'Not you, Noel,' Moira said wearily. 'You and Lisa are doing your best.'

This was astounding praise. Lisa and Noel looked at each other in shock.

'I mean, it's a hopeless situation, but at least you're keeping to the rules,' Moira admitted grudgingly.

Noel and Lisa smiled at each other in relief.

Then Moira delivered the final shock.

'It was actually about my social life that I called in,' she said. 'I'm going to be thirty-five on Friday and I was hoping, Lisa, you might join me for supper at Ennio's . . .'

'Me? Friday? Oh heavens. Well, that's very kind of you, Moira. Will there be many people there to celebrate your birthday?'

'Oh, just the two of us,' Moira said, and she gathered herself up and left.

Noel and Lisa didn't dare to speak until she had left the building.

'Why did she ask me to dinner?' Lisa said.

'She may be going mad,' Noel said thoughtfully.

Lisa had been thinking exactly the same thing. 'Why do you say that?'

'Well . . .' Noel spoke slowly and deliberately, 'it's a very odd thing to do. No one normal would invite you to dinner. You of all people.'

She looked up at him and saw he was smiling.

'Yes, you're right, Noel. The woman's lonely. That's all.'

'I was wondering . . .' Noel paused. 'I was thinking of inviting Faith to dinner. You know, to thank her for the notes and everything.'

'Oh yes?' Lisa said.

'I wonder would Friday be a good night? You'll probably be out late, hitting the clubs with Moira. I'd feel safer having a meal here. It's such a temptation to order a bottle of wine or have a cocktail in a restaurant.'

Noel rarely spoke of his alcoholism at home. He went to meetings and there was no drink in the flat. It was unusual for him to bring the subject up.

He must be interested in Faith. And it was obvious to everyone except Noel that Faith fancied him.

'That's a great idea. I'll do a salad for you before I go out and maybe you could cook that chicken in ginger you do sometimes. It's very impressive. And we'll make sure to iron the tablecloth and napkins.'

'It's only Faith. It's not a competition,' Noel protested.

'But you want her to realise you've gone to some trouble to entertain her?'

He realised with a shock that this was the first date he had planned in years.

'And in return you have to help me think of a present for Moira. Not too dear. I'm broke!'

'Ask Emily to look out something from the thrift shop for you. She finds great things—new things, even.'

'That's an idea.' Lisa brightened. 'Well, Frankie, social life around here is getting very lively. You're going to be hard pushed to keep up with us . . .'

FRIDAY EVENTUALLY CAME. Emily had found a small mother-of-pearl brooch as a gift for Lisa to give Moira. She couldn't help but like that.

Anton had laughed when Lisa said she was going to Ennio's with Moira.

'That should be a bundle of fun,' he had said dismissively.

'It will be fine,' she said, suddenly feeling defensive.

'If you want cheapo pasta, a bottle of plonk and a couple of Italians bunching up their fingers to kiss them and say "*bella signora*" . . .'

'They're nice there.'

'Are you coming round later?' he asked. 'It's Teddy's birthday too and we're having a few drinks after closing time.'

'Oh no, we'll be hitting the clubs by then.'

She had remembered Noel's expression. It was worth it to see the look of surprise and irritation on Anton's face.

Noel set the table at Chestnut Court. Lisa had left the salad in the fridge, and his chicken and ginger dish was under foil and ready to put in the oven for twenty-five minutes. The potatoes were in a saucepan.

Lisa had delivered Frankie to Declan and Fiona's: she was going to have a sleepover.

'Dada,' she had said as Noel had waved her goodbye and his heart had turned over as it always did when she smiled at him.

Now he was back in the apartment, waiting for a woman to come to supper, just as someone normal would do.

LISA HAD LOOKED very well as she set out to the birthday celebration. It was so comforting to know that Anton was jealous, that he really thought she would go to a nightclub.

At Ennio's the host was waiting for them. '*Che belle signore!*' he said. '*Marco, vieni qui, una tavola per queste due bellissime signore.*'

The son of the house bustled towards them and dusted chairs. Moira and Lisa thanked him profusely.

Lisa spotted that Maud was working there that night and Marco saw Lisa recognise her.

'I think you know my friend and colleague, Maud,' he said proudly.

'Yes, indeed I do, she's a lovely girl,' Lisa said. 'And you remember Moira Tierney who chose the restaurant for her birthday celebration?'

'Moira Tierney . . .' Marco repeated. 'Yes, and Maud has mentioned your name to me, too.'

Written all over his face was the fact that the mention had perhaps not been the most cordial, but he struggled to remember his job of welcoming guests and handed them the menus.

EMILY WENT to Dr Hat's house to check that he had his curry ready for his friend Michael. To her surprise the table was set for three.

'Will his wife be with him?' Emily asked, surprised. Only Michael had been mentioned up to now.

'No, Michael never married. Another crusty old bachelor,' Dr Hat said.

'So who is the third person?'

'I was rather hoping that *you* would join us,' he said hesitantly.

PADDY AND MOLLY CARROLL were going to the annual butchers' dinner. It was an occasion where Paddy had been known to over-imbibe, so Declan would drive them to the hotel and a taxi would take them home.

Fiona waved them off, then sat down with a big mug of tea to watch over Frankie and Johnny crawling around the floor before she had to settle them in their cots. They were both a bit restless this evening and she was going to have to separate them if they were going to go to sleep.

She was wondering if she might possibly be pregnant again. If she were it would be great and Declan would be so pleased, but it would mean that they would have to stir themselves and make sure the house was ready for them to move into before the baby was born. They couldn't put Paddy and Molly through all that business of a crying baby again.

UP IN CHESTNUT COURT the dinner was going very well.

'Aren't you a dark horse, being able to cook like this!' Faith said appreciatively. She was easy to talk to, not garrulous, but she chatted engagingly of her background. She spoke briefly about the accident that had killed her fiancé, but she didn't dwell on it. Terrible things happened to a lot of people. They had to pick themselves up.

'Where is Frankie now?' she asked. 'I brought her a funny little book of animals. It's made of cotton, so it doesn't matter if she eats it!'

'Lisa dropped her in to Fiona and Declan's on her way out to supper.'

'With Anton?'

'No, with Moira, actually.'

'A different kind of outing, certainly.' Faith knew the cast of characters.

'You could say that,' Noel beamed at her. This was all going so well.

FIONA HAD JUST brought Declan a mug of coffee when she heard running feet outside the door.

Outside was Lizzie, dishevelled and distraught.

'Can Declan come quickly? Muttie's been sick and it's all blood!'

Declan was already out of his chair and grabbing his doctor's bag.

'I'll come in a minute—I'll have to sort out the kids,' Fiona shouted.

'Fine.'

In seconds Declan was through the Scarlets' front door. Muttie was ashen-faced, and he had been vomiting into a bowl. Declan took in the scene at a glance.

'Muttie, they'll have you as right as rain in the hospital.'

'Couldn't you deal with it, Declan?'

'No, they're fierce for the backup. They'd be suing me left and right.'

'But it will take for ever to get an ambulance,' Muttie objected.

'We're going in my car. Get in there right now,' Declan said firmly.

Lizzie wanted to go with them, but Declan persuaded her to wait for Fiona. He took her back inside the house and whispered that as the hospital might need to keep Muttie in overnight, the best thing was for her to go and pack a small bag for him. Fiona would bring Lizzie up to the hospital in a taxi, and not to worry, he would make sure that Muttie was in safe hands.

By now, Fiona had arrived, and they quickly realised that they had to find somewhere for Johnny and Frankie to spend the evening. Noel was having the first real date of his life; his parents were away. Lisa had gone out with Moira—which at least would keep the social worker out of their hair; Emily would be the one to call on. Leaving Fiona to make the arrangements, Declan sped off with Muttie beside him looking pale and frightened.

MICHAEL PROVED to be a quiet, thoughtful man. He asked Emily questions about her past life. It was as if he were checking her out for his old friend Hat. She hoped that she was giving a good account of herself. Hat was such a good and pleasant companion, she would hate to lose his friendship.

She was surprised when her phone rang in the pocket of her jacket as they were at the dining table. She wasn't expecting any calls.

'Emily, big crisis. Can you do baby patrol?' Fiona sounded frightened.

Emily didn't hesitate. 'Certainly, I'm on my way!'

She quickly excused herself and hastened down the road.

Outside the Carrolls' house all was confusion. Lizzie was there crying and clutching a small suitcase; Declan had taken Muttie to hospital. The taxi was on its way for Fiona and Lizzie.

'I'm going up to the hospital with Lizzie to be with her while we wait for news of Muttie,' Fiona said as soon as Emily arrived.

'Can I move baby patrol up to Dr Hat's house? I'm sort of in the middle of a meal there.'

'Of course, Emily. I'm so sorry. I didn't mean to interrupt . . .'

'No, it's fine, don't worry. Two crusty old bachelors and myself. This will lower the age level greatly. Good luck—and let us know . . .'

'Right,' Fiona said, as the taxi pulled up outside the house. She bundled Lizzie into the back of the car. 'Emily, key under the usual flowerpot.'

'Go now,' Emily ordered.

She ran to the Carrolls' house and picked Johnny up out of his cot in the front room and fastened him into his buggy.

'We're going for a visit to Uncle Hat and Auntie Emily,' she said. She pushed the baby buggy out of the door, locked it behind her and then put the key back carefully under the flowerpot.

Dr Hat and Michael were suitably impressed with young Johnny. The little boy, exhausted from the journey, fell asleep on Dr Hat's sofa and was covered with a blanket. The meal continued seamlessly.

Hat admitted, when he produced dessert, that he had not made the meringues himself but had bought them in a local confectionery shop.

'I think he'd have got away with saying he made them himself, don't you, Michael?' said Emily.

Michael was flushed with wine and good humour. 'I'd have believed anything Hat were to tell me tonight.' He beamed at them. 'Never saw such a change in a person. If that's what retirement did for you, Hat, then lead on,

I say. And I do admire the way you all look after these children. It was never like that in our day, people were stressed and fussed and never believed that anyone else could look after a child for more than two minutes.'

'Ah, they have it down to a fine art,' Dr Hat said proudly. 'Whenever Johnny and Frankie need a minder, they're all here on tap.'

'Frankie?' Michael asked.

Emily said, 'She's my cousin Noel's daughter. He's bringing her up as a single father. Actually Noel has a date tonight. All of us have great hopes of this girl Faith. He's entertaining her in his own apartment.'

'And so Faith is meeting the baby tonight?' Michael asked.

'No, she knows the child already, she goes in to study there, you see. But the baby is out for the night to give them a bit of space, I think.'

'So who's minding Frankie tonight?' Michael asked.

His question was innocent—he was fascinated by this Toy Town atmosphere with Good Samaritans coming out of every house in the street.

Emily stopped to think. 'It can't be Lisa. She's going out with Moira. The Carrolls have gone to a butchers' dinner. Noel's parents, my uncle Charles and aunt Josie are in the West . . . Who *is* minding Frankie?'

Emily felt the first constriction of alarm in her chest.

'If you'll excuse me, I'll call Noel,' she said, 'just to set my mind at rest.'

'Noel, I'm so sorry,' she began.

'Is anything wrong, Emily?' He was alert to her tone immediately.

'No, nothing. I was just checking something. Where is Frankie tonight?'

'Lisa took her down to Fiona and Declan's earlier. I'm having a friend to dinner. Is everything all right, Emily?'

'Everything's fine, Noel,' she said and hung up immediately. 'You two mind Johnny here. I must have left Frankie in the Carrolls' house. There was only one baby in the cot.'

She was out of the door before they could ask any more. Emily ran down St Jarlath's Crescent at a greater speed than she had known to be possible. What had Fiona said? She hadn't said 'babies'. She had said 'baby patrol'.

Her hand shook as she reached under the flowerpot for the key and opened the door.

'Frankie?' she called as she ran into the house. There was no sound.

In the kitchen there was a second cot with some of Frankie's toys in it. Frankie's buggy was parked beside it. There was no sign of the child. The strength left Emily's legs and she sat down on a kitchen chair to support herself. Someone had let themselves in and taken Frankie. How could this have happened? Then the thought struck her. Of course! Fiona had come back home to check on things. Yes, that must be it.

She ran to Muttie and Lizzie's house. It was dark and closed. She knew before she started hammering on the door that there was no one in.

Now she was really frightened. She dialled Fiona's mobile number. As the number connected, she heard a phone start to ring from inside the Scarlets' house. It was Fiona's ringtone. After a few seconds the ringing stopped and she heard the voicemail message start.

Declan. She had to call Declan.

'Emily?' he said. 'Is everything all right? Is it the children?'

'Johnny's fine,' she said immediately. 'He's asleep on Dr Hat's sofa.'

'And Frankie?' Declan sounded alarmed. 'What about Frankie?'

But Emily had already started running.

Chapter Nine

They tried to be methodical about it but panic overwhelmed them; the list was checked over and over.

Signora and Aidan knew nothing about the child, but would join in any searches. It would be ages before Paddy and Molly would be home.

Who could have come into the house and spirited Frankie away? She couldn't have got out herself and Emily had been back into the house and searched the place from top to bottom. Anywhere, any small space a child might be able to crawl into—she must be here somewhere. But she wasn't.

Could somebody have been watching the house? It seemed less than possible and there was no sign of a break-in. There must be a rational explanation. Should the police be called? Having left Faith in the flat to answer any calls, Noel ran in and out of all the houses in St Jarlath's Crescent. Had anyone seen anything? Anything at all?

NOEL HAD SENT Lisa a text and asked her to call him from the ladies', out of Moira's earshot. Lisa was shocked at how frightened she felt when she heard the news. For the time being, she was *not* to come home. It didn't matter where she went, as long as she kept Moira occupied. She felt sure that Moira must be able to tell something was wrong; nailing a smile onto her face, she went back to the table.

UP AT THE HOSPITAL, Lizzie wandered up and down the corridors, asking plaintively when she was going to be able to see how Muttie was getting on. Fiona persuaded her to come back into the waiting room and sit down. They would wait for Declan to come.

He arrived twenty minutes later.

'Well, he's stable now but they're going to keep him in for a while.' His voice was grim. 'They've made him comfortable and he's sleeping,' he said to Lizzie. 'You'll probably not be able to speak to him until tomorrow but he should feel better after a good night's rest. We should all go home.'

Lizzie was pleased with the news. 'I'm glad he's getting a good rest. I'll leave his suitcase in for him for tomorrow.'

'Do that, Lizzie,' Fiona said, realising that there was something Declan hadn't told her. Could this night get any worse?

NOEL WAS ALMOST out of his mind with grief and worry and rage—what were those idiotic women doing, risking his daughter's safety like that? How could they be so stupid as to abandon her in that house, leaving her prey to—who knew what?

And as for him—it was all his own fault. Stella had trusted him with their daughter and he'd let her down, all because he'd wanted to spend some time with a woman. Now some monster, some pervert had taken his little girl and he might never see her again. He might never hold her in his arms and see her smile. He might never hear her voice calling him 'Dada'. . . If anyone had hurt her, if anyone had touched a hair of his Frankie's head . . .

LISA DECIDED to persuade Moira to go to Teddy's birthday party at Anton's.

'But I won't know anyone,' Moira had wailed.

'Neither will I. Most of them will be strangers to me—friends of April—but come on, Moira, it's free drink and it's your birthday too. Why not?'

And as Moira agreed, Lisa dragged herself together. She wished that she was at home with Noel helping to coordinate the search. There *must* be an explanation. Lisa had heard very little except a trembling hysteria from Noel about what could have happened.

SERGEANT SEAN O'MEARA had seen it all and done it all and, if he were honest, he would say that most of it was fairly depressing, but this occasion was just bizarre.

An extremely drunk man called Paddy Carroll had explained over and over that he had been at a butchers' dinner and someone had spiked his drinks. He had started to behave foolishly and so he agreed that his wife take him home in a taxi. The wife, a Mrs Molly Carroll, said that she had been delighted when her husband agreed to come home with her as her feet were killing her. But when they got home, they were bemused to find Frankie sitting on her own in the cot and their own family nowhere to be found.

They had tried to contact several people, but hadn't been able to speak to anyone who might know what was going on. They'd tried to find the child's father, Noel Lynch, but had arrived at his apartment block not knowing which flat he lived in. What sort of people don't put their names on door-bells? asked Paddy Carroll, accusingly. So what were they to do?

'So, you want us to find this Noel Lynch. Is that it?' Sergeant O'Meara had asked. 'Had you ever thought of ringing him?' And he had handed a phone to Paddy Carroll, who had suddenly looked even more confused.

FAITH PERCHED NERVOUSLY beside the phone in Chestnut Court, trying not to jump when it rang. They had agreed that if Frankie were not found within the hour, Faith would call the Guards. There wasn't long to go.

She checked her watch again. It was time. She had to call the police. Hand shaking, she reached for the phone and as she did so, it rang. Anxiously she answered. The man's voice on the other end of the phone sounded muffled and incoherent and she realised he might be drunk.

No, Noel wasn't there he was . . . No, his daughter was missing and the police were about to be called . . .

'But that's what I'm telling you,' the voice said. 'I've got his daughter here. She's with us now . . .'

And suddenly Faith heard the unmistakable sound of Frankie crying.

'SHE'S *FOUND*, NOEL! Not a hair of her head touched,' Faith said. 'She's great. She's asking for her daddy.'

'Have you seen her? Is she there with you?'

'No. They brought her to the Garda Station. It was Paddy and Molly Carroll. It was *all* a misunderstanding. They were looking for *you*.'

'What the hell did they mean by that? What do you mean, *looking for me*? We were in all night!' Noel was torn between relief and fury.

'No, it's all right, don't get angry. They got enough of a shock already.'

'*They* got a shock! What about the rest of us? What happened?'

'They came home early from their do and they found her in the cot alone in the house. They called on all the neighbours, but there was no one around. They tried to call Fiona, but she'd left her phone at Lizzie's. Declan's phone was busy, so they came to Chestnut Court to see you. Only by the sound of it they'd got the wrong flat number. By the time we knew Frankie was missing they were on their way to the Guards. She's fine and we need to get over there to pick her up.'

But Noel was still distraught. 'Frankie's in a police station. What chance will I have of keeping her once bloody Moira gets to hear of this?'

'Don't worry—I'll call Lisa as soon as I put the phone down and let her know Frankie is found. Then I'll put together some things for Frankie—why don't you collect me here and we'll go up together? Let's get her home before Moira ever knows she was missing . . .'

SERGEANT O'MEARA had no idea what they were all doing in a police station and he wished someone, anyone, would shut the screaming child up.

'Why *exactly* did you bring the child here, if you know who she is?'

Paddy tried to explain. 'It seemed like the right thing to do at the time.'

'So this Noel Lynch is on his way now, right?' Sergeant O'Meara asked wearily.

'There he is!' Paddy Carroll cried out, pointing at the glass door out into the front office. 'There he is! Noel! Noel! Come in here! We've got Frankie!'

'Frankie! Are you all right?' Noel cried, his voice muffled with emotion. 'Darling little Frankie. I'm so sorry, really I am. I'll never leave you again . . .'

Frantically, he checked that she was all right, uninjured in any way; then he wiped her face, her nose, and dried her eyes.

Behind him, meanwhile, stood a small, slim woman with green eyes and a big smile. She was carrying one of Frankie's coats and a jar of baby food, which she handed to Noel straight away.

As Noel fed his daughter, almost magically the crying stopped, the baby calmed down and peace was restored.

More and more people were arriving: a stressed-out woman with frizzy hair and a man wearing a hat like something from a black-and-white movie.

'Oh, Frankie! I'm so sorry . . .' The woman bent down to kiss the baby girl. 'I didn't know you were there. I will never forgive myself. *Never*.'

The man in the hat introduced himself as Dr Hat. 'If ever there was a case of all's well that ends well . . . it's here.' He beamed at everyone. 'And well done, Mr and Mrs Carroll. You did exactly the right thing in the circumstances. Noel, we'll all get out of here and leave Sergeant O'Meara to his business. No need to write a report at all—wouldn't you agree?'

The sergeant looked at Dr Hat gratefully. The writing of a report about this was going to be Gothic.

MUTTIE WAS ASLEEP when Lizzie arrived at his bedside. They told her that he would need a scan in the morning but that he was comfortable now; far better for her to be at home and get a good night's sleep. She left the suitcase for him beside his bed.

Lizzie pinned a note to the suitcase.

Muttie, my darling, I've gone home but I'll be back tomorrow. You're going to be fine. The next time we use this suitcase will be when we go to New York and have dinner in Chinatown.

Love from Lizzie

She felt better, she told Declan, now that she had written a letter.

His relief at the safe return of Frankie was tempered by what he had just discovered: he had spoken to the medical team that had examined Muttie. The cancer had spread all over his body.

It would not be long now.

LISA THOUGHT that the night would never end. Teddy's party at Anton's was in full swing when they got there. They had just put on music and people were beginning to dance. Lisa noticed April dancing round Anton.

'Hey, that's not dancing! That's lap dancing!' she called in a very loud voice. A few people laughed. Anton looked annoyed.

April went on weaving and squirming. 'Suit yourself,' she said to Lisa. 'You dance your way—I dance mine.'

Lisa, her rage fuelled by alcohol and jealousy, was about to engage in further conversation, but Moira interrupted quickly.

'I need a glass of water, Lisa. Can you come and get one with me?'

'You don't need water,' Lisa said.

'Oh, but I do,' Moira countered, pushing her towards the ladies' room. There she took a glass of water and offered it to Lisa.

'You're not expecting me to drink this, are you?'

'I think you should, then we'll go home.'

Lisa was only just holding herself together. Moira must never know Frankie was missing.

Moira spoke firmly. 'I'll phone us a taxi.'

'No, we can't go home. Wherever we go, we can't go home!' Lisa said.

Moira asked mildly, 'Well, where *do* you want to go then?'

'I'll think,' Lisa promised.

Just then her phone buzzed with a text message. Trembling, she read it. '*All clear. Come home any time. F safe and sound.*'

'They *found* her!' Lisa cried.

'Who?' Moira paused in the middle of talking to the taxi firm.

Lisa stopped herself in time. 'My friend Mary! She was lost and now she's found!' she shouted, with a very unfocused look on her face.

Moira began to help Lisa towards the exit.

On the way, they passed Teddy, the birthday boy, who whispered in Moira's ear, 'Well done. Anton will owe you for this. We have an unexploded bomb here,' he said, nodding towards Lisa.

'Well, it's a pity he wasn't able to do something about it!' Moira retorted.

'Not his problem.' Teddy shrugged.

'Good enough to sleep with, but not important enough to be nice to, right?'

'I just said he'd be grateful to you. She was about to make a scene.'

Moira pushed past him, supporting Lisa into the taxi. Her dismal outlook on men seemed to have been confirmed tonight.

WHEN SHE GOT HOME, Lizzie was surprised to see so many people in her house. Her sister Geraldine was there; her daughter Cathy; and Cathy's husband, Tom Feather. The twins and Marco were there, and there were constant phone calls coming in from Chicago and Australia. Everyone seemed to be making tea and Marco had provided a tray of cakes.

'Won't Muttie be disappointed to have missed all this,' Lizzie said, and people looked away before she could see the pain in their faces.

They finally persuaded her to go to bed. Cathy went upstairs with her mother and tried to reassure her.

'They're terrific in St Brigid's, Mam, don't be worrying about him. All the best consultants and everything. They'll have Da right in no time.'

'I think he's very sick,' Lizzie said.

'But he's in the right place,' Cathy said, for the twentieth time.

'He'd prefer to be in his own home,' Lizzie said, for the thirtieth time.

'And he will be, Mam, so you're to get to sleep so that you'll be up and ready for him when he *does* come home. You're asleep on your feet.'

That worked. Lizzie made a slight movement towards the bed and Cathy had her nightdress ready. Her mother looked so small and frail; Cathy wondered would she be able to bear all that lay ahead.

IT WAS CLEAR that Muttie wanted to go home so they contacted the Palliative Care Team. Two nurses would visit him each day.

After three days he was sent home, much to the delight of everyone. Two of Muttie and Lizzie's children, Mike and Marian, together with Marian's husband Harry, had come from Chicago, which shocked Muttie.

Much as Lizzie and Cathy wanted to keep him to themselves, with only the family around him, Muttie did seem to blossom when friends, neighbours and his six Associates from the pub called. Hooves sat at his feet most of the time. The dog had stopped eating and lay in his basket listlessly.

Cathy and Lizzie provided endless cups of tea as a file of people passed through each day. They called to talk to him and were given fifteen minutes at the most. And they came in their droves, first asking Lizzie what would be a good time. She kept a notebook on the hall table.

Hooves died during the night and even though they had tried to keep it from Muttie, he had known there was something wrong. Eventually, they had to tell him.

'Hooves was a great dog, we won't demean him by crying over him,' Muttie said.

'Right,' Lizzie agreed. 'I'll tell the others.'

Noel came and brought Frankie. As Frankie sat on Muttie's knee and offered him her sippy cup, Noel talked more openly than he did to anyone. He told Muttie about the terrible fright when Frankie had been lost.

'You've made a grand job of this little girl,' Muttie said approvingly.

'I sometimes dream that she's not my little girl at all and that someone comes to take her away,' Noel confessed, taking the child.

'That will never happen, Noel.'

'Wasn't I lucky that Stella contacted me. If she hadn't, then Frankie would be growing up in a different place and she'd never know any of you.'

'And wasn't she lucky that she got you,' Muttie said.

'You're a great fellow, Muttie,' Noel said unexpectedly.

'I'm not the worst,' Muttie agreed, 'but haven't I a great family around me. I'm luckier than anyone I ever heard of.'

Muttie's smile was broad at the thought of it all.

KATIE SIGHED when Lisa came into the salon. The place was already full. Had she never heard of the appointment system?

'I need something, Katie,' Lisa said.

'It will be half an hour at least,' Katie said.

'I'll wait.' Lisa was unexpectedly calm and patient.

Katie glanced at her from time to time. Lisa had magazines in her lap, but she never looked at them. Her eyes and mind were far away.

Then Katie was ready. 'Big date?' she asked.

'No. Big conversation, actually.'

'With Anton?'

'Who else?'

'You'd want to be careful, Lisa.' Katie was concerned.

'I've been careful for years and where has it got me?'

Lisa sat looking, without pleasure, at her reflection in the mirror. Her pale face and wet hair showed up the dark circles under her eyes.

'We'll make you lovely,' said Katie.

'It would help if I looked a bit lovelier all right.' Lisa smiled weakly. 'Listen, I want you to cut it all off. I want very short hair, cropped short all over.'

'You're out of your mind, you've always had long hair. Don't do anything reckless.'

'I want it short, choppy, a really edgy style. Will you do it?'

'I'll do it, but you're going to wish you hadn't asked me to.'

'Not if you give me a good cut, I won't.'

'But you said he liked you with long hair,' Katie persisted.

'Then he'll have to like me with short hair,' Lisa countered.

LISA WALKED purposefully towards Anton's. This was a good time to catch him. The afternoons were easier and less fussed.

Teddy saw her coming in. 'Fasten your seat belts,' he hissed at Anton.

'Oh God, not today, not on top of everything else . . .' Anton groaned.

When Lisa came in, she looked well and she knew it. She walked confidently and had a big smile on her face. She knew they were looking at her, Anton and Teddy, registering shock at the difference in her. The short hair gave her confidence. She smiled from one to the other.

'Ah, coffee . . .' she said, apparently delighted. 'Teddy, will you forgive me, I have to talk to Anton about something for a short while?'

Teddy looked at Anton, who shrugged. So Teddy left.

'Well, Lisa, what is it? You look terrific, by the way.'

'Thank you so much, Anton. How terrific do I look?'

'Well, you look very different, still gorgeous but different.'

'Good, so you like what you see?'

'This is silly, Lisa. Of course I like it. I like you. You're my friend.'

'Friend—not *love*?'

'Oh well, love. Whatever . . .' He was annoyed now.

'Good, because I love you. A lot,' she said agreeably.

'Aw, come on, Lisa. Are you drunk again?' he asked.

'No, Anton. Stone-cold sober and the one time I did get drunk, you weren't very kind to me. You more or less ordered Teddy to throw me out of here.'

'You were making a fool of yourself. You should thank me.' He was really irritated now.

'Calm down, Anton. It would make this discussion easier if you didn't fly into a temper. Just tell me how important I am in your life.'

'I don't know . . . very important—you do all the designs; you have lots of good ideas; you're very glamorous and I fancy you a lot. Now will that do?'

'And do you see me as part of your future?' She was still unruffled.

There was a silence. Anton looked uncomfortable. 'Don't talk to me about the future. Do you know what Teddy and I were talking about when you came in?'

'No. What?'

'The future of this restaurant. The takings are appalling, we're losing money hand over fist. The suppliers are beginning to scream. The bank isn't being helpful. Some days we're almost empty for lunch. Today we only had three tables. Punters notice these things. It needs some kind of a lift. It's going stale. You want to talk about the future—I don't think there is one.'

'Do you see *me* in your future?' Lisa asked again.

'Oh God Almighty, Lisa, I do if you could come up with some ideas rather than bleating like a teenager. That is if we *have* a future here at all . . .'

'Ideas—and what ideas do you have about me?' she asked, her voice dangerously composed.

'OK. I admire you a lot. I'm your friend . . .'

'And lover . . .' she added.

'Well, yes, from time to time. I thought you felt the same about it all.'

'Like what exactly?'

'That it was something nice we shared—but not the meaning of life or anything. Not a steady road to the altar.'

'So why did you continue to have me around?'

'As I've said, you're bright, very bright, you're lovely and you're fun. And also I think a little lonely.'

As she heard the words, something changed in Lisa's head. It was almost as if she were coming out of a dream. She could take his indifference, his infidelity, his careless ways. She could not take his pity.

'And you might be a little lonely too, Anton, when this place fails. When Teddy has bailed out and gone to another trendy place, when little Miss April has flown off to something that's successful. When people say, "Anton? Isn't he the one who used to own some restaurant . . . popular for a while but it disappeared without trace." You might well be lonely then, too. So let's hope someone will take pity on you and you'll see how it feels.'

'Lisa, please . . .'

'Goodbye, Anton.'

Lisa walked out of the restaurant jauntily. She wouldn't think about what she had just done. She would concentrate on something else. This was a city full of promise. She would tidy Anton away and hold her head high.

MUTTIE'S CHILDREN knew it would be today or tomorrow. They kept their voices low as they moved around the house. Lizzie still thought he was getting better.

'He'll go into a coma shortly,' the palliative care nurse said to Maud.

For the first time it hit Maud and she cried on Simon's shoulder.

'It's going to be hard knowing that he doesn't exist any more,' Simon said.

Father Brian Flynn was having a cup of tea with the family. 'There is a thought that if we remember someone, then we keep them alive,' he said.

There was a silence. He wished he hadn't spoken. But they were all nodding their heads. If keeping people in your memory meant that they still lived, then Muttie would live for ever.

LIZZIE SAID she was going to go in and sit with him.

'He's in a very deep sleep, Mam,' Cathy said.

'I know. It's a coma. The nurses said it would happen.'

'Mam, it's just—'

'Cathy, I know it's the end. I know it's tonight. I just want to be alone with him for a little bit.'

Cathy looked at her, open-mouthed.

'I knew for ages, but I just didn't let myself believe it until today, so look at all the happy days I had when the rest of you were worrying . . .'

Cathy brought her mother into the room and the nurse left. She closed the door firmly.

Lizzie wanted to say goodbye.

'I DON'T KNOW if you can hear me or not, Muttie,' Lizzie said. 'But I wanted to tell you that you were great fun. I've had a laugh or a dozen laughs every day since I met you and I've been cheerful and thought we were as good as anyone else. You made me think that even if we were poor, we were fine. I hope you have a great time until . . . well, until I'm there too. I know you're half a pagan, Muttie, but you'll find out that it's all there—waiting for you. Now won't that be a surprise? I love you, Muttie, and we'll manage somehow, I promise you.'

Then she kissed his forehead and called the family back in.

TWENTY MINUTES LATER, Declan arrived and went into the bedroom. He came out quickly. 'Muttie is at peace . . . at rest,' he confirmed.

They cried in disbelief, holding on to each other. Marco had arrived and he was considered family for this. Some of Muttie's Associates took out handkerchiefs and blew their noses very loudly.

Suddenly Lizzie, frail Lizzie, took control.

'Simon, will you go and pull down all the blinds, please. The neighbours will know then. Maud, can you phone the undertaker? His number is beside the phone. Tell him that Muttie has gone. He'll know what to do. Marco, can you arrange some food for us, please? People will call and we must have something to give them. Geraldine, could you see how many cups, mugs and plates we have? And could you all stop crying . . . If Muttie knew you were crying he would deal with the lot of you.'

Somehow they managed a few watery smiles.

THE WHOLE OF ST JARLATH'S CRESCENT stood as a guard of honour when the coffin was carried down the road.

Lisa, Noel and Faith stood with Frankie in her buggy. Emily stood beside her uncle and aunt with Dr Hat and Dingo Duggan. Declan and Fiona, with little Johnny in a sling, stood with Molly and Paddy. Friends and neighbours watched as Simon and Marco helped to carry the coffin.

The Associates stood in a little line, still stunned that Muttie wasn't there urging them all to have a pint and a look at the three thirty at Wincanton.

Somewhere far away a church bell was ringing. It had nothing to do with them but it seemed as if it was ringing in sympathy. The curtains, blinds or shutters of every house in the street were closed. People placed flowers from their gardens on the coffin as it passed by.

Then there was a hearse and funeral cars waiting to take the funeral party to Father Brian Flynn's church in the immigrant centre.

AT THE CHURCH, Father Flynn kept the ceremony very short. One Our Father, one Hail Mary and one Glory Be to the Father. A Moroccan boy played 'Amazing Grace' on a clarinet. And a girl from Poland played 'Hail, Queen of Heaven' on an accordion. Then it was over.

People stood around in the sunshine and talked about Muttie. Afterwards they made their way back to his home to say goodbye.

Properly.

Chapter Ten

Everyone in St Jarlath's Crescent was the poorer after Muttie's death and people tried to avoid looking at the lonely figure of Lizzie standing by her gate as she always had. It was as if she was still waiting for him. Of course everyone rallied round to make sure that she wasn't alone, but one by one her children went back home to Chicago and Australia; Cathy had to go back to her catering company, and the twins had to go back to work at Ennio's and decide on their future.

Everyone was slowly getting back to life but with the knowledge that Lizzie had no life to get on with.

Lizzie sighed a lot these days but she tried to smile at the same time. People had always found good humour and smiles in this house and it must not change now. It was when she was left alone that the smiles faded and she grieved for Muttie.

There were so many things she wanted to tell him. Every day she thought of something new: that Maud would be getting engaged to Marco and that Simon was happy about it and was still thinking about going to the US. She wanted to discuss with him whether she would stay on in the house or get a smaller place. Everyone advised her that she must make no decisions for at least a year. She wondered would Muttie think that was wise.

DR HAT SUGGESTED TO Emily that they go for a picnic as the summer had finally arrived. Emily suggested Michael come with them, though for some reason Dr Hat looked a bit odd when she raised it. She made sandwiches and filled two flasks with tea. She brought chocolate biscuits in a tin and they drove in Dr Hat's car out to the Wicklow mountains.

'It's amazing to have all these hills so close to the city,' Emily said.

'Those aren't hills, they're mountains,' Dr Hat said reprovingly. 'It's very important to know that.'

'I'm sorry,' Emily laughed, 'but then what can you expect from a foreigner, an outsider.'

'You're not an outsider. Your heart is here,' Dr Hat said and he looked at her oddly again. 'Or I very much hope it is.'

Michael started to hum tunelessly to himself as he gazed out of the window. Dr Hat and Emily ignored him and raised their voices.

'Oh, Hat, you feel safe enough saying that to me in front of Michael as a sort of joke.'

'I was never as serious in my life. I *do* hope your heart is in Ireland. I'd hate it if you went away.'

'Why exactly?'

'Because you are very interesting and you get things done. I was beginning to drift and you halted that. I'm more of a man since I met you.'

Michael's humming got louder, as if he was trying to drown them out.

'You are?' shouted Emily. 'Well, I feel more of a woman since I met you, so that has to be good somehow.'

'I never married because I never met anyone that didn't bore me before. I'd like . . . I'd like you to . . .'

'To do what?' Emily asked.

Michael's humming was now almost deafening.

'Oh, stop it, Michael,' Emily begged. 'Hat is trying to say something.'

'He's said it,' Michael said. 'He's asked you to marry him. Now just say yes, will you?'

Emily looked at Hat for some clarity. Hat drew the car to a slow stop and got out. He went round to the passenger side, opened Emily's door and knelt in the heather and gorse on the Wicklow mountains.

'Emily, will you do me the great honour of becoming my wife?' he asked.

'Why didn't you ask me before?' she wondered.

'I was so afraid you'd say no and that we'd lose the comfortable feeling of being friends. I was just afraid.'

'Don't be afraid any more.' She touched him gently on the side of his face. 'I'd love to marry you.'

'Thanks be to God,' said Michael. 'We can have the picnic now!'

EMILY AND DR HAT decided that there was no reason for delay at their age; they would marry when Betsy and Eric were in Ireland. This way Betsy would get to be matron of honour and Michael would be best man. They could be married by Father Flynn. The twins would do the catering and they could all go on honeymoon with Dingo driving them to the West.

Emily didn't want an engagement ring. She said she would prefer a nice solid-looking wedding ring and just that. Dr Hat was almost skittish with good humour and for the first time in his life he agreed to go to a tailor and have a made-to-measure suit. He would get a new hat to match it and promised to take it off in the church for the ceremony as long as it could be restored for the photographs.

Emily found her wedding outfit in the thrift shop. It arrived in from a shop that was about to close down. There were a number of pieces that had been display items and the owner said she would get nothing for them and it was better they went to some charity. Emily was hanging them up on a rail when she saw it. A silk dress with a navy and pale blue flower pattern and a matching jacket in navy with a small trim of the dress material on the jacket collar. It was perfect: elegant and feminine and wedding-like.

Carefully, Emily put the sum of money she would have hoped to get for it into the till and brought it home straight away.

Josie saw her coming through the house.

'The very woman,' Josie said. 'Will you have a cup of tea?'

'A quick one, then. I don't want to leave Molly too long on her own.'

'I'm a bit worried,' Josie began. 'It's the money Mrs Monty left to Charles.'

'Yes, and you're giving it to the Statue Fund.' Emily knew all this.

'It's just that we're worried about how much it is,' Josie said. 'You see, it's not just thousands . . . it's hundreds of thousands.'

Emily was stunned. 'That poor old lady had that kind of money! Who'd have thought it!' she said.

'Yes and that's the problem. It's too much to give to a statue. It's such a huge amount of money, you see, we wonder, have we a duty to our granddaughter, for example? Should we leave a sum for her education or to give her a start in life? Or should we give some to Noel so that he has something to fall back on if times got bad? Could I retire properly, and could Charles and I go to the Holy Land? Would St Jarlath like that better than a statue? It's impossible to know.'

Emily was thoughtful. What she said now was very important.

'What would God have wanted, I wonder?' Emily speculated. 'Our Lord wasn't into big show and splendour. He was more into helping the poor.'

'You're going off the idea of the statue, aren't you?' Josie said.

'No, I'm all in favour of the statue. It's a *great* idea, but I think it should be the smaller statue you originally thought of. Greatness isn't shown by size.'

'We could give one big contribution to the fund and then invest the rest.'

'From what you know about St Jarlath, Josie, do you think he'd be happy with that?'

Emily knew that Josie must be utterly convinced in her heart before she abandoned the cracked notion of spending all this money on a statue.

'I think he would,' Josie said. 'He was all for the good of the people and if we were to put a playground at the end of the Crescent for the children, wouldn't that be in the spirit of it all?'

'And the statue?' Emily hardly dared to breathe.

'We could have it *in* the playground, and call it all "St Jarlath's Garden for Children".'

Emily smiled with relief.

THEY DID THEIR ROSTER every Sunday night. A page was put up on the kitchen wall. You could easily read who was minding Frankie every hour of the day. Noel and Lisa each had a copy as well. Soon she would be old enough to go to Miss Keane's day nursery: that would be three hours accounted for each day. Only the name of who was to collect her would be needed for the mornings.

Lisa would take her to Miss Keane's and a variety of helpers would pick her up. Lisa wasn't free at lunchtime. She had a job making sandwiches in a rather classy place on the other side of the city. It wasn't a skilled job, but she brought to it all the skills she had. It paid her share of the groceries and little by little she told them her ideas.

A Gorgonzola and date sandwich? The customers loved it, so she suggested little posters advertising the sandwich of the week and drew them herself. She even designed a logo for the sandwich bar.

'You're much too good to be here,' said Hugh, the young owner.

'I'm too good for everywhere. Weren't you lucky to get me?'

'We were, actually. You're a mystery woman.'

He smiled at her. Hugh was rich, confident and good-looking. He fancied her, but Lisa realised that she had got out of the way of looking at men properly. She had forgotten how to flirt. She did other things to keep busy.

She joined Emily in the window-box patrol and learned a lot about plants. She picked it up quickly. Emily said she was a natural.

'I used to be bright,' Lisa said thoughtfully. 'I was really good at school and then I got a great job in an agency . . . but it all drifted away . . .'

Emily knew when to leave a silence.

Lisa went on almost dreamily, 'It was like driving into a fog really, when I met Anton. I forgot the world outside.'

She knew very clearly that if she went back to the restaurant they would all greet her warmly. They would assume she had just had a hissy fit and had now come to her senses. Anton would look at her lazily and say she was lovely and the days had been lonely and colourless since she had gone. On the surface nothing would have changed. Deep down, though, it had all changed. He didn't love her. She had just been available, that was all.

FAITH STAYED in the flat several nights a week now. She was able to look after Frankie and put her to bed on the evenings that all three of them studied. It was a curious little family grouping, but it worked. Faith said she found working like this much easier than doing it alone. Between them they went over the latest lecture and talked it out. They made notes and they revised for their exams. Now that graduation was in sight they began to imagine how it would all work out for them when they had letters after their names.

Noel would seek a better position at Hall's and if it wasn't forthcoming, then he would have the courage and qualifications to apply somewhere else. Faith would put herself forward as a manager in her office. She was doing that work in all but name and salary so they would have to promote her.

Lisa? Well, Lisa was at a loss to know what her qualifications would lead to. At one time she had hoped to be a partner in Anton's. But now? Well, she would have to return to the marketplace. It was humiliating, but she would have to contact Kevin, the boss she had left to go and work with Anton. That was last year when she had been reasonably sane and good at her job.

She picked up the phone with trepidation.

'Well, *hello*!'

Kevin was entitled to be a bit mocking. For months now Lisa had avoided him. It was very hard to call him and tell him that she had failed.

He made it fairly easy. 'You're on the market again, I gather,' he said.

'You can crow, Kevin. You were right. I should have listened.'

'But you were in love, of course,' Kevin said. There was only a mildly sardonic tone to his voice.

'That was true, yes.'

If he noticed the past tense he said nothing.

'So you're looking for a job?'

'I was wondering if you knew of anything? Anything at all?'

'Right now I can only offer you a junior place. Somewhere to settle for a while. I can't give you a top job. It wouldn't be fair on the others.'

She was very humble. 'I'd be more grateful than I could tell you, Kevin.'

'Not at all. Start Monday?'

'Can I make it the Monday after? I'm working in a sandwich bar and I'll have to give them notice . . . get someone else for them.'

'My, my, Lisa, you *have* changed,' Kevin said as he hung up.

LIZZIE FOUND the days endless. The raw pain of grief was now giving way to a gnawing ache and the void in her life was threatening to consume her.

'I'm thinking of getting a little job,' she confided to the twins.

'What work would you do, Lizzie?' Simon asked.

'Anything really. I used to clean houses.'

'Would you like to work in Marco's restaurant?' Maud asked. 'Well, his father's restaurant. They're looking for someone to come in part-time. I heard Ennio say they needed someone to supervise sending the laundry out and take in the cheese delivery and to sort yesterday's tips out from the credit card receipts. You could do that, couldn't you?'

'Well, I might be able to, but Ennio would never give me a responsible job like that,' Lizzie said anxiously.

'Of course he would,' Simon said loyally.

'You're family, Lizzie,' said Maud, smiling down at her engagement ring.

THE RELATIONSHIP between Frank Ennis and his son had been prickly from the start, and hadn't improved much during the boy's visit. Des had gone back to Australia and they kept in touch from time to time. Not often enough for Frank, who put great effort into writing weekly emails to the boy.

'You'd think he'd do more than send a postcard of the Barrier Reef,' Frank grumbled to Clara.

'Look, be grateful for what you get. My Adi only sends a card too. I don't know where she is and what she's doing. It's just the way things are.'

Then came the word they had not expected.

I find myself thinking a lot about Ireland these days. I know I was rough on you and didn't really believe you when you said you didn't know what your family had done, but it took time to get my head around it all. Perhaps we should have another go. I was thinking of spending a year there. I've been in negotiations about jobs and apparently my degree and diploma would be recognised in Ireland.

You must tell me if this is something you would be happy with and I would find myself an apartment, rather than crowd you out. Who knows, during my year there we might try the father–son thing and see how it goes.

They were both silent when they read the letter. It was the first time Des Raven had shown any sign of wanting a father–son relationship.

THE RESULTS of the examinations had been posted on the college notice board. Noel and Faith and Lisa had all done well. They celebrated with giant ice creams at the café beside the college and planned their outfits for graduation day. They would be wearing black gowns with pale blue hoods.

'Hoods?' Noel asked, horrified.

'That's just what they call them—they go over our shoulders, to mark us out as different, not engineers or draughtsmen or anything.' Lisa knew it all.

'I'm going to wear a yellow dress I have already, you won't see much of it under the gown. I'll spend the money on good shoes,' Faith decided.

'I'm going to get a red dress and borrow Katie's new shoes.' Lisa had it sorted as well. 'Now, Noel, what about you?'

'Why this emphasis on shoes?' Noel asked.

'Because everyone sees them when you go up on the stage.'

'If I polished up these ones?' He looked down dubiously at his feet.

The girls shook their heads. New shoes were called for.

'It's a lot of fuss about nothing,' Noel grumbled.

'Hours of lectures and nights of study—and you call it nothing?' Lisa was outraged.

'I'll get the damn shoes!' Noel promised.

GRADUATION DAY was very bright and sunny. That was a relief: there would be no umbrellas or people squinting into the rain. Frankie was excited to see them all dressing up.

She crawled around the floor, getting under everyone's feet, and mumbled a lot to herself about it—words that didn't make much sense until they identified 'Frankie too'.

'Of *course* you're going too, darling.' Faith lifted her up in the air. '*And* I have a lovely little blue dress for you to wear.'

Noel looked very well. He was much admired by the women, who examined his new shoes with approval. Then Emily arrived to take Frankie in the buggy wearing her new dress and they all set out for the college.

Frankie behaved perfectly during the ceremony. Noel gazed at her with pride. He had done all this for her—yes, for himself too, but all this work had been worth it for the chance to make a life for his little girl.

The new graduates filed onto the stage and the audience raked through the ranks until they found their own. Noel saw Emily holding Frankie and he smiled with pleasure and pride.

Lisa saw her mother and sister both dressed up to honour the day; she saw Garry there and all their friends. Then she saw Anton. He looked lost; as if he didn't belong there. She remembered writing down this date in his diary months back.

It didn't mean anything to her that he was there and it had all been her own fault. Anton had never loved her. It had all been in her mind.

Chapter Eleven

Emily had the spare room in Dr Hat's house beautifully decorated and she planned a series of outings to entertain Betsy and Eric. She had this ludicrous wish that they should love Ireland as she did. She hoped that it wouldn't rain and that the streets would be free of litter.

Emily and Hat were at the airport long before the plane arrived.

'It only seems the other day since you came out to meet *me* here,' Emily said, 'and you brought me a picnic in the car.'

'I had begun to fancy you seriously then, but I was terrified you'd say it was all nonsense.'

'I'd never have said that.' She looked at him very fondly.

'I hope your friend won't think I'm too old for you,' he said anxiously.

'You're my Hat. My choice. The only person I ever even contemplated marrying,' she said firmly. And that was that.

BETSY WAS BEMUSED by the size of the airport and the frantic activity all around. She had thought the plane would land in a field of cows or sheep. This was a huge sprawling place like an airport back home. She couldn't believe the traffic, the motorways and the big buildings.

'You never told me how developed it all is. I thought it was a succession of little cottages where you knew everyone that moves,' she said, laughing.

In minutes it was as if they had never been parted.

Eric and Dr Hat exchanged relieved glances. It was all going to be fine.

EMILY WAS GOING to be given away by her uncle Charles.

Charles and Josie had finally come to the conclusion that a children's playground and a *small* statue of St Jarlath would fit the bill. They had been to see a lawyer and settled a sum for Noel and one for Frankie. Charles had even arranged for Emily to have a substantial sum as a wedding gift so that she wouldn't start her married life with no money of her own. It wasn't a dowry, of course, but Charles said that so often that Emily began to wonder.

Father Flynn married them. They could have filled the church five times over, but Emily and Hat only wanted a small gathering, so twenty people stood in the sunlight as they made their vows. Then they went with Eric and Betsy to Holly's Hotel in County Wicklow and back home to St Jarlath's Crescent where the honeymoon continued for the two couples and Dingo Duggan got new tyres to make sure that they got to the West and back.

They stayed in farmhouses and walked along shell-covered shores with purple-blue mountains as a backdrop. And if you were to ask anyone who they were and what they were doing, a hundred guesses would never have said that they were two middle-aged couples on honeymoon. They all seemed too settled and happy for that.

THE HONEYMOON had been a resounding success. Emily and Betsy were like girls chattering and laughing. Hat and Eric found a great common interest in birdwatching. Dingo met a Galway girl with blue eyes and was very smitten. The sun shone on the newlyweds and the nights were full of stars.

It was over too soon for everyone.

When they got back they heard the astounding news that elegant Clara Casey, who ran the heart clinic, was now living with Frank Ennis and, wait for it, he had a son. Frank Ennis had a son called Des Raven who lived in Australia and was coming to Ireland. Fiona could talk of nothing else. Clara *live with* Frank Ennis—didn't people do extraordinary things?

THEIR FIRST CHANCE to celebrate properly as a family came when Clara's daughter Adi returned from Ecuador with her boyfriend Gerry. Des had wanted to go back to Anton's. 'It will be like starting over,' he had said.

This time, there was no need to plead for a table, even though they were nine: Clara, Frank and Des; then Adi and Gerry; Linda came with Nick. Hilary and Clara's best friend Dervla made up the party.

The restaurant was half empty and there seemed to be an air of confusion about the place. Anton said that his number one, Teddy, had gone as he needed new pastures. No, he had no idea where he had gone.

Frank Ennis, in his new suit, was in charge of the table. He poured wine readily and urged people to have oysters as the optional extra.

'I talk about my son a lot,' he said proudly to Des.

'Good. Do you talk about Clara a lot?' Des asked.

'With respect and awe,' Frank said.

'Good,' intervened Clara, 'because she wants to tell you that her clinic needs some serious extra funding . . .'

'Out of the question.'

'The blood tests take too long at the main hospital. We need our own lab.'

'I'll get your blood tests fast-tracked,' Frank Ennis promised.

'You have six weeks for us to see a real difference, otherwise the fight is on,' Clara said. 'He is amazingly generous in real life,' she whispered to Dervla. 'It's just in the hospital that his rotten-to-the-core meanness shows.'

'He's delighted with you,' Dervla said. 'He has said "My Clara" thirty times during this meal alone.'

'Well, I'm keeping my name, my job, my clinic and my house, so I'm doing very well out of it,' Clara said.

'Go on out of that, playing the tough bird, you're just as soppy as he is. You're delighted at this playing-house thing. I'm happy for you, Clara. I hope that you'll be very happy together.'

LISA WAS SURPRISED when Kevin asked her out to lunch.

She was in a junior position in the studio. She didn't expect her boss to single her out. In Quentins she was even more surprised that he ordered a bottle of wine. Kevin was usually a one-vodka person.

This looked like being something serious. She hoped he wasn't going to sack her. But surely he wouldn't take her out to lunch to give her the push?

'Stop frowning, Lisa. We're going to have a long lunch,' Kevin said.

'What is it? Don't keep me in suspense.'

'Two things really. Did Anton pay you anything? Anything at all?'

'No, he paid me nothing, but I was part of the place, part of the dream. I was doing it for *us*, not for him.'

'It's just that he's going into receivership today and I wanted to make sure you got your claim in. You are a serious victim here. You worked for him without being paid, for God's sake. You are a major creditor.'

'I haven't a notion of asking him for anything. I'm sorry it didn't work for him. I'm not going to add to his worries.'

'It's just business, Lisa. He'll understand. They'll sell his assets—I don't know what he owns and what is mortgaged or leased, but people have to be paid: you among them.'

'No, Kevin, thanks all the same.'

'You love clothes, Lisa. You should get yourself a stunning wardrobe.'

'I'm not smart enough for your office? Is that it?'

She was hurt, but she made it sound like a joke.

'No, you're too smart. Much too smart. I can't keep you. I have a friend in London. He's looking for someone bright. I told him about you. He'll pay your fare to London. And you don't want to know the salary he's offering!'

'You really *are* getting rid of me and you're pretending it's promotion.'

'*Never* have I been so misjudged! I'd prefer you to stay and in a year or two I could promote you, but this job is too good to ignore and I thought that anyway it might be easier for you.'

'Easier?'

'Well, you know, there'll be a lot of talk about Anton's. Speculation, newspaper stuff.'

'Yes, I suppose there will. Poor Anton. But in ways you're right. I couldn't bear to be in Dublin while all the vultures were picking over the place.'

'You'll go for the interview?' He was pleased.

'I'll go,' Lisa promised.

SIMON SAID it was time he and Maud talked about New Jersey. The amazing inheritance they had got from Muttie meant that Maud and Marco could put a deposit on their own restaurant and Simon could buy into the partnership of a stylish restaurant.

'I'll miss you,' Maud said.

'You won't notice I'm gone,' he assured her.

'You'll fall in love and live out there.'

'I doubt it, but I'll be home often to see Lizzie and you and Marco.'

Maud gave him a hug. 'Those American girls don't know what's coming.'

IT WAS A DAY of many changes.

Declan and Fiona and their son Johnny moved house. It was only next door but it was still a huge move. They arranged that Paddy and Molly Carroll should be part of it all so that they would realise how nothing had really changed. When Johnny was old enough to walk he would know two homes as his own.

Dr Hat and Emily decided to open a garden store. There was plenty of room still beside the thrift shop. Now that so many residents of St Jarlath's Crescent had begun to take an interest in beautifying their gardens, there was no end of demand for bedding plants and ornamental shrubs.

In the disturbed world of Anton's restaurant the staff were making their plans. They would not open next week. Everyone knew this.

April sat around the place with her notebook, suggesting places for Anton to do interviews on the difficulties of running a business during a recession. Anton felt unsettled. He wondered what Lisa would be saying.

Lisa went to London for the interview and came back very excited. When she was offered the job, she accepted immediately; now she had to move pretty quickly and there weren't enough hours in the day.

For Noel it was a good day also. Mr Hall had said that there was a more senior position in the company that had been vacant for some time. He now wanted to offer it to Noel.

'I have been impressed by you, Noel, I don't mind saying that you did much better than I would have thought at one stage. I always hoped you'd have it in you to make something of yourself, though I confess I had my doubts about you for a while.'

'I had my doubts about myself,' Noel had said with a smile.

'There's always some turning point for a man. What do you think yours was?' Mr Hall had seemed genuinely interested.

'Becoming a father,' Noel had said without having to think for a second.

NOEL AND LISA planned a first birthday party for Frankie. There would be an ice-cream cake and paper hats; Mr Gallagher from number 37 could do magic tricks and said he'd entertain the children.

Naturally, Moira got to hear of it.

'You're having all these people in this small flat?' she asked doubtfully.

'I know, won't it be wonderful?' Lisa deliberately misunderstood her.

'You should do more for yourself, Lisa. You're bright, sharp, you could have a career and a proper place to live.'

'This *is* a proper place to live.'

Noel was out at the washing machine so didn't hear.

'We have to stir ourselves from our comfort zones. What are you doing here with a man who is bringing up a child that may or may not be his own?'

'Of course Frankie's his own!' Lisa was shocked.

'Well, that's as may be. She was very unreliable, the mother, you know. I met her in hospital. She could have named anyone as the father.'

'Well, really, Moira, I have never heard anything so ridiculous,' Lisa said, blazing suddenly at the mean-spirited pettiness of Moira's attitude.

Thank God Noel had been in the kitchen while stupid, negative Moira was talking. It was just a miracle that he hadn't heard.

NOEL HAD, OF COURSE, heard every word and he was holding on by a thread.

What a sour, mean cow Moira was and he had just begun to see some good in her. Not now. Not ever again after such a statement.

He managed to shout out a cheerful goodbye as he heard the door. He wouldn't think about it. It was nonsense. He would think about the party instead. About Frankie, his little girl. That woman's remarks had no power to hurt him. He would rise above it.

First he must pretend to Lisa that he hadn't heard. That was important.

FRANKIE'S BIRTHDAY PARTY was a triumph.

Frankie had a crown and so did Johnny, since it was his birthday on the same day. Apart from the two birthday babies there were very few children coming to the party, but lots of grown-ups. Lizzie was helping with the jellies and Molly Carroll was in charge of the cocktail sausages.

Noel was glad the party went well. There were no tantrums among the children, no one was overtired. He had even arranged for wine and beer to be served to the adults. It hadn't bothered him in the least. Faith and Lisa cleared up and quietly put the unfinished bottles in Faith's bag.

But Noel's heart was heavy. A chance remark at the party had upset him more than he would have believed possible.

Dingo Duggan, who always said the wrong thing, commented that Frankie was far too good-looking to be a child of Noel's. Noel managed to smile and said that nature had a strange way in compensating for flaws.

Was it possible that Frankie was the child of someone else?

He sat very quietly when everyone had gone; eventually, Faith sat down beside him.

'Was it a strain having alcohol in the house, Noel?' Faith asked.

'No, I never thought about it. Why?'

'It's just you seem a bit down.'

She was sympathetic and so he told her about Dingo's remark. And he repeated the words that Moira had said.

Faith listened with tears in her eyes.

'I never heard anything so ridiculous. She's a sour, sad, bitter woman. You're never going to start giving any credence to anything she would say?'

'I don't know. It's possible.'

'No, it's not possible! Why would she have chosen *you* unless you were the father?' Faith was outraged on his behalf.

'Stella more or less said that at the time,' he remembered.

'Put it out of your head, Noel. You are the best father in the world and that Moira can't bring herself to accept this. That's all there is to it.'

NOEL COULDN'T SLEEP so he got up and sat in the sitting room. He got a piece of paper and made a list of the reasons why he was obviously Frankie's father and another list of reasons why he might not be. As usual he came to no conclusion. He loved that child so much—she must be his daughter. And yet he couldn't sleep. There was only one thing to do. He would get a DNA test. He would arrange it the next day.

Noel didn't want to approach either Declan or Dr Hat about the DNA test. He didn't want them to know his doubts.

He chose a doctor on the other side of the city. He brought Frankie in and swabs were taken. He would know for sure in three weeks.

THE LETTER ARRIVED at Chestnut Court.

Lisa left it on the table as she went out; in the silent flat Noel poured himself another cup of tea. His hand was too shaky to pick up the envelope. The teapot had rattled alarmingly against the cup. He was too weak to open it now. He had to get through this day without shaking like this. Perhaps he should put the letter away and open it tomorrow. He put it into a drawer.

LISA WAS STARTLED to find him there when she arrived with Dingo Duggan and his van. She was going to take her possessions to Katie and Garry's.

'Hey, I thought you'd be at work,' she said.

Noel shook his head. 'Day off,' he muttered.

'Lucky old you. Where's Frankie? I thought you'd want to celebrate a day off with her?'

'She went with Emily. No point in breaking the routine,' he said flatly.

'You OK, Noel?'

'Sure I am. What are you doing?'

'Moving my stuff, trying to give you two lovebirds more room.'

'You know, you're not in the way, there's plenty of room for all of us.'

'But I'll be going to London soon, I can't clutter your place up with all my boxes.'

'I don't know what I'd have done without you, Lisa, I really don't.'

'Wasn't it a great year!' Lisa agreed. 'A year when you found Frankie and when I . . . well, when I let the scales fall from my eyes over so many things. Anton for one, my father for another . . .'

'You never said why you came here that night,' Noel said.

'And you never asked, which made everything so restful. I'll miss Frankie though, desperately. Faith is going to send me a photo of her every month so that I'll see her growing up.'

'You'll forget all about us.' He managed a smile.

'As if I would. This is the first proper home I ever had.'

NOEL OPENED the drawer and took out the envelope. He slit it open with a knife and took out the letter inside. It was stilted and official, but it was clear and concise.

The DNA samples did not match.

A hot rage came over him. He could feel it burning round his neck and ears. There was a heavy lump in his stomach and a strange light-headedness around his eyes and forehead. This could not be true.

Stella could not have told him a pack of lies and palmed off her child on him. Surely it was impossible that she had made all these arrangements and put his name on the birth certificate if she had not believed it was true.

Perhaps she'd had so many lovers, she had no idea who might be Frankie's father. She could have picked him because he was humble and would make no fuss. Or possibly Frankie's real father was so unreliable or unavailable that he could not be contacted.

Bile rose in his throat. He knew exactly what would make him feel better. He picked up his jacket and went out.

MOIRA WAS HAVING a busy morning at the heart clinic. Once the word had got round that she was an expert at finding people's entitlements, her case load had increased. It was Moira's belief that if there were benefits, then people should avail themselves of them. She would fill in the paperwork, arrange the carers, the allowances or the support needed.

Unexpectedly Clara Casey had asked if Moira could spare her ten minutes on a personal matter.

Moira wondered what on earth it could be. The gossip around the clinic had been that Dr Casey had moved Mr Ennis into her home, but surely Clara didn't want to discuss anything quite as personal as that.

Just after midday, when Moira's stint ended, Clara slipped into her office.

'This is not on the clinic's time, Moira, it's a personal favour.'

'Sure, go ahead,' Moira said.

'It's about my daughter Linda. As you know, she and her husband are very anxious to adopt a baby and they don't know how to set about it.'

'What have they done so far?' Moira asked.

'Nothing much, except talk about it, but now they want to move forward.'

'Fine, do you want me to talk to them sometime?'

'Linda is actually here today, she came to take me to lunch. Would that be too instant?'

'No, not at all, do you want to stay for the conversation?'

'No, no—but I do appreciate this, Moira. I've realised over the last months you are amazingly thorough and tenacious. If anyone can help Linda and Nick you can.'

Moira couldn't remember why she had thought of Dr Casey as aloof and superior. She watched as Clara ushered in her tall, handsome daughter.

'I'll leave you in good hands,' Clara said and Moira felt an absurd flush of pleasure all over her face and neck.

AT LUNCH Linda was bubbling over with enthusiasm.

'I can't think why you didn't like that woman, she was *marvellous*. It's all very straightforward. You go to the Health Board and they refer you to the adoption section and fill in a lot of details, and they make home assessment visits. She asked, did we mind what nationality the child would be and I said of course not. It really looks as if it might happen.'

'I'm so pleased, Linda.' Clara spoke gently.

'So you and Frank had better polish up your baby-sitting skills,' Linda said with unnaturally bright eyes.

MOIRA LEFT THE CLINIC in high good humour. For once it appeared her talents had been recognised. It was one of those rare occasions when people actually seemed pleased with the social worker.

Her steps took her past Chestnut Court and she looked from habit at Noel and Lisa's flat. Noel would be at work, but maybe Lisa was there packing her belongings. She was heading off to London soon. Anyway, no point in going in there and talking to Lisa and being accused of spying or policing the situation. She didn't want to lose the good feeling that had come from the clinic, so she passed by.

EMILY GOT A PHONE CALL at lunchtime. It was Noel. His voice was unsteady. She thought he sounded drunk.

'Everything all right, Noel?' she asked anxiously, her heart lurching. He should have been there to pick up Frankie. What could have happened?

'Yes. Everything's fine.' He spoke like a robot. 'I'm at the zoo actually.'

'The zoo?'

Emily was stunned. The zoo was miles away on the other side of the city.

'Yes. I haven't been here for ages. They've lots of new things.'

'Yes, Noel, I'm sure they do.'

'So I was wondering, could you keep Frankie for a while longer?'

'Of course,' Emily agreed, worried.

Was he drunk? He sounded stressed. What could have brought all this on?

'And are you at the zoo on your own?'

'Yes, for the moment.'

NOEL HAD BEEN over and over it in his mind. For a year he had been living a lie. Frankie was not his daughter. God knew whose child she was.

He loved her like his own, of course he did. But he had thought she was his own child and had no one else to look after her. His name was on the birth certificate, he had loved her and looked after her and fed her and changed her. He had protected her, given her a life surrounded by people who loved her; he had made her his. Did he regret all this?

She was a year old, her mother was dead—what sort of start in life would it be if he washed his hands of her now?

Could he bring up another man's child as his own? He didn't think so. She was someone else's child, someone else had fathered her and walked away, got away with it. Should he find out who it was?

He needed a drink. Just the one, so he could see his way clearly.

IT WAS NINE O'CLOCK in the evening when Noel and Malachy turned up at Emily and Hat's house to collect Frankie.

Noel was pale but calm. Malachy looked very tired.

'I'm going to spend the night in Chestnut Court,' he said to Emily.

'That's great, Lisa's taken her things so it might be a little lonely there otherwise,' Emily said neutrally.

Frankie, who had been fast asleep, woke up.

'Dada!' she said to Noel.

'That's right,' he said mechanically.

'I've been explaining to Frankie that her granny and granda are going to build a lovely safe garden where she and all her friends can play.'

'Yes,' said Noel.

'Your parents are going to have a sod-turning ceremony for the children's garden next week. The work is going to start then.'

'Sure,' Noel said.

Wearily Malachy got them on the road. Frankie was chattering away from her buggy. Occasionally recognisable words, but not making any sense.

Noel was silent. He was there in body but not in spirit; surely people were able to guess something was different. Frankie was just the same child she had been this morning but everything else had changed and he hadn't yet had time to get accustomed to the idea.

Malachy slept on the sofa. During the night he heard Frankie start to cry and Noel get up to soothe the little girl and comfort her. The moonlight fell on Noel's face as he sat and held the child; Malachy could see there were tears on his cheeks.

FAITH HAD BEEN AWAY for three days and when she came back she rushed in to pick up Frankie.

'Have I brought you the cutest little boots?' she said to the baby as she hugged her.

'The child has far too many clothes,' Noel said.

'Ah, Noel, they're lovely little boots—look at them!'

'She'll have grown out of them in a month,' he said.

The light had gone out of Faith's face.

'Sorry, is something annoying you?'

'Just the way everyone piles clothes on her. That's all.'

'I'm not everyone and I'm not piling clothes on her. She needs shoes to go to the opening of the site for the new garden on Saturday.'

'Oh God—I'd forgotten that.'

'Are you all right? You look different somehow, as if something fell on you.'

'It did in a way,' Noel said.

'Are you going to tell me?'

'No, not at the moment. Is that all right? I'm sorry for being so rude, they're lovely shoes, Frankie will be the last word on Saturday.'

'Of course she will—now will I get us some supper?'

'You're a girl in a million, Faith.'

'Oh, much more than that—one in a billion, I'd say,' she said, and went into the kitchen.

Noel sat in the kitchen and watched Faith move deftly around, getting together a supper in minutes, something that would have taken him for ever.

'You love Frankie as much as if she was yours, don't you?' he said.

'Of course I do. Is this what's worrying you? She is mine in a way since I almost live with her and I help to look after her.'

'But the fact that she's not yours doesn't make any difference?'

'What are you on about, Noel? I love the child—don't you know that?'

'Yes, but you've always known she wasn't yours,' he said sadly.

'Oh, I know what this is all about, it's this ludicrous Moira who started this off in your head. It's like a wasp in your mind, Noel, buzzing at you. Chase it away. You're obviously her father, you're a great father.'

'Suppose I had a DNA test and found she wasn't—what then?'

'You'd insult that beautiful child by having a DNA test? Noel, you're unhinged. And what would it matter what the test said anyway?'

He could have told her there and then. He could have said that Frankie was not his. This was the only girl he had ever felt close enough to for him to even consider marrying: should he share this huge secret with her?

Instead, he shrugged.

'You're probably right, only a very suspicious, untrusting person would go for that test.'

'That's more like it, Noel,' Faith said happily.

NOEL SAT FOR A LONG TIME at the table when Faith left. He had three envelopes in front of him: one contained the result of the DNA test, one the letter that Stella had left for him before she died, and one held the letter she had addressed to Frankie.

Back in the frightening, early days when fighting to keep away from drink on an hourly basis, he had often been tempted to open the letter to Frankie. In those days he was anxious to look for some reason to keep going, something that might give him strength. Today he wanted to read it in case Stella had told her daughter who her real father was.

A year ago, what did Noel have going for him? Not much. A drunk in a dead-end job, without friends, without hope. It had all changed because of Frankie. How lonely and frightened Stella must have felt that last night.

He reached out and read the letter she had written to him in that ward.

'*Tell Frankie that I wasn't all bad . . .*' she had said. '*Tell her that if things had been different you and I would both have been there to look after her . . .*'

Noel straightened his shoulders.

He was Frankie's father in every way that mattered. Perhaps Stella had made a genuine mistake. And suppose somehow Stella was looking out for Frankie from somewhere, she deserved to know better than that the baby had been abandoned at the age of twelve months.

Noel had loved this child yesterday, he still loved her today. He would always love her. It was as simple as that.

He reached across the table and put the two letters from Stella into the drawer. The letter with the DNA results he tore into tiny pieces.

IT WAS A FINE DAY for the turning of the sod. Charles and Josie put their hands together on the shovel and dug into the ground of the small waste patch they had secured for the new garden. Everyone clapped and Father Flynn said a few words about the great results that came from a sense of community involvement and caring.

Lizzie was there with her arm round Simon's shoulder. He was going to New Jersey next week but had promised to be back in three months to tell them all what it was like. Marco and Maud stood together.

Declan, Johnny and the now visibly pregnant Fiona were there, with Declan's parents and their big dog, Dimples. Dimples had a love-hate relationship with Caesar, the tiny spaniel. It wasn't that he had anything against Caesar, it was just that he was too small to be a proper dog.

Emily and Hat were there, part of the scenery now. People hardly remembered a time when they were not together. Noel, Faith and Frankie were there, Frankie showing everyone her new pink boots. People pointed out to Noel that one of the houses in the Crescent would shortly be for sale, maybe he and Faith could buy it. Then Frankie would be near her garden. It was a very tempting idea, they said.

And as they wound their way back to Emily and Hat's house where tea and cakes were being served, Noel felt a weight lift from his shoulders. He passed the house where Paddy Carroll and his wife Molly had slaved to raise their son, a doctor, and then past Muttie and Lizzie's house, where the twins had found a better home than they could have dreamed of. He blinked a couple of times as he began to realise that a lot of things didn't matter any more.

Frankie wanted to walk the length of the road even though she wasn't really able to; Faith followed with the buggy but Frankie struggled, holding Noel's hand and calling out 'Dada' a lot. Just as they got to Emily and Hat's place her little legs began to buckle and Noel swung her up into his arms.

'Good girl, Daddy's good little girl,' he said over and over.

His chest was much less tight, the awful feeling of running down a long corridor had gone. Later tonight he would ring Malachy and then he would be ready for anything. He put his other arm round Faith's shoulder and ushered his little family into the house to have tea.

My dear, dear Frankie, my lovely daughter, I will never see you or know you, but I do love you so very much. I fought hard to live for you but it didn't work. I started too late, you see. If only I had known that I would have a little girl to live for . . . But it's all far too late for those kind of wishes now. Instead, I wish you the very best that life can give you. I wish you courage—I have plenty of that. Too much, some might say! I hope that you will not be as foolhardy and reckless as I was. Instead, may you have peace and the love of good people who will mind you and make you happy. Tonight I sit here in a ward where nobody can really sleep. It's my last night here, you see, and tomorrow is your first day here. I wish we had been able to meet.

But I know one thing. Noel will be a great father. He is very strong and he can't wait to meet you tomorrow. He has been preparing for weeks, getting things ready for you. He will be a wonderful dad and I have this very clear feeling that you will be the light of his life.

So many people are waiting for you tomorrow. Don't be sad for me, you have managed to make sense of my life eventually!

Live well and happily, little Frankie. Laugh a lot and be full of trust, not suspicion.

Remember your mother loved you with all her heart.

Stella

maeve **binchy**

'My life story would be very dull,' Maeve Binchy said recently, with wry humour. 'I was born into a happy family, got a good job, started to write books, they were successful, met a lovely man, got married to him. I mean, where's the drama in that?'

Her life may have lacked great theatrical drama, but her happiness and contentment seem to shine through in her novels. In the twenty-eight or so years that she has been writing fiction, she has created a world of fascinating and memorable characters, loved by her legions of fans around the globe. One element that her readers seem to particularly enjoy is the way in which characters from one book frequently turn up in another, just as in *Minding Frankie*. 'I get lots of letters from people saying how nice it was to know what had happened to so and so,' Maeve says. 'People do feel proprietorial about characters and they almost miss them and think of them as friends.'

She has said that she didn't set out to be a writer but became one more or less by accident. She studied history and French at University College Dublin, graduating in 1960. Her first job was teaching in a school in the city, which gave her time to indulge her love of travel in the long holidays. On one such trip, to a kibbutz in Israel, she started writing long letters home to her mother and father to reassure them that she was fine. Her parents were so impressed by the letters that her father typed them up and sent them to a newspaper. Maeve returned home from her travels to find that they had been published in the *Irish Independent*. A job as the women's editor of the *Irish Times* followed, before she moved to London to work as a features writer. This, as she says, turned out to be great training for her future career. 'On a daily paper, you learn to write very quickly; there is no time to sit and brood about what you are going to say.'

It was at this time that Maeve met, and subsequently married, the broadcaster and writer Gordon Snell, the man she describes as 'the love of my life'. The couple moved to Dalkey, near Dublin, where they bought a cottage in which they have lived ever since. Maeve had been writing fiction in her spare time and in 1982, when she was forty-two, published *Light a Penny Candle*. It was the first of many best sellers.

Her home in Dalkey is near to her family and her many friends—something in which she takes great pleasure. One of the themes in *Minding Frankie* is the importance of having good friends and of being part of a community. 'You know there's an idea where it says that it takes a village to raise a child? Well, in this case, it takes a road or a street to raise a child,' Maeve explains. In *Minding Frankie*, all the people who live in St Jarlath's Crescent—friends, family, neighbours—are so anxious that Noel should keep baby Frankie that they go out of their way to help.

Maeve describes herself as belonging to many communities. There are her neighbours, many of whom she is friendly with; her gardening friends, who offer advice on easy-to-grow plants; her foodie friends, who give her recipes for delicious, straightforward recipes; and her bridge club friends. 'When I was fifty, I decided to play bridge. Now, I cannot tell you how bad at bridge I am. We play Chardonnay bridge, a game not known in bridge clubs. It's lubricated with wine, so we don't really remember what was called, or who dealt. But we have great fun.'

She is now seventy and, in spite of health problems, her zest for life is as strong as ever. 'People might be surprised to know that even though I am big, and lame (with osteoarthritis), and have breathing problems, I don't remotely feel like that. I feel about twenty-two, and optimistic and full of adventure all the time.'

Maeve Binchy's Dublin

Maeve Binchy's fictional Dublin is a beguiling place, full of ordinary, everyday people living interesting and inspiring lives. It is clear, from the way in which she brings the city to vibrant life in novels such as *Tara Road*, *Scarlet Feather* and *Quentins*, that it is a place she loves.

As Maeve explains: 'I set all these books in Dublin because that's where I was born and that's where I grew up, so I know the feel of Dublin very well. It's a big city, rambling and spread out, and parts of it are lovely.' She appreciates the way in which Ireland's capital can seem like a village. 'It's silly to call it a village because it's not, but you do feel that if you are in Dublin you meet people over and over again. Every part of town has its own character. I hope that readers will understand it and feel affectionate towards it like I do.'

LINWOOD BARCLAY

NEVER LOOK AWAY

David Harwood is looking forward to a day's fun at the Five Mountains amusement park with his wife Jan and their four-year-old son Ethan, but his hopes of a happy family outing vanish as soon as they arrive.

Suddenly, David's role as a loving husband and father is called into question and he must use all his investigative skills as a journalist to fight his way through the maze of accusation and deceit that threatens to cut him off from those he loves.

'He's really out of it.'

'Look for a key.'

'I've been through his pockets. There's no handcuff key.'

'Maybe he wrote the combination down, put it in his wallet.'

'What, you think he's a moron? He's going to write down the combination and keep it on him?'

'So cut the chain. We take the case, we figure out how to open it later.'

'It looks way stronger than I thought. It'll take me an hour to cut through. I'm gonna have to cut it off.'

'I thought that you said it would take for ever to cut the cuff.'

'I'm not talking about the cuff.'

PROLOGUE

'I'm scared,' Ethan said.

'There's nothing to be scared about,' I said, turning away from the steering wheel and reaching an arm back to free him from the kiddy seat. I undid the buckle.

'I don't want to go on them,' he said. The tops of the five roller coasters and a Ferris wheel could be seen looming beyond the park entrance.

'We're not going on them,' I reminded him for the umpteenth time. I wondered whether this excursion was such a good plan. The night before, after Jan and I had returned from Lake George and I'd picked Ethan up at my parents' place, he'd had a hard time settling down. He'd been, by turn, excited about coming here and worried the roller coaster would derail at the highest point. After I'd tucked him in, I slipped under the covers next to Jan and considered discussing whether Ethan was really ready for a day at Five Mountains. But she was asleep, or pretending to be, so I let it go.

In the morning, however, Ethan was only excited about the trip. No roller-coaster nightmares. It wasn't until we'd pulled into the parking lot shortly after eleven that his apprehensions resurfaced.

'We're just going on the smaller rides like the merry-go-rounds,' I said to him. 'They won't even let you go on the big ones. You're only four. You have to be eight or nine. You have to be this high.' I held my hand a good four feet above the parking-lot asphalt.

Ethan studied my hand warily, unconvinced.

'It's OK,' I said. 'I'm not going to let anything happen to you.'

Ethan looked me in the eye and decided I was deserving of his trust. He worked his way out of the car-seat straps, which mussed up his fine blond hair, then slithered down to the car floor and stepped out of the open door.

Jan took the stroller out of the trunk of the Honda Accord. Once she had set it up, Ethan plopped himself into the seat. Jan leaned into the trunk again and opened a soft-sided cooler. Inside were an ice pack and half a dozen juice boxes, Cellophane-wrapped straws stuck to the sides. She handed me one of the juice boxes and said, 'Give that to Ethan.'

I took it from Jan as she finished up in the trunk and closed it. She zipped up the cooler bag and tucked it into the basket at the back of the stroller as I peeled the straw off of the sticky juice box. It, or one of the other juices in the cooler, must have sprung a tiny leak. I took the straw from its wrapper, stabbed it into the box and handed the juice to Ethan.

Jan reached out and touched my bare arm. It was a warm August Saturday, and we were both in shorts and sleeveless tops. Jan was wearing a visored baseball cap over her black hair, which she had pulled back into a ponytail and fed through the back of the cap. Oversized shades kept the sun out of her eyes.

'Hey,' she said. She pulled me towards her, behind the stroller, so Ethan couldn't see. 'You OK?'

I was about to ask her the same thing. 'Yeah, sure, I'm good.'

'I know things didn't work out the way you'd hoped yesterday.'

'No big deal,' I said. 'Some leads don't pan out. It happens. What about you? You feel better today?'

She nodded imperceptibly.

'You sure?' I asked. 'What you said yesterday, about the bridge . . . I thought you were feeling better, but when you told me that—'

She put her index finger on my lips. 'I know I've been a lot to live with lately, and I'm sorry about that.' She took a deep breath. 'I want you to know I appreciate . . . your patience.'

'I still don't think it would hurt to see someone on a regular—'

Ethan twisted round in the stroller so he could see us. He stopped sucking on the juice box and said, 'Let's go!'

Jan kissed me on the cheek. 'Let's show the kid a good time.'

'Yeah,' I said.

She gave my arm a final squeeze, then gripped the handles of the stroller. 'OK, buster,' she said to Ethan. 'We're on our way.'

Ethan stuck his hands out to the sides, like he was flying. He'd already drained his juice box and handed it to me to throw away.

We could see people lined up to buy tickets at the main gate. Jan, wisely, had bought them online and printed them out a few days earlier. I pushed the stroller while she rooted in her bag for them.

We were almost at the gates when Jan stopped dead. 'Nuts,' she said. 'The backpack. I left it in the car.'

'Do we need it?' I said. It was a long trek to where we'd parked.

'It's got the peanut-butter sandwiches and the sunscreen. I'll run back. You go ahead, I'll catch up to you.'

She handed me one adult ticket and one child and kept one for herself. She said, 'I think there's an ice-cream place, about a hundred yards in, on the left. We'll meet there?'

Jan was always one to do her research and must have memorised the online map of Five Mountains in preparation.

'That sounds good,' I said. Jan started a slow trot back to the car.

'Where's Mom going?' Ethan asked.

'Forgot the backpack,' I said.

'The sandwiches?' he said.

'Yeah.'

At the gates, I handed in my ticket and his and entered the park. The two closest roller coasters, which had looked big from the parking lot, were positively Everest-like now. I stopped pushing the stroller, knelt next to Ethan and pointed. He looked up, watched a string of cars slowly climb the first hill, then plummet at high speed, the passengers screaming and waving.

He stared, eyes wide with wonder and fear. 'I don't like that.'

'I told you, don't worry. The rides we're going on are on the other side of the park.'

The place was packed. Hundreds, if not thousands, of people moving around us. Parents with little kids, big kids.

'I think that must be the ice-cream place,' I said, spotting the stand just up ahead. I got behind the stroller and started pushing. 'Think it's too early for ice cream?' I asked.

Ethan didn't respond.

'Sport? You saying no to an ice cream?'

When he still said nothing, I stopped to take a look at him. His head was back and to the side, his eyes closed. The little guy had fallen asleep.

'I don't believe it,' I said under my breath.

'Everything OK?'

I turned. Jan had returned, the backpack slung over her shoulder.

'He's nodded off,' I said.

'You're kidding me,' she said.

'I think he passed out from fear after getting a close look at that,' I said, pointing to the coaster.

'I think I've got something in my shoe.' She navigated the stroller over to a concrete ledge, perched on the edge, nudging the stroller to her left. 'Feel like splitting a cone? I'm parched.'

'Dipped in chocolate?' I asked.

'Surprise me,' she said, putting her left foot up on her knee.

I strolled over to the ice-cream stand. It was the soft white stuff that comes out of a machine. I asked the young girl who took my order to dip it in the vat of chocolate.

She presented it to me and I took a bite, cracking the chocolate, and then regretted it. I should have let Jan have the first bite. But I'd make up for it in the week. On Monday, come home with flowers. Later in the week, book a sitter, take Jan out for dinner. This thing she was going through—maybe it was my fault. I hadn't been attentive enough. I hadn't made the extra effort. If that was what it was going to take to bring Jan round, I was up to it.

I didn't expect to see her coming straight for me when I turned. She was upset. There was a tear running down one cheek.

She came up to me quickly, 'I only looked away for a second.'

'What?'

'My shoe,' she said, her voice uneven. 'I was getting—the stone—I was getting the stone out of my shoe, and then I looked—I looked round and—'

'Jan, what are you talking about?'

'Someone's taken him,' she said. 'I turned and he—'

I was already running over to where I'd last seen them together.

The stroller was gone.

I stepped onto the ledge Jan had been sitting on. 'Ethan!' I shouted. People walking past glanced at me. 'Ethan!'

Jan was standing below me, looking up. 'Do you see him?'

'What happened?' I asked quickly. 'What the hell happened?'

'I told you. I looked away for a second and—'

'Go back to the main gate,' I told Jan, trying to keep my voice even. 'If someone tries to take him out, they'll have to go through there. There should be somebody from park security there. Tell them.' The ice-cream cone was still in my hand. I tossed it.

'What about you?' she asked.

'I'll scout out that way.' I pointed beyond the ice-cream stand.

Jan was already running. She looked back over her shoulder, did the cell-phone gesture to her ear, telling me to call her if I found out anything. I nodded and started running the other way.

I ran towards the base of the closest roller coaster, where I guessed about a hundred people were waiting to board. I scanned the line-up, looked for our stroller, or a small boy without one.

I kept running. Up ahead was KidLand Adventure, the part of Five Mountains devoted to rides for children too young for the big coasters. Did it make sense for someone to have grabbed Ethan and brought him here for the rides? Not really. Unless it was a mix-up, someone getting behind a stroller and heading off with it, never bothering to look at the kid sitting inside. I'd nearly done it myself once at the mall, the strollers all looking the same, my mind elsewhere.

Up ahead, a short, wide woman, her back to me, was pushing a stroller that looked a lot like ours. I poured on the speed, pulled up alongside her, then jumped in front to get a look at the child.

It was a small girl in a pink dress, maybe three years old.

'You got a problem, mister?' the woman asked.

'Sorry,' I said, not even getting the whole word out as I turned, scanning, scanning . . . I caught sight of another stroller. A blue one, a small canvas bag tucked into the back basket.

The stroller was unattended. I couldn't tell if it was occupied.

Out of the corner of my eye, I caught a glimpse of a man. Bearded.

Running away. But I wasn't interested in him. I sprinted in the direction of the abandoned stroller. *Please, please, please . . .*

I ran round to the front of it, looked down. He hadn't even woken up. His head was still to one side, his eyes shut.

'Ethan!' I said. I reached down, scooped him out of the stroller and held him close to me. 'Ethan, oh God, Ethan!'

I held him out where I could see his face, and he was frowning, like he was about to cry. 'It's OK,' I said. 'Daddy's here.'

I realised he wasn't upset because he'd been snatched away from us. He was annoyed at having his nap interrupted. But that didn't stop me from telling him, again, that everything was OK. I said, 'We have to find your mother, let her know everything's OK.'

I got out my phone, dialled Jan's cell. It rang five times and went to message. 'I've got him,' I said. 'I'm coming to the gate.'

Ethan had never had such a speedy stroller ride. He stuck out his hands and giggled as I pushed him through the crowds. When we got to the main gate, I stopped, looked around. I got out my phone again. I left a second message: 'Hey, we're at the gate. Where are you?'

'I'm hungry,' Ethan said. 'Didn't Mom come? Did she go home? Did she leave the backpack with the sandwiches in it?'

'Hold on,' I said. I was holding my cell, ready to flip it open the instant it rang.

Maybe Jan was with park security.

A park employee walked past. I grabbed his arm. 'You security?' I asked.

He held up a small walkie-talkie. 'I can get them,' he said.

At my request, he called to see whether anyone from security was helping Jan. 'Someone needs to tell her I've found our son,' I said.

The voice coming out of the walkie-talkie was scratchy. *'Who? We got nothing on that.'*

'Sorry,' the park employee said and moved on.

I was trying to tamp down the panic. Something was very wrong.

Someone tries to take your kid.

A bearded man runs away.

Your wife doesn't come back to the rendezvous point.

'Don't worry,' I said to Ethan, scanning the crowds. 'I'm sure she'll be here any minute. Then we'll have some fun.'

But Ethan didn't say anything. He'd fallen back asleep.

ONE
Twelve Days Earlier

'Yeah?'

'Mr Reeves?' I said. 'This is David Harwood at the *Standard*.'

'What's on your mind, David?' Reeves asked.

'Hope I didn't catch you at a bad time. I understand you just got back yesterday?'

'Yeah,' Stan Reeves said.

'And this trip was a—what? A fact-finding mission to England?'

'Yeah,' he said.

It was like pulling teeth, getting anything out of Reeves. Maybe this had something to do with the fact that he didn't like the stories I'd been writing about what could end up being Promise Falls's newest industry.

'So what facts did you pick up?' I asked.

'We found that for-profit prisons have been operating in the United Kingdom successfully for some time.'

'Did Mr Sebastian accompany you as you toured the prison facilities in England?' I asked. Elmont Sebastian was the president of Star Spangled Corrections, the multimillion-dollar company that wanted to build a private prison just outside Promise Falls.

'I believe he was there for part of the tour,' Stan Reeves said. 'He helped facilitate a few things for the delegation.'

'Was there anyone else from the Promise Falls council who made up this delegation?' I asked.

'I was the council's appointee to go to England and see their operations. There were also a couple of people from Albany.'

'So what did you take from the trip, bottom line?' I asked.

'It confirmed a lot of what we already know. That privately run correctional facilities are more efficient than state-run facilities.'

'Isn't that largely because they pay their people far less than the state pays its unionised staff?'

A tired sigh. 'You're a broken record, David.'

'That's not an opinion,' I said. 'That's a documented fact. Has Star Spangled Corrections settled on a site yet?'

'There are a number of possible sites in the Promise Falls area.'

'Star Spangled will come before council for re-zoning approval on whatever site they pick. How do you plan to vote on that?'

'I'll weigh the merits of the proposal and vote objectively.'

'You're not worried about the perception that your vote may have already been decided?'

'Why would anyone perceive such a thing?' Reeves asked.

'Well, your trip to Florence for one. Instead of coming back from England, you went to Italy for several days. Where did you stay in Florence?' I asked, even though I knew.

'The Maggio,' Reeves said hesitantly.

'I guess you must have run into Elmont Sebastian there?'

'I think I did run into him in the lobby once or twice,' he said.

'Weren't you, in fact, Mr Sebastian's guest?'

'Guest? I was a guest of the hotel, David.'

'But Star Spangled, Inc. paid for your air fare to Florence and your accommodation. You flew out of Gatwick on—'

'What the hell is this?' Reeves asked.

'Do you have a receipt for your Florence stay?' I asked.

'I'm sure I could put my hands on it if I had to.'

'So then if I were to write a story that says Star Spangled, Inc. paid for your Florence stay, you could produce that receipt to prove me wrong. My information is that your stay came to three thousand, five hundred and twenty-six euros. Does that sound about right?'

The council man said nothing.

'Mr Reeves?'

'I'm not sure,' he said quietly. 'I'd have to check. But you're way off base, suggesting that Mr Sebastian footed the bill for this.'

'I have a copy of the bill. It was charged to Mr Sebastian's account.'

'How the hell did you get that?'

I wasn't about to say, but a woman had phoned earlier in the day to tell me about the hotel bill. I was guessing she worked at City Hall or in Elmont Sebastian's office. I couldn't get a name out of her.

'Mr Reeves, when this prison proposal comes before council, will you declare a conflict of interest, given that you've accepted what amounts to a gift from the prison company?'

'You're a piece of shit, you know that?' Reeves said.

'I'll take that as a confirmation.'

'You want to know what really gets me? This high-and-mighty attitude from someone working for a newspaper that's turned into a joke. You're getting your shorts in a knot because someone might outsource running a prison, when you outsource reporting. I remember when the Promise Falls *Standard* was a paper people had respect for. Of course, that was before the Russell family farmed out some of its reporting duties, getting reporters in India to watch committee meetings over the Internet and then write up what happened at them for a fraction of what it costs to pay reporters here to do the job. Any paper that does that and thinks it can call itself a newspaper is living in a fool's paradise, my friend.'

He hung up.

I took off my headset, hit the stop button on my digital recorder. I was feeling pretty proud of myself, right up until the end there.

The phone had only been on the receiver for ten seconds when it rang. I put the headset to my ear. '*Standard.* Harwood.'

'Hey.' It was Jan.

'Hey,' I said. 'How's it going?'

'OK.' Jan paused. 'I was just thinking of that movie with Jack Nicholson where he's a germaphobe. Remember when he goes to the shrink's office? And all those people are sitting there? He says the line, from the title? "What if this is as good as it gets?"'

'I remember,' I said quietly. 'You're thinking about that?'

She shifted gears. 'So what about you? What's the scoop, Harwood?'

MAYBE THERE WERE clues earlier that something was wrong and I'd just been too dumb to notice them. But still, it seemed as though Jan's mood had changed almost overnight.

She was tense, short-tempered. Minor irritants that would not have fazed her in the past now were major burdens. One evening, while we were getting ready to make up some lunches for the next day, she burst into tears upon discovering we were out of bread.

'It's all too much,' she said to me that night. 'I feel like I'm at the bottom of this well and I can't climb out.'

At first, I thought it was a hormonal thing. But I soon realised it was more than that. Jan was down in the dumps. Depressed.

'Is it work?' I asked her one night in bed. Jan, with one other woman, managed the office for Bertram's Heating and Cooling. The latest economic slowdown meant fewer people were buying new air conditioners or boilers. And, sometimes, she and Leanne Kowalski, that other woman, didn't see eye to eye.

'Work's fine,' she said.

'Have I done something?' I asked. 'If I have, tell me.'

'You haven't done anything,' she said. 'It's just . . . I don't know. Sometimes I wish I could make it all go away.'

'Make what all go away?'

'Nothing,' she said. 'Go to sleep.'

A couple of days later, I suggested maybe she should talk to someone. Starting with our family doctor.

'Maybe there's a prescription or something,' I said.

'I don't want to take drugs,' Jan said. 'I don't want to be somebody I'm not.'

AFTER WORK on the day she called me at the paper, Jan and I drove up together to pick up Ethan at his grandparents' place.

My mother and father, Arlene and Don Harwood, lived in an older part of Promise Falls in a two-storey house built in the forties. They'd bought it in the fall of 1971 when Mom was pregnant with me. Mom had made noises about selling it after Dad retired from the city's building department four years ago, arguing that they didn't need all this space, that they could get along fine in a condo, but Dad wouldn't have any of it. He'd go mad cooped up in a condo. He had his workshop in the garage, and spent more time in there than in the house, if you didn't count sleeping. He was a relentless potterer, always looking for something to fix or tear down and do over again. A door never had a chance to squeak twice. Dad practically carried a can of WD40 with him at all times.

Jan and I knew when we left Ethan with his grandparents, as we did through the week when we both went to work, that he wouldn't be exposed to any frayed light cords or poisonous chemicals left where he could get his hands on them. And their rates happened to be more reasonable than any nursery schools in the area.

'I got hold of Reeves today, asked him about his hotel bill in Florence,' I said to Jan, who was driving in her Volkswagen Jetta wagon. It was nearly 5.30. We'd rendezvoused at our house so we could pick up Ethan in one car.

Jan said, without sounding all that interested, 'How's that story coming?'

'Some woman called me anonymously. She had some good stuff. What I need to know now is how many on the council are taking bribes or gifts or trips from this private prison corporation so that they'll give them the nod when the re-zoning comes up for a vote.'

'Even if you get the story,' Jan said, 'will they print it?'

I looked out of my window. 'I don't know.'

Things had changed at the *Standard*. It was still owned by the Russell family, and a Russell still sat in the publisher's chair. But the family's commitment to keeping it a real newspaper had shifted. The overriding concern now, with declining revenues and readership, was survival. The paper had always kept a reporter in Albany to cover state issues, but now relied on wires. We used to run two editorials a day, written by staffers. Now, we ran 'What Others Think', a sampling of editorials from across the country. We didn't think for ourselves more than three or four times a week.

But the most alarming indicator of our decline was sending reporting jobs offshore. The Russells started with the entertainment listings. Why pay someone here fifteen bucks an hour to write up what's going on around town when you could email the info to a guy in India who'd put it together for seven dollars an hour?

When the Russells found how well that worked, they stepped it up. Various city committees had a live Internet feed. Why send a reporter? Why not get a guy in Mumbai to watch it, write up what he sees, then email his story back to Promise Falls, New York?

As Brian Donnelly, the city editor and, more important, the publisher's nephew, had mentioned to me only the day before, 'How hard can it be to write down what people say at a meeting? Some of these guys in India, they take really good notes.'

'Don't you ever get tired of this?' Jan asked, hitting the intermittent wipers to clear off some light rain.

'Yeah, but I'm beating my head against the wall with Brian.'

'I'm not talking about work,' Jan said. 'I'm talking about your parents. They're nice enough, but we can never just pick Ethan up at the end of the day. You have to go through the interrogation. "How was your day?" "What's new at work?" If we'd put him in day care, they'd just kick him out of the door and we could go home.'

'Oh, that sounds better. A place where they don't actually have any interest in your kid.'

'You know what I'm saying.'

'Look,' I said, not wanting to have a fight because I wasn't sure what was going on here, 'in another month it won't matter. Ethan'll be going to kindergarten, which means we won't be taking him to my parents' every day, which means you won't have to endure this daily interrogation you suddenly seem so concerned about. It's not like we can take turns dropping him off at *your* parents' place.'

Jan shot me a look. I regretted the comment instantly.

'I'm sorry,' I said. 'That was a cheap shot.'

Jan said nothing.

'I'm sorry.'

Jan put her blinker on, turned in to my parents' driveway.

Ethan was in the living room, watching *Family Guy*. I walked in, turned off the set, called out to Mom, who was in the kitchen, 'You can't let him watch that.'

'It's just a cartoon,' she said, loud enough to be heard over running water.

'Pack up your stuff,' I told Ethan, and walked into the kitchen. Mom stood at the sink. 'In one episode the dog tries to have sex with the mother. In another, the baby takes a machine gun to her.'

'Oh, come on,' she said. 'No one would make a cartoon like that.' I gave her a kiss on the cheek. 'You're wound too tight.'

'It's not *The Flintstones* any more,' I said.

Ethan shuffled into the kitchen, looking tired.

Jan, who had come in a few seconds after me, knelt down to Ethan. 'Hey, little man,' she said. She looked into his backpack. 'You sure you have everything here?'

He nodded.

'Where's Dad?' I asked.

'He's in the garage,' Mom said. 'So, Jan, how was work today?'

I walked through the light rain to the garage. Dad was tidying his workbench when I walked in. He's taller than I am and he still has a full head of hair, which is a comfort to me.

'Hey,' he said. He was standing by his blue Crown Victoria.

Dad asked about plans for the new prison, and I had just started to fill him in when I saw Jan come out of the back door with Ethan. They walked to the Jetta and Jan strapped Ethan into the safety seat.

'Guess we're going,' I said.

I got into the Jetta next to Jan. She backed out of the driveway, pointed us in the direction of our house. She wouldn't look at me.

'You OK?' I asked.

Jan said nothing all the way home and very little through dinner. She said she would put Ethan to bed, something we often did together. I went upstairs as she was tucking our son in.

'You know who loves you more than anyone in the whole world?' she said to him.

'You?' Ethan said in his tiny voice.

'That's right,' Jan whispered. 'You remember that. If someone said I didn't love you, that wouldn't be true. Do you understand?'

'Yup,' Ethan said.

'You sleep tight and I'll see you in the morning, OK?'

I slipped into our bedroom so I wouldn't be standing there when Jan came out.

'CHECK IT OUT,' said Samantha Henry, a general assignment reporter who sat next to me in the *Standard* newsroom.

I wheeled over on my chair and looked at her computer monitor. Close enough to read it, but not so close she might think I was smelling her hair.

'This just came in from one of the guys in India, who was watching a planning committee meeting about a proposed housing development.' The committee was grilling the developer about how small the bedrooms appeared to be on the plans. 'OK, so read this para right here,' Samantha said, pointing.

'"Mr Councillor Richard Hemmings expressed consternation that the rooms did not meet the requirements for the swinging of a cat."' I grinned. '"A bedroom must be large enough that if you are standing in the centre, grasping a cat by the tail, its head will not hit any of the walls when you are spinning with your arm extended."'

'Stuff's coming in like this every day,' Samantha said. 'What do they think they're doing? Don't they care?'

I pushed away from the monitor. I always felt a little more relaxed when I moved away from Sam. The thing we'd had was a long time ago, but you started sharing a computer screen too often and people were going to talk. 'You have to ask?' I said.

'I've never seen anything like this,' she said. 'I've been here fifteen years.

I asked the ME's assistant for a new pen and she wanted to see an empty one first. Swear to God.'

'I hear the Russells may be looking to sell,' I said. It was the number one rumour going round the building.

Samantha rolled her eyes. 'I can't believe they'd sell. This place has been run by one family for generations.'

'Yeah, well, it's a very different generation running it now than ten years ago. You won't find ink running through the veins of anyone on the board these days.'

'Madeline used to be a reporter,' Samantha said, meaning our publisher.

'Used to be,' I said.

What with papers shutting down all over the country, everyone was on edge. But Sam, in particular, was worried about her future. She had an eight-year-old daughter and no husband. They'd split up years ago, and she'd never had a dime of support from him.

When she was newly divorced, with a baby, Sam put up a brave front. She could do this. Still have her career and raise a child. We didn't sit next to each other back then, but we crossed paths often enough. She let down her guard about how tough things were for her and Gillian.

I guess I thought I could rescue her.

We started spending a lot of time together. I fancied myself as more than a boyfriend. I was going to make her life OK again.

I took it pretty hard when she dumped me.

'This is too fast,' she told me. 'This is how I screwed things up last time. Moving too quickly. You're a great guy, but . . .'

I went into a funk I didn't come out of until I met Jan. And now, years later, things were OK between Sam and me. But she was still a single mother, and things had never stopped being a struggle.

She lived pay cheque to pay cheque. She reported to general assignment, and couldn't predict the hours she'd be working. She was always scrambling to find someone to watch her daughter when a last-minute assignment landed on her desk.

I didn't have Sam's week-to-week financial worries, but Jan and I talked often about what else I could do if I found myself without a job. Unemployment insurance only lasted so long. I—and Jan for that matter—was worth more dead since we each signed up for a $300,000 life insurance policy a few weeks back.

'David, you got a sec?'

I whirled round in my chair. It was Brian Donnelly, the city editor. 'What's up?'

He nodded in the direction of his office, so I got up and followed him. I wasn't forty yet, but I saw Brian was part of the new breed round here. At twenty-six, he was management, having impressed the bosses not with journalistic credentials but with business savvy. Everything was 'marketing' and 'trends' and 'synergy'.

Brian slipped in behind his desk and asked me to sit down.

'So, this prison thing,' he said. 'What have you really got?'

'The company gave Reeves an all-expenses-paid vacation in Italy after the UK junket,' I said. 'Presumably, when Star Spangled's proposal comes up before council, he'll be voting on it.'

'*Presumably.* So he's not actually in a conflict of interest yet, is he? If he abstains or something, what exactly do we have here?'

'What are you saying, Brian? If a cop takes a payoff from a holdup gang to look the other way, it's not a conflict of interest until the bank actually gets robbed?'

'We're not talking about a holdup. Do we know for sure Reeves didn't pay for the hotel? Or that he isn't paying back Sebastian? In your story, you don't actually have him denying it. We need to give him a chance to explain himself before we run this.'

'I gave him a chance,' I said. 'Where's this coming from? Are you getting leaned on by She Who Must Be Obeyed?'

'You shouldn't refer to the publisher that way,' Brian said.

'But I'm right about where this is coming from. Ms Plimpton sent the word down,' I said.

While born a Russell, Madeline Plimpton had been married to Geoffrey Plimpton, a well-known Promise Falls real estate agent, who'd died two years ago, aged thirty-eight, of an aneurysm. Madeline Plimpton, at thirty-nine, was the youngest publisher in the paper's history. Brian was the son of her older sister, Margaret, who'd never had any interest in newspapers.

Brian had never worked as a reporter, so you almost couldn't blame him for not understanding the thrill of nailing a weasel like Reeves to the wall. But Madeline had worked as a reporter alongside me more than a decade ago. It was part of her crash course in learning the family business, all designed to get her ready to be publisher once her father packed it in, which he had done four years ago. The fact that Madeline had worked in the trenches made her tiptoeing round the Reeves story all the more disheartening.

I said, 'Maybe I should talk to her.'

'That'd be a very bad idea. She's this close to—'

'To what?'

'Look, it's not all about saving the world here, David. We're trying to get out a paper that makes money, a paper that has a shot at being around a year from now. We can't afford to run anything that's not airtight, not these days, that's all I'm telling you.'

'She's this close to what, Brian?'

Brian took a few slow breaths. 'You didn't hear this from me, David, but if this prison sets up here, the *Standard* could wipe all its debts, have a fresh start. If the paper sold Star Spangled Corrections the land to build their prison that would help the bottom line.'

My mouth was open for a good ten seconds. Why had this never occurred to me? The twenty acres the Russell family owned on the south side of Promise Falls had for years been the rumoured site of a new building for the *Standard*. But that talk stopped about five years ago when earnings began to fall. 'Oh my God,' I said.

'You didn't hear it from me,' Brian said. 'And if you go out there and breathe a word of this to anyone, we're both fucked. Do you understand? Do you understand now why anything we run has to be nailed down, I mean *really* nailed down?'

I got up from my chair.

'What are you going to do, David? Tell me you're not going to do anything stupid.'

I surveyed his office. 'I'm not sure this room meets the cat-swinging code, Brian. You might want to look into that.'

I SAT AT MY DESK and stewed for half an hour. I was angry.

Maybe this was how it was going to be. You came in, you churned out your copy, didn't matter what it was, you took your pay cheque, you went home. There'd always been papers like that. I'd been naive to think the *Standard* would never turn into one of them.

I picked up the phone, dialled Bertram Heating and Cooling. If I couldn't save the state of journalism, maybe I could put a bit of effort into my marriage, which had been showing signs of wear.

A voice said, 'Bertram's'. It was Leanne Kowalski. She had the perfect voice for someone working at an air-conditioning firm. Icy.

'Hey, Leanne,' I said. 'It's David. Jan there?'

'Hang on.' Leanne wasn't big on small talk.

The line seemed to go dead, then Jan picked up and said, 'Hey.'

'Why don't we see if my parents can hang on to Ethan for a few extra hours, we'll go out for a bite to eat, just the two of us.'

'I guess,' she said.

'You don't sound very excited.'

'Actually, yeah,' said Jan, warming to the idea. 'Where were you thinking for dinner?'

'I don't know. Preston's?' A steakhouse.

'What about Gina's?' Jan asked.

Our favourite Italian place. 'Perfect. I'll pick you up.'

TAKING A SHORT CUT through the pressroom on the way to the parking lot, I spotted Madeline Plimpton.

It was the pressroom that most made this building feel like a real newspaper. I saw Madeline on the 'boards', which was pressman-speak for the catwalks that ran along the sides of, and through, the presses; these were not actually massive rollers, but dozens of smaller ones that led the never-ending sheets of newsprint on a circuitous route up and down and over and under until they miraculously appeared as a perfectly collated newspaper. The machinery had been undergoing maintenance, and an overall-clad pressman was directing Madeline's attention to the guts of one part of the presses, which ran from one end of the hundred-foot room to the other.

I didn't want to pass up this opportunity to speak to her, but I knew better than to clamber up the metal steps. The pressmen could be sensitive about people going up on the boards without their permission. I caught Madeline's eye when she glanced down.

'David,' she said. It was normally deafening in here, but the presses weren't currently in operation, so I could hear her.

'Madeline,' I said. Considering that we'd come through the newsroom together, years earlier, it never occurred to me to call her by anything other than her first name. 'You got a minute?'

She nodded and descended the metal staircase.

Once she was on the floor, I said, 'This Reeves story is solid.'

'I'm sorry?' she said.

'Please,' I said. 'I get what's going on. We like this new prison. We don't want to make waves. We play down local opposition to this thing and we get to sell them the land they need to build.'

Something flickered in Madeline's eyes. Maybe she'd figure out Brian had told me.

'But this will end up biting us in the ass, Madeline. Over time, readers will figure out that we don't care about news, that we're just a press release delivery system, something that keeps fliers from getting wet. What's the point in doing all this if we don't care what we are any more?'

Madeline looked me in the eye. 'What's happened to you?'

'I think a better question would be what's happened to you?' I said. 'Remember the time you and I covered that hostage taking, where the guy was holding his wife and kid, said he was going to kill them if the police didn't back off? And we got in between the police and the house, and we saw everything that went down, the cops storming the place, beating the hell out of that guy, even after they'd found out he didn't have a gun. Just about killed him. And the story we put together after, laying it all out just like it happened, even though we knew it was going to cause trouble with the police, which it sure as hell did when it ran. You remember the feeling?'

Her eyes went soft at the memory. 'I remember. I miss it.'

'Some of us care about that feeling. We don't want to lose it.'

'And I don't want to lose this paper,' Madeline said. 'You go to bed at night worried about whether your story will run. I go to bed worried about whether there's going to be a paper to run it in. I may not sit in the newsroom any more, but I'm still on the front line.'

I didn't have a comeback for that.

I PARKED OUTSIDE the front of Bertram's a little after 5.30 p.m. Leanne was standing in the parking lot like she was waiting for someone.

I nodded hello as I got out of the Accord and headed for the door. 'How's it going, Leanne?' I said.

'Be better if Lyall ever turns up,' she said. Leanne was one of those people who seemed to have only two moods. Annoyed, and irritated. She was skinny with black, lightly streaked short hair.

'No wheels today?' I asked. There was usually an old blue Ford Explorer parked next to Jan's Jetta any time I drove by.

'Lyall's clunker's in the shop, so he borrowed mine,' she said. 'I don't know where he is. Was supposed to be here half an hour ago.'

I offered up an awkward smile, then pulled on the office door handle. When I went inside, Jan was turning off her computer.

'Leanne's her usual cheerful self,' I said.

Jan said, 'Tell me about it.'

We happened to look out of the window at the same time. Leanne's Explorer had just careered into the lot. I could see Lyall behind the windshield, his sausage-like fingers gripped to the wheel.

Instead of getting in the passenger side, Leanne went to the driver's door, yanking it open. She was agitated, waving her hands, yelling at him. Lyall slithered out of the driver's seat and slunk round the Explorer, Leanne shouting at him the entire time.

'Must be fun to be him,' I said as Lyall opened the passenger door and got in.

'I don't know why she stays with him,' Jan said.

Leanne got behind the wheel and sped off down the road.

GINA SHOWED Jan and me to our table. Gina was a plump woman in her sixties whose eatery was a legend in the Promise Falls area.

'When did you tell your parents we'd be coming for Ethan?' Jan asked around the time we got our minestrone.

'Between eight and nine.'

Her spoon was in her right hand. As she reached with her left for the salt her sleeve slipped back an inch, revealing something white wrapped about her left wrist. 'They're good with him,' she said.

'They are,' I said. It looked like a bandage round her wrist.

Jan said, 'It's good to know that if something . . . if something happened to me—or to you—they'd be able to help out a lot.'

'What are you talking about, Jan? Nothing's going to happen to you or to me. What's that on your wrist?'

She pulled her sleeve down. 'It's nothing. I just nicked myself.'

'Let me see.'

'There's nothing to see,' she said. But I had reached across the table, taken hold of her hand, and pushed the sleeve up myself. A bandage went completely round her wrist.

'Jan, what did you do?'

She yanked her arm away. 'Let go of me!' she said, loud enough to make the people at the other tables, and Gina, glance our way.

'Fine,' I said quietly, taking my hand back. Keeping my voice low, I said, 'Just tell me what happened.'

'I was cutting some vegetables and the knife slipped,' she said. 'It's not . . . what it looks like. I swear, it was totally an accident.'

I could see injuring your finger while cutting up carrots, but how did a knife jump up and get your wrist?

'Jesus, Jan,' I said, shaking my head. 'These days, lately, I don't know . . . I'm worried sick about you.'

'You don't have to be concerned,' she said and studied her soup.

'But I am.' I swallowed. 'I love you.'

Twice she started to speak and then stopped. Finally, she said, 'I think, sometimes, it would be easier for you if you didn't have both of us to worry about. If it was just you and Ethan.'

'What are you talking about?'

Jan didn't say anything.

I was frantic with concern. 'Jan, answer me honestly. Are you having—I don't know how to put this—self-destructive thoughts?'

She kept looking at the soup. 'I don't know.'

I had this feeling that we had reached a moment. A moment when you feel the ground moving beneath you. 'You don't know,' I said. 'So you *might* be thinking about hurting yourself.'

Her eyes seemed to nod. 'These thoughts come in and I can't seem to get rid of them. I feel I'm this huge burden to you.'

'That's ridiculous. You're everything to me. I think maybe you need to talk to—'

'What, so they could put me away? Lock me up in a loony bin?'

I sensed Gina approaching.

'That's what you'd like, isn't it?' Jan said, her voice rising again. 'To be rid of me for good.'

Gina stopped and we both looked at her.

'I'm sorry,' Gina said. 'I was just going to'—she pointed at the soup bowls—'take those away, if you were finished.'

I nodded, and Gina removed them.

To Jan I said, 'Maybe we should go home and—'

But Jan was already pushing back her chair.

TWO

I didn't sleep much that night. I tried to talk to Jan on the way home, and before we went to bed, but she wasn't interested in having any further conversations with me, particularly when I brought up the topic of her seeking some kind of professional help.

So I was pretty weary the following morning, walking with my head hanging so low on my way into the *Standard* building that I didn't even notice the man blocking my path until I was nearly standing on his toes. He was a big guy, ready to burst out of his black suit. Over six feet tall, he had a shaved head.

'Mr Harwood?' he said, an edge to his voice.

'Yes?'

'Mr Sebastian would be honoured if you would join him over coffee. He's waiting down at the park. I'd be happy to drive you.'

'Elmont Sebastian?' I said. I'd been trying for weeks to get an interview with the president of Star Spangled Corrections. He didn't return calls.

'Yes,' the man said. 'My name is Welland. I'm his driver.'

'Sure,' I said.

Welland led me round the corner and opened the door of a black Lincoln limo for me. I got into the back. After Welland got behind the wheel, I asked, 'Have you worked long for Mr Sebastian?'

'Just three months,' he said, pulling out into traffic.

'And what were you doing before that?'

'I was incarcerated,' Welland said. 'I served my time at one of Mr Sebastian's facilities. I'm a product of the excellent rehabilitation programmes Star Spangled facilities offer. When my sentence ended, he took a chance on me, gave me this job.'

Welland stopped the car by the park that sits just below the falls the town takes its name from. He opened the door and pointed at a picnic table near the river's edge. A distinguished-looking, silver-haired man in his sixties was seated on the bench with his back to the table, tossing popcorn to some ducks. When he spotted me and rose from the bench, he smiled and extended a sweaty hand.

'Mr Harwood, it's a pleasure to be able to speak to you at last.'

'I've been available, Mr Sebastian,' I said. 'You're the one who's been hard to get hold of.'

He laughed. 'Please, call me Elmont. May I call you David?'

'Of course,' I said.

He pointed to the table, where two take-out coffees sat in a box filled with creams, sugars, and wooden sticks. 'I didn't know what you took in yours, so it's black. Help yourself to what you need.'

He turned himself round as I took a seat opposite him. I didn't reach for a coffee, but did go into my pocket for a pad and pen. 'I've left several messages for you. Why did you pay for Stan Reeves's trip to Florence? Is that standard policy? To reward people in advance who'll be voting on your plans?'

'You get right to it. I appreciate that. I like directness.' Sebastian prised off a coffee lid and poured in three creams. 'As it turns out, this is why I was hoping to meet with you, to show you something.'

He reached into his suit jacket and pulled out an envelope that had his name written on it. He withdrew a cheque and handed it to me.

I held it in my hand and saw that it was made out to him. And it was written on the personal account of Stan Reeves, in the amount of $4,763.09. The date in the upper right corner was two days ago.

'I know you think you were onto something with Councillor Reeves,' he said, 'that he accepted a free trip to Italy from me, but nothing could be further from the truth. I had already rented a couple of rooms in Florence, expecting to entertain friends, but they had to cancel at the last minute, so I said to Mr Reeves, while we were in England, that he was welcome to take the extra room. And he was pleased to do so, but he made it clear to me that he was not able to accept any gifts. We made arrangements that he would settle up with me upon his return. There's the cheque that proves it.'

'Well,' I said, handing it back, 'it's great that's all cleared up.'

He returned the cheque to its envelope and slipped it back into his coat. 'David, I get the sense from your stories you think there's something inherently evil about a private prison.'

'A for-profit prison,' I said.

'I'm not denying it.' Sebastian took a sip of coffee. 'Profit is not a dirty word. Nothing immoral with rewarding people financially for a job well done. And when it turns out to be a job that makes this country a better place to live, what's wrong with that?'

'You're taking what has traditionally been a government responsibility and turning it into a way to make money. And all you get out of it is, if last year is any indication, a one point three billion-dollar payoff.'

Sebastian shook his head in mock sadness. 'Do you work for free at the *Standard*?' He glanced at his watch. 'I really must be going.'

Sebastian rose from the bench and walked back to his limo. He'd brought his take-out cup with him and handed it to Welland to dispose of. Welland opened the door for him, closed it, got rid of the cup, got into the driver's seat, and the limo drove off.

TEN DAYS after our dinner at Gina's, Jan got us tickets to go to Five Mountains, the roller-coaster park.

She'd been doing her best to be herself round Ethan in the ten days since she'd said I'd be happy to be rid of her. If Ethan had noticed she wasn't well, he hadn't asked what was up. Jan had taken a few days off from work in the last week, but I'd still taken Ethan to my parents', thinking what she needed was time to herself.

The day after Gina's, I started pushing Jan to go and talk to our family doctor. She refused.

'But those thoughts you were having,' I said. 'About whether to harm yourself. Are you still having those?'

'People have all kinds of thoughts,' she said, and walked out of the room.

ON THE SAME DAY that Jan ordered the tickets, an email arrived in my in-box at work:

> We spoke the other day. I know you're looking into Star Spangled Corrections and how they're trying to buy up all the votes on council. Reeves is not the only one they've treated to trips or gifts. I've got a list of what's being paid out and who's getting it. I don't dare phone you or say who I am in this email, but I'm willing to meet you in person and give you all the evidence you need for this. Meet me tomorrow at 5 p.m. in the parking lot of Ted's Lakeview General Store. Take 87 North to Lake George. Take 9 North which goes for a ways alongside 87. There's an area where the woods opens up and that's where Ted's is. If I'm not there by 5.10, it means something has happened and I'm not coming. I'll tell you this much: I'm a woman and I will be in a white pick-up.

I read it through a couple of times, sitting at my desk in the newsroom. Rattled, I went to the cafeteria for a coffee.

'You OK?' Samantha Henry, at her desk next to mine, asked when I returned. 'I said hello to you twice and you ignored me.'

The Hotmail address the email had been sent from was a random series of letters and numbers that offered no clues about the author. I made some notes, then deleted the email. Ever since learning that the paper's owners had an interest in selling land to Star Spangled Corrections, I'd been looking over my shoulder a bit more.

My story on Reeves's Florence vacation had never made the paper. His cheque to Sebastian was obviously written after he'd found out I knew about his Florence trip, but it was enough to bury the story as far as Brian was concerned. I needed something that really nailed Reeves and possibly other council members to the wall. This anonymous email might just be it.

'I'VE BOUGHT US TICKETS to go to Five Mountains,' Jan said when she phoned in the afternoon.

'You what?'

'The park north of town we drive by with all the roller coasters?'

'I know what it is.' Everyone knew about Five Mountains. It had opened just outside Promise Falls in the spring to much fanfare.

'You don't want to go?' she asked. 'I already bought the tickets online. I don't think there's any way to take them back.'

'No, no, it's OK,' I said. 'I'm just surprised.' One minute, she was talking like someone who wanted to kill herself, the next she was booking tickets to a theme park. 'You didn't book these for tomorrow, did you?' It wasn't like Ethan was in school yet. He could go any day, and for all I knew Jan was planning to take the next day off, assuming I might be persuaded to do the same.

'No, they're for Saturday,' she said. 'Is that a problem?'

'That's perfect. It would have been hard for me to go tomorrow.'

'What's up tomorrow?'

I lowered my voice so Sam wouldn't hear. 'I have to meet somebody. I got this anonymous email, a woman claiming to have the goods on Reeves and some of the councillors. Maybe she works at City Hall or is a prison guard at one of Sebastian's facilities.'

'Oh my God, that's just what you've been waiting for. You meeting her in some dark alley or something?'

'I'm driving up to Lake George.'

Jan didn't say anything for a moment.

'What is it, hon?'

'I was just, I was just thinking of taking one more mental health day tomorrow. It's really slow in the office.'

I hesitated just for second. 'Why don't you ride up with me?' I could use the company, and given Jan's dark thoughts lately, it would be a way to keep tabs on her for the day.

'Wouldn't that freak out your contact, you not coming alone?'

'If she asks, I'll just tell her. You're my wife. We made a day of it. Combined meeting a source with a drive in the country.'

Jan didn't sound entirely convinced. 'I suppose. But if this is some secret Deep Throat kind of meeting, are we going to be safe?'

I managed a chuckle. 'Oh, it's going to be very dangerous.'

I DIDN'T THINK it would take more than an hour to drive to Lake George, but I thought it made sense to get on the road at three. The woman in the note had made it clear that there was only about a ten-minute window for us to connect. I was to be there at five, and if she hadn't shown up within ten minutes, I was to go home.

Jan decided to keep Ethan with her for most of the day, then drive over and drop him off at my parents' around two.

I got to our house about quarter to three to meet Jan, and we were on the road fifteen minutes later. For the first twenty miles, I was starting a conversation in my head that wasn't going anywhere.

'You seem better,' I wanted to say to Jan.

'You haven't been as down the last day or two,' I nearly said.

But I said nothing out of fear of jinxing things.

'Not bad traffic,' I ventured as we headed up the interstate.

Jan turned slightly sideways in her seat, alternated looking at me and the road behind us. 'There's something I should tell you,' she said.

I suddenly got that feeling again, the one I'd had in the restaurant. 'What?' I said.

'Something . . . I did. Actually, it's more like something I didn't do. You know that day we took a drive in the country?'

I shook my head. 'We do that a lot.'

'I can't remember the name of the road, but it's out in the country and it doesn't get a lot of traffic? On the way to the garden centre? And you come up to this bridge? You know where the road narrows a bit to go over it, and if there's a truck coming the other way you slow down and let it go first?'

Now I knew exactly where she was talking about.

'And it goes over the river there, and the water's moving really fast over the rocks?'

I nodded.

Jan glanced out of the back window again, then looked at me. 'So I drove up there the other day, parked the car, and I walked out to the middle of the bridge. I stood there and thought about what it would be like to jump, wondered if a person could survive a fall like that. I stood on the railing—it's made of concrete and it's quite wide. I stood there for a good thirty seconds, and then climbed down.'

I swallowed. 'Why?' I asked. 'What made you not do it?'

Because she couldn't imagine leaving Ethan and me behind.

'There was a truck coming. I didn't want to do it in front of anyone, and by the time I was back down, the moment had passed.'

I tried to conceal my alarm. 'It's good that truck came along.'

'Yeah.' She smiled, then reached out and touched my arm. 'But you don't have to worry. I feel good today. And I feel good about tomorrow, about going to Five Mountains.'

That was supposed to be reassuring? So what if she felt good right now? What about an hour from now? What about tomorrow?

'There's something else,' Jan said.

I gave her a look that said, 'What?'

'I think that blue car back there has been following us ever since we left.'

IT WAS A QUARTER of a mile behind us, too far to see what make of car it was, too far to read a licence plate. But it was a dark blue American sedan, General Motors or Ford, with tinted windows.

'It's been following us since we left?' I said.

'I'm not positive,' Jan said. 'It does kind of look like a million other cars. Maybe there was one blue car behind us when we were driving out of Promise Falls, and that's a different blue car.'

I was doing just under seventy miles per hour, and eased up on the accelerator, letting the car coast down to sixty. I wanted to see whether the other car would pull into the outside lane and pass us.

Even slowing down, we were gaining on a transport truck. The blue car loomed larger in my rearview mirror and I could see now that it was a Buick with New York plates, although the numbers were not distinct, as the plate was dirty. 'He's catching up,' I said.

'So maybe it's nothing,' Jan said, sounding slightly relieved.

I put on the Jetta's blinker to move over a lane. We overtook the truck, moved back into the right lane.

If the blue car was tailing us, it would seem to indicate that someone knew I was meeting with this anonymous source and that the email the woman had sent me had been intercepted.

Jan checked the mirror on her door. 'I don't see him,' she said.

The blue car passed the truck, moved in front of it.

'He's back,' I said.

'Why don't you speed up,' Jan said. 'See if he does the same.'

I eased the car back up to seventy. Gradually, the blue car shrank in my rearview mirror.

By the time we took the Lake George exit, I'd stopped checking my mirror every five minutes. The car had fallen from sight.

It was 4.45 p.m., and my sense of the Google map I'd printed out before we'd left told me we were only five minutes away from Ted's Lakeview General Store. We wound our way up 9 North.

It was hard to miss Ted's. It was a two-storey building set about fifty feet back from the highway, a set of self-serve gas pumps at the front. I came slowly off the main road, tyres crunching on gravel.

There were some parking spots off to one side. I backed in so I'd have a good view of the highway, then turned off the engine.

Jan rubbed her forehead.

'You OK?'

'Just getting a headache. I've had one coming most of the way up.'

'You got some aspirin or Tylenol or something?'

'Yeah, in my bag. I'm going to go in, get a bottle of water or something else to drink. You want anything?'

'An iced tea?' I said.

Jan nodded, got out of the car and went into the store. I kept my eyes on the road. A red Ford pick-up drove past.

Then a blue Buick sedan drove by. It was driving slow enough to take in what was going on at Ted's Lakeview General Store, but fast enough not to look like he was going to stop.

The car headed north and disappeared. It was 5.05 p.m.

Jan came out of the store, a Snapple iced tea in one hand, a bottle of water in the other. She opened the passenger door.

'There's been no sign,' I said. 'But there was one interesting thing. I saw what I think was our blue Buick driving by.'

Jan handed me my iced tea. 'You're kiddin' me. Do you know for sure it was the same car?'

I shook my head. 'But there was something about it as it drove past. Like whoever was inside was scanning this place.'

Jan popped some Tylenols into her mouth and chased them down with the water. She looked at the clock. 'Four minutes left.'

I nodded. 'There's still time for her to show up.'

I drank half the iced tea in one gulp. I hadn't realised how parched I was. We sat for another five minutes, saying nothing, listening to the cars go by.

'There's a pick-up,' Jan said. But it was grey and didn't turn in.

'From the north,' I said, and Jan looked.

It was the blue Buick. Maybe 200 yards away.

I opened my door.

'What are you doing?' Jan asked. 'Get back in here.'

But I was already heading across the parking lot. I wanted a better look at this car. I ran to the shoulder. The Buick was 100 yards away and I could hear the driver giving it more gas. As the car zoomed past the general store, I waited to get a look at the back bumper, but that plate was muddied up—save for the last two numbers: seven and five. The Buick moved off at high speed and disappeared round the next bend.

I trudged back to the car.

'What were you thinking?' Jan asked.

'I wanted to get the plate,' I said. 'But it was covered up.'

I got back into the car, shook my head. 'Someone knows,' I said. 'Someone found out about this meeting.'

Which was why I wasn't surprised when, by 5.20 p.m., no white pick-up had showed up. 'It's not going to happen,' I said.

'I'm sorry,' Jan said. 'I know how important this was to you.'

On the way home, Jan angled her seat back and slept most of the way. When we were almost at Promise Falls, she woke up long enough to say she didn't feel well and ask if I could drop her home before I went to get Ethan.

By the time I got back with our son, Jan was in bed, asleep.

'Is Mommy sick?' he asked, as I tucked him in.

'She's tired,' I said.

'Is she going to be OK for tomorrow?'

'Tomorrow?' I said.

'We're going to the roller coasters,' he said. 'Did you forget?'

'Yeah, I guess I did,' I said, feeling pretty tired myself.

'Do I have to go on the big ones? They scare me.'

'No,' I said. 'Just the fun rides, not the scary ones.'

I kissed him good night and went to our bedroom. I thought about asking Jan whether a trip to Five Mountains was really a good idea, but she was asleep. I undressed and got under the covers.

I slid my hand down between the sheets until I found Jan's. Even in sleep she returned the grip. I felt comforted by the warmth of it. 'I love you,' I whispered as I slept next to my wife for the last time.

THREE

'Where's my son?' I asked.

I was sitting in the reception area of the Five Mountains offices. There were a number of people there. The park manager, a thirtyish woman with short blonde hair named Gloria Fenwick, and a woman barely twenty who was the Five Mountains publicity director.

But I wasn't asking any of them about Ethan. I was speaking to an overweight man named Barry Duckworth, a police detective with the Promise Falls department.

'He's with one of my officers,' Duckworth said. 'She's down the hall with him, getting him an ice cream. I hope that's OK?'

I nodded. I was feeling numb, dazed.

'Tell me what happened after you went out to the car,' Duckworth said. Fenwick and the publicist were hovering nearby. 'I wonder if I might speak to Mr Harwood alone?' he asked them.

'Oh, sure, of course,' said Fenwick. 'If you need anything . . .'

'You have people reviewing the closed-circuit TV?' he asked.

'Of course, although we don't know who we're looking for.'

'You've got a description. Mid-thirties, five-eight, black hair, ponytail pulled through baseball cap. Red top, white shorts. Look for someone like that, anything that seems out of the ordinary.'

'Certainly, we'll do that, but you also know that we don't have all the public areas equipped yet with closed-circuit.'

'I know,' Duckworth said. 'You've explained that.' He looked at them and smiled, waiting for them to clear out. Once they had, he said, 'OK, you went out to the car. So tell me.'

'Ethan and I waited by the gate for half an hour. I'd been trying to reach my wife on her cellphone, but she wasn't answering. I wondered whether she might have gone back to the car. So I took Ethan out through the gates and we went to the car, but she wasn't there.'

'Was there any sign that she'd dropped anything off there?'

'She had a backpack with her and I didn't see it in the car.'

'OK, then what did you do?'

'We came back to the park. We showed our tickets again, then waited around just inside the gate, but she didn't show up.'

'That was when you approached one of the park employees?'

'I'd talked to one earlier, who asked security if Jan had been in touch, and she hadn't. But when we came back from the car, I found someone else, asked if they had any reports, like maybe Jan had collapsed. He got on his radio and then, when he didn't turn up anything, I called the police. Are you looking for that man?'

'The one you think was running away from Ethan's stroller?'

'That's right.'

'Did you see this man take the stroller?' Duckworth asked.

'No.'

'When you found the stroller, was he holding on to it?'

'No, I told you. I just caught a glimpse of him running through the crowd when I found Ethan,' I said.

'So he could have just been a man running through the crowd?'

I hesitated a moment, then nodded. Suddenly something occurred to me. 'Maybe she went home. Maybe she took a taxi.'

'We've already had someone go by your house and it looks like no one's home. We knocked on the door, looked in the windows.'

'Let me call my parents, see if she might have gone there.'

Duckworth waited for me to fish out my cellphone and place the call.

'Hello?' My mother.

'Mom, it's me. Listen, is Jan there?'

'What? No. Why would she be here?'

'I'm just—we kind of lost contact with each other. If she shows up, would you call me right away?'

'Of course. But what do you mean, you lost—'

'I have to go, Mom. I'll talk to you later.'

I flipped the phone shut and put it back into my pocket.

'What about her own family?' Duckworth asked.

'She's estranged from her family. Hasn't seen them in years.'

'Friends?'

'Not really. No one she spends time with.'

'Work friends?'

'There's one other woman in the office, Leanne Kowalski, at Bertram's Heating and Cooling. But they aren't close.'

The detective wrote down Leanne's name just the same.

'Has your wife ever had episodes where she wandered off, behaved strangely, anything like that?' Duckworth asked.

I took one second longer to answer than I should have. 'No.'

Duckworth caught that. 'You're sure?'

'Yes,' I said.

'How about an affair? Could she be seeing anyone else?'

I shook my head. 'No.'

'Have the two of you had any arguments lately?'

'No,' I said.

'You have a picture of her on you? Maybe on your cellphone?'

I rarely used my phone for pictures. 'I have some at home.'

'When you get home, you have some you could email me?'

'Yes.'

'Let's go back to my earlier question about whether your wife has had any episodes lately. What weren't you telling me there?'

'I was telling you the truth, she's never wandered off. But the last couple of weeks, my wife . . . she's been feeling depressed. She's said things . . .' I felt myself starting to get overwhelmed.

'Mr Harwood?'

I had to hold it together. 'The last couple of weeks, she's been having these thoughts about . . . harming herself. Suicidal thoughts. I don't think she's actually tried to do it. Well, she had this bandage on her wrist, but she swears that was just an accident when she was peeling vegetables, and she did go out to this bridge, but—'

'She tried to jump off a bridge?' Duckworth asked.

'She drove out to one, but she didn't jump.'

'Do you think it's possible she may have taken her own life?'

'I don't know,' I said. 'I hope to God not.'

'We're doing an extensive search of the grounds,' he said. 'As well, we're searching beyond the park.'

Fenwick, the park manager, had reappeared. 'Detective?' she said. 'We have something you might want to see.'

She led Duckworth, with me following, to a cubicle. The publicist was at a computer looking at some grainy black-and-white images.

She said, 'Our people in security were reviewing some images from the gate around the time the Harwoods arrived.'

I looked at the screen. The image showed a ticket booth, and there, in the crush of people arriving, were Ethan and I.

'It was not that tricky,' the young woman at the keyboard said. 'They entered the name 'Harwood' into the system, which brought up the ticket info, and that showed the time of entry.'

'Yeah, that's us,' I said, pointing.

'Where's your wife?' Duckworth asked me.

'She wasn't with us when Ethan and I entered the park.'

Duckworth's eyes narrowed. 'Why was that, Mr Harwood?'

'She forgot the backpack. We were almost at the gate, and then she remembered, and she told us to go on ahead, we'd meet up later by the ice-cream place.'

'That's what you did? But that's not the last time you saw her.'

'No, she came in later and joined us.'

Duckworth nodded, then said to the publicist, 'Can your people get some pics from the area of the ice-cream stand?'

She half turned in her chair. 'No,' she said. 'We don't have any cameras there at this point. Just on the gates and the rides.'

Duckworth studied me for a moment before saying he wanted to check in with his people. He was moving for the door.

'I want to get Ethan,' I said.

'Absolutely.' He went into the hall, closing the door behind him.

DUCKWORTH WALKED down the hall and turned into a room gridded with cubicles. He guessed that on a weekday these desks would be filled with people conducting business for Five Mountains. But today there were only two people in this office. Didi Campion, a uniformed officer in her mid-thirties, and Ethan Harwood. They were sitting across from each other.

'Hey,' Duckworth said.

All that remained of an ice-cream treat Ethan had been eating was an inch of cone. His tired eyes found Duckworth. The child looked bewildered and very small. He said nothing.

'We're going to get you back with your dad in just a minute,' Duckworth said. 'Would you mind if I talked with Officer Campion over here for just a second? We're not going any place.'

Ethan looked at Campion and his eyes flashed with worry. Duckworth could see that the boy had formed an attachment to her.

'I'll be right back,' Campion assured him and touched his knee.

She got out of the chair and joined Duckworth a few feet away.

'Well?' he asked her.

'He wants to see his parents. Both of them. He's asking where they are.'

'What about the person who took him away in his stroller?'

'He doesn't know anything about it. I think he slept through it.'

Duckworth leaned in. 'Did he say when he last saw his mom?'

Campion sighed. 'I don't know if he quite got what I was trying to ask him. He just keeps repeating that he wants his mom and dad.'

'I'll take the kid to his father in a second.'

Campion took that as a sign that they were done and went back to sit with Ethan.

The door edged open. It was Fenwick. 'Detective, I know your people are out combing the grounds, but Five Mountains personnel have searched every inch of them and they're reporting that they haven't found any sign of this woman in any kind of distress. No woman passed out in any rest rooms, no indication that she fell or came to any harm. I think it would be best if the police presence in the park were scaled back. It's making our guests nervous. They'll think terrorists have put bombs on the roller coasters.'

Duckworth's cell rang. He put it to his ear. 'Yeah.'

'It's Gunner here, Detective. I'm down in the security area. We patched that video of the guy and his kid going through the gates a few minutes ago up to the main office.'

'I just saw it.'

'They couldn't pick out the wife in those, right?'

'That's right. Mr Harwood says his wife had gone back to the car to get something and told him to go on ahead.'

'OK, so she would have come into the park a few minutes later then, right? Because the Harwoods ordered their tickets online, we were able to pinpoint at what time those tickets got scanned at the gate. So we thought, we'll look for when the third ticket, the wife's, got processed at the gate, and then when we had that we could find the closed-circuit image for that time. But nothing's coming up.'

'What do you mean? You saying she never came into the park?'

'I don't know. I've got them checking their ticket sales records, that got bought in advance online, and they show only two tickets being purchased on the Harwoods' Visa. One adult and one kid.'

THE DOOR OPENED and Ethan ran in. I scooped him up in my arms.

'You OK?' I asked. He nodded. 'They were nice to you?'

'I had an ice cream. Where's Mommy?' Ethan asked.

'We're going home now,' I said.

'Is she home?'

I glanced at Duckworth, who had followed Ethan into the room. There was nothing in his expression.

'Let's just go home,' I said.

Still holding Ethan, I said to Duckworth, 'What do we do now?'

'You head home and send me a picture. If you hear anything, get in touch with me.' He had already given me his card. 'Tell me again how you bought your tickets for today?'

'I told you. From the website. Jan ordered them.'

'So it wasn't actually you who sat down at the computer to do it, it was your wife?'

'That's what I just said. Is there something wrong?' I asked.

'Only two tickets were bought online. One adult, one child.'

I blinked. 'Well, that doesn't make much sense. She was in the park. They wouldn't have let her in the gate without a ticket.'

'And I'm asking them to look into that. But if it turns out only one adult ticket was purchased, does that figure?'

It didn't. 'Maybe Jan made a mistake,' I offered. 'Ordering online, it's easy to do that. I was booking a hotel online once, and the website froze up for a second, and when I got the confirmation it said I'd booked two rooms when I only wanted one.'

Duckworth's head went up and down. 'That's a possibility.'

The only problem with my theory was that, on the way into Five Mountains, Jan had taken all our tickets out of her bag. She had handed me mine and Ethan's, and kept one for herself so she could get into the park after she went back to the car for her backpack. She hadn't mentioned any ticket problem when she'd found us.

I suddenly had another theory that was too upsetting to discuss aloud, certainly not in front of Ethan. Maybe Jan never bought a ticket because she was thinking she might not be around to use it. *No point buying a ticket if you know you're going to kill yourself.*

'Something?' Duckworth said.

'No,' I said. 'I really need to get Ethan home.'

'Absolutely,' he said and moved aside to let me leave.

LEAVING FIVE MOUNTAINS was a surreal experience.

Once I had Ethan in his stroller, we exited the offices and were back in the park, not far from the main gate. We were surrounded by the sounds of children and adults laughing.

I held on tight to the stroller handles and kept on pushing.

Ethan swung round and tried to eye me from his stroller seat. 'Is Mommy home?' It had to be the fifth time he'd asked.

I didn't answer. I couldn't shake the feeling that something bad had happened to Jan. That Jan had done something bad to herself.

AS WE CAME IN the door of the house Ethan shouted, 'Mom!'

'I don't think she's home,' I said. 'You go in and watch some TV and I'll just make sure.'

He trundled off to the family room while I searched the house. I ran up to our bedroom, checked the bathroom, Ethan's bedroom. Back to the ground floor, I went down the steps into our basement. It didn't take more than a second to realise she wasn't there.

In the kitchen, I found our laptop by the phone. I opened the photo program. We'd gone to Chicago last fall, and it was the last time I had moved pictures from the digital camera into the computer. I looked through the photos and zeroed in on one shot that was particularly good of Jan. Her long black hair, her brown eyes, soft cheekbones, small nose. At her throat, a necklace with a small pendant designed to look like a cupcake, with diamond-like frosting and cake of gold, something Jan had had since she was a child.

I dug Detective Duckworth's card from my pocket and sent the picture to the email address that was embossed on it. I also printed out a couple of dozen copies of that first shot.

I reached for the phone. I wanted Duckworth to know he had the photos now. I dialled his cellphone.

'Duckworth,' he said.

'It's David Harwood,' I said. 'I just sent you the pictures.'

'You're home? Any sign of her? Phone message, anything?'

'Nothing,' I said.

'OK, we'll get those pictures of your wife out right away.'

'I'll talk to the *Standard*,' I said. There was still time to get Jan's picture in the Sunday edition.

'Why don't you let us handle that?' Duckworth said. 'It might be better if any releases about this are funnelled through a single source. Plus it's only been a few hours. Your wife might walk in the door tonight and this will all be over. That happens, you know.'

'You think that's what's going to happen this time?'

'We don't know. I'm just saying we might want to give this a few more hours before we issue a release. I'll be in touch.'

I found Ethan on the floor watching *Family Guy*.

'Ethan, you're not watching that.' I picked up the remote and killed the TV. 'I've told you not to watch that!'

He whispered, 'I'm sorry.' His lower lip protruded.

I took him into my arms. 'I didn't mean to yell at you.'

He nodded, sniffing. 'When's Mommy coming home?' he asked.

'I just sent a picture of Mommy to the police, so if they see her they can tell her we're here waiting for her,' I said. 'You know what I think we should do? Let's go and see Nana and Poppa.'

'I just want to stay here in case Mom comes home.'

'I'll tell you what,' I said. 'We'll write her a note so she knows where we are. Would you help me with that?'

Ethan ran up to his room and returned with some blank paper and his box of crayons. 'Can I write it?' he asked.

'Sure,' I said.

I set him up at the kitchen table. He'd been working on his letters. He printed several capital letters, some of them backwards.

'Great,' I said. 'Now let's go.' I wrote at the bottom of the page: *Jan. Gone to my parents with Ethan. PLEASE call.*

I got him into the car again and we drove to my parents' house.

'When we get there, you go in and play,' I said to Ethan. 'I need to talk to Nana and Poppa for a while.'

My mother happened to be looking out of the front window when we pulled into the driveway. Dad was holding the door open by the time Ethan was bounding up the porch stairs. He ran into the house.

Dad stepped out, Mom behind him. 'Where's Jan?' he asked.

I collapsed into my father's arms and began to weep.

ONCE I'D PULLED MYSELF together, Mom and Dad and I sat in the kitchen to talk. Ethan was playing in the living room.

'Maybe she's just gone to think things over,' Dad said. 'You know how women can be sometimes.'

Mom placed her hand over mine. 'Perhaps if we put our heads together, we can think about where she might have gone.'

'I've been doing that,' I said. 'I don't know where to begin.'

Dad said, a little too loud, 'I just can't believe she'd kill herself.'

'For God's sake, Don, keep your voice down,' Mom hissed at him. 'Ethan's just in the other room.'

'Sorry,' Dad said. 'But still, she doesn't seem the type.'

'The last couple of weeks,' I said, 'this change came over her.'

Mom wiped away a tear running down her cheek. 'I know what your father is saying, though. I just didn't see any signs. Tell me again what she said to you at the restaurant.'

It was hard to say these things out loud without getting choked up. 'She said something like I'd be happy if she was gone. That Ethan and I would be better off. Why would she say that?'

'She wasn't in her right mind,' Dad said. 'For the life of me, I can't figure what she'd be unhappy about. She's got a good husband, a wonderful boy, you both got good jobs. I just don't get it.' It was then that I noticed his eyes were welling up with tears.

'Dad,' I said, clutching his hand.

He pulled it away, got up, and walked out of the kitchen.

'He doesn't want to show how upset he is,' Mom said. 'Any time you have problems, it tears him apart.'

In the other room, I heard him say to Ethan, 'Hey, kiddo. Did I show you the train catalogues I picked up?'

Ethan said, 'I'm watching TV.'

A few minutes later, Dad came back into the dining room, composed. 'You know what I was thinking? Jan didn't leave a note. If she was going to do something to herself, she'd have left a note.'

'People don't always do that,' I said. 'Only in the movies.'

'Maybe there were some other people she wanted to see before she did anything too rash. Like, maybe her own family.'

'She doesn't have any family. At least not any that she talks to.'

'Could be she felt she needed to look them up after all these years,' Dad said. 'Tell them what she thinks of them.'

'Say that again?' I said.

'She could be trying to find her family. You know, after all these years, she wants to clear the air. Give them a piece of her mind.'

I walked over and surprised him with a pat on the shoulder. 'That's not a bad idea,' I said.

ERNIE BERTRAM, owner of Bertram's Heating and Cooling, was sitting on the front porch of his home, nursing a bottle of beer, when an unmarked police cruiser pulled up at the kerb. An overweight man in a white business shirt with tie askew got out and glanced up at the porch. 'Mr Bertram?' he said.

Bertram stood up. 'What can I do for you?'

'Detective Duckworth, Promise Falls police,' he said, mounting the steps. 'Hope I'm not disturbing you.'

Bertram pointed to a wicker chair. 'Have a seat.'

Duckworth did. 'Get ya a beer?' Bertram sat back down.

'Thanks, but no,' Duckworth said. 'I need to ask you a couple of questions. Jan Harwood works for you, isn't that right?'

'That's right,' he said.

'I don't suppose you've heard from her today?'

'Nope. It's Saturday. Won't be talking to her till Monday.'

The front door eased open. A short, wide woman in blue stretch trousers said, 'You got company, Ern?'

'This is Detective Duckworth with the police, Irene. He can't have beer, but maybe you could have a lemonade or something?'

'I've got some apple pie left over,' Irene Bertram said.

Duckworth considered. 'I could be persuaded to have a slice.'

'With ice cream? It's just vanilla,' she said.

'Sure,' he said. 'I wouldn't mind that at all.'

Irene retreated. Ernie said, 'It's just a frozen one you heat up in the oven, but it tastes like homemade. So what's this about Jan?'

'She's missing,' the detective said. 'She hasn't been seen since about midday, when she was with her husband and son at Five Mountains. When's the last time you talked to her?'

'That'd be Thursday,' he said.

'Not yesterday?'

'No, she took Friday off. She's been taking a few days off here and there the last couple of weeks.'

The door opened. Irene Bertram presented Duckworth with a slab of pie that had a scoop of ice cream next to it the size of a softball.

'Oh my,' he said.

'Jan's missing,' Ernie said to his wife.

'Missing?' she said, plonking herself down in a third chair.

'Yup,' Ernie said. 'She was up at that new roller-coaster park and she just disappeared.'

Duckworth put a forkful of pie into his mouth, then followed it with some ice cream. 'This is amazing.'

'I made it myself,' Irene said.

'I already told him,' Ernie said.

'You bastard,' she said.

'How would you describe Ms Harwood's mood the last few weeks?' the detective asked. 'Did she seem a bit down, or troubled?'

Bertram took a drag on his beer. 'I don't think so. Although I'm on the road a lot. I'm not in the office much.'

'So if, say, Jan Harwood had been depressed of late, you might not have noticed?' Duckworth said between forkfuls.

'Only one depressed in that office is Leanne,' Bertram said. 'If anything, I'd say Jan was excited, acting like something was just around the corner. When she came to me, asking about taking a day off here and there, it was—I don't know how to describe it—like she was looking forward to something.'

'How much time had she taken off lately?' Duckworth asked.

'Let me think . . . there was yesterday, and another day earlier in the week, and a couple the week before.'

Duckworth had taken out his notepad and was writing things down. When he was done, he said, 'I want to go back to something you said about Jan being excited. Tell me more about that.'

Ernie thought. 'Maybe it was a bit like when women are getting ready for something. Like a trip, or having relatives in to visit.'

Duckworth finished the last of the pie and ice cream in three more bites.

'Where did they go yesterday?' Ernie asked.

'Where did who go yesterday?' Duckworth asked.

'Jan and David. They went on some outing yesterday. Jan mentioned it before she left work on Thursday.'

'You sure you don't mean their trip to Five Mountains today?'

He shook his head. 'She said David was taking her somewhere on Friday. It was all really mysterious, she said she couldn't talk about it. I got the idea that maybe it was a surprise or something.'

Duckworth scribbled on his pad. He was about to thank Ernie for his time and Irene for the pie when a phone rang inside the house.

Irene jumped up and went inside.

When Duckworth rose out of his chair, Ernie did the same. 'David must be beside himself,' Ernie said. 'Wondering what's happened to his wife. I sure hope you find her soon.'

Irene was at the door. 'It's Lyall,' she said. 'He hasn't seen Leanne all day. Actually, not since yesterday.'

Duckworth felt a jolt. 'Leanne Kowalski?'

Ernie went into the house and picked up the receiver sitting by the phone on the front-hall table. Duckworth followed him in.

'Lyall?' Ernie listened for a moment, then said, 'Nope, I didn't. Since when? . . . That's a long time to be shopping, even for a woman. Did you hear about Jan? Police are here—'

'May I take that?' Duckworth said and took the phone away from Ernie. 'Mr Kowalski, this is Detective Barry Duckworth with the Promise Falls police department. What's this about your wife?'

'She's not home. She went out shopping hours ago. At least that's what she usually does on a Saturday. What's this about Jan?'

Duckworth had his notepad out again. 'Mr Kowalski, what's your address?'

FOUR

There was something I'd never been totally honest about with Jan.

It wasn't that I'd lied to her. But there was something I'd done I'd never told her about.

About a year ago, I'd driven by her house, the house she grew up in, her parents' place, a nearly three-hour drive from Promise Falls. It was in Rochester, on Lincoln Avenue. The white paint was peeling from the walls and a couple of the shutters hung crookedly.

I had been driving back from Buffalo, where I'd interviewed a source. It was on the way back that I decided to take 490 North off 90 and head into the Rochester neighbourhood where Jan grew up.

It never would have been possible for me to take this detour if we hadn't had the leak behind the bathroom basin several days earlier.

Jan was at work and I had taken the day off as payback for several late-night city council meetings I'd recently covered—this was before we'd turned that beat over to Rajiv or Amal or whoever in Mumbai. I'd gone down to the unfinished side of our basement, where the boiler and hot-water tank are, and noticed a steady drip of water coming down from between the studs. That was where the copper pipes turned north to feed the upstairs bathroom.

I did what I always did when I had a household emergency. I called Dad.

'Sounds like maybe you've got a pinhole leak in one of your pipes,' he said. 'I'll be right over.'

He showed up half an hour later with his tools.

'It's going to be in the wall,' he said. 'The trick is finding it.'

We thought we could hear a hissing sound behind the bathroom basin. Dad pulled out a saw with a pointed end on the blade that would allow him to stab right into the plaster and start cutting.

'Dad,' I said, looking at the floral wallpaper, 'would it be worth going in from the other side?'

'What's over there?' he asked.

'Hang on,' I said. As it turned out, the linen closet was on the opposite side of the wall from the basin. I opened it and cleared out everything on the floor below the first shelf—a laundry basket, a stockpile of toilet paper. Then I got down on my hands and knees, crawled into the closet and listened for the leak. The baseboard that ran along the inside looked loose along the back. I got my fingers in behind it, and felt something.

It was the top edge of a letter-sized envelope, hidden behind the baseboarding. I worked the envelope out. There was nothing written on it. I opened it, and inside I found a piece of paper and a key. I removed the paper. It was a 'Certificate of Live Birth'.

Jan's birth certificate. All the details she had never wanted to share with me were on this piece of paper. Of course, I already knew her last name was Richler, but she'd gone to great lengths never to speak her parents' names or even say where they lived.

Now, at a glance, I knew that her mother's name was Gretchen and that her father's name was Horace. There was an address for a house on Lincoln Avenue. I put the document back into the envelope. I didn't know what to make of the key. It didn't appear to be a house key. I left it in the envelope and put it back where I'd found it.

By the time I got round the other side of the wall, Dad had made a hole. 'I'm in!' he said. 'And there's your leak right there!'

Before the Buffalo trip, I went to the online phone directories and found a Horace Richler living in Rochester on Lincoln Avenue.

It was hard not to be curious about the Richlers when Jan had so steadfastly refused to talk about them.

'I don't want anything to do with them,' she'd said over the years. 'I don't ever want to see them again.'

What I'd learned since meeting Jan at a jobs placement office, when I was interviewing some unemployed people for a story six years ago, was that her father was a miserable son of a bitch and her mother spent most of her time drunk and depressed. The story of her life with her parents spilled out in bits and pieces over the years.

'They blamed me for everything,' Jan said one Saturday night two years ago when my parents had taken Ethan for a sleepover. We'd gone through three bottles of wine—a rare event—and Jan began to talk about a part of her life she'd never shared with me.

'What do you mean, they blamed you?' I asked.

'Him, mostly,' Jan said. 'For screwing up their lives. Dad had a nickname for me. Hindy.'

'Like the language?'

She looked at me through glassy eyes. 'No, short for "Hindenburg". He thought of me as his own personal disaster.'

'That's horrible.'

'Yeah, well, that was true love compared to my tenth birthday. He promised to take me to New York to see a Broadway musical. I'd always dreamed of going there. He said he'd got tickets for *Grease.* That we were going to take the bus down, stay in a hotel. I couldn't believe it. My father, he'd been so indifferent to me for so long . . .'

She had another sip of wine. 'So the day came that we were supposed to go. I got my bag all packed. I picked out a red dress and black shoes to wear to the theatre. And my father, he wasn't doing anything to get ready. I told him to get moving and he said, "There's no trip. No tickets for *Grease.* Never was. Disappointment's a bitch, isn't it? Now you know how it feels."'

I was speechless. Finally, I found some words. 'How'd you deal with that?'

She said, 'I went to another place.'

'Where? Relatives?'

'No, no, you don't get it,' she said. Jan put her hand to her mouth. 'I think I'm going to be sick.'

The next morning she refused to talk about it.

She did tell me, over time, that she left home at seventeen and for nearly twenty years had had no contact with her parents.

I'd never told Jan about what I'd found behind the baseboard. I didn't want her to know I'd violated her privacy.

Driving back from Buffalo, I found the Lincoln Avenue home, and stared at its peeling paint and shutters askew. But looking at the house really didn't tell me anything. Then her parents showed up.

I had been parked across the street and two houses down, so I didn't attract the attention of Horace and Gretchen Richler as they got out of their twenty-year-old Oldsmobile.

Horace opened his door slowly. It took some effort for him to bring himself out. He was in his late sixties or early seventies, a few wisps of hair, a couple of liver spots. He was short and stocky.

Horace was going round to the trunk as Gretchen got out. She moved slowly, too, although she wasn't quite as creaky as her husband. She got to the trunk first and waited for him to unlock it.

She was tiny, under five feet. She reached into the trunk for half a dozen plastic grocery bags, lifted them out and headed for the door. Her husband closed the trunk and followed, carrying nothing.

They went into the house and they were gone.

They didn't appear to have spoken a word between them.

Was there anything I could read into what I'd seen? No. And yet I was left with the impression that these were two people going through the motions, living out their lives a day at a time without purpose. I detected an overall sadness about them.

When the Oldsmobile had pulled into the driveway, I'd had an impulse to get out, march over, and tell Horace Richler that a man who would abuse his daughter—even if that abuse was limited to emotional—didn't deserve to be called a father. I wanted to tell him that his daughter had turned out well despite his attempts to sabotage her. But I didn't tell him anything.

I drove home and never told Jan about the stop I had made.

SITTING IN MY PARENTS' living room, it was getting dark outside. I thought about my visit to the Richler home.

What if Jan had been wanting to say to her parents what I'd wanted to say when I'd parked close to their house? What if the way her father had treated her had been eating her up for years? I tried to put myself in her position, knowing how fragile and self-destructive she'd been feeling. *I'm thinking about taking my own life. Before I do it, do I confront my father, tell him what I think of him? Tell my mother she should have stood up for me? Tell both of them how they ruined my life before I end it?* I shuddered.

'You OK there?' Dad asked.

'Yeah,' I said.

'So, you've been thinking about my idea?' Dad asked. 'About Jan looking up her parents?'

'Yeah, I have.'

'You got any way to get in touch with them?'

'I think I could find them,' I said. 'They live in Rochester. I know the address. Their names are Horace and Gretchen Richler.'

Mom's eyes widened. 'Jan told you about her parents?'

'I figured it out.'

'I'd give them a call,' Dad said, 'see if she's been in touch.'

'I'm afraid the moment I say Jan's name, they'll hang up on me.'

He shook his head. 'How can parents be like that? You didn't always do what we wanted but we never disowned you. You have to let your children make their own decisions in life, good or bad.'

I went into the kitchen to use the phone. I had Detective Duckworth's card in my hand and dialled his cell.

'Duckworth.'

'It's David Harwood,' I said. 'I wanted to check in.'

'I don't have any news,' Duckworth said guardedly.

'You still have people searching?'

'We do.' He paused. 'I think, if there are no developments overnight, we should put out a release in the morning.'

'I might not be here in the morning,' I said.

'Where are you going to be?'

'Jan's parents are in Rochester. She hasn't had any contact with them in twenty years. But what if she decided to go and see them? Maybe she wanted to finally tell them what she thinks of them.'

Duckworth was quiet, saying only, 'I suppose.'

'I'd phone them, but they've never set eyes on me. What are they going to think, some guy phones them and says he's their son-in-law and oh, by the way, their daughter's missing and is there any chance she might have dropped by? And if Jan *is* there, and doesn't want me to know, I'm worried that if I call, she'll take off.'

'Maybe,' Duckworth said with little conviction. 'Tell me again about your wife and Leanne Kowalski.'

The question threw me. 'They work together. That's about it.'

'What time did you and your son get to Five Mountains?'

Why did he ask it that way? Why didn't he ask when Ethan and I and *Jan* got to Five Mountains?

'It was about eleven. Is something going on?' I asked.

'If I have any news, Mr Harwood, I'll be in touch.'

I hung up the phone.

BARRY DUCKWORTH closed the phone and said to Lyall Kowalski, 'Sorry about that.'

'Was that Jan's husband?' he asked. He and the detective were sitting in his living room. Lyall was in a black T-shirt and dirty knee-length shorts with pockets all over them.

'Yes, that was him,' Duckworth said.

'Has he seen my wife?'

'No,' Duckworth said, but thinking, *At least he's not saying he has*. 'Tell me again what time your wife left the house.'

'She was actually gone before I got up. I got in kind of late last night and was sleeping in.'

'Where had you been?'

'I was at the Trenton.' A local bar. 'With some friends.'

'So you got home when?'

Lyall scrunched up his face, trying to remember. 'Three? Or maybe five.'

'And your wife was here when you got home?'

'As far as I know,' he said. 'I didn't actually talk to her. I didn't make it as far as the bedroom. I camped out on the couch.'

'Why'd you do that?'

'Leanne gets kinda bitchy when I come home drunk. I didn't want to have to deal with that, so I didn't get into bed with her.'

'Did you see your wife in the morning?'

'I think I might have heard her saying something to me while I was sleeping it off, but I can't exactly swear to it.'

'So what does your wife usually do on a Saturday?'

'She has a routine. She goes out around eight thirty. She goes out by herself to the malls. Every one between here and Albany.'

'What time would you be expecting her back?'

'Three or four? Five at the latest.'

'And did you try calling your wife at all?'

'I tried her cell but it goes straight to message.'

Duckworth nodded slowly. He asked, 'When was the last time you actually saw or spoke to your wife, Mr Kowalski?'

'I guess, middle of yesterday? She called me from work.'

'Do you have a list of the bank and credit cards your wife uses?' Duckworth asked. 'We could check, see where she used them.'

'When Leanne buys anything, she tends to use cash. We're on a limited budget and kinda had our cards cancelled.'

'Has Leanne done this before? Gone out and not come back until late? Is it possible that she might have a boyfriend?'

'No, she wouldn't do that. She's not going to mess around on me. No way.' The man was on the verge of tears. 'I'm real scared something's happened to her. Like maybe she had a car accident or something. Have you checked on that? She drives a Ford Explorer. It's blue and it's, like, a 1990, so it's kind of eaten up with rust.'

'I don't have a report of an accident involving that make of car,' Duckworth said. 'How close are your wife and Jan Harwood?'

Lyall blinked. 'They work together.'

'Are they friends? Do they get together after work?'

'No,' he said. 'Leanne thinks Jan's a bit stuck-up, you know?'

After the interview, before Duckworth pulled away from the Kowalski house, he got out his phone, waited for someone to answer, and said, 'Gunner, you still at Five Mountains?'

'I've been here all day,' he said. 'Just finishing up now.'

'How'd it go?'

'OK, so, the first thing we did was see if we could track down that third ticket bought online. We thought maybe there was a glitch in the system, but we've pretty much ruled that out. If she came into the park, she didn't do it with a ticket purchased over the Internet.'

'Right,' Duckworth said.

'Then, with the picture the husband provided, we spent the rest of the day looking at the people coming in and going out through the gates, trying to spot the wife. It's not easy. There's so many people, sometimes you can't make them out, sometimes they're wearing hats that cover half their face, so she might have been there and we didn't see her. We looked for a woman dressed the way the husband described her. Nothing. If she's there, we can't find her.'

'OK, look, thanks, I appreciate it. Go home.'

'You don't have to tell me twice,' Gunner said.

'Can you put Campion on?'

Duckworth heard Gunner put down the phone and call out to Officer Didi Campion. She picked up the phone. 'Campion here.'

'It's Barry Duckworth. I want to ask you again about the kid this morning. Did he actually say the mother was with them at the park?'

'He was asking about her. I got the sense he'd seen her there.'

'Do you think—how do I put this—he could have been convinced his mother had been there even if she hadn't?'

'You mean like, the dad says we're just going to meet your mom now, your mom just went into the bathroom, something like that?'

'That's what I was thinking,' Duckworth said. 'The kid's only four years old. Maybe the dad made him think his mother was there even if she wasn't. Harwood says the three of them are going to Five Mountains, but he only gets two tickets. He says his wife has been talking suicide. But her boss says he didn't see any signs that she was depressed. If anything, she was excited about something.'

'Weird. So the husband, he's laying the groundwork.'

'This Bertram guy, the wife's boss, said Harwood took his wife for a drive some place on Friday. When Bertram asked her where they were going, she said it was a secret or something, a surprise.'

'So where are you going with this, Detective?'

'You've put out news releases before, right?'

'I've worked that end, yeah.'

'I told Harwood we'd put out a release tomorrow, but I think we need to put one out tonight. Shake the bushes. We've still got time to make the eleven o'clock news. A picture of Jan Harwood, believed last seen in the vicinity of Five Mountains. Police seeking any information about her whereabouts, contact us, the usual drill.'

'I'm on it,' Campion said.

Duckworth thanked her and closed the phone. He was wondering whether Jan Harwood ever made it to Five Mountains and just what her husband might have done with her. How that fitted in with Leanne Kowalski, he had no idea. He decided to focus, for now, on Jan Harwood. Maybe he'd turn up Leanne Kowalski along the way.

EVEN THOUGH I was exhausted, I decided to leave immediately for Rochester. I left Ethan to spend the night with my parents.

I was about a half an hour out of Rochester when my cellphone rang.

'It was on the TV news,' Mom said. 'A picture of Jan, and that the police were looking for help to find her. That's good, right?'

'Yeah,' I said. 'But the detective said they'd make a decision about that tomorrow. You'd think if he was deciding to change the timing of the release, he would have let me know.'

I wondered how long it would be before someone from my own paper called, asking how the *Standard* could get scooped on the disappearance of the spouse of one of its own staff members.

'Are you almost there?' Mom asked.

'Pretty close,' I said. 'I'm thinking maybe I should just knock on Jan's parents' door tonight. I can't stay in a hotel all night thinking about her. I have to do something right away. How's Ethan?'

'He's asleep. Your father and I are going to turn in now. But if you have any news, you call us, OK?'

'I will. You too.'

I put the phone back into my jacket. I was almost at Rochester.

Just after midnight I got off 90 and headed north on 490. Not long after that, I found my way to Lincoln Avenue. The streetlamps were the only thing casting any light at 12.10 a.m. I stopped outside the front of the house I had seen only once before. The place was dark.

I got out of the car, walked up the driveway and onto the porch. I rapped five times with the brass knocker on the door. When I didn't see any lights going on after fifteen seconds, I did it again. Finally, I could see, through the window, light cascading down the stairs.

In another moment, Horace Richler appeared, in a bathrobe and pyjamas. Before he got to the door, he shouted, 'Who is it?'

'Mr Richler?' I called out. 'I need to speak to you.'

'Who is it? You know what time it is?'

'My name is David Harwood! Please, it's very important.'

There was someone else coming down the stairs now. It was Gretchen Richler, in a nightgown and robe, her hair in disarray.

'It's about Jan,' I said.

I thought I saw Horace Richler hesitate for a second as he reached for the door, perhaps wondering if he heard me correctly. I heard a deadbolt turn back, a chain slide, then the door opened about a foot.

'What the hell is this all about?' Horace Richler asked.

'I'm so sorry to wake you. I wouldn't do this if it weren't an emergency. My name's David Harwood. I'm Jan's husband.'

The two of them stared at me.

'Jan's missing and I'm trying to find her. I thought, maybe, there was a chance she might come here to see you.'

They were both still staring. Horace Richler's face, at first frozen, was turning into a furious scowl. 'You've made some kind of mistake, mister,' he said. 'You better get off my porch.'

'I know that you haven't talked to your daughter in a long time, but I'm worried that something bad has happened to her,' I said.

Horace Richler's face grew red with fury. 'I don't know who you are or what your game is. I may be an old man, but I'll kick your ass all the way down Lincoln Avenue if I have to.'

I wasn't ready to give up. 'Tell me I haven't got the right house. You're Horace and Gretchen Richler and your daughter is Jan.'

'That's right,' Gretchen whispered.

'My daughter's dead,' Horace said through gritted teeth.

The comment hit me like a two-by-four across the side of the head. Something horrible had happened. I'd got here too late.

'My God,' I said. 'When? What happened?'

'She died a long time ago,' he said.

I breathed out. I assumed he meant that because he and his daughter were estranged, it was as though Jan was dead to him. 'I know you may feel that way. But if you ever loved her, you need to help me now.'

Gretchen said, 'You don't understand. She really is dead. She died when she was only five years old. It was a terrible thing.'

FIVE

The woman opened her eyes. She blinked a couple of times, adjusting to the darkness.

She was in bed, on her back. It was warm in the room and in her sleep she had thrown off her covers. She reached down and touched her stomach. Her skin was cool, but slightly clammy. She was taken aback for a moment to discover she was naked. She'd stopped sleeping in the nude a long time ago. Those first few months of marriage, sure, but after a while, you just want something on.

Light from the tall streetlamps out by the highway filtered through the bent and twisted window blinds. She listened to the relentless traffic streaming by. Big trucks roaring through the night.

She slipped her legs out from under the covers, sat up, and placed her feet on the floor. The cheap industrial carpet was scratchy beneath her toes. She sat on the side of the bed for a moment, leaning over, head in her hands.

She had a headache. She glanced at the bedside table, as if some aspirin and a glass of water might magically be there, but all she could see in the dim light were some crumpled notes and change, a digital clock that was reading 00:10, and a blonde wig.

That told her she'd only been asleep for an hour at the most. She'd got into the bed around half past ten, tossed and turned until well after eleven. At some point, clearly, she'd nodded off, but the last hour of sleep had not been a restful one.

She stood up, padded softly across the room and pushed open the door to the bathroom. She went inside and felt for the light switch. The intense illumination stung her eyes. She squinted until she got used to it, then gazed at her reflection in the mirror. 'Yikes,' she whispered. Her black hair was stringy, her eyes dark, her lips dry.

There was an open toiletries bag by the basin. Inside the bag, she found a travel-sized bottle of aspirin. She tapped two tablets into her palm. She put them in her mouth, then leaned over a running tap to scoop some water into her hand before swallowing the pills.

Her stomach growled. Maybe that's why she had the headache. She was hungry. She'd had very little to eat the whole day. Too on edge. But hungry as she was, she wasn't going to venture out of this motel room. She might end up drawing more attention to herself at night, a woman alone, than she would during the day.

She flicked off the light before turning the bathroom doorknob.

She walked over to the window and looked out at the motel's parking lot, half expecting to see the blue Ford Explorer out there. But that had been ditched long ago, and far from here. Lyall probably would have called the police by now. Useless as he was, he'd notice eventually that his wife hadn't returned home.

She turned away from the window. There wasn't much else to do but try to get back to sleep. She sat gently on the side of the bed, raised her legs ever so slowly, lowered her head onto the pillow, trying her best not to disturb her partner's sleep.

But the person on the other side of the bed stirred, turned over and said, 'What's going on, babe?'

'Shh, go back to sleep,' she said. 'I had a headache. I was looking for aspirin.'

'You're just stressed out. It's going to take you a while to get over this whole Jan thing.'

The woman said, 'What's to get over? She's dead.'

'So you better hit the road,' Horace Richler said to me, starting to close the open front door.

'Wait!' I said. 'Please! This doesn't make any sense.'

'No kidding,' Horace said. 'You wake us up in the middle of the night asking for our dead daughter, you're right it makes no sense.'

He nearly had the door closed when Gretchen said, 'Horace, hang on a minute.' She said to me, 'Who did you say you are?'

'David Harwood,' I said. 'I live in Promise Falls.'

'And your wife's name is Jan?'

I said, 'That's right. Before we got married she was Jan Richler.'

'There must be lots of Jan Richlers in the world,' Gretchen said.

'But her birth certificate says her parents are Gretchen and Horace, that she was born in Rochester on August 14, 1975,' I said.

It was as if the air had been let out of both of them. Horace acted like he had taken a blow to the chest. He folded in on himself and his head drooped. He let go of the door, took a step back into the house. Gretchen's face had fallen, but she held her spot at the door.

'I'm sorry,' I said. My knees felt weak and I was trembling slightly. 'This is as much a shock to me as it is to you.'

Gretchen shook her head sadly. 'This is very hard on him. Why would your wife have our daughter's birth certificate?'

Before I could even attempt to come up with an explanation, I said, 'Would it be all right if I came in?'

Gretchen turned towards her husband. 'Horace?' she said. All he did was raise his hand dismissively, an act of surrender.

'Come in then,' she said, opening the door wider. She led me into a living room filled with old furniture. I took a seat in one of the chairs. Gretchen sat on the couch. 'Horace, come on, sit down.'

There were some framed family photos in the room, most of them featuring one or both of the Richlers, often with a boy. There was one picture of him—as an adult—in uniform.

Gretchen caught me looking. 'That's Bradley,' she said.

Reluctantly, Horace Richler came over to the couch and sat down next to his wife. Gretchen rested her hand on his pyjama-clad knee.

'He's dead,' Horace said, seeing that I'd been looking at the picture of the young man.

'Afghanistan,' Gretchen said. 'An IED almost two years ago.'

'I'm so sorry,' I said.

The room was quiet for several seconds.

'So that's both our children,' Gretchen said.

Hesitantly, I said, 'I don't see any pictures of your daughter.' I was desperate to see what she had looked like, even as a five-year-old. If it was Jan, I was sure I'd know it.

'We . . . don't have any out,' Gretchen said. 'It's . . . hard. Even after all these years. To be reminded.'

Another uncomfortable silence ensued, until Horace, whose lips had been going in and out in preparation, blurted, 'I killed her.'

I said, barely able to find my voice, 'What?'

He was looking down into his lap, seemingly ashamed. Gretchen put her other hand to his shoulder. 'Horace, don't do this.'

'It's true,' he said.

Gretchen said to me, 'It was a terrible, terrible thing. It wasn't Horace's fault.' Her face screwed up, like she was fighting back tears. 'I lost a daughter and a husband that day. My husband's never been the man he was once, not in thirty years.'

I asked, 'What happened?'

Gretchen started to speak but Horace cut her off. 'I can tell it,' he said. Horace reached inside himself for the strength to continue. 'It was the 3rd of September, 1980. It was after I'd come home from work, after Gretchen had made dinner. Jan and one of her little friends, Constance, were playing in the front yard.'

'Arguing more than playing,' Gretchen said. 'I'd been watching them through the window. You know how little girls can be.'

Horace continued, 'I was going to meet my friends after dinner. Bowling. I was in a league back then. The thing is, I'd got home late, ate my dinner fast as I could, because I was supposed to be meeting up with everyone at six, and it was already ten past when I finished dinner. So I ran out to the car and jumped in and backed out of the driveway like a bat out of hell.'

'It wasn't his fault,' Gretchen said again. 'Jan . . . was pushed.'

'If I hadn't been going so fast,' Horace said, 'it wouldn't have mattered. You can't go blaming this on that other little girl.'

'But it is what happened,' Gretchen said. 'The girls were having a fight, standing by the driveway, and Constance pushed Jan into the path of the car just as Horace started backing up.'

'Oh my God,' I said.

Horace said, 'I knew right away I'd hit something. I slammed on the brakes and got out, but . . .' He made his hands into tight fists, as though that could keep the tears from welling up in his eyes.

'The other little girl started to scream,' Gretchen said. 'It was her fault, but can you really blame a child?'

'I was the one behind the wheel,' Horace said. 'I should have been watching. And I wasn't. I was too worried about getting to a bowling alley on time. They never did a thing to me. Said it wasn't my fault, it was an accident. I wish they'd done something to me, but anything they might have done, short of killing me, wouldn't have stopped me from wanting to punish myself even more.'

'Horace tried to take his life,' Gretchen said. 'A few times.'

He looked away, embarrassed by that revelation.

'That child who pushed Jan, her life was ruined that day, too,' Gretchen said. 'I know she deserves some pity. But I never had any for her, or her parents. Not surprising, they moved away after that.'

'There's not a single time I get in the car I don't think about what I did,' Horace said. 'Not a single time, not in all these years.'

This was the saddest room I'd ever been in.

Listening to Horace Richler tell how he ran over his own daughter with his car would have been devastating enough. But he was talking about Jan. The Jan on my wife's birth certificate. But Horace's Jan had been dead for decades. And my Jan was, at least up until today, alive. But it was glaringly obvious that they could not be the same person. I was so numbed by what I'd been told that I didn't know what to ask next.

'Mr Harwood?' Gretchen said. 'Are you OK? You've got bags under your eyes and don't look like you've slept in a long time.'

'I don't . . . I don't know what to make of this.' I tried to focus. 'Could I please see a picture of Jan?'

Gretchen got up, opened an old-fashioned roll top desk, and reached in. It was a black and white, slightly faded, portrait shot. She handed it to me. 'This was taken about two months . . . before.'

Jan Richler had been a beautiful child. An angelic face, dimples, curly blonde hair. I searched for any hints of my wife. Maybe something in the eyes, the way the mouth turned up at the corner.

There was nothing.

I handed the photo back to Gretchen. 'Thank you,' I said quietly. 'May I show you a picture?' I reached into my jacket for one of the copies I'd printed out of the snapshot I'd emailed to Duckworth.

Horace took the picture first, gave it nothing more than a glance, then handed it to Gretchen. She studied the picture at arm's length, then brought it up close, giving it a microscopic examination.

'Anything?' I said.

'I was just . . . noticing how beautiful your wife is,' she said. She picked up the photo to hand it to me, then reconsidered. 'If your wife is using our daughter's name, maybe she has ties to this area. In case I saw her, should I hang on to this?'

It was possible Jan might show up here, and it would be good for her image to be fresh in the Richlers' minds. 'Sure,' I said.

She took the picture and put it in the drawer with her daughter's.

Horace said, 'And that woman, she says we're her parents?'

'She's never talked about you by name,' I said. 'I figured it out from her birth certificate.'

'Would you excuse me for a minute?' Gretchen asked shakily.

After she had climbed the stairs and we heard a door close, Horace said to me, 'You think you're over it, and then something comes along and opens up the wound all over again.'

'I'm sorry,' I said. I attempted to stand up. I was a bit shaky.

'I hope you're not thinking of getting behind the wheel of a car,' Horace said.

'I'll stop for a coffee on the way,' I said. ' I need to get home to see my boy.'

From the top of the stairs, Gretchen said, 'How old is your son?'

I watched as she descended. She seemed to have pulled herself together. 'He's four,' I said. 'His name is Ethan.'

'How's it going to help your son if you fall asleep at the wheel and go into a ditch?' Gretchen pointed to the couch, where Horace still sat. 'You'd be more than welcome to stay here.'

The couch looked very inviting. 'I don't want to put you out,' I said.

'Please,' she said.

I nodded gratefully. 'I'll be gone first thing in the morning.'

Horace had his face screwed up tight. 'So if your wife says she's Jan Richler but she's not, then who is she? And how could she do that to our little girl? Take her name? Hasn't she suffered enough?'

ON SUNDAY MORNING at 6.30 a.m., Barry Duckworth was asleep in bed when the phone rang.

His wife, Maureen, who was already awake, picked up the receiver on her side of the bed. 'Hello . . . Yeah, hi . . . No, don't worry about it, I was already up. . . . Sure, he's here.'

She woke Barry up and held out the phone. Barry grabbed it.

'Duckworth,' he said.

'Hey, Detective. You got a pen?'

Barry grabbed the pen and paper that were sitting by the phone. He made a couple of notes. 'Great, thanks,' he said and hung up.

Maureen looked at him expectantly. She knew that yesterday he had put in an extra-long day, looking for that woman who went missing at the roller-coaster park.

'We got something,' he said.

DUCKWORTH GOT DRESSED and had a cup of coffee in his hand before he dialled the number from the phone in the kitchen.

Someone picked up after two rings. 'Ted's,' a man said.

'Is this Ted Brehl?' Duckworth asked.

'That's right.'

'This is Detective Barry Duckworth, Promise Falls police. You called in about half an hour ago?'

'Yeah, I saw that thing on the news last night. When I came in to open the store this morning, I thought I should give you a call.'

'Where's your store?'

'Up by Lake George.'

'I know the area. Real pretty up there.'

'So, I saw that woman, Jan Harwood. She was in here on Friday afternoon. She came in to buy some water and iced tea.'

'Was she alone?'

'She came into the store alone, but she was with a man, her husband, I guess. He was out in the car.' Ted Brehl's description of it matched the vehicle owned by David Harwood.

'So they just stopped to buy some drinks and then left?'

'No, they sat out there for a while, talking. I looked out a few times. I looked out again around five thirty and they were gone.'

'You're sure it was her?'

'Oh yeah. I might normally have forgotten, but she struck up a conversation with me. She said she'd never been up this way before. I asked her where she was going and she said she didn't exactly know. She said her husband wanted to take her for a drive up into the woods. She said maybe it was some sort of surprise, because he'd told her not to tell anyone they were going.'

'How was her mood? Was she happy? Depressed? Troubled?'

'She seemed just fine, you know?'

'Sure. Listen, thanks for calling.' Duckworth hung up.

I WOKE EARLY on the Richlers' couch. I'd slept in my clothes, taking off only my jacket and shoes before I'd put my head down on a pillow Gretchen had provided.

I grabbed my travel kit, went into the bathroom and shaved. When I came out, Gretchen was in the kitchen. I went in to say goodbye. Just in case Jan somehow turned up here, I wrote down my home and cellphone numbers and address, as well as my parents' number and address. 'Please get in touch,' I said to Gretchen.

The interstate's a pretty good place to let your mind wander. My thoughts were all over the place. And they all circled round one thing. Why did my wife have the name and birth certificate of a child who had died years ago at the age of five?

There must be some explanation. I wondered if maybe Jan had been required to take on a new identity. And the name she had to take happened to be Horace and Gretchen Richler's daughter.

It was hardly a secret that if you could find the name of someone who'd died at a young age, there was a good chance you could build a new identity with it. I'd worked in the news business long enough to learn how it could be done. You applied for a new copy of the deceased's birth certificate, since birth and death certificates were often not cross-referenced. With that, you acquired other forms of identification: a Social Security number, a driver's licence.

What was the most likely reason for someone to shed a past life and start a new one? Two words came to mind: *witness protection.*

Maybe that was it. Jan had witnessed something, testified in some court case. Against whom? The mob? It had to be someone, or some organisation, with the resources to track her down and exact revenge if they managed to do it. If that was the case, the authorities would have had to create a new identity for her.

It was the kind of secret she might feel she could never tell me. If she was a protected witness, living out a new life in a new location, what did it have to do with her disappearance? Had someone figured out where she was? Did she run to save herself? Maybe—

My cellphone rang on the seat next to me. 'Yeah?'

'Dave, you're the biggest story on the news and you don't let your own paper know about it?' Brian Donnelly, the city editor.

'Brian,' I said.

'Man, this is terrible,' he said.

'Yeah,' I said. 'Jan's been gone since about—'

'By the time the cops issued their release, the paper had gone to bed, so TV and radio have it, but we haven't got anything, and it's about one of our own people! You couldn't call us with this?'

'Brian, I don't know what I was thinking,' I deadpanned.

'I'll put Samantha on to get some quotes from you for the main story, but I want you to write a first-person. "Mystery Hits Close to Home for Reporter." This kind of play, might help, uh, find . . .'

'Jan,' I said.

'Exactly. So if you—'

I flipped the phone shut. A few seconds later it rang again. I flipped it open and put it to my ear.

'Dave? It's Samantha here.'

'Hi, Sam.'

'I just heard what Brian said to you. I can't believe he said those things. I am so sorry. Is Jan still missing?'

'Yes.'

'Is there anything you can say, for the record?' Sam asked.

'Just . . . that I'm hoping she'll be home soon.'

'The cops are being weird about it. The head of the investigation, Duckworth, is releasing very few details and not saying much.'

'Sam, I'm on the way home. I'm going to see Duckworth when I get back, and maybe then we'll have a better idea what we're dealing with. I honestly hadn't expected them to release anything until this morning.'

'OK, off the record. How are you holding up?'

'Not so good.'

'Listen, I'll call you later, OK?'

'Thanks, Sam.'

I DECIDED TO STOP at my house before picking up Ethan at my parents. I pulled into my driveway shortly before noon.

For the last twenty miles, all I could think about was the birth certificate I had found. I needed to see it again. I needed to prove to myself that I hadn't imagined it.

I went upstairs. I opened the linen closet and dragged out everything from the bottom. I crawled into the closet and prised away the baseboard along the back wall with a screwdriver.

The envelope was gone.

SHE HAD ACTUALLY been asleep when the man in the bed next to her threw back the covers and padded to the bathroom. She'd stared at the ceiling for a long time after getting back into bed. Thinking about what she'd done, the life she'd left behind. The body they'd buried. But at some point, her anxiety surrendered to weariness.

Like her, Dwayne had slept naked. Dwayne Osterhaus was a thin, wiry man, just under six feet tall. His lean, youthful body was betrayed by his thinning grey hair. Maybe prison did that to you, she thought, watching him cross the room. Turned you grey early.

He closed the bathroom door but she could still hear him taking a leak. The toilet flushed and the bathroom door opened.

'Hey,' he said. 'You're awake.' He crawled back into the bed and slipped his hand down between her legs.

'Hey,' she said. 'You've been away so long you think you have to get to the main event right away. No one's marching you back to a cell in five minutes.'

'Sorry,' he said and moved his hand away.

She turned to face him. Why not be a bit accommodating? she thought. Play the role. She touched him. She wondered what he might have done in prison. Had he had sex with men? She knew he wasn't that way, but half a decade was a long time to go without.

Dwayne figured thirty seconds of foreplay was more than enough to get her motor running. He threw himself on top of her. The whole thing was over in a minute, and for that she was grateful.

'Wow, that was great,' she said.

'You sure?' he asked.

'You were terrific,' she said.

He propped himself up on his elbow. 'What should I call you now? I need to get used to something other than your regular name. Like if we're in public. I guess I could call you Blondie.' He nodded towards the wig on her bedside table and grinned. 'You look hot when you're wearing that, by the way.'

She thought a moment. 'Kate. From now on, I'm Kate.'

Dwayne flopped onto his back. 'Well, *Kate*, sometimes I can't believe it's over. Seemed more like a hundred years. Other guys just did their time, day after day. It wasn't like they had anything waiting for them when they got out. Me, every day I just kept thinking about what my life would be like when I finally got out.'

'I guess not everybody had waiting for them what you had waiting,' said Kate.

Dwayne glanced over. 'No shit,' he said. 'Plus, I had you waiting, too.'

Kate had not been foolish enough to think he'd been talking about her in the first place.

'I know you think I'm the stupidest son of a bitch on the planet,' he said. 'We were all set, and then I get picked up for something unrelated. You don't think I wasn't kicking myself every day, asking myself how I could be so stupid? The thing is, that guy provoked me. A guy swings at you with a pool cue, what are you supposed to do?'

'If you'd paid him the money you owed him, he wouldn't have taken a swing at you, and you wouldn't have picked up the eight ball and driven it right into his forehead,' she said.

'Good thing the guy came out of his coma before sentencing,' Dwayne said. 'They'd have sent me away for ever.'

Neither of them said anything for a couple of minutes. Dwayne finally broke the silence with, 'I have to admit, babe, every once in a while I got worried that you wouldn't wait. I mean, it's a long time.'

'I don't want to make it sound like I had it as bad as you,' Kate said, 'but I was in a prison of my own while you were in yours.'

'You were smart, I gotta hand it to you, the way you did it, getting a new name, disappearing so fast.'

The thing was, she'd already had that in place, even though she hadn't started using it right away. Just seemed like a good idea.

Dwayne had been going by another name when it all went down and was confident that if that guy started asking around, things wouldn't get traced back to him. When he got arrested for the assault, it was his real name that went in the paper, so no major worries there. But once things went west, she started playing it safe. With so much waiting for her at the end of the rainbow, she didn't want to leave anything to chance. Not when she realised the courier had lived.

'So this guy you married,' Dwayne said. 'What was he like?'

'He's . . . never realised his potential.'

Dwayne nodded. 'That's what I'm about. Realising my potential. You're going to have a brighter future with me, that you can count on. You know what I'd like to do? I'd like to live on a boat. You're free. You don't like where you are, you go some place else. You want to live on a boat?'

'I've never really thought about it,' she said. 'I think I might get seasick. I like the idea of an island, though. Some place with a beach, where you could sit all day and watch the waves roll in. A piña colada in my hand. No one to bother me, ask me for anything.'

Dwayne hadn't listened to a word. 'I'd like to get a big boat with whaddyacallems, staterooms. Every night, when you go to sleep, you hear the water banging up against the boat, it's real relaxing.'

Kate threw back the covers. 'I'm going to take a shower.'

Walking to the bathroom, she wondered what had happened in the years since she'd last been with Dwayne. Something was different. Sure, he was no rocket scientist when she was with him before, but there'd been compensations. Living on the edge, the almost constant, awesome sex, the thrill of taking chances.

It was no surprise that he'd be different now. A guy gets sent down for a few years, he's not going to be the same guy when he gets out.

Maybe it wasn't just him. Maybe someone else had changed.

'I need some breakfast,' he said. 'Like a Grand Slam, you know? The whole thing. Eggs, sausage, pancakes. I'm starving.'

AT DENNY'S, they got a low-rise booth next to a man who was taking two small children out for breakfast. The man, his back to Dwayne, was telling the boys—they looked to be twins, maybe six years old—to sit still instead of getting up and standing on the seat.

The waitress handed them menus. 'You know what you want?'

'I want a donut!' one of the boys shouted behind Dwayne.

'We're not getting donuts,' the father said. 'You want some bacon and eggs? Scrambled the way you like them?'

'I want a donut!' the boy whined.

Dwayne was grinding his teeth as he ordered his Grand Slam while Kate ordered pancakes with syrup on the side.

As the waitress walked away, Dwayne leaned towards Kate and whispered, 'I think your wig's a bit cockeyed.'

She reached up and adjusted it.

'You look good like that,' he said. 'You should dye your hair.'

'And if the cops figure out they're looking for a blonde, what do I do? Dye it again? I'd rather get myself a couple more wigs.'

Dwayne smiled lasciviously. 'You could wear a different one every night.'

'That how they do it inside?' she asked. 'Guy's a redhead one night, brunette the next, takes your mind off the fact he's a man?'

She couldn't believe she'd said it.

Dwayne's eyes narrowed. 'Excuse me?'

'Forget it,' she said.

'There something you want to ask me?' he asked.

'I said forget it.'

The twins were jabbing at each other. The father yelled at them both to stop it.

Dwayne's eyes were boring into Kate. 'You think I'm a faggot? You want to go places you shouldn't? I can do that, too. How's it feel putting your friend in the ground?'

'She wasn't my friend,' she said.

'You worked in the same office together.'

'She wasn't my friend. And I get it. We're even. I'm sorry.'

'He did it first!' one of the boys whimpered.

Dwayne closed his eyes and gritted his teeth. 'Damn kids.'

'It's not their fault,' she said. 'They have to be taught how to behave in a restaurant. Their dad should have brought something for them to do, a colouring book, a video game. That's what you do.'

The waitress served the father and twins, and a moment later brought plates for Kate and Dwayne.

'Eat your breakfast,' the father said behind Dwayne.

'I don't *want* to,' said one twin.

The other one showed up at the end of Kate and Dwayne's table. He inspected their breakfast until Dwayne said, 'Piss off.' Then the boy strolled up to the cash register.

The father twisted in his booth and said, 'Alton, come here!'

Kate poured some syrup on her pancakes, cut out a triangle from one and speared it with her fork. She had a feeling that she needed to eat fast, that they might not be staying here much longer.

Dwayne shovelled food into his mouth. 'What were the odds that we'd run into her?' he asked.

'Alton, come back here right now!'

'My eggs are icky!' said the twin still at the table.

Dwayne spun round, put one hand on the father's throat, drove him down sideways and slammed his head onto the bench. The man's arm swept across the table, knocking eggs and bacon all over himself and the floor. His eyes were wide with fear as he struggled for breath. He batted pitifully at Dwayne's muscled arm, pinning the man like a steel beam. The boy at the table watched, horrified.

Dwayne said, 'I was going to have a word with your boys, but my girl here says it's your fault they act like a couple of wild animals. You need to teach them how to behave when they're out.'

Kate was on her feet. 'We need to go,' she said.

SIX

Barry Duckworth had just left Gina's restaurant. Gina had called the police after seeing a story on the TV news about Jan Harwood's disappearance. When Duckworth came by to interview her, she said that the Harwoods had dined in her restaurant recently.

Gina said that they had been talking about something that couldn't have been good because they both looked distressed. She was going over to the table when Jan Harwood said to her husband something like 'You'd be better off if something happened to me'.

Duckworth quizzed Gina on the exact words Jan had used.

Gina had replied, 'Maybe she said he'd be happy if she was dead. Or he was rid of her. Something like that.'

But Gina said that she didn't hear any of David Harwood's part of the conversation. At any rate, Jan looked upset. She got up from the table and they left without having the rest of their dinner.

After sampling a slice of Gina's astonishing cheese-and-Portobello-mushroom pizza, Duckworth got into his car. He was thinking he might need to take a drive up to Lake George before the day was over, but there was one other stop he wanted to make first.

ARLENE HARWOOD TRIED TO keep busy. Her husband was entertaining Ethan with an old croquet set in the back yard. Just whacking the balls in any old direction was keeping Ethan occupied, and Don quickly abandoned plans to teach Ethan the game's finer points.

Arlene, meanwhile, did some dishes, she ironed, she paid some bills online. She did not use the phone. She didn't want to tie up the line. David might call. Maybe the police. Maybe Jan.

She racked her brain trying to figure out where Jan might have gone, what might have happened to her. She'd always had a feeling that there was something about Jan that wasn't quite right. David had fallen for her soon after he'd met her while doing a story for the *Standard* on people looking for jobs at the city employment office. Jan was new to town, looking for work, and David tried to coax some quotes out of her. But Jan didn't want her name in the paper or to be part of the piece.

Something about her touched David. She seemed, he once disclosed to his mother, 'adrift'. Although she wouldn't be interviewed for the piece, she did disclose to David that she lived alone, didn't have anyone in her life, and had no family here.

David had once said if it hadn't been so corny, he would have asked her how a woman as beautiful as Jan could be so alone. Arlene Harwood had thought it a question worth asking.

When David finished interviewing other, more willing subjects at the employment office, he spotted Jan outside waiting for a bus. He offered her a lift and, after some hesitation, she accepted. She had rented a room over a pool hall.

'That's really—I mean, it's none of my business,' David said, 'but that's not really a good place for you to live.'

'It's all I can afford at the moment,' she said.

'What are you paying?' he asked.

Jan's eyes widened. 'You're right, it's none of your business.'

'Tell me,' he said.

She did.

David went back to the paper to write his story. After he'd filed it, he made a call to a woman he knew in Classified. 'You got any rentals going in tomorrow I can get a jump on? I know someone looking for a place. Let me give you the price range.'

She emailed him copies of four listings. He drove to the pool hall, went upstairs and down a corridor, knocking on doors until he found Jan.

He handed her the list he'd printed out. 'These won't be in the paper until tomorrow. At least three of these are in better parts of town than this, and they're the same as what you're paying now.'

That weekend, he helped her to move.

Someone new to rescue, his mother thought, after Samantha Henry had made it clear she could manage on her own. It was a short courtship. They were married in a matter of months.

'Why wait?' David said to his mother. 'If she's the right one, she's the right one. I've been spinning my wheels long enough.'

'Jan wants to rush into this, too?'

'Remind me how long you knew Dad before you got married?'

'Got you there,' Don said, walking in on the conversation. They'd gone out for five months before eloping.

The thing was, Don had loved Jan from the first time David brought her home. Jan ingratiated herself effortlessly with David's father and it struck Arlene that Jan had a natural way with men. She was unquestionably desirable with the full lips and eyes, the pert nose. Her long legs looked great in everything from a tight skirt to jeans. And she had a way of communicating her sex appeal without it being tarty. No batting of the eyelashes, no baby-girl voices. Arlene, however, was immune to that kind of charm.

Not that Jan had ever been anything but cordial with her. But what kind of girl, Arlene wondered, cuts off all ties with her family? How bad did parents have to be not to let them know they had a grandson? Jan must have had her reasons, Arlene told herself. But it just didn't seem right.

The doorbell rang. Startled by the sound, Arlene went into the hall. There, through the glass in the front door, Arlene spotted an overweight man in a suit and loosened tie. She opened the door.

'I'm Detective Duckworth. You're David's mother?'

'Yes.'

'I'm heading the investigation into your daughter-in-law's disappearance. I'd like to ask you some questions.'

'Oh, of course, please come in.' As Duckworth crossed the threshold she asked, 'You haven't found her, have you?'

'No, ma'am,' he said. 'Is your son home?'

'No, but Ethan's here. Did you want me to get him?'

'That's OK. I met Ethan yesterday. He's a handsome fellow.' Duckworth sat down on the living-room couch and waited for Arlene to do the same. 'Your son . . . this must be terrible for him.'

'It's dreadful for all of us. Ethan doesn't really understand how serious it is. He just thinks his mother has gone away for a while.'

Duckworth found an opening. 'You have some reason to think that's not the case?'

'Oh, I mean . . . I mean, we are hoping that's all this is. But it's so unlike Jan to just take off. She's never done anything like that before, or if she has, David's never mentioned it.' She bit her lip, thinking that came out wrong.

'Have you noticed anything out of the ordinary with Jan lately?' Duckworth asked. 'A change in mood?'

'Oh my, yes. David's been saying the last couple of weeks Jan has seemed very depressed. It's been a tremendous worry to him.'

'So you observed this change in Jan's mood?'

Arlene stopped to consider. 'Well,' she hesitated. 'I think Jan always puts on her best face when she's around her in-laws.'

'So you can't point to any incident where Jan acted depressed?'

'Not that I can think of.'

'That's OK. I'm trying to nail down Jan's movements the day before she went missing. Do you know what Jan was doing on the Friday before she went to the Five Mountains park?'

'I don't really know. Oh wait, she and David went for a drive. David asked if we would look after Ethan longer that day, because he had to go some place and Jan was going to go along with him.'

'Do you know where they were going?'

'I'm not sure. You really should ask David. Do you want me to get him on the phone? He's on his way back from Rochester.'

'No, that's OK. I just wondered if you had any idea.'

'I think it had something to do with work. He's a reporter.'

'So, he asked you to babysit Ethan until they got back?'

'That's right. Before it got dark David picked up Ethan.'

'David and Jan,' Duckworth said.

'Actually, just David,' Arlene said. 'He came by on his own.'

Duckworth nodded, like there was nothing odd about this, but he had a tingling in the back of his neck. 'Wouldn't it make sense for both of them to drop by on the way home and pick up Ethan?'

'David said Jan wasn't feeling well during the drive back, so he dropped her at their place and then he came over here for Ethan.'

'I see,' Duckworth said. 'But I guess she felt well enough in the morning to go to Five Mountains. How did she seem to you then?'

'I didn't see her in the morning. They went straight to the park.' Outside, the sound of a car door closing. Arlene got up, went to the window. 'It's David. He'll be able to help with these questions.'

Duckworth got to his feet. 'I'm sure he will.'

WHEN I PULLED UP in front of my parents' house, I spotted an unmarked police car at the kerb. My pulse quickened. I was out of the car in a second and took the steps up to the porch two at a time. As I swung open the door, I found Duckworth standing there.

'Has something happened?' I asked.

'No, no, nothing new,' Duckworth said. Mom was standing just behind him, her eyes desperate and sorrowful. 'I was driving by and decided to stop. Your mother and I were having a chat.'

I felt deflated. But the truth was, I was the one with news.

'I need to talk to you,' I said to him. 'But I want to see Ethan first.' I could hear his laughter coming from the back yard. I started to move past the detective but he reached up and held my arm.

'I think it would be good if we could talk right now,' Duckworth said. 'It would help if you'd come down to the station with me.'

Trying to keep the anxiety out of my voice, I said, 'OK.'

He let go of my arm and went out of the door. Mom came up and hugged me. She must not have known what to say because she said nothing.

'It's OK, Mom,' I said. 'I'm sorry. I was going to take Ethan off your hands.'

'Don't be stupid,' she said. 'Just go with him.' She let go and I could see tears welling up in her eyes. 'David, that detective looked at me funny when I said that Jan—'

'Mr Harwood!'

I looked over my shoulder. Detective Duckworth had the passenger door of his unmarked car open, waiting for me.

'I have to go,' I said. I ran down to Duckworth's car, hopping into the front seat. When he got into the driver's seat and put the car into drive, I asked, 'Why are we going to the station?'

Duckworth ignored my question. 'So you came back from Rochester this morning?' he asked.

'Yes.'

'And you went out there why again?'

'I was looking for Jan's parents.'

'Did you find them?'

I hesitated. 'That's what I want to talk to you about. But let me ask you something first. If the FBI or some other organisation puts someone in the witness protection programme, and they resettle them in your own back yard, do they give you a heads-up about it?'

'Generally speaking, the FBI views local law enforcement as a bunch of know-nothing hicks, so my guess is they'd not be inclined to share that kind of information. You're asking this because . . .'

'I think it's just possible that—'

'Wait, let me guess,' Duckworth said. 'Your wife is a witness in hiding. Her cover's been blown and now she's taken off.'

'Is this a joke to you? Jan may not be who she says she is.'

Then, 'And just who is she, really? Tell me, I'm listening.'

'I don't know,' I said. 'I've—I've found out some things in the last day that don't make a whole lot of sense to me. I went to Rochester and found Horace and Gretchen Richler, the people who are listed on Jan's birth certificate as her parents. They had a daughter named Jan, but she died when she was five. Her dad accidentally hit her with the car, backing out of the driveway.'

'Man. How do you live with that the rest of your life?'

'Yeah.' I gave Duckworth a minute for it to sink in. 'What do you make of that?'

'Let me make a call when we get to the station. And while someone's looking into that, we can talk about some other things.'

'HAVE A SEAT,' he said, pointing to the plain chair at the plain desk in the plain room.

'Isn't this an interrogation room?' I asked.

'It's a room,' Duckworth said. 'A room is a room. I want to talk to you privately, it's as good a place as any. Hang on while I make a call about that witness protection thing. You want a coffee or a soft drink or something?'

I said I was OK.

'Be right back, then.' He slipped out of the room, closing the door behind him. I sat down on one of the metal chairs. This didn't feel right.

There was a mirror on one wall. I wondered whether Duckworth was on the other side, watching through one-way glass. I stayed in the chair, tried to calm down. But inside I was churning.

After a few minutes, the door opened and Duckworth came in.

'I'm not an idiot,' I said. 'The way this is going. Leaving me in here to sweat it out for a while on my own. I get it. You think I'm a suspect.'

'I never said that.' Duckworth pulled up a chair.

'So tell me you don't think I have anything to do with this.'

'How about you tell me about this trip you took up to Lake George two days ago?'

'What?'

'You've never mentioned it. Why's that?'

'Why would I? Jan went missing the following day.'

'Why don't you tell me about it now?'

'Jan and I drove up to Lake George to meet with a source for a story I've been working on.'

'What story is that?'

'I've been working on stories about Star Spangled Corrections wanting to come to Promise Falls. The company has done favours for at least one council member that I know of. Someone sent me an email, that there were others taking payoffs to buy their votes when the prison comes up before council for zoning approvals.'

'Who sent you the email?'

'I can't tell you that.'

'Oh,' said Duckworth. 'Confidentiality. Protecting your source.'

'No,' I said. 'The email was anonymous and the person didn't show up. The email said that I was to look for a woman in a white truck. She would come at five to Ted's, a general store/gas station north of Lake George. No woman in a white truck showed up.'

'So you drove up there? And you took your wife with you?'

'Yes.'

'Why'd you do that? Do you normally take your wife along when you're going to interview someone?'

'Not usually. But like I told you, she's been feeling depressed the last few weeks, and she was going to take Friday off, so I suggested she come along for the ride. What's the point of this, Detective?'

'I'm just getting a full picture of the events that led up to your wife's disappearance.'

'Going to Lake George did not "lead up" to her disappearance. It's just something we did the day before Five Mountains. Unless—'

Duckworth cocked his head to one side. 'Unless?'

The car. The one Jan had spotted following us.

'Jan saw a car following us up,' I said. 'Then, when we were waiting in the parking lot for this contact to show up, the car drove by a couple of times.'

'Who would have followed you?' Duckworth asked.

'At the time, I figured it was someone who found out this woman had arranged to meet me. But now I don't know. Maybe that car was following Jan. She's a relocated witness, someone figured out who she was, was following her, and she had to disappear.'

'I guess you wouldn't have any trouble producing that woman's email for me,' Duckworth said. 'When did you receive it?'

'Last Thursday,' I said. 'And . . . I deleted it.'

'That seems like an odd thing to do. Why'd you do it?'

'I don't think everyone at the *Standard* shares my enthusiasm for pursuing this story. I've learned not to present stories unless they're completely nailed down. I like to play my cards close to the chest. So I don't leave emails around for my superiors to read.'

Duckworth looked unconvinced, but went in another direction. 'Tell me about this car that was following you. Make, model?'

'It was a dark blue Buick with tinted windows.'

'Did you happen to get a plate number?'

'I tried, but it was covered with mud.'

'Was the whole car covered in mud, or just the plate?'

'The car was pretty clean, actually. Just the plate was dirtied up. Doesn't that tell you they probably did it deliberately?'

'Absolutely,' Duckworth said.

'Don't patronise me,' I said. 'You don't believe a word I'm saying. I can see it in your face. But we were there. Talk to whoever was working in the store that day. Jan went in to buy something to drink. Someone there might remember her.'

Duckworth looked at me. 'I believe you were there. So when did you drive home?'

'I stayed until around five thirty, and when I was sure the woman wasn't going to show, we drove back.'

'Both of you,' Duckworth said.

'Of course both of us.'

'Any stops along the way?'

'Just to my parents' place. To pick up Ethan.'

'So both of you went to get your son.'

'No,' I said. 'I went alone to get Ethan. Jan had a headache. She asked me to drop her off at our house first.'

Duckworth nodded. 'But isn't your parents' place on the way home? You'd have to pass your parents' house to get to yours coming back from Lake George, then double back to get your son.'

'That's true,' I said. 'But my parents like to talk. And Jan wasn't up to that. That's why I took her home first. What are you getting at? You think I left her up in Lake George?'

When Duckworth didn't say anything, I said, 'You should go up there. Talk to whoever was working at Ted's store that day.'

'Mr Harwood, your wife's been identified as being in the store at the time you say. Trouble is what she had to say when she was in there. She said you'd driven up there for some sort of surprise. She said she had no idea what she was doing up there.'

'What? That's crazy. Jan knew why we were going up there. Whoever told you that is lying.'

'Why would someone lie about that?' Duckworth asked.

'I have no idea. But Jan wouldn't have said that.'

'Why did Mrs Harwood tell you that you'd be happier if she was gone?' Duckworth asked. 'Maybe even dead?'

'What?' I said again. 'What the hell are you talking about?'

'Are you denying she ever said that?'

I opened my mouth to speak, but nothing came out. Finally, I said, 'Gina's. Almost two weeks ago. We were having dinner at Gina's. Jan was distraught through dinner. She said some crazy things. Then she had this outburst—loud enough for anyone in the restaurant to hear—that I'd be happy to be rid of her. But she never said I wanted her dead. I don't know why she'd think that I'd be happier without her, unless it's tied in to her depression.'

'About Jan's depression,' Duckworth said. 'It's interesting that the only one who noticed your wife suffering from that is you. And why were only two tickets charged to your wife's card at Five Mountains? One adult, one child. Was it because you knew you wouldn't be taking your wife with you?'

'I didn't order them,' I said. 'Jan ordered them. And she was there, at the park. I can't explain the ticket thing. Maybe . . . maybe, when she came back from the car, she realised she'd printed out the wrong thing, that there wasn't a ticket for her, and she paid cash to get in.'

'We've looked at all the security footage at the gates and we can't find her. Not coming in and not going out.'

'Look, I see what you are doing here and you've got it wrong,' I said. 'The first thing you need to do is to check out Jan's birth certificate, and these people I thought were her parents, but who turned out not to be.'

'So show it to me,' Duckworth said.

'I don't . . . have it. It had been hidden in an envelope, behind a baseboard in the linen closet, at our house. But I looked today, when I got back from Rochester, and it was gone.'

'Well.'

'Come on. Can't you call those things up anyway? The state has records. You can get a copy of it. But you're not going to. Because you don't believe anything I've told you.'

'Which story would you like me to believe? The one about your wife wanting to kill herself, or the one about her being in the witness protection programme? Or have you got a third one?'

I put my elbows on the table and my head in my hands. 'My wife's out there somewhere and you need to be looking for her.'

'You know what would save me a lot of time in that regard?' Duckworth asked. 'You could tell me where she is. What did you do with her, Mr Harwood? What did you do with your wife?'

'I DIDN'T DO ANYTHING with her!' I shouted at Duckworth. 'I swear I didn't. Why the hell would I want to hurt her? I love her. She's my wife, for God's sake. We have a son!'

Duckworth sat expressionless, unruffled.

'I am not lying to you!' I said. 'I am not making this up! Jan's been depressed. I don't know how to explain that no one else noticed how Jan was feeling. Maybe she could only be herself with me.' I shook my head in frustration. Then, an idea. 'You should talk to Leanne Kowalski. They work together. Even if Jan was able to hide how she was feeling with most people, Leanne would pick something up.'

'Leanne.' Duckworth said the name slowly. 'I'll have to check that out. How would you describe Jan's relationship with Leanne?'

'They just worked together.'

'They ever do things together? Lunch, shopping?'

'No.'

'They didn't hang out sometimes after work?'

'How many times do I have to tell you? No. Just talk to her. Talk to every person you can find. You're not going to come across anyone who thinks I have anything to do with Jan's disappearance. I love her.'

'I'm sure.'

'You have this so completely wrong.' I pushed back my chair and stood up. 'Am I under arrest?'

'Absolutely not,' Duckworth said.

'I'm going to need a ride back to my car and—no, forget it. I'll find my own way back to my parents' place.'

'About that,' Duckworth said. 'Before we sat down for our little chat, I popped out to see about search warrants. We're seizing both of your cars, and we're conducting a search of your house.'

'You're searching my house?' I said. 'Are you serious?'

As if on cue, my cellphone rang. I flipped it open. 'Hello?'

'David?' My mother. 'They're towing away your car!'

'I know, Mom, I just found out that—'

'I went out and told them they couldn't do that, that you can park for free for three hours on that side of the street, but—'

'Mom, there's nothing you can do about it. I'm at the police station and I need a ride—'

'One of my men can give you a lift,' Duckworth said.

I glanced at him. 'Go screw yourself.'

'What?' said Mom.

'Send Dad down here,' I said. 'Can you do that?'

'Are you OK? Are you in some kind of—'

'Mom, just send Dad and I'll explain it when I get there.' I closed the phone and slipped it back into my coat.

'I'm not the bad guy,' I said to Duckworth. 'You're having people search my house when they should be searching all over Promise Falls. What if my wife's somewhere and needs help?'

Duckworth opened the door for me and I went through it. I was heading for the main lobby, with Duckworth following, when I stopped suddenly, turned, and said to him, 'You didn't even ask anyone to check the witness protection thing, did you?'

Duckworth said nothing.

'You *have* to look into Jan's background. I know, at first, I thought maybe Jan had killed herself. That's the way it was looking to me. But there's more going on here than I realised.'

'I can assure you, Mr Harwood, I'll be following this investigation wherever it goes.'

'I'm telling you,' I said, leaning in close to him, getting right in his face, 'I did not kill my wife.'

'Well,' said a familiar voice off to one side.

Duckworth and I both turned to see Stan Reeves, the City Hall councillor, standing there. A grin was creeping across his face.

'I'll be damned,' he said, looking at me. 'If it's not the holier-than-thou David Harwood of the *Standard*,' he said. 'The things you hear when you're paying a parking ticket.'

I BROKE AWAY from Duckworth and headed for the door.

Dad pulled up at the kerb in his blue Crown Victoria about five minutes later. I got in the passenger side and slammed the door.

'Watch it, you'll shatter the glass,' he said.

'Dad, take me by my house. What's happening at your house?'

'It's like your mother told you on the phone. They took the car away. It wasn't parked illegally,' Dad said.

'That's not why they towed it,' I said.

Dad looked at me with disappointment. 'They repossessed it? You didn't keep up your payments?'

I suppose it was a sign of faith in me that Dad would suspect me of being a deadbeat before he'd think of me as a murderer.

'Dad, the police are looking for evidence. The police think that maybe I did something with Jan.'

'She's your wife, David! What's wrong with them? You'd never hurt Jan.'

'Cops always look at the husband when a wife's missing,' I said. Was I trying to make Dad feel better, or myself? Maybe my interrogation by Duckworth was just standard operating procedure.

No. There was more to it than that. The circumstances of Jan's death were working against me. The fact that only two tickets had been ordered online. The fact that Jan had not disclosed to anyone else how depressed she'd been feeling the last couple of weeks.

I believed these things could be explained. What I couldn't figure out was why the person working at Ted's Lakeview General Store was lying. Why would someone tell police Jan had said she didn't know where she was going, that her husband had brought her up there for some sort of surprise? That was crazy. Jan had gone in to buy a couple of drinks. How likely was it that she would strike up a conversation with whoever was behind the counter about anything, let alone why she was up there with her husband? If that's what the proprietor at Ted's had told the police, he or she was lying.

Unless, of course, Detective Duckworth was lying. Was he making the whole thing up to see how I'd respond? But how did he know in the first place that we'd been up there? The person Jan had bought drinks from must have contacted the police, after seeing the news reports about her.

'What?' Dad said. 'What are you thinking?'

'I don't know what to think,' I said. 'Just get me home.'

I saw police cars outside the house as we turned the corner. Jan's car was no longer in the driveway, so they must have scooped it at the same time as they were taking mine from my parents' house. Dad barely had the car stopped before I was out of the door, running across the lawn and up the steps. The front door was open. 'Hello!' I shouted.

A woman, in uniform, appeared at the top of the stairs. I recognised her as the officer who'd looked after Ethan at Five Mountains yesterday while I talked to Duckworth. Campion, her name was.

'Mr Harwood,' she said.

'I want to see the warrant,' I said.

'Alex!' she called, and a small, slender man emerged from the bedroom I shared with Jan. 'This is Mr Harwood,' she told him.

He came down the stairs. 'Detective Alex Simpson,' he said. He handed me a paper. 'This is a warrant to search the premises.'

I took the paper from him and glanced at it, unable to see through my anger to the words on the page. 'Just tell me what the hell you're looking for and I'll show it to you,' I said.

'I'm afraid it doesn't work that way,' Simpson said.

I bounded up the stairs. Campion was looking through my and Jan's drawers, rooting through underwear. 'Is this necessary?'

Campion did not answer. I noticed that our laptop was in the middle of the bed. 'What's that doing there?' I asked.

'I'm going to be taking that with me,' Campion said.

'That's got all our finances and addresses and everything—'

'David.' I turned. My father was standing in the doorway. 'David, you have to see what they've done with Ethan's room.'

I crossed the landing. My son's bed had been stripped. The bins where he kept his toys had been dumped and strewn across the floor. I was speechless with rage. I was about to say something to Detective Simpson when the cellphone in my jacket rang. 'Yeah?' I said.

'Hey, Dave, it's Samantha. What is going on?'

'I can't talk right now, Sam.'

'Dave, listen, I've got to be up-front with you. This isn't just a friend calling. I'm looking for a quote. I need something now.'

What I felt most like saying was that the Promise Falls police were a bunch of morons who were wasting time harassing me while my wife remained unfound. But instead I said, 'Go ahead, Sam.'

'Is it true that you're a suspect in this investigation into what happened to your wife?'

It hadn't been thirty minutes since I'd left the station. How could the *Standard* already know that—

Reeves.

I doubted Duckworth would have told the councillor anything. But my stupid overheard comment would be all Reeves needed to put in an anonymous call to the paper to say that one of the *Standard*'s own people had been spotted at police headquarters, angrily denying that he'd killed his wife. The moment Reeves was finished with the *Standard*, his next calls were probably to the TV stations.

'Sam, where did you get this?'

'Dave, come on,' Samantha Henry said. 'You know how this works. We got a tip and I'm following it up. I'm sorry, but I have to ask: is it true? Are you about to be arrested? Are you a suspect?'

Outside, I heard the squeal of brakes. Still holding the phone to my head, I slipped past my father and downstairs to the front door. It was a TV news van.

'I have to go, Sam,' I said, and ended the call.

'Isn't that News Channel 13?' Dad said.

'Yeah, Dad,' I said. 'We need to get out of here. If they start showing up at your place, I don't want them bothering Ethan. We're just going to walk out calmly and get in your car.'

'Gotcha.'

We walked out, as a driver and reporter got out of the van.

'Excuse me,' the reporter called. 'Are you David Harwood?'

I pointed to the house. 'The cops may know where to find him.'

On the way, Dad said, 'I don't know if you've thought of this, son, but maybe you need to talk to a lawyer or something.'

'Yeah,' I said. 'I might have to do that.'

'You could try Buck Thomas. When we had that trouble with the Glendons' driveway encroaching onto our lot? He's a good man.'

'I might need someone with a different area of expertise. The thing is, the police haven't charged me with anything. If Duckworth had something on me, he wouldn't have let me leave that station.'

Dad nodded again. 'You're probably right. And since you haven't done anything wrong, it's not like they're going to find any evidence against you after tearing apart your house and your cars.'

If that comment was meant to put me at ease, it didn't work.

SEVEN

They were cruising along the Mass Pike in Dwayne's tan pick-up, which his brother had lent to him when he was released from prison. It was a fifteen-year-old Chevy that sucked gas, even with the air conditioner off, which was all the time, because it didn't work.

'Are you sure it's not working?' Kate asked.

'Just put the fan on.'

'I did and it's nothing but hot air,' Kate said. 'Maybe we should have hung on to the Explorer. It was old but the air worked.'

Dwayne shot her a look. 'What's with you? You still pissed about what happened back there?'

At Denny's. She'd given him hell for that as soon as they'd got into the truck and were on the highway. 'What were you thinking?' she'd said. 'Probably somebody's called the cops.'

'It was no big deal,' Dwayne had said. 'I did that guy a favour. From now on, he'll get those kids to behave.'

For thirty miles she kept looking back, expecting to see flashing red lights. This habit Dwayne had of losing it just when they needed to keep a low profile, was a problem. She hoped he could keep a lid on things until they got their business done in Boston.

They didn't speak for several miles. She was the one to break the silence. 'What was it like?' she asked. 'Everyday life in prison.'

'Wasn't so bad. You always knew what to expect. You knew when to get up and when to go to bed and when it was lunchtime. You didn't have to make a lot of decisions. What should I wear? What should I eat? That kind of stuff wears you down, you know?'

Wasn't that what her life had been like the last few years? Decisions? Having to make decisions not just for herself but other people? The thing was, she felt like she'd just got out of prison, too. Here she was, heading down the highway, feet up on the dashboard, the wind blowing her hair.

She wondered why she didn't feel better about it.

THE PLAN WAS pretty simple. First, they had to go to the two banks. Then, once they had the merchandise from the safe-deposit boxes, they'd find this guy Dwayne had heard about who'd assess the value of their goods, then make them an offer. She hoped it would be worth the wait. She—they—were going to be rich. It was the only thing that had kept her going all these years. Knowing that there was going to be—in all likelihood—millions of dollars.

Maybe, if she and Dwayne hadn't swapped keys, and the moron hadn't got himself thrown in jail, she'd have found a way to move the process along, even if it had meant only getting a chance at her half. But when he got arrested, and the key to her safe-deposit box got tossed in with his personal effects where she couldn't get at it, what choice did she have, really, but to hang in and hide out?

That last part was important. Because she knew someone was going to be looking for her. She knew the courier had lived. Once he recovered, he'd surely go looking for the person who'd not only relieved him of a fortune in diamonds, but his left hand as well.

She'd always figured she was more at risk than Dwayne. The courier had seen her face. He'd looked right into her eyes before he passed out. She hadn't expected him to wake up. *The blood.*

The courier would have figured out how she'd got onto him. It had been through his girlfriend, or rather, his ex-girlfriend, Alanna. Kate had worked with Alanna at a bar outside Boston. Grabbing a smoke during breaks, Alanna would rag on about how this guy was always going to Africa, and how he was mysterious about what he did for a living. One time they're in his Audi, he has to pop into a building to meet somebody. He tells her he'll be back in ten minutes, so she decides to check out this gym bag behind the driver's seat, and finds these velvet-lined boxes. One of them has half a dozen diamonds in it, and she's thinking, Is this stuff real? He comes out sooner than expected, catches her, has a fit, hasn't called her since.

And the woman who now called herself Kate thought, *Diamonds*?

She'd been hanging out with this guy Dwayne for a few weeks, told him what she'd heard. They found Alanna's ex, watched him, figured out his routine. Planned a bait-and-switch. They'd meet him with a limo when he came up from New York on Amtrak.

It wouldn't take the courier long, once the painkillers started wearing off, to figure Alanna was the leak.

A couple of months after it all went down, there was a story on the *Globe* website about a woman named Alanna Dysart found floating off Rowes Wharf. There was every reason to think that before she died, she gave her killer the names of everyone she might ever have blabbed to about his line of work.

She might very well have given him the name Connie Tattinger.

And so she vanished.

ETHAN RAN into my arms as I walked through the front door of my parents' house. I hoisted him into the air and kissed his cheeks.

'I want to go home,' he said.

'Not yet, sport,' I said. 'Not yet.'

Ethan shook his head. 'I want to go home and I want Mom.'

'Like I said, not right yet.'

He squirmed angrily in my arms to the point that I had to put him down. He strode down the hall, then vanished into the kitchen, where I heard him open the fridge. Ethan usually enjoyed being here, but he hadn't been in his own house since yesterday morning. And as much as my parents loved Ethan, he was probably wearing out his welcome.

'Sorry,' I said to Mom.

'He just misses his mom. David, why did they take your car away?'

Dad, who'd just come in, said, 'You should see what they're doing at his house. Tearing the place apart, that's what they're doing.'

I steered Mom outside onto the porch where Ethan couldn't hear. 'The police think I did something to Jan,' I said.

'Oh, David,' she said. 'Why would they think such a thing?'

'Things are . . . things seem to be pointing in my direction,' I said. 'Some of it's coincidence, like the fact that no one's actually seen Jan since I took her to Lake George on Friday. But then there's other things that don't make sense, where people have been telling lies. Like up in Lake George, whoever runs that store up there.'

'David, I don't know what you're talking about. Why would people tell lies about you? Why would someone want to get you in trouble?'

'The boy needs a lawyer,' Dad said through the screen door.

'I need to go there and find out why that person at Ted's Lakeview General Store is lying,' I said.

'Is anyone listening to me?' Dad said through the screen door.

'Dad, please,' I said. 'I don't have time. I have to find Jan, and I have to find out why things are being twisted to look like I did it.'

I HIT THE ROAD an hour later in my father's car. Before I left, I told my parents what I had learned in Rochester. Dad had gone into a rant about incompetent civil servants who'd probably issued Jan the wrong birth certificate.

Mom was deeply troubled by the news. She said, 'What will we tell Ethan? Who are we supposed to tell him his mother really is?'

Dad was still going on about how I needed to get a lawyer even as I got behind the wheel of his car. On this, I had to admit he was talking sense, but I couldn't bring myself at this point to explain everything that had happened in the last two days to someone new. I had too much to do.

To placate him, I said, 'You want me to get a lawyer? Go ahead and find me one. Just not someone who handles driveway disputes.'

I kept watching my rearview mirror all the way to Lake George. I wasn't expecting to see the blue Buick Jan had spotted the last time I'd driven up here, but I did have a feeling that Duckworth, or one of his minions, would be keeping an eye on me. If I was being followed, they were doing a good job. No car caught my eye the entire drive up. I pulled into the parking lot of Ted's shortly after 3 p.m.

The door jingled as I went in. A thin man in his late sixties or early seventies was behind the counter. He nodded as I came in.

I said, 'Are you *the* Ted?'

'That's me,' he said. 'What can I do for you?'

'I'm a reporter for the Promise Falls *Standard*,' I said. 'Detective Duckworth told me he was speaking to someone here about that woman who's gone missing. Would that be you?'

'One and the same,' he said with a lilt in his voice. The suggestion that he was about to be interviewed had brightened him.

'So this woman, Jan Harwood, she was in here?'

'I'm as sure it was her as I am that you're standing right there.'

'And you called the police? Or were they in touch with you?'

'Well,' he said, 'I saw her on the news the night before, them saying she was missing, and right away I recognised her.'

'Wow,' I said, making notes on a pad that I'd taken from my pocket. 'But how could you recognise someone who was just in here for a minute?'

'Normally, you'd be right about that. But she was pretty chatty. She said that she was up here for a drive with her husband.'

'She just came out and said that?'

'Well, first she said how beautiful Lake George was, and I said are you staying around here? And she said no, she was just up for a drive with her husband. She bought some drinks and asked me if there were any fun things to do around here because her husband had brought her up on a little car trip and she was wondering why. She thought maybe he was planning to surprise her with something.'

'Did she give any other reason why they were up this way? Like, I don't know, that they were meeting someone?'

Ted thought about that. 'I don't think so. Just that her husband had brought her up this way and wouldn't tell her why.'

I set my pad and pen on the counter. 'Why are you lying, Ted?'

'What the hell are you talking about? I'm telling you the truth.'

'I don't think so. I don't believe she said those things to you.'

'If you don't believe me, get the police to show you the tape. Look.' Ted pointed to a small camera hung from a bracket on the wall. 'We got sound, too. It's not great, but you listen close you can hear what people say. I got robbed back in 2007. That's when I got the camera and microphone.'

'It's all recorded?' I said.

'Ask the cops. They came here earlier today, made a copy of it.'

'Why would she say those things?' I said, slipping the pad back into my jacket. But I was talking to myself, not Ted. I was looking down as I went out of the door, trying to come up with a reason why Jan would have told someone she didn't know that I'd brought her up here for a surprise.

Maybe, had I not been so preoccupied, I would have had some inkling that Welland, Elmont Sebastian's ex-con driver, was waiting to ambush me the moment I came outside.

WELLAND GRABBED ME by my jacket and threw me against the wall of the store hard enough to knock the wind out of me.

'What the—'

It was all I managed to say before Welland had his face in mine. 'Hey, Mr Harwood,' he said.

'Get your hands off me,' I said. Welland's arms, like a couple of shock absorbers, had me pinned to the building.

'Mr Sebastian was hoping,' he said with exaggerated politeness, 'you might be able to have a word with him.'

I glanced over and saw the limo only a few feet away.

The door of the store opened and Ted stuck his head out. 'Everything OK out here?'

Welland shot him a look. 'Get lost, old man.'

Ted walked back inside.

Welland eased off me, but placed a vicelike grip on my arm and led me to the limo. He opened the back door, shoved me through the opening and closed the door again. Elmont Sebastian sat on the far side of the thickly padded leather seat. 'Mr Harwood, a pleasure,' Sebastian said.

Welland came round the car and got behind the wheel. He sped out of the lot so fast I felt myself thrown back into the seat. He headed north.

'I never saw you following me,' I said.

Sebastian nodded. 'We were a couple of miles back. We were sloppy last time, having you followed up here with one car, which you spotted. So this time, we used several to keep track of you. Once you stopped here again, that information was relayed to me.'

'This'll make quite a story. "Prison Boss Kidnaps Reporter".'

'I don't think you'll write that. Once you've heard my proposal, I think you'll be feeling more kindly towards me. I understand if you don't give me an answer today. I know you have a lot on your plate right now, what with this unfortunate business of your wife.'

'You know all about that,' I said.

'It would be difficult not to. Some news reports are calling you a "person of interest", which strikes me as a nice way of saying "suspect". The only thing that travels faster than good news is bad news. But, in your line of work, you know that. Why do the media only focus on the negative? Here I am, offering to bring jobs and prosperity to your town, and all I get is grief. At least from you.'

'But not my paper,' I said. 'It's been very kind. Have you made a deal yet with Madeline to buy her land?'

'Star Spangled Corrections is exploring a number of options,' Sebastian said. 'What I'd like to do now is get to my proposal. I wonder how you'd feel about a career change? When Star Spangled Corrections sets up here we're going to need someone to deal with the press. I'd like you to be my media relations officer. I can guess what you're being paid at the *Standard*. Seventy, eighty thousand?'

Less.

'Your starting salary would be double that. I'll be honest. If you take this job, your editorial campaign against my facility ends, and I end up with a bright young man with a lot of media savvy.'

I said, 'As you said, I have a lot on my plate. But I can still give you an answer now. No.'

Sebastian looked saddened, but it seemed feigned. 'I had hoped, had you accepted my proposal, this next item of business would be a simple matter. But now I suspect it may be more difficult.'

'What's that?'

'Who's your source? Who was it you came up here to meet?'

'I didn't come up here to meet with anyone,' I said.

Sebastian smiled at me as though I were a child who had disappointed him. 'Please, David. I know that's why you came up here Friday. I know a woman was in touch with you. And I know she didn't show up. Now you're up here one more time. Were you stood up again?'

'I'm not here to meet with anyone.'

Sebastian sighed. 'Do you have time for a story, David?'

'I'm something of a captive audience,' I said.

'One time, at our facility outside Atlanta, we were having trouble with an inmate who went by the nickname of Buddy.'

Welland glanced at his mirror.

Sebastian said, 'He got that name because everyone wanted to be his friend and thought it was in their interests to stay on his good side. He was tough, a member of the Aryan Brotherhood, a white supremacist gang.' Sebastian called up to his driver. 'Welland, would you like to tell this? I'm afraid when I do it sounds boastful.'

Welland collected his thoughts, and then said, 'Mr Sebastian had a problem with Buddy. He was an expert at piss-writing.'

'At what?' I asked.

'You can use piss to write and it's like invisible ink. When you hold the paper up to the light or heat it, you can see the message. Mr Sebastian found out Buddy was communicating with his associates this way and he didn't want him to do it. It wasn't conducive to the smooth operation of the facility. So Mr Sebastian had Buddy brought to his office, keeping him cuffed, of course. A guard undid Buddy's trousers, pulled 'em down.' Welland cleared his throat, like maybe he didn't enjoy telling this story. 'And Mr Sebastian put fifty thousand volts to his package.'

'A Taser,' Sebastian said. 'A stun gun.'

I looked at Sebastian. 'You stun-gunned the man's genitals?'

'I explained to Buddy that when you have blood in your urine, it's trickier to use it for invisible ink. I never would have thought it was possible to make a member of the Aryan Brotherhood cry.'

'I think it would be hard not to, having that done to you.'

'Oh, it wasn't that,' Sebastian said. 'Once he'd recovered from the shock, I showed Buddy a picture of his six-year-old son and explained how unfortunate it would be if any of the recently released inmates he'd terrorised were to find out where his little boy lived. That's when I saw that solitary tear run down his cheek.'

'Well,' I said.

'Indeed,' said Sebastian. 'So, I would very much appreciate it if you would tell me who invited you up here to meet with her.'

'I don't know how you know about that email,' I said. 'But since you clearly do, you know it was anonymous.'

He nodded. 'Although your first rendezvous was not successful, it's probable that this woman found another way to contact you.'

'She didn't,' I said. 'I think she must have had second thoughts.'

'Then what are you doing back here again?'

'I drove up to talk to the manager of that store. My wife went in there to buy some drinks when we came up on Friday. I thought she might have said something to him that would help me find her.'

'David, I have to assume that email came from within my organisation, or within Promise Falls City Hall. It's important to me to find out who would contact you and suggest any kind of malfeasance on my company's part.'

Welland was slowing the car. He had the turn signal on, and a moment later was driving down a gravel road into a thick forest.

Welland brought the car to a stop.

We were in the middle of nowhere, surrounded by trees.

'It's beautiful out here,' Sebastian said. 'Only a mile off the main road and it's like you're a hundred miles from civilisation. But being out here, in the open, can be as dangerous as being kept behind bars in one of my facilities. Certainly for you. Right now.'

We locked eyes. I was determined not to be the first to look away, even though I was pretty scared. He could have Welland kill me and dump me here and my body might never be found.

Finally, Sebastian sighed, broke eye contact, and said to Welland, 'Find a place to turn round and head back.' To me, he said, 'This is your lucky day, David. I believe you. About your source.'

I felt, briefly, tremendously relieved.

'But we're not done,' he said. 'While you may not know who this source is, I would be most grateful if you'd make an effort to find out and then let me know. You may be contacted again.'

I said nothing. The limo was moving again. Welland found a narrow intersection up ahead and managed to turn the beast round, then headed for the highway that would take us, I hoped, back to Ted's.

'So was it Madeline?' I asked.

'I'm sorry?' Sebastian said.

'Madeline Plimpton, my publisher. Did she feed you the email from that woman? It's not much of a stretch to think that she has clearance allowing her to read every message attached to one of the paper's email addresses. I deleted it as quickly as I could, but I guess I wasn't fast enough. Is that the deal? She betrays her staff, keeps the heat off you, and in return you buy her land?'

Sebastian's eyes seemed to twinkle. 'That's the trouble with you newspaper types,' he said. 'You're so incredibly cynical.'

'WHY DO YOU KEEP staring at that picture?' Horace Richler asked.

Gretchen was sitting on the front step of their home, holding the picture David Harwood had left with them of his wife. Horace noticed that on the step next to Gretchen was the framed photo of their daughter, Jan.

'I'm just thinking,' she said, and looked up. She could see the two little girls playing in the front yard, laughing one minute, arguing the next. Then Horace, running out of the front door, getting into his car, throwing it into reverse and hitting the gas.

'Hey, what's going on inside your head?' Horace asked.

When Gretchen didn't reply, Horace sat himself down on the steps and leaned his shoulder into his wife's.

He said, 'I had a dream about Bradley last night. That Afghanistan never happened. That he never went over there. I was dreaming that you and I were sitting right here, and I looked down the street and I saw him walking up the road in his uniform.'

A tear ran down Gretchen's cheek.

'And he had Jan with him,' Horace said, his voice breaking. 'She was still a little girl, and she was holding on to her big brother's hand, and the two of them were coming home. Together.'

Gretchen held on to the photo with one hand and dug a tissue out of her sleeve with the other. She blew her nose, dabbed her eyes.

'It was that fella coming here,' Horace said, 'that's what triggered it. He shouldn't have come here, bringing his troubles into our house when we got enough of our own.' He picked up the photo of his daughter. His body seemed to crumple round it.

'It wasn't your fault,' Gretchen said for probably the thousandth time. She stared again at the printout picture of Jan Harwood. 'I haven't stopped looking at this all day. I knew, when he first showed it to me last night . . .'

'You seemed kind of upset,' Horace said. 'You went upstairs.'

Gretchen was struggling to say something. 'Horace . . . Horace, look at the picture.'

'I've seen the picture.'

'Look, look right here.' She pointed.

'Hang on,' he said, then reached into the front pocket of his shirt, where he kept a pair of wire-rimmed reading glasses. He opened them up and slipped the arms over his ears. 'Where do you want me to look?'

'Right here.'

He grasped the picture with both hands. He studied it for a moment and then his face began to fall. 'I'll be damned,' he said.

WELLAND HAD GOT back on the highway. As we approached Ted's, I sensed the car slowing, but then it sped up. 'You passed it,' I said to Welland. I glanced at Sebastian. 'What's going on?'

He didn't seem to know any more than I did. 'Welland?' he said.

His driver said, 'Didn't look safe to pull in, sir. Looked like someone was waiting for Mr Harwood.'

'Pull over once we get round that bend,' Sebastian said.

The car maintained its pace for a few seconds, then Welland steered it onto the shoulder. Once the car was stopped, Sebastian said, 'I hope you'll give due consideration to everything I've said.'

I opened the door, got out and started walking back to Ted's.

AS I WALKED along the shoulder my cellphone rang. It was my mother.

'It's getting bad here,' she said. 'TV trucks and reporters. Everyone wants to talk to you or get a picture of Ethan.'

'Mom, what's tipped everyone off?'

'I've been checking the websites, first your paper's, then others. It's starting to spread. The headlines say things like "Reporter Questioned in Wife's Disappearance" and "Reporter Tells Police: I Didn't Kill My Wife". It's just terrible. It's all innuendo and suggestions and—'

'Tell me about Ethan. Does he know what's going on?'

'We're keeping him inside. He's watching some Disney DVDs.'

'OK, that's good.'

'Hang on, your father wants to talk to you.'

'Son?'

'Hi, Dad.'

'I got a lawyer for you. Her name's Natalie Bondurant. I called her office, and they had this weekend emergency number and I got hold of her. She said she's willing to talk to you.'

'Thanks. That's great, Dad.'

'I got her number. Can you write something down?'

I had my notepad in my pocket. 'All right.' I got out the pad, flipped it open, wrote down the number Dad dictated to me.

Ted's had come into view. Leaning up against Dad's car was Detective Barry Duckworth.

'NICE DAY for a walk,' Duckworth said as I approached. 'What are you doing here?' His unmarked cruiser was parked to one side. That must have been what Welland saw before he decided to keep on driving.

'I might ask you the same thing. I came up to talk to Ted.'

'What were you doing leaving your car here and strolling down the highway? Not much down there to see.'

I wanted to tell him about my ride with Sebastian. But the prison boss had intimidated me to the point that I wasn't sure that was a good idea.

'I was just walking and thinking.'

'About what Ted told you?'

'So you've already spoken to him.'

'Briefly,' Duckworth said. 'You shouldn't be approaching witnesses, giving them a hard time. That's bad form.'

'He says it's on the security video. What Jan said to him.'

'That's right. What he said basically checks out. Who was it took you for a ride and dropped you off down the road?'

Ted must have told him about seeing Welland grab hold of me.

'It was Elmont Sebastian,' I said. 'And his driver. He wanted to talk to me. I've been trying to get some quotes from him.'

'And he drove all the way up here to give them to you?'

'Look, I want to get home. Things don't sound good there.'

'There's a bit of a media frenzy building,' Duckworth said. 'I want you to know, I didn't set it off. I think it was your pal Reeves. It's not my style, to get something like this going.'

'For what it's worth, thank you. So you followed me up here?'

'Not exactly. I was on my way up to something else and decided to pop in and have a face-to-face with Ted myself. Ted mentioned you'd just been in and that your car was still here.'

'So you decided to wait for me. What was the other thing you came up here for?' I asked.

Duckworth's cellphone rang. He put it to his ear and said, 'Duckworth . . .

OK . . . Is the coroner there yet? . . . I don't think I'm any more than a couple of miles away. See you shortly.'

He ended the call and put the phone away.

'What is it?' I asked. 'What was that about the coroner?'

'Mr Harwood, there's been a discovery just up the road from here.'

'A discovery?'

'A shallow grave off the side of the road. Freshly dug and covered over.'

I reached out and used the car to support myself. My throat went dry and my temples began to pulse. 'Whose body's in it? Is it Jan?'

'Well, they don't know anything for sure yet,' Duckworth said. 'Why don't we take my car?'

WE HEADED NORTH, the way I'd been taken by Sebastian and Welland, but Duckworth turned down a gravel road that went down, then up. Not far ahead, several police cars blocked our path.

'We'll walk in from here,' Duckworth said, slowing to park his car.

'Who saw this grave?' I asked.

'A couple of hours ago, a guy who lives in a cabin at the end of this road spotted something suspicious at the side, went to check it out, realised what was buried there, and called the police. Local cops secured the scene, then contacted us. We'd already put them on alert about your wife.' Duckworth opened his door. 'You can stay here if you'd like.'

'No,' I said. 'If it's Jan, I have to know.'

We got out of the car and started up the road. A uniformed officer coming from the direction of the crime scene approached.

'You Detective Duckworth?' he said.

Duckworth nodded and extended a hand. 'This is Mr Harwood. He's the one whose wife is missing.'

'Mr Harwood,' the cop said. 'My name is Daltrey.'

'Is it my wife?' I asked.

'We don't know that at this stage.'

'But it's a woman?' I asked. 'A woman's body?'

Daltrey replied, 'Yes, it's a woman.'

'I need to see her,' I said.

Duckworth lightly touched my arm. 'I really don't think that's a good idea. Let me go there first. You wait with Daltrey. If there's a reason for you to come up, I'll come and get you.'

'OK,' I said.

Duckworth went ahead. He was back in about five minutes. 'If you're up to it, I think it would help if you make an identification.'

'Oh God,' I said. I felt weak in the knees.

He gripped my arm. 'I don't know that this is your wife, Mr Harwood. But I think you need to be prepared for that fact. Take a minute.'

I took a couple of breaths, swallowed, and said, 'Show me.'

He led me between two police cars that had acted as a privacy shield. I looked to the left and saw that where the opposite side of the ditch sloped up, there was a five-foot ridge of earth. Draped over the ridge was a dirt-splotched white hand and part of an arm.

Duckworth led me up to the grave. I could feel him watching me.

I looked at the dirt-smeared face of the dead woman lying in that grave and fell to my knees. 'Oh God,' I said.

Duckworth knelt down next to me. 'Talk to me, Mr Harwood.'

'It's not her,' I whispered. 'It's not Jan. It's Leanne Kowalski.'

EIGHT

In the short time she'd been going by the name Kate, she'd never got used to it. Maybe she needed a few more days for it to feel like her own. The funny thing was, she couldn't even think of herself by her original name these days. If someone called out 'Hey, Connie!' she wasn't even sure she'd turn round. It had been years since anyone had known her as Connie.

Her worry now was if someone shouted out 'Jan!' she'd turn round reflexively, wouldn't even think about it. You spend six years with a name, you start to get comfortable with it. That was the name she'd been answering to for a long time. That, and 'Mom'.

When she'd told Dwayne Jan was dead, she'd been telling herself more than him. She wanted to put that person, that life, behind her. She reached up and made an adjustment to the wig as they continued on to Boston.

It was the same wig Jan had worn when she walked in—and out—of Five Mountains. She'd worn it long enough to get through the gates, then went into a ladies' room stall to remove it before rejoining Dave and Ethan.

The wig and a change of clothes had been in the backpack. The moment Dave had run off in search of Ethan, she'd gone into the closest ladies' room, taken a stall and stripped down.

She'd switched from shorts to jeans and traded the sleeveless top for a long-sleeved blouse. But the blonde wig was the accessory that really pulled it all together. She jammed her discarded outfit back into the backpack and strolled out of that ladies' room. Walked, real cool-like, through those gates, through the parking lot, met up with Dwayne, got into his car, and they'd left the park.

She'd never had to worry about Ethan. She knew that if Dave didn't find him, someone else would. She hoped the Dramamine-spiked juice box she'd given Ethan put him out for most of it.

Having a kid, becoming a mother, that had never been part of the plan. But then, neither had getting married.

She'd picked Promise Falls at random. Nice, anonymous upstate New York town. She had no ties there. She could go there, find a job, a place to live, and bide her time until Dwayne had done his time. When he was out, they'd go back to Boston, exchange keys, open the safe-deposit boxes and make their deal.

So she came to Promise Falls, found a room over a pool hall, and went looking for work at the employment office at City Hall. And ran into David Harwood, Boy Reporter. He was adorable. She didn't want any part of his story, however. If you gave an interview, the next thing they were going to ask you for was a picture.

But she chatted with him a little, and he ended up finding her a new apartment. Then she let him take her to dinner.

After a short courtship, David proposed. Jan sensed an opportunity presenting itself. The only thing more anonymous than living as a single woman in Promise Falls was living as a married woman in Promise Falls. As the wife of a small-town newspaper reporter, she didn't fit the profile of a diamond thief.

No one was going to find her here. She could play this role. Wasn't that what she'd been doing since she was little? Imagining herself to be someone she wasn't was the only way she'd got through her childhood. Her father blaming her all the time for screwing up their lives, her mother too self-absorbed to tell him to lay off. Imagining she was someone else had got her through until she'd walked out of that door and never gone back.

For some time, she was actually Connie Tattinger. But even as Connie, she could be whoever she needed to be. She could be a good girl, and she could be a bad girl. You did what you had to do to get a roof over your head and some food in your stomach.

When she met David, she fell easily into the role of small-town wife. It didn't take a lot of effort. It was actually fun to play. And when the time came to pack it in, she could do that, too.

The thing Jan hadn't counted on was the kid.

They hadn't been married long before she suspected she was pregnant. Couldn't believe it, sitting there in the bathroom one morning after David had gone to work. Got out the test, waited ten minutes, looked at the result, thought, Shit.

Great day for David to have forgotten some notes. Suddenly appears upstairs. He caught something in the way she looked, saw the pregnancy-test packaging. She ended up telling him she was pregnant.

This doesn't have to be a bad thing, he says.

Part of her decision was calculating. A child would make her blend in even more. And being a loving mother, wasn't it just another role? Once she looked at it this way, Jan wanted the child. She didn't think about what she would do when Dwayne got out.

But now Dwayne was out. And she'd stayed with the plan. She was going for the money and, once she had it, she'd move on to her final role. The independent woman, who didn't need anyone else for anything. She was going for the beach and piña colada. No more David. No more Dwayne.

But there was a hitch. *Ethan.*

She'd really got into that whole mother act. What she hadn't anticipated was how hard this role would be to walk away from.

JAN KNEW FIVE MOUNTAINS was going to be tricky to pull off. But she'd been out there on her days off, scoped out where all the CCTV cameras were. There was the remote chance she'd see someone they knew, but Jan figured she wasn't going to be there long, and for much of the time she wasn't going to look anything like Jan Harwood. It never occurred to Jan she'd run into someone she knew *after* they got away from Five Mountains.

If only Dwayne had picked some place else to get gas. Outside Albany, he gets off the highway near one of those big malls. And guess who's filling up right next to them?

'Jan?' Leanne Kowalski said. 'Jan, is that you?'

The dumbass . . .

On cue, like he knew she was thinking about him, Dwayne said, 'We're making good time. Should be in Boston pretty soon.'

'Great,' Jan said. But the closer they got to Boston, the more on edge she felt. She told herself it was a big city. What were the odds anyone would recognise her? 'When's the last time you talked to your guy who wants to buy our stuff?'

'The day after I got out,' Dwayne said. 'I call him, I say, "You're never going to guess who this is." He can't believe it. He says he gave up on me long ago. So I say, I'm back and ready to deal. He goes, "Are you kidding me?" The other thing he said was, "There was never anything in the news about the diamonds going missing".'

'That's not surprising,' Jan said. 'You don't go reporting illicit diamonds stolen. There's not even supposed to be any of them any more, not since that whole diamond certification thing got going back in 2000. You never saw that movie because you were in jail, the one with Leonardo DiCaprio, all about Sierra Leone and—'

'Don't you mean the Sierra Desert?' Dwayne asked.

'That's the Sahara Desert. Anyway, even with the certification thing going on, and the whole industry clamping down, there's still a big market in illicit diamonds and you don't go to the cops whining about having some ripped off. So who is this guy?'

'His name's Banura,' he said. 'He's black. I think he's from that Sierra place you mentioned. I'll call him tonight and tell him we'll be there tomorrow about noon. The banks open at nine thirty, ten. We hit mine, we hit yours. We'll be done pretty quick.'

OSCAR FINE had parked his black Audi on Hancock Street in Beacon Hill. He was watching an address on the other side of the street. It was early evening, about the time that Miles Cooper got home from work. He had been watching him for a few days now.

Oscar knew that Cooper was stealing from the man they both worked for. And the man had figured out what Miles was up to.

'I'd like you to look after this for me,' the man had said to Oscar.

'Not a problem,' Oscar said.

So he'd tracked Miles's movements for the better part of a week. If Miles

Cooper followed his usual routine, he'd be walking down the street any moment and—

There he was. Late fifties, overweight, balding.

He reached his home, unlocked the door and went inside.

Oscar Fine got out of his Audi. He crossed the street and rang the doorbell. Miles opened the door.

'Hey, Oscar,' Miles said.

'Hi, Miles,' Oscar said. 'Can I come in?'

Something flickered in Miles's eyes. Oscar could see it. It was fear. Oscar had got better at reading people the last five years. Back then, he'd been a bit overconfident. Sloppy. At least once.

'Sure, yeah, come on in,' Miles said. 'Good to see you.'

Oscar stepped in and closed the door.

'What can I get you?' Miles asked. 'I was just going for a beer.'

'I'm good,' Oscar said. He followed Miles into the kitchen.

Miles opened the fridge, leaned down, reached in for a bottle, and by the time he turned round, Oscar was pointing a gun at him, holding it in his right hand, his left arm stuck down into the pocket of his jacket. The gun had a silencer at the end of the barrel.

'Oscar, what the hell? You scared me half to death there.'

'He knows,' Oscar said.

'Who knows? Christ, put that thing away. I nearly wet my pants.'

'He knows,' Oscar said again.

Miles moved to a wooden kitchen chair and sat down. He had to put the bottle on the table because his hand was starting to shake.

'You need to know why this is happening,' Oscar said. 'It would be wrong for you to die not knowing why this is happening.'

'Oscar, you got to cut me some slack here. I can pay it back.'

'No,' Oscar said.

'But I can, with interest. I've got some other cash set aside—'

The gun went *pfft, pfft*. Oscar Fine put two bullets in his head. Miles Cooper pitched forward, hit the floor, and that was it.

Oscar let himself out, got in his Audi and drove away.

OSCAR FINE ONLY HAD to slow as he approached the security gate at the shipping-container yard. The guard in the booth recognised the car and the driver and hit the button to make the gate shift to the right.

There were thousands of the rectangular boxes in the compound, stacked like monstrous colourful Lego blocks. Oscar parked his car and got out. He walked over to a green container and unlocked the door. About four feet inside was a secondary wall and a regular-sized door, which he unlocked with a second key. He reached along the inside of the wall with his right hand and found a bank of switches. He flipped them all up and instantly the inside of the container was bathed in light. Just inside the door were a leather couch, a leather reclining chair, and a forty-six-inch flat-screen TV mounted to the wall. About halfway down the container was a narrow, gleaming kitchen. Beyond that, a bathroom and bedroom.

Oscar took the gun from his jacket and set it on the kitchen counter beside a silver laptop, its screen black. He sat down on a stool by the counter and hit a button on the side of the laptop. While he waited for the machine to get up and running, he reached for a remote and turned on the TV. It was already on CNN. He checked his email first, then went to a couple of his favourite sites. He glanced up occasionally at the TV while he surfed around.

The news anchor was saying, '. . . a person who makes his living reporting the news finds himself at the centre of it. Police are refusing to say whether they believe Jan Harwood is alive or dead, but they have indicated that her husband, David Harwood, a reporter for a newspaper in Promise Falls, north of Albany, is a person of interest. The woman has not been seen since she accompanied her husband last Friday on a trip to Lake George.'

Oscar Fine glanced at the television for only a second, not really interested, then back to his computer. Then he looked up again.

They had flashed a picture of this missing woman. Oscar only caught a glimpse of the image before the newscast moved on to a shot of a house where the Harwoods lived. Oscar kept waiting for them to show the woman's picture again, but they did not.

He returned his attention to the laptop, and with his right hand did a Google search of 'Jan Harwood' and 'Promise Falls'. That took him to the Promise Falls *Standard* website, where he found a story as well as a picture of the missing woman. He stared at it. He remembered the woman's hair as red, but now it was black. And she'd worn heavy make-up. This woman here, she had a toned-down look.

He clicked on the picture, blew it up. There it was. The small scar on her cheek. She probably thought she'd pancaked it enough to make it invisible the one and only time they'd met. But he'd seen it.

That scar was all the proof he needed. That, and the throbbing at the end of his left arm, where his hand used to be.

Oscar Fine had some calls to make.

DUCKWORTH AND I had moved away from the open grave containing the body of Leanne Kowalski. I was shaking.

I said, 'I'm gonna be sick.' And I was. Duckworth gave me a few seconds to make sure I wasn't going to do it again.

'Let's go back to my car,' Duckworth said.

He opened my car door for me and helped me in, then got in on the other side. Neither of us spoke for the better part of a minute.

'When you came up here on Friday with your wife, did you bring Leanne Kowalski with you?' Duckworth finally asked.

I closed my eyes. 'No,' I said. 'Why would we do that?'

'Did she follow you up here? Did you arrange to meet her here?'

'No and no.'

'You don't think it's odd that Leanne Kowalski's body turns up within a mile or two of the place where you claim you were meeting this source of yours?'

'Do I think it's odd? You're damn right I think it's odd that Leanne Kowalski is lying dead over there. You want me to list the odd things that have happened to me in the last two days?'

Duckworth nodded slowly. Finally, he said, 'And would you think it odd if I told you that a preliminary examination of your car—the one you used to drive up here on Friday with your wife—has turned up samples of blood and hair in the trunk? I got the call just before you came back for your car. It'll be a while before we get back the DNA tests. Want to save us some trouble, tell us what we're going to learn?'

It was time to get help.

DRIVING HOME from Lake George, I reached Natalie Bondurant, the lawyer my father had been in touch with, on my cellphone. Once we got the preliminaries out of the way, and she was officially going to act on my behalf, I said, 'There's been a development since you spoke to my father. Actually, a few.'

'Tell me,' she said.

'Leanne Kowalski, the woman who worked in the same office as my wife, her body was found not far from where I had driven on Friday with Jan.'

'So the cops already like you for this thing,' she said, 'and now they've got this. Are they going to find your wife, too?'

'I hope to God not,' I said. 'And Detective Duckworth said they've found blood and hair in the trunk of my car.'

'He may be trying to rattle you. Can you explain those things?'

'The hair? We're in and out of the trunk, I suppose some stray hairs could fall in, but I don't know why there'd be blood there.'

'There's a lot of circumstantial evidence building up round you. But what the police don't have is a body. They've got Leanne Kowalski's, but they don't have your wife's. That's good news. It means the police don't have a solid case yet. That doesn't mean they might not be able to build one without a body. Plenty of people have gone to jail for murder where a body was never found.'

If I hadn't been driving, I would have closed my eyes. I was nearly home. It was just after eight.

A thought occurred to me.

'There was something weird about where they found Leanne's body. It was right by the side of the road. It wasn't much of a grave. Just enough to put somebody into it and cover it with a bit of dirt. All somebody had to do was go a few more feet into the woods and they could have buried her where she wouldn't have been seen.'

'You're saying she was meant to be found?' Natalie said.

'It hadn't occurred to me until now, but yeah. I wonder.'

'Come to my office tomorrow morning at eleven,' she said. 'Bring your cheque book.'

'OK,' I said. I was in my parents' neighbourhood.

'And don't have any more conversations with the police without me present,' she said.

'Got it.' I turned into my parents' street.

There was a mini media circus in front of the house.

Two TV news vans. Three cars. People milling about.

'And,' Natalie Bondurant said, 'no talking to the press.'

'I'll see what I can do,' I said, and ended the call.

I parked and got out of my father's car. A reporter and cameraman jumped out of each of the news vans and called out my name. Young people with notepads and digital recorders got out of the three cars. Samantha Henry emerged from a red Honda Civic. She wore an apologetic look on her face.

The reporters swarmed me, shouting out questions.

'Why do the police consider you a suspect?'

'Did you kill your wife, Mr Harwood?'

I pushed past them and went up the stairs to my parents' front door.

BY THE TIME I pulled into the driveway of my own house with Ethan in the back seat, it was 9 p.m. Ethan had fallen asleep on the way home. I lifted him out of his seat and he rested his head on my shoulder as I took him into the house. The moment I came through the door, I was reminded that the house had been searched by the police earlier in the day. Sofa cushions were tossed about, books removed from shelves, carpets pulled back.

I laid Ethan on the couch. Then I went upstairs and made some sense of his room. I put the toys back in bins, clothes in drawers.

I went back down, picked Ethan up and carried him to his bed. I placed him on his back, undressed him, put his pyjamas on him, slipped him under the covers and kissed him on the forehead.

Without opening his eyes, he whispered sleepily, 'Good night, Mommy.'

ROLLING OFF HER, Dwayne said to Jan, 'I always like to start a big day like this with a bang.'

She got out of the motel bed, slipped into the bathroom and shut the door.

Dwayne, on his back, laced his fingers behind his head and smiled. 'This is it, baby. A few hours and we'll be set. You know what I think we should do later today? We should look at boats.'

Jan hadn't heard anything after 'baby'. She had turned on the shower after taking a moment to figure out how the taps worked in this one-star joint, which was five miles from downtown Boston.

Dwayne stood up. He grabbed the remote and turned on the television. He was flipping through the channels at high speed when he said, 'What the hell?' He went back a couple of stations and there was a photo of Jan. 'Hey!' he shouted. 'Get out here!'

She didn't hear him from under the shower.

Dwayne banged the door open and shouted, 'You're on TV!'

The anchor was saying, '—the journalist for the Promise Falls *Standard* says his wife went missing on Saturday, yet police sources have said that no one has actually seen Jan Harwood since late Friday afternoon. And there's a new development this morning. The body of a coworker of the missing woman was found in the Lake George area, not far from where Jan Harwood and her husband were seen before she went missing. Looks like we're going to have some sunshine this afternoon in the greater Boston—'

Dwayne reached through the shower curtain and turned off the water. Jan's hair was in full lather.

'Dwayne!'

'Didn't you hear me? It was on the news. They were shouting questions at your husband, and they found the body.'

Jan squinted at him through soapy eyes. She was instantly feeling cold as the water dripped from her naked body. She said, 'OK.'

'That's good, right?'

'Let me finish up in here,' Jan said. She pulled the curtain shut and fiddled with the taps. She stuck her face into the spray to get the shampoo out of her eyes. But they'd been stinging before this.

She'd found herself crying at one point in the night. Not that she was sobbing uncontrollably. But there was a moment when she felt *overwhelmed.* A few tears got away before she fought them back.

As she'd lain there in bed, she'd imagined putting her hand on Ethan's head, feeling his silky hair on her palm. She'd imagined the smell of him. The sounds his feet made padding on the floor when he got up in the morning and walked into their room to see if she was awake.

Think about the money. She tried to push him out of her thoughts.

From the moment she'd started going out with David, she'd convinced herself it was about the money. This façade, this marriage, this raising a child, it was all part of how she was earning her fortune. She just had to do the time, until Dwayne got out, and she'd be out of there. And once she'd exchanged the diamonds for cash, she'd be rid of Dwayne, too.

The way she'd left things in Promise Falls, no one would be looking for her. At least not alive. When they didn't find her body, the police would figure David had done a good job disposing of it. Oh, he'd tell them he was innocent, but wasn't that what all guilty men said? When it finally dawned on David that his wife had set him up, what exactly was he going to do about it from a jail cell?

At least Ethan would be OK. His grandparents would look after him. Don's heart was in the right place. And while Jan never cared for how Arlene looked at her sometimes, there was no doubt she loved Ethan to death. Jan struggled to find some comfort in that.

Maybe, once she had her money, she'd forget about the last few years, make believe the people she'd known—and the one she had brought into the world—during that time never really existed. Once she had the money. The money would change everything. That's what she'd always believed.

DWAYNE STOPPED THE TRUCK in Beacon Street. 'Here you go,' he said.

Jan looked to her right. They were parked outside the front of a MassTrust branch between a Starbucks and a high-end shoe store.

'This is it?' she said.

'This is it. Your key opens a box right here.'

This had been the way they'd worked it. They'd each picked a safe-deposit box to store their half of the diamonds, kept the location secret, and then swapped keys. That way, they'd need each other when they wanted to cash in.

'Let's do it,' she said.

They got out of the truck together, walked through the front doors of the bank and went up to a service counter.

Jan said, 'We'd like to get into our safe-deposit box.'

'Of course,' said a middle-aged woman. She needed a name, and for Dwayne to sign in a book, and then she led them into a vault where small, rectangular mailbox-like doors lined three walls.

'Here's yours right here,' the woman said, producing a key and inserting it into a door. Jan took out the key she'd been holding on to for five years, inserted it into the accompanying slot. The door opened and the woman slid out a long black box.

'There's a room for your convenience,' she said, opening the door so that Dwayne and Jan could enter. She set the box down on a counter and withdrew, closing the door on her way out.

Dwayne lifted the box lid. Inside was a black fabric bag with a drawstring. Jan loosened the drawstring and tipped the bag over the counter. Diamonds spilled out. Dozens and dozens of them.

'Oh my God,' Dwayne said, like he'd never seen them before.

Jan was shaking her head slowly in disbelief.

'And this is just half of them,' Dwayne said. 'We are so rich.'

'I didn't remember there was this many,' she whispered.

She started collecting them, slipping them back into the bag. 'I think one of them fell on the floor,' she said.

Dwayne dropped down to his hands and knees. 'Got it,' he said, and then he wrapped his arms round Jan's legs, pulling her towards him. 'We should do it in here.'

'We can celebrate later,' she said. 'After we get our money.'

Dwayne stood up, took the bag from Jan's hand.

'I'll put it in my handbag,' she said.

'No, it's OK,' he said, stuffing the bag into the front pocket of his jeans, which created an unsightly, off-centre bulge. 'I got it.'

JAN GAVE DIRECTIONS to Dwayne that took them to a bank in Cambridge. He parked the truck and felt in his pocket for his safe-deposit box key.

He had his hand on the door when Jan reached over and held his arm. 'This time,' she said, 'I'll hold on to them.'

'Yeah, sure, no big deal,' he said, pulling his arm away.

They entered the bank and followed the same routine. They were led into the vault, then ushered into a private room so that they could inspect the contents of the box. Once the bag of diamonds was safely tucked into Jan's handbag, they walked out of the bank and back to the truck.

I HAD A LOT to do that Monday. I woke Ethan shortly after eight. After breakfast, I dropped him off at my parents' house, then drove to the newspaper. I had time to pop in before my appointment with Natalie Bondurant. I went up to the newsroom. As I walked to my desk, what few people were there stopped whatever they were doing to watch me. No one said anything.

When I tried to sign in to my computer, my password was rejected. 'What the hell?' I said.

Then, a voice behind me. 'Hey.' It was Brian. I spun round in the chair. He said, 'I didn't expect you in today. Got a sec?'

Once we were both inside his office, he closed the door, pointed to a chair. I sat down and he settled in behind his desk.

'I hate to do this,' he said, 'but I—we're—they're putting you on suspension. Actually, more like a leave. A leave of absence.'

'Why's that? Did you think I wanted to write a book?' It was a reporter's usual reason for taking a leave. I knew what was going on, but it was hard to pass up an opportunity to make Brian squirm.

'No, not anything like that,' he said. 'It's just your current predicament kind of compromises your ability as a journalist at the moment.'

'Am I on a paid suspension or unpaid?'

Brian couldn't look me in the eye. 'Things are kind of tight. It's not like the paper can afford to pay people for not doing anything.'

'I've got three weeks' vacation,' I said. 'Why don't I take that now? I still get paid, but I'm not writing. If my problems haven't gone away in three weeks, you can suspend me then without pay.'

Brian thought about that. 'Let me bounce that off them.'

'Them' meaning Madeline.

'Thanks,' I said. 'Do you want me to ask *them* myself?'

'What do you mean?'

I stood up and opened the door. 'See you later, Brian.'

On the way out of the newsroom, I went past the bank of mailbox cubby-holes, scooped a couple of envelopes out of my mailbox—one of them was my payslip. I wondered whether it would be my last. I stuffed the envelopes into my pocket and went to the publisher's office. I opened the door to Madeline's oak-panelled room, despite her executive assistant's protests.

Madeline sat behind her desk, looking at something. She raised her eyes and took me in, not even blinking. 'Hello, David.'

'I just dropped by to thank you for your support,' I said.

'Sit down, David.'

'No, thanks, I'll stand. I saw Brian, found out I'm on the street.'

'I'm not without sympathy,' Madeline said. 'Assuming, of course, that you had no involvement in your wife's misfortune.'

'If I told you I didn't, would you even believe me?'

She paused. 'Yes,' she said. 'I would.'

That threw me. I sat down.

'I've heard the whispers,' Madeline said. 'I've asked around. I know people in the police department. You're much more than a person of interest. You're a suspect. They think something has happened to your wife and they think you did it. So I feel doubly bad for you. I feel badly that something may have happened to Jan. But it's not possible for you to work as a reporter at the moment. You can't be doing stories when you are a story.'

'I asked Brian if I could take all the vacation that's owed to me.'

She nodded. 'That's a good idea. Of course, do that.'

'I have to ask you something else. Did you go into my emails, find one from a source offering to tell me about Star Spangled payoffs to council members, and pass it on to Elmont Sebastian?'

She held my stare for several seconds. 'No. And, when and if you get back to work, if you get something on him or anyone whose votes he's allegedly buying, I'll see that it makes the front page. I don't like that man, and I don't want to do business with him.'

I got up and left.

JAN HAD NEVER actually killed anyone, at least not on purpose.

But she knew the law would already see her as a murderer. Even though she hadn't been the one who clamped a hand over Leanne's mouth and nose and kept it there until she stopped flailing about, she didn't do anything to stop it, either. Jan watched it happen. And it was her idea to take Leanne's body to Lake George—a way to tighten the noose on David, who police would know had been in that neck of the woods with her—and bury it in that shallow grave in plain view, using a shovel in the back of Dwayne's brother's pick-up. Any jury would see that they hung for that together.

And she knew it was only luck that Oscar Fine hadn't died when she cut off his hand to steal the briefcase he had cuffed to his wrist.

That had been a pretty desperate moment. They thought he'd have a key on him. Or a combination to the briefcase. And the chain that linked the case to his cuff was high-tensile steel that their tools wouldn't cut. But they could go through flesh and bone.

So, once he was out cold—and that hadn't taken long after Dwayne shot the dart into him—she did it. If you'd asked her the day before whether she had it in her to cut off a man's hand, she'd have said no way. But then there you are, in a limo parked in a vacant lot, not knowing whether someone's going to come by, and you're doing things you'd have never thought yourself capable of.

Too bad he got that look at her face before passing out. Even tarted up with enough lipstick and eye shadow to paint a powder room, she never stopped worrying that he might remember her. Would have been a lot better if the son of a bitch had bled to death. Then she wouldn't have had to marry a guy, have a kid, live a lie—

Focus, she told herself. *Let's just take this one step at a time. We have all the diamonds. Now we just have to convert them to cash.*

They'd driven out of downtown, south out of Boston. They had to find this Banura dude, find out what the jewels were worth, negotiate a price, get their cash, start their new life together.

Start *her* new life. Dwayne was going to be history.

Not that he didn't have his merits. When she'd got wind of the diamond courier he had helped her to set it up, getting the dart gun, driving the limo. So maybe she was the only one with the balls to cut the guy's hand off. You couldn't have everything.

But she'd needed him to get into the safe-deposit boxes. And she needed him now to connect with Banura. But after that, well, Dwayne really wasn't what Jan was looking for in a man. Once she had her money, she'd invest in a foolproof passport and then go off to Thailand, or the Philippines. Some place where the money would last for ever.

THEY FOUND the house. A small storey-and-a-half with white siding. Dwayne parked in the driveway behind a minivan.

'He said come in around the back,' Dwayne said.

'You're not worried, us walking in here with everything we've got?' Jan asked. Half the diamonds were still tucked into Dwayne's jeans, while Jan had her share in her bag. 'What if he decides to take the diamonds off us?'

'Hey, he's a businessman,' Dwayne said. 'You think he's going to throw away his reputation, screwing over a client like that?'

Jan wasn't convinced.

'OK, if you're worried . . .' Dwayne reached under the seat and pulled out a small, short-barrelled revolver.

'How long have you had that?' Jan said.

'Got it from my brother when he let me have the truck.'

Another thing that could have sunk us if we'd been pulled over, Jan thought. But knowing they had a weapon offered some comfort.

Dwayne tucked the gun into the pocket of his jacket. 'Let's get rich.'

They got out of the truck and walked round to the back of the house, where Dwayne found a door with a peephole and pressed a white button to the left of it. Seconds later there was the sound of a deadbolt being turned.

A tall, wiry man with very dark brown skin opened the door. He smiled, exposing two rows of yellowed teeth. 'You are Dwayne.'

'Banura,' Dwayne said, shaking hands. 'This is . . . Kate?'

She smiled nervously. 'Hi.'

Banura extended a hand to her and drew them both into the house. Inside the door was a flight of stairs heading down. Banura returned to position a bar that spanned the width of the door. He led them downstairs, hitting a couple of light switches on the way.

The stairway wall was lined with cheaply framed photos—some in colour and some, mercifully, in black and white. Most were of young black men, some just children, barefoot and dressed in tattered clothes, photographed against bleak African landscapes of ruin and poverty. They were wielding rifles, raising hands in victory, grinning for the camera. In several, the men posed over corpses.

Banura took them into a crowded room with a long, brilliantly lit workbench. Spread out on the bench was a black velvet runner, and over it three different magnifiers on metal arms.

'Have a seat,' Banura said in his thick African accent, gesturing to a tatty couch that was half covered in boxes.

'Sure,' Dwayne said, dropping onto a narrow spot on the couch.

'You won't be needing your gun,' Banura said, his back to Dwayne as he sat at the workbench. 'The one in your right pocket. I'm not going to take anything from you. And you are not going to take anything from me. That would be totally foolish.'

'Sure, I get that.' Dwayne laughed nervously. 'I just like to be cautious.'

'Let me see what you have,' Banura said.

Jan reached into her handbag and withdrew her bag. Dwayne fished out his from his jeans. They presented them to Banura.

He opened both bags, emptied them onto the black velvet. He examined half a dozen stones with his magnifiers, then said, 'These are very good. Where did you get these? I'm just curious.'

'Come on, Banny Boy, I'm not telling you that.'

Banura nodded. 'That's fine. Sometimes it is better not to know. What counts is the quality of the merchandise. And this is superb.'

'So, what do you think they're worth?' Jan asked.

Banura studied her. 'I am prepared to offer you six.'

Jan blinked. 'I'm sorry?'

'Million?' Dwayne said, sitting up at attention.

Banura nodded solemnly. 'I think that's more than generous.'

Jan had never expected to be offered six million dollars. She thought maybe two or three million, but this, this was unbelievable.

Dwayne stood up, trying not to look excited. 'I think that's a figure my partner and I can work with. But we'll need to talk about it.'

'We'll take it,' Jan said.

'So where's the money?' Dwayne said.

'I don't keep funds of that nature around here,' Banura said. 'I will have to make arrangements. You may take your product with you, and later this afternoon we can make an exchange. For a transaction of this size, I will have an associate present, and you will not be permitted to enter my premises with that gun on you. Come back at two.' Banura gathered the jewels and returned them all to one bag, since they fitted easily enough.

He held out the bag and Jan took it before Dwayne could get his hands on it. She put it into her handbag. 'So, two o'clock, then,' Jan said.

Banura followed them up the stairs, then pulled back the bar across the door. 'Goodbye,' he said.

The bar could be heard clinking in place once they were outside.

'Six mil!' Dwayne said. 'Did you hear the man?' He threw his arms round her. 'It was all worth it, baby.'

Jan smiled, but she wasn't feeling it. It was too much money.

WHEN HE WAS BACK at his workbench, Banura picked up a cellphone, dialled a number. He put the phone to his ear. It rang once.

'It was them,' Banura said.

'When?'

'Two o'clock.'

'Thank you,' Oscar Fine said and ended the call.

NINE

Natalie Bondurant said, 'Either somebody's setting you up, or you killed your wife.'

'I didn't kill my wife,' I said. I was in my new lawyer's office. 'I don't know for sure something's even happened to her.'

'*Something* has happened to her,' Bondurant said. 'She's gone. She may very well be alive, but *something* has happened to her.'

I'd told her everything that had happened to me in the last few weeks, including my chats with Elmont Sebastian. It had occurred to me that if something had happened to Jan and I got framed for it, I wouldn't be able to write any more stories about Star Spangled Corrections' bid for a prison in

Promise Falls. Could Sebastian be manipulating things behind the scenes to have me neutralised?

Natalie sat behind her desk. 'I think it's a stretch that Sebastian is setting you up to take the fall for this. From everything you've told me, Sebastian has a more direct approach. First, a cash inducement. The job offer. When you turned that down, he moved on to simple scare tactics. I think there's a more obvious answer. Let's review a few things. The tickets going into Five Mountains. One child ticket, one adult ticket ordered online. You're the only one who seems to know about your wife's recent bout of depression. No one sees Jan from the time you left that store in Lake George. She tells that shopkeeper some tale about not knowing why you've driven there.'

'Supposedly.'

Natalie ignored that. 'And Duckworth wasn't lying to you. They've found hair and blood in the trunk of your car. And guess what they found in the history folder of your laptop? Sites that offered tips on how to get rid of a body.'

I blinked. 'How do you know this?'

'I chatted with Duckworth before you arrived. Full disclosure.'

'That's crazy,' I said. 'I never looked up anything like that.'

'There's also a life insurance policy you took out on your wife.'

'It was Jan's idea. She thought it made sense and I agreed.'

'Jan's idea,' Natalie repeated, nodding.

'What?' I said.

'You're not getting this, are you?' She shook her head. 'How well do you really know your wife?'

'Really well. Very well. You don't spend more than five years with someone and not know them.'

'Except you're not even sure what her real name is. Clearly it's not Jan Richler. Jan Richler died when she was a child.'

'There has to be an explanation. She might be a relocated FBI witness. Maybe she testified against someone and had to take on a new identity.'

'You told this to Duckworth,' she said.

I nodded. 'I don't think, when I told him, he believed a word of it. I'd already told him about Jan's depression, but that story was falling apart whenever he talked to anyone else.'

'How do you explain the fact that you're the only one who witnessed your wife's change in mood?'

'Maybe I was the only one she felt she could be honest with.'

'Honest?' Natalie said. 'We're talking about a woman who's been hiding from you, since the day you met, who she really is. What if her depression was an act just for you?'

Slowly, I said, 'Go on.'

'OK, let's forget this business about the FBI getting your wife a new name and life. The FBI doesn't have to look for people who died as children to create new identities for people. They can make them right out of thin air. So has it occurred to you that your wife might have gone about getting a new identity on her own?'

'I can't come up with a reason why she'd do such a thing.'

'David, it wouldn't surprise me that as we sit here the police are drawing up a warrant for your arrest. Finding Leanne Kowalski's body a couple of miles from where you were seen with your wife will have shifted them into overdrive. All they've wanted is to find a body, and now they've got one. They probably figure you killed Jan, that Leanne found out or witnessed it, so you killed her, too. They don't even need to find your wife's body now. They'll be able to put together some kind of case with Leanne's.'

'I didn't kill Leanne,' I said.

'You're in a mess, and there's only one person I can think of who could have put you there.'

My head suddenly felt very heavy. I let it fall for a moment, then raised it and looked at Natalie. 'Jan,' I said.

'Bingo,' she said. 'She was the one who ordered the Five Mountains tickets. She was the one who fed you—and you alone—a story about being depressed. Why? So when something happened to her, that's the story you'd tell the cops. A story that would look increasingly bogus the more the police looked into it. Who had access to your laptop to leave a trail of tips on how to get rid of a body? Who could easily have put her own hair and blood in the trunk of your car? Who told the Lake George store owner that she had no idea why her husband was taking her for a drive up into the woods? Who persuaded you to take out life insurance, so that if she died you'd be up three hundred grand?'

I felt the ground starting to swallow me up. 'But why?' I asked. 'I mean, if she wanted out of the marriage, why not just leave?'

'Because it isn't enough for her to get away. She doesn't want anyone to come looking for her. No one's going to come looking for her if they figure she's dead. She wanted to get away, and she wanted you to be her cover story. Her patsy. Her fall guy.'

'Why would she do this to me?' I whispered. But there was a bigger question. 'Why would she do this to Ethan?'

Natalie crossed her arms and thought about that a moment.

'Maybe,' she said, 'because she's not a very nice person.'

'SOMETHING'S WRONG,' Jan said.

They were sitting in a McDonald's. Dwayne had ordered two Big Macs, a chocolate shake and a large order of fries. Jan had bought only a coffee and even that she wasn't touching.

His mouth full, Dwayne said, 'What's wrong?'

'It's too much money. The stuff is hot. You're never going to get retail value for it. Best you can expect is ten or twenty per cent.'

'That's probably what he was offering us,' Dwayne said.

'He didn't even look at all the diamonds,' Jan said.

'He did a random sampling, and he was impressed,' Dwayne said. 'OK, what is the downside? So maybe he's offering us more than you were expecting. What are you worried about? That he's going to come after us later and ask for some of his money back?'

'No, I don't think he's going ask for some of his money back,' Jan said. 'Did you see the photos on his wall?'

'I didn't notice. Couple of hours, we go and pick up our money. I was thinking, to kill time, we go and find some place that sells boats.'

'I want to find a jewellery store. I want a second opinion.'

'THIS IS A dumb idea,' Dwayne said as they sat in the truck outside the front of a jewellery store with black iron bars over the windows and door.

'I want someone else to have a look at them,' Jan said. 'If the guy in here looks at a few and says they're worth such and such, then I'll know what we're being offered isn't out of whack.'

Jan still had the bag of diamonds in her bag.

'Don't you go thinking about sneaking out of the back door,' Dwayne said. 'Half those diamonds are mine.'

'Why would I run off with them now when someone has promised to give us six mil for them?' Jan got out of the truck, opened the outer door of the jewellery store and stepped into a small alcove. There was a second door that was locked. Through the iron bars and glass, Jan could see a middle-aged woman behind the counter. The woman suppressed a button and suddenly her voice filled the alcove. 'May I help you?' she asked.

'Yes,' said Jan. 'I need a quick appraisal.'

There was a buzz, Jan's cue to pull on the door handle. Once inside, she discreetly picked half a dozen diamonds from the bag.

'I was wondering if you could give me an idea what these might be worth. Do you have someone who can do that?'

'I can do that,' the woman said. 'Let's see what you have.'

On the counter was a desktop calendar pad, a grid of narrow black rules and numbers on a white background. The woman reached for a jeweller's eyepiece, adjusted a lamp so it was pointing down onto the calendar, then asked Jan to put the stones onto the lit surface.

The woman leaned over and one by one studied each of the six stones. When she was done, she said, 'Where did you get these?'

'They're in the family,' Jan said. 'They've been passed down to me. So what would you say they were worth? Individually, that is.'

The woman sighed. 'Let me show you something.' She placed one of the diamonds on its flattest side on one of the black rules on the calendar. 'Look at the stone directly from above.' Jan did as she was told. 'Can you see the line through it?'

Jan nodded. 'Yes, I can.'

The woman took a single diamond from a drawer. She straddled it on the black line beside Jan's stone. The two diamonds looked identical. 'Can you see the line through this stone?' she said.

Jan leaned over a second time. 'I can't make it out,' she said.

'That's because diamonds reflect and refract light unlike any other stone or substance. The light's being bounced in so many directions in there, you can't see through it.'

Jan felt a growing sense of unease. 'What are you saying?' she asked. 'That my diamonds are of an inferior quality?'

'No, I'm not saying that. What you have here is not a diamond. It is cubic zirconium, a man-made substance. It looks like diamond. They even use it for advertisements in diamond trade magazines.'

Jan wasn't hearing any of this. She hadn't taken in anything after the woman said what she had were not diamonds. 'It's not possible,' she said under her breath. 'My diamonds, my cubic . . .'

'Cubic zirconium.'

'They must be worth something,' Jan said, unable to hide the desperation in her voice.

'Of course,' the woman said. 'Perhaps fifty cents each?'

DUCKWORTH PULLED HIS CAR over to the shoulder. Fifty yards ahead, police cars were parked on either side of this two-lane stretch of road northwest of Albany, which was built along the side of a wooded hill. Beyond the shoulder where Duckworth had parked, the ground dropped off steeply into more forest. That was where a passing cyclist had noticed something. An SUV.

When the first rescue team had shown up, ropes were used to get down to the vehicle safely. There was no one in the Ford Explorer and nothing to indicate that an occupant had been injured inside it.

A check of the plates showed that the Explorer belonged to Lyall Kowalski, of Promise Falls. Soon the locals learned that the wife of the man who was the registered owner of the vehicle had been killed. And that was when someone put in a call to Duckworth.

Standing at the top of the hill, Barry Duckworth could see the path the SUV had taken. Grass had been flattened. The Explorer had nicked a couple of trees on the way down, judging by the missing bark.

The first thing Duckworth thought was, Huh?

What was the Explorer doing here? If you looked at a map, Promise Falls was in the middle, Lake George was up to the north, and Albany was down here to the south. How did Leanne's car end up at the bottom of this hill, but her body up in Lake George?

'Someone ditches the car here hoping it won't be found,' he said to himself, 'but leaves Leanne's body so somebody will find it.'

BY THE TIME I walked out of Natalie Bondurant's office, I was so shaken by her interpretation of recent events I was in a walking coma. I was traumatised, shell-shocked, dumbstruck.

Jan had set me up. At least that was how it looked.

I started my father's car, drove it home, pulled into my driveway, unlocked my front door and stepped into my house. As I stood in that place, it suddenly felt very different. If everything that had happened here for the last five years was built on a lie—on Jan's false identity—then was this a real home?

I mounted the stairs and went into our bedroom, which I'd so carefully tidied after the house had been turned upside-down by the police. I stood at the foot of the bed, taking in the whole room.

I started with the closet. I reached in and hauled out everything of Jan's. I tore blouses, dresses and trousers off their hangers and threw them on the bed. I don't know what I was looking for. But I felt compelled to take everything of Jan's, disrupt them and expose them to the light.

When I was done with the closet, I yanked out all the drawers in Jan's half of the chest of drawers. I flipped them over, dumped their contents onto the bed—underwear, socks, hosiery. I walked out of the bedroom—leaving it in a worse state than the police had—and went down to the basement. I grabbed a screwdriver and a hammer, then came back up.

I opened the linen closet, hauled everything out that was on the floor, got on my knees and, with the screwdriver and hammer, ripped out the baseboards. When I was finished with that closet—having found nothing—I started in on the one in Ethan's room. When I struck out there, I tackled our bedroom and came up empty.

I tapped on the wooden floors throughout the house, looking for any planks that appeared disturbed. A few boards looked as though they might have been tampered with, so I drove the screwdriver between them and prised them up. The flooring cracked as the nails were ripped out. I got my nose right into the hole I'd created. Nothing.

In the kitchen, I emptied every drawer. Pulled out the fridge, looked behind it, dumped out flour and sugar containers. Nothing.

I was desperate to find anything that might tell me who Jan really was or where she might have gone. And I didn't find a single thing.

Maybe that birth certificate and the envelope that had been hidden behind the baseboard in the upstairs linen closet had been the only thing Jan had hidden in this house. There'd been a key in that envelope, too. A strange-looking key, not a typical door key.

Then it hit me what it probably was. A safe-deposit box key.

Before Jan had taken up with me, she'd put something away for safekeeping. And the time had come for her to go and get it.

Slowly, I walked through our home. The house looked like a bomb had hit it. There weren't many places to sit save for the stairs. I sat on a lower step, put my face into my hands, and began to cry.

If Jan really was dead, my life was shattered.

If Jan was alive and had betrayed me, it wasn't much better.

If Natalie Bondurant's take on everything was right, it meant Jan was alive and, to save my own neck, I needed to find her.

But it didn't mean I wanted her back. As I wiped the tears from my cheeks, I looked for something in all of this that was good. Something that would give me some hope, some reason to carry on.

Ethan. I had to keep going for Ethan. I had to find out what was going on, and stay out of jail, for Ethan. I couldn't let him lose his father. And I wasn't about to lose my son.

WHEN JAN CAME OUT of the jewellery store and got into the pick-up truck, her face was set like stone and her hand seemed to shake when she reached for the handle to pull the door shut.

'What's going on?' Dwayne asked. 'What'd they say?'

Jan said, 'Just go.'

Dwayne turned the ignition and threw the truck into drive.

'What's wrong?' Dwayne said as he drove. 'You look like you just saw a ghost. What'd they say in that store?'

Jan turned and looked at him. 'It's all been for nothing. All of it.'

'Connie, what the hell are you talking about?'

'They're worthless!' she screamed. 'They're fake! They're all cubic something or other! They're not diamonds!'

He pulled over, slammed on the brakes. 'What are you saying?'

'Are you deaf, Dwayne? Are you hard of hearing? Let me tell you real slow so you'll understand. They. Are. Worthless.'

Dwayne's face was crimson. He turned to face Jan. 'Tell me.'

'I showed this woman half a dozen of the diamonds. She got out her eye thing and studied them all and said they were all fake.'

'That is *not* possible,' Dwayne said through clenched teeth. 'She's playing some sort of game. Figured if she said they were worth next to nothing, she could make you a lowball bid.'

'You're not getting it! She didn't make any offer. She didn't—'

He lunged across the seat and grabbed her round the throat.

Jan choked. 'Dwayne—'

'I don't care what you were told by some stupid bitch back there. A guy is prepared to give us six million for these diamonds, and I am prepared to accept his offer no matter what you say.'

'Dwayne, I can't brea—'

'Or maybe . . . let me guess. Did she say the diamonds were actually worth more? But you figure, you'll come back out and tell little ol' Dwayne that they're worth nothing, so I'll say, let's forget the whole thing and hit the road, while you go back and negotiate an even better deal and keep all the money for yourself?'

Jan gasped for air as Dwayne maintained his grip on her neck.

'You were able to play your little husband for all these years, so how hard could it be to play me for a few days, am I right?'

Jan felt herself starting to pass out.

Dwayne took his hand away. 'Fuck this,' he said. 'I'm trading these diamonds for our six million, and when I've got the money I'll make a decision about what your share is going to be.'

Jan coughed and struggled to get back her breath as Dwayne put the truck in gear and sped off down the street.

It was the closest she'd ever come to dying. Two thoughts had flashed across her mind before she thought it was all over.

I could do it. I could kill him. And: *Ethan.*

DWAYNE WAS DRIVING round in circles. Jan had sat quietly in the seat next to him, waiting until she thought he'd calmed down.

Finally, she whispered, 'You need to listen to me. I know you think I'm lying about what that lady said. But let's just say I'm telling the truth. If I am, why did Banura say they were first rate?'

Dwayne shook his head. 'OK, if you're not lying, then maybe that woman doesn't know squat.'

'It is her business,' Jan said. 'It's what she does.'

'Then maybe Banura doesn't know squat.'

Now Jan was shaking her head. 'It's his business, too.'

'Well, one of them doesn't know what they're talking about.'

'I think they both know what they're doing,' Jan said. 'But one of them's lying. And it doesn't make any sense that the woman in the jewellery store is lying.'

'You think Banny Boy is lying about how much he's going to give us? You think he'll have three million for us instead of six?'

'He's not going to pay anything for stones that are worthless.'

Dwayne's face was darkening again. The anger was returning. Jan knew what was going on. He was so close to the money he could taste it. He didn't want anyone ruining his dream.

'If they're worthless, then why didn't he tell us that when he first saw them?' Dwayne said. 'Why make us come back at two?'

'I don't know,' Jan said.

'I'll tell you why,' Dwayne said. 'It's not safe to keep that kind of cash around. He probably had to go some place to get it.'

Jan knew that Dwayne was beyond convincing at this point.

He said, 'When I get my boat, I'm using you for a damn anchor.'

FOR OSCAR FINE, it was about redemption. He had to set things right, restore some personal order, and the only way he could do that, no matter how long it took, was to find the woman who took his hand.

It was more than an injury. It was a humiliation. He had always been the best. When you wanted something done, he was the man you called. He took care of things. He didn't screw up. But then he did. Big-time.

The thing was, he knew something might be up. That was the whole point of toting a briefcase full of bogus jewels. They were worried about a leak, that their system for moving jewels into the country, and then to their various markets, had been compromised.

It had been Oscar Fine's idea. Do a decoy delivery, he said. For theatrical effect, he hooked himself to a briefcase with a handcuff. Any other time, he transported goods in a gym bag. A handcuff, it was like carrying a sign that said 'Rob me'.

Oscar Fine knew something was up when the limo arrived and the driver did not get out to open his door. Let him do it himself.

OK, he said to himself, *I can play along. That's the whole point of this.*

So he opened the door on his own, and there she was. A woman with red hair, all lipstick and low-cut top and a skirt up to here and sheer black stockings and hooker heels, and right away he knew this was a trap.

She said, 'They said you deserved a bonus.'

Yeah, like that would happen. But he could play along with this. Let them think they're pulling a fast one. Pretty soon a gun will come out, he gives up the code and the briefcase, lets them drop him off somewhere.

Too bad about the dart.

It came from where the driver was sitting. Caught him below the right nipple, went through his jacket, pricked the skin. The effect was almost instantaneous. As he began to weave, the woman lurched towards him, grabbed the briefcase. Since he was attached to it by the wrist, he stumbled forward and into the back of the car. His arms and legs started going numb. He started to say 'What the hell' but all that came out was 'Wawawa'.

While the dart made it difficult to speak, it hadn't totally slowed his thought process. They were going to want the briefcase. And he was happy to let them have all the cubic zirconium that it held. But if he couldn't talk, how would he tell them the combination? The case had five numbers that had to be lined up for it to open.

The driver and the woman, once they couldn't open the case or release it from the handcuff that attached it to his wrist, started yelling at each other. First, he heard metallic clinking. They'd brought tools. His wrist, being grabbed, examined, thrown down, picked up again. A search of his pockets, the inside of his jacket. Then they were both shouting at him, asking for the combination. He tried to say something, but the words would not come.

'He's really out of it,' the woman said.

'Look for a key,' said the driver.

'I've been through his pockets. There's no handcuff key,' said the woman.

'Maybe he wrote the combination down, put it in his wallet,' said the driver.

The woman: 'What, you think he's a moron? He's going to write down the combination and keep it on him?'

'So cut the chain,' the driver said. 'We take the case, we figure out how to open it later.'

'It looks way stronger than I thought,' the woman said. 'It'll take me an hour to cut through. I'm gonna have to cut it off.'

'I thought you said it would take for ever to cut the cuff,' the driver said.

The woman: 'I'm not talking about the cuff.'

Oscar had a pretty good idea now what they were going to do.

He tried to form the word 'Wait'. If they could hold off long enough for the tranquilliser to wear off slightly, he could articulate the numbers they needed to open the briefcase. 'Wu,' he said.

'What?' said the woman.

'Dwer,' he said.

She shook her head and looked at him. A change seemed to come across her face, like a mask. He would never forget that face. 'Sorry,' she said.

And then she began to cut.

THE INJURY WAS so horrendous, so traumatic, it had the effect of rousing Oscar Fine from the effects of the mild tranquilliser.

Once the woman and the driver had bolted with the case, he managed to slip off his necktie and, with his remaining hand, wrap it a few inches above the ragged stump to staunch the blood flow.

It wasn't enough. The blood was still coming.

He was going to die.

He didn't have the strength to open the door, get to his feet, try to flag someone down.

This was it.

'Would you step out of the car, please?'

Huh?

Banging on the window. 'Hello? Police! You can't park your limo here. Would you step out of the car, please?'

HE WASN'T ABLE to offer the cops much help.

Didn't see them, he said.

Never mentioned the briefcase.

Said he had no idea why they cut off his hand. His guess? Mistaken identity. They must have thought I was someone else.

HIS RECOVERY took several months. Sure, Oscar felt pain. But mostly, he felt shame. He'd screwed up a job. He'd been outwitted.

But in many ways, even minus a hand, he was better at his job than he'd ever been before. Less cocky, more cautious.

And there was never a moment when he wasn't looking for her. He only had one lead. A name: Constance Tattinger. He'd got it from Alanna, the one who'd gone snooping in his gym bag. He needed to know who she might have talked to. And before she died, Alanna came up with that one name.

The only Constance Tattinger he was able to find any record of was born in Rochester, but her parents moved when she was a little girl to Tennessee, then Oregon, then Texas. The girl had left home when she was sixteen or seventeen, and her parents, speaking to Oscar Fine in their El Paso home, had told him that they'd never heard from her again.

He was pretty sure they were telling him the truth, considering the mother and father were bound to kitchen chairs at the time and Oscar Fine was holding a knife to the woman's neck.

He slit both their throats.

Oscar Fine figured she'd been going by other names since his encounter with her. He was pretty sure she and her accomplice had never tried to unload the fake diamonds. Oscar Fine and the rest of the organisation he worked for had put the word out to everyone they knew to be on the lookout for them. And years had gone by without anyone trying to turn them into cash. But Oscar never gave up hope that, some day, they'd try.

When he saw the face of Jan Harwood—all scrubbed up and wholesome—on television, he just knew. It was *her*.

And knowing the kind of person she was, he was betting she was fit as a fiddle and that she was going to be needing some cash.

That was when Oscar Fine started making some calls.

TEN

I heard someone trying the front door, which I had locked behind me when I'd come home. I was still sitting on the stairs.

'David?' It was my father, shouting through the door.

I got up and opened the door.

His eyes went wide when he saw the damage. 'David, what the hell happened here?' He stepped in. 'Have you called the police?'

'It's OK, Dad,' I said. 'I did it.' I led him through the debris into the kitchen. 'You want a beer or something?' I asked him.

'There's thousands of dollars in damage. Your insurance isn't going to cover it if you did it yourself. Are you nuts?'

I opened the fridge. 'I got a Coors in here. You want that?'

Dad shook his head and looked at me. 'Yeah, sure.' He took the can, popped the top and took a swig. 'Why did you do this?'

I found one more can and opened it. After I took a long drink, I said, 'I thought Jan might have hidden something else here. She hid that birth certificate and a key in an envelope behind a baseboard.'

The phone rang. I picked up. 'Hello.'

'Mr Sebastian would like to speak with you.' It was Welland.

I sighed. 'Sure.'

'Not on the phone. Out front.'

I replaced the receiver, ignored Dad's quizzical look, and went out of the front door and down the steps to the limo. Instead of following me outside, Dad went upstairs, no doubt curious about just how much damage he was going to feel obliged to help me fix.

Welland came round the front of the car to greet me. He reached for the rear door handle to open it for me.

'I'm not getting inside and I'm not going anywhere,' I said. 'If he wants to talk to me, he can put his window down.'

Welland, evidently prepared to accept that, rapped the window lightly with his knuckle and a second later it powered down. Sebastian leaned forward slightly in his seat so he could see me.

'Good day, David.'

'What do you want?'

'The same thing I wanted to know last time we spoke. I want to know who was going to meet with you.'

'I told you. I don't know.'

'You need to find out. That woman is a threat to me.'

'My plate is full,' I said. 'But I do have an idea for you.'

Sebastian's eyebrows went up a notch.

'You could go screw yourself.'

Sebastian nodded solemnly and put the window up.

Welland looked at me. 'He's not going to ask you again.'

'Good,' I said.

'No, not good. It means that Mr Sebastian is prepared to *escalate*.'

Welland got back behind the wheel and took off down the street. I walked back into the house and found Dad upstairs, on his hands and knees, straddling an open stretch in the floor where I'd ripped up a board.

'You can't let Ethan come back here,' Dad said. 'There's a hundred places where he could get hurt. David, I know you're going through a lot, but there's some really nice hardwood here you've gone and ruined.'

'It was a stupid thing to do,' I conceded.

Dad was putting boards to one side. 'I should be able to figure out which boards go where. But some places, you're going to have to spring for some new wood. I can go home and get my tools.'

'You don't have to do that right now,' I said.

Dad turned and yelled, 'What the hell else am I supposed to do? Tell me that! What the hell else!' He padded further up the hall, watching for nails as he approached the linen closet.

'That was where I started,' I said, feeling defeated. 'That was where I found the envelope, in there.'

'But you didn't find anything else,' he grumbled. He reached for a piece of baseboard I'd prised away from inside the linen closet, turned it over to look for nails, and said, 'Hello, what's this?'

It was an envelope taped to the back of the baseboarding. When I'd ripped the boards off, I'd been looking for what might be left behind them, not what might be taped to the back of them.

Dad peeled the tape away. When he had the envelope free, he handed it to me. I opened it and pulled out a single piece of paper.

It was a birth certificate, for a child named Constance Tattinger.

'What is it?' Dad asked.

'A birth certificate,' I said.

'Whose?'

I said, 'I'm not sure.' I knew I'd heard that name. At least the first name. Recently, within the last couple of days. I tried to think.

The name had come up at the Richlers'. Constance was the name of Jan's playmate. The little girl who had pushed Jan into the path of the car Horace backed too quickly out of the driveway.

I looked back at the birth certificate, looking for a date of birth for Constance Tattinger. April 15, 1975. Just a few months before the date of birth on the Jan Richler birth certificate.

I scanned the rest of the document. Constance Tattinger had been born in Rochester. Her parents' names were Martin and Thelma.

'Oh my God,' I said. 'It all fits. If you were the grown-up Constance Tattinger, and you needed a new identity, and you were looking for someone who'd died as a child, you could save yourself a lot of time by picking one you already knew about.'

'I don't know what you're talking about,' Dad said.

I needed to confirm this. I went to the phone, got the number again for the Richlers in Rochester, and dialled.

'Hello?' Gretchen Richler.

'Mrs Richler,' I said. 'It's David Harwood. I'm sorry to bother you, but I have a question. You mentioned the first name of the girl who was playing in your yard when . . . the accident happened.'

'Constance,' she said. Gretchen made the name sound like ice.

'What was her family's name?'

'Tattinger,' she said without hesitation.

'Didn't you say her family moved away?'

'That's right. Not long after.'

'Do you know where they moved to?'

'I have no idea,' she said. 'Have you found your wife?'

'Not yet,' I said.

'You sound hopeful. You think she's alive?'

'I do. But I don't yet understand all the circumstances behind why she disappeared. Thank you, Mrs Richler. I'm sorry to have disturbed you. Please pass on my regards to your husband.'

'Perhaps I can do that when he gets home from the hospital,' Gretchen said coldly. 'He tried to kill himself this morning. I think your visit, and your news, were a bit too much for him.'

'I'M NOT GOING DOWN into that basement,' Jan said.

They were sitting in the pick-up, parked in Banura's driveway. A couple of houses down, a black Audi was parked at the kerb.

'Look,' said Dwayne. 'Is it because I lost my cool back there? If that's what this is about, I'm sorry.' He laid it on so thick she could tell he wasn't. 'We're minutes away from becoming millionaires. You gotta keep your eye on the prize.'

'I'll keep watch here,' she said. 'If there's a problem, I'll lay on the horn.'

'If you want to sit here and be a big pussy, that's fine.' Dwayne glanced at his watch. It was five minutes to two. He grabbed the bag of diamonds, opened the truck door and started getting out.

'Wait,' Jan said. 'Take the gun.'

Dwayne looked at her scornfully. 'You heard what the man said. He said not to bring any weapons into his house.'

Jan leaned across the front seat and reached under it. She pulled out the gun. 'Seriously, you should take it.' If things went south in that basement, it was best that Dwayne took care of them before someone came charging out looking for her. And she'd rarely handled guns. At least Dwayne knew how to point and shoot.

Dwayne said, 'You need to lighten up.' He got out of the truck.

Jan shifted over behind the wheel and kept the gun next to her.

'I APPRECIATE THIS,' Oscar said to Banura, sitting in his basement workshop. 'You're sure this is the stuff I've been looking for?'

'No question.'

'And they're expecting how much?'

'Six.'

Oscar Fine smiled. 'I'll bet he got excited when he heard that.'

Banura nodded. 'The girl, though, she looked a bit . . .'

'Dubious?'

'Yeah, dubious. I was thinking, maybe I oversold it.'

'Not to worry.' Oscar looked at his watch. 'Almost two.'

Banura grinned. 'Showtime.'

There was a rapping on the door above them. Banura went upstairs. He moved the bar out of position and opened the door.

'Hey,' Banura said.

'How's it going,' said Dwayne.

'Raise your arms, please.' Dwayne did as he was told, allowing Banura to pat him down. 'Where is your friend?' Banura asked.

'She's waiting in the truck,' he said. 'You got the money?'

'Everything is all set to go,' Banura said, closing the door and putting the bar back in position.

They came down the stairs. As Dwayne entered the room, he glanced right, saw Oscar Fine standing there, left arm tucked into his pocket, right arm extended, pointing the gun directly at his head.

'Hey, whoa, what the hell is this?' To Banura, Dwayne said, 'You said you might have an associate here, but you got no call to threaten me.'

'Do you remember me?' Oscar Fine asked.

'I got no idea who you are,' Dwayne said.

The man with the gun took his left arm out of his pocket. Dwayne looked down and noticed the missing hand. He paled instantly. A moment later, the crotch of his jeans darkened.

'I take that to mean that you do remember me,' Oscar Fine said, pointing the gun below Dwayne's waist.

'Yes,' Dwayne said.

'Tell me your name.'

'Dwayne. Dwayne Osterhaus.'

'Well, Dwayne Osterhaus, it's nice to meet you at last. Although we didn't have a real face-to-face, I believe you were the driver.'

'You shoulda had a combination or something,' Dwayne said. 'Then, you know, things would have been different.'

'It was difficult to communicate a combination to you once you'd shot me with the dart,' he said.

'I'm really sorry, man,' Dwayne said. 'You understand, I wasn't the one who actually did it, you know that, right?'

'I remember who did it,' Oscar Fine said. 'Where is she?'

Dwayne hesitated.

Oscar Fine said, 'Dwayne, you must see where this is going. It's in your interests to be cooperative. Where is she?'

Sweat droplets had formed on Dwayne's forehead. 'In the truck.'

'Why didn't she come in with you?'

'She's nervous,' Dwayne said. 'She thinks Mr Banura was offering too much money. She got suspicious. She took some of the diamonds to someone else to look at. They said they're worthless.'

Oscar Fine nodded. 'But yet you're here.'

Dwayne appeared close to tears. 'I took Mr Banura here at his word.'

'Does she suspect I am here?' Oscar Fine asked.

'She never said that. She's just spooked.' Dwayne brightened, wiped the tears from his eyes. 'I got an idea. You let me walk away and I'll go out to the truck and tell her there's a problem, that some of the money, it's in some weird currency, like euros or Canadian, and she needs to help me count it, and I'll get her in here, and then you can let me go. Swear to God, I never wanted her to cut your hand off. I was all, hey, let's get stronger tools to cut through the chain, so you wouldn't get hurt. But she got caught up in the moment and went crazy.'

Oscar Fine nodded, as though considering the proposal. 'I have some questions,' he said.

'Oh yeah, sure, no problem.'

In fact, Oscar had quite a few. About where the two of them had been the last six years. About who Constance Tattinger had become. Where she'd been living. Dwayne told Oscar all he knew.

'You've been very helpful,' Oscar Fine said.

'Yeah, well, it's the least I can do.' Dwayne attempted another smile. 'So, whaddya say, I bring her in here and you let me go?'

'I don't think so,' Oscar Fine said, and shot Dwayne in the face. 'There's no reason I can't go out and talk to her myself.'

OSCAR FINE OFFERED his apologies to Banura. 'I have made a mess and I accept full responsibility for that.'

Banura was looking at the blood on the wall behind where Dwayne had been standing. 'I seen worse,' he said.

Oscar wrote a number on a piece of paper. 'Call that number, tell them Mr Fine told you they'd handle things. They'll come and take care of all this. Clean-up as well as removal.'

'Appreciate it,' Banura said.

'But you might as well wait a few minutes until I have the other one,' he said, and Banura nodded.

'Do you have an alternative way out of here?' Oscar Fine asked. 'Someone could be watching this door.'

'No,' Banura said. 'This is all walled off from the rest of the house, only access is from the back door. But there are cameras.'

'Show me.'

Banura led Oscar over to the workbench, where, in addition to his jeweller's tools, there was a keyboard and a monitor. Banura tapped some keys. The screen divided into quadrants, each offering a different view of Banura's property. 'There's a camera on each side of the house,' he said.

Oscar looked at the upper-right corner, which was a view of the street at the front of the house, with the driveway off to the far right. He could see the pick-up truck but, given the way the light was reflecting off the windshield, it was difficult to make out if anyone was inside.

The camera mounted at the back door showed no one in the yard.

Banura pointed to the upper-right image. 'You see that?'

The pick-up truck was starting to back up.

THE MOMENT AFTER Dwayne disappeared into the house, Jan was working out possible scenarios in her head for what was going on:

Banura didn't know the first thing about diamonds. Unlikely.

Banura knew they were fake, didn't like being conned, and was going to teach them a lesson when they returned. Possible, but why wait until 2 p.m.?

Could he have been in touch with Oscar Fine? After all these years, could that man still be reminding those in the business to be on the lookout for a large quantity of fake diamonds? And a particular woman who matched her description? *Get out of here*, she told herself.

Her hand was on the key. All she had to do was start the engine, back up, get on the interstate. And go where? All these years, she'd had a plan. Get out of Promise Falls, head to Paradise. But she needed the cash from those diamonds to buy her ticket.

Worthless. She'd waited all that time to get what she wanted, never stopping to think for a moment she might already have something.

That phoney life was a real life. A real husband. *A real son.*

She took her fingers off the keys, reached into her bag. She took out a creased and tattered photo, looked into the face of her son. 'I'm sorry,' she whispered. She set it on the seat next to her.

She was ready to bail. But there was part of her that still wondered: *What if.* What if, by some fluke, Dwayne had called it right? What if he walked out with the money and she wasn't there?

She needed a sense of how things were going.

Jan left the keys in the ignition, got out of the truck, grabbing the gun. She walked down the side of the house, rounded the corner and went up to the door. Very faint noises, muffled by the heavy door, came from inside. The hint of a voice, high-pitched, whiny. She caught a few phrases.

'. . . swear to God, I never . . . I was all, hey, let's . . . get some stronger tools . . . so you wouldn't get hurt. But she . . . went crazy . . .'

Jan didn't need to hear any more. She'd been sold out. They'd be coming for her next. Any second now that door would be opening.

She bolted, rounded the corner of the house, grabbed the handle on the driver's door with her left hand, the gun still in her right. She jumped in, dropped the gun onto the seat and turned the ignition.

The engine didn't catch the first time.

As she turned the key a second time, she noticed a figure coming out from behind the house. A man in a long jacket, wielding a gun in his right hand. It was pointed in her direction.

The engine caught. She shifted into reverse and had her foot on the gas even before she'd turned to make sure no one was there. She bounced from the driveway to the street and cranked the wheel.

The windshield shattered.

For a millisecond she looked back in the direction of the shot, saw the man with the gun. Saw the left arm with no hand at the end.

As Jan put the truck into drive, Oscar Fine fired again. The shot went in through the passenger window and out through the driver's door.

Oscar was running into the street. Jan stomped on the accelerator, raced past the black Audi, guessing that was his car. She heard a sharp ping, above and behind her head. Sounded like a bullet had gone into the cab.

It just made her drive faster. She glanced into her mirror, saw the man running for the black car. It was the last image she had of him before she hung a hard right and kept on going.

She never noticed that, in all the excitement, the wind had swept up her picture of Ethan and carried it out of the window.

Oscar saw the piece of paper fluttering through the air. He was almost glad for an excuse not to get in the car and go after Jan Harwood. Chases invariably ended badly. And with only one hand, it was difficult for Oscar Fine to perform quick steering manoeuvres.

If he could find her once, he could find her again. Especially with everything Dwayne had told him. He walked up the street to pick up the piece of paper. It was a photo. A picture of a small boy.

NOT LONG after my talk with Gretchen, there was an unexpected call. I grabbed the phone before the first ring was finished. 'Hello?'

'Mr Harwood?' A woman's voice. 'You're not the person to do this story any more.'

'What? Who is this?'

'I sent you the information about Mr Reeves's hotel bill. So you could write about it. Why didn't you do a story?'

'He paid Elmont Sebastian back. My editor felt that killed it.'

'Well, then give that list to someone else who can get the story done. I called the paper and they told me that you were suspended because your wife is missing. I don't want anyone who might have killed his wife working on this story, no offence.'

'List? What are you talking about?'

She sighed at the other end of the line. 'The one I mailed to you.'

I patted my jacket pocket, felt the envelopes I'd stuffed in there when I'd passed my mailbox at the *Standard*. I dug them out. One was from payroll, the other was an envelope addressed to me, with no return address. I tore it open, took out a single sheet of paper. It was a list of names of people on Promise Falls council, with dollar amounts written next to them, ranging from zero up to $25,000.

'Is this for real?' I said. 'Is this what Elmont Sebastian's been paying these people?'

'You're just looking at this now?' the woman said. 'That's why someone else should be investigating this. Elmont has screwed me over one time too many and I want to see him nailed.'

I asked, 'Why didn't you show up at Lake George?'

'What?' she said. 'What are you talking about?'

'The email you sent me. To meet you up there.'

'I don't know what you're talking about,' she said. 'I'm not meeting you or anyone else face-to-face. You think I'm stupid?'

She hung up. I sat there a moment, slid the paper back into the envelope and stuffed it back into my pocket. Any other time, this would have made my day, but getting a great story wasn't a priority at the moment. But one thing my anonymous caller had said stuck with me. She had not emailed me to meet her in Lake George. Someone else had lured me up there. *Jan.*

I SPENT THE REST of that day trying to find out everything I could about Constance Tattinger. I explained to Dad that I had some work to do, and he said he did as well. He was going to get started on repairing all the damage in the house. He phoned my mother and explained, quietly, what had happened, and that he was going to stay there for the rest of the day, if that was OK with her. She'd have to look after Ethan without any assistance.

Mom said that was fine. She asked to speak to me. 'Tell me how you are,' she said. 'Your father says you've ripped your house apart.'

'Yeah, I felt pretty stupid about it, until Dad found something I missed. I think I have a lead on Jan. I could really use a computer. I need to search for people named Tattinger.'

'Your father says he's coming home for tools. I'll send him back with my laptop.'

I thanked her for that, and hung up.

I told Dad to make sure he came back with Mom's laptop. He added 'laptop' to the bottom of his list. 'Be back in a jiff,' he said.

I called Samantha Henry at the *Standard.* 'Can you do me a favour?' I asked her. 'I need you to check with the cops, see what you can get on the name Constance Tattinger.'

'Spell it.'

I did.

'And who's this Constance Tattinger?'

'I'd rather not say,' I said.

'Oh, OK,' she said. 'So, you're on suspension, the cops think you may have killed your wife, and you want me to start trying to dig up info for you without telling me why.'

'Yeah, that's about right,' I said.

'OK,' said Sam. 'I'll call you if I get anything.'

'Thanks, Sam. One more thing. The story about Sebastian and Reeves I've been working on? It's yours. I've got something that'll break this story wide open. A list of payouts to various councillors.'

'What?'

'I can't sit on it. I don't know when I'll be back. This story needs to be told asap. I'll give this list to you next time I see you.'

'Where'd you get the list?'

'I can fill you in later, OK? I've got to go.'

'Sure,' Sam said. 'I appreciate this. I'll nail this thing for you.'

'Right on,' I said and hung up.

Dad was back within the hour. He dragged in his toolbox, a table saw, some scraps of baseboarding he must have been keeping in his garage since God invented trees, and went upstairs.

I got Mom's laptop and started with the online phone directories. There weren't that many people with that name in the US—about three dozen—and only four listings for an 'M. Tattinger'. They were in Buffalo, Boise, Catalina and Pittsburgh. I started dialling.

People answered at the Buffalo and Boise numbers. The Buffalo Tattinger was a Mark, and the Boise Tattinger was a Miles.

I asked if they knew of a Martin Tattinger, who, with a woman named Thelma, had a daughter named Constance. No, and no.

No one answered at the Catalina and Pittsburgh numbers.

I figured I might be able to raise someone later in the day at the other numbers, once people were home from work.

The day dragged on. In the late afternoon the phone rang.

Mom said, 'Ethan wants to talk to you.'

Some receiver fumbling, then, 'Dad?'

'Hey, sport, how's it going?'

'I wanna come home. I've been here for days.'

'Ethan, it's only been a couple.'

'When's Mommy coming home?'

'I don't know,' I said. 'What are you doing?'

'I'm playing with the bat.'

'Bat?'

'The OK bat.'

I smiled. 'Are you playing *croquet* with Nana?'

'No. She says it makes her back hurt to hit the ball.'

'So how do you play by yourself?'

'I hit the ball through the wires. I can make it go really far.'

'OK,' I said. 'Is Nana making anything for dinner?'

'I think so. I smell something. Nana! What's for dinner?' I heard Mom talking. Then Ethan said, 'Pot roast.'

'What time's Nana serving dinner?'

Ethan shouted out another question. 'Seven,' he said.

'OK, I'll see you then, OK? I love you,' I said.

'I love you, too,' he said. 'Bye, Dad.' And he hung up.

I TRIED THE Pittsburgh listing for M. Tattinger again.

'Hello?' A man. Sounded like he could be in his sixties or older.

'Is this Martin Tattinger?' I asked.

When the man didn't respond right away, I asked again.

'No,' the man said. 'This is Mick Tattinger.'

'Is there a Martin Tattinger there?'

'No, there isn't. I think you must have the wrong number.'

'I'm sorry,' I said. 'But maybe you can help me. My name is David Harwood. I'm trying to find a Martin Tattinger, who's married to Thelma. They have a daughter Constance. Last I heard, they were living in Rochester, but that was some time ago. You wouldn't by chance be a relative, know how I might find Martin?'

'The Martin Tattinger you're looking for is my brother,' he said flatly. 'He and Thelma moved around a lot, ending up in El Paso. Why you trying to get in touch with him?'

'It's about their daughter, Constance,' I said. 'She might be in trouble, and I'm trying to contact her parents.'

'That's going to be hard,' Mick said. 'They're dead.'

'Oh,' I said. 'I'm sorry. I didn't realise they'd passed on.'

Mick snorted. 'Yeah, passed on. That's a nice way to put it. They were murdered. Throats slit. Four, five years ago.'

'Did they catch who did it?' I asked.

'No,' Mick Tattinger said. 'What's this about Connie?'

'Constance—Connie is missing,' I said.

'There's nothing new about that. She's been missing for years. When they died, Martin and Thelma hadn't heard from her for ages. She took off when she was sixteen or seventeen. Not that I could blame her. She probably doesn't even know her parents are dead.'

'I think you might be right,' I said.

'She might get some satisfaction from knowing,' Mick Tattinger said. 'Martin was my brother, but he and Thelma wouldn't have won any Parent of the Year awards. His bitchin' and her drinkin' and mopin' about, they were a pair. But that doesn't mean they deserved what they got. Martin was fixing cars, running a garage in El Paso. Far as I know, he was keeping his nose clean. So why does someone kill them? Nothing was stolen. But Connie's alive? I figured she was probably dead, too.'

'Why do you say that?'

'She was so screwed up. It all goes back to something that happened when she was little, but no sense getting into that.'

'The girl that got run over in the driveway?'

'You know about that? Martin was a prick even then, but after the accident, things went sour. He was working for a dealership that was owned by the dead girl's uncle. He took it out on Martin, fired him. Martin blamed Connie, but she was just a kid, right? He found a job at another dealership in another town, took the fall when someone stole some tools. Martin didn't do it, but management thought he did and fired him. He found other work, but it didn't matter, he always blamed Connie, like she was their bad luck charm.'

'How'd she handle it?' I asked.

'The few times I saw them together, it was like . . . like she was in another place. Like she was imagining she was *someone* else. I think it was her way of surviving . . . Who'd you say you were?' I told him my name again. 'What are you? A private investigator?'

'A reporter,' I said. 'I'm a reporter.'

DAD CAME DOWN to the kitchen.

'It must be dinnertime,' he said, looking at the clock. It was 6.40 p.m. 'When did your mother say we were supposed to go over?'

I said, 'Huh?'

'What's wrong with you? You look like you've seen a ghost.'

'Something like that.'

The phone rang. I glanced down at the display. Mom. Or possibly Ethan, who had learned some time ago how to use the speed dial on his grandparents' phone.

I picked up. 'Yeah.'

'I can't find him,' Mom said, her voice shaking. 'I can't find Ethan.'

ELEVEN

For half an hour, Jan drove randomly. Go a few miles, turn left. Go a few more, turn right. Get on the interstate, get off. She hoped the more randomly she drove, the harder she'd be to follow. And she hadn't noticed any black Audis in her rearview mirror. When she got on the interstate, and there was no sign of the Audi behind her, she started to feel more confident that Fine was not on her tail.

But that was not a great comfort. If he could find her once, it seemed likely he could find her again. Dwayne had to be dead. No way Oscar Fine was letting him out of that basement alive.

The question was, how much had Dwayne said before he died?

Think, she told herself, heading west on the Mass Pike. *Think.*

One thing was a no-brainer. Banura had turned them in. Once they'd been to see him, and he'd examined what they had to sell, he must have tipped off Oscar Fine. But why was Oscar on alert now, after all this time? Had he seen a news report about her disappearance? Even if he had, those stories carried pictures of her looking like Jan Harwood, and Jan didn't look anything like that girl in the back of the limo. But maybe, someone cuts off your hand, you remember a little more than hair colour and eye shadow . . .

Jan let go of the steering wheel long enough to bang it with her fist. Was there any part of this that she hadn't screwed up?

Pulling the stupid job in the first place. Hooking up with Dwayne Osterhaus. Not knowing the value of the goods they'd stolen. Coming back to Banura's when she knew the deal was too good to be true. *Walking away from what she had.*

She glanced down at the dash, saw that the truck was nearly out of gas.

She took the next exit, put thirty dollars' worth into the tank. When she got back into the truck, she was shaking.

And thinking. Thinking back to the very beginning. Back to when she pushed the Richlers' daughter into the path of that car.

She never meant to kill the Richler girl. She was just angry about something she'd said. Constance Tattinger was jealous of Jan, of the things she had and of how much her parents adored her. Gretchen and Horace Richler bought her Barbies and pretty shoes. They'd even bought their girl a necklace that looked like a cupcake. It was the most beautiful necklace Constance had ever seen.

One day, when Jan Richler wore it to school, and took it off briefly when it was itching her neck, Constance Tattinger reached into her jacket pocket and took it. Jan Richler cried and cried when she couldn't find her necklace, and became convinced Constance had taken it. Two days later, on Jan Richler's front lawn, she told Constance what she believed she'd done, and Constance, angry and defensive, shoved the girl out of her way.

Right into the path of the car.

All these years, the woman who would steal Jan Richler's identity hung on to that necklace. She'd been tempted many times to throw it away, but could never bring herself to do it.

One day, Ethan would see it in her jewellery box and ask if he could have it—cupcakes were his favourite snack—and his mother would say no, it really wasn't something a boy would wear, so he begged her to wear it when they went on a trip to Chicago.

She agreed to wear it for a day, and then never wore it again.

She thought about all these things as she sat in that truck. She thought about the life she'd had with Ethan and David and—

Focus.

The woman known as Jan gave her head a small shake. There'd be time later to wallow in self-pity. Something more urgent was nagging at her.

There was every reason to believe Oscar Fine knew that she had been living the last few years as Jan Harwood. He could have learned this from Dwayne, or he could have figured it out from the news reports of her disappearance where she was from. If she were Oscar Fine, wouldn't Promise Falls be her next stop?

She reached down next to her, looking for the photograph of Ethan she had taken from her bag. It wasn't there.

Jan started the engine. Without realising it, she'd been driving in the direction of the place she'd called home for the last five years. She had to go back. And she had to get there before Oscar Fine did.

She wondered where Ethan would be. David, if he hadn't been arrested, would probably be at the police station, or meeting with a lawyer, or driving all over trying to figure out what had happened to her.

Jan almost laughed when it hit her: *I wish I could talk to David about this.* She knew that wasn't possible. There would be no room for forgiveness there, even though all she had to do was walk into a police station to put him in the clear. The things she'd done—you didn't put that kind of stuff behind you and start over. Maybe, some day, some evidence might come along that would clear him.

By then she and Ethan would be gone. Ethan was her son. She was going to come out of all this with something that was hers. It was most likely he was with Nana and Poppa. She'd go there first.

BARRY DUCKWORTH was driving back from Albany in the late afternoon, approaching Promise Falls, when his cellphone rang.

He'd been thinking. From the beginning, he'd liked David Harwood for this. There were so many parts of his story that didn't hold together. His wife's so-called depression. The ticket that was never purchased. The evidence from Ted, the store owner in Lake George. For motive, there was that $300,000 life insurance policy.

It looked like Harwood took his wife to Lake George and killed her. After all, no one had seen her since, so long as you didn't count the boy, Ethan. But Duckworth had been having doubts about his initial theory ever since the discovery of Leanne Kowalski's body. From the moment Harwood had looked into that shallow grave and seen her there. Duckworth had watched closely for the man's reaction.

Duckworth had not anticipated what he saw. *Genuine surprise.*

If David Harwood had killed that woman and put her into the ground, he might have been able to feign shock. He could have put on an act and looked shattered. But why had Harwood looked so surprised? The eyes went wide. There was a double take. Leanne's body was not the one he had been steeling himself to see.

That told Duckworth that Harwood was not Kowalski's killer. And it wasn't very likely that he'd killed his wife, either.

If Harwood had killed Jan, and disposed of her elsewhere, he wouldn't have looked so taken aback. He'd have known he was going to be looking down at someone other than his spouse.

And then there was the business of the Explorer. Harwood might have had time to kill Leanne between taking his wife up to Lake George and going to Five Mountains the next day, but Duckworth couldn't figure out how the Explorer got all the way down to Albany and ended up at the bottom of an embankment. When did Harwood have time to do that? How did he manage it alone? Wouldn't you need one person to drive the Explorer, and another for the car that you'd need to get back to Promise Falls?

His cellphone rang. 'Duckworth.'

'Yeah, Barry, it's Glen.'

Glen Dougherty. Barry's boss. The Promise Falls police chief.

'It wouldn't normally be me calling you with this, but some lab results just got copied to me and I wondered if you had them yet.'

'I'm on the road.'

'This Jan Harwood disappearance. You asked for tests on some hair and blood samples in the trunk of the husband's car. They're back. They match the missing woman, based on hair samples you took from the house when you had it searched. I think you need to move on this. Looks like this clown moved her body in the trunk.'

'Maybe,' Duckworth said. 'But there's parts of this I don't like.'

'Looks to me like you've got this son of a bitch dead to rights now. Time to bring him in again, sweat him out.'

'I can bring him in again, but I'm not sure.'

'Barry, I'm getting a lot of pressure on this one. From those amusement park people and the mayor's office. Five Mountains makes a lot of money for the area. People start thinking someone snatching kids there, they're going to stay away. You hearing me?'

'Absolutely,' Duckworth said. 'I—'

But the chief had ended the call.

DAD AND I drove over in two cars as fast as we could. Mom was standing on the porch, waiting for us, and ran over to the driveway as we each pulled in. She was at my door as I was getting out.

'There's still no sign—'

'Start from the beginning,' I said as Dad got out of the other car.

Mom took a moment to catch her breath. 'He'd been in the back yard whacking the croquet ball around. I was in the kitchen, checking on him every few minutes, but I was hearing *whack*, *whack*, *whack*, so I knew what he was up to. Then I realised it had been a while since I heard it. I went outside and couldn't find him.'

'Dad,' I said, 'call the police.'

He nodded and headed for the house.

Mom reached out and held my shoulders. 'I swear I was watching him. I only let him out of my sight for a few minutes. I'm sorry, I'm so sorry, David, I'm just so—'

'It's OK. We'll keep looking. Have you tried the neighbours?'

'No, I've just been looking everywhere. I thought maybe he was hiding in the house, under a bed. But I can't find him any place.'

I pointed to the houses next door and across the street. 'You start knocking on doors. I'll make one last check of the house. Go. Go.'

Mom ran to the house on the left as I ran into the house.

'His name is Ethan Harwood,' Dad was saying into the phone. 'He's four years old.'

I shouted, 'Ethan! Ethan, are you here?'

I ran downstairs, checked behind the boiler and the storage area under the stairs. Satisfied that Ethan was not in the basement, I scaled the stairs and came into the kitchen. Dad was off the phone.

'They said they'll have a car swing by in a while,' he said.

'A while?' I said. '*A while?*'

Dad looked shaken. 'They asked how long he'd been gone and when I said under an hour, they didn't seem all that excited.'

I moved Dad aside and grabbed the phone, and punched in 911.

'Listen,' I said once I had hold of the dispatcher who'd spoken to my father. 'We don't need some car coming by in *a while* to help us find my son. We need someone right *now*.' And I slammed the receiver down. To Dad I said, 'Go help Mom knock on doors.'

For the second time, Dad turned and did what I told him.

I ran upstairs, opened closet doors, looked under beds. Nothing.

By the time I got out to the front of the house, a dozen neighbours were in the street, milling about. My parents' door-knocking had brought people out, wondering whether they could help.

'Everyone!' I shouted. 'Please, can you listen up for a second?'

They stopped gossiping among themselves and looked at me.

'We can't find my boy, Ethan. He was in my parents' back yard. Now he's gone. Could you check your back yards and garages?'

Some of them nodded, but they weren't moving with any speed.

'Now!' I shouted.

They started to disperse, save for one man in his twenties, a tall but doughy, unshaven lout. He said, 'So what'd you do, Harwood? Getting rid of the wife wasn't enough? You got rid of the kid, too?'

Something snapped.

I ran at him, got him round the waist and brought him down. All the others who'd been heading off to hunt for Ethan stopped to watch the show. I took a swing and caught the corner of his mouth, drawing blood. Before I could take another swing, Dad had his arms round me from behind. 'Son!' he shouted. 'Stop it.'

'You jerk!' the man said, feeling his mouth for blood.

Dad shouted at everyone, 'Please, just look for Ethan.'

The man got up and started to walk off, but not before looking at me and saying, 'You watch it. They're going to get you.'

I turned away, my face flushed. Dad came up alongside me. 'You OK?'

I nodded. 'We have to keep looking.'

At the end of my parents' street, and a block to the left, was a 7-Eleven. Could Ethan have wandered there on his own, looking to buy a packet of his favourite cupcakes? Did he even have any money on him?

Running flat out, it only took a minute to reach the store. I burst through the front door and breathlessly asked the guy behind the counter if a small boy had been in within the last hour, all by himself, to get a package of cup-cakes. The man shook his head.

I ran back to my parents' house, both of them standing outside the front.

'Anything?' I asked.

They shook their heads no.

'Would he try to go to your house?' Mom asked.

I looked at her. 'That's brilliant,' I said. 'He kept asking me if he could come home. Maybe he just decided to start walking.'

Although only four, Ethan had already demonstrated a keen sense of direction, correcting me from his back-seat perch any time I took us on a route to my parents' that wasn't the most direct. He'd probably be able to find his way to our house. And the thought of him crossing all those streets . . .

'We need to trace our way back,' I said.

'I didn't see him on the way over,' Dad said.

'We were in such a rush to get here, we might not have noticed.'

I had the keys to Dad's car in my hand and was heading over to it, when an unmarked police car came tearing up the street.

'Good,' I said. 'Cops.'

The car pulled over to the kerb, blocking the end of my parents' driveway, and Barry Duckworth got out, his eyes fixed on me.

'They sent *you*?' I said to him. 'I thought they'd send a regular car and uniformed officers. But, whatever.'

'What?' he said.

'Aren't you here about Ethan?'

'What's happened to Ethan?' Duckworth asked.

My heart sank. The cavalry hadn't arrived after all. 'He's missing,' I said. 'Since the last hour or so.'

'You've called it in?'

'My dad did. Look, you need to get your car out of the way. He might have gone back to our house.'

'We need to talk,' Duckworth said. 'I need you to come downtown. I want to go over a few things again.'

My jaw dropped. 'My son is missing. I'm going to look for him.'

'No,' said Duckworth. 'You're not.'

MY FIRST IMPULSE was to start shouting, but I knew if I overreacted, Duckworth might have me in handcuffs in a matter of seconds. So I tried to keep my voice even and controlled. 'Ethan may be wandering round all by himself, trying to get from one side of town to the other, crossing streets he's not old enough to cross.'

Duckworth nodded. 'When other officers get here, they'll be able to mount a systematic search. They're good at this sort of thing.'

'I'm sure they are, but he's my son, and if you'll move your car out of the way, I'm going to try to find him myself.'

Duckworth's jaw tightened. 'I have to bring you in.'

The air round us was charged, like an electrical storm was imminent. 'This is not a good time,' I said. 'I'm not going.'

'I'm not asking,' Duckworth said firmly.

'Come on,' Dad said. He and Mom were standing just behind me. 'What the hell are you doing? You have to let him find Ethan. What's so important that you have to talk to my son now?'

Instead of looking at Dad, Duckworth spoke to me. 'There are developments in the case that we need to talk about at the station.'

There was no way I was going to that station. I had a feeling if Duckworth managed to get me there, I wouldn't be leaving.

'Hey!' someone across the street shouted.

We all looked. It was the guy I'd punched in the mouth. There was still blood on his chin. He looked at Duckworth. 'You a cop?'

'Yes,' the detective said.

'That jerk assaulted me,' he said, pointing a finger my way.

Duckworth tilted his head at me.

'It's true,' I said. 'We asked neighbours to help look for Ethan, and he . . . he accused me of killing my son. And my wife. I lost it.'

Duckworth turned back and said to the man, 'I'm sure an officer will be along shortly and he can take your statement.'

'Screw that,' the man said, walking across the street towards us. 'You need to put the cuffs on him right now. I got witnesses!'

The guy was ready to get into it with me all over again, striding right up to me, close enough to poke me in the shoulder. I hadn't noticed it when I'd tackled him, but this time I was getting a strong whiff of booze off him.

Duckworth quickly pulled the man's arm down and off me and said, forcefully, 'Sir, if you'll just go stand over there and wait for the officers to arrive, they'll be happy to take your statement.'

'I seen this guy on the news,' he said. 'He's the one killed his wife. Why isn't he in jail already?'

Duckworth said, 'What's your name?'

'Axel. Axel Smight.'

'How much have you had to drink tonight, Mr Smight?'

He looked offended. 'What's that supposed to mean? If I've had a bit to drink, I'm not entitled to police protection?'

'Mr Smight, I'm only going to tell you this one more time. Go and stand over there and wait for the officers to arrive.'

'You're not going to arrest him? I'm telling you, the guy attacked me.' He touched his hand to his bloody chin. 'What do you think this is? Strawberry milkshake?' He was shouting now.

Duckworth pulled back his jacket, revealing handcuffs clipped to his belt.

'There you go!' Smight said. 'Cuff the son of a bitch!'

Duckworth took hold of Smight, spun him round and forced him down onto the hood of his unmarked cruiser. He twisted Smight's left arm behind him, slapped one cuff on the wrist, and then grabbed the right arm to do the same.

I didn't stay to watch the whole procedure. I ran for Dad's car, put the key into the ignition and turned over the engine. There looked to be enough room to squeeze past Duckworth's car if I ran onto the grass.

'Mr Harwood!' Duckworth shouted, trying to hold a squirming Axel Smight onto the hood. 'Stop!'

I put the car in reverse and hit the gas, clipping the corner of the front bumper of Duckworth's vehicle on the way out. I got the car onto the street, stopped with a screech, threw it into drive and sped off.

The moment I turned the corner I slowed down, scanning both sides of the street, looking for any signs of Ethan.

'Come on,' I said under my breath. 'Where are you?'

I was turning into my street when my cellphone went off. I nosed the car in to the kerb and was getting out as I put the phone to my ear. 'Yeah?'

'Dave, it's Sam. I need you to come by the paper.'

'I'm kind of busy, Sam,' I said. 'I can't.' I was walking down the side of the house. Ethan didn't have a key to the house. I supposed it was possible he'd taken the one my parents keep on a nail at their place. I stood in the back yard and shouted, 'Ethan!'

'You just blew out my eardrum,' Sam said.

I used my key to open the back door, and called his name again.

There was no answer.

'Dave?' Sam asked. 'I need you to come by the paper. It's important. Elmont Sebastian is here. He wants a word with you.'

I felt a chill run the length of my spine. I remembered the story about the Aryan Brotherhood prisoner whose genitals he'd Tasered. The one nick-named Buddy. The one Sebastian had made cry when it was suggested to him something might happen to his six-year-old son on the outside if he didn't play by Sebastian's rules.

IT WAS GETTING DARK when I wheeled into the *Standard* parking lot. I spotted Elmont Sebastian's limo near the doors to the production end of the newspaper building, where the presses were housed. I parked near the limo and got out. As I did, Welland appeared from behind the driver's seat and opened the rear door.

I was expecting to see Sebastian, and he was there, but sitting next to him was Samantha. She appeared to have been crying. She got of the car and said to me, 'I'm sorry. I was doing it for my kid.'

'What are you talking about?'

'Do I have to tell you times are tough? I've got bills. I'm raising a child. I know it was wrong, David, but what am I supposed to do? End up on the street? And newspapers are screwed, anyway. There's no future here. It's only a matter of time before we all lose our jobs. I'm looking out for myself and my kid while I can. Mr Sebastian's offered me a job with Star Spangled Corrections.'

'Writing press releases or midnight guard duty?' I asked.

'Deputy assistant media relations officer,' she said.

'It was you,' I said. 'You saw the email before I deleted it.' She'd have had time. When the anonymous email landed, I went for a coffee before making the decision to delete it. 'You went on my computer and told Sebastian about it.'

'I said I was sorry,' she said. 'I told him you're trying to find someone named Constance Tattinger, that she's probably the one who just sent you that list. That's what he wants to talk to you about.' She walked away, got into her car and drove out of the lot.

My face felt hot.

'Come on in,' Sebastian said, patting the leather seat. 'Help me out and I might still be able to find a spot for you, too. It might not be media relations. I've promised that to Ms Henry. But you'd be perfect for writing up proposals. You have a nice turn of phrase.'

'Do you have my son?' I asked.

Sebastian's eye twitched. 'I'm sorry?'

'If you have him, just tell me. If there's something you want in exchange, name it. I'll tell you anything I know.' I allowed myself to get into the car, the door still open, one foot still on the ground outside.

'All right, then,' he said. 'Tell me about Constance Tattinger. You asked Ms Henry to check into that name. That's your source? I'm puzzled, because I've never heard of her.'

'She's not the source,' I said. 'Constance Tattinger is my wife.'

'I don't follow. Why would your wife have a list of names—'

'She didn't,' I said. 'I called Sam about two different things. I guess she thought they were related when she called you.'

'I'm a bit confused. I thought your wife's name was Jan.'

'Jan Richler's the name she was using when we met, but I think she was born Constance Tattinger. I'm pretty sure she set up the Lake George meeting. But it was a trick. She wouldn't know the first thing about what you're doing to buy votes on council. Now what about my son?'

'I don't know a damn thing about your kid. And I don't care.'

I felt deflated. As frightening as it would be for Ethan to have been picked up by this pair, I was hoping they had him to trade.

'If you don't know anything about my son, then we're done here,' I said, swinging my other leg back out of the car.

'I don't think so. Regardless of whoever your wife is, something was mailed to you. Something you have no business possessing.'

The list in my pocket. The one I'd foolishly told Sam about.

'I think you're mistaken,' I said, now fully out of the car.

It would have been easy to give him the envelope and walk away. But I knew there was a chance I might come out the other side of this hell I was living through, and return to work as a reporter. And if I did, I wanted to bring down Sebastian. There wasn't any chance of that happening if I handed over what was in my jacket.

'David, you need to consider your position,' Sebastian said.

Welland was coming round the car. When he reached the open door, he and Sebastian exchanged a look. Sebastian said, 'If you're not going to hand it over, I'll have to ask Welland to get it for me.'

I bolted.

Welland's right arm got hold of me by the wrist, but I was moving fast enough that my hand slipped out of his grasp. I hightailed it across the parking lot towards the *Standard* building. Welland was closing in on me. He was snorting like an angry bull in pursuit. While he beat me in the muscle and bulk department, he wasn't all that fast, and I had the back door open before he could get hold of me. I was overwhelmed by the sound of running presses, a heavy, loud, humming that went straight to the centre of my brain. This time of night, only one of the three presses was running, producing some of the weekend sections.

I was running wildly at this point, heading down any path that presented itself to me. Ahead and to the right was a set of steep metal stairs leading up onto the boards that ran through the presses. I grabbed hold of the tubular handrails and scurried up them. Even over the din, I heard some pressmen shouting, telling me to get down.

Once up on the boards, I had a good fifty feet of catwalk ahead of me. I stopped, looked back, expecting to see a pressman or Welland appear at the top of the stairway, but no one materialised. I debated doubling back, then concluded it was safer to keep going in the same direction, to the set of stairs at the far end of the presses.

To my left, the press was going at full bore, endless ribbons of newsprint going past at blinding speed. Every few feet there was an opening where the boards cut through to the other side.

I started moving again, and then Welland appeared at the top of the other set of stairs.

I whirled round planning to double back, but standing where I'd been seconds earlier was Elmont Sebastian. He wasn't young, but he'd scaled those steps in no time. I thought I had a better chance of bulldozing my way past him than heading towards Welland.

I started running at Sebastian. He broadened his stance, but I didn't slow down. I slammed into him, but instead of just him going down, he grabbed me round the neck and we went down together.

'You son of a bitch!' he shouted. 'Give it to me!'

We rolled on the boards. I brought up a knee and tried to get him in the stomach. I must have hit something, because he loosened his hold on my neck long enough for me to get back onto my feet.

But Sebastian was up almost as quickly and leapt on my back. The tackle threw me to one side, into one of the walkways that went through the presses. Newsprint flew past us on both sides.

As I stumbled to one side, Sebastian was pitched against the railing. He was facing it, and his upper body leaned over with the impact. He threw his hands in front of himself, but there was nothing to catch on to.

But there was something to catch on to him.

It happened so blindingly fast that if you'd caught it on video, and had the chance to play it back in slow motion, you still probably wouldn't be able to see how it went down. But what happened, basically, is Sebastian's right hand bumped up against the speeding newsprint, which flung his arm upward and into the spinning press.

His arm was torn off in a second. And it just disappeared.

Elmont Sebastian screamed and collapsed onto the boards, reaching over with his left arm, hunting for his right.

I looked down, horrified and aghast.

Welland came up behind me, saw his boss. 'Oh my God.'

Sebastian thrashed about for a second, then stopped. His eyes were open, but I wasn't sure that he was dead. Not yet.

I said to Welland, 'We've got to call an ambulance.'

I started to move, knowing no one would be able to hear me on my cell-phone with the roar of the press—which had not stopped—in the background.

'No,' Welland said. 'Let's wait a bit.'

Down below, pressmen were pointing, shouting. I wasn't sure they could see what had happened to Sebastian.

'We're gonna let him go,' Welland said. 'He never should have zapped me in the balls or threatened my son.'

I stared at him, speechless.

He added, 'We didn't take your boy. I'd never have let him do that.'

SOMEONE HAD KILLED the press. It was slowing, the noise receding.

Welland—or Buddy, as I now knew him to be—squeezed past me on the catwalk. 'I'm outta here,' he said.

An alarm was ringing now, and pressmen were coming up on the boards.

'Where are you going?' I asked Welland.

'I got people who can help me disappear.' He glanced up, pointed. 'Those look like cameras. Whole thing's probably on closed-circuit. You're in the clear. By the time they start looking for me, I'll be gone.' He didn't waste another word on me. He made for the stairs, slid down them, ran for the door and was gone.

One of the pressmen said, 'What happened?' Then he spotted Sebastian, and looked away almost as quickly. 'Oh man.'

'Call an ambulance,' I said. 'I don't think it'll matter, but . . .'

'I've seen guys lose fingers, but never anything like that.' He shouted down to someone to call 911.

I didn't want to hang around and explain. I made my way down the stairs and was about to head for the door to the parking lot when I saw Madeline Plimpton striding in my direction. 'Talk to me.'

'Elmont Sebastian's up there,' I said, pointing at the rollers. 'If he's not dead yet, he will be before anyone gets here.'

'Dear God,' she said. 'Why—'

'It may be on the monitors,' I said. 'I hope it is.' I moved round her, heading for the door. 'And I guess I owe you an apology. Sam Henry was reading my emails. She's sold out you and me and everyone else at the paper.'

'David, start from the beginning.'

I shook my head. 'Ethan's missing. I have to go.'

'David, what's going on?' Madeline said. 'You come back—'

I didn't hear the rest as the door closed behind me. After I got into my car and turned the key, I had to think about where I was going to go next. I'd been left shaken by what had just happened.

Samantha's phone call luring me to the *Standard* had prevented me from doing a search of my house for Ethan. I'd got the door open, and I'd called out his name, but I hadn't been through the house room by room. I also had no memory of locking the house after getting Sam's call. It was possible that even if Ethan hadn't been in the house when I was last there, he could be there now.

It made sense to check in with my parents to see whether anything had happened since I'd fled in such a hurry. I took out my phone and saw there was one message. I checked it.

'Mr Harwood, this is Detective Duckworth. Look, I'm willing to overlook what happened, but I'm not kidding around. You have to come in. There are things about this case that don't make sense, things that are in your favour. But we need to sort them out if—'

I deleted the message, then speed-dialled my parents' house. Mom answered on the first ring.

'Has Ethan turned up?' I asked.

'No,' Mom whispered. She sounded as though she'd been crying. 'Where are you? That detective, he was gone and now he's back. I think he's going to arrest you if you show up.'

'I just have to keep looking,' I said. 'If you hear anything—*anything*—let me know.'

'I will,' she said.

I slipped the phone back into my coat and headed for home.

I WAS WORRIED Duckworth might be watching my place, so I parked round the corner. I saw no suspicious cars in the street.

I entered through the back door. As I'd suspected, I'd left it unlocked. I came in through the kitchen. The house was dark and I was reluctant to flip on a light just in case someone was out there that I'd missed. There were still several boards out of place. I was suddenly worried that if Ethan had come home, he might have caught his foot in one of the holes where boards were missing.

'Ethan!' I said. 'It's Dad! It's OK! You can come out!'

I listened, hoping to catch some faint sound of movement in the house. I thought I heard a board creak, overhead, in Ethan's room.

I went through the kitchen, stepping carefully. I mounted the stairs slowly in the dark. 'Ethan?' I said. 'Are you up here?'

The door to Ethan's room was ajar. I pushed it open. A glow from a streetlamp fell through Ethan's window.

There was a dark shadow on the far side of his bed. Someone was standing there, someone far too tall to be Ethan.

I reached over to the wall switch and flipped it up.

It was Jan. She had a gun in her hand, which she was pointing directly at me. 'Where's Ethan?' she asked. 'I've come for Ethan.'

TWELVE

I couldn't recall Jan looking worse. Her hair was scraggly, her eyes bloodshot. The gun was shaking in her hand.

'Put that down, Jan,' I said. 'Maybe you'd rather I called you Constance, but it's hard for me to think of you as anyone but Jan.'

She blinked. The gun didn't move.

'I guess I can understand why you never wanted to introduce me to your parents,' I said. 'One set was fake and the other was dead.'

Her eyes widened. 'What?'

'Martin and Thelma? Your real parents?' Something in her eyes said yes. 'You don't know? Someone killed them a few years ago.'

If she was troubled by this news, she didn't show it. 'Where's Ethan?' she asked. 'Is he with Don and Arlene?'

'No,' I said.

'Oh no . . .' she said. 'No, no . . .'

I took a step closer to her. 'Put that gun down, Jan.'

She shook her head. 'No, he has to be here,' she said dreamily. 'I've come for him. We're going away.'

'Even if he was here,' I said, 'I would never, ever let you take him. Give me the gun.' I inched closer.

'You don't understand,' she said. 'I need it. I need this gun.'

'You don't need it with me.' I took another step towards her.

Jan stifled a laugh. 'You're not the one I'm worried about. So my parents are dead. He must have thought they knew where I was. He must have killed them when they couldn't tell him anything.'

'Are you talking about who killed your parents? Is that who you're worried about?'

'I did a bad thing,' Jan told me. 'I did something . . .'

'What did you do?' I was less than two feet away from her now.

'Everything's been for nothing. The diamonds weren't real.'

'Diamonds?' I said. 'What diamonds?'

'They were worthless.' She stifled a laugh. 'Fucking worthless.'

I grabbed her wrist. I tried to twist the gun out of her hand, but she began to pull her arm away. I wouldn't let go. She swung at me with her left hand, hitting me in the face. I swung my right arm up, knocked her hand away as I held on to her right. Then I turned in to her and got both hands on her wrist, doubling the pressure to make her drop the weapon. I threw my body into it, forcing Jan against the wall, hard, knocking the wind out of her. While the move may have weakened her, it also prompted her to pull the trigger.

The shot, which sounded like a sonic boom in Ethan's small bedroom, went into the floor. I jumped, but I didn't loosen my grip. I slammed her wrist against the wall. Once, twice. The third time, the gun clattered to the floor. I let go of Jan's hand, scrambled to get hold of the gun, grabbed it, then rolled and pointed it at her.

'Who are you?' I shouted, both hands wrapped round the gun.

She sat on the bed, tears running down her cheeks. 'I'm Connie Tattinger. I'm also Jan Harwood. No matter who I am, I'm Ethan's mother. And I was your wife. I've been . . . waiting. And hiding.'

'Waiting for what? Hiding from whom?'

Jan took a few breaths. 'We hijacked a diamond shipment in Boston. Six years ago. Then, my partner, he got sent away for something else. The diamonds were in a safe place but it was going to be a few years before we could get at them. The man we took them from . . . he's been looking for us, for me, all that time.'

I was trying to take it all in. Those few sentences, summing up years of deception. I grabbed on to something Jan had already said. 'But you said they were worthless. Why would this man want them back?'

'Because of what I did to him. I cut off his hand to get the briefcase he was attached to.' She sniffed. 'He lived.'

I was so stunned that I lowered the gun. 'So you had to hide out. You came to Promise Falls. And married me. You figured I could help you blend in. Who'd guess the nice little wife down the street had anything to do with a diamond heist?'

She nodded.

I had more questions. 'So let me figure this out. When your partner got out of jail, you'd recover the diamonds?'

'Yeah, we expected to get a lot of money for them.' She wiped away a tear. 'But they weren't worth anything. The man whose hand I cut off—his name's Oscar Fine—he'd been putting the word out. Dwayne, the one I stole the diamonds with, knew a man who'd give us cash for them. But when we went back for the money, Fine was there. He must have killed Dwayne. And he tried to kill me.'

I rested my head up against Ethan's closet door.

Jan said to me, 'What happened to the floors?'

'I found the birth certificate, the one for Jan Richler. Behind the baseboard in the linen closet.'

'You couldn't have,' she said. 'I took it with me.'

'I found it a long time ago, but put it back. After you disappeared, I found your real one. Why didn't you take that, too?'

'I needed the other envelope for the key that was in it. It didn't occur to me to get the other one. So you knew about the Richlers?'

'I knew of them, but I only went to see them after you disappeared. I found out about their daughter. You have any idea what you've done to those people? Bad enough what happened when you were a little girl. But to use their daughter's name now, all these years later, that—'

'I'm poison,' Jan said. 'Anyone who comes in contact with me, their life goes into the toilet. Jan, her parents, my parents, Dwayne.'

'Me,' I said. 'Ethan.'

Jan met my eye and looked away again.

'I was the perfect patsy. Your sole audience. So when you disappeared, it looked like I was lying. Like I was trying to make them think you killed yourself, and the cops would figure I'd killed you. The trip to Lake George, the stuff you told that guy in the store. Everything pointed to me. And it was you who sent the email.'

Half a nod. 'You'd already heard from that woman. I knew you'd fall for the email.'

'The tickets you ordered online. How'd you get into the park?'

'I paid cash,' she whispered. 'I had a change of clothes, a wig, in the backpack. When you ran after Ethan, I went into the rest room and changed, then walked out of Five Mountains.'

'The thing I don't get is why. *Why* would you do this to me? How could you do this to me? How could you do this to Ethan?'

Her eyes moved about for a second, as if searching for the answer. Then they stopped abruptly, as though the answer had been right in front of her. She said, 'I wanted the money.'

'WHAT DID YOU THINK was going to happen?' I asked. 'After I ended up going to jail for killing you?'

'I figured because there was no body, you'd get off. But they'd still think you did it, and they wouldn't come looking for me.'

'And if they convicted me?'

'Your parents would look after Ethan. They love him.'

I nodded. 'And what about me? Did you love me?'

'If I said yes, would you even believe it?' she asked.

'No,' I said. 'What about Leanne? How'd she end up dead?'

Jan shook her head tiredly. 'Dwayne and I, we ran into her, outside Albany. She saw me in the truck, came over, wondered what I was doing there, who Dwayne was. Dwayne did what he had to do. We took her to Lake George, in the pick-up, under the cover.'

'That meant a lot of backtracking.'

'I had this idea,' she said, 'that if we left her body up there, it would . . . it would build the case against you.'

'I never knew you for a minute,' I said. 'Why did you have Ethan? When you got pregnant, why didn't you get an abortion?'

'I was going to. Having a child wasn't part of the plan. I'd taken precautions, but . . . I lay awake at nights, convinced I was going to do something about it. I went to a clinic in Albany.' She wiped tears from her eyes. 'I couldn't do it. I wanted to have a baby.'

I shook my head. 'You're a monster. A psychopath. The devil in a dress. I loved you. But it was all an act. None of it real.'

Jan struggled to find the words she wanted to say. 'I came back because of love. I came back for Ethan. With Oscar Fine out there, looking for ways to get to me, I knew I had to come back for Ethan, to protect him. He's my son. I'm his *mother*, for God's—'

I'd had enough. I raised the gun, pointed it and pulled the trigger. Jan screamed as the shot filled the room.

The bullet went into the wall over Ethan's headboard.

'That's what kind of mother I think you are,' I said.

Shaking, Jan said, 'It's true. I came here for him. I drove by your parents' house, didn't see any sign of him, then I came here. I let myself in. When you came home, I was going to leave with him.'

'Jan, it's over. You have to turn yourself in, tell the police how you set me up. If you love Ethan, the only way to prove it is to make it possible for me to raise him. You're going to go to jail for a long time. But if you mean what you say, if you love your son, you have to make things right so that he has his father there for him.'

A calm seemed to come over her. 'OK,' she said quietly.

'But the first thing we have to do,' I said, 'is find him.'

It was as though I'd thrown cold water on her. She became, suddenly, focused. 'You don't know where he is? He's missing?'

'This afternoon. He was playing with the croquet set in the back yard and Mom stopped hearing—'

'When?' Jan asked. 'When did she notice he was gone?'

'Late. Like, five or six o'clock.'

'He could have got there by then,' Jan said.

'Tell me,' I said. 'Are you talking about this Oscar person?'

She nodded. 'I think he knows who I've been these last six years. Either from the news, or from Dwayne, before he killed him.'

'Jan, how would he even know where to find Ethan?'

'You think he's stupid? All he has to do is look up your name. He'll find this address, your parents' address, plus . . .'

'Plus what?'

Jan's face crumpled. 'He may even have a picture of Ethan.'

It was all dizzying. Encountering Jan, learning about her past, coming to grips with the realisation that Ethan might not just be missing, but in real danger. As I got up off the floor, my hand caught on the edge of a long piece of hardwood flooring shaped like a jagged icicle.

I cursed. Tucking the gun under my butt, I prised out a splinter with my thumb and forefinger. Then I picked up the gun and got to my feet. 'This guy, what would he do with Ethan if he had him?'

Jan shuddered. 'I think he'd do anything to get back at me.'

'I'll call Duckworth,' I said. 'He's the detective who's been trying to find you. He can get everyone looking for Oscar Fine. If the police find him, they find Ethan. Fine probably figures that as long as he has Ethan, alive, he'll have leverage with you.'

Jan nodded. 'I'll tell the detective anything he needs to know.'

I took out my phone, flipped it open, and had started to dial Duckworth's number, when a voice said, 'Stop.'

I looked up. There was someone in the doorway. A man with one hand.

'DROP THE GUN and the phone,' Oscar Fine said to me. He had a weapon of his own pointed at me. It had a long barrel, slightly wider at the end. I was guessing that was a silencer. There'd already been two unsilenced shots fired. With any luck, maybe the neighbours had heard them and dialled 911.

My gun was aimed at the floor and I was pretty sure I'd be dead before I could raise my arm to use it. So I let the gun fall to the floor and I tossed the phone, still open, onto the bed.

'Kick it over here,' Oscar Fine said. 'Carefully.'

I slid the gun towards him with my shoe. He knelt down and, using his stump and the weapon in his one hand like a set of chopsticks, picked up the gun, then slipped it into his pocket.

The colour had drained from Jan's face.

'Where's my son?' I asked.

Oscar Fine didn't look at me. His eyes were fixed on Jan. 'It's been a long time,' he said.

'Please,' Jan said. 'You have the wrong person.'

He smiled wryly. 'Really. Show a little more dignity than your boyfriend did at the end. You know what he did? He pissed himself. I'm guessing you're made of stronger stuff. After all, you were the one who had it in you to cut off my hand. He just sat up front.'

Jan said, 'You should have had a key on you. If you'd had a key, we could have taken the briefcase without hurting you.' She nodded in my direction, 'Please let him go. Tell him where our son is so he can go and get him.'

Oscar Fine looked like he was thinking something over. Then, in an instant, his arm went up and the gun in his hand went *pfft*.

I shouted, 'No! God, no! *Jan!*'

Jan was tossed back against the wall. Her mouth opened, but she didn't make a sound. She looked down at the blossom of red above her right breast and touched it. I ran to her, tried to hold her as she started her slide down the wall. I eased her down. Her eyes were already glassy.

'Ethan,' she whispered to me. Her breathing was short and raspy.

'I know,' I said. 'I know.'

I looked at Oscar Fine, who hadn't moved since firing the shot. 'I have to call an ambulance,' I said. 'My wife . . . she's losing a lot of blood.'

'No,' he said.

'She's dying,' I said.

'That's the idea,' Oscar Fine said.

Jan struggled to raise her head. 'Ethan. Where is Ethan?'

Oscar Fine shook his head. 'I have no idea. But if you'd like, I'd be happy to look for your son. Once I find him, who would you like his hands sent to?' He smiled sadly at me. 'It won't be you.'

Jan's eyelids fell shut. I slipped my arm round her, pulled her to me.

In the distance, we heard a siren. Oscar Fine cursed as the sound grew louder. 'Change of plan.' He waved the barrel at me. 'Come.'

I took my arm from Jan and walked across the room and through the door. I could hear steps pounding on the front porch. Fine stayed close behind me. I could feel the barrel of the gun touching my back.

From downstairs, I heard Duckworth yell, 'Mr Harwood?'

'Up here,' I said in a voice loud enough to be heard.

'Are you OK?' Lights started coming on downstairs.

'No. And my wife's been shot.'

'I've called an ambulance.' Duckworth had reached the bottom of the stairs. Oscar Fine and I were standing behind the low first-floor railing.

Duckworth had his weapon drawn. I could see the puzzlement in his face, wondering who the man with me could be.

Oscar Fine said, 'I'm going to shoot Mr Harwood if you don't let us leave together.'

Duckworth took a moment to assess things. 'There's going to be a dozen officers out front in about two minutes,' he said.

'Then we have to move quickly.' Oscar moved me down a step at a time. 'Lower your weapon or I'll shoot Mr Harwood now.'

Duckworth, seeing the gun at my back, lowered his gun, but held on to it.

We reached the ground floor and Fine eased me towards the kitchen. He was going to take me out of the back door.

We were beneath the first floor railing when I noticed Duckworth glancing up. Oscar Fine and I craned our necks upwards at the same time, too.

It was Jan. She was standing at the railing, leaning over it at the waist. A drop of blood touched my forehead like warm rain.

She said, 'You will never hurt my son.'

And then she pitched her body forward over the railing. As she started to come down, I saw that she was clutching firmly, in both hands, the dagger-like plank of hardwood flooring I'd caught my hand on.

Fine had no time to react before its sharp, ragged end caught him where neck meets shoulder. The force of Jan's fall rammed the plank into his torso, and that, combined with the weight of Jan's body, put him down on the floor in an instant. Neither of them moved after that.

Jan and Oscar Fine were declared dead at the scene.

I spent the better part of an hour with Barry Duckworth, explaining everything to him as best I could. I had the sense he believed me. But even before we got into that, I had something more urgent to discuss with him.

'Ethan's still missing,' I said. 'Jan was certain Oscar Fine had taken him, but upstairs there, just before everything happened, he said he didn't know anything about him.'

'Was he lying, do you think?' Duckworth asked.

'I don't think so,' I said. 'If he'd had Ethan, I think he would have enjoyed taunting us with the fact.'

But to be certain, we found a black Audi—registered to Oscar Fine—one street over. We checked the back seat and trunk for any signs of Ethan. We came up empty.

'Everyone is working on this,' Duckworth assured me as we sat at the kitchen table. 'Every available member of the department is looking for your boy. We're interviewing everyone on your parents' street and your street, doing a door-to-door right now.'

None of this made me feel any better.

'She did it for Ethan,' I said. 'And for me. She pulled it together long enough to kill that man, so I'd be there for Ethan.'

'I guess she did,' Duckworth said.

Mom and Dad arrived shortly after that. There was hugging and crying. I tried to tell them what I knew about the events of the last three days. And the last six years. And even before that.

While Duckworth went off to help oversee the crime scene, the three of us sat at the table, not knowing what to do. Some time around midnight, the phone rang. I picked up. 'Hello?' I said.

'Mr Harwood, I've done a terrible thing.'

I WAS THERE by 3 a.m.

Duckworth put up some objections at first. First, he didn't want me leaving the crime scene. Second, if I knew who had taken my son, if he'd been kidnapped, Duckworth had to send in the police.

'I don't know that it's exactly a kidnapping,' I said. 'It's kind of complicated. Just let me go and get my boy and bring him home.'

He mulled it over a moment, then finally said, 'Go.'

When I pulled up in front of the Richlers' house in Rochester, Gretchen was standing at the door waiting for me.

'Let me see him,' I said as I came up the porch steps.

She nodded. She led me upstairs and pushed open the door to what I presumed to be the bedroom she shared with her husband.

Ethan was under the covers, sound asleep.

'I'll let him sleep for a bit more,' I said.

'I've put on coffee,' Gretchen said. 'Would you like some?'

'Yes,' I said, following her downstairs. 'Is your husband . . .'

'Still in the hospital,' she said. 'They have him in the psychiatric ward, I guess they call it. They've got him under observation.'

She filled two mugs with coffee and set them on the kitchen table. Gretchen Richler took a seat across from me. 'I know what I did was wrong,' she said.

I blew on the coffee, took a sip. 'Tell me what happened.'

'We were looking at that picture you left with us of your wife. It was the necklace she was wearing. The cupcake. It had been our daughter's. She'd lost it before she died. She'd accused Constance of stealing it. When I saw it on your wife, I knew.'

'It was the only time I remember seeing her wear it,' I said. 'She had it in her jewellery box but never put it on. But just before that trip, Ethan found it. He loves cupcakes and begged her to wear it.'

'That last time you called, just after Horace tried to take his own life, when you said you thought your wife was still alive, that you thought maybe you were going to find her, I went . . . I went a little crazy. I was so angry. This woman, she'd taken my daughter's life not once but twice. I wanted her to know how it felt. So, with Horace in the hospital, I drove to Promise Falls. I found your parents' house and I saw your son in the back yard. I told him I was his Aunt Gretchen, and that it was time for him to come home.'

I had another sip of coffee. 'And he went with you in the car?'

She nodded. 'I'd stopped round the corner, before I got to your place, and bought some treats to keep him happy. Then I started driving back and he told me I was going the wrong way. I had to explain to him that he was going to stay with me for a little while.'

'How'd he take that?'

Gretchen choked up and a tear formed in her eye. 'He started to cry.'

'What were you planning to do?' I asked.

'On the way to Promise Falls, I'd made up my mind. I was going to . . . get even, make things right. But once he was in the car . . .'

'You couldn't do it,' I said. 'You wouldn't have hurt him.'

'He's a lovely boy,' she said, looking at me again. 'He really is.'

'So you just came back to Rochester?'

She nodded sadly. 'I'm very ashamed of myself. I am.'

'You have no idea what you've put us through,' I said. 'My mother may never forgive herself for letting Ethan out of her sight.'

'I'll tell her I'm sorry. I will. Don't you get a chance to make some sort of statement to the family when they sentence you?'

I felt so tired. 'I don't think that will be necessary,' I said.

Gretchen was confused. 'I don't understand. I kidnapped your son. I have to be punished for that.'

I reached across the table and put a hand on hers. 'I think you've been punished enough. You and your husband. By my wife. All that matters to me is that my son is OK, and that he's not in danger. I'll do what I can to persuade the police not to charge you.'

'I made him dinner,' Gretchen said, not hearing me. 'He settled down after a while, and I made him some macaroni and cheese.'

'He likes that.'

'I knew I was going to have to call you. I was going to do it in the morning. But I knew you wouldn't be able to sleep, not knowing where he was, so I decided to call when I did.'

'I'm glad. I'd like to get my son now.'

Gretchen led me upstairs. I sat on the edge of the bed.

'Ethan,' I whispered, touching his shoulder gently. 'Ethan.'

He opened his eyes slowly. 'Hi, Dad,' he said.

'Time to go,' I said.

I pulled back the covers. He was still dressed, his shoes on the floor next to the bed. As I helped Ethan sit up, Gretchen handed me his shoes. While I was slipping them on his feet, he said, 'That's Aunt Gretchen. She picked me up at Nana's.'

'I hear she made you macaroni and cheese.'

'Yup.'

Once I had his shoes on, I picked him up and went downstairs. 'I hope Horace will be OK,' I said as Gretchen opened the door.

'Thank you,' she said. She patted Ethan on the head. 'Bye-bye.'

'Bye, Aunt Gretchen,' he said, rubbing his eyes.

I carried him to Dad's car and belted him into the safety seat in the back. I was about to turn the key when Ethan asked, 'Did you find Mommy?'

'Yes,' I said.

'Is she home?' he asked.

I got out of the front seat and into the back. I closed the door behind me and snuggled close to Ethan, taking his hands into mine.

'No,' I said. 'She's gone away. She won't be coming back to us. But you have to know she loves you more than life itself.'

'Is she mad at me?' he asked.

'No,' I said. 'She could never be mad at you.' I paused, then found the words I wanted. 'The last thing she did, she did for you.'

Ethan nodded tiredly, cried a little, then fell back asleep. I kept holding him. We were still there like that when the sun came up.

linwood **barclay**

In 2007, Canadian author Linwood Barclay's *No Time for Goodbye* was chosen as a Richard & Judy Summer Read for Channel 4, and we were delighted to include it as one of our best choices for Select Editions. The story revolved around an adolescent girl who wakes one morning to find that her entire family has disappeared without trace, seemingly for ever, and it became the UK's biggest-selling novel of 2007.

Barclay's newest thriller, *Never Look Away*, also opens with a chilling scene that will generate fear and sympathy in the hearts and minds of all parents—the nightmare of discovering that your toddler has disappeared in a frenetically busy amusement park. But does the author believe that people without children will also relate to this?

'I think so. And I'm not the kind of guy who writes about terrorists trying to unleash a biological weapon or smuggling plutonium across the border. I don't really connect with that. I don't identify. I tap into the more common anxieties like, It's three in the morning, why isn't my kid home in bed? I don't know anybody who lies awake at night worrying about biological terrorism, but they do lie awake worrying about why their kids aren't home . . . or about their mortgage.'

The twists and turns in *Never Look Away* come thick and fast from the first page, which must make it hard for Barclay to explain how he set about plotting the book without giving too much away.

'Yes, I do find *Never Look Away* a tricky book to talk about because it has a twist even in the prologue. You think it's going to be a missing kid story, but it's not. I wanted to throw out the urban myth that's going around about kids being abducted at theme parks so I thought, Let's start with that and then let's turn it around.'

When Linwood Barclay was a toddler, he lived in the United States but was taken to live in Canada just before his fourth birthday, when his father, a commercial artist whose illustrations of cars appeared in *Life*, *Look* and *Saturday Evening Post*, accepted a position with an advertising agency in Canada. From the time he was in Grade 3 at school, Linwood could be found filling notebooks with stories.

'It was television—and I watched a lot of it—that really got me interested in writing.

A single episode a week of my favourite show was not enough, so I wrote more stories featuring these characters created by other people. When I reached Grade 5, I found it was taking me too long to write out my stories, so my father gave me a five-minute typing lesson. We had an old Royal typewriter and Dad said, "This finger goes here, this one here, this one hits these keys, and so on." That was it.'

Linwood was just sixteen when his father died, and he spent the next few years helping to run the family business—a cottage resort and trailer park—before getting his first newspaper job at the *Peterborough Examiner*, a small Ontario daily, at the age of twenty-two. In 1981 he joined the *Toronto Star*. It surely comes as no surprise, then, that the character of David Harwood in *Never Look Away*, is a journalist.

'Well, I wanted to avoid that occupation really, but then I thought, Harwood has to be a journalist so he can figure out where to start and what questions to ask. Another reason why I wanted to do a journalist in this book was because I wanted to write about what's happening to newspapers, not as the main story but as the backdrop.'

Over the course of his career, Barclay has written thousands of newspaper articles and columns, as well as a memoir that he's very proud of: *Last Resort*: *Coming of Age in Cottage Country*, and three other nonfiction titles. In 2004 he launched a mystery series around a character named Zack Walker, but it was the publication of his stand-alone thriller, *No Time for Goodbye*, that first catapulted him to international fame. Why was it, though, that he chose to write crime fiction?

'The first books I ever read were the adventures of the Hardy Boys. From there I went on to Agatha Christie and Nero Wolfe, then graduated to the harder stuff, like Chandler and Hammett and Macdonald. The crime novel that made a huge impression on me, around Grade 9 or so, was *The Goodbye Look* by Ross Macdonald. I thought then, Why would you want to write any other kind of book? What appeals to me about crime fiction is it demands a strong plot. Plots move stories. Simple as that.'

Apart from his many years experience as a newspaperman, which furnishes the character of David Harwood, the author has witnessed the kind of depression that Jan Harwood is seen to be suffering from in the early chapters of *Never Look Away*.

'I've had moments where I would get really down . . . and I have a brother who has struggled with illness, too, so I have been able to observe a lot. I hope that the first quarter of the book, where I'm establishing what Jan is going through, is convincing.'

Writing, touring and book-promotional commitments take up much of Linwood Barclay's time, so how does he choose to unwind and relax?

'Movies, walking, visiting different cities. And I'm a model train nut. My son and I have built, over the years, a huge layout in our basement. And I just love cars. I wish I could have a dozen of them.'

THE GENESIS PLAGUE

MICHAEL BYRNES

Mesopotamia, 4004 BC

An exotic stranger appears in a remote village. Mesmerising in her beauty and authority, she is venerated as a goddess—until she unleashes a terrible curse.

Iraq, present day

A mercenary unit led by Sergeant Jason Yaeger stumbles upon a mysterious cave in the desert, lined with ancient carvings. Strangely, the cave's tunnels also hold a high-tech surveillance system.

It will take the courage of Yaeger's soldiers, the assistance of the FBI, and the scholarship of archaeologist Brooke Thompson to discover the link between the cave's contents and a very devious and sinister present-day plot.

PROLOGUE

Mesopotamia, 4004 BC

Nightfall was darker now, more ominous, thought Enliatu. And with the darkness had come great misfortune for his people, which could be attributed to a malevolent force: the outsider who had mysteriously emerged from the forbidden realm over the eastern mountains, the beautiful woman who was now being marched to her death.

The captive was flanked by eight warriors carrying spears and bitumen torches. Two of the men gripped the ropes fastened to the leather collar around her neck. Her hands were unbound so that she could carry the mysterious clay jar that had been in her possession since her arrival six moons ago. She cradled the vessel as if it were her child.

Her exotic fair skin and gemlike eyes were nothing like those of the dark-coloured tribes that inhabited the known lands. The women of the village were captivated by her. They'd competed to stroke her strange soft hair and smooth skin. The men's attraction was far more feral. They had vied for her attention, and her fierce indifference merely intensified the rivalry. Eventually the men had agreed to share the prize.

On the third moon the conspirators had crept into the hut where she slept. They had covered her mouth, restrained her limbs, stripped away her coverings. Then they had had their way with her until each man's carnal appetite had been sated.

By sunrise the first man had fallen ill. First came sweating, then chills and quaking limbs . . . and the blood. So much blood.

All were dead before sunset.

As the procession moved swiftly along the bank of the swollen river,

Enliatu noticed that the flood had swallowed the circular granaries up to their rooftops. Soon the mud bricks would soften and dissolve beneath the churning water. Not a trace would remain.

Surely a cleansing was underway. Perhaps the creator was seeking to reclaim mankind itself, for just as men had formed bricks to build dwellings, the gods had moulded men from earthen clay.

THE PROCESSION BROKE AWAY from the riverside and disappeared through a line of towering cedars. The warriors carried on in silence, while the prisoner began to hum a soft sensual melody.

Overhead, the night owls screeched, as if in response to her call. This caused the men to stop suddenly. They held the torches high and, with terror-filled eyes, searched the darkness with spears at the ready. The handlers tugged the ropes, choking the prisoner into submission. When she fell silent once more, the unearthly chorus above abruptly ceased.

The ground rose sharply; the cedars thinned and yielded to the scrubby foothills leading up to the jagged mountains. Enliatu led them towards a fire pit. The two boys he had sent ahead to prepare the site knelt beside the pit, stirring two clay bowls that simmered over low flames.

The handlers goaded the prisoner ahead.

Keeping a safe distance, Enliatu instructed the boys to confiscate her burden. When they advanced towards her, she pulled the jar close to her breast, screaming wildly as they tried to tug it free. Finally, the boys stripped the jar from her. She fell limp to the ground, retching.

Enliatu instructed the older boy to open it.

The boy curled his trembling fingers under the lid, swiftly pulled it away. Immediately the dancing fire glow captured movement deep inside the vessel. He recoiled and stumbled backwards.

Undeterred, Enliatu stepped forward and extended his torch over the opened jar. Upon seeing the hideous form nestled within the jar, he scowled in revulsion. It would end here tonight, Enliatu vowed silently. He instructed the boys on what to do next.

The older boy returned to the fire pit and slid wooden rods through the handles on the simmering clay bowls. Then his partner helped him to lift the first bowl. Steadying it over the woman's jar, they decanted the glutinous, steaming liquid—kept pouring until the resin bubbled over the rim.

The prisoner shrieked in protest.

Again the owls screeched from the dark forest.

Enliatu studied the concentric ripples billowing across the resin's shimmering surface. The wicked dweller was trying to emerge.

The petrified older boy replaced the lid, held it firmly in place until the thumping within the jar slowed, then ceased.

The prisoner was on her hands and knees, growling like a wolf. Their eyes locked. Enliatu was convincd that this was a creature of the night. All the while she kept her fingers wrapped around her beaded necklace. Was this how she communicated with the other realm?

Enliatu signalled to the warriors. They forced the prisoner to the ground, face up, and restrained her splayed limbs. The largest warrior came forward, tightly gripping the haft of a formidable axe, its bronze blade glinting in the firelight. He crouched beside her, grabbed a fistful of hair at the crown, and yanked her head back to expose the smooth flesh of the neck. A momentary assessment just before he raised the axe high, then brought it down in a precise arc aimed directly above the collar.

Grunting with satisfaction, the warrior tossed the axe aside and grabbed the severed head by its soft locks. But his smile vanished when he looked into the glowering eyes that still seemed alive. Even the lips remained frozen in a taunting grimace.

Enliatu pointed to the second clay bowl simmering on the fire pit. Extending the ghastly head away from his body, the warrior dropped it into the boiling resin. Enliatu watched it sink lazily into the opaque sap amid a swirl of blood—its dead eyes still glaring defiantly, as if promising that its curse had only just begun.

CHAPTER ONE

Northeast Iraq, present day

'I'm empty!' Jam called over to Sergeant Jason Yaeger, his unit commander, who was crouched behind a massive limestone boulder, four metres away.

Keeping his right eye pressed to the rifle scope, Jason pulled out a fresh magazine and tossed it to Jam. The unit's mishmash of Russian weapons, scrounged from a wandering Afghani arms dealer, gave each man's rifle a unique report that helped Jason to keep a rough count on expended rounds. Jam was heavy on the trigger of his AK-74—more pull than squeeze.

'Slow it down or you're going to lock it up!' Precisely the reason Jam had earned his nickname, Jason thought.

Though the ten remaining Arab militants had superior numbers and a high-ground advantage, the art of the kill was heavily weighted in favour of Jason's seasoned team. The dwindling ammo supply, however, couldn't have come at a worse time. If the bad guys were to call for back-up, Jason's unit could be attacked from the rear. Worse yet, the enemy might head deeper into the Zagros Mountains—a rebel's paradise filled with caves and rugged passes.

Over the border and into Iran.

He whistled to Jam, made a sweeping hand motion that sent him scrambling up the hill and to the right. He fought the urge to scratch at the prickly heat beneath his scruffy beard, which, along with contact lenses that transformed his hazel eyes to muddy brown, an unflattering *galabiya* robe and a *kaffiyeh* head wrap, had passed him off as a Bedouin nomad.

It took less than a two-count before a red-and-white checked *kaffiyeh* popped up over the rock pile, a Kalashnikov semiautomatic sweeping into view an instant later. Jason squeezed off three shots that would've left a perfect dime grouping on a bull's-eye and adjusted the remaining target tally downwards: nine.

Ducking from sight, he grabbed his rucksack and scrambled away just as a pomegranate-shaped grenade arced over the boulder, landed in the sand and popped. A ten-metre uphill dash brought him to a rocky hillock covered in scrubby brush.

While the militants screamed back and forth to one another in Arabic, Jason brought out his Vectronix binoculars and scanned the two enemy positions. The device's laser automatically calculated GPS coordinates while recording live images onto its micro-sized hard drive.

Dipping beneath the hillock, he flipped open a laminated field map to verify the correct kill box on the grid. From his vest pocket he fished a satcom that looked nearly identical to a civilian cellphone. He placed a call to the air base at Camp Eagle's Nest, north of Kirkuk. A barely perceptible delay followed by a tiny digital chirp confirmed that the transmission was being securely encrypted, just before the command operator responded with the first authentication question:

'Word of the day?'

He pressed the transmitter button. 'Cadillac.'

'Number?'

'One-fifty-two.'

'How can I help, Google?'

Even under fire, Jason had to smile. He'd earned his new nickname a few months ago, after joining the boys at the air base for a drink-while-you-think version of Trivial Pursuit. Jason had circled the game board and filled his pie wheel without ever cracking open a beer. Obtuse facts—'things no self-respecting 29-year-old should know'—were Jason's forte.

'We're low on ammo,' Jason reported loudly over the persistent rat-a-tat-tat-tat in the background. 'Nine militants pinned down. Some light artillery. Need a gunship ASAP.' He provided the operator with coordinates.

'Roger. I'll have Candyman there in four minutes.'

Noting the time, Jason slid the sat-com back into his vest and mopped the sweat from his eyes with his sleeve. He needed to make sure that the others weren't too close to the intended strike zones. First he glanced over to Jam, who was now a good fifteen metres farther up the slope, curled up in a gulch, cursing at his weapon's stuck slide bolt. Vulnerable, but adequately covered.

Along the roadway at the hill's base, Camel was still dug in behind a felled, bullet-riddled Arabian one-humper. For the past few months, former marine sniper Tyler Hathcock had shared a strange bond with the beast, which, coupled with his preferred cigarette brand, helped to inspire his nickname. Earlier, Camel had used the beast as a decoy by riding it bareback down the narrow roadway to block the approaching enemy convoy. When the ambush began, he'd been trapped in the open. So he'd dismounted, shot his humped buddy through the ear and used it as a surprisingly effective shield.

Crazy bastard.

Not far from Camel's position, Jason spotted Dennis Coombs—dubbed 'Meat' for his imposing stature that was pure Oklahoma farm-boy muscle—still pinned down behind the severely strafed Toyota pick-up that had been the convoy's lead vehicle. In the driver's seat was the slumped body of an Arab male. Behind the Toyota were three more trucks left abandoned by the enemy. Eight dead Arabs littered the ground around them.

Bobbing in and out of view over the hood of the second truck was the red turban of Jason's last man, Hazo. The 42-year-old Kurd acted as the unit's eyes and ears: translator, facilitator, go-to man. Hazo was simultaneously their best asset and worst liability since, like most Kurdish Christians, he refused to handle a weapon. All brain, no brawn—but a helluva nice guy.

Jason crawled farther up the rise to survey the enemy. He didn't like what he saw. Behind a formidable rock pile, three white-turbaned Arabs were assembling a long fat tube with Soviet markings. A fourth man wearing a black *kaffiyeh* was readying its first mortar shell.

'Damn.'

Jason positioned himself behind a natural V in the rock. Not the best sight line and only the targets' head scarves were visible . . . but he'd make it work. With the stock of his SVD sniper rifle nestled comfortably on his right shoulder, Jason took aim at the black *kaffiyeh* and sprang up slightly until the target's bearded face panned into view.

Pop-pop-pop.

The mortar dropped from the dead man's hand and the three white turbans scrambled to recover it. Jason sank back below the ridge.

The sat-com vibrated in his waistcoat pocket. He pulled it out.

'It's Candyman. Talk to me, Google.'

'Three targets remaining in position one . . . guns and an RPG. Five gunmen in position two.'

After pocketing the sat-com, Jason took up his rifle and rucksack then kept moving farther up the hillock, hoping to get a better angle on the white turbans. With limited rounds to spare, it was head shots or nothing at all. He only hoped the men wouldn't succeed in loading the RPG-7 before the air strike commenced.

His new vantage point let him monitor the gunmen who were pinned down in the second position: four men surrounding one tall guy in the centre. Jason steadied the cross hairs of his rifle over a chunky Arab with a patchy grey beard. The Arab made an abrupt move that granted Jason a clear facial on the central figure. His heart skipped a beat.

'Can't be,' he murmured. However, that hard dark face was unmistakable. What the hell was he doing here? The visceral urge to pull the trigger was overwhelming.

But if he knowingly took down terrorism's newest, most wanted man, he'd whip up an unimaginable shit storm. Directives were black and white for a reason, he reminded himself. Not yet. Let it go. He quickly zoomed in on the face with his binoculars and recorded the image.

Snatching up the sat-com, he used the analogue walkie-talkie channel to radio the other unit members, 'Nobody fire on position two.'

The thumping rotors of an AH-64 Apache were getting louder. Dropping back, Jason watched the gunship sweeping in.

A second later, the sat-com vibrated. 'That you, Candyman?'

'You ready for me, Google?'

'Yes, but do not, repeat, do not fire on position two. Over.'

'Got it. How 'bout position one?'

Jason peeked over the rocks, saw one of the white turbans pop up then disappear. The rocket tube came in and out of view. No clear shot.

'Hydras on position one. Have at it,' Jason replied urgently.

'Roger that. Stay low and cover your ears.'

Fifteen seconds later, the Apache was in strike range. The laser sensor on its nose cone locked on the rock pile's GPS coordinates. An instant later, a pair of Hydra 70 missiles launched from the chopper's stub-wing pylons.

Jason stole a final glimpse of position one. The RPG-7 launch tube jutted out from the rock with a mortar affixed to its tip. It was going to be close.

Ducking down, he tossed his rifle to the ground and covered his ears. He watched the missiles stream in along sharp trajectories that laced the crystalline blue sky with two crisp lines of exhaust smoke—a fearsome sight. As the missiles hissed overhead, the rocket launcher's mortar sliced upwards and glanced one of them—not hard enough to detonate the Hydra's warhead, but enough to push it off its intended path.

The first Hydra slammed position one and threw a reverberating blast wave over the mound that made Jason's teeth rattle. A rush of intense heat came right behind it. A split second later, the second Hydra struck and the ground quaked even harder. The explosion echoed off the mountains.

Jason watched the chopper bank hard to avoid the wobbling mortar, which stayed airborne for five seconds before plummeting into an orchard of date trees and exploding in an orange fireball.

Snatching up his rifle, Jason scrambled down the hillside. With the rifle high on his shoulder, he swept the muzzle from side to side, waiting for any movement near the decimated rock pile. But the smoke and dust made it impossible to see what was happening, so he took cover behind a boulder and waited while a westerly wind thinned the smoke.

Down below, Camel broke cover and sprinted up the slope. Jason covered him with suppressive fire until he did a home-plate slide through the gravel and came to a stop at Jason's feet.

'Safe!' Camel called out, grinning ear to ear like a schoolkid.

Some guys are born for this. Then Jason got a good look at Camel's face. It appeared as if he'd stuck his head in a bucket of gore. 'You all right?'

'I'm fine. My camel isn't. Why the cease fire on the second position?'

'Fahim Al-Zahrani is with them.'

'What!' Camel's brow crinkled, cracking the congealing camel blood like dry clay. 'Can't be. Intel said he's in Afghanistan.'

'Show you the pictures later,' Jason said, tapping his binoculars. 'He's the tall one in the middle. Remember, the Pentagon wants him alive.'

Suddenly, Jam screamed over, 'They're heading uphill!'

Jason and Camel went storming out on opposite sides of the boulder with weapons drawn.

The black smoke was still thick enough to provide cover for the Arabs, but Jason was relieved to see Al-Zahrani's tall form being pulled up the slope by a pair of cronies. The remaining two Arabs trailed behind them, hauling a polyethylene case.

As Jason and Camel closed in behind them, Meat broke cover to pull up the rear. Then Jam popped out from the gulch and began sprinting along the ridge in a perpendicular intercept. He had his now-useless AK-74 clutched menacingly in his right hand, knowing the best he could do was intimidate the Arabs, maybe slow their advance.

When Jason broke through the smoke, he saw that the Arabs were heading for a sizable opening in the cliff face. Judging by the flames licking the rocky outcropping and the fresh scars above it where an entire section of the mountain had sheared away and tumbled down the slope, Jason figured that it had been the impact point for the deflected Hydra missile.

Once the Arabs had funnelled into the opening and disappeared from sight, Jason slowed his advance and signalled to the others to take cover. Chasing after them into a cave wouldn't be smart.

From behind a boulder, Jason scanned the opening with his binoculars. No sign of the jihad quintet, but when he zoomed in, he did notice something peculiar: about two metres into the opening the black void was framed by a rectangular enclosure like an open doorway. Tighter magnification revealed bolt heads lining the unnatural shape.

'What do we have here?' he muttered.

Someone whistled loudly. Meat was pointing to a smoking object that lay not far from where he'd taken cover. Even from a distance, Jason could tell that the mangled and blackened metal was the door that had been blown clear off the frame he'd just spied. Scoping the object, he determined it to be roughly one by two metres, fat as a phone book, with a wide circular turn crank like he'd expect to find on a submarine hatch. The door's unmarred sections showed that it had been painted to match the mountain's earth tones. Around its edges were remnants from military-grade camouflage netting. Must have been quite effective, he thought, since no one had spotted it earlier.

Maybe the militants hadn't intended to slip through the mountains. Maybe they were heading to this place all along. Perhaps it was a bunker.

He'd read in his field manual that the Zagros Mountains stretched 1,500 kilometres from northern Iraq down to the Straits of Hormuz in the Persian Gulf, with peaks reaching 4,500 metres. The Zagros range's most bittersweet contribution to the region was the sedimentary deposits trapped beneath its eastern foothills—Iran's massive oil fields.

From out of the cave came a muffled fizzy sound, like a freshly cracked bottle of pop releasing its carbonation. Just as Jason's eyes found the opening, a blinding glow flashed in the black void beyond the doorframe . . . the silhouette of a projectile . . . a resounding whump. In the next instant, a roiling fireball billowed out from the opening, throwing heat waves that rippled down the slope. Huge rock fragments shot out in all directions.

A softball-sized stone plummeted down and struck Jason squarely between the shoulder blades, knocking him flat to the ground. Pain jolted up his spine, down his arms. He rolled onto his back, groaning in pain, seeing nothing but white for a five-count. Had he not been wearing a Kevlar vest under his robe, the stone might have paralysed him.

'You OK, Google?'

He blinked his eyes and drew a steady breath. 'Yeah, I'll live.'

Jam helped him to his feet. Jason noticed that Jam's left cheek was red and blistered, the curly black scruff sizzled away.

'I was a bit too close when the missile went off.' Jam stroked the tangle of toasted hairs. 'I needed a shave anyway.'

Jason looked up at the grey smoke cloud spewing out from the ridge. The doorframe was lost behind the collapsed cliff face.

'That was an RPG . . . right?'

'Yeah, it was.'

Meat, Camel and Hazo jogged over to join them.

'Everybody all right?' Jason asked the trio.

'Super,' Meat grumbled. When he got a good look at Jam, he stepped closer and cringed. 'What's with your face?'

'You're one to talk, Dracula. That blood mask really brings out your eyes.'

'All right, fellas,' Jason cut in. For front-line fighters, adrenaline surges always came with euphoria—at least if you were still standing when the bullets stopped flying. It was the junkie high that kept them coming back for more. But it also made the hyped-up men tougher to rein in. 'Good to see that everyone's all right. I'm sure you've noticed that we've got a new problem on our hands.' He motioned to the smoking cliff.

'Seems to me they don't want us coming in after them,' Jam said.

'These caves . . .' Hazo chimed in. 'The tunnels can lead anywhere. They could find a way out. Maybe on the other side of the mountain . . . maybe a kilometre away.'

'Or they went and buried themselves,' Camel said.

Jason was inclined to agree with both assertions. 'Let's have a closer look at that door.' He waved for them to follow.

Kneeling beside the blackened metal, Jason could feel heat radiating off it. He carefully hunted the surface for any telling marks: manufacturer's stamps, engraved plates or Arabic scrawls. He found nothing. 'Let's flip it. Cover your hands. This thing's smokin' hot.'

It took all five men to heave the thing up and over. It landed on the gravel with a crunching thump. The twisted hinges looked like they'd been lifted from a bank vault.

'That's definitely military construction,' Meat observed. 'I'm guessing that's one of the old regime's hide-outs. A fallout shelter, maybe.'

'Shit, maybe we'll finally find some WMDs squirrelled away up there,' Jam added.

Jason got to his feet. 'Whatever's inside that mountain must be mighty important to have been covered up like this.'

'Hey wait. You missed something there, Sarge,' Jam said, pointing to the corner where some camouflage netting had melted into the metal. 'Here . . .' He moved closer and tapped it with his knife.

Jason leaned in for a better look. Sure enough, there was a rectangular object caught up in the netting, slightly bigger than a credit card, thicker too. Whatever it was, it had taken a beating, just like the door. Curling his fingers under its edges, Jason tried to prise it free. But it had a plastic casing that had glued to the hot metal. He felt a tap on his shoulder.

'Here,' Jam said, handing over his knife.

'Thanks.' Working the blade under the object, Jason managed to cut it away. Strings of melted plastic stretched behind it like gum.

Jason turned the object over a couple of times. It was taupe, lightweight, with a now-indiscernible picture on its topside—what might have been a passport photo. There was a long keyhole slit centred on its short edge where a clip or strap could be affixed. 'Looks like a library card, or something.'

'ID badge,' Meat said. 'There's probably a chip inside that casing, like a swipe card.'

Jason proffered the card to Meat, who moonlighted as the group's techie. 'Think you can open it up . . . see if there's any useful data that might tell us who this belonged to?'

'I'll see what I can do,' he replied noncommittally.

'Make it happen,' Jason said. 'Now, we need to get into that cave. Fast. Unfortunately, we're going to need some help.'

Everyone knew what he meant. No one was thrilled about the proposition, yet no man could find adequate reason to oppose it. Jason pulled out his sat-com and radioed the command operator with instructions to dispatch a marine platoon to his position immediately.

CHAPTER TWO

Las Vegas, Nevada

Wrapping up a business call, Pastor Randall Stokes discreetly eyed the attractive female reporter from the *Vegas Tribune* seated on the other side of his mammoth mahogany desk. Ms Ashley Peters was too busy taking inventory of the inner workings of Our Savior in Christ Cathedral to notice.

'Look, a cathedral without a carillon is like an angel without wings . . .' he told the caller.

He noticed that Ms Peters was jotting copious notes as her gaze swept the bookcase brimming with treatises on evangelism and military biographies. Her attention shifted to the opposite wall where Stokes's citations and war medals were framed together with a display of photos. She went to take a look. There was plenty of biographical material on that wall to please any reporter, Stokes thought: Randall Stokes front and centre with international dignitaries, rubbing elbows with Hollywood power brokers, shaking hands with secretaries of state, presidents and generals.

She continued along the wall to the portrait of a teenage marine cadet in dress blues. Then came the photos of a twenty-something Stokes with his war buddies, armed to the teeth amid the ravaged backdrop of half a dozen battle zones—Kuwait, Bosnia and Baghdad among them. She finished with the stills capturing Stokes in his most familiar role: preaching to his ever-swelling evangelical flock. In two other frames, those photos had morphed into *Time* magazine covers.

As he put down the phone, Stokes let out an exasperated sigh. 'My apologies,' he said to the reporter. 'Where were we?'

'The megachurch,' she reminded him, pointing with her pen out of the window at the nearly complete glass, steel and stone construction superimposed over the distant backdrop of the Mojave Desert Valley's sprawling casino metropolis.

'Many call you a modern-day Joseph Smith,' she said.

Stokes made a dismissive gesture. 'Ms Peters, I didn't transcribe the Word of God from golden tablets scrawled in hieroglyphics.' Not exactly, he thought. 'We'll let the Mormons make those proclamations.'

The interview continued with innocent questions about the church's tremendous growth and Stokes's ambitious mission to transform faith, not only in America but in countries around the world. The reporter tactfully solicited his perspective on the lecture series he'd parlayed into a global ministry, and why his message of revelation proved so timely for Christians who saw the US invasion of Iraq as fulfilment of End Times' prophecy heralding Christ's return.

As Stokes anticipated, Ms Peters turned her queries to the contributions that funded both his global mission and this extraordinary construction project. Venturing into the minefield, the reporter had smartly turned up her charm. It began with some innocent nibbling on the tip of her pen—a mildly seductive act that Stokes had to admit was a potent distraction.

'As you know, your past and current political affiliations have many speculating as to how the church raises its funds.'

'Our benefactors choose to remain anonymous,' Stokes replied. 'Just how Christ himself would have wanted it.'

'I see.' She made more notes. 'Off the record . . . do you miss all that?' She pointed with the pen at the military photos. 'The action, the glory?' Spoken like a true civilian.

'Memories of war aren't like fond recollections of one's first love.'

'True. An ex-girlfriend might take your favourite sweatshirt and CDs . . . but not your leg.'

It was common knowledge that Stokes's military career had derailed in 2003 when a bomb in the road outside Mosul claimed his right leg just below the knee. However, Stokes could tell by her reddening cheeks that she was well aware that the thin line of etiquette had just been crossed. Smiling tightly, he replied, 'I suppose you're right. Every soldier leaves a piece of himself on the battlefield. Some of us literally so.'

She back-pedalled with, 'It's just so amazing how after all of that you found God. I've read that it was after your . . .' a pause to hunt for the right word '. . . accident . . . that He began speaking to you. Is that true?'

'That's right. And I have no doubt you've also read that my critics attribute my revelation to post-traumatic stress disorder.' Stokes's critics didn't merely cite the mental and physical trauma he'd suffered from his violent disfigurement. They went as far as blaming the drug pyridostigmine bromide, or PB, which had been given to US troops during the 1st Gulf War to counteract the effects of chemical agents, such as nerve gas. 'Utter nonsense,' he said loudly.

'So you were chosen by God? You're a prophet?'

'Something like that, I suppose.' His posture became more guarded.

The manner in which she now set down her pen implied that her next question would be off the record. 'But you hear Him? When He talks to you, I mean.'

'Loud and clear,' Stokes soberly confirmed, casting his eyes heavenwards.

She stared at him in wonderment for a long moment.

'Wow.'

Now he could see her subtly assessing him in impure ways. Charisma was like catnip for ambitious women like Ms Peters. Despite forty-six years and his mild 'handicap', he'd vigilantly maintained a physique that was nothing but lean muscle stretched over a wide six-foot frame. Strong jaw, a full head of hair and a bronze tan that made his green eyes flash. No doubt Ms Peters's article would make note of his commanding presence. After all, there was no denying that the right image had buttressed his star power.

She snatched up the pen again. 'Are the End Times here?'

'Best to assume that judgment can come at any day, any hour.'

'Do you think God's judgment will fall on terrorists like Fahim Al-Zahrani for past atrocities and the recent attacks orchestrated against religious monuments around the world?'

The preacher's expression turned severe.

Two months previously, Fahim Al-Zahrani—al-Qaeda's top lieutenant and the man rumoured to be Osama bin Laden's heir apparent—had claimed responsibility for the most fearsome terror attacks since 9/11.

Stokes's voice went down an octave as he replied, 'Any man who sends suicide bombers into holy places like St Peter's Basilica and Westminster Abbey should expect eternal punishment beyond human comprehension. Regardless of what happens here, on this earth . . . whether perceived as justice or injustice . . . no manhunt, no supreme court, will ever compare to the wrath of God.'

The reporter had to catch her breath before continuing. She skimmed her list of questions. 'With the tide reversing on the recent troop withdrawals in the Middle East, some say we may soon embark on a modern Holy War. A new crusade between West and East. In your opinion, will military intervention ever change the dynamic in the Middle East?'

His reply was anything but direct.

'Not until every human being has accepted Christ as humankind's saviour will the war for souls end.'

Stalemate.

The desk phone buzzed quietly—a ringtone assigned to a secure, dedicated line. 'Excuse me.' Hiding his alarm, Stokes stiffly picked up the phone. He listened as the caller calmly reported without preamble, 'They've found the cave.'

'I see,' he replied. 'Hold a moment.'

Stokes glanced at the reporter and covered the receiver. 'I'm afraid we need to stop here.'

WHILE CAMEL AND JAM scoured the interiors of the four pick-up trucks the Arabs had abandoned on the roadside, Jason strode towards the mobile command shelter his team had erected at the bottom of the foothill. From a distance, the structure's black goat-hair sheathing and simple wood framework were easily confused for Bedouin—an effective ruse since Arabs usually shunned nomads.

Jason pulled back the door flap and dipped inside the tent's cool interior.

Provisions were stacked around its interior perimeter, leaving just enough room to accommodate sleeping mats. A section of the roof had been peeled back to let in some light. Crammed into a camping chair, Meat sat in front of a folding table that hosted his laptop and techno gear.

Jason swilled some water from his canteen and watched Meat tap away on the laptop's keyboard. 'Any luck?'

'Yeah, actually. The outside was cooked but the inside was raw.' He held up a pair of tweezers with a wafer-thin computer chip pinched between the jaws.

He examined each side of the chip with a magnifying loupe. 'No stamps. Nothing. The data's probably encrypted too. I'm thinking it's an IPS chip.'

The Identity and Passport Service data chip, Jason recalled, was a smart card for biometric access systems—encrypted files containing a user's retinal scan, fingerprints and other unique identifiers.

'No worries, though,' Meat said. 'I'm sure we can crack it.'

Jason watched as Meat hooked a rectangular USB device, no bigger than a deck of playing cards, into his laptop—a high-tech data reader developed by the NSA. What looked like a passport photo came up on the screen—the face of an attractive, thirty-something female. Meat whistled. 'Yummy.'

Leaning in, Jason's brow rumpled with confusion. 'How can that be right?' he said. The green-eyed brunette with a flawless complexion looked like a model for Revlon. 'That's no Iraqi.'

'Nope.' Meat scrolled the data. 'That's Ms Brooke Thompson. Sorry, make that Professor Brooke Thompson. Female, as you can see . . . US citizen . . . Born April the 19th, 1975 . . . last clocked in 15.02, May the 2nd, 2003. No social security but her passport number's here.'

'What would she have been doing here?' Jason aired his thoughts aloud.

'And right after the Battle of Baghdad. This place was a battle zone back then.'

'Transmit that data to the home office and ask them to send an agent immediately to find her and vet her.'

'Got it.'

Jason waited for him to wrap up the call on his sat-com, then encrypt the data file and bounce it off a satellite to Global Security Corporation's Washington DC headquarters.

'Anything else?' Meat asked.

Jason unclipped the binoculars from his neck strap, handed them to Meat. 'Let's have a closer look at some of the video I took earlier.'

Meat patched the binoculars' hard drive into the laptop with a fire wire. A new program launched onscreen. 'Tell me what you're looking for and I'll freeze the image,' Meat said.

Jason leaned in close to review the playback. The high-resolution images were crystal clear. The frames skipped backwards until Jason spotted what he wanted. 'There.'

Meat hit a key to pause the image.

'Zoom in on the tall guy in the middle.'

'That Al-Zahrani?'

'You tell me.'

For a good minute, Meat replayed and advanced the footage. Satisfied that he'd found the best full-frontal view of the guy's face, he froze the image, dragged a frame over the head, and zoomed in. The enlargement pixellated before sharpening on the screen.

Meat slumped back in his chair and gave his beard a long, hard stroke. 'You're right. That's definitely him.'

'Humour me and run facial recognition on it.'

Meat leaned forward again to work the keyboard. Using an encrypted signal, he linked to the military's satellite network and routed an inquiry to the FBI. Meat's clearance enabled him to pull Al-Zahrani's biometric statistics from the agency's database. He instructed the program to compare the stats.

'As close as I've ever seen to a precise match. See for yourself.'

As Jason verified the results, excitement and concern came in equal measure.

'Imagine if we catch this raghead alive,' Meat said. 'We'd be goddamn heroes. Not to mention the bounty. Shit. Ten mil? We could all retire.'

'Right. You wouldn't know what to do with yourself,' Jason scoffed.

Meat considered the dream, then dickered it down in his mind to settle for something more realistic. 'I'd at least take some R&R . . . eat some cheese steaks instead of MREs and vermin roast.'

'I'd settle for a proper shower,' Jason said, scratching his beard. Getting back to business, he asked, 'Hey, where's the Snake?'

'Over there.' Meat pointed to a bulky case covered by a goatskin.

'Give me a hand. I want to see if we can't peek inside the cave.'

IT TOOK A LOT to fluster Randall Stokes. However, when the caller had conveyed what had transpired in Iraq, a sour taste rose in his throat.

There'd always been the possibility that someone might accidentally stumble upon the cave installation—precisely the reason so many security protocols had been built. But what had just happened was something Stokes could not dream up. The caller had indicated that a US helicopter gunship had misfired a missile—a freak accident. But Arab militants storming into the tunnels? Certainly this was God's plan. It was the only plausible explanation. Had the time come?

Seated at his desk, Stokes drafted a secure email. The brief message stated in cryptic terms that countermeasures were to commence immediately.

Step one: a comprehensive cleanup.

There was an outside chance that some random clue left behind might trigger an investigation. Regrettably that meant that outside contractors who'd worked on the project—the most vulnerable links—would need to be eliminated quickly. Stored on his computer's encrypted hard drive were the statistics for each scientist—everything from passport information, credit history and social security numbers to work history, family contacts and last-known addresses. Stokes attached all eight 'A-list' profiles to the email. Just as he was about to click the SEND button, the phone's intercom came to life.

'Sorry to disturb you, Randy.'

'What is it, Vanessa?'

'Mr Roselli is insisting on seeing you . . . He's acting strange,' she added.

'Give me a minute, then send him in.'

Stokes focused again on the draft, removed profile number 4 labelled 'ROSELLI, FRANK'. Verifying the content one last time, he clicked a command that encrypted the message and pushed it out into the ether. He leaned back and considered how to handle the surprise visitor. When he peered at the open door in the rear wall of the office, an idea came to him. A brilliant idea.

Fifteen seconds later, Roselli lumbered into the room. The portly project manager looked even more ruddy than usual.

'Frank.' Stokes greeted him with presidential style. 'What a surprise. What's the emergency?'

Roselli huddled on the edge of the leather visitor's seat, elbows propped on knees. Sweat peppered his brow and deep worry lines cut parallel tracks across his forehead.

'Haven't you heard?' he said. 'The alarm in the cave? For God's sake. They'll find—'

Stokes raised a hand to stop him. 'I've heard,' he replied levelly.

'I told you this might happen!' Roselli pointed a pudgy index finger at Stokes. 'We should've permanently sealed the opening.'

'And how do you suppose what's in the cave could be released without a doorway?'

Rolling his eyes, Roselli didn't have an answer.

'Let me remind you that it was a missile, Frank. A missile that accidentally veered off course. Sorry, but we didn't plan for that.' Stokes got up. 'Let's not have someone overhearing this conversation,' he said and, waving for Roselli to follow, led the way to the open door in the rear of the office.

Roselli hesitated at the entry threshold to assess the keypad on the doorframe. His head tilted to calibrate the thickness of the door—five, maybe six, inches. Then he peeked inside. 'What is this place?'

'My private gallery. We can talk more freely in here.' Stokes placed a hand on the man's shoulder and urged him inside.

The spacious, windowless gallery housed an impressive collection of ancient artefacts in sturdy display cases—mostly Middle Eastern, as far as Roselli could tell. No surprise, since Stokes was obsessed with anything remotely linked to Mesopotamia or Persia, both past and present. Floor-to-ceiling shelves lined the walls; dozens of compact clay tablets were neatly laid out behind thick glass doors.

Mounted atop a wide granite plinth was an enormous limestone slab, maybe six feet high, four feet wide, he guessed. On its face were intricate etchings of two winged beasts, spirits facing one another in profile, as if courting for a dance—each half-human, half-lion. It was the stone seal they'd removed from the cave entrance and replaced with a heavy-duty metal door.

In the display cases beside the seal, Roselli spotted some of the artefacts they'd recovered from deep within the labyrinth: a beautiful necklace of glossy shells, a clay jar painted in symbols and whose bizarre contents remained locked within rock-hard resin. But the most prominent display case was covered with a veil. The thought of what might be inside it made him shudder.

Stokes paced over to the stone slab and admired it for a moment. 'When God expelled Adam and Eve from Eden, the cherubim were posted outside the entrance so that the humans could never return to paradise. The sacred guardians . . .'

'Now is not the time for Bible thumping,' Roselli fumed. 'We need to focus on the cave. What are we going to do?'

Stokes shrugged and contemplated the situation. 'The cave being discovered like this . . . well, it can only be considered divinely inspired, wouldn't you agree?'

'Bullshit.'

'Let me get us drinks. Then we'll figure things out. Scotch?' Another of Roselli's Achilles' heels.

In Pavlovian fashion, Roselli licked his lips. 'That'd be good.'

Stokes patted him on the back. 'It'll be OK. I promise. Be back in a minute.' He pivoted on his good foot and made his way outside.

Roselli turned back to the centre of the room and stared at the veiled display case. The loose ends of the silky cover billowed against air pumping in from overhead vents. Or maybe something beneath it was stirring. Curiosity got the better of him and he stepped cautiously towards it. Cringing, he reached out and began to lift the cover. But the sudden sound of the door closing made him jump in fright. His eyes snapped to the door.

'Stokes?'

The door's locking mechanism turned over with a clunk.

'Stokes!'

On the other side of the door, Stokes punched a code into the keypad and activated the hermetic seal. Roselli's screams barely permeated the dense walls. But soon, all would be silent.

ROSELLI'S FISTS THROBBED as he pounded on the door. The ceiling vents hummed. Instead of the climate-control system scrubbing away contaminants, however, it was now sucking oxygen from the room.

Finally, he turned and put his back against the door in defeat, slid down to the carpet. He loosened his tie, unbuttoned the shirt collar. Each laboured breath became more shallow, more painful. It felt as if he was being slowly strangled by invisible hands. The grim reality quickly settled over him: this vault was to be his tomb.

'Devious bastard,' he said in a thin, wheezy voice.

Perhaps this was a fitting end for what he'd done to assist Stokes these past years—to enable his ambitious plan for Armageddon, or whatever name might be ascribed to the delusional end game.

Determined not to go down without a fight, Roselli tried to think of how he could warn the others whom Stokes would consider a threat. From his jacket pocket, he pulled out his BlackBerry, confirmed that not one signal bar showed on the screen.

Roselli navigated his address book and began drafting a mass email—a warning to all who'd worked on the project, plus an admission of his participation in a most egregious act with consequences that potentially threatened humankind's existence. That should get their attention, he thought. Maybe then they would rally together and seek justice. The possibility gave Roselli hope.

Next, he prepared a second email message, but assigned it a later delivery time. This one was meant for Stokes. When he finished the draft and read it over a final time, he couldn't help but grin, despite the bleakness of his predicament.

Roselli edited delivery instructions for the messages to ensure completion of two tasks: attempt delivery every minute until a signal is obtained and delivery confirmed; autodelete the messages upon transmission.

The wheezing was heavier now, his vision spotty.

From his pocket, he withdrew a tiny glass vial filled with white powder. With utmost care he sprinkled the tacky granules over the PDA's keyboard and control buttons. Then he slipped the empty vial back into his pocket.

He let his arms drop limply to the floor. The room seemed to be crushing in around him. A minute later, darkness crept in from the corners of his vision. Then everything slipped into oblivion.

'KEEP BACK from the opening,' Jason reminded Jam. 'Let's not have you catch a bullet with your face.'

'Yes, mother,' Jam replied.

Having clambered to the high point of the rubble heap that blocked the cave entrance, Jam had pulled away enough debris and stone to enable Camel to punch five feet of three-inch-wide conduit clear through to the other side.

Not hard for Jason to imagine someone on the other side attempting to put a few bullets through the PVC pipe.

'Good to go,' Camel reported. 'Pass the line up.'

The sand-coloured armoured flex cable hung in long loops from Hazo's crooked elbow. The Kurd passed Camel the business end of the line—a shielded optical lens tip. The cable's other end connected to a toaster-sized portable command unit that was mostly lithium battery.

Camel began threading the Snake through the PVC. 'It's going through,' he said. 'Keep it coming, Hazo.'

Meat flipped back the device's lid, which doubled as the LCD viewing screen, and powered on the unit. The set-up was similar to a compact laptop: full-size keyboard, touchpad mouse, some simple controls. From the carrying case, he retrieved what looked like a video-game joystick, plugged it into a port on the unit's rear panel. With the touch of a button, the halogen floodlight mounted on the Snake's tip lit up. The streaming video came through bright and clear.

'We have eyes,' Meat reported. He reached into the case again, grabbed the unit's headphones and put them on. Then he adjusted the audio level on the integrated microphone.

Jason crouched beside him to get a look at the images from inside the cave.

As Camel pushed more flex cable through the pipe, the camera advanced farther down the bumpy slope of rocks until it found gravel.

'Hold it there,' Meat said. He pulled back on the joystick while pressing his thumb on the control button. The first pictures immediately shone bright and clear.

Just behind the blocked entry, smooth parallel walls set roughly two metres apart tapered off into the darkness.

Jason studied the image, saw no sign of activity. 'All right, Camel, keep it moving . . . slow and steady.'

'Hear anything yet?' Jason asked.

'Nothing,' he reported. 'It's quiet in there. Really quiet.'

A few metres in, Meat spotted something on the walls. 'Hey, see that?'

'Hold up,' Jason called up to Camel. The picture steadied. 'What is it?' he asked Meat.

'Something on the left wall.' He toggled the joystick to get a better angle, then zoomed out for a wide shot. 'Looks like a mural.'

When the picture came into focus, Jason was amazed at what he was seeing: the entire left wall was filled with narrative scenes carved in pristine bas-relief. The central figure depicted was a shapely woman holding a cylindrical object that emanated wavy lines. Assembled around her were men and women presenting gifts and food. There was even a group genuflecting as if in worship. Beneath her feet was a repeating pattern of nautilus-shaped swirls.

'Hazo, come take a look at this.'

Hazo's brow rumpled. After ten seconds, he shook his head. 'I don't know this . . . but this rosette here?' He pointed to a bracelet on the woman's wrist. 'This means she is like a god, or how you say . . . ?'

'Divine?' Jason surmised.

'Yes, divinity. This says divinity.'

'So she's a goddess. Some kind of religious image.'

'I think so. But not Christian. And Muslims would never allow these pictures. Very blasphemous.'

Pointing to the swirls, Jason asked, 'Is this supposed to be a river?'

'Um, yes. I'd agree with that. And I think it's rising.'

'And what's this in her hands?'

'Maybe a container. These lines . . .' Hazo tilted his head sideways to ascertain a meaning.

'Maybe a light?'

'Or something radiating from it.'

Meat gave Jason a surprised look. 'What, like magic?'

Jason shrugged. 'All right, let's document everything. Meat, take some still shots, then keep the camera moving along this wall.'

'Got it,' Meat said.

For the next ten minutes, Camel worked more cable through the pipe to push the camera deeper and deeper into the passage. The images on the left wall had become progressively more disturbing. The swirls rose with each 'frame', and Hazo's early guess that this portrayed rising flood waters proved correct, when later images showed bodies and animals being swept 'downstream' in elongated swirls.

Most disturbing, however, was how the story's depiction of the woman progressed. Her devotees from frame one had obviously had a change of heart, because the final frames showed men binding her, then leading her away with spears to the mountains. The final frame depicted the woman's beheading.

At the end of the storyboard, the wall was covered from top to bottom in wedge-shaped hashes laid out in neat rows. Jason asked Hazo what it might mean.

This time Hazo was quick to respond, 'That looks like a very ancient alphabet. Maybe from Sumer.'

'Sumer?' Meat asked.

'The southern region of ancient Iraq,' Jason told him.

'So what is this place?' Meat asked. 'One of Saddam's old bunkers?'

Jason shook his head. 'We've seen plenty of bunkers. Nothing like this.' He rubbed his neck while glancing over at what remained of the optical cable. 'Let's push the camera in as far as we can. See if we can spot anything else.'

The hewn passage walls abruptly transitioned to rough, uncut stone. Three metres deeper, the camera approached a split.

'Wait . . .' Meat said, pressing a finger against the headphone speaker. 'I hear something.'

He punched a button on the keyboard and the audio feed played over the unit's built-in speakers. Sliding the headphones off, he raised the volume and listened intently.

First came the distinct chatter of voices, the dialect unmistakably Arabic. Two, maybe three different men, Jason guessed. The Arabs had yet to find a way out. Maybe this tunnel wasn't so extensive after all.

'They see the light,' Hazo translated. 'They don't know what to do.'

The next sounds were metallic bolts sliding and clicking—weapons being readied.

'Maybe we should pull the camera . . .' Meat started.

On the screen, a glossy shape poked out from around the corner and winked in the light.

'Is that a mirror?' Jason said.

'I think so,' Meat said. 'We should pull the camera out.'

'Good idea,' Jason said. 'All right, Camel,' he called out loudly, 'let's pull it back.'

But before Camel could react, the tiny flicker dropped off the unit's screen just before one of the Arabs popped into view and stormed towards the camera. His rifle was safely slung over his shoulder, but between his hands was a melon-sized rock. His dirt-smeared face twisted into a snarl as he raised the rock up high over his head and lunged at the camera. The last image was a shot of the man's sandals. The last sound was a resounding thwack that rattled the unit's speakers. Then the image snapped offline and turned to snow.

'Ouch,' Meat said, cringing.

Camel began pulling out the flex cable and Jam coiled the line back into neat loops. A minute later, the flattened tip popped out from the conduit, smoking and crackling.

'At least we know they're still in there, Sarge,' Jam said.

'Guys,' Camel said, peering off in the distance. He spit a gob of chewing tobacco onto the ground and pointed out along the flatland.

Three kilometres out, a military convoy whipped a billowing dust cloud up into the blazing orange sunset. A UH-60 Black Hawk was flying random crisscrosses above it to scout the terrain.

'Cavalry's here,' Camel grunted.

RANDALL STOKES sauntered to the wet bar, pulled a tumbler off the shelf, and poured two fingers of very expensive single malt Scotch. He raised the glass.

'Cheers, Frank.'

It hurt when good men—loyal men—were sacrificed for the greater good. Roselli was an extremely valuable asset. He'd perfectly coordinated the project in Iraq, which, given the mission's complex logistics and broad scope, had been no easy task. Though it was Stokes's brainchild, Roselli had recruited the multidisciplined talent who took the project from concept to reality. He'd assembled a team of renowned archaeologists and anthropologists from around the globe and brought them into the middle of a war zone to unlock the greatest discovery in human history.

It was Roselli who'd designed the ingenious security protocols and ensured each scientist working on site knew only a piece of the cave's intricate puzzle.

Most impressive was Roselli's brilliant handling of high-ranking members of Congress, the FBI and the armed forces, to bring together the funding and technological know-how. As far as the stakeholders were concerned, it was all an anonymous debit against the defence budget in the name of national security.

Stokes and Roselli had been together since the beginning: through twelve weeks of boot camp at Parris Island, side by side at the Emblem Ceremony—receiving their eagle, globe and anchor pins—at Marine Special Operations School learning the tactical art of irregular warfare. Best friends. Brothers.

Roselli was one tough mother who never gave up the fight. He'd even saved Stokes's life by bayoneting an Iraqi soldier who tried to attack him with a knife.

Now Stokes had repaid the deed by locking Roselli in an airless room. He drained the Scotch.

Stokes reminded himself that nothing could deter the mission's success. So much was at stake. There was a new battlefront now—a new killing field. The last generation of fanatics was mostly desperate, idealistic kids blinded by radical religious teachings with no regard for human life—infidels and innocents alike. The leaders behind the scenes manipulating these foot soldiers were by far the most dangerous enemy he'd ever encountered—a societal cancer that strove to destroy civilisation. One thing was certain: in the end, only one side would remain standing.

'It's for the best,' a soothing voice said from behind.

Startled, Stokes spun around in his chair.

There was no one in the room.

When would He present Himself?

'Yes, it is for the best,' Stokes agreed. 'Frank's work was vital . . . but he didn't understand the grand design to which we aspire.'

'Few do, my son.'

Stokes's eyes darted back and forth, searching for an apparition. 'They found the cave. You know that, of course. Will this jeopardise our work?'

'Have faith. All is in accordance.'

'And when will I know that it has begun?'

'It has already begun. Do you not see the signs?'

There are no accidents, thought Stokes.

'Yes, I see the signs. And the Rapture? When will it come?'

No answer.

CHAPTER THREE

Boston, Massachusetts

Global Security Agent Thomas Flaherty turned his '95 Chrysler Concorde off Huntington Avenue onto Museum Road. The promo banners along the museum's neoclassical granite edifice were dusted with snow, but the words 'Treasures from Mesopotamia, September 21–January 4' were easy enough for him to make out.

He steered to a parking place, grabbed his BlackBerry and accessed the urgent find-and-deliver order from GSC's Boston office. Only ten minutes ago, he'd received a terse phone call confirming that the museum was the asset's current location.

The woman's profile was a bit lengthy, so he read aloud to himself to drive home the key points: 'Brooke Thompson. Thirty-three. Single.' He looked at the attractive photo. Single? He could assume only that she came with an ex-husband, excessive emotional baggage and two cats. Otherwise, the facts didn't compute.

He continued down the list. 'PhD in palaeontology, Boston College . . . professor at same . . . Middle East antiquities curator, Boston Museum of Fine Arts . . . award, award, award . . . blah, blah, blah . . .' Satisfied, he dropped the BlackBerry into his coat pocket.

He threw open the door and the chill immediately cut into his bones. Stuffing his hands into his pockets, he set a brisk pace towards the visitors' entrance. At the information desk he asked where he might find Professor Thompson.

'You're in time, she's just gone up to present. Here, take this.' The assistant handed him a glossy programme and pointed the way.

Flaherty slipped through the auditorium door and a museum employee waved him to an empty seat. There was a huge viewing screen above the stage that made him feel like he'd come to watch an IMAX movie. However, the image projected onto the screen—some skull with a heavy brow ridge—wasn't exactly blockbuster material.

When Flaherty's gaze finally settled on the lecturer whose sultry voice buttered the sound system, his eyebrows went up.

'Whoa!' he exclaimed to himself.

Roaming freely in front of the stage's central podium, clicker in her hand, clip-on microphone wired to the lapel of a form-fitting navy trouser-suit, was Professor Brooke Thompson. What he'd seen of her on the BlackBerry was only a head shot that showed wavy hair shaped to the shoulder, a long graceful neck and a face straight off a magazine cover. The complete picture was even more impressive.

Finally he began to focus on what she was saying. Brooke Thompson was an engaging speaker. Though Flaherty thought he wouldn't give a rat's ass about the seemingly arcane topic—'Mesopotamia and the Origins of Written Language'—she immediately hooked him.

'It's around 10,000 years ago,' Brooke Thompson was saying, 'when the most recent Ice Age finally comes to a close. The massive glacial sheets retreat to uncover the land, while the rapid melt-off causes a dramatic rise in sea levels. The Neanderthals have long since vanished'—she pointed up to the skull on the screen—'and by 6000 BC, modern humans are thriving. They domesticate livestock for food, milk and clothing. They plant seeds along the river banks to grow their own food. They are the world's first farmers. Around 5500 BC they begin to irrigate the land with canals and ditches, allowing them to spread from the fertile north to the arid south. This agricultural revolution spawns large organised settlements throughout the Middle East in modern Egypt, Israel, Syria and Iraq—a region referred to as the Fertile Crescent, or the Cradle of Civilisation.'

She pointed the clicker and the projector brought up a detailed map centred on the Middle East.

'Surplus foods allow extensive trading over wide areas. To manage this new way of life, humans develop a systematic means of communication that doesn't rely on memory or oral transference. Enter the first written language. Which leads us to the epicentre of it all—right here . . .'

Brooke used the clicker's laser pointer to place a bright red dot at the map's centre, just north of the modern Persian Gulf.

'Here is where archaeologists have unearthed the ruins of the world's earliest hierarchical societies. This once lush and peaceful paradise was known as the "land between two rivers", or "Mesopotamia". Hard to imagine since today it is a war-torn nation known as Iraq.'

Some quiet chatter rippled through the crowd.

'The earliest known written communication dates to around 3500 B.C.'

Brooke hated suppressing the real truth about the ancient writings she'd uncovered in Iraq only a few years ago—the truth that would upend every established theory about the emergence of Mesopotamian culture, the discovery of an ancient language that would push back the time line by at least five centuries. But she'd signed an airtight confidentiality agreement.

If only she could tell the world how irrefutable evidence showed that around 4000 BC a cataclysm took place in northern Mesopotamia—an event so profound that progress and humankind itself were thrown back in time, forced to start anew. The first Dark Ages. Instead, she forged on as expected.

'Around 3500 BC, the Mesopotamian elite began using stamped seals to identify their property. Here you have a typical cylinder seal,' she said, pointing the clicker to the next image, a small stone tube covered in geometric depressions.

For the next few minutes, she elaborated on a series of slides that showed a steady 2,000-year evolution from crude pictographs to schematic wedge-shaped forms called cuneiform—a slow march towards standard word symbols that borrowed and refined the old elements.

'It wasn't long before writing was used to record legends and mythology. Thousands of years before Adam and Eve appear in the Hebrew book of Genesis, Mesopotamian creation myths—the world's first true literature—feature a garden paradise, a tree of knowledge and humanity's first man and woman. Long before Noah's great flood, a cuneiform epic written in clay around 2700 BC tells the story of the Babylonian hero Gilgamesh, who'd built a boat to escape a cataclysmic flood. And in 2100 BC Abraham leaves Ur to become the Old Testament patriarch, founder of monotheism and progenitor of the twelve tribes of Israel.

'From these primitive languages emerge the early Semitic languages: Assyrian, Aramaic, Hebrew. Then come Greek, Latin, the Romance languages and English. Not until the Macedonian army led by Alexander the Great conquered Mesopotamia and Persia around 325 BC did cuneiform begin its rapid decline,' Brooke concluded. 'So be sure to visit the gallery and enjoy this incredible exhibit—a true time capsule of human history written in clay.'

AGENT THOMAS FLAHERTY stood stage left, patiently waiting while Professor Thompson autographed copies of her latest book, *Mesopotamia —Empires of Clay*. Flaherty observed how she interacted with her admirers and decided that her charm seemed genuine. Fifteen minutes later, the professor sat back to flex the fingers on her left hand.

Flaherty moved in, saying, 'And I thought the Middle East was all about oil.'

Brooke smiled courteously.

'Really enjoyed your lecture,' Flaherty said. 'You know your stuff. And you actually make it interesting. Too bad I didn't have more professors like you when I was at BC.'

'Ah, a fellow alumnus. What year did you graduate?'

'A couple years ahead of you. Ninety-five.' Sensing by her reserved expression that he was being pegged as creepy, he skipped to the formal introduction: 'Special Agent Thomas Flaherty, Global Security Corp.' He flashed his ID. 'I know this isn't the best time, but I need to ask you some questions about your work in Iraq back in 2003.'

'Let me see that,' she said, motioning for the ID.

Brooke studied the laminated card closely: the data, the agency's holographic imprint, the not-so-flattering photo of Agent Flaherty before he'd shaved away an unruly goatee. Then she passed it back to him. 'Never heard of Global Security Corporation.'

He kept it simple. 'We work for the Department of Defense.'

'Sounds very official,' she said. 'So what can I do for you?'

'Actually, this might take a while. Maybe I can buy you a coffee in the café downstairs?'

'All right,' she said. 'But tea. Green tea.'

JASON USED HIS BINOCULARS to survey the approaching military convoy. With all the dust being kicked up, he wondered why they even bothered painting the vehicles in desert camouflage.

The lead vehicle was a six-wheeled, twenty-ton behemoth with a V-hull—a Mine Resistant Ambush Protected armoured transport, or MRAP. Affixed to its front end was a huge mine roller that scraped the ground to pre-detonate any pressure-triggered improvised explosive devices, or IEDs, that might be buried in the roadway. On the MRAP's roof, Jason could make out a telescoping optics mast—infrared, heat sensors, the works. Trailing like ducklings behind the MRAP were five flat-bellied Humvees.

The Black Hawk's side doors were open. Inside, as well as the pilot and copilot, he spied six marines. A conservative tabulation meant that twenty-five to thirty jarheads would be arriving in the next five minutes. Marines weren't always keen on cooperating with contractors. But circumstance dictated that a team effort would be critical to getting into that cave . . . and fast. Play nice, an inner voice told Jason.

'Hey, Meat,' Jason called out. 'Print out those pictures pronto. I need to send Hazo on a field trip.'

Hazo came over with a nervous look on his face. 'Field trip?'

'You know the locals,' Jason explained. 'I want you to show those pictures around, figure out what those images on the wall can tell us. And find out if anyone knows this woman whose ID we found. No way she was here alone.'

Tentative, Hazo nodded. 'But how will I get to the city?'

'You'll fly, of course.' Jason pointed to the chopper.

While twenty-eight marines busily pitched camp, Jason convened with Colonel Bryce Crawford in the makeshift Bedouin command tent. Before he set out to brief the colonel on what had transpired, Jason persuaded Crawford to loan out his chopper for a fact-finding mission.

'Make it fast,' Crawford warned Hazo. 'No goofing around out there.'

Jason could tell that the forty-something, no-nonsense Texan intimidated Hazo. The Kurd cowered from the colonel's tough, grey eyes and jutting square chin.

'Yes, Colonel,' Hazo replied sheepishly. 'I promise to work quickly.'

'Then why are you still standing here? Get moving!' Crawford barked.

Jason watched Hazo scramble out from the tent, down the hill to the chopper.

'A Kurd?' Crawford grumbled, shaking his head with incredulity. 'You sure he's on our side, Sergeant?'

'Hazo's been thoroughly vetted. We'd be dead in the water without him.'

'If he screws up, it's on your head, Yaeger. Not mine.'

Jason nodded.

They watched as the copilot helped Hazo into the jump seat and secured his flight helmet. The rotors wound up and the chopper lifted into the air, spinning sand in its wash.

'So tell me what we've got.'

'Four kills on the hill, eight more on the road. Five more holed up in that cave.' Then Jason took a breath and dropped the bomb, 'And we suspect that Fahim Al-Zahrani is in there with them.'

Crawford's eyebrows shot up. 'You expect me to believe that?'

'See for yourself,' Jason said, moving over to Meat's laptop and bringing up the side-by-side pictures. 'Took these myself. Ran facial rec on them. Perfect match.'

Crawford gave each image a critical stare. Then he said, 'This raghead is supposed to be in Afghanistan.'

'They were trying to move him through the mountains.'

'And he's not buried under all that stone?'

'Already pushed a Snake through the rubble. All clear on the other side. So far, we've seen no blood or bodies. And one of the hostiles managed to smash the camera. We're pretty sure they're all still trapped in there.'

Crawford nodded. 'All right, Yaeger.' His covetous eyes stayed glued to Al-Zahrani's digital portrait. 'I need this one alive.'

And there it was, thought Jason—the colonel's subtle jockeying to claim the prize as his own.

Then in the reflection of the computer monitor, Jason caught Crawford staring at the ID badge casing and chip that Meat had left beside the laptop. He saw the colonel's eyes widen with alarm. It lasted only a fraction of a second.

'You should know that's no ordinary cave up there,' Jason said.

Crawford stood up. 'How so?'

Jason told him about the blown-out security door and the strange images carved into the entry tunnel's wall. For now, he refrained from telling him about the badge.

Crawford took fifteen seconds to mull the facts. 'All right, Yaeger. I get it. What do you say we go ahead and plunge this toilet?'

THIRTY KILOMETRES SOUTH of the cave, Candyman set the chopper down in a vacant parking lot on the edge of As Sulaymaniyah, Kurdistan's economic hub. With an escort of two US marines, Hazo jumped into the waiting Humvee, which sped them to his cousin Karsaz's restaurant in the city centre, a hot spot for tourists and the military.

'Choni!' Karsaz greeted him with delight. 'You look like hell.'

'And you still need to lose weight,' Hazo jabbed back.

Karsaz burst out laughing. 'This is true! My wife tells me this every day.' He hooked a heavy arm over Hazo's shoulder and held him tight. 'Come, let us sit and talk.'

Karsaz towed him into the bustling dining room where they settled into a booth set off in a quiet corner. Karsaz asked the waitress to bring coffee.

'Really, Hazo, you're not looking so good. Makes me think you're still patrolling the mountains with those American mercenaries. Why do you bother with them?'

'I try to help them so that innocent lives may be spared,' Hazo explained. 'It was you who said, "See with your mind, but hear with your heart."'

The waitress returned and set down a saucer and mug for each of them. Hazo sipped the Turkish coffee, savouring the spicy cardamom.

'The reason I am here . . . I was hoping you might help.'

In a low voice Karsaz replied, 'I do have a family, so I trust you won't put me in harm's way. You know what they do to informants?'

'I understand.' From his pocket, Hazo pulled out the photos. 'If you could take a look at these pictures.' He began with the head shot of the female scientist. 'This woman was here a few years back. Perhaps with others. Do you recognise her?'

'Many people walk through these doors,' Karsaz replied with obvious scepticism. Retrieving a pair of bifocals from his suit-jacket pocket, he put them on and gave the photo a cursory glance. A surprised look came over him. 'Ah . . . yes.' He held up an index finger and tapped it at the air. 'I remember this one. She did eat here a few times. Very friendly, polite.'

'Do you remember when?'

'Not long after the Texas cowboy blew up Baghdad.'

'Was she alone?'

'No, there were others too.' He took a moment to juice the memory. 'The others were all men. Five, maybe six. Some military men, yes . . . and two wearing Levi jeans.'

Hazo moved on to pictures from inside the cave. 'And these . . . Any idea what these images might mean?'

'What is this?' Karsaz said to himself, as he studied the haunting images. 'Looks like something you might find in the temple ruins of Babylon . . . or Ur, perhaps. You remember? Back in school we saw things like this on our trips, yes?'

Hazo tried to keep him on track. 'These etchings are different from anything I've ever seen in Babylon. See this woman?' He tapped the picture. 'This goddess figure is highly unusual.'

'Maybe it is Ishtar?' Karsaz guessed.

The Assyrian goddess of sex and war. Hazo considered, contemplating the picture again. 'It's possible.'

'What is this she carries in her hands?' Karsaz said, scrunching his eyes. 'And why does it glow like this?'

'I thought you might know, cousin.'

'The woman in the photo . . . did she find these things?'

Perceptive, as always, thought Hazo. 'It would be best that I not say too much about it.'

'I see,' Karsaz said. 'I suppose if anyone were to know about them, it would be the monks. There is that monastery in the mountain north of Kirkuk. You know the place?'

'I do.'

Karsaz handed the photos back to Hazo. 'I would suggest you go there. See if the monks can answer your questions.'

STOKES PUNCHED his security code into the keypad and the bolts disengaged. The door whispered open. Roselli was sprawled face up on the carpet in the centre of the room, his complexion blue and his murky eyes frozen wide open. A foul stench drifted from the post-mortem bowel release staining the carpet.

'Oh, Frank. Why couldn't you just keep your cool, like the old days?' Stokes said. He crouched and rummaged through the corpse's pockets until he found a key ring and Roselli's PDA. 'All right fellas,' he called. 'Get in here.'

A broad-shouldered man came in wearing a sour expression. Behind him a second man, shorter by at least five inches, entered pushing a tilt truck. Both men were wearing baseball caps and overalls embroidered with a logo for a fictitious security company. The truck parked near the service entrance bore the same insignia.

'How do you want to do this?' the taller one asked, all business.

'Let's go with heart attack at the wheel.' Stokes tossed the keys over.

'Like a telephone pole . . . something like that?'

'Sure. Just nothing too dramatic,' Stokes said. 'And no witnesses.' He slipped Roselli's PDA into his inside breast pocket.

The two men hoisted the body up on a three-count, then dropped it into the tilt truck with a thud. Stokes stared at the wide brown stain left behind on the rug. A call to housekeeping would raise too many questions. He settled on cleaning the mess himself.

As he made his way out of the vault, a small ringtone chirped inside his jacket. Stokes paused in confusion and pulled out Roselli's PDA. A confirmation flashed on the display: '2 MESSAGES DELIVERED.'

Liberated from the vault's thick walls, the PDA had finally caught some airwaves.

'Great,' Stokes huffed.

Navigating the BlackBerry's menus, he hunted for the draft copy of Roselli's first message. But he found nothing. Almost immediately, however, 'undeliverable' error messages started bouncing back from the intended recipients' email accounts. Stokes was relieved to see that the addressees were the scientists who'd taken part in the 2003 cave excavation. Roselli's message began with a warning about Stokes's malicious intentions. Next came a rally call for each recipient to contact the authorities with all information pertaining to his or her time spent in Iraq. What Roselli hadn't anticipated was that Stokes's NSA contact had already deactivated and emptied said email accounts—stage one of the clean sweep that would be complete only when each name on the list wound up the subject of an obituary. That task was well underway.

'Nice try, Frank. Always a step ahead of you.'

The PDA's grimy keyboard was making his fingers sticky, some tacky white powder that could only have come from the doughnuts that had led to Roselli's doughy belly. Disgusted, Stokes paused to wipe his hands with his handkerchief before hunting for the second stealth email.

But sifting through the SENT and DELETED items, he could not find a second draft. After two more minutes, however, Stokes did manage to determine the email address to which the second message had been sent. The domain was registered to Our Savior in Christ Cathedral—Stokes's own account. He checked his emails. Nothing from Roselli.

Cursing, Stokes tossed the PDA in his desk drawer.

'YOUR GREEN TEA with honey.' Agent Flaherty set a paper cup in front of Brooke Thompson.

'Thanks. You're pretty good at table service.'

'Got me through college.' He set down a second cup for himself—black coffee—then sat in the chair on the opposite side of the café table. He took a second to peer out the floor-to-ceiling window at the wind whipping the snow drifts. 'God, I hate the cold.'

Brooke thought the guy looked like he could use some time at the beach, like many pallid Bostonian Irish. Though that same UV avoidance probably accounted for his unblemished complexion. If he'd graduated in '95, she assumed him to be thirty-six, maybe thirty-seven. But he could easily pass for thirty. Brooke was a stickler for a good nose and ears, and he had both, the right mix of pretty boy and man's man. Despite the bad one-liner he'd opened with back at the auditorium, Agent Thomas Flaherty had passed her first-ten-seconds test with flying colours.

He sipped some coffee, then took out a small notepad. 'Let's talk about Iraq, starting with when you were there and why.'

'Hold on, Agent Flaherty . . .'

'Tommy.'

'Right. Tommy. First you need to tell me why I should be talking to you.'

'Fair enough. There was an incident in the Iraqi mountains. Some of our guys were working under cover, patrolling the area. They got into a shooting match with some hostile locals. An ID card with your name on it was found in the middle of it all.'

'ID card?' She considered this. 'Oh yeah. I did lose one of those. It was more like a security badge.'

'That's a good start. So tell me how you lost it. That way I can explain to my boss how you weren't associated with the other side.' His deadpan expression showed he wasn't joking.

'Look . . . I'd received an offer to assist in an excavation in the northern mountains. I accepted. I arrived there in September 2003. The fourteenth, to be exact.'

This did jibe with the passport activity provided to him. To keep her honest, he jotted down the date anyway.

'All expenses paid,' she added. 'It was an incredible opportunity, especially since Western archaeologists hadn't turned a shovel in that region for decades—thanks to politics, of course. Since this was only months after the US invasion, everything was very hush-hush. And I wasn't told anything specific until I'd arrived in Baghdad.'

'Who made you this offer and handled the arrangements?'

'A guy named Frank took care of everything.'

'Frank . . .?'

She shrugged. 'Just Frank. He was a middleman.'

'He funded the project?'

'I was never told who funded the project. Benefactors sometimes want to keep a low profile. But shouldn't you guys know this?'

'Sorry?'

'You know, the military, some obscure part of Homeland Security, the CIA, or whatever it goes by nowadays. I mean, I'd been given a military escort—US soldiers wearing desert fatigues with American flag arm patches, the works. You might want to ask your boss about that.'

This temporarily stumped Flaherty. If his boss knew anything about it, this visit wouldn't be taking place. 'And what kind of work were you asked to perform?'

'What I do best: decipher ancient languages. I was brought up north to the mountains to a tunnel, a cave actually, that dated back a few thousand years. The walls were covered in ancient picture carvings and cuneiform. Wasn't easy, either. That language pre-dated anything I'd ever seen. Really incredible stuff.' She checked to make sure nobody was listening in, then said in a low tone, 'The kind of stuff that would challenge every established theory on the emergence of writing.'

'And what did it say?'

'You'll have to talk to Frank. Because if I can't publish in the *American Journal of Archaeology*, you'll have to wait your turn.'

'You have a number for this Frank?'

She shook her head. 'Everything was handled by email. The times he did call, the number came up "restricted".'

'You can give me this email address?'

'When I'm back to my computer, I suppose.'

He dug in his pocket and pulled out a business card. 'If you could forward it to me, that'd be great. And try not to lose the card, please,' he taunted.

'Funny,' she said. 'I remember when I lost that ID. Frank freaked out. There was so much equipment in the cave, debris too. Lord knows where it wound up. But he got me a new card within minutes. Super-tight security there. Guys with guns outside, the works.'

'Any other scientists?'

'A handful. Archaeologists, mostly. But we were kept apart, no consorting or information sharing. A really frustrating way to work. The others had higher clearance than me. I was allowed only in the entry passage—the first of what was probably a maze of tunnels. There was a guard stationed where the entry tunnel forked, scanning IDs. Like a checkpoint.'

He needed to fish for a connection to the Arabs who were now holed up in the cave. 'Any chance it had something to do with Islamic militants?'

'You're kidding, right?'

Flaherty shook his head sharply.

'What I saw in that cave had been there over 4,500 years before Muhammad was even born. Terrifying, yes. Terrorism, no.'

A few tables away, Flaherty noticed a man with a thin face and Dumbo ears, sipping coffee. The guy seemed preoccupied with their discussion, but quickly diverted his attention back to a museum map laid flat on the table. Flaherty lowered his voice. 'Anything else?'

'I was there only a few days, taking pictures, making rubbings of the walls. Once I cracked the alphabet, I was asked to give all the materials back. Then they put me back on a plane, no pictures, no records, no copies, nada. The most incredible thing I've ever seen and all I've got to show for it is up here.' She tapped her temple. 'I'm not in any trouble, am I?'

Flaherty's eyes didn't move from the notepad. 'I'll need to report back to my boss, see what she has to say. There'll be some fact checking, of course.' He finally looked up. 'I'll keep you posted. But we'll probably need to meet again. So try not to skip town,' he said with a smile.

WHEN HE'D FINISHED scrubbing the carpet, Stokes took a breather next to a metre-high display case shaped like an obelisk. The artefact contained in its glass tip captured his attention: a clay tablet, no larger than a hymnal, etched in lines, pictograms and wedge-shaped cuneiform. An amazing work created by the first masters of celestial study—the ancient Mesopotamians.

He'd never divulged to anyone how he'd procured this treasure map to the origins of Creation hidden deep within the Zagros Mountains. The tablet represented Stokes's pledge to those who'd bestowed the artefact upon him. The pledge that had transformed a warrior into a prophet.

It all began on a day in 2003 . . .

While US forces bombed Baghdad, Stokes's Force Recon unit was still routing out Taliban from the Afghan mountains, just like they'd been doing since October 2001. Shortly after Iraq's capital had been seized, his unit had been redeployed to northern Iraq to pursue Saddam loyalists who were fleeing Mosul and heading over the mountains for Syria and Turkey.

The Department of Defense had issued a list of Iraq's most-wanted men in the form of a deck of playing cards. In the first two weeks, Stokes and his six-man unit had captured two diamonds, one heart and one club. By the end of the first month, they'd hunted and killed fifty-five insurgents, without one civilian casualty.

Things had gone smoothly.

Perhaps that should have clued Stokes that his luck was sure to turn.

Stokes and fellow special operative Corporal Cory Riggins were heading south to Mosul for a weekly briefing with the brigadier general. Their Humvee was forced to a stop in a congested pass where a group of Iraqi boys had turned the dusty roadway into a soccer field. The kids made no effort to move.

'I should just run over them,' Riggins said. 'A few less fanatics in our future.'

'Never did like kids, did you?' Stokes said, hopping out from the Humvee. 'I'll take care of it.'

Stokes had made it only four paces from the truck when one of the boys scored a goal that sent the soccer ball rolling up to Stokes's feet. He didn't think much about the fact that the kid playing goalie didn't come running after it. The kids simply jumped up and down, waving their arms for Stokes to kick it back. Grinning, Stokes planted a swift kick on the ball.

That was the last time he'd seen the lower half of his right leg.

What Stokes hadn't known was that the soccer ball had been packed with C4 and had been remotely armed the moment it rolled to a stop, waiting for the force of Stokes's kick to compress its concealed detonator.

The explosion was fierce, lifting Stokes into the air and throwing him back against the Humvee. There was no pain. Just the woozy haze from shock and an overwhelming urge to vomit.

The boys scattered as a trio of militants broke cover to ambush the Humvee. They shredded the Humvee's interior with machine guns, before Riggins could escape or return fire.

Then they circled around Stokes, jeering him as he spat bile into the sand. Since his eardrums had been blown out, he couldn't hear what they were saying, and his eyes, coated in blast residue, struggled to focus.

Then came the beating.

The Arabs mercilessly kicked him about the face until he spat out teeth. Next, they pummelled his ribs and testicles. When they began stomping on his bloody stump, Stokes passed out.

They'd done everything possible to maim him. Yet for some reason, no doubt wicked, they let him live. Perhaps they'd determined that his mutilation was punishment far greater than death.

For hours he lay there, bloodied and beaten, cooking in the sun. Onlookers came and went, going about their business, some stopping to spit on him. All he could think was how he'd given his life to save these people and not one came to his aid.

Finally, when he'd given up hope, one person did come for him: the man who would forever change Stokes's life, the man who would guide him down the path to ultimate retribution.

CHAPTER FOUR

'Give it some more gas!' Jason yelled down to the driver.

The MRAP's 450-horsepower Mack diesel engine rumbled. The winch's steel cable stretched even tighter, straining to pull free a mammoth mountain chunk that easily weighed ten tons. The rock was wedged in tight, anchoring the debris pile that had slid down to block the entrance.

Finally, the rock did a drunken lurch then teetered forward.

'Everybody back!' Jason screamed. He motioned for Crawford and the dozen or so marines watching at the bottom to clear off to the sides. Then he yelled to the MRAP driver, 'Move out!'

Once Big Mama got going, the huge pile dammed up behind her erupted into a landslide—huge, sharp rocks bouncing and tumbling end over end.

Jason cupped his hands around his mouth and screamed, 'Move it! Go! Go! Goooo!' The driver was quick to respond, but Jason could tell that the MRAP wasn't accelerating fast enough. Big Mama struck the vehicle's rear with a huge clang, denting the rear doors and fracturing the windows.

Jason's attention returned to the cave. Despite the mishap, what he saw had him grinning. Once again a wide opening yawned in the cliff face.

TO AVOID MORTAR FIRE reported in northern Kurdistan, the Black Hawk maintained a westerly flight path high above the Iraqi plain. On approach to Mosul it curled right, keeping the city to the west, then headed for its next destination, thirty-five kilometres northeast.

As he gazed out towards the distant city, a great sadness came over Hazo. It had been over thirty years since Saddam Hussein's regime had forced hundreds of thousands of Kurds—Hazo's family among them—to relocate from Mosul to camps in the desolate southern deserts. Those who hadn't cooperated were attacked with Sarin nerve gas.

While in the resettlement camp, Hazo's asthmatic mother had been denied access to critical medicine. She died from the desert's oppressive dry heat. His father, a robust, jovial man and once Mosul's most industrious carpet retailer, had been executed by a firing squad and tossed into a mass grave. Hazo's two older brothers had been killed by a suicide bomber while travelling to seek work in Baghdad, shortly after the US invasion.

Hazo's sombre gaze traced the wide curves of the Tigris to the outskirts of Mosul where mounds and ruins scattered over 1,800 acres marked the site of ancient Nineveh. The Bible said that the prophet Jonah had come here after being spat out from the great fish's belly to proclaim God's word to the wicked Ninevites. But long before Jonah's mission, the city was a religious centre. Hazo pulled out the pictures from the cave, studied the woman who'd been depicted on the wall. Had she been a living being? Or might this be a tribute to the Assyrio-Babylonian goddess Ishtar, as Karsaz had suggested?

An eight-pointed star was Ishtar's mythological symbol, and the woman depicted on the cave wall wore a wristband bearing an eight-petalled rosette. Like most Iraqis, he could recall bits and pieces of the goddess's lore: how the cunning seductress would cruelly annihilate her countless lovers; how, after failing to bed the Babylonian hero Gilgamesh, she'd persuaded the supreme god Anu to release the Great Bull of Heaven to deliver apocalyptic vengeance upon the Babylonians.

Could this really be Ishtar? he thought. He flipped to an image that showed a warrior presenting the female's disembodied head to an elder. He couldn't recall anything about Ishtar being executed so cruelly.

The chopper dipped and began its descent.

Ahead Hazo spotted Mount Maqloub jutting skywards along the fringe of the Nineveh plain. Only as the chopper closed in over the craggy sandstone mountain did the angular lines of the Mar Mattai monastery seem to materialise from the cliff face. Nestled behind the modern façade, with its onion dome marking the main entrance, was one of the world's oldest Christian chapels, founded in AD 363.

The Chaldean monks who resided within the monastery's walls proclaimed to be direct descendants of the Babylonians. They were the earliest Arab Christian converts, the preservers of Aramaic, 'Christ's language'. Here they safeguarded the world's most impressive collection of Syriac Christian manuscripts and ancient codices chronicling Mesopotamia's lesser-known past.

None knew ancient Iraq better.

CLIMBING THE MONASTERY'S precipitous front steps, Hazo pulled the olive wood crucifix from beneath his *galabiya* to display it prominently on his chest. Before he could knock on the main door, a bespectacled young monk with a black beard opened it.

'Shlama illakh,' the monk said, peering over at the unorthodox sight of the Black Hawk plunked down in the parking lot. He glanced at Hazo's crucifix. Switching to English, he said, 'How may I help you, brother?'

Hazo introduced himself. 'I was hoping that one of your brothers might help me. You see, I have these pictures . . .' He held out the photos.

The monk kept his hands folded behind his back as he examined the top photo. His lips drew tight. 'You must talk to Monsignor Ibrahim about these things,' and he set off in a steady shuffle.

The monk led Hazo through the modern corridors of the main building and out a rear door that fed into a spacious courtyard. The humble stone building they entered next was much older—the original monastery. Hazo noticed that the inscriptions glazed into its intricate friezes and mosaics were not Arabic; they were from a language that the world outside these walls considered dead—Aramaic.

The monk continued to a staircase that cut deep beneath the nave. The subterranean atmosphere was disorienting. It seemed as if he was being led into the mountain itself. Hazo's anxiety eased when up ahead he saw bright light coming from a glass doorway fitted with steel bars.

The monk stopped at the door and entered a code into a keypad. He led Hazo into a vast, windowless space divided into aisles by floor-to-ceiling cabinets. The air was sterile and dry. Trailing behind the monk past the long tables that lined the room's centre, Hazo glimpsed spines of countless ancient manuscripts behind glass panels.

Deep in the library, they found the elderly monsignor. Wearing a black robe and hood, he was stooped over a drawing board equipped with a goose-neck LED lamp, sweeping a saucer-sized magnifying loupe horizontally across the open pages of a thick codex.

The monk whispered in the monsignor's ear. The elderly man's suspicious eyes appraised Hazo over his bifocals and he dismissed the monk with a curt nod.

Hazo approached the table and bowed slightly. 'Thank you, Monsignor Ibrahim. I was asked to—'

'Let me see your pictures,' the monsignor demanded. He held out his hand, the severely arthritic fingers quivering. The moment he laid eyes on the first picture, Hazo noticed the creases in his brow deepen.

The monsignor cleared his throat then said, 'Where did you find these?'

'A cave . . . to the east, in the Zagros Mountains. Those images were carved into a wall. There was writing too and—'

The monsignor stopped him. 'I suppose you want to know who this is?' he said, almost as an accusation.

'Well, yes.'

The monsignor eyed Hazo's crucifix. 'Come. I will show you.' He stood up and set off down the aisle.

THE INTERIOR OF HIS CAR was so cold that Thomas Flaherty's breath crystallised the instant it came into contact with the windshield. He started the engine and clicked on the defrosters, then grabbed his trusty scraper. He cursed the Boston winter while he swept snow off the windows. It took him another three minutes to chip away at the ice encrusted on the windshield's wiper blades. Back inside, he pumped the accelerator to speed things along.

Once his fingers had thawed to an itchy tingle, he took out his BlackBerry and started thumbing his preliminary findings into a secure email message addressed to his boss, Lillian Chen, with a CC to Jason Yaeger.

He'd met Jason at GSC only two years ago. In Flaherty's opinion, that high school valedictorian from New Jersey was meant to teach some arcane history course at an Ivy League university or find a cure for cancer—not scour the Middle East for terrorists. But Jason Yaeger was out for vengeance. Hard determination glimmered like a razor's edge in his eyes. To lose a brother the way he had . . .

Composing the email helped Flaherty formalise his initial assessments: Professor Brooke Thompson had been forthright in answering questions about her involvement in an excavation that had taken place in northern Iraq in 2003; though Ms Thompson was unwilling to breach her confidentiality agreement about her findings, the nature of her involvement seemed consistent with her expertise in deciphering ancient languages; and though her back story would require verification, he would not consider her a flight risk should further enquiries be warranted. Flaherty did, however, emphasise that the excavation's implied covert coordination by the US military merited further investigation.

He sent the report off, pocketed the BlackBerry and put the car in drive. The mounting snow constricted the street, making a U-turn impractical. So he continued straight on Museum Road and made a right at the T intersection. As he started along The Fenway, a splash of happy pastel colours set against the dreary grey museum edifice caught his eye. He recognised the sky-blue ski jacket and pink cap that had been hanging on the back of Brooke Thompson's chair.

The sidewalks had yet to be shovelled and she was having a tough time getting the wheels of her rolling attaché case to spin. She had settled for dragging the case over the fresh powder. En route to her car, he guessed.

As Flaherty continued slowly along the slippery roadway, he noticed the door of the museum open. Out came another familiar face: the nosy guy with the Dumbo ears from the café. The guy's beady eyes immediately went to Brooke Thompson, scanned the area, then snapped back to Brooke.

REVELLING IN THE BEAUTY of the fresh fall that blanketed the park, Brooke plodded through the snow. To her right, she noticed that the snow now reached up to the nose of a monumental bronze head. If there was aesthetic intent in plopping a huge head onto the museum's lawn, the message was lost on her. Nonetheless, it jogged memories about the etchings Brooke had studied in that Iraqi cave, which included a graphic retelling of a woman's beheading. Those images, though masterfully crafted, were not intended to elicit artistic appreciation. They were meant to convey a warning.

Maybe if she had been allowed to decipher all the writing on the walls, she'd know the whole story. She had figured out enough to know that whoever the beheaded woman had been, the devastation that followed her was on a grand scale.

During the dig, one of the archaeologists had come outside the cave entrance to get a clear satellite signal for a phone call. She'd overheard his conversation concerning some carbon-dating results. Though he'd not specified the types of organic specimens that had been dated, she'd guessed at some traces of food, flowers or maybe bone.

The archaeologist had specifically mentioned 'a tight confidence interval around 4004 B.C.' In the context of Iraq, this date was impossible for Brooke to forget since a seventeenth-century Irish archbishop named James Ussher had meticulously reconstructed the chronology of biblical events to come up with a very precise date for Creation: Sunday, October 23, 4004 BC. And, like most theologian scholars, Ussher placed Eden in ancient Iraq.

What could they have found inside the cave that could be so important . . . and so ancient?

She clambered over the snow that lined the kerb along Forsyth Way. Across the street, the only car that remained was her green Toyota Corolla. Thanks to a snow plough, the car had practically been buried beneath ice and snow. Luckily, she'd learned to keep a shovel in her trunk for just such occasions.

She went to the rear of the car and tried the frozen trunk lock. But she fumbled the keys and they plopped into the snow. When she dipped down to fish them out, she heard a small popping sound. Something whisked overhead and the lamppost behind her let out a resounding clang.

Startled, she remained in a low crouch. 'What the hell . . .?'

Another small pop sounded and something thwacked into the Corolla's rear quarter panel, dimpling the sheet metal outwards right in front of her face. She screamed and tumbled back into the snow.

Somebody was shooting at her.

THE MARINE COLONEL stood at the base of the slope glaring up at the reopened cave where Jason's men were helping the marines clear more debris. With the sun dropping fast over the horizon, they were working double-time against the imminent nightfall.

'Once the sun's down, we'll need to keep any lighting to a minimum,' Crawford told Jason. His eyes combed the surrounding mountains. 'No need to draw more attention to ourselves.'

'Should be clear skies tonight,' Jason said. 'We'll have plenty of moonlight. The guys probably won't even need their NVGs. The only place we'll need some lighting is in the tunnels.'

Crawford circled his gaze to the two snipers posted outside the cave entrance. 'If it was up to me, I'd skip the formalities and firebomb the bastards. Al-Zahrani or not.'

Jason knew the colonel was only half sincere. 'Washington wants him alive. Intel says he's plotting to—'

'Don't preach the rhetoric to me, Yaeger. I know the score. This war's got too goddamn civil for my taste, is all I'm saying. The prick killed almost 500 civs in one day in those cathedrals last month. In less than a year he's racked up another thousand or so by sending his martyrs into subways, bus stations and malls strapped with C4. And this psycho's just getting warmed up. Wants to make a nice impression on his boss. That way when bin Laden's diseased kidneys finally give out, he can take al-Qaeda to the next level. If we still had some balls in Washington maybe we'd get this done the old-fashioned way.'

Avoiding a political debate, Jason pointed his chin up at the cave. 'Think we should gas them out?'

'Not sure how effective that'll be if we don't get in there first and see how deep those tunnels go. Wouldn't be smart sending men in there.'

Jason agreed. 'You fellas bring a SUGV?'

The Small Unmanned Ground Vehicle, or SUGV, was a thirty-pound compact radio-controlled reconnaissance robot equipped with a single articulating arm, cameras and dual rotary tracks for climbing stairs and rolling over rubble—invaluable for infiltrating terrorist hide-outs and diffusing roadside bombs.

'I was getting to that, Yaeger. We've got a shiny new PackBot in the truck. Not sure how she'll respond in a cave—transmissions might get sketchy.'

'We'll use a fibre-optic line,' Jason replied.

'Worth a try, I suppose. Tell me, where's your Kurd sidekick?'

'Had to go north of Mosul. Shouldn't be much longer.'

'You said he needed to look into something. That was two hours ago. What exactly is he doing?'

'He's following up on a very important lead.'

When Hazo had called earlier, he'd indicated that his cousin had positively identified the American scientist, who'd apparently been chaperoned by a number of military types. Only minutes ago he'd also received an email from Thomas Flaherty, which summarised an initial interview with the archaeologist in Boston—facts that perfectly corroborated Hazo's story. The question was: did Crawford already know something about the excavation that had taken place here in 2003?

'Hazo's got contacts—influential people who know things.'

'Don't diddle my pie hole, Yaeger. What "things"?'

Jason squared off with the colonel. 'The kind of things that lead us to trapping Fahim Al-Zahrani in a cave when every branch of the military thinks he's in Afghanistan. So I tend not to bust his balls for staying out late on a fact-finding mission. Capeesh?'

Crawford's jaw jutted out. 'I'm warning you—don't mess with me. If I find out there's something you're not telling me . . .' For maximum effect, he let the threat linger.

But Jason wasn't backing down. 'Info sharing is a two-way street, Colonel. We're both fighting the same enemy.'

THE REALISATION that someone was trying to kill her made Brooke Thompson respond in the way her mom had drilled into her head since childhood, 'Help!' she screamed. 'HELP!'

With the snowstorm having driven everyone home early, there was no one close by to hear. The nearest pedestrian was almost a block away, a guy in a hooded fleece. She tried again, louder this time, 'Heeeelp!'

The guy kept moving.

Both shots seemed to have come from the same direction, which meant the gunman was somewhere along the path she'd walked from the museum. Brooke scrambled on all fours along the kerb to keep the Corolla between them.

She pulled off her pink cap, then popped her head up over the four inches of snow that covered the Corolla's hood. The shooter was easy to spot: a thin man wearing a grey overcoat and a black snowcap. She fully expected the face to belong to Agent Thomas Flaherty, but the big ears and aquiline features weren't his. The man swung a handgun directly at her head and the muzzle flashed white.

As she ducked, the shot glanced the snow on the Corolla's hood and zipped out perilously close to her scalp.

'Heeeeeeeeelp!'

In less than five seconds, she guessed, he'd be circling the car to close in for the kill. And there was nothing she could do about it.

WHEN FLAHERTY SAW DUMBO pull out a Glock, he pushed down hard on the Concorde's accelerator. The car fishtailed in the snow before finding traction on a patch of rock salt and shooting forward. The gunman fired off two shots that kept the archaeologist pinned down behind her car.

Christ, did he hit her? was all Flaherty could think.

Then the guy dashed out in the roadway on Forsyth Avenue and managed a third shot.

'No, no, no!'

Sliding a wide right onto Forsyth Avenue, Flaherty fought the steering wheel to straighten the car on the slick road. He leaned on the horn and depressed the accelerator again. Now he had Dumbo's attention. The guy planted himself in the centre of the street at twenty metres, levelled the Glock at the Concorde's windshield.

Dipping below the dashboard, Flaherty jammed down on the brakes while cutting the wheel hard to the left. The round thwunked into the passenger-side doorframe. The Concorde swung into a sideways skid, but the forward momentum kept it on a direct line for the shooter.

Still low, Flaherty reached for his underarm holster and unsnapped his Beretta.

There was a thump that continued over the car's rear window, then trunk, that was certainly the gunman. Flaherty immediately popped up and saw the Corolla directly ahead. He braced himself for the impact. The Concorde's bumper clipped the side of the Corolla and the car spun another ninety degrees so that he was now looking at the erratic tyre tracks he'd left in the snow. The downed gunman was already making a move for his fumbled Glock, his right leg hobbling from the car-jumping stunt.

Flaherty threw open the driver's door, thrust the gun into the opening and pulled the trigger. The shot wasn't well aimed, but it forced Dumbo to abandon the Glock and go scrambling for cover behind a construction barricade that cordoned off the sidewalk.

Keeping his eyes on the barricade, Flaherty reached across to the passenger door and pushed it open.

'Brooke, it's me, Agent Flaherty! Get in the car!'

He heard feet crunching through snow. She bounded into the seat beside him then pulled the door shut.

'Stay down,' he told her.

Flaherty shifted the car into reverse and pushed down on the accelerator, spinning the tyres. As soon as the car got moving, he flipped the gun to his left hand and powered down his window.

Sure enough, Dumbo jumped out over the barricade and began running at the car. He was gripping a back-up pistol. Flaherty shot at him. His left-handed aim was lousy and the assassin sensed it—he didn't break stride or deviate to either side, just kept coming.

'Damn, he's fast,' Flaherty grumbled. He fired again and saw the round spit snow close to the assassin's feet. He pushed harder on the accelerator, trying like hell to keep the car on a straight line. Another quick glance in the rearview showed that the intersection was directly behind. No time for a three-point turn. Blindly racing into traffic wouldn't be smart, either. That meant another fancy manoeuvre.

Flaherty jerked the wheel all the way to the left while at the same time easing off the gas. With the tyres grabbing nothing but ice and powder, the car initiated a wicked spin. At the ninety-degree mark, he cranked the wheel in the opposite direction and pushed down on the accelerator. The timing was good, but the result was far from perfect. The car slid more than the 180 degrees he intended, and caught the kerb and the snow heaped along it.

Flaherty got the car moving again and didn't look back.

THE MONSIGNOR SLID OPEN the glass door of a bookcase and pulled out a leather-bound codex. 'I presume you know the Creation story?'

Hazo nodded.

The monsignor's lips twisted into a wry smile. He set the richly illustrated manuscript on a bookstand and, using a flat-tipped stylus, began leafing through the ancient pages.

'Ah, yes. See here,' he said, stopping on a page and tapping the tip of the stylus on its central drawing. He straightened and took a step to the side. 'Look familiar?'

Hazo leaned in to examine the drawing, which replicated images in his photos. The detail was incredibly accurate. So accurate that he could believe only that the artist must have seen the cave itself. 'It is the same.'

'The words speak of the beginning of recorded history. A time when God cleansed the earth with water to begin anew. When the first woman created by God had returned to paradise to seek retribution.'

'This has to do with Eve?' Hazo said, now completely perplexed.

The old man shook his head and smiled knowingly. 'No, not Eve.' He whispered conspiratorially, 'Lilith.'

'Lilith?' Hazo scrutinised the ancient drawing. 'I don't understand.'

'Eve was not the first woman created by God,' the monsignor explained. From a nearby bookshelf, he retrieved a bible and turned to the first page. 'If you read Genesis 1 and Genesis 2 carefully, you will discover two separate accounts of God's creation of humans. In Genesis 1, man and woman are created simultaneously. Listen.' He traced the lines of the Bible with the stylus then read, '"So God created man in his own image, in the image of God he created them; male and female he created them."' His eyes shifted from the page. 'Just like He created every creature in duality to facilitate procreation.'

'Simultaneously,' Hazo said in a low voice.

'That is right. Yet it is the second account told in Genesis 2 that most remember. When a lonely Adam wanders the garden of paradise, and God, in afterthought, decides that man needs a spiritual companion.'

'When God takes Adam's rib to make Eve.'

The old man smiled. 'Not literally a rib. A better translation would refer to "his side". Eve was Adam's second partner, his consummated wife, who the Bible tells us was destined by God to be dominated by her husband. Lilith, the first woman created by God, was the opposite. She had a voracious sexual appetite, always demanding to be, how shall we say . . . on top of Adam. She was anything but subservient.'

'But it doesn't say those things in the Bible, does it?'

The monk smiled. 'Any references to Lilith were long ago removed from Genesis by the patriarchal Catholic Church, which didn't like the idea of such a dominant female figure. However, I can show you another picture that will help you understand this.'

The monk disappeared behind the stacks and returned with a modern coffee-table book titled *Masterpieces of the Vatican Museums*.

'In 1509, Michelangelo painted Lilith's picture on the ceiling of the Sistine Chapel—the fresco called *The Temptation of Adam and Eve*.'

He turned the book to Hazo so he could see the photo.

'Michelangelo based this narrative painting on an apocryphal text called "The Treaty of the Left Emanation", which said that after God had banished Lilith from Eden, she'd returned in the form of a serpent to coax her replacement, Eve, into eating the forbidden fruit.'

Hazo studied the image that combined two scenes: the half woman, half serpent, entwined around the tree, reaching out to Adam and Eve, and, beside it, the angel expelling the couple from paradise.

'This is the pivotal event in Christianity that speaks to Original Sin and the downfall of humankind. All attributed, of course, to the sin of a woman.'

'Amazing,' Hazo said.

'There is one obscure reference to Lilith in the Old Testament as well. When Isaiah speaks of God's vengeance on the land of Edom, warning them that the lush paradise will be rendered infertile and pestilence will bring desolation.'

'So she is specifically mentioned in the Bible,' Hazo said.

'Indeed. Lilith is also mentioned throughout Jewish apocrypha, the Dead Sea Scrolls, the Talmud, the Kabbalah, the Book of Zohar, and the medieval *Alphabet of Ben Sira*. All portray her as a demonic seductress who tortured men and made them impotent. But Lilith's story goes back much further than this.'

The monk explained that when the Babylonians destroyed Jerusalem in 586 BC, King Nebuchadnezzar II exiled the Jewish priests to Babylon. Having lost the Jerusalem temple and its sacred texts, the priests recreated a written account of their heritage, borrowing heavily from Mesopotamian mythology. Many of those stories had been traced to the third millennium BC, to cuneiform texts that spoke of the Lilitu—demons of the night, bearers of pestilence who wandered desolate places to wreak havoc on humankind.

'The legend of Lilith may be the most ancient tale ever told,' the monsignor said. 'How old, no one really knows. But most would agree that Lilith is the progenitor of all female demons that later emerge in Mesopotamian, Greek and Roman mythology.'

The monk removed his glasses and his expression turned severe.

'Perhaps now you know too much, my son. Because these photos of yours . . . these are very ancient images of the story of God's creation of the first woman. The story of paradise lost. And though it may sound crazy, if not impossible, it appears to me that you've stumbled upon a legendary place.'

'Tell me,' Hazo beseeched.

The monk pointed to the last photo showing men busily preparing a headless body for burial.

'Lilith's tomb.'

CHAPTER FIVE

'What the hell was that all about?' Brooke fumed, as she tried to buckle her seat belt with tremulous fingers. 'Who was that guy?'

'Damned if I know,' Flaherty said, checking the rearview mirror again.

'Who do you work for again? CIA?'

He shook his head. 'Global Security Corporation. Just like it says on my business card. We're a US defence contractor, among other things.'

'Other things?'

He sighed, then told her, 'GSC provides the staffing services every civilised country needs: mercenaries, spies, bodyguards, counter-terrorist agents, cyber defence techs. Those kinds of "things".' He glanced over at her to gauge her response.

'How do I know that guy with the gun wasn't one of your men?'

'Definitely not. Our assassins are a helluva lot better than that. You'd have been dead, probably from a car bomb. Or at least a discreet sniper shot,' he said after giving the logistics momentary consideration.

'Thanks. That's comforting.'

'Hey, if you didn't notice, those bullets were coming in my direction too,' he reminded her.

'I suppose,' she relented. 'You know, you weren't exactly a marksman back there, either.'

He couldn't help but grin. This woman was definitely feisty. 'For the record, that's the first time I've ever had to fire a gun at something other than a range target. And in my defence, shooting with my left hand while speeding in reverse on snow wasn't in my training repertoire.'

'So what exactly is your repertoire?'

'I'm an information guy. Intelligence. Glorified desk jockey. I interrogate witnesses and suspects . . . that sort of thing.'

'Sounds like you're a paid conversationalist.'

'Or a bullshit detector.' He smiled.

She tried to suppress a laugh, but failed. The adrenaline buzz was abating and her muscles were starting to go limp again.

'God, that was scary.'

'Amen, sister. That was wicked crazy back there.'

Running her fingers through her wet hair, she blew out a long breath. 'So now what? Are you supposed to protect me or something?'

'Our local office is next to the Federal Building downtown. We'll head there, figure out what to do.'

Brooke stared out the frosty window.

'Look. Here's the deal. A colleague asked me to find you. He's a deep-cover operative in Iraq. He's the one who found your ID badge. I know that if he suspected you were in danger, he'd have told me.'

'How do I know he didn't call that guy too?'

'Not a chance,' he said.

'Well, someone wants me dead. And the timing can't be a coincidence. It's got to be someone in the military, right?' she insisted.

Flaherty said nothing, because on that point, he'd have to concur. It had him wondering who else besides Jason could possibly have known about Brooke's involvement in Iraq and could also be capable of coordinating a kill order so quickly. Why had she suddenly become a threat?

'We need to find this Frank guy you were talking about. I need that email address.' Flaherty pulled out his BlackBerry. He keyed in his security code and held it out for her. 'You said his address was on your computer, right?'

Staring at the device, she asked, 'Why didn't you give this to me earlier?'

'Basic psychology. I ask you for information, and your future response, your compliance or lack thereof, indicates your propensity to cooperate.'

'Or maybe you just wanted to give me your card so I'd call you. I have a bullshit detector too.'

She took the BlackBerry and tried logging into her email account. 'Huh. That's weird.'

'What?'

'Says my username and password are invalid. Like my account is gone. That's impossible.'

Flaherty sighed. 'No, actually, it's not.'

'What do you mean?'

'NSA. That's my guess. Thirty thousand computer scientists and cryptographers under one roof in Fort Meade, dedicated to cracking data and voice communications, can do just about anything when they have your number. Remember those geeks in high school, the video-game junkies? Imagine a building full of 'em.'

'God,' she groaned. 'I like video games too, but I'm not snooping around people's private information.'

'You've got to have something else from this guy, right? A business card, a pay cheque . . .?'

She shook her head. 'No card. And the money was wired to my account.' Then she thought back to eavesdropping on the archaeologist who'd performed the carbon studies. 'Wait. There was this archaeologist who was at the cave when I was there. He was outside the cave, making a cellphone call. Something about test results on samples he'd sent out. I overheard him mention an AMS lab where he'd sent samples for testing.'

'AMS lab?'

'Accelerator Mass Spectrometer. The machine used for carbon-dating studies.'

'Remember the name of the place?'

'No. Damn.' Then she remembered something else. 'But there were other test results he'd mentioned. Biological cultures or something. He was reading from a report that had an official seal on its cover. Some kind of weird insignia. I remember it had a symbol representing a DNA helix, or chromosomes. And it had a long acronym that began with USA . . .'

Flaherty feared he knew what she meant. 'Type in this web address.' He had to repeat the tricky URL three times.

Once Brooke brought up the home page, she immediately recognised the insignia. 'Yeah, that's it!'

For Flaherty, this was anything but good news. 'Great,' he grumbled.

There was a long acronym beside the insignia: USAMRIID.

'I remember the two "I's" in the name too,' she said. 'Reminded me of Roman numerals. Says here "United States Army Medical Research Institute of Infectious Diseases".'

'Exactly,' Flaherty said. He let out another sigh. This assignment was fast snowballing into something much bigger. 'Among other things, that's America's bioweapons division.'

'WHAT DO YOU MEAN she got away?' Crawford snapped into the sat-com's microphone.

'There was someone else there. A detective, I think,' the caller replied.

'So?' He circled around the MRAP to avoid being overheard by the marines milling around the camp.

'I had her pinned down. Was moving in to finish her. The guy came out of nowhere. Took me down with his car, started shooting. He managed to take her away.'

'You listen to me, you incompetent scumbag . . . You find her, you kill her. Or I'll have your head, you hear me?' Crawford terminated the call.

Deliberating on how to inform Stokes about the mishap, he finally settled on sending a text message—short and sweet.

Who was this detective who had beaten them to the archaeologist? Only someone on the inside could have sent him. The fact that the woman's ID badge had been sitting next to Yaeger's computer left little doubt as to the culprit.

Crawford bounded over to the command tent where Yaeger and his tech were helping the marines prepare the recon robot. He reined in his fury and considered how to approach Yaeger. This kid was no automaton—wouldn't be doing this kind of work if he was. Any guy who passed the psych profile to go deep cover wouldn't be the type to back down. If Yaeger had an agenda, he certainly wasn't going to divulge it.

'Sergeant,' Crawford called out.

The mercenary looked up. 'Yeah.'

'Walk with me,' Crawford said, pacing away from the tent. 'I need to know if you've spoken to anyone about what's happening here.'

Jason's response was forthright, 'You, air command . . .'

'Don't be coy with me, Sergeant,' Crawford warned. He needed to be direct, without raising undue suspicion. 'Someone on the outside. Did you communicate with non-military, civilians perhaps?'

'Why would I do that?'

Crawford tried to decipher Yaeger's gaze, but read nothing.

'Until we confirm exactly who's holed up in that cave, I want all communication running through me. I know you want this guy in there to be Al-Zahrani but, until we're absolutely certain, this operation has to be airtight. Let me have your sat-com.' He held out his hand.

Jason merely stared at the hand. 'You know I can't do that, Colonel.' He looked deep into Crawford's hard eyes. 'Don't make me remind you that I'm accountable to a different authority. So if you have a concern, best for you to voice it. I don't like playing games—especially not when the stakes are so high.'

Crawford shook his head like a disappointed parent. 'Yeah, the stakes are high. Ten million high for you, isn't that right? Free agents like you don't get it. True soldiers aren't motivated by bonuses. And don't cry to me about your story, 'cause I've already heard how your brother died in the Towers. This little vendetta of yours seems too personal. One might say it compromises your objectivity.'

Jason kept his cool. 'Since you've done your homework, you should know that my psych examination suggests otherwise. Don't forget that I have people too. And I'm starting to feel that I need to check your background.'

Crawford flashed a sardonic grin. 'Until we know what and whom we're dealing with up there I'd appreciate it if you did not stir the hornets' nest, is all I'm saying.'

Staring into the colonel's shifty eyes, Jason counted to five to decompress. 'The bot's prepped and ready,' he replied calmly. 'I've got work to do.' He didn't wait to be dismissed—just sidestepped Crawford and strode to the tent.

RANDALL STOKES STARED at the computer screen wondering when Frank Roselli's elusive email would make an appearance in his inbox.

This morning's cleanup had Stokes's lower left eyelid twitching and his neck muscles quaking in spasm—his body's most recurrent stress valves. Even the skin on his hands was breaking out in an itchy rash. No doubt that was due to Crawford's blunt update concerning the botched kill order on the Boston mark. Normally, this wouldn't overly concern Stokes. Except this time the mysterious white knight who'd thwarted the assassin had been overheard asking the mark probing questions about Iraq.

Three kill confirmations had already arrived: an archaeologist in Geneva, a biocontainment engineer in Munich, a microbiologist in Moscow. No complications or interference. No interloper. Therefore, the archaeologist was an isolated problem that, in all probability, linked directly to the ID card the deep-cover unit had found near the cave.

Turning his attention back to the business at hand, Stokes brought up a new window and entered three pass keys. A chequerboard of live video feeds came online—sixteen closed-circuit cameras, equipped with audio and infrared, transmitting interior shots of the labyrinth via an encrypted digital signal.

Fourteen cameras showed no movement—only still shots of winding passageways walled by jagged rock glowing in emerald night vision. The scene on cameras '01E' and '11G', however, were far from static.

Stokes double-clicked the grid box for '11G' and the window enlarged on the screen. The live shot showed five heavily armed Arabs funnelling single file through the tunnel, moving deeper into the mountain, still frantically searching for an alternative exit.

No one knew better than Stokes that the cave had only one accessible opening—precisely the reason the ancient Mesopotamians, and Stokes himself, had chosen the site. After all, the lair's primary purpose was to contain evil, both then and now.

Stokes grinned widely. 'Hello, gentlemen. Welcome to Armageddon. So glad you could make it. Those weapons aren't going to help you now. Nothing can help you now.' He put both elbows on the desk and cradled his chin on folded hands, beaming.

When the tall man in the middle came close to the camera, Stokes paused the feed and minutely studied the infamous face. Fahim Al-Zahrani. The odds were incredible, on the outer fringe of impossible, yet the picture didn't lie. The Lord had brought the Dark Prince into the lion's den for ultimate judgment. How poetic, thought Stokes.

He heard a pecking sound and turned to see a white dove perched outside his window. An untrained observer might consider this a miracle since doves weren't native to the Mojave Desert. However, it wasn't uncommon for local hotels to release flights of doves during wedding ceremonies. But surely this lone messenger had been sent for Stokes.

He has given me a sign that the time has come.

'Thank you, Lord. I am your servant. I am your avenger.'

With renewed vigour, Stokes turned back to the computer and input the encryption keys that brought up the Remote Systems Interface. Using this simple command module, Stokes could manage the critical systems installed in the cave's deepest, most protected chamber. He stared at the main panel where seven indicator icons blinked 'SEALED'. He moved the pointer over the first icon and let his index finger hover over the mouse button.

'Is it time, Lord? Give me a sign.'

The sign he received was not what he expected: a new message alert chimed over the computer speakers.

Stokes immediately switched to check his inbox. An absurd thought came to him: might God be so bold as to communicate through email?

But the message was from Crawford. 'NEED MORE TIME.'

Stokes turned to the window but the dove was no longer there. The rash on his hands suddenly flared and he scratched at it incessantly with a letter opener, with little relief.

'I DON'T UNDERSTAND. How could the Infectious Disease guys have anything to do with the cave?' Brooke asked.

'We've had bioweapons teams in Iraq since we first set foot there,' Flaherty replied. 'Remember, Iraq supposedly had a huge cache of WMDs.'

Brooke keyed USAMRIID into Wikipedia and scrolled the entry. The more Brooke read, the more the military's biodefence division sounded like a biological bakery that specialised in the most unsavoury recipes. She wasn't sure whether to praise or fear its existence. 'Who runs this place?'

'USAMRIID'—Flaherty pronounced the acronym phonetically: you-sam-rid—'answers to the US Army Medical Research and Materiel Command. An army colonel oversees the operation.'

'So why would an archaeologist have been talking to these people?'

'Probably wasn't an archaeologist, is my guess.'

'If samples had been sent to this agency for testing, there'd be a record of it, right?'

'Maybe.'

'Can you call one of your people to check it out . . . to see if tests were performed on samples from Iraq during that time?'

'That's a good idea,' he said. 'But first, I need to call my guy in Iraq . . . let him know what happened back at the museum.'

In the side mirror, Flaherty eyed the illuminated headlights of a Ford Explorer that had turned in behind him three blocks earlier. The SUV trailed at a comfortable distance, occasionally falling back two or three car lengths. Nothing to worry about . . . yet.

Flaherty pulled out his sat-com and called Yaeger.

'Hey, Jason,' Flaherty said loudly into the sat-com's microphone. 'It's Tommy. Can you hear me?'

'Yeah. What's up?'

'Found your scientist in Boston.'

'She as cute as her picture?'

'Actually, she's in the car with me. Let me put you on speaker.'

Once the introductions were over, Flaherty said, 'Brooke was there in 2003. Part of an excavation team that studied that cave you uncovered. She deciphered an ancient language . . . some writings found on a wall.'

'I've seen the writing,' Jason confirmed. 'Pictures, too . . . carved into the left wall of the entry tunnel.'

'Beautiful, aren't they?' she said.

'What does it all mean?'

'It's a bit complicated. But it's the earliest recorded specimen of ancient Mesopotamian mythology . . . a story about a woman who came from another land.' Having almost been murdered, Brooke was comfortable with throwing her confidentiality agreement to the wind.

'The woman who was decapitated?' Jason asked.

'That's the one.'

'Why did they kill her?'

'The story implies that many people died shortly after her arrival. Similar to a witch hunt, I suppose,' Brooke guessed. 'She was different, came from a faraway place. They didn't understand her.'

'And they blamed her for the deaths,' Jason said.

'Correct.'

There was a pause, and Brooke knew that Jason was trying to understand the military's interest in this archaeological discovery.

'What was her name?'

'Actually, it wasn't specified in the writings I studied.' Evil didn't really need a name, she thought.

Flaherty recapped Brooke's story. He explained her role in the excavation sponsored by none other than the US military, the tight security procedures, the mysterious facilitator known only as 'Frank'.

Brooke held up the BlackBerry and tapped on the USAMRIID logo.

'I'm afraid it gets even stranger,' Flaherty warned. 'It wasn't just the military that watched over the excavation. Seems USAMRIID was involved.'

'What? You mean the biochem guys?'

'Yeah.'

Another pause.

'All right,' Jason said. 'We're prepping a recon bot to send into the cave. I've got enough surprises to worry about.'

'I'm afraid there's something else. Right after I spoke to Brooke, some guy with a gun came after her.'

'Christ,' Jason groaned in frustration.

'Yeah, we barely got out of there alive,' Flaherty painted a quick picture of the incident outside the museum.

'That's too much of a coincidence for my taste,' Jason said.

'Not sure who the gunman was or who might have sent him,' Flaherty said. 'But it seems USAMRIID sent out some samples for processing. If our guys can dig through their records, we might find out what they were studying and who ordered the tests.'

'Smart thinking. Look, Tommy, you two need to keep safe until we figure out what's going on here.'

'I know. I'm taking Brooke to the office now.' Flaherty said. 'You watch over your shoulder too.'

The line went dead. Flaherty pocketed the phone.

'Sounds like a clever fellow,' Brooke said.

'If only you knew,' Flaherty said. In the rearview mirror, the angular headlights swooped in from behind—the vehicle a mere shadow. Checking the wing mirror, Flaherty saw a Hyundai sedan in the fast lane, three car lengths back. Then the vehicle tailing him made another abrupt manoeuvre and eclipsed the Hyundai. Flaherty glimpsed the driver's silhouette. When he discerned the driver's big ears, his heart jumped into his throat.

'Red light!' Brooke yelled, throwing both hands onto the dashboard. Instead of slowing, Agent Flaherty stomped on the accelerator and blew through the intersection.

'Are you crazy?' she cried.

'That's him behind us in the Explorer.'

He considered a U-turn along the wide avenue, but the traffic coming in the opposite direction was too heavy.

'Here we go,' he warned Brooke and cut a hard right that threw her up against his legs, hard enough to make her see stars.

The Concorde careened through a line of construction barricades, giving the Explorer the split second needed to close the gap. The roadway fed into a wide tunnel with tiled walls and began a sharp descent beneath Copley Place. The Concorde's tyres squealed as Flaherty steered into the bend.

Brooke was disoriented by what little she could see: ceiling tiles and lights. 'You turned into a garage?'

'Not a garage. I'm taking a short cut to the Mass Pike.'

'You're going down into the tunnel?'

He nodded.

She'd driven this ramp many times—a main exit for Interstate 90, which snaked deep below the city centre. Problem being that she knew the traffic flow only went up. 'This tunnel is a one-way exit! You're going the wrong—'

'I know! It's OK.' He checked the mirror and could see the Explorer's headlights skimming the curved wall behind him. 'The ramp's closed for construction.'

But up ahead, where the ramp merged at a Y, he spotted a hulking utility truck and workers in hard hats. Not OK, he thought.

The truck was at a standstill in the centre of the roadway with barely any room to spare to its right. But there was no stopping now. Flaherty punched the accelerator and leaned on the horn. Seeing the headlights racing towards them, the befuddled workmen barely had time to react. They hit the deck and grabbed hold of the safety rail. Flaherty pulled slightly to the right to aim for the narrow opening. He clenched his teeth.

The wide-bodied Concorde slipped cleanly through the gap with inches to spare on either side. But not fifteen metres ahead, a second truck blocked his lane. Flaherty corrected the wheel hard to the left and slalomed around the vehicle, so close that the passenger-side wing mirror sheared off.

His heart was in overdrive and adrenaline had all his senses buzzing. Knowing that the most dangerous leg of this obstacle course still lay ahead only added to his anxiety.

In his remaining side mirror he saw the Explorer bob and weave to avoid the second truck, grinding the Explorer's side panels along the tunnel wall in a plume of orange sparks.

'Son of a bitch. Can't shake him,' Flaherty grumbled.

The tunnel arced downwards like the curl of a question mark and he braked lightly along the sharp bend until it yielded to a long and empty stretch. He hit the gas hard and the surreal sensation of rocketing through the tunnel's tight confines made him feel like a bullet being shot through the barrel of a gun.

Ahead Flaherty spotted construction barriers topped with flashing amber lights. Immediately beyond the cordon, the ramp joined the interstate tunnel at an extremely tight Y. However, with Flaherty coming the wrong way down the ramp the turn would be treacherous. He could see the headlights of vehicles zipping through the tunnel at highway speed.

He stamped on the brake pedal. The car bowled through the barriers, flinging them up and out. He pulled the wheel all the way to the right and the car commenced a runaway spin into the oncoming traffic.

The next second was a blur of screeching tyres and blaring horns.

The Concorde dragged heavily across the roadway, avoided a sedan cruising along the slow lane, but careened sideways into a yellow removals truck in the fast lane. Flaherty felt the Concorde's front end crumple and snap. The collision was bone-crunching, but prevented the Concorde from striking the cement median, even managed to pull the car straight with forward momentum.

Flaherty's heart nearly gave out when he heard a bellowing air horn that could belong only to a very large truck. His eyes snapped to his side mirror and he saw the Explorer cut blindly into the roadway—a grave miscalculation that put the assassin directly into the path of a hulking semitrailer. The big rig locked its brakes and the cab jostled madly from side to side, its tyres churning grey smoke.

But the Explorer couldn't accelerate fast enough and the semi struck with brute force. The Explorer seemed to explode into a thousand pieces—glass and metal shooting out in all directions.

Flaherty barely glimpsed the assassin's body as it was catapulted through the windshield. In the wing mirror, he stole a final glimpse of the jackknifed trailer and the mangled Explorer. Then he sped off through the tunnel.

CHAPTER SIX

The Black Hawk bounced to a rest in a moonlit field just beyond the perimeter of the encampment. Hazo unbuckled himself and hopped out. By the time he was clear of the rotorwash, Jason had come down the slope to meet him.

'Glad you're back,' Jason said. He hooked Hazo by the arm and led him past a dozen marines gathered nearby. Once they were out of earshot, he asked, 'How did you make out?' Glancing back to the command tent, he saw Crawford standing stiffly with arms crossed, leering over at him.

'I discovered many things. Many disturbing things,' Hazo clarified. 'As I told you, my cousin recognised the woman on the ID badge.'

'Not long after you left, my guy in the States found this woman. Had a talk with her. It all agrees with what your cousin told you. How about your visit to the monastery? Were the monks able to help you with the pictures from the cave?'

'Oh yes,' Hazo said. He told Jason about the conversation he'd had with Monsignor Ibrahim—the incredible story of Creation and a wicked woman named Lilith. 'The monsignor told me that this cave . . . The legends say that it is Lilith's tomb.'

'Tomb?' Brooke Thompson hadn't mentioned this.

'That is right. These monks are very smart. They know many secrets, many hidden truths.' He gazed warily at the cave opening. 'The monsignor told me that she is buried beneath the mountain,' he said in a whisper. 'This place is evil, Jason. Cursed.'

'Buddy, don't let the monk's stories scare you. Last I checked, ancient tombs don't have steel security doors. And the only evil inside that mountain is still alive and kicking and armed with a rocket launcher. All right?'

Hazo nodded.

'You did great,' Jason said. 'But right now, we've got a much bigger problem to deal with. This guy Crawford hasn't said one word about the military having been in that cave.'

'But would he know about it?' Hazo said.

'I'm thinking yes, he does. And I'll tell you why.' He detailed the call he'd received from Thomas Flaherty—the thwarted assassination attempt on Brooke Thompson.

Hazo was deeply disturbed. 'Crawford sent an assassin to find her?'

'The timing is too convenient for me to think otherwise.' Jason glanced across to the lights of the command tent. Crawford had his back to them, talking furtively into his satellite phone. 'And he's been on that phone an awful lot.' He shook his head. 'We've got to watch our backs on this one.'

Suddenly something else caught Jason's eye—a dark form sweeping in and out of the moonlight high up near the mountain's crest. A watcher was skulking in the darkness. 'We've got company.'

Hazo's eyes shifted up to the mountaintop and panned slowly back and forth. 'Yes. I see him.'

'I don't like this one bit,' Jason said. 'Let's walk over here.' With Hazo keeping pace beside him, Jason headed for the terrorists' four abandoned pick-up trucks, which the marines had parked in a neat row beside the road. When they'd reached the vehicles, Jason reached into his pocket and pulled out a marker pen. He began drawing a circle on the hood of the first Toyota.

Not seeing any ink coming out from the marker's tip, Hazo was confused. 'I don't understand. It doesn't do anything.'

'That's the point. The ink is invisible to the naked eye,' Jason explained. 'But not to military satellites.'

'Ah,' Hazo said. 'Very clever.'

'Makes it easy to track vehicle movements from the sky.' He casually moved to the next pick-up and scrawled an invisible star on its hood. Another glance to the camp, and Jason stepped up to the third pick-up. This time, he traced out a square. On the hood of the fourth pick-up, he drew an invisible triangle. Capping the marker, he slipped it back inside his pocket. Then he pointed to each pick-up in turn, saying, 'Circle . . . star . . . square . . . triangle,' committing each pick-up to memory.

'Very good,' Hazo said, impressed.

'And since we're on the topic of satellites . . .' Jason pulled out his binoculars, activated the infrared, and discreetly spied Crawford's position in the tent. The colonel was still on his call, pacing in small circles. 'Who are you talking to, Crawford?' Jason muttered to himself. He used the laser to calculate Crawford's GPS grid. Then he flipped open his sat-com and put out a call of his own—one that Crawford certainly would not approve.

'Mack, it's Yaeger. I need a big favour,' Jason said. On the other end of the line, he could hear Macgregor Driscoll, GSC's star Communications and Remote Weapons Specialist, crunching away on some potato chips. 'I've got a guy here in Iraq who's been making lots of calls with the intent of undermining our mission. If I give you his coordinates, can you see if you can listen in on him?'

'I'll give it a go.'

Jason twice repeated the GPS data for Crawford's current position. Then he heard Mack tapping away on a keyboard, linking in to the commercial satellite network to triangulate the signal.

'Hmm. Got the signal . . .' More tapping. 'Oh yeah, that's gonna be a problem. Your caller's not using a voice channel . . . and he's transmitting in digital, not analogue. It's all bouncing through military satellites. Nice of you to say you want me to eavesdrop on the marines.'

'Sorry,' Jason said. 'Can you crack the encryption?'

'Four-thousand-ninety-six-bit RSA secure-key encryption?' Mack cackled. 'Don't think so. That shit was invented because of guys like me.'

'All right,' Jason said. There had to be another way. 'So the caller and the person he's calling each have a key cipher?'

'That's right. Both phones use the same key encryption software.'

'How about this: can you locate the second key?'

'Yeah, sure,' Mack replied matter-of-factly.

Jason listened to fifteen seconds of click-clacking accompanied by Mack's heavy breathing.

'Well helloooo . . .' Mack sang in pleased revelation. 'You just got very lucky, Yaeger.'

'How's that?'

'This call's being routed through a ground station in San Francisco. Still can't tell you what they're talking about. But I can tell you exactly where the other caller's phone is plugged into a wall jack.'

'That would be great.'

'Huh. I think your guy might be calling his bookie.'

'Come again?'

'Your marine is talking to someone in Vegas.'

'Las Vegas? You sure about that?'

'Yup. And it gets even weirder. Seems his bookie is an evangelist.'

AGENT THOMAS FLAHERTY and Professor Brooke Thompson had arrived at the branch office of Global Security Corporation. Brooke now sat alone in Flaherty's spartan cubicle, peering out of the east-facing window that provided a spectacular tenth-floor view of downtown Boston.

The past half hour had been a whirlwind. After their harrowing escape, Flaherty had exited the Mass Pike and continued on to downtown. His wrecked car had been ignored by the police cruisers, which sped past in response to the fatal collision blocking the interstate tunnel.

News of the assassin's failed attempt would take time to disseminate back to the unknown client, Flaherty had told her. And that precious time 'off the grid' provided them a fleeting tactical advantage.

'Brooke,' a voice squawked over the intercom on the desk phone. 'It's me. Flaherty. Look to your left.'

She saw Flaherty's head above the cubicles of the open-plan office.

'Come on over here,' he said. 'There's someone I'd like you to meet.'

The person to whom Flaherty was referring stood from her chair as Brooke approached. Barely reaching the agent's shoulder, the petite woman had bobbed grey hair and wore a tasteful flannel trouser-suit.

'Annie is our resident expert on satellite surveillance. Our eye in the sky.'

'Hi, Brooke. Tommy's told me you've had a crazy day.'

She rolled her eyes. 'It's been like a bad movie.'

'Take a look at this,' Flaherty said, pointing to the images on the display that they'd been reviewing.

Easing into the chair, Brooke stared at the monitor, which showed a detailed aerial shot of a highly diverse terrain. There were mountains to the top and right of the screen, green flatlands in the middle and to the left, and brownish tans blending in at the bottom. Roadways appeared as thin lines, and webbed throughout the land to connect a disparate matrix of dense cities. Though for Brooke, the rivers snaking through the plains were the region's true fingerprint.

'Just want you to confirm something for us,' Flaherty said. 'We're looking at—'

'Northern Iraq,' she said.

Annie smiled. 'Right.'

Brooke anticipated Flaherty's request. 'The cave was right here, in the mountains.' She pointed to the exact spot. 'There.' She looked up at Flaherty. 'Did I pass the test?'

He smiled. 'Yup.'

Annie leaned in to get a closer look. 'That's it,' she confirmed, and zoomed in on the cave.

'With the eight-hour time difference, it's night there right now,' Flaherty said. 'So this isn't a live shot. It was taken earlier today.'

Bending over Brooke's shoulder, Flaherty used a pen as a pointer. 'A few hours ago, our deep-cover field agents ambushed four trucks on the roadway here,' he said, pointing to the winding gravel ribbon running along the bottom of the screen. 'Some of the militants escaped . . . went up this slope.' Using the pen, he traced the approximate path to the cave.

'Wow,' Brooke said, staring at the mini war zone. 'It's hard to imagine that this area was once a lush paradise.'

'Really?' Annie said.

'Back in 4000 BC there was a huge village here.' With her finger Brooke indicated the plain to the west of the foothills. 'A trading outpost. The major trade routes for ancient Persia ran through the mountain passes.' She indicated the deep valleys connecting Iran and Iraq in the screen's extreme upper right. 'That's how they brought in stone, timber and copper.'

'So what happened to the people that lived there?' Annie asked.

'The simple explanation points to climate shift. Massive floods silted the soil, destroyed practically everything . . . made northern Mesopotamia unsuitable for crops. The survivors were forced to migrate east and west across Eurasia, and to the south as far as Egypt. In fact, starting around 4000 BC, the archaeological remains of human occupation completely disappear for nearly a thousand years in this entire region. It's often referred to as the Dark Millennium.'

'So how do you explain that the cave seems to have been occupied during that time?' Flaherty asked.

'According to the inscriptions on the cave wall, the floods were just beginning. Floods of epic proportion.'

'Flaherty!' a stern female voice called from somewhere beyond the cubicles.

Instantly, Flaherty's expression soured.

The voice called again at the same time as his cellphone rang. 'Flaherty here.'

'Tommy, it's Jason.'

'Flaherty! I see you!' said the faraway voice.

Operations Chief Lillian Chen, a petite 45-year-old Korean in a severe trouser-suit, made a summoning gesture.

'Be right there,' Flaherty said, holding up his hand, then pointing to his phone. Clearly short on patience, Chen executed a crisp about-face and disappeared.

'Sorry, Jason,' Flaherty said into the phone. 'What's up?'

Flaherty listened intently as Jason told him about encrypted calls Colonel Crawford had been exchanging with someone inside an evangelical church in Las Vegas. The background check Mack had run through the NSA database indicated that the church's leader, Randall Stokes, was a former Special Ops commando who'd served time with Crawford in Beirut, Kuwait, Afghanistan and Iraq.

Jason said, 'I'm guessing he's somehow involved in what's happening over here in Iraq. Stokes might even have something to do with the hit order on Brooke Thompson. I already spoke to Lillian, explained the situation.'

'I can see that.'

'One other thing . . . I asked Lillian to check out that USAMRIID lead. She's got people at Fort Detrick sifting the archives for anything sent in from Iraq back in 2003. If biological tests were performed, we should have confirmation within a couple hours. In the meantime, I need you to talk to Stokes . . . in person. Lillian's already made arrangements to get you to Vegas, leaving immediately. They're preparing a file for you with everything we know about Stokes. So get to Logan ASAP and you can study up on him on your way out there. I don't think I need to tell you that there's a lot riding on this, Tommy.'

'You can count on me.'

'I knew I could. I'll be in touch,' Jason said, then ended the call.

'AREN'T YOU READY YET?' Bryce Crawford's eyes traced the fibre-optic cable from the PackBot's rear to a large spool that patched into a suitcase-sized remote command unit, painted in desert camouflage. The unit's cover was inset with a seventeen-inch LCD viewing screen; its base hosted a computer hard drive, keyboard and toggle controls. 'I could have invaded North Korea by now.'

'Almost there, sir,' replied the engineer—an attractive 28-year-old female with the fringes of a pageboy haircut sticking out from beneath her helmet.

Crawford surveyed the tight perimeter his marines had formed around the encampment. Everyone was on high alert after Sergeant Yaeger claimed to have spotted an Arab watcher. His gaze shifted to Hazo. Yaeger had yet to disclose fully what his sidekick had discovered during his fact-finding mission. But the copilot who'd escorted the Kurd had told Crawford about the visit to a restaurant in As Sulaymaniyah, which had led to an excursion to a monastery near Iraq's northeastern border. This confirmed for Crawford that Yaeger knew much more than he was letting on. And the implications were highly unnerving.

The bot came online with a sudden jerk of its articulating arm, and Crawford gave a start.

'OK. We're good to go,' the engineer reported.

Crawford and Jason knelt either side of her, intently watching the live transmissions from the bot. 'Right or left?' she asked, bringing the bot to a stop at the end of the entry passage.

'Go right,' Crawford immediately blurted, before Jason could give it a thought.

Pressing forward on the joystick control, she advanced the bot forward into the junction. Then she toggled right and the onscreen image rotated until the camera was directed down the tunnel branch. It was evident that this winding, craggy passage, approximately two metres wide according to the laser measurements coming back from the bot, had not been altered from its natural state.

'Here we go.'

As the bot advanced beyond the dimly lit entry passage, rising and falling over the undulating ground, the light quickly melted away and the camera's night vision automatically compensated for the darkness. On the command unit's viewing screen, the live feeds transformed to green-tinted monochrome. The glowing airborne dust swirling in the camera made it seem like the bot was trapped inside a snow globe.

'It's quiet in there,' the engineer said. She adjusted the volume slide control upwards. The only sounds over the audio feed were the bot's low humming gears and the crunching of gravel beneath its rotary tracks.

'Too quiet,' Crawford added.

'The air quality in there is surprisingly good,' the engineer reported, glancing at the data readings from the bot's onboard sensors.

'Wait,' Jason interrupted. 'Back it up a bit.' Eyes narrowed to slits, Jason attempted to discern something in the image. 'Can you shine some light?'

The engineer pressed a button that shut off the infrared. The screen went black for a split second before the bot's floodlight snapped on. The crisp image showed the tunnel's raw features.

'There,' Jason said, pointing to an unnatural form partially hidden along the ceiling. 'Can you get a better shot of that?'

'Sure.' The engineer worked the controls to angle the camera up and zoomed in on the compact object fitting snugly into a hole in the rocky ceiling. It had an angular body and a circular eye.

There was no doubt what they were looking at. 'A camera?' Jason gasped. 'What the hell is that doing in there?'

'What . . . like a surveillance camera?' Meat said, coming over for a better look.

Crawford finally spoke up. 'First the metal door, now this. It has to be a bunker.'

'Could be.' Jason studied him. Crawford seemed to be feigning surprise. Why?

'Let's kill the light and keep moving,' Crawford suggested.

For another five minutes, they all watched in silence as the robot wound through the mountain's stark bowels. Twice, the engineer needed to swivel the camera sideways to study openings in the wall. But both times, the floodlight revealed dead ends. Along the way, they'd spotted two more surveillance cameras. The bot went deeper, until the fibre-optic cable spool nearly emptied.

Then the passage's structure changed. The jagged walls widened before falling away. Only the ground was discernible at the bottom of the screen.

'What do we have here?' Jason said, squaring his shoulders.

'Looks like . . . a cave?' The engineer paused the bot and its audio feed went eerily silent. Pushing another button, she said, 'Let's try sonar.'

A small panel popped up in the monitor's lower right corner. Within seconds, the sonar data-capture was complete and a three-dimensional image representing the interior space flashed on the screen.

'Wow. It's pretty big,' the engineer said, interpreting the data. 'Like the inside of a movie theatre.' She studied the sonar image. 'It's not picking up any exit tunnels. Looks like a dead end. Nothing throwing off a heat signature in there either.'

'So no one's in there?'

'Nothing living.' Her eyes narrowed as she studied the image more. 'There's some strange formations along the outer edges of the cave. See here?' She pointed to the anomalies for Crawford and Jason and they each had a long look at them.

'Probably just stones,' Crawford said dismissively.

'No,' Jason disagreed. Atop the strange mounds, he could make out plenty of orblike shapes. 'Those aren't stones. Let's turn on some lights.'

The engineer clicked off the infrared, turned on the floodlight.

On screen, the immense space came to life.

'My God . . .' she gasped.

The space was a cavernous hollow deep within the mountain. And heaped like firewood along its perimeter were countless human skeletons.

STOKES NOTED THE TIME. Over an hour ago, the assassin Crawford had dispatched to Boston was supposed to have provided a kill confirmation on Brooke Thompson. Twenty minutes earlier, he'd tried to take matters into his own hands by calling the assassin directly. The call had immediately gone to voicemail. That meant the pesky professor could still be alive—a very sloppy loose end.

He scratched nervously at his raw palms before turning his attention to the computer monitor, where the cave's camera feeds were showing plenty of activity. As Crawford had indicated during their last phone conversation, the PackBot was being sent into the cave to explore the passages and pinpoint the Arabs' location.

To buy some time, Crawford had cleverly diverted the robot down the passage leading away from the Arabs. The bot was now parked in the cave's burial chamber, panning its camera left to right. For those viewing the bot's video transmission, the macabre sight would be nothing less than terrifying—like glimpsing Hell itself.

On another panel, Stokes honed in on the Arabs slowly making their way deeper into the tunnel, determined to find a way out. They were very close to the cave's most secret chamber now. Too close. And Stokes was concerned that if they were to stumble upon the installation that was the heart of Operation Genesis, they might try to destroy his precious handiwork.

'It is time,' a voice suddenly called out to him.

Startled, Stokes sat bolt upright and scanned the room.

'Let loose the fury,' the voice commanded.

'Yes . . .' Stokes said, hoping the Lord would reveal His countenance. The voice was all around him. It seemed to permeate his skull. How would God eventually manifest Himself?

'I understand.'

Stokes brought up a new window on his monitor to access the cave's command interface module.

He stared at the seven icons blinking 'SEALED'. With trembling fingers, he clicked each icon in turn, and the flashing indicators flipped from red to green; 'SEALED' now changed to 'OPEN'. When the a box came up to confirm the changes, he paused, then slowly typed in the password—ARMAGEDDON.

Stokes's eyes glimmered with pleasure as he watched his unwitting Arab detainees reacting to the eerie noises emanating from deep within the mountain's belly. In the background, mechanical sounds echoed through the passage—gears engaging, pistons whining, a droning whoosh. The Arabs had mistaken the noises for artillery. A man with a patchy beard was trying to hush the others, but to little avail.

While the four underlings, huddled around the dim cellphone light, attempted to hash out a hasty defence strategy, Al-Zahrani was surprisingly cool. The infrared showed him studying the exchange: assessing behaviour, mentally separating the strong from the weak. Clearly he wasn't pleased with what he was hearing.

There was a solemnity and drive about Al-Zahrani that commanded respect—qualities typical of a general. The fact that this revolutionary was a star Oxford University graduate and hailed from a wealthy Saudi oil family was intriguing. Most men could only dream of the luxurious life that Al-Zahrani had abandoned. Such indifference to material things required incredible inner strength and, to Stokes, underscored the potency of the new enemy that threatened the modern world. Tainted ideology was a most fearsome force.

Lord, show me the righteous way, he thought.

Suddenly, Al-Zahrani commanded the men to move forward—towards the commotion. They disappeared from view for a few seconds before the next camera picked up their trail.

The man with a patchy beard was at the front, cellphone light extended in his left hand, AK-47 clutched tight in the crook of his right arm. The other three men trailed in his wake, weapons at the ready, and Al-Zahrani pulled up the rear, swinging a handgun at his side. Even he was visibly tense, because the metal-on-metal sounds they'd been hearing had given way to something much different.

Ahead in the darkness, something was moving.

Writhing.

'Best to turn around, my friends,' Stokes muttered, his left eyebrow tipping up.

The audio picked up scratching and clicking.

The procession halted abruptly as the leader made the first visual confirmation.

When he spotted the horror that lay ahead, he screamed out in terror and wheeled around so fiercely that he barrelled into the two men behind him.

He stumbled, and the cellphone fumbled out of his grasp and clattered along the rocky ground.

Panic infected them.

As the leader regained his footing he shoved at the others, trying to speed them along. He attempted to retrieve the phone, but it disappeared beneath the slithering mass that crashed into him like a violent wave. He recoiled, levelled the AK-47, and opened fire.

Al-Zahrani was in the previous camera frame, blindly clawing his way through the darkness. But something scurried beneath his feet and caused him to trip and fall. He screamed as it took a chunk of flesh out of his hand.

Stokes looked at the other frame and saw the gunman lose his footing and tumble backwards, the assault rifle swinging up over his head, spraying bullets along a wild arc. The lethal barrage strafed the two men trailing behind him, sending the pair crumpling to the ground.

An instant later, a ferocious explosion ripped through the passage and obliterated the camera.

THE ENGINEER GASPED as the bot's camera swept slowly from side to side for the second time, panning over the ghastly bone pile that formed a ring ten feet high.

'Looks to me like another hiding place for evidence of Saddam's genocide,' Crawford said.

'No,' Jason said. The only similarity he saw here was the sheer number of bones. 'Doesn't look anything like Saddam's handiwork.'

'How so?' Crawford challenged.

'First off, not one of the skulls we've seen on that screen shows signs of execution. No bullet holes, fractures—'

'Hey, smart guy, Sarin doesn't leave its mark on bones,' Crawford countered quickly.

'Wait . . .' the engineer interjected.

Crawford and Jason turned their attention back to the screen.

'See this?' she said, pointing to something on the wall just to the right of where the bot had entered the cave. 'Looks similar to the pictures and writing on the wall of the entry tunnel.'

'More pictures and scribble,' Crawford said. 'Let's cut the—'

But the colonel was cut short by a bellowing blast that echoed out from the cave and shook the ground.

CHAPTER SEVEN

As the sleek white Cessna Citation X jet with no markings flew over Missouri en route for Nevada, Brooke Thompson stared out of the cabin window at the patchwork of farmland that blanketed the flat Midwest landscape in squares and circles of russet and ochre. The layout repeated itself as far as the eye could see.

Lillian Chen had given Flaherty the green light to take Brooke along with him to Vegas and to brief her on Stokes. It made sense, since Brooke was the only person who'd actually met the conspirators face to face, and her visual confirmation could certainly expedite matters.

'With the high stakes involved, we need to be certain,' Lillian had said. 'Any slip-ups could cost us dearly.'

A phone rang and Flaherty spotted the handset mounted in the fuselage wall. 'I guess that's for us,' he said. 'Agent Flaherty here,' he responded.

Brooke watched him as he kept the phone to his ear and jotted in a notepad. She caught herself examining his fingers for a wedding ring.

Flaherty ended the call and grinned. 'Remember back in 2008 when the FBI nailed that guy for mailing anthrax-tainted letters to a couple of senators right after 9/11?'

She nodded.

'OK. Well, turns out he had been a senior biodefence researcher at USAMRIID. Anyway, after the investigations implicated USAMRIID, Fort Detrick set out to account for every vial in the Infectious Disease Unit's inventory. Took them four months. By June 2009, over 70,000 samples had been catalogued, 9,000 of which had not been previously documented in the database. And among the overlooked samples were some interesting specimens procured by one Colonel Frank Roselli.' He looked at her and smiled.

'Frank? Our Frank?'

He held up a hand. 'It gets better. The specimens Roselli brought in all originated from a cave excavation in northern Iraq.'

'No way.'

Flaherty leaned forward. 'When my office tried to contact him at home, they were told that just this morning Frank Roselli wrapped his car around a telephone pole in Carver Park, Nevada. Only a few miles from Vegas.'

'My God . . .' she gasped. 'That's awful.'

But Flaherty had more to tell. 'So my office contacted the coroner, who said that no official cause of death has been determined. They suspect he had a heart attack at the wheel. But I think we'd both agree that foul play shouldn't be dismissed.'

'Exactly what samples did Frank send back from the cave? Had to be organic specimens, right?'

'Definitely. But not the kind USAMRIID normally collects. Seems Frank was studying bone samples. Lots and lots of bones.'

Brooke felt her blood curdle. 'Like, animal bones?'

Flaherty shook his head, 'Human. And strangely enough, the samples were mostly teeth. Almost a thousand of 'em. The inventory indicated that every tooth had been drilled to perform genetic analysis.' He checked his notes again. 'Oh, and every tooth was from a male.'

Why teeth? she wondered. 'That's all the description said?'

'No. It also said that Frank's tooth collection was incinerated.'

'SOMEONE TELL ME what the hell just happened in there!' yelled Crawford.

The engineer held up her hands. 'Everything's clear here,' she said, pointing to the PackBot's remote display.

'All right,' Crawford said. 'Let's back that lawn mower up and send it down the other passage.'

In less than three minutes the bot was back at the entry tunnel. As it roved through the tight rocky walls of the other passage, the audio picked up the distinct echoing of fast footfalls. The engineer speeded up the bot. A few metres ahead, it began rising and falling sharply over heavy debris strewn about the tunnel floor. Dense dust began swirling around the camera lens. The footsteps stopped abruptly.

'Let's shed some light,' Jason said. 'See what we've got.'

When the floodlight went on, a figure sharpened onscreen. A man huddled in a foetal position beneath a pile of rubble that completely blocked the narrow passage from floor to ceiling. He was using his head scarf to shield his mouth and nose from the dust.

'Looks like he's not going anywhere,' Crawford said. 'Is he armed?'

The engineer zoomed in on the bloody hands, down along the body. 'Doesn't appear to be, sir.'

'Good.' Crawford called to a pair of marines near the cave entrance. 'Holt. Ramirez—put your respirators on, get in there and pull him out!'

Tensions were high as everyone waited for Crawford's men to re-emerge from the cave. Jason's anxiety was particularly acute. Five hostiles had gone into the cave. Only one was in the process of being extracted, the fate of the remaining four unknown.

Then three figures emerged: two marines wearing respirators flanking a tall, bedraggled prisoner. At first, Jason couldn't make out the Arab's identity since the man had his bound, bloody hands raised up to shield his face.

Crawford pulled the man's hands down and pointed a flashlight into his face. Though the captive was smeared with blood and grime, Jason immediately recognised him.

'Look who we have here. Fahim Al-Zahrani. Mr Jihad himself,' Crawford said, full of glee. He snapped off the light, put his hands on his hips. 'As salaam alaikum, asshole.'

The prisoner didn't reply, glaring defiantly at the colonel. Confirmation of his identity rippled through the ranks. The excited marines at the bottom of the slope began whooping.

ON A NEIGHBOURING MOUNTAINTOP to the south, the watcher peered through a night-vision monocular. The moment the captive's face came into view, the watcher's instant elation gave way to terror. Our leader has been captured!

The watcher scrambled up over the ridge. In the pale moonlight, he could see the rescue team's trucks parked in the valley below. He stood high up on the outcropping designated as the signal relay spot. Then he pulled a plastic glow stick from under his tunic, cracked it, and waved the luminescent green tube in wide arcs.

CENTRAL TO CRAWFORD'S ENCAMPMENT were two Compact Allweather Mobile Shelter Systems, or CAMSS—barn-shaped tents ten and a half feet high at the eaves, twenty feet wide, thirty-two feet long, which four men could assemble in less than thirty minutes. The first tent served the dual role of central command and billeting Crawford and his staff sergeant. Normally, the second tent stored boxed rations, and accommodated ten sleeping mats, used on rotation by the platoon detail. But Crawford had ordered the marines to clear out the sleeping area so that the space could be used for Fahim Al-Zahrani's temporary detainment.

The prisoner sat on an empty munitions crate, his hands bound tight with a nylon double-loop security strap. A second strap looped snugly around his ankles. Two marines with M16s stood to either side of him.

The company medic, Lance Corporal Jeremy Levin—a scrawny 31-year-old family-practitioner reservist who was five months into his third tour in Iraq—sat on a crate facing Al-Zahrani. He'd already flushed the wound on Al-Zahrani's hand with Betadine and cleaned the prisoner's face with sanitising wipes. But he was concerned by Al-Zahrani's condition: clammy complexion, despondency and wheezing.

He inserted an otoscope in Al-Zahrani's left ear, which was perforated, then the right ear, which was leaking blood and clear fluid.

Crawford watched over his shoulder. Jason and Hazo stood behind him.

'Hey, asshole,' Crawford said loudly to Al-Zahrani. 'I know you speak English. Just want to let you know that I think the Geneva Convention is a load of camel shit. So don't expect me to respect your civil liberties.'

Levin flicked on the light of an ophthalmoscope and moved close to examine Al-Zahrani's unblinking eyes. 'Pupils are responding just fine . . . no apparent neurological damage. Doesn't appear that he's in shock.'

'So he's just pretending to be mute?' Crawford asked.

'I'm sure he's a bit overwhelmed, Colonel,' the medic replied curtly as he went back to the case for an aural digital thermometer. He took the temperature in both ears and made a sour face. 'Hmm. He seems to be running a high fever. That could explain the apathy.'

'You telling me he caught a cold?' Crawford said.

'More than a cold,' Levin replied.

Apathy was an understatement, thought Jason. The world's premier terrorist seemed lifeless. His dark, emotionless gaze remained fixed on the ground. What could he be thinking? Was he humiliated or afraid? Jason wanted him to fight . . . wanted him to react.

Levin swabbed some mucus from Al-Zahrani's dripping nostril. 'Not sure if this is due to the dust he inhaled, or if it's something else. I'll test him for the flu, just in case.'

Crawford backed up a step. 'If this son of a bitch gets me sick . . .'

'I'm sure you'll be just fine,' the medic said. He wrapped a pressure cuff around Al-Zahrani's left arm, put the earbuds of a stethoscope in his own ears, and used the rubber bulb to inflate the cuff. Everyone remained silent as he assessed the patient's vitals.

'Given all the excitement, his blood pressure is awfully low.' He placed the stethoscope's chestpiece over Al-Zahrani's heart and listened intently. He moved it to the ribs and monitored the pulmonary functions. 'He's got a lot of obstruction in there. Fluid. Probably inhaled a lot of dust.'

Not as much dust as the innocent civilians who'd been at Ground Zero, thought Jason, trying to reconcile how men like this were capable of evil on such a grand scale. 'What do you think happened to his hand?' he asked.

The medic studied the deep, ragged puncture wound. Already, it appeared worse than only minutes ago.

'Probably caught some shrapnel, or a ricochet. Could be a wound he already had. Not sure. But I don't like how the tissue looks—this discoloration and swelling.' He rolled up the sleeve of Al-Zahrani's tunic, turned the arm over, and traced his gloved finger along the protruding, dark veins in the wrist and forearm. 'Seems he's got a nasty infection. I'll give him some antibiotics . . . some ibuprofen for the fever.'

'Why don't you boil him some tea while you're at it?' Crawford barked.

The medic's face twisted in a knot.

Jason spoke for the medic, 'If Washington wants to interrogate him, he won't be very useful if he's dead.'

'You mean he might not be worth ten million?' Crawford jabbed.

Jason was fast losing patience. 'The Department of Defense's bounty specifies "dead or alive",' he replied tartly. 'I'm sure we'd agree that "alive" would be preferred.'

'You and your boys get to keep that money, isn't that right, Yaeger?'

'That's right. It's part of our incentive plan. Keeps us all motivated. So yeah, the money will be ours to keep.'

'You're a disgrace, Yaeger.' The colonel's words seethed with loathing. 'Nothing but a sellout. And just remember that it was the US marines who pulled that cocksucker out from the cave. That's the story everyone here knows. So I wouldn't suggest spending your money just yet.'

'I've already sent plenty of video and pictures back to my office . . . make a nice documentary about the six-month manhunt that led us all here. Not to mention all the thrilling images of my unit's ambush, which feature this guy's ugly mug all over them. Funny thing is, there aren't any marines in those shots. So don't you worry about us,' Jason said, grinning smugly.

Levin pulled a blood-filled syringe from a thick vein snaking up Al-Zahrani's forearm. 'We'll need to lay him down.'

Crawford took a few seconds to decompress before saying, 'Fine. Set up a bed for him. But you be sure to hang an American flag next to him. Remind him that he's ours now. When you're done, I want you to set up a video camera in here too.' He turned his attention back to Jason. 'All right, Yaeger. Time for you and your boys to earn your money.' He pointed to Hazo. 'He stays with me, just in case Al-Zahrani decides to scribble some Arabic. You speak Arabic, isn't that right?'

Hazo nodded. 'I do, Colonel.'

'Of course you do. You're no millionaire yet, so go fetch a pen and paper. We've got work to do.' He turned to Yaeger. 'In the meantime, we've got another goddamn tunnel to unclog. And we still need to figure what in hell blew up in that cave. Wrangle up your boys and get working on that. I'll have Staff Sergeant Richards help you.'

'Fine. But now that we've confirmed his identity'—Jason tilted his head to the prisoner—'I need your assurance that back-up is on the way. We can't risk losing him now.'

'Don't cry . . . You'll get your money—'

'I'm not worried about the money, Crawford!' Jason snapped. 'For Christ's sake! We've just captured Fahim Al-Zahrani! And up in those mountains, I saw someone who might already have called for help to set him free. As I see it, the entire battalion should be here!' He snatched the sat-com off the colonel's belt and held it up. 'Make the call to General Ashford . . . or I will.'

Crawford's baleful eyes grew wide. 'I don't take kindly to insubordination, soldier,' he hissed.

Jason stepped closer, so that his nose practically touched the colonel's. 'And I don't take kindly to incompetence.'

Without breaking eye contact, Crawford plucked his phone from Jason's hand. 'That'll be all, Sergeant.'

'Make the call,' Jason repeated. He took two steps back and paused. Before he turned to leave, he added, 'And just so we're clear, Crawford—I'm not your soldier.'

THOUGH JASON WASN'T FOND of Crawford's leadership style, he had to admit that the colonel's platoon was a well-oiled machine. In less than fifteen minutes Staff Sergeant Richards had a human chain of twenty marines ferrying blast debris from the cave, helped by Camel, Meat and Jam.

Jason was intent on having a closer look at the cave's burial chamber.

He grabbed a flashlight and moved swiftly through the winding passages, drawing lessons from the PackBot's earlier exploration.

The subterranean atmosphere was completely disorienting, the air cool and loamy, thin on oxygen. It felt as if the earth had swallowed him whole. Imagining Al-Zahrani groping through the pitch black with no hope of escape gave Jason bitter satisfaction. It was hard to believe that after so many months chasing ghosts, the A-list madman was now their prisoner.

Over the past months, the intelligence Jason's unit had pieced together had pointed to a band of heavily armed operatives moving furtively from south to north. Shortly after Jason had requested surveillance support from a Predator drone flying reconnaissance rounds over the northern plain, the caravan had been spotted heading towards the Zagros Mountains. Jason's unit had staged a hasty ambush, cornering Fahim Al-Zahrani himself.

Now Jason was certain that the Arabs had been trying to smuggle Al-Zahrani over the mountains and he feared that Al-Zahrani was plotting an escape. Crawford had better call for back-up, he thought.

Finally, the passage widened and yielded to the cave. Jason paused and moved the light beam left to right. All along the walls the bone piles were stacked high—a circle of death.

There was a story to be found in these bones, but what could it be? Upon closer examination, he discovered that none of them had teeth.

Then something on the ground glinted in the light. Jason bent down for a better look and saw a silver edge covered in heavy dust. He swept the dust away and picked up an object that was definitely not from long ago. It was a tool that resembled a high-tech surgical instrument. Something a dentist might use. Had to have been left behind by one of the scientists brought in for the 2003 excavation. He pocketed it.

Jason remembered the bot had spotted something to the right of the exit. Jason shone the flashlight along the curve of the wall until he found the spot that had clearly been smoothed by tools to prepare the surface for etching. And the image etched into stone made his jaw drop.

AS THE CESSNA made the final descent into Las Vegas International Airport, Thomas Flaherty's BlackBerry chimed. 'It's from Jason,' he told Brooke. When he brought up the text message, he noted a handful of icons for picture attachments. 'Says: "Al-Zahrani in custody. Have Brooke review pix from inside cave. Is this Lilith?"'

Brooke sat bolt upright, not sure what to be most excited about. 'Is he saying that Fahim Al-Zahrani has been captured?'

Flaherty briefly explained how Jason's team had been tracking al-Qaeda operatives for the past few months, leading up to the ambush that forced Al-Zahrani and his surviving posse to take cover in the mountain.

'Wow. That is huge,' she said, mouth agape. 'That's like catching the Devil himself.'

Flaherty tried to wrap his brain around it too. 'It's ten million dollars huge,' he murmured.

'What?'

'Nothing.' He shook his head.

'So let's see those pictures,' she said, eyeing the BlackBerry.

Flaherty read aloud the name Jason had assigned the first attachment, 'Mass Grave'. The picture clearly showed a dense pile of human bones. Brooke wasn't sure how to react. 'This is what Frank's team had been studying?'

'Seems so. There are a few other pictures,' he said, showing her how to open the files.

The next picture Brooke brought up hit her like a sledgehammer. 'Look at this,' she said.

He squinted to make out the details. 'What are those?'

'Jawbones,' she said.

'There aren't any—'

'Teeth!' she exclaimed. 'Of course! This is where Frank got the teeth. From these bones.'

The next image took Brooke's breath away.

'Hubba hubba. Who's that?' Flaherty said.

Brooke didn't respond. She was absorbed in the image—a wall etching that depicted a voluptuous, naked woman. Flaring out from beneath her raised arms were birdlike wings and she wore an elaborate conical headdress. In her left hand, she held a serpent. Perched on her right hand was some kind of bird. And beneath her feet was a pile of human skeletons.

Flaherty said, 'This supposed to be the same woman whose head got lopped off?'

'Looks that way.'

'Why would they behead an angel?'

Brooke shook her head. 'Not an angel. Protective spirits—the good spirits—are always shown with upward-pointing wings. See here how her wings are pointing down.'

'So what does that mean?'

'It implies that she is a demon. And see this rosette?' Brooke pointed. 'It's an ancient symbol of divinity. This conical headdress she's wearing is also a symbol of godliness.' She panned across the image to the wide-eyed bird perched on the goddess's right hand. 'It's an owl. God, how did I not think of this? Jason's right. Of course this is Lilith. The serpent, the owl, the wings . . .'

'And who, pray tell, is Lilith?'

'In the pantheon of ancient Mesopotamian deities, she was the goddess of storms and pestilence. Lilith was even said to be the first woman God created alongside Adam. But because she was seductive and mischievous, God banished her from paradise. In exile, she found a new lover to satisfy her carnal desires—one of God's fallen archangels named Samael. Better known as the Angel of Death or the Grim Reaper.'

'You don't say,' Flaherty said.

'By copulating with Samael, Lilith became immortal and acquired supernatural powers. Ancient texts say that she morphed into a serpent and slithered back into Eden and persuaded Adam and Eve to disobey God so that they, too, lost favour with Him and were banished. It's a common mythological theme,' she explained. 'Curiosity and forbidden knowledge leading to humankind's downfall. Usually at the hand of a woman.'

'Just like Pandora's Box.'

She grinned. 'In the original Greek myth of Pandora, the vessel containing all the world's evils is described as a pithos—a large clay jar, just like the one Lilith brought into that village.'

'So maybe Pandora was inspired by Lilith too,' Flaherty said.

'Maybe.'

'Let's have a look at the other pictures Jason sent,' he suggested, reaching out to open the remaining file. 'Any idea what this is?'

Brooke snatched the BlackBerry back from him. 'Writing,' she said, excited. 'The same kind of text I deciphered in the cave's entry tunnel.'

'What does it say?'

She shrugged. 'I'm sure I can decipher it. But I'll need to enlarge it.'

Flaherty glanced out the window and was surprised to see that the jet was already gliding in low over the runway. 'I'll transfer the file to my laptop,' he said, patting his carry-on bag. 'You can read it in the car.'

'Awesome,' she said, beaming. 'We might just get Lilith's story after all. Do you know what that means?' She looked like a kid on her birthday.

'Not really, but I'm sure you'll tell me.'

LANCE CORPORAL LEVIN estimated that fifteen minutes had elapsed since the marines had hung an American flag behind his patient's head and set up a tripod-mounted camcorder to record the interrogation. As Colonel Crawford fired his questions, the patient was highly uncooperative, though not by choice, Levin was certain. He could tell by Al-Zahrani's withdrawn and hazy gaze that his condition was deteriorating at an alarming rate. Only five minutes ago, he had begun coughing. Now that cough was accompanied by heaving lungs that wheezed and gurgled. Coupled with fever, malaise and runny nose, Levin suspected that the prisoner had come down with flu, although tests had shown that Al-Zahrani was 'negative' for both influenza A and B, and for avian and swine flu.

Crawford still hadn't called for back-up. There was little hope that he would heed a request to have Al-Zahrani airlifted to the nearest hospital for proper treatment, which was what Levin's gut was telling him the situation might warrant.

Suddenly Crawford's growing frustration with his prisoner hit a crescendo. He kicked over a crate and stormed out.

'Lunatic,' Levin mumbled. He made eye contact with the Kurd, who shrugged, set down the marker and notepad, then made his way outside.

REACHING THE TOP of the slope, Crawford summoned Staff Sergeant Richards from the cave entrance. 'How much longer till it's cleared?'

'Maybe a couple hours,' he guessed. 'I'm pushing the men as hard as I can.'

'Push harder,' Crawford insisted. 'I want to find out exactly what they brought into that cave.' He looked over at Jason Yaeger, who was hauling buckets and dumping them down the slope.

Richards picked up on the colonel's preoccupation. 'He was on his phone again,' the staff sergeant said. 'Didn't seem to be talking to anyone . . . just fiddling around. And before that, I saw him go into the other tunnel. Disappeared for a good fifteen, twenty minutes.'

'Nothing but trouble,' Crawford said.

Yaeger was making his way over. 'Find anything interesting while you were poking around in there?' asked Crawford.

'Plenty,' Jason replied with defiant eyes. 'But something tells me it wouldn't be news to you.'

'Is that so?'

'Call it instinct.'

Crawford stood his ground. 'You should be careful jumping to rash conclusions. Could get you in a world of trouble.'

'I agree. Just like I've already concluded that you didn't call for back-up. Isn't that right?'

Crawford grinned. 'That's my call to make, not yours. As soon as that tunnel is clear, shouldn't take long to pull those other ragheads out. Then we'll be on our way. I'm guessing it might take another hour or so. About the same time it would take for a support platoon to get here. Besides, my men have been monitoring the airwaves and haven't heard a peep.'

'An hour?' Jason repeated. 'We don't even know what's behind those rocks. How can you be sure it won't take a lot longer?'

'Call it instinct. And let's face it, Yaeger,' he said with forced diplomacy, 'if there were miles of tunnel behind that rubble, Al-Zahrani wouldn't have been heading for the front door. We're close to extracting these sons of bitches and you know it. You've done your part, now let me do mine.'

Jason studied Crawford for a few seconds. Something wasn't right. 'One hour,' he said.

Crawford nodded. 'If we're not done by then, you can make the call yourself. Call in the entire brigade for all I care.'

SUDDENLY, AL-ZAHRANI VOMITED over himself, filling the tent with a putrid smell. The two marines standing guard immediately backed away. 'Jesus, Doc,' the first marine said. 'What the hell's wrong with this guy? It's like he's dying or something.'

The second marine craned his head to get a look at what came up from Al-Zahrani's stomach. 'Not sure what he ate last, but there's an awful lot of blood in there. That can't be good.'

'We've got to get him to a hospital, immediately,' Levin addressed the first marine. 'You need to convince Crawford to transport him. Tell him what's happening in here.'

'I'll see what I can do.' The marine hurried from the tent.

Frantic now, Levin was trying to figure out what else to try. Whatever was making Al-Zahrani haemorrhage internally might be visible under a microscope, he reasoned. He unpacked a battery-powered microscope, turned on his laptop and connected the scope's USB cable. Then he pulled on a fresh pair of gloves and peeled open a lancet. Grabbing a glass specimen slide, he pricked Al-Zahrani's finger and squeezed a blood drop onto the slide.

Levin hastened back to his makeshift lab table and centred the specimen over the microscope's diffusion screen. Then he used the software controls to adjust magnification. A darkfield condenser lit the specimen from the sides, so that bands of light fluoresced the blood's living components.

As he adjusted the resolution, Levin immediately spotted anomalies. Many of the red cells were misshapen and coagulated into clumps, plus many spiny platelets' and ovoid white cells' membranes had also been compromised and were lysing—proof that a foreign invader was aggressively killing the cells from the inside out.

'What in God's name . . .?'

He set the microscope to its maximum magnification. In microscale, an invading force was engaged in a fight to the death. But he'd need an electron microscope to analyse the virions effectively. Whatever it was, its primary objective was plainly replication.

'Jesus,' he gasped.

'Everything all right, Doc?' the guard nervously inquired.

'No,' Levin replied grimly, his complexion ashen. Would the troops' inoculations protect against this elusive killer? If not, the repercussions were unimaginable. 'My God, we could all be infected.'

'Infected?' The marine shifted uneasily. 'What do you mean?'

But before Levin could respond, the sound of gunfire pierced the night.

CHAPTER EIGHT

Agent Flaherty checked the GPS on the dashboard of the rented silver Dodge Charger. Eight miles to go.

The GPS registered Our Savior in Christ Cathedral as an unknown lot along North Hollywood Boulevard. So Flaherty chose a random street number that was in the same range as the cathedral.

In the passenger seat, Brooke held Flaherty's laptop and was studying an enlargement of one of the pictures transferred from his BlackBerry. He'd given her his notepad and a pen to jot down her transcriptions. She'd already filled one page and was starting on a second.

'Anything useful in those pictures?'

'Oh yeah,' she said. 'Hang on just a minute . . . almost finished.'

He drove on in silence for a solid minute and Brooke exhaled, sat tall in her seat and folded the laptop shut.

'All done,' she said. 'My God, Tommy. You're not going to believe this.'

'Try me.'

Brooke cleared her throat. 'It starts with this passage:

> "She came from the realm of the rising sun
> She who holds dominion over beasts and men
> She who is the Screech Owl, the Night Creature
> She who sows vengeance and retribution on all men
> Before the moon had twice come
> Fathers and sons, all, were dead
> Her hand touched them not
> Bathed in blood they perished, destroyed from within
> No mother or daughter did she punish
> She commanded the rivers to consume the land
> The demon who killed the many
> The one sent by the great creator to end all."'

'OK,' said Flaherty. 'That is creepy.'

'Tommy, those skeletons Jason found in that cave were all the men in that village. And this is saying Lilith killed them.'

'How?'

'If she didn't use physical force, then I'd assume she spread some kind of disease that made them bleed to death.'

'What kind of disease kills everyone in two days? And only males? At least it explains why those teeth at Fort Detrick all came from males.' When he looked over, he saw that she was deep in thought. 'Brooke?'

Teeth. Pestilence. Males. 'Oh my God,' she said suddenly. 'Just recently, I read in an archaeology journal about excavations of mass graves in France where plague victims had been buried. In ancient specimens, plague leaves an imprint in the pulp of victims' teeth. These archaeologists had found perfectly preserved *Yersinia pestis* DNA in the teeth.'

'Yurwhat DNA?'

'*Yersinia pestis* is the bacterium that causes bubonic plague. It gets into your lymph nodes, replicates like crazy, and makes you slowly haemorrhage to death,' she explained.

'Pleasant.'

'Remember from history class when in the fourteenth century the Black Death killed half the population of Europe?'

He nodded. 'Actually, I do.'

'That was bubonic plague. It became a pandemic and killed over a hundred million people worldwide. Almost a quarter of the world's population at that time.'

'So you think something like the Black Death killed these guys?'

'With such a high mortality rate, probably something worse, but I'm no epidemiologist.'

Flaherty slowed to make a left. 'All right, let's hold off on this for a little while, because we're almost there. We need to talk about how we're going to handle this Stokes character.'

'He may not even be here, Tommy.'

'He'll be here,' Flaherty replied confidently. 'He needs that encrypted phone line to talk with Crawford.'

JASON WAS INSIDE the tunnel entrance when he heard the rat-tat-tat-tat of automatic gunfire. He dropped the rubble-filled bucket he'd just taken from the marine in front and ran to the opening, squatting low.

In the moonlight, he could see a marine crossing the roadway—presumably the shooter. On the other side of the road, the scout rounded a hillock with the stock of his M16 raised up against his shoulder. The other marines stayed back and hunkered down to cover him.

Then the scout lowered his weapon and shook his head, pointing to something on the ground. Jason couldn't hear clearly what was said, but saw five marines go out to have a look. When the scout reached down and held up a limp fox by its tail, they all lowered their weapons and gave him a good ribbing.

Jason didn't like the fact that the scout was so quick to shoot a suspicious target. He turned to the others. 'False alarm.'

As he dumped rubble down the slope, he was surprised to see that the carefree marines stayed out on the open road, heckling the shooter. 'Not smart, fellas,' he grumbled to himself.

Jason scanned the area, but Crawford and his officers were nowhere to be found. Probably back in the tent grilling Al-Zahrani, he guessed. Ten minutes ago, one of the marines who'd been assigned to watch over the prisoner came looking for Crawford, visibly distressed. But another man had redirected him down the hill to where Crawford had gone to check on the men working inside the MRAP. Now Jason was wishing he'd asked the guard if there was a problem. Something wasn't right.

'Guys, I'll be back in a few minutes,' he called to the men in the cave.

As he loped down the steep incline, a whump-hsssss sound—like fireworks being shot up into the sky—made him stop dead in his tracks. His eyes locked on to a fiery orange light streaming through the night . . . on a direct path for the loitering marines.

Jason cupped his hands and yelled, 'Get off the road!'

But it was too late.

The marines had no time to react. The RPG mortar tore them to pieces in a billowing fireball. Shrapnel spray took down three more marines posted nearby. Jason looked over his shoulder and saw men streaming out from the cave. 'We're under attack!' one of them yelled to others still inside the cave. 'Everyone out!' Down below, chaos broke out as the marines tried to determine where the enemy was positioned.

Another mortar was fired at the camp. Jason traced the exhaust trail and pinpointed a gunman sinking below a hummock fifty metres south. The grenade struck one of the Humvees and threw out a huge fireball, sending marines dashing for cover.

At the same time, automatic gunfire started raining down from elevated positions along the neighbouring mountaintop. Through his night-vision binoculars, Jason spotted trucks less than a klick south along the roadway. He scrambled down towards the camp.

THE CHAOS OUTSIDE the tent rang loud and clear, but inside Levin was adamant as he pleaded with Crawford, 'We can't move him now! He's infected!'

'Stand down, Corporal,' Crawford said. He turned to the two guards. 'You two go outside and make sure no one comes near this tent.'

'Colonel . . .' Levin pleaded, grabbing Crawford's arm. 'This man is very, very sick! He's got—'

'Get your mangy paw off me, Corporal. I know damn well what he's got.'

Crawford forcefully shoved the medic back into the table, sending the laptop and microscope hurtling to the ground.

Levin picked himself up. 'What do you mean you know what he's got?'

A malevolent expression came over Crawford. 'Don't you worry about that,' he hissed. 'Just get Al-Zahrani ready for transport.'

'Look at him!' Levin screamed. 'It's too late! He needs to be quarantined! We all need to be quarantined!'

Crawford smirked. 'No we don't.'

The colonel's response confused Levin. 'But anyone who touches him . . . anyone who goes near him—'

Crawford snatched the M9 pistol off his belt holster and fired a single shot into Levin's chest. As the medic crumpled to the ground, the tent's rear door opened. Crawford wheeled instantly and aimed his pistol.

'Easy,' Staff Sergeant Richards said. 'It's just me.'

Crawford holstered the pistol. 'Let's go, we don't have much time.'

Striding towards Al-Zahrani, Richards eyed the dead medic, sprawled face down in a pool of blood. 'What did you—?'

'Just keep moving,' Crawford replied dismissively.

Making a sour face, Richards positioned himself at the head of the bed and reluctantly hooked his arms under the prisoner's armpits. 'Grab his feet,' he told Crawford.

Crawford hesitated at the prospect of touching Al-Zahrani. He glanced at Levin's body and, for the first time, felt doubt. What if the medic was right? What if Stokes didn't really know how the contagion would respond in a real-world setting?

'Sir! Please . . . I can't do this alone,' Richards insisted.

Snapping out of his funk, Crawford rushed over to the bed and hooked his hands under Al-Zahrani's ankles. He counted to three. They hoisted the prisoner from the bed, carried him out the back door, and loaded him into the passenger seat of a pick-up truck idling outside.

'I NEED TO SPEAK with Crawford . . . Now!' Jason insisted to the two marines who blocked the door to the tent. 'So step aside!' He had to yell to compete with the barrage of gunfire throughout the camp. The marines aimed their M16s at his chest.

'Sorry. We have our orders,' the shorter one replied.

'And we have ours!' a deep voice blasted over the din.

In unison, Jason and the marines turned to the voice.

Meat, Camel and Jam stepped up in a V formation, pointing M16s at the marines.

The taller man lowered his weapon, then motioned his partner to step aside.

Jason made his way through the door. He was shocked to find Al-Zahrani gone and the medic dead. He registered a tiny blinking red light. It was the camcorder Crawford had set up to record his interrogation. Jason hit the eject button and pocketed the mini-DVD disc.

Then his eyes caught the splotchy blood trail that snaked from the bed to the rear door. Out back there were no guards and Crawford was nowhere to be found. In the sand, tyre tracks curled around the side of the tent. Dust from a moving vehicle still hung in the air.

Jason traced the tyre tracks to the roadway, heading north. Despite the danger from flying bullets, he ran out near the road and ducked behind the confiscated pick-up trucks—now three instead of four. Looking north through the binoculars, he found the fourth pick-up racing along the winding roadway. The passenger's slumped head, wrapped in a turban, was just visible through the blown-out rear window. He had no doubt it was Al-Zahrani.

There was no way a militant could have broken the perimeter, snuck Al-Zahrani from the tent and stolen the truck unnoticed. And why hadn't Crawford had guards posted at the tent's rear door? Because an insider orchestrated the grab, Jason quickly concluded. 'Crawford, you motherfucker.'

Where could they be taking Al-Zahrani? Something told him that Crawford wasn't concerned about protecting the prisoner. So what was his motive?

'Yaeger, get out of there!' a distant voice screamed. 'Grenade!'

Jason ran for the shallow ravine that cut along the opposite side of the road. He glimpsed the mortar arcing through the air on a direct line for the trucks, just before he dived for cover.

He was midair when the mortar struck. Amid a spray of heat and glass, a tyre rim hurtled directly for his head like a frisbee. He was certain he would be decapitated. But the blast wave cartwheeled his body forward an instant before that could happen.

Jason landed on his back at the bottom of the muddy ditch. He slowly opened his eyes and assessed his body, fully expecting to see some missing parts. Amazingly, everything moved fine, nothing felt broken. Just some ringing in his ears.

'Google!' a concerned voice yelled.

Jason looked up.

'Dude! I thought you were dead!' Meat slid down into the ditch. 'I saw you running out here. What are you, nuts?'

'They took Al-Zahrani. Moved him out in one of the pick-up trucks . . . heading north.' Jason pointed.

'Who?'

'Pretty sure it was Crawford or one of his men.'

'Why would he do that?'

'Don't know. But we've got to get Al-Zahrani back.'

Meat clasped Jason's hand and tugged him to his feet. 'The trucks are toast. And there's only one Humvee left . . . but it's got two flat tyres.'

'So we'll follow them in the MRAP,' Jason replied hastily.

'Way too slow. I've got a better idea.'

NESTLED BEHIND A HILL on the camp's northern limit, the Black Hawk had yet to sustain bombardment. 'You still know how to fly one of these things?' Jason asked.

Meat gave the chopper a sideways glance. 'No worries, bro,' he said. He hopped in the pilot's seat.

Camel and Jam crested the hill and scrambled down.

Seeing them alive gave Jason relief. At the onset of the attack, they'd all been safe inside the cave helping to clear debris.

'It's pandemonium back there!' Jam said.

'Where's Hazo?' Jason asked.

'He said he'll stay here and keep an eye on things,' Camel said.

With Crawford unaccounted for, Jason wasn't thrilled about the idea. But there was no time to deliberate. 'Fine. Let's go!'

The Black Hawk's engines fired up and the rotors began gathering momentum.

'Get us clear!' Jason yelled, pointing out over the plain. 'Then move into firing range!'

'Roger,' Meat said.

'Firing range?' Camel muttered over the intercom.

'We can't abandon the platoon,' Jason said. 'They won't be able to hold off those gunners. We've got enough firepower to take them down.'

Safely out over the plain, Meat banked the chopper along a wide arc and headed south to allow for the first glimpse of the enemy convoy.

'Holy shit!' Jam said. 'Look at them all!' There were maybe a dozen trucks visible on the road south of the camp.

'All right,' Meat said, flipping down his night-vision lenses. 'I'll take us two klicks out so we can line up for a nice shot.'

THE ROADWAY CUT horizontally along the targeting display on Jason's weapons console, and the convoy lined up onscreen like a shooting gallery. Jason decided to use the same tactic that roadside bombers frequently employed when assaulting US convoys—strike the lead vehicle first, then the rearmost vehicle second to immobilise everything in between.

Jason felt his stomach knot as he zoomed in and panned the cross hairs over one of the trucks fanned out in the front of the convoy.

He squeezed the trigger control and a flashing red dot appeared on the display. He adjusted the aim, held the dot steady, and the cross hairs flashed from red to green. He slid his thumb over the red firing button and pressed down.

The first missile shot out in front of the chopper along a high arc, then bobbed and weaved as its onboard guidance system synchronised with the laser's coordinates. Jason kept his eyes nailed to the cross hairs and made slight adjustments for the side-to-side rocking caused by Meat's less-than-graceful attempt to hover the Black Hawk. Onscreen the missile struck with a brilliant flash.

'Nice!' Meat said.

The second missile hissed out from the weapons pylon. Within seconds, it hit—decimating the target.

Jam and Camel high-fived.

'Now pop 'em in the middle,' Meat said.

'Roger that,' Jason said. He fired a third missile.

As the chopper pulled away, Jason's nerves were buzzing with adrenaline, his fingers trembling. He briefly allowed himself to embrace the primal urge awakened deep in his core—the lust for vengeance. 'That's for Matthew. Burn in Hell . . . all of you.'

But the vendetta was far from complete.

'Now let's get Al-Zahrani back,' Jason said.

'YOU THINK IT'S smart just to barge in there?' Brooke said, peering at the building as Flaherty parked near the cathedral's entrance. 'Shouldn't the police be here or something?'

'The pastor might make a break for it the second he spots a police car.'

'So how do you propose we handle this?'

'I propose we get married,' he said.

'Excuse me?'

'Just follow my lead.' Flaherty turned off the engine. 'Let me come around and get you.'

Baffled, Brooke waited for him to circle to her door. He proffered a hand. 'Come, darling. I think you'll love this church. I hear the wedding ceremony is breathtaking.'

She caught on to the ruse. 'Very clever. We're posing as customers.' Peering at him with doting eyes, she added, 'Let's make it look genuine, shall we?' and kissed him on the lips. 'Just in case anyone's watching.'

For a moment, he revelled in the magic. 'Good,' he replied finally, trying to pass it off as meaningless. 'Very authentic.'

She threaded her arm through his and rested her head on his shoulder. 'Shall we?'

RANDALL STOKES'S MIND was in a fog as he listened to Crawford's account of a siege staged against the encampment by Al-Zahrani's supporters. The death toll among the platoon was remarkable, given the fact that the militants had only guns and RPGs.

'Where is Al-Zahrani now?'

'I had him moved, just like you wanted. Problem is I don't think he'll make it.' His next words were tinged with dissension. 'This isn't good, Randall. You should have waited to—'

'Let's not play the blame game,' Stokes warned, his voice hoarse. A coughing fit came over him. During the past three hours, his breathing had become progressively strained, as if his chest had been filled with pebbles. Out of the window he saw a silver sports sedan arrive in the parking lot.

'This plan of yours has gone to shit!' Crawford blasted. 'I'm calling for back-up.'

'You'll do no such thing,' Stokes said. Another coughing fit came over him, more intense this time. He snatched a handkerchief from his pocket and held it over his mouth. When he pulled it away, he was stunned to see the crisp white linen was speckled with red dots. As he stared at the blood, a chilling realisation hit him: this was no mere physical response to stress.

'Randall? You there?'

He pressed the receiver to his ear. 'Do nothing until that cave is cleared out. Understand?'

'Let's be sensible about this. Al-Zahrani's been infected . . .'

Infected. The word lingered in Stokes's mind as he stared at the handkerchief. Infected?

'So maybe we can use that to our advantage.'

'After all our preparation and planning, there is no way in hell that I'm going to rely on one catalyst. You heard what Frank told us: rapid transmission is critical. It's the whole purpose of what we've done inside that cave. If Al-Zahrani is isolated, the whole thing fizzles out. There'll be no backpedalling now.'

Outside, the driver had just got out from the silver car and was making his way around to the passenger side. 'There's no such thing as a perfect plan,' Stokes said. 'Now get your men together and open that tunnel. Anyone asks questions, you tell them you've got four more terrorists to pull out of that hole. That's all anyone needs to know.'

As the female got out from the car, Stokes did a double take. Even from a distance she looked awfully familiar.

'I'll see what I can do,' Crawford said, exasperated.

Stokes slammed the receiver back on its base. He went to his email screen and opened a JPEG attachment.

A perfect match.

'What in God's name is she doing here?' It was insult enough that the miserable prick of an assassin had botched his assignment. But her showing up on the doorstep? He slid open the desk drawer and pulled out his Glock. Clicking the safety off, he dropped it into his jacket pocket.

The computer let out an alert; a new email message had arrived. When he saw who'd sent it, his heart faltered. 'It's about time, Frank,' he muttered.

> How ironic that I'd come to your office to kill you. But, as always, you were a step ahead. Congratulations, Randall! If there is justice in this godforsaken world, you will no doubt confiscate my PDA. If so, you may have noticed the thin residue coating its keyboard. See that rash on your hand?

Pulse accelerating, Stokes turned over his hand and assessed the raw, inflamed skin on his palm.

> Since you're so obsessed by disease, it's only fitting that you die from pestilence. That was a highly concentrated strain of anthrax you touched. Death comes swiftly, but not before two to three days of intense suffering as your respiratory system bleeds out and chokes you. Or maybe you'll choose to hasten your demise by your own hand? Good riddance. See you in Hell.

Stokes crumpled in his chair and turned to the window. On the other side of the glass, a black dove stared back at him.

CHAPTER NINE

From the sky, the rogue pick-up truck was easy to spot as it sped along an open ribbon of dusty roadway leading west over the plain. The Black Hawk was closing the gap fast. 'That's them,' Jason said, lowering his night-vision binoculars.

'Where do you think they're taking him?' Meat asked. 'Kirkuk?'

'Probably. And we can't let that happen. The road crosses a bridge up ahead. Think you might be able to set us down on the other side, block them in?'

'Hell yeah,' Meat said. 'We could just take out the bridge.'

'That would be a waste of taxpayers' dollars,' Jason said with a smile.

As the Black Hawk swooped low over the truck on a direct path for the bridge, Jason suddenly noticed activity—Arab men scurrying out from under the trusses with weapons. Jason screamed, 'Pull up!'

Through his night-vision lenses, Meat saw an RPG tube aimed directly at him. 'Oh shit,' he gasped. He pulled hard to the left. At close range, the chopper was hopelessly caught in the gunner's sight. He decreased altitude.

The grenade launched in under a second, and the gunner—whether by luck or design—anticipated the helicopter's movement.

The mortar struck high behind the cabin with the mast and rotors taking the brunt of the explosion. Hot metal shot through the chopper.

Through the cracked windshield Jason saw the moonlit horizon tilt like a seesaw. Then the Black Hawk's nose dropped. The ensuing freefall happened so fast, Jason had no time to brace for impact. In an instant, there came a deafening crunch of metal and shattering glass. Jason's head whipped forward.

For a good ten seconds, he saw nothing but white.

The chopper had come to a standstill at a thirty-degree forward pitch so that the harness dug into his ribs. Knifing pain radiated across his chest. He felt a warm, wet sensation over his feet and legs, which he assumed to be his own blood. When his vision finally came into focus, however, Jason was surprised to see that he was submerged in water up to his shins.

Over his right shoulder he saw the moon. The landscape was cleaved by a wide irrigation canal with steep embankments that snaked through the fields covering the plain. Water flowing through the canal churned around the downed Black Hawk.

'Are we dead yet?' Meat groaned, rubbing his neck.

'We will be if we don't keep moving,' Jason said. He tried to think how far the chopper had flown from the bridge. 'They're going to come for us.' He unclipped his helmet and tossed it into the shallow pool that covered the floor, worked the harness buckles next. Meat did the same.

'Camel? Jam?' Jason called. 'You guys OK?'

No answer.

Jason slid off his seat and peered into the rear to check. What he saw was horrifying. Both men were hanging limply from their harnesses. Camel's helmet had been blown clear off, along with half his skull. A foot-long metal rod speared through the top of Jam's helmet and out through his face.

Jason fought to remain focused, called upon his training to override the threatening emotional storm. You won't survive unless you keep it together. He closed his eyes for a moment and cycled a deep breath.

'Jesus, Google,' Meat said, distraught. 'How could this happen?'

Jason didn't have an answer.

The distant sound of a truck engine echoed through the canal, gaining in intensity. 'Now what?' Meat said.

Jason reached around his seat and grabbed the M16s stowed there. He tossed one to Meat.

'Now we make them pay for this.'

JASON AND MEAT climbed the embankment and crawled into a dense barley field that bordered the canal.

Fifteen seconds later a lone pick-up truck made a slow approach through the canal, heading straight for the flames shooting up from the fallen Black Hawk.

Scanning the enemy, Jason counted five men—the driver, a passenger, three men with machine-guns in the cargo bed. When the truck came to a stop, all five jumped out and gathered around the crash site. They raised their hands to the sky and began chanting 'Allahu Akbar!'

When they started posing for victory pictures, however, something inside Jason snapped. He stood up, raising his M16 with lightning speed, and opened fire. Meat followed Jason's lead. Neither stopped firing until their ammo clips had emptied. When it was finished, the river ran red.

Wordlessly, Jason and Meat collected the weapons from the dead Arabs and loaded them into the truck. Jason snatched the camera from the ring-leader's grip. He snapped some pictures of his own and slipped the camera into his pocket. Inside the truck he found paperwork on the dashboard that bore a familiar Arabic insignia.

Meat climbed into the seat beside him and saw it too. 'Al-Qaeda. They're like cockroaches.'

A disturbing realisation settled over Jason: this ambush was no coincidence. These men who'd been lying in wait were no mere splinter group. 'These guys had been tipped off that Al-Zahrani was driven out from the camp,' he said.

Keeping the truck's lights off, he backtracked through the canal towards the roadway. Within two minutes, the silhouette of the bridge came into view.

As he moved in cautiously, he spotted a dark form tangled on the rocks underneath the span.

'What is that?' Meat said. 'Is that—?'

Jason flipped on the headlights. Now the form was easy to identify. 'Yeah. It's a body.'

Making a slow approach, Jason scanned the immediate area. No vehicles. No men. They slogged over to the dead man.

'Staff Sergeant Richards,' Jason said, shaking his head. 'Figures.'

'Hate to state the obvious, Google. But there must've been more of those guys under this bridge. 'Cause they killed this guy,' he pointed at the dead staff sergeant, 'and the truck he was driving isn't here any more. I think that means Al-Zahrani is gone.'

'Not exactly,' Jason replied confidently.

BROOKE THOMPSON and Thomas Flaherty strolled up the cathedral's centre aisle. Shafts of sunlight penetrated the gravity-defying geodesic dome. The altar dominated the rear wall, resembling a concert stage with its huge viewing screens, speaker clusters and spotlighting arrays. Thousands of seats arranged in tiered arcs had already been installed on the main floor, but the balcony was still an unfinished piece of curved concrete.

'Welcome,' a cheery voice called to them, and a gaunt man with a pure white pompadour headed to greet them.

He proffered a hand, first to Brooke. 'Minister Edward Shaeffer, at your service.'

'Hi, I'm . . . Anna,' she said.

'May Christ's love shine upon you, Anna,' he said with Broadway flair, clasping his other hand over hers.

'And this is my fiancé, Thomas.'

'Fiancé. How exciting. Such a joyous time. Congratulations.'

Shaeffer relinquished her hand and took Flaherty's.

'We've just moved into town,' he explained, 'and we were hoping to have our wedding ceremony here.'

'The cathedral won't be open for another three or four months.'

'We were thinking about next October,' Brooke said.

'That should do just fine.'

'While we're here, would it be possible to meet Pastor Stokes?' Flaherty asked.

The request caught Shaeffer off guard. 'I'm afraid he's indisposed at the moment. Though for wedding arrangements, you'll need to speak directly to our Minister of Ceremonial Rites, Maureen Timpson.'

'That won't be necessary, Edward,' a warm voice called out.

A tall figure materialised from the shadow beneath the balcony.

Brooke immediately recognised Randall Stokes from the picture in Flaherty's file.

'Did I hear "wedding"?' Stokes said with a well-rehearsed smile. Striding down the aisle, his artificial leg limped slightly.

Brooke immediately understood how Stokes had achieved celebrity status. The man had presence. He was tall, handsome and meticulously dressed—though she noticed his complexion was pallid and his eyes showed fatigue.

'Edward, I'll talk to Anna and Thomas so you can finish what you're doing.'

The minister knew not to question Stokes. 'Splendid. It was nice to meet you both.' He half bowed before ambling back towards the altar.

'Please, walk with me,' Stokes said, leading them towards the lobby. 'We can talk in my office,' he said, pressing the button for the elevator. 'I'm sure you have many questions.'

Unsure of the context of his remark, Brooke and Flaherty remained silent.

'However, if we're all going to be honest,' Stokes added, 'shouldn't you use your real name, Ms Thompson?' He looked deep in her eyes. 'Ms Brooke Thompson. Isn't that right?'

Brooke gave Flaherty an uneasy glance.

The elevator doors slid open. 'Please,' Stokes motioned them inside. The doors glided shut, and the elevator began its imperceptible ascent. Gospel music pumped in from overhead speakers.

'How was your flight from Boston?' Stokes asked.

'Smooth sailing,' Flaherty said. He noticed Stokes was wheezing. And the overhead lighting highlighted a film of perspiration on the preacher's face.

'Are you CIA or FBI?' Stokes asked.

'Neither,' Flaherty replied truthfully.

Stokes gave him an appraising stare. 'I'm not surprised. Feds love to travel in pairs and wave their credentials around. Makes them feel special. You're not the cowboy type. So let me guess . . . You've got a Boston accent and Bostonians prefer to stick to their own.' Simple deduction led to only one conclusion: must work for the same outfit as the mercenaries who'd found the cave. 'Therefore, I'd say you're with Global Security Corporation.'

'Lucky guess,' Flaherty replied flatly. 'Agent Thomas Flaherty.'

The elevator came to a stop. Stokes led them into his office.

'Please, have a seat,' Stokes said, indicating the wingback chairs on the guest side of his desk. 'You actually would make a handsome couple, but why are you really here?'

Flaherty got to the point. 'Our intelligence shows that during the past twenty-four hours you've been communicating with US Marine Colonel Bryce Crawford. He's been making encrypted calls to a land line in this building. That one, perhaps?' He pointed to the phone on Stokes's desk.

'Perhaps,' Stokes replied.

'So you're aware that Colonel Crawford's platoon is assisting an extraction effort currently underway in the Iraqi mountains?'

'I am.'

Stokes's candour surprised Brooke.

'I assume you're also aware that Frank Roselli was killed in a freak car crash today. Not far from here, in fact.'

Stokes paused before replying. 'Very unfortunate.'

'You don't seem too broken up for a man who just lost a close friend,' said Flaherty.

'I've seen plenty of death in my day. After a while, one gets numb to it.'

'Seems you've killed plenty in your day too.'

'I killed lots of bad guys so kids like you could eat McDonald's, drive SUVs and have 3.2 children. The only thing I'm guilty of is being a die-hard patriot.'

'But why did you try to kill me?' Brooke asked.

Stokes grinned.

'Hold on, Brooke,' Flaherty said. 'You see, Stokes, at roughly the same time Frank Roselli was killed, an assassin tried to kill Ms Thompson in Boston. But he died trying. Our office had a tough time working through the guy's multiple identities. He did, however, have a marine tattoo on his arm. So we tried running his prints through the CIA database instead and found that Corporal Lawrence Massey trained at Camp Pendleton—under Bryce Crawford.'

'Go on,' Stokes encouraged.

'In 2003 Ms Thompson was hired by Frank Roselli to assist in a covert excavation in the Iraqi mountains, a project of which the Department of Defense has no formal knowledge. The same cave, as it turns out, that Crawford is so intent on protecting. Everyone commissioned to work on that dig, present company excluded'—he tipped his head towards Brooke—'has turned up dead in the past twenty-four hours. And of course there are those bone samples Roselli had brought back from the dig and studied at Fort Detrick. All those teeth.' Flaherty got up from his chair and pointed to the framed picture of Stokes, Roselli and Crawford on the trophy wall. 'You're a smart man. So I'm sure you see where I'm going with this.'

A coughing fit struck Stokes. He held a handkerchief over his mouth. When he was done, he stared at the bloodied linen and struggled to catch his breath. He shook his head and laughed.

'Are you all right?' Flaherty couldn't help but ask.

'Actually I'm not. By tomorrow, I'll be dead. Which means I have no reason to hide anything from you. So you'll get your answers. You'll hear things you'll wish you had never heard. But first I need to show you a few things.'

Stokes ushered the two guests across the office to an ordinary-looking door centred between two floor-to-ceiling bookcases. He punched a pass code into a keypad mounted on the doorframe to disengage the vault's pneumatic locking system. He clasped the door handle and turned to Brooke and Flaherty. 'Few have ever been in this room,' he confided in a whisper. 'This is where I keep my personal collection.'

'After you,' Flaherty said to Brooke. As she slipped past him, he paused at the threshold and gave the formidable security door closer consideration. He noted the dead bolt on the door's inside face. Giving the spacious vault a cursory once over, he detected no other doors or windows. The air in here was thin. One word came to mind: asphyxiation.

As she moved deeper into the vault, Brooke was rendered speechless by the incredible assortment of Mesopotamian relics Stokes had amassed. She stared in wonder at the huge monolith carved in bas-relief with two winged Mesopotamian protective spirits, half human, half lion, facing one another in profile. Raised wings and ceremonial dress adorned with rosettes depicted their divinity.

'Is this from Babylon?'

'No. That was the seal that we removed from the cave entrance.'

She quickly tabulated that it pre-dated Babylonian works by at least fourteen centuries. 'It's magnificent.'

'Indeed. Even more impressive than what came centuries after it. Just like the writing you transcribed for us—far more sophisticated than anyone ever expected.'

In the obelisk-shaped display case next to the seal, Brooke spotted a highly unusual clay tablet etched not only in writing, but schematic designs.

'This text . . . these images,' she said in awe. 'Is this what I think it is?'

Stokes nodded. 'The world's oldest map. Given to me by a dear friend.'

It had been Monsignor Ibrahim himself who had overseen Stokes's physical recovery and spiritual rehabilitation after he'd lost his leg. The monsignor had brought Stokes to the looming mountain that marked Lilith's ancient tomb and imparted to him a haunting tale of civilisation's first Apocalypse, which had devastated a lush paradise. By torchlight, they'd stood side by side in the cave's entry passage as the monsignor recounted Lilith's journey, immortalised in stone. He'd shown Stokes the chamber where Lilith's victims had been buried en masse. Then he'd brought Stokes to the demon's tomb, deep inside the mountain.

'Like you, Lilith's bold venture into the unknown realm has not been in vain,' the monsignor had told him. 'Her predestined journey merely marked the beginning for changes yet to come. Now it is time for your destiny to begin.' And from that humble beginning Operation Genesis had sprung.

Stokes punched a code into the base of the display case, then unhinged the lid. He removed the tablet and offered it to her.

'This, Ms Thompson, is the map to what later mythology would call Eden. A treasure map that points to the beginning of humanity and civilisation. A thriving city in the northern mountains of ancient Mesopotamia. It is how we found the cave.'

As she held the tablet, Brooke was overcome.

'You can see,' Stokes said, 'the river that once led to the Zagros Mountains. But the real clues are written here.' He indicated the wedge-shaped symbols.

The way the symbols repeated suggested to Brooke that it was a numbering system. If so, the established time line of recorded history had been turned upside-down. The earliest known numeral system had been developed in southern Mesopotamia in 2000 BC by the Sumerians using Y-shaped wedges and sideways Vs. What appeared on this tablet looked very different, and much more sophisticated than the Sumerian system.

'These are numbers?' Brooke said.

'Yes. Geographic coordinates based on astrological measurements,' Stokes said. 'Ingenious for its time.'

'Is that possible, Brooke?' Flaherty asked.

She considered it, then nodded. 'The Mesopotamians were obsessed with the celestial cycles. So I'd say yes.' But without fully transcribing and testing the number system she had to accept what Stokes was saying. 'And this was what led you to the cave?' she asked Stokes.

'Yes.'

Flaherty was losing his patience. 'This is all very nice, Stokes. But let's talk about the other things you found in the cave. The real reason behind your excavation. We know about the skeletons. So why did you study all their teeth?'

'Yes, the teeth,' Stokes said. He reflected for a moment then directed his response to Brooke. 'As you know, the emergence of civilisation has been marked by false starts and setbacks. And every major turning point, every conquest in history, has been determined by nature's most potent equaliser: disease. The story you deciphered on the wall of that cave chronicled one of the most profound events that shaped modern civilisation. It told of a thriving, technologically advanced people who'd effectively been wiped out shortly after the arrival of a foreign visitor.'

'Lilith,' Brooke said.

'That's one of the names later mythology ascribes to her,' he conceded. 'Lilith was responsible for a wholesale extermination at the dawn of civilisation.'

'But only the males died, right?' Brooke said.

'Every one of them. Which begged the question: how could pestilence afflict only men? It seemed impossible. But the remains found in that cave substantiate the story. At that time Frank Roselli was overseeing Fort Detrick's Infectious Disease lab. His top virologists and geneticists studied specimens from the cave—traces of ancient DNA left behind from a most unusual virus. I'm not a scientist, so the nuances are lost on me. However, I do understand the basic mechanics.'

Stokes paused to marshal his thoughts. 'The majority of conventional viruses are coded in RNA and replicate within the cytoplasm of host cells. But some viruses, like Lilith's plague, are coded in DNA and penetrate deeper into the host cell's nuclear core to replicate. When Lilith's virus enters the host cell's nucleus, replication can occur only when the viral DNA successfully binds to a matching gene sequence found on the male Y chromosome. And we believe that that gene sequence is specific to males of distinct Arab ancestry. In the absence of this specific Y chromosome gene marker, the virus remains dormant. So a female, or a male of non-Arab descent, can carry the virus, but not manifest its symptoms.'

Stokes continued, 'The skeletons we found in that cave were among the earliest ancestors of modern Arabs. When we compared their Y chromosomes to modern Middle Eastern men, the similarities were startling. So that brings us to a most compelling crossroads.' He held out his hands like a magician. 'You're a smart man, Agent Flaherty. I'm sure you see where I'm going with this.'

Flaherty certainly understood what Stokes was implying, though he wasn't buying it. 'You're hoping to recreate Lilith's plague.'

'Bravo,' Stokes said.

Brooke was incredulous. 'You're saying you've created a plague that kills only males of Arab ancestry?'

'Give or take,' Stokes said.

'But you developed a vaccine, right?' Brooke said.

'There is no vaccine, Ms Thompson. And by the time one is developed, the balance of humankind will be reset, just as God intended when he sent Lilith over those mountains so long ago. It's a perfect solution to solve the hostilities in the Middle East. No soldiers or weapons needed. We let Mother Nature do what she does best.'

'The DNA would have degraded,' Brooke said with conviction. 'The DNA in those teeth wouldn't have been any good.'

'You're missing the point, Ms Thompson. The teeth from the skeletons in the burial chamber only confirmed the genetic profiles of the plague victims. And you're absolutely correct: the viral DNA found in those specimens wasn't well preserved. However, there was some perfectly preserved viral DNA. Let me show you.'

Brooke and Flaherty watched Stokes step over to the veil-covered display case in the room's centre. 'You see, it wasn't only Lilith's victims we discovered in that cave.' Stokes pulled the veil away, revealing the most prized item in his collection, locked within a rectangular glass case. 'It was Lilith herself.'

MOUNTED ON A GLASS BASE inside the case was a translucent sphere, flat on top and bottom, no bigger than a medicine ball. Frozen within it was a human head.

Cold prickles shot down Brooke's spine. Lilith's head was both beautiful and ghastly. Wisps of golden hair intermingled with swirls of blood spun through the honey-coloured sphere. The flesh remained intact so that even now, millennia later, the face seemed locked in time, a snapshot of death that bore testament to a brutal execution. The lips remained in a taunting smile. But it was the inescapable stare of the eyes that was most frightful.

'As you can see, she has been perfectly preserved,' Stokes said. 'After the executioners cut off her head, they immediately sealed it away, hoping that Lilith's evil would be trapped for eternity. But it wasn't Lilith's soul that had been the source of her malevolence. It was her DNA. And you can see how we got to it by drilling through the resin.' He pointed to thin bore holes that extended through the resin to penetrate the skull's crown. 'All we had to do was extract the dormant virions and culture them.'

'If it's so simple, why are you so concerned about the cave?' Flaherty said.

'Come now, Agent Flaherty,' Stokes said, feigning disappointment. 'A virus in a dish is useless. For a plague to have any effect, it must be spread—widely and rapidly. It needs a catalyst.'

Then Flaherty remembered Jason saying how sick Al-Zahrani had been when they pulled him out from the cave. 'You infected Al-Zahrani, didn't you? Is he your catalyst?'

'He's infected, yes. But I can't rely on him. He's only one man, after all.' Stokes stepped up to the display case, pressed his hand against the glass, and stared reverently at Lilith. 'The beauty of plague is that, once it is introduced into a population, nature itself provides the most reliable delivery system.'

Stokes's breathing was getting shallower. 'Once the infection begins, no one will be able to stop it. In under an hour this virus rips through cells, gets into the blood and the lymph nodes. In less than two hours, it strikes the lungs and becomes pneumonic.'

'Nu-what?' Flaherty said.

'It becomes airborne. Someone can catch it just by breathing it in,' Brooke said in horror.

'Very good, Ms Thompson,' Stokes said. 'When all is said and done, an entire generation of Arabs will be wiped out and the threat of Islamic fanaticism along with them. And there will be zero accountability for the United States.'

'Why do this?' Brooke challenged. 'What's the point?'

'The point? Come now, Ms Thompson,' Stokes said. 'This is no ordinary enemy. They don't wear uniforms. They don't respect innocence. They hate civilisation and everything we stand for. Flying planes into buildings is only the beginning for them.'

'You're a real nut job, Stokes,' Flaherty said. 'I'm giving you one more chance to answer my question. What's in the cave?'

'I could tell you, but that would only ruin the surprise,' Stokes replied.

'I don't have time to play games with you.' Flaherty's fuse had burned out. If there was something in the cave, Jason would need to be warned. He went for his gun, but Stokes managed to draw his own gun first. To Flaherty's horror, the pastor levelled it at Brooke's chest.

'I've had lots more practice than you, Agent Flaherty,' Stokes said as another coughing fit struck. He covered his mouth with the crook of his arm and when he pulled it away, blood and bile covered his jacket sleeve. 'Let's not make this messy. I told you, I'm already a dead man. Don't you see?' He held out the gory sleeve. 'I've got nothing to lose.'

'You don't look dead to me,' Flaherty said.

'Roselli managed to infect me with one of his lab experiments,' Stokes said. 'Some home-grown variety of anthrax, apparently. So if that's the case, I won't last another day. With that in mind, I'm determined to witness the results of all my hard work. And right now, you're making that very difficult for me. Give me your gun.' He extended his free hand.

Flaherty knew that despite Stokes's hopeless condition, the former Special Ops commando was fully capable of pulling the trigger at least once before going down. 'Fine,' he said, passing his Beretta to Stokes.

Stokes pocketed the gun. 'Now, while I attend to business, you can make yourselves comfortable.' He stepped backwards towards the door. 'Behave yourselves and I'll have someone let you out after this is over.'

Helpless, Flaherty and Brooke watched as Stokes pulled the door closed.

CHAPTER TEN

'You're sure these coordinates are right?' Meat asked, checking his handheld GPS unit. 'I mean, this thing's pretty accurate.'

Twenty minutes earlier, the satellite trace Jason had called in to Mack had pinpointed the square he'd marked on the hood of the truck Staff Sergeant Richards had used to spirit Al-Zahrani away from the camp. The grid had led them here, to a desolate region less than a twenty-kilometre drive from the downed Black Hawk. The perfectly flat terrain provided long-range visibility over wheat fields extending in every direction. An occasional ramshackle structure poked up into the landscape. But there was no sign of the hijacked truck.

'They must be on the move again,' Jason guessed. 'I'll have Mack request another—'

'Whoa . . . hang on,' Meat said. 'See that shit box over there?'

A two-storey house constructed from cinderblock glowed in the moonlight.

'What about it?'

Meat pointed to a crude overhang attached to the side of the house. 'There she is.'

Only a corner of the scratched-up bumper and a sliver of the sky-blue tailgate stuck out from beneath the camouflage netting that covered the stolen pick-up.

Jason eased the truck forward and stopped five metres from the house. In the upstairs window he saw two silhouettes moving behind drawn shades.

'Get ready. There's our host,' Meat said, pointing to the porch.

An Arab with an AK-47 was trying to see inside the truck.

'Ta' âl huna!' Meat called in Arabic. Come over here, stupid.

The Arab came up to Meat's window and leaned in for a better view.

Meat plunged his K-bar knife through the man's Adam's apple and then sliced the blade upwards. He let the body drop to the ground out of view of the house.

Jason grabbed one of the AK-47s they'd stripped from the al-Qaeda gang. 'Let's go,' he said. As Meat headed straight for the house he shadowed him with his weapon drawn.

Inside, Jason turned right and swept the first room. Nothing but a wooden table and two metal folding chairs.

Jason heard frenzied voices overhead. Three distinct tones. He dropped to one knee, raised his AK-47, and strafed the ceiling in a wide 'G', followed by a tight 'X'. The voices had gone silent, but a single set of footsteps pattered fast towards the centre of the house before Jason could line up for another sweep.

Meat also heard the runner and bolted to the staircase. He spotted his target and opened fire.

An agonising scream rang out just before a rifle came cartwheeling down the stairs.

Meat charged up the stairs. Three seconds later, he yelled, 'Google, get up here!'

CRAWFORD SHONE the floodlight up at the gaping hole the marines had opened on top of the rubble that dammed the tunnel passage. Emerging from the other side, a grimy face capped by a sand-coloured helmet appeared in the light.

'Colonel, there's a lot of blood on this side,' Corporal William Shuster reported matter-of-factly. 'Some fingers and tissue too. I don't see how anyone could've survived the explosion.'

Crawford remained stone-faced. 'Al-Zahrani managed to walk out of here. Let's make sure no one else does.'

Shuster scuttled down the rocks, a flashlight in his right hand. His left was balled up in a fist and he opened it to reveal a palm full of metal ball bearings covered in a tacky film—trademark shrapnel used in padding suicide vests. 'Found these on the ground,' he said. 'They're covered in C4 residue. Not sure why one of them would have detonated himself in there. You'd think he'd have waited for a few of us before pushing the button . . . take a few infidels with him on his way to paradise.'

None of this surprised Crawford. Stokes had been quick to inform him about the clumsy gunman who'd let loose some rounds into the man who'd been strapped with plastic explosive. More troubling was the quiet on the other side of the blockage. Crawford anticipated activity. Lots of activity. And not from the holed-up Arabs.

He turned to the six men congregated in the passage behind him. 'Ramirez . . . Holt. You two get in there with Corporal Shuster and see what we've got.' The marines looked at one another in a way that clearly suggested dissension. 'This isn't a democracy, gentlemen. Get your weapons and get in there! And where's that damn Kurd?'

'Here, sir,' a quiet voice called from the rear.

The four marines made room for Hazo to shuffle through.

Crawford had to make a conscious effort not to react to the Kurd's appearance. The man looked haggard and feverish, his eyes bloodshot. The similarity to Al-Zahrani's early symptoms was alarming.

'If we have any survivors in there,' Crawford said, 'I'll need you to talk some sense into them. Tell them to be smart and surrender. Can I count on you to do this?'

'Colonel,' Shuster said defiantly. 'He's in no condition to—'

Crawford stepped up to Shuster and put his face so close, the two men touched noses. 'Corporal, you are way out of line.'

'Please,' Hazo said, putting an appeasing hand on Shuster's arm. 'I will help you.'

Shuster unstrapped the M9 pistol from his side holster and proffered it to Hazo. 'If you're going in there, take this.' He gave him a quick tutorial on how to flip off the safety and fire the gun. 'And stay behind us,' he added.

THE INSTANT Stokes attempted to close the vault's door, Flaherty snatched the clay map from Brooke and bolted after him. He was only four steps away when the door stopped short from sealing against the frame. On the other side, Stokes tried pulling harder on the handle, yet the dead bolt was slightly engaged, protruding just enough to keep the door from sealing. Flaherty had tampered with it on entering.

It took mere seconds for Stokes to detect the problem and he raised his gun to prepare for a cautious re-entry.

Flaherty launched the five-pound tablet at Stokes's head. Stokes bobbed sideways and the tablet skimmed his right ear. In the process, he managed to fire one shot that sailed past Flaherty and thwacked into the thick security glass on the front of the display case containing Lilith's head.

Before Stokes could regain his footing, Flaherty charged forward and buried his right shoulder in the preacher's abdomen. The tackle lifted Stokes, brought him crashing down on to the floor with his chest catching the brunt of the impact.

Yet Stokes was quick to respond and the gun came arcing towards Flaherty's face. With both hands, Flaherty grabbed at Stokes's wrist and forced the Glock sideways. A second shot rang out and punched through the wall.

Flaherty was certain that getting into a wrestling match with Stokes was a losing proposition. But Stokes had two things working against him: a missing leg and anthrax-tainted lungs. With the struggle escalating, Flaherty could hear bubbling sounds coming from Stokes's chest.

Stokes responded with a head-butt that caught Flaherty on the bridge of the nose and made him see stars but he managed to hold on to the gun. At the same time, he buried his shoulder in Stokes's face.

Choking, Stokes struggled to push Flaherty away.

Then Stokes let out a muffled scream and Flaherty felt the gun pinned hard against the floor. He glimpsed a chunky black boot grinding down on the gun.

'Let it go, Stokes!' Brooke yelled. She stomped down a second time and the gun fell from his mashed fingers. A swift kick sent it skittering across the carpet.

Like riding a bronco, Flaherty couldn't control the flailing and bucking pastor. To regain his balance, he had to relinquish his grip on Stokes's wrist and another forceful buck sent Flaherty tumbling onto the floor. Stokes rolled on to his elbows and retched blood and bile on to the carpet.

It was the opportunity Brooke had been waiting for. In her hand, she clutched the nearest solid object she could find—the clay tablet. With all her might, she swung the map of Eden down at Stokes's head. It connected. The pastor collapsed onto the floor.

JASON HAD TO COVER his mouth and nose with his sleeve to fight off the fetid stench. Sprawled atop a mattress that was the room's only furnishing, the corpse of Fahim Al-Zahrani lay in a gory mire. Blood streamed like tears from his lifeless eyes—the orbs solid red. And the entire mattress beneath his lower half was completely saturated, suggesting that blood and liquefied organs had found their way out of every possible exit.

'Man,' Meat said, 'what did these guys do to him?'

'They didn't do this. They couldn't have.'

'Then who did?'

As if on cue, Jason's sat-com vibrated. He dug in his pocket to find it, saw that it was Flaherty.

'Everything all right in Vegas?'

'No. Not by a long shot, I'm afraid.'

Jason listened as Flaherty rehashed the candid tell-all discussion he and Brooke had had with Pastor Randall Stokes—the discovery of an ancient contagion that USAMRIID scientists under Frank Roselli's guidance had weaponised for mass transmission throughout the Middle East. Staring over at Al-Zahrani, Jason felt his nerves turn to ice. When Flaherty detailed Stokes's sinister objective—to annihilate the Arab male population—he could feel a dark cloud settling over him. He'd had a similar response back in September 2001, when his sister had called to report that their brother, Matthew, was officially missing at the World Trade Center.

'Not sure if I buy what Stokes said about this virus he and Roselli concocted,' Flaherty said.

'He's right, Tommy. We just found Al-Zahrani and he's dead.'

'But you pulled him out of that cave only a few hours ago.'

'That's right. We thought he had a fever. But it looks like something minced his organs and pushed them out his throat. We killed a few others that had been in contact with him . . . it's a long story. But they weren't looking too good either. If you ask me, I'd say they were showing early signs of being infected with this virus.'

'These men you've killed . . .' Flaherty said, thinking it through. 'You've got to get rid of the bodies. Burn them or something. Until we find out what's really happening, we can't risk letting this thing get out in the open.'

'Agreed.'

'There's something else too. However Stokes was planning to spread the virus, it's in that cave. He referred to it as a "delivery system". Our friend Crawford has been in on this thing all along. And he's determined to finish this, understand? So you've got to wrap things up there quickly and find a way to get back to that cave and stop Crawford.'

'HOW LONG till Candyman's chopper gets here?' Meat asked, uncapping another of the five-gallon gas cans they'd liberated from the shed where the stolen truck had been hidden.

'Ten minutes,' Jason replied. He snapped a dozen photos of Al-Zahrani's corpse, including close-ups of the face.

'Show time,' Meat said. He handed Jason one of the matchbooks he'd found in the downstairs kitchen. 'I'll give you the honour. The downstairs is ready to go. We just need to light it on the way out.'

When Meat left, Jason set the gas can down and filed the image of Al-Zahrani in his memory. He tore off a match and struck it.

'Burn in Hell,' Jason said, and flicked the match onto the mattress.

THE TUNNEL CURVED GENTLY from left to right, then back again, the ground rising and falling along a general downward trajectory. The air quality was degrading quickly, and Shuster worried that if something were not found soon, he'd need to abandon the exploration. One thought kept cycling through his mind: why would Fahim Al-Zahrani have retreated back towards his enemy? If Al-Zahrani had met a dead end, they had to be nearing it—which coincided all too well with the strange noise that was growing stronger with every step. The persistent churning sounds were difficult to place, but didn't seem to indicate a human source. Perhaps an underground water source.

He paused to try to decipher the noise.

'Sounds like something's alive down there,' Holt said.

No one challenged the idea.

'Wait here,' Shuster suggested. 'I'll go check it out.'

'Good idea,' Ramirez said.

They watched in silence as Shuster disappeared around the bend.

Hazo braced himself against the tunnel wall. He was ashen and sluggish, and his chest heaved every time he inhaled.

'Hey, Hazo,' Ramirez said. 'You know anything about this place?'

Hazo shrugged. 'Just legends.'

'That's a start,' Ramirez said. 'What legends?'

Hazo paused. 'A demon was buried here,' he explained bluntly. 'This is what some say.'

'Demon?' Holt jumped in. 'Exactly what kind of demon?'

There was no reason to keep secrets at this juncture, thought Hazo. 'Those are her pictures on the wall near the entrance. Her name is Lilith. Thousands of years ago, she came to this place. She killed every man and boy.' The conversation quickly exhausted his lungs, forcing him to cough.

'Guys!' Shuster's voice echoed up from the mountain. 'Get down here . . . I found something!'

Holt set off on a brisk pace through the tunnel, Ramirez and Hazo bringing up the rear. The passage curled sharply before spilling into a cavernous black hollow. Holt stopped dead in his tracks. 'What the . . .?' he gasped.

'Over here,' Shuster called to him from deep within the hollow.

He spotted Shuster's flashlight, now mounted on the muzzle of his M16, floating in the darkness. The light played over the surface of a massive angular form that resembled an unhitched trailer or a railroad boxcar plonked down in the middle of the cave.

And it seemed that the sounds they'd been hearing—now clearly recognisable as the whirring of mechanical parts—were coming from inside it.

'Come on, Holt!' Shuster shouted. 'Get over here!'

'Am I seeing what I think I'm seeing?' Ramirez said.

'This ain't no dream,' Holt said, pointing his light down to illuminate the ground. He was surprised to see that a section of the cave floor had been levelled into a two-and-a-half-metre-wide path, definitely not by natural means, but by some kind of excavating machine. Around the cave's walls, his light glinted off enormous stainless-steel holding tanks shaped like inverted baby bottles.

Holt and Ramirez trotted over to Shuster, while Hazo paused to catch his breath.

'How did this get down here?' Holt asked.

'Must have been brought in here in pieces, assembled on site. Modular construction. See there,' Shuster said, moving his rifle muzzle up and down so that the light emphasised one of many riveted seams connecting the container's outer steel panels.

Holt and Ramirez kept their M16s at the ready. A pale purple light glowed on a grooved ramp that led down from the side of the container. The container's short side, two and a half metres square, partially enclosed a central entry-way. Beside it, a mechanical door mounted on rails had been slid open. Semitransparent plastic flaps dangled like a curtain from the top of the entry-way to provide an air barrier. The flaps provided enough visibility to suggest that there was no one inside.

Ramirez spotted six more containers lined neatly in a row behind this one. 'Seven containers?'

'That's right,' Shuster said. 'And take a look up there.' He traced the beam along the tubular flex duct leading out from the top to join a central trunk that rose like a chimney for fifteen metres before disappearing through the cave's lofty vault. Six identical ducts branched off the main feed and patched into the tops of the other containers. The gentle breeze pushing out between the entry-way flaps confirmed that fresh air was being pumped in from above ground.

'It's a ventilation system,' Shuster said.

'Detainment cells?' Holt guessed.

'Maybe Saddam's weapons lab,' Ramirez said.

'Only one way to know for sure,' Shuster said, noting PVC pipes snaking down beside the duct work. Water lines, he guessed. 'Stay here. I'll take a look inside. See what we've got.'

WHILE THE MARINES were preoccupied with the strange structures, Hazo had made a discovery of his own. His flashlight had caught a spot where the rock face had been smoothed flat around an arched opening in the rock maybe a metre up from the ground.

He considered calling out to the others. But he needed to conserve his energy. A profound lethargy was settling into his limbs and his fever was spiking. Perspiration was welling out from his pores.

Mindful of his footing on the uneven ground, Hazo made his way to the wall in stops and starts. He squared his body with the niche and directed his light inside it. It ran much deeper than he'd thought, extending maybe two metres into the rock like a small tunnel. A deep lip the width of his hand had been carved around the rim of the opening, probably to keep a thick seal in place—a seal that had been removed. It stood to reason that the contents had also been looted. The design of the niche best suited something long and narrow that could be slid inside.

As he thought about the cave's known mythology, the realisation hit him like a wrecking ball.

'A body,' he whispered.

This niche had been a tomb. Lilith's tomb.

ON FINAL APPROACH to the camp, the Black Hawk glided low and hovered over the roadway precisely where Jason's unit had initiated its ambush only nine hours earlier. To Jason it seemed as if he'd fired that first shot a lifetime ago.

'Jesus,' Candyman said as he surveyed the ravaged camp. 'What a mess.'

On the southern perimeter, five Humvees had been rendered smouldering heaps of twisted metal. The two tents at the camp's centre had fared no better—each burned bare to the ribs. Laid neatly beside the roadway, he counted fifteen body bags ready for airlift.

'I'm still not seeing any back-up down there,' Meat said.

'They'll be here,' Candyman said decisively. 'I'd give it another forty-five minutes or so. When they radioed the camp, Crawford told them that everything was fine . . . that the camp was secure. So they were heading back to Camp Eagle's Nest. I had to convince them to turn around again.'

Candyman set the Black Hawk down on the roadway and said, 'Good luck, fellas. I've got orders to keep moving.'

Before the Black Hawk had even lifted in the air, Jason was halfway up the slope with Meat scrambling to keep up with him.

WHILE AGENT FLAHERTY was making phone calls to arrange for Stokes to be taken into custody, Brooke decided to have a closer look at the artefacts in the vault. First, she approached the case containing a sizable clay jar, just to the left of the case that accommodated Lilith's macabre severed head. Before commencing her analysis, she gave the head a sideways glance, certain that the demon's dead eyes were evaluating her every move.

'I'm just going to have a quick look,' she explained to it. 'Nothing to worry about.' Best to play nice with the evil temptress, she thought.

The bulbous clay vessel was roughly a third of a metre wide at its base, and stood about half a metre tall. Posted behind it was an enlarged photo board containing various pictures documenting its careful extraction from deep inside the cave.

The first photo showed one of the bas-reliefs Brooke had herself studied in the entry-way, depicting Lilith carrying this very jar. The second and third photographs showed Lilith's tomb in two stages: first covered by an ornately carved seal with two protective spirits (she glanced at the real-life version standing on the plinth only a little way away), second with the seal removed to show the contents. The tomb was simple enough: a deep niche carved into a rock wall. The prone skeleton's rib cage and arm bones were barely visible behind a squat clay pot positioned at the front of the niche. The top of the jar could be seen poking up from behind the pot.

Now she focused on the pot's construction. The vessel's irregular form clearly showed that this jar had been handmade without the aid of a pottery wheel, which was strange since pottery wheels had been in use centuries before 4000 BC. And the jar's neatly painted lines and decorative slashed incisions all resembled similar relics she'd studied from Hassuna and Samarra—sites that dated to 5500 BC.

Another case contained a reconstructed necklace, also recovered from Lilith's tomb. The necklace's beads were of two varieties: glossy obsidian, a black volcanic glass found in eastern Turkey, and smooth cowry shells, which in antiquity would have been found along the ancient shores of the Persian Gulf. Brooke had seen similar pieces from Arpachiyah and Chagar Bazar, all dating to the Ubaid period, around 5500 BC.

How could Lilith have acquired a jar and jewellery from fifteen centuries earlier? she wondered.

Tantalising possibilities streamed through her mind.

Then she had a shocking realisation. The stout clay pot shown in the photo had been cut precisely in half, probably with a laser, so as to free the hardened core that encased Lilith's head. The halves had been put back together and were on display to the right of the case holding the head. Similar razor-sharp lines ran down both sides of the jar, suggesting that it had also been cut in two to study the contents.

Could the original contents still be inside the jar? Or was this just the reassembled vessel? Brooke's heart began racing at the thought of it.

She studied the case containing the jar. It had a hinged top and a keypad, like the case from which Stokes had removed the clay map. She'd seen the numbers Stokes had used to access the map. Odds were the code was the same for this box. She punched in the code. The keypad flashed and the top's locking mechanism snapped open.

Brooke opened the case. She held her breath as she reached inside.

CHAPTER ELEVEN

The container's high-tech interior baffled Corporal Shuster. Overhead, the fluorescent tubes looked like the ultraviolet lights used in plant nurseries to mimic sunlight. The air was redolent with an ammonia-like scent.

Mounted like cubbyholes along the side walls were seven adjoining Plexiglas cells. Each was the size of a footlocker and had a hinged front panel vented with a dense grid of tiny air holes.

Cages? wondered Schuster.

All the front panels were held open by a mechanised piston—whatever inhabited the cages seemed to have been set free. When was anyone's guess. Inspecting one of the cages, he saw a thick wire mesh bottom with a tray liner that angled towards a slot on the side wall. Perforated tubes looping around the tray's edges were likely intended to flush away waste.

But there was plenty of waste on the floor—grape-sized pellets, black against the purple light. He crouched down for a better look, but recoiled from the acrid stench. Coating almost every surface were short black hairs, as straight as pins. Millions of them.

Along the back side of each cage, a dozen short metal tubes with rolling ball ends protruded from the wall like nipples. He used his index finger to push one of the tips. Milky fluid streamed out over his fingertips. Oddly, it smelled like wheat beer. A feeding system, he guessed, probably linked into the PVC supply lines he'd seen running up to the ceiling.

Air and food pumped in from above. It seemed as if the whole operation was automated from the outside.

Ramirez made his way inside. He came to a stop after two steps. 'What kind of freaky shit is this?' He buried his nose in his sleeve.

'Breeding kennels, I think,' Shuster said.

Ramirez wasn't buying it. 'For what?'

'Don't know.'

'Maybe al-Qaeda's selling puppies on the black market to fund the jihad.'

'Funny.'

'Who could have built this?' Ramirez asked.

Shuster shook his head. 'Got me.'

'Creepy,' Ramirez muttered. He paced slowly along the aisle, trying to make sense of it all.

Outside the container, Holt could see Ramirez and Shuster. The ventilation system's motor turned off with a loud thunk, startling him.

'Hey,' he called, 'did you guys switch the air off?'

'It's probably on a timer,' Schuster replied. 'Nothing to worry about.'

'Right,' Holt said. But when the fan whirred to a stop, other sounds masked by the humming motor suddenly came to the foreground. It took a moment for his ears to adjust, but the sounds were definitely there—subtle scratching noises. The vast space made it difficult to discern where they were coming from, but they seemed loudest towards the rear of the cave. 'Guys, I hear something weird out here.'

No answer.

Holt aimed his M16 towards the disturbance, moved the light slowly from right to left through the soupy darkness, but saw nothing.

The more he listened to the sounds, the more he tried to convince himself they were nothing at all. Probably some other piece of machinery buried deeper in the cave that was in need of a little grease.

Holt moved stealthily down the path, pausing outside the door of each container and glancing into its interior. There was no movement inside any of them. What exactly were these things? he wondered.

As he cornered the final container, the noises grew louder. Much louder.

He deliberated on whether to investigate or turn back. Then his light settled on an opening in the cave's rear wall.

He stood perfectly still and angled his right ear for a better listen.

Now he was certain that the noises were coming from inside the burrow. What if the terrorists were holed up in there waiting to make a move?

Holt levelled his rifle and advanced towards the opening. Once inside, he hesitated and shone the light into the tunnel. The ground pitched steadily downwards into a sharp bend that curved out of sight about ten metres from where he was standing. Whatever was causing the disturbance was definitely in there.

As he followed the bend, he raised his M16 higher on his shoulder, stared down the light beam mounted on the muzzle. The sounds intensified, throwing his senses into high gear. Definitely didn't sound like a machine. Or a terrorist, either.

Ssssst.

Chssst.

Something tapped his shoulder from behind and he let out a bloodcurdling scream. In the same instant, he whirled fiercely and tweaked his ankle. When he tried to bring the rifle up for a shot, the muzzle hit the wall hard enough to shatter the element in his light.

'Whoa! Relax!' Ramirez yelled out, holding out his hand.

Holt took a few seconds to compose himself.

Ramirez couldn't help but laugh.

Holt laughed too, and it felt good. 'Scared the crap outta me, you—'

The droning from deep within the tunnel suddenly whipped up like a raging tempest. Ramirez's smile went flat. He took a step back and brought his rifle up high. 'What the . . .'

Before Holt could turn to see what was emerging from the shadows, he saw Ramirez's eyes fill with terror. 'Holy shit! Get out of the way!'

Fully panicked, Holt refused to look back. He scrambled towards Ramirez, clumsily barrelling into him. Both men went down.

'What the fuck!' Ramirez shouted.

Holt's hands swept the ground, probing for his weapon. His fingers registered something. But it wasn't steel—it was spongy. And it bit him. Then came another deep bite on his thigh. 'Ahh!'

Ramirez was back on his feet and shone the light on Holt. His blood went cold as thousands of eyes glared back at him.

ANXIOUS TO SHARE his discovery of Lilith's tomb with Shuster, Hazo made his way towards the cave's centre and along the row of containers. He spotted Shuster inside the fourth one. Best not to disturb him, Hazo thought.

He aimed his light up to a truck-sized motor housing mounted on a steel platform atop the container, directly above the door. Amber lights blinked on its control panel. Bolted alongside the doorway was the platform's access ladder.

A shrill scream rang out and Hazo spun towards it, sweeping his light from side to side.

Shuster responded in an instant, bounding down the short ramp with his M16 at the ready. 'What the hell was that?' he asked Hazo.

'Back there.' Hazo pointed to the cave's rear.

'Stay here,' Shuster told him then bolted off to investigate.

When the corporal disappeared around the container at the end of the row, Hazo decided to climb up to the control platform for a better view. Gripping the ladder rungs, he began his ascent. Halfway to the top, he paused to catch his breath.

Off in the distance, he heard Ramirez laughing, Holt joining in shortly thereafter. Must have been a false alarm, he reasoned.

The wheezing in his lungs had given way to something much worse. Suddenly something ruptured beneath his breastbone. Within seconds, he felt like he was drowning. He coughed violently and a hot viscous liquid swelled into the back of his throat, bringing with it the taste of copper.

Blood.

Fighting the dread that threatened to paralyse him, he spat out the vile phlegm and managed to catch his breath. Clambering topside, he was overtaken by a bout of dizziness that forced him to his hands and knees. He cleared his lungs again, spat up more blood. If he'd been sickened by the same disease that afflicted Al-Zahrani, he realised, it wouldn't be long before the lethargy would give way to complete immobility and delirium. And after that . . .

Ramirez and Holt had stopped laughing and begun screaming. Hazo came to his senses. Getting to his feet, he was able to see shifting light coming from the tunnel they'd gone into.

'Get out of there!' he heard Shuster yell.

Hazo saw Ramirez's helmet bob in and out of view, Holt's next.

Three seconds later, all hell broke loose as the cave filled with the deafening clack-clack-clack of machine-gun fire.

Then Ramirez zigzagged up the path, his weapon angled low. 'Get away from me, get away from me!' he yelled.

Hazo leaned over the platform's safety rail, trying to discern what he was shooting at. At first, he couldn't spot the enemy. Then the threat became all too clear.

An undulating black wave spilled out from the rear of the cave, spreading over the ground as if a colossal oil drum had tipped over. With it came unearthly squealing that filled the cave. In the darkness the pulsing crests twinkled with countless ruby specks that shimmered like sequins.

Hazo's skin crawled at the sight of a churning sea of eyes, whiskered snouts, rubbery bodies covered in black hair. Layers upon layers of them.

Rats.

'Up here!' Hazo screamed to Ramirez. 'There is a ladder!' But his weak scream was lost in the brood's high-pitched squealing.

In less than fifteen seconds, Ramirez's ammo clip ran dry. Wasting no time with a pointless reload, he unclipped the light from the weapon's muzzle and whipped the M16 like a scythe at the advancing horde. Then he broke into a sprint and headed for the entry tunnel. The rats weren't far behind.

More screams came from the rear of the cave. Hazo hunted the darkness with his flashlight and spotted Holt knee-deep in the squirming black mass.

'STOP SNOOPING AROUND,' a gruff voice whispered over Brooke's shoulder.

Brooke flinched. Her fingers lost their grip and the jar's lid clattered back into place. Spinning around, she came face to face with Flaherty.

'Jesus, Tommy,' she said, clutching her chest. She eyed his swollen nose, the bloodstains on his shirt. 'You nearly scared me to death!'

'Just thought I'd tell you we can't leave until the infectious disease folks come and scrub us down. We'll need to be quarantined.'

'Great.' Rolling her eyes, she turned back to the jar.

'What are you looking at?' he said.

'It's the jar Lilith was carrying just before she was executed. It's supposed to have some kind of magical power. I thought I'd take a look . . . see what's inside it.'

'And?'

'I haven't got that far yet, thanks to you.'

'So what are you waiting for? Let's see if there's a rabbit in the hat.'

'All right.' She rubbed her fingertips together, then reached into the case. With utmost finesse, Brooke curled her fingertips around the lid's thick rim. She lifted away the platelike clay disc and gave it to Flaherty. 'Hold this.'

Brooke tapped a fingernail on the solid glossy layer just below the jar's rim. It made the clink-clink sound of glass.

'I'm not seeing anything inside it,' Flaherty said. 'You?'

'No.' But if the ancient Mesopotamians had preserved the jar's contents employing the same method used on Lilith's head, then deep inside the jar something was trapped inside a viscous substance that over the centuries had hardened like glass. They just couldn't see it yet.

'Maybe we can shine a light in there, or something,' he suggested.

'I've got a better idea.' Closely studying the cut lines that split the circular rim into two equal arcs, Brooke could see paper-thin slivers of light squeezing through the fine gaps. 'I don't think this is glued.'

Reaching in with both hands, she pinched the top of the rim at the middle of each half and applied gentle outward pressure on the opposing sides.

It was sticky at first. She bit her lip and put some more push behind her fingers. The pottery yielded with a gritty creak. 'Hah . . . there we go.'

Flaherty tilted his head sideways for a better look, but refused to get any closer to the relic. With the bulbous core still masked in the jar's shadows, he couldn't yet decipher the contents.

Brooke was grinning from ear to ear. 'Oh, this is amazing.'

Flaherty's eyes twinkled with admiration as he watched how she worked the pieces apart with patient dexterity. There was an endearing innocence lurking beneath Brooke Thompson's sophisticated exterior, and in this moment her passion for archaeology burned like the sun.

Brooke spread the pottery halves so that their crescent-shaped surfaces slid out from under the solidified inner mass. The liberated core clunked against the bottom of the display case. 'My God, Tommy . . . look at this!' she gasped. 'It's beautiful.'

'Beautiful?' Flaherty said. What had been inside the jar resembled a solid, honey-coloured crystal ball, much the same as the one containing Lilith's head. And coiled inside the opaque mass was a large snake whose jaws were hinged open and frozen in place, as if it had been drowned. Like its beheaded charmer, the snake's malevolent eyes were wide open in a threatening glare. Its hooked fangs were easily five centimetres long. The black, ropey body—thick as a beer can—was covered in scales the size of a thumbnail. Flaherty guessed that if he could stretch the thing out, it would be nearly two metres long.

'Think it was poisonous?' he asked, fixated on the fangs.

'Sure looks like it,' Brooke said, slowly circling the case to see the snake from all angles.

'Why the hell would she be carrying this thing around?'

'I don't know. But think about it, Tommy—a snake is one of the central figures in Creation mythology, just like in the story of Adam, Eve and Lilith.'

Halfway around the case, she froze.

'Look here,' she said, tapping on the glass to indicate a bulge in the snake's midsection. 'Looks like the snake's last meal wasn't fully digested.'

AS RAMIREZ TORE THROUGH the tunnel, the squealing din faded and he became confident he'd make it out from the mountain unscathed. In fact, it sounded as if the rats had stayed inside the cave.

However, Ramirez's relief vanished in an instant when a series of bright flashes up ahead coincided perfectly with the hammering of automatic gunfire.

The bullets struck him low—one shattering his left kneecap, six more to the groin and thighs. His legs instantly went from under him and his face slammed into the ground. It was so fast, he didn't even scream. With all the adrenaline pumping through his system, the pain was slow coming.

But when the gunman emerged into the glowing cone of his fallen flashlight, the sting of treachery was instantaneous.

'Crawford?' he groaned, blood streaming into his right eye from a ragged gash that split his forehead. 'Wh—why?'

There was no answer. The colonel simply pressed the M16's muzzle against Ramirez's head and delivered the kill shot.

THE RODENTS were all over Holt. Hazo watched in horror as the marine flailed his arms violently, flinging rats in every direction. Trudging knee-deep through the teeming brood, it looked as if Holt were slogging through wet cement.

'Up here!' Hazo screamed. The coughing seized his voice. Spitting up more blood and bile, Hazo watched helplessly as Holt tried to quicken his pace. Then desperation and frustration got the better of him and he raised his knees to try to run. It was a costly mistake.

Trampling the rats underfoot caused Holt to lose his footing. He faltered, caught himself, faltered again. The rats piled onto him. He got back up again and shook some of them free, before slipping and going down a final time.

Hazo shone his light on the spot, praying that Holt would get up.

He didn't.

The rats swarmed over their prey.

'Hazo!' a voice called out over the maddening squeals.

Hazo turned and saw Shuster pulling himself up over the edge of the neighbouring container. He'd lost his helmet and his trouser legs were torn up and bloody. Otherwise, he seemed unharmed.

'Are you all right?' Hazo called back.

Shuster rolled onto his back. 'I'm OK,' he said, panting.

Hazo looked towards the entry tunnel and saw that the glow of Ramirez's light seemed to be growing stronger—coming back towards the cave.

YEARS HAD PASSED since Bryce Crawford last walked these tunnels, yet he still recognised every oddity and anomaly inside the mountain as if they were the birthmarks of a former lover.

Once Frank Roselli had declared the installation 'complete' the previous spring, the single entrance to Operation Genesis's self-sustaining breeding facility had been sealed. Every mechanical part of the gnotobiotic isolator cells that housed the rats had been designed for remote operation. The facility generated its own power from a compact nuclear reactor capable of churning out electricity for ten years before needing refuelling.

Even replenishment of the feeding tanks was handled by a cleverly concealed pipeline to a dairy farm situated a kilometre to the west. The milky nutrient solution manufactured there was a potent brew infused with plague virions and gonadotropin hormone that stimulated the brood's pituitary development to promote aggressive behaviour. What they'd built inside this mountain was the most sophisticated installation of its kind. Such a pity that not long from now, not a trace of it would remain, Crawford thought.

As he neared the cave, his apprehension intensified with the sounds of squealing.

These are no ordinary rats, he thought.

In one year, the typical female black rat—sexually mature at three months—gestated every twenty-four days, gave birth to twelve pups and spawned 16,000 offspring. But thanks to Roselli's ingenious breeding technique, the birthing rate had been increased to an average of sixteen pups. Therefore, the growth algorithm for Operation Genesis conservatively assumed that each female in the initial set would account for an astounding 24,000 descendants in the first year alone. Naturally, the descendants would carry that trend forward exponentially.

Much of the epidemiological detail was lost on Crawford. But he remembered Roselli referring to the rats as a natural 'intermediate host' for plague transmission. Stokes preferred to call them a 'delivery system'. All Crawford knew was that once the brood had reached critical mass, they'd be released from the cave into the Zagros Mountains.

Once unleashed on their new habitat, the rat population would spread out in all directions. According to Roselli, there'd be numerous ways the rats would transmit the Genesis Plague virions to humans. Crawford could recall only the top three: contamination of food and water supplies via blood, urine, faeces or saliva, primary contact through a bite (less likely), or, most potently, through bloodsucking sand flies and mosquitoes that would feast on the rats, then relay the virus to humans and livestock through bites. The perfect transmission vector.

At first, Crawford thought Stokes's plan to settle the score in the Middle East sounded insane. Now that the mission was nearing completion, however, he felt nothing but reverence for the man. Stokes was a visionary, a crusader, a saviour. Stokes would rewrite human history.

And Crawford was determined to play his part. At this juncture, all he needed to do was act the role of the Pied Piper and herd the critters out the front door. Though he wasn't counting on that being the easiest of tasks. If rats felt threatened, they would defend themselves—exactly the reason Crawford had brought along the rodent repeller, a transmitter that had been cleverly integrated into Crawford's walkie-talkie. He powered on the transmitter and a steady ultrasonic signal began transmitting in the 45,000 Hz range. For the rats, the high-frequency waves were like Kryptonite to Superman.

The tunnel walls fell away from his light, giving way to the cave's soupy black void. Without pause, Crawford stormed inside, machine gun raised high on his shoulder, ready to cut down any moving target larger than a rat.

HAZO WATCHED the luminescent beam sweep from side to side. Certain that the light would attract the rats, Hazo was confused when the writhing brood cowered back like ebbing surf. It looked as if an invisible wall were pushing out in front of the light to repel them, like some kind of fantastical force field.

Advancing to within fifteen metres of the containers, the light swung up to spotlight Shuster. The rats' squeals were suddenly drowned out by the clamour of automatic gunfire and Hazo saw the spitting of tiny white flashes.

In the same instant, Shuster's face ripped open and the back of his head exploded in a spew of blood and brains. The force from the impact threw him backwards and he tumbled off the container.

Dropping to his knees, Hazo flashed his light down at the body. The rats were already swarming over it.

Then the light shifted to Hazo.

Penned in by the platform's railings, there was nowhere for him to go. He scrambled for the handgun that Shuster had given him and sprang to his feet. Squinting in the light, he failed to make visual confirmation of a target, but blindly fired three shots. The light didn't budge.

'Drop the gun, Hazo!' the gunman yelled up at him.

Hazo wasn't surprised that it was Crawford's voice. 'No!' he replied.

'I'll shoot you dead right now if you don't drop the gun,' Crawford threatened.

'You do what you must,' Hazo screamed. 'I'm already dead.'

A pause.

'Get off that platform,' Crawford yelled.

Get off the platform? Why would Crawford want him to come down if he had no problem shooting Shuster…?

There was no way Hazo was willing to sacrifice himself to the rats. Best to take a few bullets and avoid the suffering.

Hazo turned his back and shut his eyes. 'Shoot me!' he yelled out. 'Shoot me in the back like the coward you are!' He gritted his teeth and waited for the end—waited for Crawford's bullets to finish the job his microscopic assassins had already started.

No shots came.

Confused, Hazo eased his eyes open. 'What are you waiting for!' But directly in front of his face, he saw the answer to his own question. A sticker was plastered onto the metal housing covering a huge, tubular machine. The ominous symbol—a circle cut like a pie into six alternating yellow and black slices—carried a universal warning: radiation.

'This is your last chance!' Crawford screamed.

Hazo ignored him, as he tried to process this new information. Could this be a nuclear reactor? Clearly, if Crawford wanted him to back away, it could mean only that he feared a stray bullet might pierce its volatile core.

He pointed the gun directly at the reactor. 'You move, I shoot.'

For ten seconds there was no response. Then the light beam shifted.

Without warning, something hurled out from the light—glinting as it pinwheeled directly towards Hazo. It struck him in the chest like a fist, pushing him back against the reactor. He crumpled onto the platform and all feeling in his right hand turned to pins and needles. The gun slipped from his grip and skittered to a stop at the edge of the platform.

This time, Hazo found it impossible to catch his breath. He looked down and saw a black handgrip, buried to the hilt, sticking out beneath his right clavicle, close to the shoulder. When he tried to move towards the gun, bolts of pain shot down his arm and over his chest, making him see pure white.

Then he heard Crawford's boots clanging up the ladder rungs.

CHAPTER TWELVE

It hadn't taken much effort for Jason to persuade Crawford's disenchanted marines to step aside so that he and Meat could get into the tunnel. After squirming through the opening above the debris pile, they'd progressed quickly through tight winding passages until Jason abruptly dropped to one knee with his M16 directed straight. He signalled to Meat to halt.

Jason shone his light low to the ground less than ten metres ahead.

A body in desert camouflage blocked their path. Though the face was turned away from them, a glinting crucifix dangling from the corpse's neck left little doubt as to the marine's identity.

'Ramirez,' Jason whispered softly to Meat.

Jason eased back to a standing position, listened intently for any activity. He turned to Meat. 'Hear that?'

Meat nodded. 'Sounds like rusty wheels.'

Jason proceeded and Meat followed close at his heels. As he stepped over the body, he caught a glimpse of the dime-sized hole drilled through Ramirez's temple.

The tunnel curved yet again. After cautiously rounding the bend, Jason saw the slightest trace of light softening the darkness. He also heard screaming over the growing din of tinny squeals. One of the voices belonged to Crawford, the other, unmistakably, Hazo. It sounded as if the two were arguing.

Jason looked back at Meat and said in an urgent tone, 'Let's do this.'

HAZO WAS AMAZED how quickly Crawford had made it up to the platform. It seemed like mere seconds had elapsed since the colonel threw the knife into his chest. Not enough time for Hazo to muster the strength to make a play for the gun. But even the slightest movement tweaked the blade against nerves and zapped him like a taser.

Crawford gave the handgun a swift kick and it sailed off into the darkness. 'Nice try. But your aim was lousy.'

Hazo's gaze burned with contempt. 'You are an evil man,' he said. Wincing, he tried to prop himself up against the reactor.

'Don't be such a bad sport. You're no match for me. None of you Arabs is a match for me.'

'I am a Kurd,' said Hazo.

Crawford reached into his pocket, pulled out a foot-long plastic zip-tie and strapped Hazo's wrist to the rail. Hazo screamed in agony, coughed up a wad of mucus and blood.

'Sounds like you've got a hairball in there. Oh, sorry . . . that's just the plague.' Crawford eyed the huge generator. 'You aren't stupid—this sure is a nuclear reactor. A couple of puny bullets won't do it much harm.' Then he squatted beside a luggage-sized box bolted to the base of the reactor. 'But this baby, here, packs enough punch to vaporise everything inside this mountain.'

Crawford patted the boxy shell that protected the W54 Special Atomic Demolition Munition, the plutonium equivalent of twenty-two tons of TNT.

'Before that happens, I'm going to push these rats out of here, using my little whistle here.' Crawford tapped his walkie-talkie. 'That way they can swarm over this godforsaken sandbox you call a country to set things straight once and for all.'

Horrified, Hazo watched the colonel unhinge the bomb's lid to access a control console. When Crawford inserted a key card into a slot on the panel, a digital display illuminated.

'Please, think about what you are doing,' Hazo pleaded. 'Destroy the cave . . . me . . . That is fine. But you can't spread this disease. Think of all the innocent people. Even you can't do such a thing.'

'I can do anything I damn well please,' Crawford replied, entering an eight-digit code on the console's number pad. He pressed a button and a digital display illuminated with numbers: 00:20:00. Crawford hit another key and the countdown began. 'You've got less than twenty minutes. Meantime, I've got some work to do.'

'Crawford!' a deep voice bellowed out from the darkness.

The colonel's bravado instantly turned to alarm. He wheeled and drew his M16—all in one motion. His light lanced the darkness and found one of those damn mercenaries near the entrance tunnel—the Goliath-sized guy they called Meat.

'Don't you assholes know when to die?'

He opened fire before the man could raise his weapon but Meat managed to duck into the tunnel.

WITH CRAWFORD'S ATTENTION focused on Meat, Jason crept up the ladder leading to the platform. As he'd advanced through the shadows, Jason had seen the marine tap the device on his belt and refer to it as a 'whistle'. Judging from the way the rats stayed far away from Crawford, he guessed it was a variant of an ultrasonic transmitter used to ward off pests from camp provisions.

Nearing the top of the ladder, Jason peeked over the edge of the platform. Crawford was facing sideways, using his light to probe the entry-way for Meat. Though Crawford was wearing a helmet and a flak jacket, Jason could easily put a bullet through his face. But, however tempting that might seem, he'd have to try to take him alive. Crawford was the lone survivor of the twisted cabal who'd masterminded Operation Genesis. There were plenty of questions still unanswered.

'You're finished, Crawford,' Hazo whispered, smiling grimly.

'Not even close,' he said, turning to face Hazo.

Glowering, he pressed the M16's muzzle against Hazo's head.

It was exactly what Hazo expected Crawford to do. And it drew his attention away from Jason, who was now quietly stepping up onto the platform. But Crawford was alerted to Jason's presence by the subtle shift in the metal grating under his feet. By the time Crawford turned, Jason had lunged, burying a shoulder into Crawford's abdomen and thrusting him back against the safety rail that looped in front of the reactor.

Jason drove his elbow up into Crawford's jaw, then landed a smashing head-butt on the bridge of his nose. Blood sprayed everywhere. Jason grabbed for Crawford's right forearm and pushed the M16 away. Shots sprayed wildly into the cave's vault. Then, with all his might, Jason pressed the forearm longways over the metal rail—kept pushing down until he heard bones snap. Crawford yelped in pain, thrashing viciously. The M16 slipped from his grip and tumbled over the railing.

Crawford brought his left elbow down between Jason's shoulder blades directly on the spine. He followed it up with a knee to Jason's face.

Jason reeled, stumbled backwards and collapsed onto the platform.

Crawford used his left hand to yank the knife from Hazo's shoulder. Hazo screamed in anguish.

Jason sprang to his feet and squared off with Crawford.

'Still got some fight left, eh?' Crawford said, grinning deviously. His misshapen right arm dangled limply at his side, and he clutched the knife in his left hand.

'Plenty,' Jason said, wiping blood from a gash over his eye.

'You're gonna need it, boy,' Crawford warned, with a menacing thrust of the knife. He eyed the spinning numbers on the nuke's console. 'You can't stop this now,' he said. 'Even I can't override the countdown.' Crawford stepped closer, forcing Jason to backstep to the open edge of the platform near the ladder.

'I'm not asking you to stop it,' Jason replied.

'You're a cocky son of a bitch, aren't you? Tell me, when you found Al-Zahrani drowned in his own filth, didn't you just love it? After what he did to your brother, it must've tickled your dick.'

'You don't know shit about my brother.'

Crawford tested Jason's reflexes with another thrust of the knife but Jason pulled back nimbly.

'I know plenty about you, Yaeger. You want revenge and here I am handing you retribution wrapped in a bow . . . and you're fighting me? You want this just as bad as me. These rats and this plague—it's the answer.'

'A plague is not an answer. Nothing that can kill so many innocent people is a solution.'

'That's not the way I see it.' Crawford stepped closer.

Then something popped up over the lip of the platform and a bright light suddenly flashed in Crawford's eyes.

Jason sprang at Crawford, grabbed his flak jacket with both hands and planted his foot in his stomach. He tugged the colonel forward while dropping back in a somersault and using the momentum to launch Crawford over the edge of the platform.

Clinging to the ladder with the flashlight in his hand, Meat ducked as Crawford went airborne.

'Noooo—!' Crawford yelled as he landed hard.

Meat pointed the light down at him. The colonel's body was contorted into a pretzel shape. The left leg was bent completely sideways, the right arm pinned beneath the torso.

'Thanks,' Jason said, holding a hand out for Meat.

'What are friends for?' Meat said, stepping up onto the platform.

Jason knelt beside Hazo. 'Hey, buddy,' he said, using his knife to cut Hazo's wrist free from the railing. The Kurd's complexion was sickly and trickles of blood were dribbling from his nostrils and ears.

'I do not feel so well, Jason,' Hazo muttered.

'We're going to get you out of here. Meat will carry you.'

Hazo managed a thin smile, waved his hand dismissively. 'Is it true that Al-Zahrani is dead?' he asked.

Jason couldn't lie. 'Yeah, buddy. He's dead.'

'This disease killed him? This plague that is inside me?'

Jason hesitated. 'We didn't find him in time.'

'Is there a treatment, Jason?' Hazo asked, his voice weak.

Jason didn't know what to say. The medic was dead and according to Tommy Flaherty, Stokes had indicated that there was no vaccine. Finally, with his heart in his throat, he shook his head.

'Can I spread this to others?'

Jason swallowed hard and felt a surge of emotion fill his chest. He could tell that Hazo already knew the answer, but needed him to make peace with it. 'Yes.'

'Then I must stay here. You know that.'

A feeling of utter helplessness wrenched Jason, made his head numb. He'd already lost two men today.

'Jason, we've got a problem,' Meat said, monitoring the scene below. 'The rats. They're moving closer.' He also noticed that the tiny yellow light on Crawford's walkie-talkie that had been blinking in a steady rhythm had now turned to a sporadic pulse. 'I think Crawford's gizmo got a good jolt when he hit the ground. Looks like it's fading out.'

Jason glanced at the nuke's digital counter. Fifteen minutes, eight seconds. There was no way they could carry Hazo outside in time. And Crawford wouldn't be making it out either.

'Hazo's right,' Meat said. 'We don't have much time. And there's no way we can allow these rats to get out of here. Let the nuke do its job. It's the best option we've got to stop this thing from spreading.'

Jason nodded. 'You're a great man, Hazo. Your family will be very proud when I tell them what you've done.'

'Thank you, Jason,' Hazo said. 'Thank you for showing me hope when I saw nothing but despair. When I meet my father again, it will be with dignity. Now you must go. Please.'

Meat descended the ladder while monitoring the scene directly below: rats streaming up and down the ramp leading into the container, as if staging a raid. Reaching the lowest rung, he leaped out over the horde and landed safely in the shrinking circle of clear ground that surrounded Crawford.

When Jason looked down at the colonel, he couldn't believe what he saw. Crawford was now trying to smash his walkie-talkie. 'Meat! Stop him!'

Meat grabbed the thrashing arm with both hands. 'Give it up, Crawford!'

Jason jumped down off the ladder and came up behind Meat.

Crawford's entire body quaked from the adrenaline coursing through his system. 'You don't know what you're doing!' he ranted madly. 'It's them or us! Don't you see?'

'Yeah, yeah . . .' Meat said, snatching the walkie-talkie from Crawford's belt. 'I'll take this, thanks.' He tossed it to Jason.

'Take his grenades too,' Jason said.

Meat plucked the three grenades from Crawford's flak jacket and clipped them to his own belt.

Meanwhile, Jason went over to retrieve Crawford's fumbled Bowie knife.

'You're responsible for quite a few deaths today, Crawford,' Jason said. 'Good men who trusted you. That's a lot of blood on your hands. As far as I see it, it's high time for you to pay for what you've done.' He dropped the knife onto Crawford's chest. 'You can keep that, tough guy. See how well you do against them.' He motioned to the rats.

Crawford's jaw jutted out, his eyes boiling with rage.

'Come on, Jason. Let's get outta here,' Meat said.

'Just a sec,' Jason said. He unclipped the light from Crawford's M16 and set it on the ground to illuminate the spot.

'What are you doing?' Crawford demanded.

Slowly backing away, Jason grinned while holding up the walkie-talkie. With each step, the ultrasonic barrier retreated from Crawford and the hungry rats encroached a few inches more into the circular void—countless hungry eyes glinting red in the light.

'Can you see this, Hazo?' He glanced up at the platform and saw the Kurd's head pop into view.

'Yes.'

'This is for you, buddy. Godspeed, my friend.' Jason took another step back. The rats spilled over Crawford's paralysed legs.

Crawford screamed. 'Damn you, Yaeger!'

Jason dashed towards the tunnel where Meat was waiting.

The black wave crashed over Crawford's body.

'Feel better now?' Meat said.

'Much,' Jason said, setting the transmitter on the ground just inside the narrow entry-way. 'That should hold them back long enough. Now let's get the hell out of here!'

JASON SECURED the MRAP's rear doors. 'All clear. Go!' he yelled.

The engine roared and the hulking troop carrier lurched forward.

'How much longer?' Meat asked.

He glanced at his watch again. 'Less than a minute.'

Jason hoped that the walkie-talkie had enough juice left in it to hold back the rats. But even if the brood managed to break through the ultrasonic barrier, they'd have a tough time squeezing through the rubble pile Meat had plugged up using Crawford's three grenades.

He scanned the worried faces of the marines huddled tight along the side-wall benches. One of the soldiers had his left arm in a sling, two others had bandaged heads, and the cute robot operator with the pageboy haircut had a makeshift splint wrapped tight over her right shin. 'Everybody OK?'

Some nods, some affirmative responses.

'Good,' Jason said.

The MRAP gathered speed as it climbed on to the roadway and headed south.

'Jesus, what happened in there?' one of the marines asked.

Casting his eyes to the floor, Jason wasn't sure how to respond. Would anyone really believe the truth?

Meat answered for him, 'A weapons stash. It was booby-trapped. Crawford must've hit some kind of tripwire that activated a timed detonator.'

Five seconds later, a brilliant white light flashed through the rear window, accompanied by an ear-splitting explosion like a thunderclap. There was a deceptive delay that preceded the shockwave. When it hit, the MRAP groaned and bucked, jostling everyone inside. Arms and legs flailed and bodies rolled. The hull filled with screams and expletives.

A barrage of heavy debris pounded the roof, clanging the vehicle's thick armour plating like a gong. The white light dissipated and a second wave of pelting debris came raining down over the truck's exterior.

Then came an eerie calm.

EPILOGUE

'I feel like I'm hanging from a noose,' Meat grumbled as he tugged at the starched white collar.

'What do you mean?' Jason said, fixing his own bow tie and taking extra-long strides to keep up with Meat. 'Nothing wrong with looking classy once in a while.'

Jason gazed up to admire the cerulean sky through the dome of triangular glass panels which covered the Great Court that was the heart of the British Museum.

'Doesn't look like Tommy's here yet,' he said.

A lithe brunette wearing a skimpy cocktail dress and high heels strode by, gazed at Meat appraisingly, then flashed him an approving smile. Meat smiled back, and miraculously the tuxedo felt comfortable. He reconsidered his position, saying, 'I suppose classy isn't so bad. I'm just not used to getting all dressed up like some rich socialite.'

'Funny you should say that,' Jason said. He slid his hand under his lapel and pulled out a white envelope.

Meat looked at it suspiciously. 'If that's another goddamn subpoena—'

'Calm down . . .' Jason said.

There'd been plenty of court requests over the past weeks since they'd returned home from their mission. Accompanied by an army of counsellors from GSC's Legal Affairs division, Jason and Meat had endured exhaustive questioning at a Congressional hearing. They'd quickly been absolved of any formal charges, thanks largely to the video captured on the disc Jason had recovered from the camcorder in Crawford's tent.

The day after he'd been taken into quarantine, Randall Stokes had suffered a miserable demise. NSA cryptographers succeeded in cracking the sophisticated encryption on Stokes's computer hard drive and retrieved all the operational details for Operation Genesis. Auditors had forensically reconstructed the money trail for the project's financing, most of it misappropriated from defence money earmarked for biochemical research at Fort Detrick shortly after the 2001 terror attacks. The balance of funding came from charitable donations to Stokes's evangelical mission.

'It's not a subpoena,' Jason said. He held the envelope out. 'Come on . . . it won't bite.'

Meat took it reluctantly.

'After that fire at the safe house burned out,' Jason explained, 'the skeletons were recovered from the ashes. One of the skeletons had a unique dental implant.'

'All right,' Meat said, not grasping the connection. He peeked into the envelope and saw the back of a cheque.

'Turns out the FBI matched the dental work with records already in its database,' Jason explained.

Meat looked at Jason in disbelief. 'Al-Zahrani?'

Jason nodded. 'The only positive ID. Of course, those photos I took before we set the place on fire helped too.'

Meat flipped the cheque over. His jaw dropped. For once, he was speechless.

'Your cut of the bounty. And Lillian agreed to send Jam's and Camel's widows their cut. Hazo's sister, Anyah, got his share. I've got an envelope for Tommy, too. How's that for classy?' He patted Meat on the shoulder.

'Hey, Google!' a Bostonian voice called out.

Jason turned to see Flaherty strutting towards him with a confident swagger. When he saw the beauty on Flaherty's arm, he almost swooned.

'That the archaeologist?' Meat said.

'That's her.' Wearing an elegant evening gown that accentuated nothing but curves, Professor Brooke Thompson looked like she'd taken a detour off the red carpet at the Oscars.

'Hey, fellas,' Flaherty said cheerily. He shook hands and introduced Brooke.

'By the way, Tommy,' Jason said, taking another white envelope out from his pocket, 'I've got something for you.'

'It can wait, though, right? I mean, this is Brooke's night.'

'Sure.' Jason pocketed the envelope and turned to Brooke. 'This must be pretty exciting.'

'It's a bit nerve-racking, actually,' she admitted.

The evening's main event would be her highly anticipated speech that would retell an ancient story of mysticism, betrayal and retribution written in what proved to be the world's oldest documented language. Included would be Brooke's in-depth analysis of the cache of Mesopotamian tomb relics on display that bore testament to elaborate funerary rituals pre-dating Egyptian mummification by over 1,500 years.

'I'm finally going to get to tell my story,' Brooke said. 'I'm just not sure if the world is ready to hear it.'

'Speaking of which,' Flaherty said, reaching into his pocket, 'I've got an envelope too.' He handed it to her.

'What is this?' she asked.

'Your carbon dates,' Flaherty replied.

Anticipation glinted in her eyes.

'Dates for what?' Meat asked.

'The organic stuff we found in Stokes's vault,' Flaherty explained. 'Lilith's head, of course, plus the snake and the rat it ate.'

'Actually, the rat wound up being the key to everything,' Brooke explained. 'We found out that the rat was also carrying the plague. In fact, it was the primary host. So we think that while Lilith was feeding infected rats to her pet snake, she was bitten and became a carrier, too.'

'That is gross,' Meat said. 'Sounds like Lilith was a real prize.'

Brooke fished out the papers, unfolded them and scanned the report. 'OK, Lilith dates between 4032 BC and 3850 BC. Just what we expected. And her DNA matches closest to ancient Persia,' she said, feeling a chill creep over her skin. Persia, where Lilith and the Angel of Death, Samael, became lovers. She flipped to the next page. 'The rat is in about the same date range. And the snake . . .' Her face blanched. She shook her head. 'No, this can't be right . . . they couldn't date it.'

Flaherty shrugged. 'I guess that can happen, right?'

'Shouldn't,' she said. 'Any organic substance from 4000 BC should have plenty of carbon-14 in it.'

'But isn't there an age limit for those tests?' Jason said.

She drew her lips tight and raised her eyebrows. 'Typically the test is good for up to 50 or 60,000 years. After that, whatever carbon-14 is left in the specimen is usually too minuscule to measure.'

It was Meat who cast rationale to the wind. 'So maybe the snake is over 60,000 years old.' Then he grinned and made his eyes go wide, saying in his best spooky voice, 'Or maybe the demon snake was never alive to begin with.'

michael **byrnes**

RD: What first triggered the idea for *The Genesis Plague*? Did you start with the idea of the cave and the ancient carvings, perhaps, or with the fanatical evangelist and his sinister plot?

MB: My inspiration for *The Genesis Plague* came from ancient Mesopotamian myths about creation and demons, and how those stories coincided with the rise and fall of civilisations in that region—known today as Iraq.

RD: This is your third novel about things biblical and ancient. Do you think that you will continue to mine this interesting seam of ancient history? Can you disclose what the next book will be about?

MB: For me, a balanced blend of ancient secrets and modern conspiracy makes for compelling plot hooks. I will continue to incorporate these elements into future novels. I'm sorry to say that the subject of my next book is still under lock and key.

RD: What was the most difficult aspect of *The Genesis Plague* to get right?

MB: The logistical and tactical aspects of current military intervention in Iraq required considerable research. Luckily, I have friends who serve with the US military in Iraq and they graciously provided me with considerable insight.

RD: Have you ever been into the desert in southern Iraq? And, if so, what were your impressions of the country?

MB: Though I haven't travelled to Iraq, my military friends, plus an abundance of research material, helped me form clear impressions of the region's terrain, people, politics, culture and history.

RD: How do you do the research that your plots require? For *The Genesis Plague*, for example, you must have had to find out how a plague virus can get into DNA?

MB: My research consists of a lot of reading, web searching, videos, and consulting with knowledgeable people. When I wrestle with daunting topics like DNA and viruses, I filter the science to keep it simple for the reader. I feel that science adds plausibility to my stories; however, I can, and do, take liberties where I see fit. That's the beauty of writing fiction!

RD: Where do you live, and are you happy there?

MB: I've lived in Florida for over three years now and my family and I love calling it home. We are part of a very family-friendly community and there are plenty of outdoor activities to enjoy year-round.

RD: Are you still working as an insurance broker? Is selling an art that can be fully mastered, or is there always something new to learn?

MB: Yes, I still work as an insurance broker. With technology radically reshaping every industry, including insurance, the art of selling is evolving at hyperspeed. Like writing, selling is a continuous process of growth and learning—an art likely never to be mastered.

RD: What's a typical working day for you?

MB: I typically write in the early morning, when all is quiet and my creative mind is most uninhibited. The remainder of my workday is dedicated to my insurance business.

RD: Do you have particular hobbies, other than writing, that you've stuck to for many years?

MB: In my free time, my wife and three children get most of my attention. However, I still make time for guitar and basketball.

RD: Do you travel outside the States a great deal? What destination is top of your wish list?

MB: This year, my trips were limited to the US and Canada, but I would love to travel more extensively throughout the Middle East.

RD: When are you at your happiest, and when are you at your most annoyed?

MB: I'm happiest spending time with my wife and three children, riding bikes, going to the beach, and visiting family and friends. I'm probably most annoyed when I have to stop writing when I'm in the zone. But that's life!

RD: Can you name five famous people, dead or alive, who you would choose to invite to your ultimate dinner party?

MB: 1. Jesus (philosopher), 2. Alexander the Great (conqueror), 3. Malcolm Gladwell (author), 4. Eddie Van Halen (guitarist), 5. Warren Buffet (mogul).

RD: If your wife and two small daughters and son had to pick five adjectives to describe you, which do you think they would choose?

MB: Attentive, moody, creative, funny and smart.

RD: And, last but not least, if you won the lottery, would it change your life in any way and, if so, how?

MB: For me, a windfall would certainly shake things up a bit. I think I'd share the bulk of lottery winnings with family and friends. Then I'd establish a free international workshop for aspiring writers, instructed by best-selling authors. Of course, I'd be sure to save some. Finally, I'd definitely splurge on lavish family vacations.

COPYRIGHT AND ACKNOWLEDGMENTS

Spine: Shutterstock. Front cover (from left) and page 4 (from top): © Caro/Alamy; www.anne-smith.net; Juergen Stein/STOCK4B/Getty Images; cave: Getty Images; skull: www.istock-photo.com. Page 5 (top) © Simon Wilson/*Toronto Star*; 6–8: images: Shutterstock; illustration: Kate Finnie; 142 © Adrian Housten; 143 © Apex. 144–6: illustration: Andrew Rowland@ Advocate-Art; 274 © Liam White; 275 © Tupungato/www.istockphoto.com. 276–8 image: © Zarathustra/Fotolia; illustration: James Kessell; 434 © David Cooper. 436–8 image: Shutterstock; illustration: Rick Lecoat@Shark Attack. 574 © courtesy of Simon & Schuster.

Printed and bound by GGP Media GmbH, Pössneck, Germany

020-270 UP0000-1